PELHAM

PELHAM

or

THE ADVENTURES
OF A GENTLEMAN

Edward George Bulwer-Lytton

Edited with an introduction by

Jerome J. McGann

UNIVERSITY OF NEBRASKA PRESS · LINCOLN

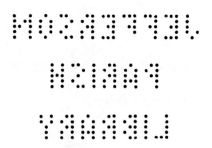

Publishers on the Plains

UNP

Copyright © 1972 by the University of Nebraska Press

All rights reserved

International Standard Book Number 0–8032–0703–4

Library of Congress Catalog Card Number 77–88085

Manufactured in the United States of America

This edition of PELHAM *is dedicated to*

Virgil Burnett

CONTENTS

VOLUME ONE

VOLUME TWO

INTRODUCTION

Edward George Earle Lytton Bulwer-Lytton (1803–73), the first Lord Lytton, is generally remembered today as the author of *The Last Days of Pompeii* (1834). But among his contemporaries his fame began and was always connected with another sort of novel altogether—*Pelham*, the acknowledged "hornbook of dandyism" throughout nineteenth-century Europe. Published in 1828, just after the great days of Byron and Brummell were over and just before the long reign of Victoria had begun, *Pelham* was one of the most popular novels of the century. It ran through numerous editions in England and America and appeared in French, German, Italian, and Spanish translations.

One of the reasons for the novel's tremendous vogue was its strongly topical flavor. More than anything else, Bulwer was a man of his age, much involved in its politics, active in society. Thus one is not surprised to discover in all his writings a fine sensitivity to current tastes and interests. Bulwer had, as well, a brilliant, curious, and eclectic mind. But these real intellectual virtues often produced serious weaknesses in many of his writings, which are justly felt to be somewhat shallow and have hardly endured the passage of time. Yet if Bulwer's urban habits—a set of qualities which Italians define in the word *mobilità* and Englishmen in the idea of dandyism—served only to weaken much of his so-called serious writing, *Pelham* not only survives these qualities intact, it is, as a work of art, enriched by them. Remarkably sensitive to everything current, elegant, and busy, Bulwer immobilizes for one brief moment the marvels of those swiftly passing scenes of early nineteenth-century England. In *Pelham*, the polished life of the Regency and its immediate aftermath rises to the surface of Bulwer's finest prose, its all but fatal instrument and symbol.

Bulwer was the author of a large body of novels, plays, poetry, history, criticism, and philosophy, and it was for his literary efforts, rather than his public life, that he wished to be remembered. But today only a carefully guided tour of his works will do justice to his various talents. Of his plays, *Money* (1840), a comedy of manners, is probably the best. If his poetry deserves the oblivion into which it has fallen, his discursive prose, especially the candid and witty study of national character, *England and the English* (1833), preserves its strengths. Among the novels, besides *Pelham,* only *The Last Days of Pompeii* sustains any sort of achievement. Parts of *Zanoni* (1842) and *Lucretia* (1846) are good—both illustrate Bulwer's passion for gothic effects—while the short story "The Haunters and the Haunted" (1862), obviously in a similar vein, is one of the finest single pieces he ever wrote. Of the strictly historical fiction, into which Bulwer put so much labor, only *The Last of the Barons* (1843) can hold one's attention.

Yet a book like *Pelham* succeeds not only because its author aspired to literary fame, but because he was much involved in the public life of his time and widely connected in society. Bulwer was always a highly personal novelist, and the world of *Pelham,* an exclusive but by no means parochial one, he knew perfectly and moved in at ease. Lying just below the highly polished surface of his novel is a variety of persons, attitudes, and events which were drawn directly from Bulwer's own life. Pelham, for example, was partly modeled on Bulwer's college friend George William Frederick Villiers (1800–70), the fourth earl of Clarendon, a man noted for his brilliance, gay conversation, and epicurism; and whatever Villiers may have lacked, we can be sure Bulwer was able to supply from his own habits and tastes. Even Bedos, Pelham's valet, was based on the character of Bulwer's valet of his bachelor days, and the author told his son that the Lords Vincent and Guloseton were both taken from life. Nearly everyone in the novel has his historical counterpart, though some of them we are now unable to identify. Only Glanville seems to have been a wholly imaginative invention, but when we recall how obsessed Bulwer was with the character of the Byronic hero, we realize how personal even this figure was for him.

Two love stories dominate the action of *Pelham,* and though both must be traced back to Bulwer's own life, the one is a product of his imagination, the other of an experience only too painfully real. The doomed love of Reginald Glanville and Gertrude Douglas is clearly modeled on the thwarted youthful love affair Bulwer invented for himself in his romanticized autobiography. According to the story, Bulwer's unnamed love was forced to marry another and then died a few years later, in 1824. Bulwer said the incident "coloured the whole of his life." His persistence in maintaining the truth of this fiction fully justifies his otherwise ingenuous remark. The other love story began in real joy and ended in real tragedy. Bulwer met, fell in love with, and married the beautiful and clever Rosina Doyle Wheeler (1802–82). The extent of the disaster—they were married in 1827, against the wishes of Bulwer's mother, and separated in 1836—can only be measured when we recall how happy they were when they began their lives together and how bitter they had become by the time of the separation. The love story of Henry Pelham and Ellen Glanville is Bulwer's representation of the early days of his relationship with Rosina. Fortunately, *Pelham* was finished before their life together began to turn sour.

Rosina nursed an implacable enmity against her estranged husband until her death. The separation hurt her terribly and she always laid the fault for it at his feet. She accused him of many things, including unfaithfulness, but the only certainty is that he treated her very cruelly at times and often left her alone for protracted periods. All that can be said in his defense is that, at the time, he was under extreme pressure to keep his family financially solvent—both he and Rosina were anything but careful with the little money they had—and he was forced to spend almost all of his time writing and selling his work. During the years that saw the gradual erosion of his marriage, Bulwer did succeed in establishing a solid literary reputation.

II

We read *Pelham* today because it is a witty and entertaining book. It has other recommendations as well, less aesthetic, perhaps, but by no means insignificant. It contains, for example, the first permanent record of some of Beau Brummell's most celebrated exploits, it changed fashions of dress and dictated styles of behavior, and it was repeatedly consulted by later writers seeking to formulate philosophic and aesthetic systems of dandyism. It was also the most popular "fashionable novel," as it is still the finest example of the genre, which was just then gaining an immense vogue. Disraeli's *Vivian Grey* (1826–27), the only serious competitor, cannot match it.

In its heyday the fashionable novel had a reputation for inconsequence and triviality, and *Pelham* naturally came in for some sharp criticism. Carlyle dignified one of his greatest aversions, the genre as a whole and *Pelham* in particular, with a famous satiric attack in *Sartor Resartus,* and Bulwer was also to feel the critical contempt of Hazlitt for his dandified tastes. Himself a moralist by no means lukewarm, Bulwer was peculiarly susceptible to attacks of this sort. As a result, when he set about correcting and revising his novel, he introduced a set of alterations which were designed to silence his critics by reducing *Pelham's* naughty and impudent tone. Many of his revisions were, of course, merely technical, and thus morally innocent, yet in the mass of major and minor changes one can discern few, if any, that add to the book's dandiacal and brazen tone, but a good many which tend to weaken it. All such changes strike at the vital center of the novel, whose fundamental seriousness, and even morality, is at all times a direct function of its pointedly supercilious tone.

Thus, perhaps the quickest way to understand the special quality of this novel is to examine briefly some of the alterations which Bulwer introduced into the book in order to modify its tone. The first alteration we find, for example, is a dropped paragraph—rather brief—toward the conclusion of the marvellous initial anecdote about Pelham's parents.

> I have, however, often thought that it was better for me that the affair ended thus,—as I know, from many instances, that it is frequently exceedingly inconvenient to have one's mother divorced. (p. 4)

We understand why Bulwer removed the passage: to a superficial reader Pelham might, from this, seem monstrously cavalier about marriage and divorce, and hardly a respectful son. Moreover, Bulwer's own marital troubles, and the possible consequences for his children, could not have been altogether out of his mind when he made this revision around 1840. Yet Pelham's commentary on his parents shows the nicest of moral judgments. "Exceedingly inconvenient" is precisely what the divorce of Pelham's parents might or even could be. To describe it any differently would be to indicate in Pelham a misjudgment not only of their characters but of his own as well.

This paragraph, indeed, the entire anecdote, is brilliantly satiric just because it seeks to call up in certain readers a sense of moral outrage that a son should speak so brazenly about his parents. A society which treats marriage with such insouciance is certainly being ridiculed here. But Pelham regards his parents with a tolerant and even fond amusement, and as the reader goes on he discovers that this extraordinary young man can give to his mother's worldly opinions the respect they actually deserve. Pelham is always precise. What the reader may fail to notice is that the principal objects of attack here are neither Pelham's parents nor their manner of life, but the sentimental moralist who cannot stomach such honesty and precision in the son of no matter what sort of parents, and those undiscriminating moralists whose sense of outrage at such goings-on, and at Pelham's own bantering tone, indicates their inability to judge morals and human conduct as exactly and dispassionately as Pelham does.

xiv

Consequently, the numerous minor changes of phrase designed to make Pelham appear less impudent and cavalier can only serve to undermine the entire basis of his critical position. Originally he had "adjusted [his] best curl" after reading the first of his mother's inimitable letters. The phrase was dropped. Very late in the novel, when he escapes to the country to clear his mind, he had taken with him "a volume of Bishop Berkeley and a bottle of wrinkle water." This exact information is kept from us in the later editions, and similar revisions were introduced through the entire length of the novel. By this type of change Bulwer tried to emphasize for the reader the basic moral worth of his dandified hero. But to reduce in any way our sense of Pelham's resolute elegance is to make his moral earnestness at once less astonishing to us, less significant for the objects of his criticism, and less admirably purposeful for himself. Pelham is an effective moralist because he is also a scrupulous and brazen fop. To smooth away this quality in his character at all is to make certain criticisms impossible for him. Thus, he and Lord Vincent originally proceed to the duel with D'Azimart "as silently as Christians should." Later this becomes "as silently as philosophers" because the entire process of revision has aimed to make Pelham less critical and distant from the commonplace and "Christian" manners of his time.

The alterations also purified Bulwer's novel of its deep and recurrent strain of sensuality. *Non sum qualis eram,* Pelham might well have observed had he read his own revised history. For example, after living in Paris for only "several weeks," Pelham says he is pleased with what he has accomplished.

> I had enjoyed myself to the utmost, while I had, as much as possible, combined profit with pleasure; viz. if I went to the Opera in the evening, I learned the dance in the morning; if I drove to a *soirée* at the Duchesse de Perpignan's, it was not till I had fenced an hour at the *Salon des Assauts d'Armes;* . . .

But the brilliant, if mildly daring, conclusion to this little catalogue was removed from every edition after 1828:

> and if I made love to the duchesse herself it was sure to be in a position I had been a whole week in acquiring from my master of the graces. (p. 72)

The negative effect of such omissions cannot be too strongly emphasized, for the original novel achieves its moral purpose because the original hero is such a complicated phenomenon. Were it not for his contrived foppery, natural decadence, and healthy sensuality, his moral earnestness would be insufferable. To be sure, the revised novel does not obliterate the original character of its hero, but it does represent a book in which the balance of tone has been shifted from what it was in the earlier versions. It is for this reason that the present edition has returned to 1828 for its text.

III

Very much influenced by the fiction of William Godwin, Bulwer always insisted that intellectual seriousness was the highest quality of a novel. As he says in that entirely characteristic essay "Art in the Novel" (1838): "We estimate the artist, not only in proportion to the success of his labours, but in proportion to the intellectual faculties which are necessary to that success." Flaws in execution are minor blemishes if the supervening idea, or moral, is sublimely conceived.

The governing moral purpose of *Pelham* is the definition of a form of intellectual heroism, and the exposure of the variety of ways in which men succeed in deviating from the ideal. Pelham narrates, after the fact, his own *Bildungsroman*. Quite simple in its basic form despite its episodic nature, the novel portrays Pelham moving through a three-stage moral development. The first two are essentially quests for knowledge of himself and the world. His education is initially undertaken in the most agreeable of forms, the pursuit of pleasure and amusement. This part of his development concludes when he leaves Paris for England and the prospect of a political career. As in the two subsequent stages, the conclusion of this one involves the testing of his intellectual growth. Since Pelham must ultimately become master of his person and the circumstances of his life, he must make all things subject to his mental and spiritual powers. As soon as he learns that he must leave Paris, he makes a series of intellectual gestures which prove how completely he has mastered his own legitimate desires for an amusing life, and how thoroughly he is able to analyze and discriminate the moral values of the people involved in such a life. The great encounter with Brummell, alias Russelton, at Calais, climaxes this period of testing, for in that scene we realize that the dandy Pelham is not only the intellectual and moral superior of the king of fashionable life, but his equal in elegance and wit as well.

The power to control and direct his emotions and intellectual desires with an all but superhuman purposefulness is radically increased when Pelham is thrust into the even more difficult period of his political engagement. During this stage he suffers his only serious moral lapse: seeking election to Commons for the Borough of Buyemall, he behaves in a wholly indiscriminate and contemptible fashion. Though we still admire his mental agility, he reveals a dangerously shallow and thoughtless ambition in his conversations with the electors. Narrow-mindedly self-satisfied and indifferent to these admittedly less than perfect individuals, he fails as an intellectual hero on two counts: he does not see the moral significance of the event, and he sullies his own honor. Afterwards, by a stroke of fortunate poetic justice, the seat he has won is suddenly taken from him. When he reflects upon his conduct in this affair he condemns it as mere "viciousness." His mistake thus becomes an intellectual benefit to him, for he comes to understand that power, ambition, and self-mastery may acquire negative moral dimensions when they are not consciously enlisted in the service of noble ends.

Thus the education in self-discipline gained in the first stage of his growth is revealed as a possible source of danger in the first part of his second period of development. This discovery heightens Pelham's self-consciousness even more as it is made clear to him that his mastering power must be not his detached rationality but his engaged spiritual self. He does not repudiate his coolly efficient intelligence any more than he gives up his natural inclination to pleasure and amusement. What he does do is set all these human functions in their proper order and subordination. The cherished need for pleasure ensures a human quality in his sublime spiritual ideal of life, while his carefully cultivated intelligence enables him to strike out toward that ideal in the most efficient way possible.

The conclusion of the second stage of his life, like that of the first, is at once a culmination and a new beginning. The moment comes when he receives, in a letter from the epicure Guloseton, the power to revenge himself upon Lord Dawton, who has broken a promise of political preferment for Pelham. Dawton, who has behaved contemptibly despite his position and enormous political prestige, shows himself to be the moral inferior equally of the generous and happily unpolitical Guloseton and the sincere, if dilettantish, Lord Vincent. But Dawton, though immoral himself, is supporting political measures which Pelham actually favors. Pelham, therefore, solidifies his friendships with Guloseton and Vincent and refuses the temptation to overthrow the political power of a man who is unworthy even of Pelham's anger. The decision is paralleled to an earlier one at the end of the first part of Pelham's adventures, when he took revenge, in a cutting letter, upon the insolence of Mr. Howard de Howard. In neither case does he act immorally or incorrectly—the circumstances surrounding each incident are quite different—but the implicit comparison of the two events is Bulwer's way of indicating an advance in Pelham's moral consciousness. The difference is that between a spirited, if self-disciplined, youth, and a precise, though passionate, man. Bulwer uses this same technique a number of times in the book: Pelham's pragmatic relations with Guloseton and the Clutterbucks, for example, are implicitly compared to his crass behavior toward the voters of Buyemall in order to point up, again, the extent of Pelham's growth.

The final stage of Pelham's career begins in earnest immediately after he has made his decision about Dawton and the crucial vote in Parliament. Henceforth, as Pelham says, he thinks only of Ellen and Reginald Glanville, the two beings closest to him and his life's ideals. The final period is concerned with the unraveling of the murder mystery and the exculpation of Glanville's character. It represents the consummation of his moral development, since these events do not involve so much a process of personal growth as the revelation of an achieved condition. The quest here is undertaken primarily for the benefit of another rather than himself, though as such it calls into play all the virtues and capabilities which he has acquired. The climactic scene in this part of the book is Pelham's descent into the criminal haunt of Brimestone Bess to get the evidence that will clear Glanville of the murder charge. Though it has all the trappings of a descent into an underworld for truth and self-discovery, it is not this at all. Pelham already knows the truth and only goes on the adventure to prove it to the world. Moreover, Pelham has nothing further to discover about himself. The journey is, rather, an apocalyptic ritual designed to prove publicly what is already plain fact: that Glanville is not a murderer and that Pelham is a marvel. The scene is particularly effective because it is deliberately equated with an earlier underworld journey—Glanville's descent into the madhouse to find Gertrude. Unlike Pelham's, that quest was for self-knowledge: by it Glanville comes to see in horrible detail not only what Tyrrell is guilty of, but what he must himself bear a great responsibility for. By paralleling the two journeys Bulwer measures the moral distance between Pelham and his friend (though the fact that Glanville undertook the journey at all is the beginning of *his* vindication).

What we have been describing in *Pelham* Bulwer called, in "Art in the Novel," the "Conception" of a work of fiction, that is, its principle of design. Careful structuring was one of Bulwer's two fundamental requisites for any good novel, and *Pelham* was clearly planned with a forethought equal to his own highest principles. From a closer perspective the book might not appear so consciously wrought. Indeed, some of the novel's earliest reviewers found fault with what they regarded as an excessively episodic form. A fine piece of Bulwer's own criticism answers the objection.

> The mechanism and conduct of the story ought to depend upon the nature of the preconceived design . . . . It is by not considering this rule that critics have often called that episodical or extraneous, which is, in fact, a part of the design. Thus, in "Gil Blas," the object is to convey to the reader a complete picture of the surface of society: the manners, foibles, and peculiarities of the time. . . . Hence, the numerous tales and nouvelettes scattered throughout the work, though episodical to the adventures of Gil Blas, are not episodical to the design of Le Sage. . . . They are not passages which lead to nothing, but conduce to many purposes we can never comprehend, unless we consider well for what end the building was planned.

The argument applies equally well to Bulwer's novel. Pelham's adventures bring him into contact with a wide variety of life from the highest to the lowest reaches of society. Constantly we are testing Pelham's character against these others and, in the process, discovering not only the weaknesses and strengths of everyone, including the hero, but also the particular reasons for their behavior to each other and, often, the probable or actual consequences which their actions entail. It is only in this picaresque fashion that we, like Pelham, can arrive at viable principles of judgment. Along with the hero, we must have our intellectual dexterity and spiritual substance constantly tested in the difficult disorder of circumstantial, if also providentially designed, historical reality.

Bulwer calls the second fundamental quality of all good fiction the "Sentiment," that is, a pervasive tone or mood which "emanates from the moral and predominant quality of the author." It is, he says again, "a pervading and indescribable harmony in which the heart of the author seems silently to address our own." We must not suppose that this "sentiment" or tone supporting the action of *Pelham* is merely some vague or impalpable atmosphere. It entails a conscious pattern of devices aimed to dramatize the central themes treated in the book. The "Sentiment" of *Pelham* has been called, variously, exuberant high spirits, youthful vigor and freshness, vitality. This sort of critical description, though currently out of fashion, describes very well perhaps the most important theme or moral of *Pelham,* which is constantly telling us that human life is a varied and wonderful thing to the man of feeling and wit, and that keen physical and intellectual sensitivity can be cultivated. The world is all before us, and by the example of Pelham's life we are urged to open the doors of our perceptions.

Pelham is a man of generous parts and many roles, and his history conducts him through a multitude of scenes entirely worthy of him. He describes himself as one who loves to observe and remember, two qualities which ensure not only the exercise and development of his own marvellous capacities, but the preservation of all his energies as well. An epicure and a philosopher, a dandy and a man of feeling, equally pleased with the life of the mind and a life of adventure, nothing is lost upon him. *Semper paratus,* he has a totally uncircumscribed life in the present and for the future, and his capacious "memory" is a sign that his entire past is virtue preserved. He is the book's chief symbol of the central theme of unlimited vitality, as his devotion to Ellen Glanville emphasizes. Attempting to define her lovable uniqueness, Pelham can only exclaim: "She was alive!" Ellen Glanville is Pelham's *beau idéal.*

But of course in one sense Ellen Glanville is *not* alive. As a realistic character she is hopelessly dead. If we observe the novel closely we cannot fail to see that none of the characters, not even Pelham, is alive by any realistic standards. They are all morality figures of one sort or another: Frances Pelham is worldly wisdom, Guloseton is the epicure, Ellen, Ideal Love, Glanville, a Byronic hero, Thornton is the dissipated man, and Pelham, the intellectual hero. When an author tells us that a "book itself should be a thought," we should be neither surprised nor critical of such a procedure. Nor does it mean that his characters will necessarily be reduced to simplified and uninteresting abstraction. In fact, Bulwer remains throughout devoted to his theme of the complex vitality of life even in his representation of character.

Bulwer's brilliant analyses of artistic characterization in "Art in the Novel" can help to explain this apparent contradiction. He says that an author must take "advantage of the multiform inconsistencies of human nature." A weak novelist, when portraying avarice, will make his character "not the avaricious miser, but abstract avarice itself." He goes on to contrast Shakespeare:

Not so Shakespeare when he created Shylock. Other things, other motives occupy the spirit of the Jew besides his gold and his argosies; he is a grasping and relentless miser, yet he can give up avarice to revenge. He has sublime passions that elevate his mean ones.

It is the *method* of Bulwer's analysis here which reveals his own artistic procedure. Shakespeare is a consummate realistic artist, but Bulwer's criticism emphasizes not a mimesis but an ideational content. At the simplest intellectual level Shylock is avarice, but, at a more profound level, he is an image or idea of a specific type of fully human life. All art must remain true to the "multiform inconsistencies of life." At the same time, Bulwer will make the purpose of his novels rigorously moral and intellectual: *Pelham* exists to express an *awareness* of complex realities, appeals to the mind, and seeks to transfer to the reader the intellectual forms which are the artist's insights into the significance of life. The difference between a mimetic and an intellectual novelist is the difference between Jane Austen and William Godwin—or Bulwer-Lytton.

Take Lady Frances, Pelham's "affectionate and incomparable parent" and one of the book's minor triumphs of characterization. At the simplest level she represents worldly wisdom. But Bulwer enslaves her so completely to this idea, makes her represent it with such an arbitrary thoroughness, that our awareness of his design in her becomes enormously heightened. She grows, paradoxically, not abstract but unique. Hearing that her son has been ill, she sends him one of her wonderful letters.

> How dreadfully uneasy I am about you: write to me directly. I would come to town myself, but am staying with dear Lady Dawton, who wont hear of my going; and I cannot offend her for *your* sake. By the by, why have you not called upon Lord Dawton? but, I forgot, you have been ill. My dear, dear child, I am wretched about you, and how pale your illness will make you look! just too, as the best part of the season is coming on. How unlucky! Pray, don't wear a black cravat when you next call on Lady Roseville; but choose a very fine *baptiste* one—it will make you look rather delicate than ill. (p. 295)

And so on. Everything in her life is governed by considerations of position and worldly advancement. Even when her son is ill she can think in no other terms. Nevertheless, though she is constantly ridiculed in her own words, letters like these also underline the genuine human aspects of her worldly character. She is vain and absurd, but also exceedingly shrewd and, in her own fashion, scrupulously moral. In this letter her maternal affections are emphasized for us by her own untoward manner of expressing them. Bulwer's method as a novelist is to make us conscious of these facts, not so much responsive to a complex reality as aware of a complex meaning within his own intellectually purposeful design.

Bulwer suggests a human meaning in most of his other morality figures not by intensifying their slavery to a hobbyhorse but by adding other dimensions. Tyrrell is weak and profligate, but not without a certain honor and emotional sincerity. He is a negative image of Glanville, just as Glanville is a negative image of Pelham, and Job Jonson a lower-class analogue. The point is that Bulwer creates figures which constantly, in themselves and in their interactions with each other, suggest the *idea* of the world's variousness, of specific likenesses and distinctions which can be discovered everywhere. Bulwer would say that his characters were manifestations of Sentiment, expressions alike of the author's attitudes toward his subjects and of his most cherished spiritual preoccupations.

All this does not mean that readers must identify an author with his fictional works. Certain sensible distinctions must be drawn. In the first place, if an artist's works do express aspects of his mind, they may very likely express no more than that. Lady Frances is a great deal besides worldly wisdom. To see a novel as the image of the artist is to forget that men change with their histories whereas their works remain fixed beyond time. All this Bulwer asserts in the 1848 Preface to *Pelham* (see Appendix B). It is also a fact that time wrought serious changes in Bulwer's own life, not the least of which was the collapse of his marriage. The later Bulwer is at once a more sober and romantic artist, a fact clearly reflected in his works. He would never again publish anything like *Pelham*.

The verve of this novel, its expression of a spirited intellectual delight in living, is further developed through Pelham's acute mental powers. In a book which places so high a value upon intelligence, Pelham is the appropriate hero. To see through appearances with Pelham's exactness is to possess an all but divine perspective, and we are Pelham's fortunate inheritors. Nor does his constant exposure of folly and vice diminish his sense of enjoyment. To understand the harmless pedantry of Vincent, as well as his political naïveté, only heightens Pelham's sense of the man's fundamental worth, both as an intellectual and as a man. The same is true of Pelham's other charming companion, Guloseton, the happy epicure and simple friend. We, like Pelham, cherish these men all the more for seeing them for what they are. Less complicated characters, like Wormwood or Dawton, also expand Pelham's engagement with life. Not only do they instruct Pelham further in seeing life steadily and entirely, they increase his emotional range. It is a joy to observe the foolish vanity of Wormwood, "the dandy venomous" as Bulwer calls such a person in *England and the English.* As for Dawton, he too ministers to Pelham by increasing the hero's concern for what is noble and just. Pelham's moral condescension toward him is no unworthy emotion, and when Pelham makes Dawton squirm in a self-conscious awareness of his base behavior, Pelham's virtuous amusement is justly to be relished. This is the human equivalent of what Empson once called, accurately if superciliously, "God's laughter." Yet both Milton's God and Bulwer's Pelham have a perfect right to such amusement.

Pelham tells us that he frequently obeys a rule to treat serious things lightly and trivial things seriously. Though not absolute, the principle is a good one for sharpening clear-sightedness and enlarging sensitivities. A finely cut jacket, scrupulously clean linen, a perfectly prepared mushroom, all are possible sources of wonder. What Baudelaire said of another dandiacal genius, Constantin Guys—"He was an ego, incapable of being satisfied with the non-ego"—applies perfectly to Pelham. No reverses of fortune can interrupt the march of his imperturbable existence. He is equal to all things. Submitting both serious and trivial matters to the most careful scrutiny, Pelham preserves himself from what he calls *grossièreté.* To be exact in this way is to be tasteful, a response mechanism of remarkably precise calibre. The most subtle of registers, Pelham can perceive important values in the most ephemeral things, and is sensitive alike to all trumpery and falsehood. Only by protecting himself from manufactured illusions of pleasure and goodness, of emotion and intellect, can he preserve the exquisiteness of his delicate machinery. This is one of the most important ideas in *Pelham:* that dandyism, or what Bulwer calls, in *England and the English,* the possession of "certain correct, general notions about that indefinable thing, 'good taste,'" is, in its achieved condition, a striking symbol of a fundamental human ideal. In this respect, dandyism is an unlimited intellectual and emotional responsiveness manipulated with perfect ease and control by a mastering self.

Finally, we should see that Bulwer's insistence upon the need for severe self-discipline is by no means intended to circumscribe Pelham's energies. On the contrary, all perfection and vital plenitude depend upon such discipline. Speaking about a proper method of education, Vincent asserts one of the book's central ideas when he tells us that the intellect and the reason must be trained before the imagination. First teach a child "to *reflect*, before you permit him full indulgence to *imagine*." To reverse this process—to excite the imagination before judgment has been acquired—is to produce, at best, a Reginald Glanville, a man self-condemned as a "melancholy and dreaming enthusiast." The man of pure imagination cannot control the world of dull and ignorant actuality, nor, in the face of its intransigence, can he live completely alone with his ideals. Like Byron's heroes, like the youth in Shelley's *Alastor,* all are either crippled or destroyed. Not so Pelham, who is able to create an ideal romantic way of life within the very dungeons of this palatial world. Pelham never forgets that, in a human world, every West End implies an East End, and that no hero can afford to ignore either, or to miss the weaknesses of the one and the energies of the other. One of the novel's finest effects is achieved through Bulwer's deliberate equation of the manners adopted in London East and London West. Fully, if subconsciously, aware of this, Pelham exposes the tasteless and ignoble vulgarities of *ton* as well as the honor, daring, and intellectual gifts which can be found even among thieves. Nothing coarse or ignoble can touch Pelham because he is armed beforehand with the most acute perception and complete self-discipline. These powers let him metamorphose himself at will, to the frustration of all his enemies, and arrange his sensorium with such delicacy that the highest pleasures of mind and body are always his. Sublimely rather than restrictively economical, Pelham discovers the earthly paradise.

IV

Pelham is Bulwer's finest novel because the themes and moral purpose are advanced, with a remarkable thoroughness, both in the style and the controlling design. The book retails the development of an intellectual hero: not *the* intellectual hero, but a hero of his own time, and modified further by the peculiar qualities of his own character; and not anything but an *intellectual* hero. Lermontov's story of that classic Russian intellectual hero, Pechorin, is a nice analogue. Both Pelham and Pechorin are dandies—elegant, brazen, and unremittingly self-conscious beings bent upon preserving their uniqueness amidst the conventional milieux which they exist to expose and analyze. Both books employ an episodic form, both describe the moral development of their heroes, and both are the occasion for trenchant commentaries upon the manners of the times. But the comparison is even more instructive for the marked differences between the two novels. The narrative of *A Hero of Our Own Time,* convoluted and symbolic, is the appropriate vehicle for a tale of a severe grace gained through the extreme experience of desolation. *Pelham,* on the other hand, is picaresque and associational, a form which perfectly enacts the beneficent moral adventures of a cultural messiah. Pechorin, an extreme fatalist, leaves us as a man with no hope left for himself or his society, though, paradoxically, this end is for him really a sort of triumph, and for his society a revelation. Pelham, a meliorist, leaves us with the most auspicious signs for his own future and, because of this, for his society as well. Like all dandies—like the hero of Gautier's *Mlle de Maupin,* for example—both Pechorin and Pelham are idealists. But while Lermontov's hero is gloomy and self-conscious, and Gautier's sensual and curious, Bulwer-Lytton's is gay and moral. All three trace a common parentage in different aspects of Byronism.

In the later editions of *Pelham* Bulwer's dandified world is noticeably less resolute. Not quite so impudent and a bit more conventional, the later Pelham sometimes even seems an insufferable moral prig showing off manners and tastes which he does not take quite seriously. To see how seriously Pelham should take such matters we must return to the novel published in 1828. Unlike Bulwer's Russelton, a dandy by anxiety who conquers fashionable life out of fear, Pelham is a dandy out of natural inclination. Not to be seriously concerned about his curls, not to discriminate exquisite food, not to possess good taste in all things and to demand such taste as an ideal, would be to deny not only the specifics of his own personality (he was born to such circumstances and codes), but the highest values he is capable of conceiving. For those ideal values can only be defined in the particular terms and forms of thought which Pelham's own upbringing permit. A bohemian may attain human perfection, but he can never be a dandy. It is simply a matter of definition. One law for the lion and the ox is oppression.

Thus, in *Pelham,* dandyism is the symbol of an important human truth: that in the quest for perfection each man can gain only what is specifically his own. Dandyism enlarges upon the importance of personality, of uniqueness, in a world waging an increasingly fierce war upon the minute particulars of life. No democrat, Bulwer argued the impossibility of large-scale social amelioration except through the encouragement of personal virtues. His lifelong political ideas are represented, clearly if only implicitly, in this early novel.

University of Chicago   JEROME J. McGANN

BIBLIOGRAPHY

This bibliography offers a few basic sources for further information about Bulwer-Lytton in general and *Pelham* in particular. The standard edition of Bulwer-Lytton's works is the Knebworth (37 vols., 1873–77). For a list of the principal editions of *Pelham* consulted, see A Note on the Text and Editing.

Bell, E. G. *Introduction to the Prose Romances, Plays and Comedies of Edward Bulwer, Lord Lytton*. Chicago: W. M. Hill, 1914.

Howe, Susan. *Wilhelm Meister and His English Kinsmen*. New York: Columbia University Press, 1930.

Lytton, Edward R. B., First Earl of Lytton. *The Life, Letters, and Literary Remains of Edward Bulwer, Lord Lytton*. 2 vols. London: Kegan, Paul, Trench, and Co., 1883.

Lytton, Victor A. G. R. B., Second Earl of Lytton. *The Life of Edward Bulwer, First Lord Lytton*. 2 vols. London: Macmillan and Co., 1913.

McGann, Jerome J. "The Dandy." *Midway* (Summer 1969): 3–18.

Moers, Ellen. *The Dandy. Brummell to Beerbohm*. London: Secker and Warburg, 1960.

Rosa, Matthew W. *The Silver-Fork School*. New York: Columbia University Press, 1936.

Sadleir, Michael. *Bulwer: A Panorama. I. Edward and Rosina, 1803–1836*. London: Constable and Co., 1931.

Vincent, Leon Henry. *Dandies and Men of Letters*. Boston: Duckworth and Co., 1913.

Watts, James C. *Great Novelists. Scott, Thackeray, Dickens, Lytton*. London: Ward, Lock, and Co., 1880.

A NOTE ON THE
TEXT AND EDITING

The text of the present edition of *Pelham; or, The Adventures of a Gentleman* reprints, with the modifications specified below, the second edition, published in three volumes by Henry Colburn (London, 1828). It has been preferred to the first edition, also published in 1828, chiefly because it prints Pelham's famous "Maxims," which did not appear in the first edition, and because it incorporates Bulwer's corrections of misprints and misspellings in the first edition. Later editions were ruled out because many of the emendations introduced in 1835 and 1840 weakened the force of the novel, as I have discussed in the Introduction. All the variant readings from the texts of the first edition and the 1835 and 1840 editions are reprinted in the Textual Notes, which begin on page 459 and are signaled in the text by an asterisk. An annotated list of the principal nineteenth-century editions up to and including the Knebworth edition of the *Collected Works* is given in the second section below.

In preparing this edition of *Pelham* I have adhered as closely as possible to the text of the second edition. Consequently, I have retained obsolete forms and unusual usages which were acceptable at the time the novel was written. They are listed in the first section below. If Bulwer himself changed a form in a later edition (as when he changed *ancle* to *ankle*), the original has been retained and the alteration recorded in the Textual Notes. Original punctuation has been altered only when an obvious misprint occurred or when it interferes with easy reading. For example, I have transposed commas placed next to and inside close parentheses—), for ,)— and in several cases I have normalized the use of single and double quotation marks. Such changes in punctuation and other minor textual alterations—corrections of misprints, misspellings, and some instances of inconsistent usage—have been made silently.

Words which appear to have been accidentally omitted from the text are restored and enclosed in brackets.

When necessary, I have referred to the 1840 edition to help distinguish a misprint from an unusual usage; in doubtful cases, I have also consulted the Knebworth edition of the *Collected Works*. Similarly, I have used these editions to help determine whether the apparent misspelling of a foreign word was an authorial lapse or a form acceptable at the time. I have not altered any of the corrupt foreign-language or English quotations when it was evident that Bulwer, perhaps trusting to memory, had simply misquoted; but I have silently corrected spelling errors and supplied diacritical marks. Wherever a misquotation occurs, it is indicated in a footnote. Throughout the book the French particle was treated inconsistently (e.g., *Compte D'A——* and *Compte d'A—*) and I have allowed both forms to stand; but in a few cases I have regularized inconsistent spelling and treatment of place names: e.g., I have used consistently *dispatch* for *despatch* and *Mont Orgueil* for *Mont-orgueil*. In two instances I have transliterated Greek forms: Ευρηκα into its common English form *Eureka* and Θοιναι into *Thoinai*.

Bulwer's own notes, which appear on the text page as numbered footnotes in the same series as my critical and explanatory notes, are indicated by bracketed initials [B-L] and the date of the edition in which the note was added, if it is other than the second edition of 1828. I have included all the notes which Bulwer retained in the 1840 edition. Notes which appeared only in the first edition and the 1835 edition have been placed among the variants in the Textual Notes.

Since the novel is highly topical, I have annotated all references to contemporaneous persons, places, events, etc. which are not explained in the text itself. Obvious exceptions are made in the case of famous persons and events, like Byron and Waterloo. I have also included notes supplementing the information in the Introduction regarding the historical figures who stood behind many of Bulwer's characters. Some historical references—e.g., the date of the Council of Pisa—have also been annotated. Unusual verbal forms, like *unked*, have been glossed.

The other large group of explanatory notes aims to identify the literary quotations—mainly Latin, French, and English—which appear throughout the novel. Unfortunate though it may be, I have not been equal to Bulwer's extraordinary eclecticism, and some of his quotations remain unidentified, as my notes indicate. Except for the simplest or most familiar foreign phrases, the quotations are translated in the notes. The novel also contains a good deal of proverbial wisdom. Since, by its very nature, such material cannot be said to have a specific source, I have not annotated it beyond an initial directory note. Similarly, Bulwer sometimes puts common phrases, like "sweet and holy," in quotation marks. These too I have generally passed without comment, for similar reasons.

Obsolete Forms and Unusual Usages Retained in the Text

ante-revolutionary, anti-room, *appartemens,* ar'n't, cachmere, cachemire, chace, chesnut, *connoissance,* controul, coquets, dependant, develope, drank (as past participle), duchesse, *egaremens,* faultered, forestal, hacknied, hobbydehoy, instil, jackall, Parmasan, *porte cocher,* potatoe, recal, recompence, *remercîmens,* Rochefoucault, *savan,* scissars, sha'n't, superintendant, trowsers, villany, Werter, ycleped.

Principal Editions Consulted and Textual Bibliography

The important bibliographies in textual matters are Michael Sadleir's *XIX Century Fiction,* 2 vols. (London: Constable and Co., 1951), the British Museum Catalogue of Printed Books, and the *Cambridge Bibliography of English Literature,* Volume 3 1800–1900, ed. George Watson (Cambridge: Cambridge University Press, 1969). All, including the recently published *CBEL,* are inadequate in one way or another. Only Sadleir lists an edition for 1833, for example, and he suggests that it was never published, which is not the case. None lists the 1849 edition which, though not significant textually, deserves special notice here since it contains the hitherto unrecorded "Advertisement," Bulwer's third and final preface to *Pelham* (see Appendix B).

1828. London: Henry Colburn. Three volumes. The first edition.

1828. London: Henry Colburn. Three volumes. With a preface and emendations. See Introduction. The second edition.

1833. London: Henry Colburn. Three volumes. Colburn's Modern Standard Novelists (on title page). A reprint of the 1828 second edition, and the novel's first appearance in Colburn's Modern Standard Novelists series.

1835. London: Henry Colburn. Two volumes. With a new preface and emendations. See Introduction. Published as one of Colburn's Modern Standard Novelists.

1839. London: Henry Colburn. Two volumes. A reprint of the 1835 edition.

1840. Volume two of the first edition of Bulwer's *Collected Works*. 10 volumes. London: Saunders and Otley. With a new preface and further emendations. See Introduction. All subsequent editions have returned to this text as their standard.

1849. London: Chapman and Hall. One volume. With an "Advertisement."

1873. Volume seven of the Knebworth edition of the *Collected Works*. 37 volumes. London: G. Routledge and Sons. Reprints the preface and text of 1840.

PELHAM;

OR, THE

ADVENTURES OF A GENTLEMAN.

" Je suis peu sévère, mais sage—
" Philosophe, mais amoureux—
" Mon art est de me rendre heureux,
" J'y réussis—en faut-il davantage ?"

" A complete gentleman, who, according to Sir Fopling, ought
to dress well, dance well, fence well, have a genius for love letters,
and an agreeable voice for a chamber."

ETHEREGE.

SECOND EDITION.

IN THREE VOLUMES.
VOL. I.

LONDON :

HENRY COLBURN, NEW BURLINGTON STREET.

1828.

The first epigraph on the title page may be translated thus:

"I am somewhat austere, but sensible; philosophical yet amorous too; my aim is to please myself. I am successful—What more do I need?" The quotation has not been traced.

The second epigraph is from Sir George Etherege's *The Man of Mode,* I, 1, 441–44.

N.B. The asterisk symbol (*) signals a textual note. The textual notes begin on page 459.

PREFACE
TO THE SECOND
EDITION OF *PELHAM*

I believe if we were to question every author upon the subject of his literary grievances, we should find that the most frequent of all complaints, was less that of being unappreciated, than that of being misunderstood. None of us write perhaps without some secret object, for which, the world cares not a straw: and while each reader fixes his peculiar moral upon a book, no one, by any chance, hits upon that which the author had in his own heart designed to inculcate. It is this impression, in my individual case, that calls forth for the present edition of "PELHAM," that prefatory explanation, which I deemed it superfluous to place to the first.

It is a beautiful part in the economy of this world, that nothing is without its use; every weed in the great thoroughfares of life, has a honey, which observation can easily extract; and we may glean no unimportant wisdom from folly itself, if we distinguish while we survey, and satirize while we share it. It is in this belief that these volumes have their origin. I have not been willing that even the common-places of society should afford neither a record nor a moral; and it is therefore, from the common-places of society that the materials of this novel have been wrought. By treating trifles naturally, they may be rendered amusing, and that which adherence to *Nature* renders amusing, the same cause also may render instructive: for Nature is the source of all morals, and the enchanted well, from which not a single drop can be taken, that has not the power of curing some of our diseases.

I have drawn for the hero of my Work, such a person as seemed to me best fitted to retail the opinions and customs of the class and age to which he belongs; a personal combination of antitheses—a fop and a philosopher, a voluptuary and a moralist—a trifler in appearance, but rather one to whom trifles are instructive, than one to whom trifles are natural—an Aristippus[1] on a limited scale, accustomed to draw sage conclusions from the follies he adopts, and while professing himself a votary of Pleasure, in reality a disciple of Wisdom. Such a character I have found it more difficult to portray than to conceive: I have found it more difficult still, because I have with it nothing in common,[2] except the taste for observation, and some experience in the same scenes in which it has been cast; and it will readily be supposed that it is no easy matter to survey occurrences the most familiar, through a vision, as it were essentially and perpetually different from that through which oneself has been accustomed to view them. This difficulty in execution, will perhaps be my excuse in failure, and some additional indulgence may be reasonably granted to an author who has rarely found in the egotisms of his hero, a vent for his own.

To the narrator of the following "Adventure," I have not scrupled to attribute, even to a degree which some (perhaps with too literal a judgment) have censured as excessive, the fopperies and flippancies of those respectable individuals, classed under the common appellation of *Dandy:* first, because of that class my hero is, albeit an unworthy, a devoted member; and my Novel professes to describe manners, not as they ought to be, but as they are. Secondly, because I designed to show that even with the most appropriate occupations of the said illustrious individuals, a taste for knowledge may be advantageously combined—and that imbecility and prejudice are, though frequent, by no means necessary ingredients in the composition of a fine gentleman, even though his nostril be delicate in perfumes, and his taste oracular in dress. Thirdly, and principally, because with the generality of those into whose hands a novel upon manners is likely to fall, the lighter and less obvious the method in which reflection is conveyed, the greater is its chance to be received without distaste and remembered without aversion. Nor have I indulged in frivolities for the sake of the frivolity: under that which has most the semblance of levity I have often been the most diligent in my endeavours to

---

1. Aristippus (425?–366? B.C.): Greek philosopher, founder of the Cyrenaic School.

2. I regret extremely that by this remark I should be necessitated to relinquish the flattering character I have for so many months borne, and to undeceive not a few of my most indulgent critics, who in reviewing my work have literally considered the Author and the Hero one flesh. "We have only," said one of them, "to complain of the Author's egotisms; he is perpetually talking of himself!"—Poor gentleman! from the first page to the last, the Author never utters a syllable. [B-L]

inculate the substances of truth. The shallowest stream, whose bed every passenger imagines he surveys, may deposit *some* golden grains on the plain through which it flows; and we may weave flowers not only *into* an idle garland, but, like the thyrsus of the ancients, *over* a sacred weapon. I have dwelt the longer upon this point, because it is one to which the most frequent animadversion has been attracted. My other faults as an author I will not attempt to excuse. I consider, on the contrary, that the best return I can make for the general liberality and kindness of criticism which I have received is—frankly to confess them, and to leave in that present confession a hostage for future improvement. It now only remains for me to add my hope that this edition will present the "ADVENTURES OF A GENTLEMEN" in a less imperfect shape than the last, and in the words of the erudite and memorable Joshua Barnes[3]—"So to begin my intended discourse, if not altogether true, yet not wholly vain, nor perhaps deficient in what may exhilarate a witty fancy, or inform a bad moralist."

THE AUTHOR

October, 1828.

---

3. In the Preface to his Gerania. [B-L] Joshua Barnes (1654–1712): English scholar and antiquarian, author of the imaginary voyage *Gerania* (1675).

VOLUME ONE

CHAPTER I

Où peut-on être mieux qu'au sein de sa famille?
French Song[1]

I AM AN ONLY CHILD. MY FATHER WAS THE YOUNGER son of one of our oldest earls; my mother, the dowerless daughter of a Scotch peer. Mr. Pelham was a moderate whig, and gave sumptuous dinners; —Lady Frances was a woman of taste, and particularly fond of diamonds and old china.

Vulgar people know nothing of the necessaries required in good society, and the credit they give is as short as their pedigree. Six years after my birth, there was an execution in our house. My mother was just setting off on a visit to the Duchess of D———; she declared it was impossible to go without her diamonds. The chief of the bailiffs declared it was impossible to trust them out of his sight. The matter was compromised—the bailiff went with my mother to C———, and was introduced as *my tutor*. "A man of singular merit," whispered my mother, "but *so* shy!" Fortunately, the bailiff was abashed, and by losing his impudence he kept the secret. At the end of the week, the diamonds went to the jeweller's, and Lady Frances wore paste.

I think it was about a month afterwards that a sixteenth cousin left my mother twenty thousand pounds. "It will just pay off our most importunate creditors, and equip me for Melton,"[2] said Mr. Pelham.

"It will just redeem my diamonds, and refurnish the house," said Lady Frances.

The latter alternative was chosen. My father went down to run his last horse at Newmarket, and my mother received nine hundred people in a Turkish tent. Both were equally fortunate, the *Greek* and the *Turk;* my father's horse *lost,* in consequence of which he pocketed five thousand pounds; and my mother looked so charming as a Sultana, that Seymour Conway fell desperately in love with her.

---

1. Translation of epigraph: "Where can one better be than in the bosom of his family?"

2. Melton: a great sporting center, especially for foxhunting and cockfighting.

Mr. Conway had just caused two divorces; and of course, all the women in London were dying for him—judge then of the pride which Lady Frances felt at his addresses. The end of the season was unusually dull, and my mother, after having looked over her list of engagements, and ascertained that she had none remaining worth staying for, agreed to elope with her new lover.

The carriage was at the end of the square. My mother, for the first time in her life, got up at six o'clock. Her foot was on the step, and her hand next to Mr. Conway's heart, when she remembered that her favourite china monster and her French dog were left behind. She insisted on returning—re-entered the house, and was coming down stairs with one under each arm, when she was met by my father and two servants. My father's valet had discovered the flight (I forget how), and awakened his master.

When my father was convinced of his loss, he called for his dressing-gown—searched the garret and the kitchen—looked in the maids' drawers and the cellaret—and finally declared he was distracted. I have heard that the servants were quite melted by his grief, and I do not doubt it in the least, for he was always celebrated for his skill in private theatricals. He was just retiring to vent his grief in his dressing-room, when he met my mother. It must altogether have been an awkward *rencontre*,* and, indeed, for my father, a remarkably unfortunate occurrence; for* Seymour Conway was immensely rich, and the damages would, no doubt, have been proportionably high. Had they met each other alone, the affair might easily have been settled, and Lady Frances gone off in tranquillity;—those d——d* servants are always in the way!

I have, however, often thought that it was better for me that the affair ended thus,—as I know, from many instances, that it is frequently exceedingly inconvenient to have one's mother divorced.*

I have observed that the distinguishing trait of people accustomed to good society, is a calm, imperturbable quiet, which pervades all their actions and habits, from the greatest to the least: they eat in quiet, move in quiet, live in quiet, and lose their wife, or even their money, in quiet; while low persons cannot take up either a spoon or an affront without making such an amazing noise about it. To render this observation good, and to return to the intended elopement, nothing farther was said upon that event. My father introduced Conway to Brookes's,[3] and invited him to dinner twice a week for a whole twelvemonth.

---

3. Brookes's: a famous club in St. James's Street.

Not long after this occurrence, by the death of my grandfather, my uncle succeeded to the title and estates of the family. He was, as people justly* observed, rather an odd man: built schools for peasants, forgave poachers, and diminished his farmers' rents; indeed, on account of these* and similar eccentricities, he was thought a fool by some, and a madman by others. However, he was not quite destitute of natural feeling; for he paid my father's debts, and established us in the secure enjoyment of our former splendour. But this piece of generosity, or justice, was done in the most unhandsome manner: he obtained a promise from my father to retire from Brookes's,* and relinquish the turf; and he prevailed upon my mother to take* an aversion to diamonds, and an indifference to china monsters.

CHAPTER II

Doctrina sed vim promovet insitam
Rectique cultus pectora roborant.
                                    HORAT[1]*
Tell arts they have no soundness,
    But vary by esteeming;
Tell schools they want profoundness,
    And stand too much on seeming.
If arts and schools reply,
Give arts and schools the lie.
                    The Soul's Errand

AT TEN YEARS OLD I WENT TO ETON. I HAD BEEN educated till that period by my mother, who, being distantly related to Lord———, (who had published "Hints upon the Culinary Art"), imagined she possessed an hereditary claim to literary distinction. History was her great *forte;* for she had read all the historical romances of the day, and history accordingly I had been carefully taught.

---

1. "Instruction increases inborn worth, and right discipline strengthens the heart" (Horace *Carmen* 4.433–34). The English epigraph, below, is actually from Sir Walter Raleigh's poem "The Lie," lines 61–66.

I think at this moment I see my mother before me, reclining on her sofa, and repeating to me some story about Queen Elizabeth and Lord Essex; then telling me, in a languid voice, as she sank back with the exertion, of the blessings of a literary taste, and admonishing me never to read above half an hour at a time for fear of losing my health.

Well, to Eton I went; and the second day I had been there, I was half killed for refusing, with all the pride of a Pelham, to wash tea-cups. I was rescued from the clutches of my tyrant by a boy not much bigger than myself, but reckoned the best fighter, for his size, in the whole school. His name was Reginald Glanville: from that period, we became inseparable, and our friendship lasted all the time he stayed at Eton, which was within a year of my own departure for Cambridge.

His father was a baronet, of a very ancient and wealthy family; and his mother was a woman of some talent and more ambition. She made her house one of the most *recherché** in London. Seldom seen at large assemblies, she was eagerly sought after in the *well winnowed soirées* of the elect. Her wealth, great as it was, seemed the least prominent ingredient of her establishment. There was in it no uncalled for ostentation—no purse-proud vulgarity—no cringing to great, and no patronizing condescension to little people; even the Sunday newspapers could not find fault with her, and the querulous wives of younger brothers could only sneer and be silent.

"It is an excellent connection," said my mother, when I told her of my friendship with Reginald Glanville, "and will be of more use to you than many of greater apparent consequence. Remember, my dear, that in all the friends you make at present, you look to the advantage you can derive from them hereafter; that is what we call knowledge of the world, and it is to get the knowledge of the world that you are sent to a public school."

I think, however, to my shame, that notwithstanding my mother's instructions, very few prudential considerations were mingled with my friendship for Reginald Glanville. I loved him with a warmth of attachment, which has since surprised even myself.

He was of a very singular character: he used to wander by the river in the bright days of summer, when all else were at play, without any companion but his own thoughts; and these were tinged, even at that early age, with a deep and impassioned melancholy. He was so reserved in his manner, that it was looked upon as coldness or pride, and was repaid as such by a pretty general dislike. Yet to those he

6

loved, no one could be more open and warm; more watchful to gratify others, more indifferent to gratification for himself: an utter absence of all selfishness, and an eager and active benevolence were indeed the distinguishing traits of his character. I have seen him endure with a careless goodnature the most provoking affronts from boys much less than himself; but directly I, or any other of his immediate friends, was injured or aggrieved, his anger was almost implacable. Although he was of a slight frame, yet early exercise had brought strength to his muscles, and activity to his limbs; and his skill in all athletic exercises whenever (which was but rarely) he deigned to share them, gave alike confidence and success to whatever enterprise his lion-like courage tempted him to dare.*

Such, briefly and imperfectly sketched, was the character of Reginald Glanville—the one, who of all my early companions differed the most from myself; yet the one whom I loved the most, and the one whose future destiny was the most intertwined with my own.

I was in the head class when I left Eton. As I was reckoned an uncommonly well-educated boy, it may not be ungratifying to the admirers of the present system of education to pause here for a moment, and recal what I then knew. I could make twenty* Latin verses in half an hour; I could construe, *without* an English translation, all the easy Latin authors, and many of the difficult ones, *with it:* I could *read* Greek fluently, and even translate it through the medium of a Latin version at the bottom of the page.* I was thought exceedingly clever, for I had only been* eight years acquiring all this fund of information, which, as one can never recal it in the world, you have every right to suppose that I had entirely forgotten before I was five and twenty. As I was never *taught* a syllable of English during this period; as when I once attempted to read Pope's poems, out of school hours, I was laughed at, and called *"a sap;"* as my mother, when I went to school, renounced her own instructions; and as, whatever school-masters may think to the contrary, one learns nothing now-a-days by inspiration: so of everything which relates to English literature, English laws, and English history (with the exception of the said story of Queen Elizabeth and Lord Essex), you have the same right to suppose that I was, at the age of eighteen, when I left Eton, in the profoundest ignorance.[2]

2. It is but just to say that the educational system at public schools is greatly improved since the above was written. And take those great seminaries altogether, it may be doubted whether any institutions more philosophical in theory are better adapted to secure that union of classical tastes with manly habits and honourable sentiments which distinguishes the English sentiment. [B-L; 1840 ed.]

At this age, I was transplanted to Cambridge, where I bloomed for two years in the blue and silver of a fellow commoner of Trinity. At the end of that time (being of royal descent) I became entitled to an *honorary* degree. I suppose the term is in contradistinction to an *honourable* degree, which is obtained by pale men in spectacles and cotton stockings, after thirty-six months of intense application.

I do not exactly remember how I spent my time at Cambridge. I had a piano-forte in my room, and a private billiard-room at a village two miles off; and between these resources, I managed to improve my mind more than could reasonably have been expected. To say truth, the whole place reeked with vulgarity. The men drank beer by the gallon, and eat cheese by the hundred weight—wore jockey-cut coats, and talked slang—rode for wagers, and swore when they lost—smoked in your face, and expectorated on the floor. Their proudest glory was to drive the mail—their mightiest exploit to box with the coachman—their most delicate amour to leer at the barmaid.[3]

It will be believed, that I felt little regret in quitting companions of this description. I went to take leave of our college tutor. "Mr. Pelham," said he, affectionately squeezing me by the hand, "your conduct has been most exemplary; you have not walked wantonly over the college grass-plats, nor set your dog at the proctor—nor driven tandems by day, nor broken lamps by night—nor entered the chapel in order to display your intoxication—nor the lecture-room, in order to caricature the professors. This is the general behaviour of young men of family and fortune; but it has not been yours. Sir, you have been an honour to your college."

Thus closed my academical career. He who does not allow that it passed creditably to my teachers, profitably to myself, and beneficially to the world, is a narrow-minded, and illiterate man, who knows nothing of the advantages of modern education.

---

3. This, at that time, was a character that could only be applied to the gayest, that is, the worst, set at the university—and perhaps now the character may scarcely exist. [B-L; 1840 ed.]

CHAPTER III

Thus does a false ambition rule us,
Thus pomp delude, and folly fool us.
SHENSTONE[1]
An open house, haunted with great resort.
BISHOP HALL'S *Satires*

I LEFT CAMBRIDGE IN A VERY WEAK STATE OF HEALTH;
and as nobody had yet come to London, I accepted the invitation of
Sir Lionel Garrett to pay him a visit at his country seat. Accordingly,
one raw winter's day, full of the hopes of the reviving influence of air
and exercise, I found myself carefully packed up in three great coats,
and on the high road to Garrett Park.

Sir Lionel Garrett was a character very common in England, and,
in describing him, I describe the whole species. He was of an ancient
family, and his ancestors had for centuries resided on their estates in
Norfolk. Sir Lionel, who came to his majority and his fortune at the
same time, went up to London at the age of twenty-one, a raw, uncouth
sort of young man, in* a green coat and lank hair. His friends in
town were of that set whose members are *above ton,* whenever they
do not grasp at its possession, but who, whenever they do, lose at once
their aim and their equilibrium, and fall immeasurably below it.
I mean that set which I call *"the respectable,"* consisting of old peers
of an old school; country gentlemen, who still disdain not to love
their wine and to hate the French; generals who *have served* in the
army; elder brothers who succeed to something besides a mortgage;
and younger brothers who do not mistake their capital for their income. To this set you may add the whole of the baronetage—for I
have remarked that baronets hang together like bees or Scotchmen;
and if I go to a baronet's house, and speak to some one whom I have
not the happiness to know, I always say *"Sir John———."*

---

1. William Shenstone, "The Price of an Equipage," lines 23–24. The second
epigraph is from Joseph Hall, *Satires,* 3, 7, 9.

It was no wonder, then, that to this set belonged Sir Lionel Garrett—no more the youth in a green coat and lank hair, but pinched in, and curled out—abounding in horses and whiskers—dancing all night—lounging all day—the favourite of the old ladies, the Philander of the young.

One unfortunate evening Sir Lionel Garrett was introduced to the celebrated Duchess of D. From that moment his head was turned. Before then, he had always imagined that he was somebody—that he was Sir Lionel Garrett, with a good-looking person and eight thousand a-year; he now knew that he was nobody unless he went to Lady G.'s, and unless he bowed to Lady S. Disdaining all importance derived from himself, it became absolutely necessary to his happiness, that all his importance should be derived solely from his acquaintance with others. He cared not a straw that he was a man of fortune, of family, of consequence; he must be a man of *ton;* or he was an atom, a nonentity, a very worm, and no man. No lawyer at Gray's Inn, no galley slave at the oar, ever worked so hard at his task as Sir Lionel Garrett at *his. Ton,* to a single man, is a thing attainable enough. Sir Lionel was just gaining the envied distinction, when he saw, courted, and married Lady Harriett Woodstock.

His new wife was of a modern and not very rich family, and striving like Sir Lionel for the notoriety of fashion; but of this struggle he was ignorant. He saw her *admitted* into a good society—he imagined she *commanded* it; she was a hanger on—he believed she was a leader. Lady Harriett was crafty and twenty-four—had no objection to be married, nor to change the name of Woodstock for Garrett. She kept up the baronet's mistake till it was too late to repair it.

Marriage did not bring Sir Lionel wisdom. His wife was of the same turn of mind as himself: they might have been great people in the country—they preferred being little people in town. They might *have* chosen *friends* among persons of respectability and rank—they preferred *being* chosen *as acquaintance* by persons of *ton.* Society was their being's end and aim, and the only thing which brought them pleasure was the pain of attaining it. Did I not say truly that I would describe individuals of a common species? Is there one who reads this, who does not recognize that overflowing class of the English population, whose members would conceive it an insult to be thought of sufficient rank to be respectable for what they are?—who take it as an honour that they are made by their acquaintance?—who renounce the ease of living for themselves, for the trouble of living for persons who care not a pin for their existence—who are wretched if they are

10

not dictated to by others—and who toil, groan, travail, through the whole course of life, in order to forfeit their independence?

I arrived at Garrett Park [with] just time enough to dress for dinner. As I was descending the stairs after having performed that ceremony, I heard my own name pronounced by a very soft, lisping voice, "Henry Pelham! dear, what a pretty name. Is he handsome?"

"Rather *distingué** than handsome," was the unsatisfactory reply, couched in a slow, pompous accent, which I immediately recognized to belong to Lady Harriett Garrett.

"Can we make something of him?" resumed the first voice.

"Something!" said Lady Harriett, indignantly; "he will be Lord Glenmorris! and he is son to Lady Frances Pelham."

"Ah," said the lisper, carelessly; "but can he write poetry, and play *proverbes?*"[2]

"No, Lady Harriett," said I, advancing; "but permit me, through you, to assure Lady Nelthorpe that he can admire those who do."

"So you know me then?" said the lisper: "I see we shall be excellent friends;" and disengaging herself from Lady Harriett, she took my arm, and began discussing persons and things, poetry and china, French plays and music, till I found myself beside her at dinner, and most assiduously endeavouring to silence her by the superior engrossments of a *béchamelle de poisson.*

I took the opportunity of the pause, to survey the little circle of which Lady Harriet was the centre. In the first place, there was Mr. Davison, a great political economist, a short, dark, corpulent gentleman, with a quiet, serene, sleepy countenance, which put me exceedingly in mind of my grandmother's arm-chair*; beside him was a quick, sharp little woman, all sparkle and bustle, glancing a small, grey, prying eye round the table, with a most restless activity: this, as Lady Nelthorpe afterwards informed me, was a Miss Trafford, an excellent person for a Christmas in the country, whom every body was dying to have: she was an admirable mimic, an admirable actress, and an admirable reciter; made poetry and shoes, and told fortunes by the cards, which *came actually** true.

There was also Mr. Wormwood,[3] the *noli-me-tangere* of literary lions—an author who sowed his conversation not with flowers but thorns. Nobody could accuse him of the flattery generally imputed

---

2. *Proverbes:* a parlor game involving the execution of a skit to illustrate and develop a proverb.
3. The poet Samuel Rogers (1763–1855), "with his habit of saying ill-natured things, was glanced at in Wormwood" (*The Life, Letters, and Literary Remains of Edward Bulwer, Lord Lytton,* II, 193).

to his species: through the course of a long and varied life, he had never once been known to say a civil thing. He was too much disliked not to be *recherché;** whatever is once notorious, even for being disagreeable, is sure to be courted in England.* Opposite to him sat the really clever, and affectedly pedantic Lord Vincent, one of those persons who have been *"promising young men"* all their lives; who are found till four o'clock in the afternoon in a dressing-gown, with a quarto before them; who go down into the country for six weeks every session, to cram an impromptu reply; and who always have a work in the press which is never to be published.

Lady Nelthorpe herself I had frequently seen. She had some reputation for talent, was exceedingly affected, wrote poetry in albums, ridiculed her husband, who was a fox hunter, and had a great *penchant pour les beaux arts et les beaux hommes.**

There were four or five others of the unknown vulgar, younger brothers, who were good shots and bad matches; elderly ladies, who lived in Baker-street, and liked long whist; and young ones, who never took wine, and said *"Sir."*

I must, however, among this number, except the beautiful Lady Roseville, the most fascinating woman, perhaps, of the day. She was evidently *the* great person there, and, indeed, among all people who paid due deference to *ton,* was always sure to be so every where. I have never seen but one person more beautiful. Her eyes were of the deepest blue; her complexion of the most delicate carnation; her hair of the richest auburn: nor could even Mr. Wormwood detect the smallest fault in the rounded yet slender symmetry of her figure.

Although not above twenty-five, she was in that state in which alone a woman ceases to be a dependant—widowhood. Lord Roseville, who had been dead about two years, had not survived their marriage many months; that period was, however, sufficiently long to allow him to appreciate her excellence, and to testify his sense of it: the whole of his unentailed property, which was very large, he bequeathed to her.

She was very fond of the society of *literati,** though without the pretence of belonging to their order. But her manners constituted her chief attraction: while they were utterly different from those of every one else, you could not, in the least minutiae, discover in what the difference consisted: this is, in my opinion, the real test of perfect breeding. While you are enchanted with the effect, it should possess so little prominency and peculiarity, that you should never be able to guess the cause.

12

"Pray," said Lord Vincent to Mr. Wormwood, "have you been to P——— this year?"

"No," was the answer.

"I have, my lord,"* said Miss Trafford, who never lost an opportunity of slipping in a word.

"Well, and did they make you sleep, as usual, at the Crown, with the same eternal excuse, after having brought you fifty miles from town, of small house—no beds—all engaged—inn close by? Ah, never shall I forget that inn, with its royal name, and its hard beds—

"'Uneasy sleeps a head beneath the Crown!' "[4]

"Ha, ha! Excellent!" cried Miss Trafford, who was always the first in at the death of a pun. "Yes, indeed they did: poor old Lord Belton, with his rheumatism; and that immense General Grant, with his asthma; together with three 'single men,' and myself, were safely conveyed to that asylum for the destitute."

"Ah! Grant, Grant!" said Lord Vincent, eagerly, who saw another opportunity of whipping in a pun. "He slept there also the same night I did; and when I saw his unwieldly person waddling out of the door the next morning, I said to Temple, 'Well, *that's the largest Grant I ever saw from the Crown.*' "[5]

"Very good," said Wormwood, gravely. "I declare, Vincent, you are growing *quite* witty. Do you remember Jekyl?* Poor fellow, what a really good punster *he* was—not agreeable though—particularly at dinner—no punsters are. Mr. Davison, what is that dish next to you?"

Mr. Davison was a great gourmand: "*Salmi de perdreaux aux truffes,*" replied the political economist.

"Truffles!" said Wormwood, "have *you* been eating any?"

"Yes," said Davison, with unusual energy, "and they are the best I have tasted for a long time."

"Very likely," said Wormwood, with a dejected air. "I am particularly fond of them, but I dare not touch one— truffles are so *very* apoplectic—you, I make no doubt, may eat them in safety."

Wormwood was a tall, meagre man, with a neck a yard long. Davison was, as I have said, short and fat, and made without any apparent neck at all—only head and shoulders, like a cod-fish.

---

4. A parody of a line in *II Henry IV,* III, 1, 31. Punning on famous quotations is one of Lord Vincent's favorite conversational gambits.

5. It was from Mr. J. Smith that Lord Vincent purloined this pun. [B-L] James Smith (1775–1839): English parodist who frequently collaborated with his brother Horace.

Poor Mr. Davison turned perfectly white; he fidgeted about in his chair; cast a look of the most deadly fear and aversion at the fatal dish he had been so attentive to before; and, muttering "apoplectic," closed his lips, and did not open them again all dinner-time.

Mr. Wormwood's object was effected. Two people were silenced and uncomfortable, and a sort of mist hung over the spirits of the whole party. The dinner went on and off, like all other dinners; the ladies retired, and the men drank, and talked indecorums.* Mr. Davison left the room first, in order to look out the word "truffle," in the Encyclopaedia; and Lord Vincent and I went next, "lest (as my companion characteristically observed) that d————d Wormwood should, if we stayed a moment longer, 'send us weeping to our beds.' "[6]

CHAPTER IV

Oh! la belle chose que la Poste!
Lettres De Sévigné[1]
Ay—but who is it?
As You Like it

I HAD MENTIONED TO MY MOTHER MY INTENDED VISIT to Garrett Park, and the second day after my arrival there came the following letter:—

"MY DEAR HENRY,

"I was very glad to hear you were rather better than you had been. I trust you will take great care of yourself. I think flannel waistcoats might be advisable; and, by-the-by, they are very good for the complexion. Apropos of the complexion: I did not like that green* coat you wore when I last saw you—you look best in black—which is a great compliment, for people must be very *distingué** in appearance, in order to do so.

---

6. Richard II, V, 1, 45.

1. "Oh! What a beautiful thing is the Post Office!" (*Letters* of Marie de Rabutin-Chantal, marquise de Sévigné [1626–96]). The second epigraph is misquoted from *As You Like It*, III, 2, 197.

14

"You know, my dear, that those Garretts are in themselves any thing but unexceptionable; you will, therefore, take care not to be *too* intimate; it is, however, a very good house: all* you meet there are worth knowing, for one thing or the other. Remember, Henry, that the acquaintance (*not* the friends) of second or third-rate people are always sure to be good: they are not independent enough to receive whom they like—their whole rank is in their guests: you may be also sure that the *ménage* will, in outward appearance at least, be quite *comme il faut,* and for the same reason. Gain as much knowledge *de l'art culinaire* as you can: it is an accomplishment absolutely necessary. You may also pick up a little acquaintance with metaphysics, if you have any opportunity; that sort of thing is a good deal talked about just at present.

"I hear Lady Roseville is at Garrett Park. You must be particularly attentive to her; you will probably now have an opportunity *de faire votre cour* that may never again happen. In London, she is so much surrounded by all, that she is quite inaccessible to one; besides, there you will have so many rivals. Without flattery to you, I take it for granted, that you are the best looking and most agreeable person at Garrett Park, and it will, therefore, be a most unpardonable fault if you do not make Lady Roseville of the same opinion. Nothing, my dear son, is like a *liaison* (quite innocent of course) with a woman of celebrity in the world. In marriage a man lowers a woman to his own rank; in an *affaire de coeur* he raises himself to her's. I need not, I am sure, after what I have said, press this point any further.

"Write to me and inform me of all your proceedings. If you mention the people who are at Garrett Park, I can tell you the proper line of conduct to pursue with each.

"I am sure that I need not add that I have nothing but your real good at heart, and that I am your very affectionate mother,

"FRANCES PELHAM.

"P.S. Never talk much to young men—remember that it is the women who make a reputation in society."

"Well," said I, when I had read this letter, and adjusted my *best curl,** "my mother is very right, and so now for Lady Roseville."

I went down stairs to breakfast. Miss Trafford and Lady Nelthorpe were in the room talking with great interest, and, on Miss Trafford's part, with still greater vehemence.

"So handsome," said Lady Nelthorpe, as I approached.

15

"Are you talking of me?" said I.

"Oh, you vanity of vanities!" was the answer. "No, we were speaking of a very romantic adventure which has happened to Miss Trafford and myself, and disputing about the hero of it. Miss Trafford declares he is frightful; *I say* that he is beautiful. Now, you know, Mr. Pelham, as to *you*——"

"There can," interrupted I,* "be but one opinion—but the adventure?"

"Is this!" cried Miss Trafford, in a great fright, lest Lady Nelthorpe should, by speaking first, have the pleasure of the narration.—"We were walking, two or three days ago, by the sea-side, picking up shells and talking about the "Corsair,"² when a large fierce—"

"Man!" interrupted I.

"No, *dog,* (renewed Miss Trafford) flew suddenly out of a cave, under a rock, and began growling at dear Lady Nelthorpe and me, in the most savage manner imaginable. He would certainly have torn us to pieces if a very tall—"

"Not so very tall either," said Lady Nelthorpe.

"Dear, how you interrupt one," said Miss Trafford, pettishly; "Well, a very short man, then, wrapped up in a cloak—"

"In a great coat," drawled Lady Nelthorpe. Miss Trafford went on without noticing the emendation,—"had not with incredible rapidity sprung down the rock and—"

"Called him off," said Lady Nelthorpe.

"Yes, called him off," pursued Miss Trafford, looking round for the necessary symptoms of our wonder at this very extraordinary incident.

"What is the most remarkable," said Lady Nelthorpe, "is, that though he seemed from his dress and appearance to be really a gentleman, he never stayed to ask if we were alarmed or hurt—scarcely even looked at us—"

("I don't wonder at *that!*" said Mr. Wormwood, who, with Lord Vincent, had just entered the room;)—"and vanished among the rocks as suddenly as he had appeared."

"Oh, you've seen that fellow, have you?" said Lord Vincent: "so have I, and a devilish queer looking person he is,—

> "'The balls of his broad eyes roll'd in his head,
> And glar'd betwixt a yellow and a red;
> He looked a lion with a gloomy stare,
> And o'er his eyebrows hung his matted hair.'³

---

2. Byron published "The Corsair" in 1814.   3. Unidentified.

Well remembered, and better applied—eh, Mr. Pelham?"

"Really," said I, "I am not able to judge of the application, since I have not seen the hero."

"Oh! it's admirable," said Miss Trafford, "just the description I should have given of him in prose. But pray, where, when, and how did you see him?"

"Your question is religiously mysterious, *tria juncta in uno,*" replied Vincent; "but I will answer it with the simplicity of a Quaker. The other evening I was coming home from one of Sir Lionel's preserves, and had sent the keeper on before in order more undisturbedly to——"

"Con witticisms for dinner," said Wormwood.

"To make out the meaning of Mr. Wormwood's last work," continued Lord Vincent. "My shortest way lay through that churchyard about a mile hence, which is such a lion in this ugly part of the country, because it has three thistles and a tree. Just as I got there, I saw a man suddenly rise from the earth, where he appeared to have been lying; he stood still for a moment, and then (evidently not perceiving me) raised his clasped hands to Heaven, and muttered some words I was not able distinctly to hear. As I approached nearer to him, which I did with no very pleasant sensations, a large black dog, which, till then, had remained *couchant,* sprung towards me with a loud growl,

> " 'Sonat hic de nare canina
> Litera,[4]

as Persius has it. I was too terrified to move—

> " 'Obstupui—steteruntque comæ—'

and I should most infallibly have been converted into dog's meat, if our mutual acquaintance had not started from his reverie, called his dog by the very appropriate name of Terror, and then slouching his hat over his face, passed rapidly by me, dog and all. I did not recover the fright for an hour and a quarter. I walked—ye gods, how I *did* walk—no wonder, by the by, that I *mended* my pace, for as Pliny says truly—

---

4. The Latin tags in this paragraph are, respectively: "Don't you hear the bark of a dog?" (Persius *Satires* 1.109–10); "I was appalled, and my hair stood on end" (Virgil *Aeneid* 2.774 and 3.48); and "Fear is the harshest corrector" (Pliny the Younger *Epistles* 7.17).

Mr. Wormwood had been very impatient during this recital, preparing an attack upon Lord Vincent, when Mr. Davison entering suddenly, diverted the assault.

"Good God!" said Wormwood, dropping his roll, "how very ill you look to-day, Mr. Davison; face flushed—veins swelled—oh, those horrid truffles! Miss Trafford, I'll trouble you for the salt."

CHAPTER V

Be she fairer than the day,
Or the flowery meads in May;
If she be not so to me,
What care I how fair she be?
                    GEORGE WITHERS[1]
It was a great pity, so it was,
That villanous saltpetre should be digged
Out of the bowels of the harmless earth,
Which many a good tall fellow had destroyed.
                    First Part of King Henry IV

SEVERAL DAYS PASSED. I HAD TAKEN PARTICULAR PAINS to ingratiate myself with Lady Roseville, and so far as common acquaintance went, I had no reason to be dissatisfied with my success. Any thing else, I soon discovered, notwithstanding my vanity, (which made no inconsiderable part in the composition of Henry Pelham) was quite out of the question. Her mind was wholly of a different mould from my own. She was like a being, not perhaps of a better, but of another world than myself; we had not one thought or opinion

5. Most of the quotations from Latin and French authors, interspersed throughout the work, will be translated for the convenience of the general reader; but exceptions will be made where such quotations (as is sometimes the case when from the mouth of Lord Vincent) merely contain a play upon words, which are pointless, out of the language employed, or which only iterate or illustrate, by a characteristic pedantry, the sentence that precedes or follows them. [B-L; 1840 ed.]

1. George Withers (1588–1667), English poet and pamphleteer, "The Lover's Resolution." The second epigraph is from *I Henry IV*, I, 3, 59–62.

in common; we looked upon things with a totally different vision; I was soon convinced that she was of a nature exactly contrary to what was generally believed—she was any thing but the mere mechanical woman of the world. She possessed great sensibility, and even romance of temper, strong passions, and still stronger imagination; but over all these deeper recesses of her character, the extreme softness and languor of her manners, threw a veil which no superficial observer could penetrate. There were times when I could believe that she was inwardly restless and unhappy; but she was too well versed in the arts of concealment, to suffer such an appearance to be more than momentary.

I must own that I consoled myself very easily for my want, in this particular instance, of that usual good fortune which attends me *auprès des dames;** the fact was, that I had another object in pursuit. All the men at Sir Lionel Garrett's were keen sportsmen. Now, shooting is an amusement I was never particularly partial to. I was first disgusted with that species of rational recreation at a *battue,* where, instead of bagging anything, *I was nearly bagged,* having been inserted, like wine in an ice pail, in a wet ditch for three hours, during which time my hat had been twice shot at for a pheasant, and my leather gaiters once for a hare; and to crown all, when these several mistakes were discovered, my intended exterminators, instead of apologizing for having shot at me, were quite disappointed at having missed.

Seriously, that same shooting is a most babarous amusement, only fit for majors in the army, and royal dukes, and that sort of people; *the mere walking* is bad enough, but embarrassing one's arms moreover, with a gun, and one's legs with turnip tops, exposing oneself to the mercy of bad shots and the atrocity of good, seems to me only a state of painful fatigue, enlivened by the probability of being killed.

This digression is meant to signify, that I never joined the single men and double Mantons that went in and off amongst Sir Lionel Garrett's preserves. I used, instead, to take long walks by myself, and found, like virtue, my own reward, in the additional health and strength these diurnal exertions produced me.

One morning, chance threw into my way *une** bonne fortune,* which I took care to improve. From that time the family of a Farmer Sinclair, (one of Sir Lionel's tenants) was alarmed by strange and supernatural noises: one apartment in especial, occupied by a female member of the household, was allowed, even by the clerk of the parish, a very bold man, and a bit of a sceptic, to be haunted; the

19

windows of that chamber were wont to open and shut, thin airy voices confabulate therein, and dark shapes hover *thereout,* long after the fair occupant had, with the rest of the family, retired to repose. But the most unaccountable thing was the fatality which attended *me,* and seemed to mark me out, *nolens volens,* for an untimely death. *I,* who had so carefully kept out of the way of gunpowder as a *sportsman,* very narrowly escaped being twice shot as a *ghost.* This was but a poor reward for a walk more than a mile long, in nights by no means of cloudless climes and starry skies; accordingly I resolved to "give up the ghost"[2] in earnest, rather than in metaphor, and to pay my last visit and adieus to the mansion of Farmer Sinclair. The night on which I executed this resolve was rather memorable in my future history.

The rain had fallen so heavily during the day, as to render the road to the house almost impassable, and when it was time to leave, I inquired with very considerable emotion, whether there was not an easier way to return. The answer was satisfactory, and my last nocturnal visit at Farmer Sinclair's concluded.

CHAPTER VI

Why sleeps he not, when others are at rest?[1]
BYRON

ACCORDING TO THE EXPLANATION I HAD RECEIVED, THE road I was now to pursue was somewhat longer, but much better, than that which I generally took. It was to lead me home through the churchyard of ————, the same, by the by, which Lord Vincent had particularized in his anecdote of the mysterious stranger. The night was clear, but windy; there were a few light clouds passing rapidly over the moon, which was at her full, and shone through the frosty

---

2. Cloudless climes and starry skies: Byron, "She Walks in Beauty," line 2. The phrase "give up the ghost," a common one, appears in Job 14:10 and John 19:30.

1. Byron, *Lara,* 1, 147.

air, with all that cold and transparent brightness so peculiar to our northern winters. I walked briskly on till I came to the churchyard; I could not then help pausing (notwithstanding my total deficiency in all romance) to look for a few moments at the exceeding beauty of the scene around me. The church itself was extremely old, and stood alone and grey, in the rude simplicity of the earliest form of gothic architecture: two large dark yew-trees drooped on each side over tombs, which from their size and decorations, appeared to be the last possession of some quondam lords of the soil. To the left, the ground was skirted by a thick and luxuriant copse of evergreens, in the front of which stood one tall, naked oak, stern and leafless, a very token of desolation and decay; there were but few grave stones scattered about, and these were, for the most part, hidden by the long wild grass which wreathed and climbed round them. Over all, the blue skies and still moon shed that solemn light, the effect of which, either on the scene or the feelings, it is so impossible to describe.

I was just about to renew my walk, when a tall, dark figure, wrapped up, like myself, in a large French cloak, passed slowly along from the other side of the church, and paused by the copse I have before mentioned. I was shrouded at that moment from his sight by one of the yew trees; he stood still only for a few moments; he then flung himself upon the earth, and sobbed, audibly even at the spot where I was standing. I was in doubt whether to wait longer or to proceed; my way lay just by him, and it might be dangerous to interrupt so substantial an apparition. However, my curiosity was excited, and my feet were half frozen, two cogent reasons for proceeding; and, to say truth, I was never very much frightened by any thing dead or alive.

Accordingly I left my obscurity, and walked slowly onwards. I had not got above three paces before the figure rose, and stood erect and motionless before me. His hat had fallen off, and the moon shone full upon his countenance; it was not the wild expression of intense anguish which dwelt in those hueless and sunken features; nor their quick change to ferocity and defiance, as his eyes fell upon me, which made me start back and feel my heart stand still! Notwithstanding the fearful ravages graven in that countenance, then so brilliant with the graces of boyhood, I recognized, at one glance, those still noble and chiselled features. It was Reginald Glanville who stood before me! I recovered myself instantly; I threw myself towards him, and called him by his name. He turned hastily; but I would not suffer him to escape; I put my hand upon his arm, and drew him towards me.

"Glanville!" I exclaimed, "it is I! it is your old—old friend, Henry Pelham. Good God! have I met you at last, and in such a scene?"

Glanville shook me from him in an instant, covered his face with his hands, and sunk down with one wild cry, which went fearfully through that still place, upon the spot from which he had but just arisen. I knelt beside him; I took his hand; I spoke to him in every endearing term that I could think of; and roused and excited as my feelings were, by so strange and sudden a meeting, I felt my tears involuntarily falling over the hand which I held in my own. Glanville turned; he looked at me for one moment, as if fully to recognize me: and then throwing himself in my arms, wept like a child.

It was but for a few minutes that this weakness lasted; he rose suddenly—the whole expression of his countenance was changed—the tears still rolled in large drops down his cheeks, but the proud, stern character which the features had assumed, seemed to deny the feelings which that feminine weakness had betrayed.

"Pelham," he said, "*you* have seen me thus; I had hoped that no living eye would—this is the last time in which I shall indulge this folly. God bless you—we shall meet again—and this night shall then seem to you like a dream."

I would have answered, but he turned swiftly, passed in one moment through the copse, and in the next had utterly* disappeared.

CHAPTER VII

You reach a chilling chamber, where you dread
Damps—

CRABBE's *Borough*[1]

I COULD NOT SLEEP THE WHOLE OF THAT NIGHT, AND the next morning, I set off early, with the resolution of discovering where Glanville had taken up his abode; it was evident from his having been so frequently seen, that it must be in the immediate neighbourhood.

---

1. Crabbe, *The Borough*, letter 11, "Inns."

I went first to Farmer Sinclair's; they had often remarked him, but could give me no other information. I then proceeded towards the coast; there was a small public house belonging to Sir Lionel close by the sea shore; never had I seen a more bleak and dreary prospect than that which stretched for miles around this miserable *cabaret*.* How an innkeeper could live there is a mystery to me at this day—I should have imagined it a spot upon which anything but a sea-gull or a Scotchman would have starved.

"Just the sort of place, however," thought I, "to hear something of Glanville." I went into the house; I inquired, and heard that a strange gentleman *had* been lodging for the last two or three weeks at a cottage about a mile further up the coast. Thither I bent my steps; and after having met two crows, and one officer on the preventive service,[2] I arrived safely at my new destination.

It was a house very little better, in outward appearance, than the wretched hut I had just left, for I observe in all situations, and in *all* houses, that "the public" is not too well served. The situation was equally lonely and desolate; the house, which belonged to an individual, half fisherman and half smuggler, stood in a sort of bay, between two tall, rugged, black cliffs. Before the door hung various nets, to dry beneath the genial warmth of a winter's sun; and a broken boat, with its keel uppermost, furnished an admirable habitation for a hen and her family, who appeared to receive *en pension,* an old clerico-bachelor-looking raven. I cast a suspicious glance at the last-mentioned personage, which hopped towards me with a very hostile appearance, and entered the threshold with a more rapid step, in consequence of sundry apprehensions of a premeditated assault.

"I understand," said I, to an old, dried, brown female, who looked like a resuscitated red-herring, "that a gentleman is lodging here."

"No, Sir," was the answer: "he left us this morning."

The reply came upon me like a shower bath; I was both chilled and stunned by so unexpected a shock. The old woman, on my renewing my inquiries, took me up stairs, to a small, wretched room, to which the damps literally clung. In one corner was a flock-bed, still unmade, and opposite to it, a three-legged stool, a chair, and an antique carved oak table, a donation perhaps from some squire in the neighbourhood; on this last were scattered fragments of writing paper, a cracked cup half full of ink, a pen, and a broken ramrod. As I mechanically took up the latter, the woman said, in a charming *patois,*

---

2. Preventive service: the Coast Guard.

which I shall translate, since I cannot do justice to the original: "The gentleman, Sir, said he came here for a few weeks to shoot; he brought a gun, a large dog, and a small portmanteau.* He used to spend all the mornings in the fens, though he must have been but a poor shot, for he seldom brought home anything; and we fear, Sir, that he was rather out of his mind, for he used to go out alone at night, and stay sometimes till morning. However, he was quite quiet, and behaved *to us* like a gentleman; so it was no business of ours, only my husband does think———"

"Pray," interrupted I, "why did he leave you so suddenly?"

"Lord, Sir, I don't know! but he told us for several days past that he should not stay over the week, and so we were not surprised when he left us this morning at seven o'clock. Poor gentleman, my heart bled for him when I saw him look so pale and ill."

And here I *did* see the good woman's eyes fill with tears: but she wiped them away, and took advantage of the additional persuasion they gave to her natural whine to say, "If, Sir, you know of any young gentleman who likes fen-shooting, and wants a nice, pretty, quiet apartment—"

"I will certainly recommend this," said I.

"You see it at present," rejoined *the landlady*, "quite in a litter like: but it is really a sweet place in summer."

"Charming," said I, with a cold shiver, hurrying down the stairs, with a pain in my ear, and the rheumatism in my shoulder.

"And this," thought I, "was Glanville's residence for nearly a month! I wonder he did not exhale into a vapour, or moisten into a green damp."

I went home by the churchyard. I paused on the spot where I had last seen him. A small gravestone rose over the mound of earth on which he had thrown himself; it was perfectly simple. The date of the year and month (which showed that many weeks had not elapsed since the death of the deceased) and the initials G. D. were all that was engraven upon the stone.* Beside this tomb was one of a more pompous description, to the memory of a Mrs. Douglas, which had with the simple tumulus nothing in common, unless the initial letter of the surname corresponding with the latter initial on the neighbouring gravestone, might authorize any connection between them, not supported by that similitude of style usually found in the cenotaphs of the same family: the one, indeed, might have covered the grave of a humble villager—the other, the resting-place of the lady of the manor.

I found, therefore, no clue for the labyrinth of surmise: and I went home, more vexed and disappointed with my day's expedition than I liked to acknowledge to myself.

Lord Vincent met me in the hall. "Delighted to see you," said he, "I have just been to ———, (the nearest town) in order to discover what sort of savages abide there. Great preparations for a ball—all the tallow candles in the town are bespoken—and I heard a most uncivilized fiddle,

> "'Twang short and sharp, like the shrill swallow's cry.'[3]

The one milliner's shop was full of fat squiresses, buying muslin ammunition, to make the *ball go off;* and the attics, even at four o'clock, were thronged with rubicund damsels, who were already, as Shakspeare says of waves in a storm,

> "'Curling their monstrous heads.' "[4]

CHAPTER VIII

Jusqu'au revoir le ciel vous tienne tous en joie.
MOLIÈRE[1]

I WAS NOW PRETTY WELL TIRED OF GARRETT PARK. LADY Roseville was going to H—t—d, where I also had an invitation. Lord Vincent meditated an excursion to Paris. Mr. Davison had already departed. Miss Trafford had been gone, God knows how long, and I was not at all disposed to be left, like "the last rose of summer,"[2] in single blessedness at Garrett Park. Vincent, Wormwood, and myself, all agreed to leave on the same day.

The morning of our departure arrived. We sat down to breakfast as usual. Lord Vincent's carriage was at the door; his groom was walking about his favourite saddle horse.

---

3. Unidentified.

4. *II Henry IV*, III, 1, 23.

1. "Heaven keep you merry till we meet again" (*Tartuffe,* V, 4). [Bulwer-Lytton's translation; 1840 ed.]

2. Thomas Moore, "'Tis the Last Rose."

"A beautiful *mare* that is of your's," said I, carelessly looking at it, and reaching across the table to help myself to the *pâté de foie gras.*

"Mare!" exclaimed the incorrigible punster, delighted with my mistake: "I thought that you would have been better acquainted with your *propria quae maribus.*"[3]

"'Humph!" said Wormwood, "when I look at you I am always at least reminded of the *as in praesenti!*"

Lord Vincent drew up and looked unutterable anger. Wormwood went on with his dry toast, and Lady Roseville, who that morning had, for a wonder, come down to breakfast, good naturedly took off the bear. Whether or not his ascetic nature was somewhat mollified* by the soft smiles and softer voice of the beautiful countess, I cannot pretend to say; but he certainly entered into a conversation with her, not much rougher than that of a less gifted individual might have been. They talked of literature, Lord Byron, conversaziones, and Lydia White.[4]

"Miss White," said Lady Roseville, "has not only the best command of language herself, but she gives language to other people. Dinner parties, usually so stupid, are, at her house, quite delightful. I have actually seen English people look happy, and one or two even almost natural."

"Ah!" said Wormwood, "that is indeed rare. With us every thing is assumption. We are still exactly like the English suitor to Portia, in the Merchant of Venice. We take our doublet from one country, our hose from another, and our behaviour every where. Fashion with us is like the man in one of Le Sage's novels, who was constantly changing his servants, and yet had but one suit of livery, which every new comer, whether he was tall or short, fat or thin, was obliged to wear. We adopt manners, however incongruous and ill suited to our nature, and thus we always seem awkward and constrained. But Lydia White's *soirées* are indeed agreeable. I remember the last time I dined there we were six in number, and though we were not blessed with the company of Lord Vincent, the conversation was without 'let or flaw.'[5] Every one, even S——— ———, said good things."

---

3. Parody of Quintilian *Institutio oratoria* 5.12.18. The phrase puns on *maribus*: "what is proper to the ocean [*mares*]." The Latin phrase, below, is also a parody, this time of an everyday expression meaning "cash down." The pun is on *as.*

4. Written before the death of that lady. [B-L] Lydia White died in 1827 at her home in Park Street, after a successful career as one of the most famous of the Regency hostesses.

5. Perhaps recalling *Love's Labour's Lost*, V, 2, 415.

26

"'Indeed!" cried Lord Vincent; "and pray, Mr. Wormwood, what did you say?"

"Why," answered the poet, glancing with a significant sneer over Vincent's somewhat inelegant person, "I thought of your lordship's figure, and said—*grace!*"

"Hem—hem!—'*Gratia malorum tam infida est quam ipsi,*' as Pliny says,"[6] muttered Lord Vincent, getting up hastily, and buttoning his coat.

I took the opportunity of the ensuing pause to approach Lady Roseville, and whisper my adieus. She was kind and even warm to me in returning them; and pressed me, with something marvellously like sincerity, to be sure to come and see her directly she returned to London. I soon discharged the duties of my remaining farewells, and in less than half an hour, was more than a mile distant from Garrett Park and its inhabitants. I can't say that for one, who, like me,* is fond of being made a great deal of, that there is any thing very delightful in those visits into the country. It may be all well enough for married people, who, from the mere fact of *being* married, are always entitled to certain consideration, put—*par exemple*—into a bed-room, a little larger than a dog kennel, and accommodated with a looking-glass, that does not distort one's features like a paralytic stroke. But we single men suffer a plurality of evils and hardships, in entrusting ourselves to the casualties of rural hospitality. We are thrust up into any attic repository—exposed to the mercy of rats, and the incursions of swallows. Our lavations are performed in a cracked basin, and we are so far removed from human assistance, that our very bells sink into silence before they reach half way down the stairs. But two days before I left Garrett Park, I myself saw an enormous mouse run away with my almond paste,[7]* without any possible means of resisting the aggression. Oh! the hardships of a single man are beyond conception; and what is worse, the very misfortune of being single deprives one of all sympathy. "A single man can do this, and a single man ought to do that, and a single man may be put here, and a single man may be sent there," are maxims that I have been in the habit of hearing constantly inculcated and never disputed during my whole life; and so, from our fare and treatment being coarse in all matters, they have at last grown to be all matters in course.

6. "The thankfulness of a bad man is as treacherous as himself" (Pliny the Younger *Epistles* 1.5).

7. A cosmetic used to soften the skin.

CHAPTER IX

Therefore to France.
Henry IV[1]

I WAS REJOICED TO FIND MYSELF AGAIN IN LONDON. I
went to my father's house in Grosvenor-square. All the family, viz. he
and my mother, were down at H—t—d; and, *malgré** my aversion to
the country, I thought I might venture as far as Lady S———'s for a
couple of days. Accordingly, to H—t—d I went. That is really a noble
house—such a hall—such a gallery. I found my mother in the drawing-
room, admiring the picture of his late Majesty. She was leaning on
the arm of a tall, fair young man. "Henry," said she, (introducing
me to him) "do you remember your old schoolfellow, Lord George
Clinton?"

"Perfectly," said I, (though I remembered nothing about him) and
we shook hands in the most cordial manner imaginable. By the way,
there is no greater bore than being called upon to recollect men, with
whom one had been at school some ten years back. In the first place,
if they were not in one's own set, one most likely scarcely knew them
to speak to; and, in the second place, if they *were* in one's own set,
they are sure to be entirely opposite to the nature we have since acquired: for I scarcely ever knew an instance of the companions of
one's boyhood being agreeable to the tastes of one's manhood: a strong
proof of the folly of common people, who send their sons to Eton and
Harrow to *form connections.*

Clinton was on the eve of setting out upon his travels. His intention was to stay a year at Paris, and he was full of the blissful expectations the idea of that city had conjured up. We remained together
all the evening, and took a prodigious fancy to one another. Long
before I went to bed, he had perfectly inoculated me with his own
ardour for continental adventures; and, indeed, I had half promised
to accompany him. My mother, when I first told her of my travelling

---

1. *Henry V*, II, 3, 58, is misquoted.

28

intentions, was in despair, but by degrees she grew reconciled to the idea.

"Your health will improve by a purer air," said she, "and your pronunciation of French is, at present, any thing but correct. Take care of yourself, therefore, my dear son, and pray lose no time in engaging Coulon[2] as your *maître de danse.*"

My father gave me his blessing, and a check on his banker. Within three days I had arranged every thing with Clinton, and, on the fourth, I returned with him to London. From thence we set off to Dover—embarked—dined, for the first time in our lives, on French ground—were astonished to find so little difference between the two countries, and still more so at hearing even the little children talk French so well[3]—proceeded to Abbeville—there poor Clinton fell ill: for several days we were delayed in that abominable town, and then Clinton, by the advice of the doctors, returned to England. I went back with him as far as Dover, and then, impatient at my loss of time, took no rest, night or day, till I found myself at Paris.

Young, well-born, tolerably good-looking, and never utterly destitute of money, nor grudging whatever enjoyment it could produce,* I entered Paris with the ability and the resolution to make the best of those *beaux jours* which so rapidly glide from our possession.

CHAPTER X

Seest thou how gayly my young maister goes?
BISHOP HALL's *Satires*[1]
Qui vit sans folie, n'est pas si sage qu'il croit.
LA ROCHEFOUCAULT

I LOST NO TIME IN PRESENTING MY LETTERS OF INTRO-duction, and they were as quickly acknowledged by invitations to

---

2. Coulon was a famous *maître de danse.* He later moved to London, taught in Marlborough Street, and published the widely used *Coulon's Handbook* of fashionable dances.

3. See Addison's Travels for this idea. [B-L]

1. Joseph Hall, *Satires*, 3, 7, 1. The French epigraph may be translated: "Who lives without folly is not so wise as he thinks." (François, duc de la Rochefoucauld, *Maximes* [1665], maxim no. 209). La Rochefoucauld (1630–80) was a moral philosopher, celebrated for his epigrammatic wisdom.

balls and dinners. Paris was full to excess, and of a better description of English than those who usually overflow that reservoir of the world. My first engagement was to dine with Lord and Lady Bennington,[2] who were among the very few English intimate in the best French houses.

On entering Paris I had resolved to set up *"a character;"* for I was always of an ambitious nature, and desirous of being distinguished from the ordinary herd. After various cogitations as to the particular one I should assume, I thought nothing appeared more likely to be remarkable among men,* and therefore pleasing to women, than an egregious coxcomb: accordingly I arranged my hair into ringlets, dressed myself with singular plainness and simplicity (a low person, by the by, would have done just the contrary), and putting on an air of exceeding languor, made my maiden appearance at Lord Bennington's. The party was small, and equally divided between French and English: the former had been all emigrants, and the conversation was chiefly in our own tongue.[3]

I was placed, at dinner, next to Miss Paulding, an elderly young lady, of some notoriety at Paris, very clever, very talkative, and very conceited. A young, pale, ill-natured looking man, sat on her left hand; this was Mr. Aberton, one of the *attachés.*

"Dear me!" said Miss Paulding, "what a pretty chain that is of your's, Mr. Aberton."

"Yes," said the *attaché,** "I know it must be pretty, for I got it at Brequet's,[4] with the watch." (How common people always buy their opinions with their goods, and regulate the height of the former by the mere price or fashion of the latter.)

"Pray, Mr. Pelham," said Miss Paulding, turning to me, "have you got one of Brequet's watches yet?"

"Watch!" said I: *"do* you think *I* could ever wear a watch? I know nothing so plebeian. What can any one, but a man of business, who has nine hours for his counting-house and one for his dinner, ever possibly want to know the time for? An assignation, you will say:

---

2. The originals of Lord and Lady Bennington were Mr. and Mrs. Charles Cunningham, an English couple living in Paris when Bulwer visited there in the early 1820's, and intimate with the best circles. Bulwer struck up a close friendship with Mrs. Cunningham, and they carried on a lively correspondence.

3. The emigrants were Royalist adherents who fled France and the victorious revolutionaries of 1789.

4. Brequet's: the shop of a fashionable French watchmaker.

true, but (here I played with my best ringlet)* if a man is worth having, he is surely worth waiting for!"

Miss Paulding opened her eyes, and Mr. Aberton his mouth. A pretty lively French woman opposite (Madame D'Anville) laughed, and immediately joined in our conversation, which, on my part, was, during the whole dinner, kept up exactly in* the same strain.

"What do you think of our streets?" said the old, yet still animated Madame de G————s. "You will not find them, I fear, so agreeable for walking as the *trottoirs* in London."

"Really," I answered, "I have only been once out in your streets, at least *à pied,* since my arrival, and then I was nearly perishing for want of help."

"What do you mean?" said Madame D'Anville.

"Why, I fell into that intersecting stream which *you* call a kennel, and *I* a river. Pray, Mr. Aberton, what do you think I did in that dangerous dilemma?"

"Why, got out again as fast as you could," said the literal *attaché.*

"No such thing, I was too frightened: I *stood still, and screamed for assistance.*"*

Madame D'Anville was delighted, and Miss Paulding astonished. Mr. Aberton muttered to a fat, foolish Lord Luscombe, "What a damnation puppy,"—and every one, even to the old Madame de G————s, looked at me six times as attentively as they had done before.*

As for me, I was perfectly satisfied with the effect I had produced, and I went away the first, in order to give the men an opportunity of abusing me; for whenever the men abuse, the women, to support alike their coquetry and the conversation, think themselves called upon to defend.

The next day I rode into the Champs Elysées. I always valued myself particularly upon my riding, and my horse was both the most fiery and the most beautiful in Paris. The first person I saw was Madame D'Anville. At that moment I was reining in my horse, and conscious, as the wind waved my long curls, that I was looking to the very best advantage, I made my horse bound towards her carriage, which she immediately stopped, and speaking in my natural tone of voice, and without the smallest affectation, I made at once my salutations and my court.

"I am going," said she, "to the Duchesse D————g's this evening—it is *her* night—do come."

"I don't know her," said I.

31

"Tell me your hotel, and I'll send you an invitation before dinner," rejoined Madame D'Anville.

"I lodge," said I, "at the Hôtel de ———, Rue de Rivoli, *au second** at present; next year, I suppose, according to the usual gradations in the life of a *garçon,* I shall be *au troisième:** for here the purse and the person seem to be playing at see-saw—the latter rises as the former descends."

We went on conversing for about a quarter of an hour, in which I endeavoured to make the pretty Frenchwoman believe that all the good opinion I possessed of myself the day before, I had that morning entirely transferred to her account.

As I rode home I met Mr. Aberton, with three or four other men; with that glaring good-breeding, so peculiar to the English, he instantly directed their eyes towards me in one mingled and concentrated stare. *"N'importe,"* thought I, "they must be devilish clever fellows if they can find a single fault either in my horse or myself."

CHAPTER XI

Lud! what a group the motley scene discloses,
False wits, false wives, false virgins, and false spouses.
GOLDSMITH's *Epilogue to the Comedy of the Sisters*[1]

MADAME D'ANVILLE KEPT HER PROMISE—THE INVITATION was duly sent, and accordingly at half past ten to the Rue D'Anjou I drove.

The rooms were already full. Lord Bennington was standing by the door, and close by him, looking exceedingly *distrait,* was my old friend Lord Vincent. They both came towards me at the same moment. "Strive not," thought I, looking at the stately demeanour of the one, and the humourous expression of countenance in the other— "strive not, Tragedy nor Comedy, to engross a Garrick."[2] I spoke first to Lord Bennington, for I knew he would be the sooner dispatched, and then for the next quarter of an hour found myself over-

---

1. Goldsmith, "Epilogue to *The Sister,*" lines 13–14.
2. David Garrick (1717–79): English actor, theater manager, and author.

32

flowed with all the witticisms poor Lord Vincent had for days been obliged to retain. I made an engagement to dine with him at Véry's[3] the next day, and then glided off towards Madame D'Anville.

She was surrounded with men, and talking to each with that vivacity which, in a Frenchwoman, is so graceful, and in an English-woman would be so vulgar. Though her eyes were not directed towards me, she saw me approach by that instinctive perception which all coquets possess, and suddenly altering her seat, made way for me beside her. I did not lose so favourable an opportunity of gaining *her* good graces, and losing those of all the male animals around her. I sunk down on the vacant chair, and contrived, with the most un-abashed affrontery, and yet with the most consummate dexterity, to make every thing that I said pleasing to her, revolting to some one of her attendants. Wormwood himself could not have succeeded better. One by one they dropped off, and we were left alone among the crowd. Then, indeed, I changed the whole tone of my conversa-tion. Sentiment succeeded to satire, and the pretence of feeling to that of affectation. In short, I was so resolved to please that I could scarcely fail to succeed.

In this main object of the evening I was not however solely em-ployed. I should have been very undeserving of that character for observation which I flatter myself I peculiarly deserve, if I had not during the three hours I stayed at Madame D———g's, conned over every person remarkable for any thing, from rank to a ribbon. The duchesse herself was a fair, pretty, clever woman, with manners rather English than French. She was leaning, at the time I paid my respects to her, on the arm of an Italian count, tolerably well known at Paris. Poor O———i! I hear he is just* married. He did not deserve so heavy a calamity!

Sir Henry Millington was close by her, carefully packed up in his coat and waistcoat. Certainly that man is the best padder in Europe.

"Come and sit by me, Millington," cried old Lady Oldtown; "I have a good story to tell you of the Duc de G———e."

Sir Henry, with difficulty, turned round his magnificent head, and muttered out some unintelligible excuse. The fact was, that poor Sir Henry was not that evening *made* to sit down—he had only his *standing up coat* on. Lady Oldtown—heaven knows—is easily consoled. She supplied the place of the dilapidated* baronet with a most superbly mustachioed German.

---

3. Véry's: celebrated restaurant in the Palais Royal.

"Who," said I, to Madame D'Anville, "are those pretty girls in white, talking with such eagerness to Mr. Aberton and Lord Luscombe?"

"What!" said the Frenchwoman, "have you been ten days at Paris and not been introduced to the Miss Carltons? Let me tell you that your reputation among your countrymen at Paris depends solely upon their verdict."

"And upon your favour," added I.

"Ah!" said she, "you *must* have had your origin in France; you have something about you *presque Parisien.*"*

"Pray," said I, (after having duly acknowledged this compliment, the very highest that a Frenchwoman can bestow) "what did you really and candidly think of our countrymen during your residence in England?"

"I will tell you," answered Madame D'Anville; "they are brave, honest, generous, *mais ils sont demi-barbares.*"

CHAPTER XII

Pia mater,
Plus quam se sapere, et virtutibus esse priorem
Vult, et ait propè vera.

HOR. SAT.[1]

Vere mibi festus atras
Eximet curas.

HOR. OD.

THE NEXT MORNING I RECEIVED A LETTER FROM MY mother.

"My dear Henry," began my affectionate and incomparable parent—

"MY DEAR HENRY,   .

---

1. "A doting mother wants him wiser and more virtuous than herself, and says to him what is pretty nearly true" (Horace *Epistles* 1.8.26–27). In the second epigraph Bulwer is punning on *Vere*: "Festive Véry's shall banish my moody cares" (Horace *Carmen* 3.14.13). Bulwer wrongly located the first epigraph.

"You have now fairly entered the world, and though at your age my advice may be but little followed, my experience cannot altogether be useless. I shall, therefore, make no apology for a few precepts, which I hope may tend to make you a wiser and better man.

"I hope, in the first place, that you have left your letter at the ambassador's, and that you will not fail to go there as often as possible. Pay your court in particular to Lady ———. She is a charming person, universally popular, and one of the very few English people to whom one may safely be civil. Apropos, of English civility, you have, I hope, by this time discovered, that you have to assume a very different manner with French people than with our own countrymen: with us, the least appearance of feeling or enthusiasm is certain to be ridiculed every where; but in France, you may venture to seem not quite devoid of all natural sentiments; indeed, if you affect enthusiasm, they will give you credit for genius, and they will place all the qualities of the heart to the account of the head. You know that in England, if you seem desirous of a person's acquaintance you are sure to lose it; they imagine you have some design upon their wives or their dinners; but in France you can never lose by politeness: nobody will call your civility forwardness and pushing. If the Princess De T———, and the Duchesse de D———, ask you to their houses (which indeed they will, directly you have left your letters), go there two or three times a week, if only for a few minutes in the evening. It is very hard to be *acquainted* with great French people, but *when* you are, it is your own fault if you are not *intimate* with them.

"Most English people have a kind of diffidence and scruple at calling in the evening—this is perfectly misplaced: the French are never ashamed of themselves, like us, whose persons, families, and houses are never fit to be seen, unless they are dressed out for a party.

"Don't imagine that the ease of French manners is at all like what *we* call ease: you must not lounge on your chair—nor put your feet upon a stool—nor forget yourself for one single moment when you are talking with women.

"You have heard a great deal about the gallantries of the French ladies; but remember that they demand infinitely greater attention than English women do; and that after a month's incessant devotion, you may lose every thing by a moment's *impolitesse.**

"You will not, my dear son, misinterpret these hints. I suppose, of course, that all your *liaisons* are platonic.

"Your father is laid up with the gout, and dreadfully ill-tempered and peevish; however, I keep out of the way as much as possible. I

35

dined yesterday at Lady Roseville's: she praised you very much, said your manners were particularly good, and that you had already quite the *usage du monde.** Lord Vincent is, I understand, at Paris: though very tiresome with his learning and Latin, he is exceedingly clever and *répandu;** be sure to cultivate his acquaintance.

"If you are ever at a loss as to the individual character of a person you wish to gain, the general knowledge of human nature will teach you one infallible specific,—*flattery!* The quantity and quality may vary according to the exact niceties of art; but, in any quantity and in any quality, it is more or less acceptable, and therefore certain to please. Only never (or at least very rarely) flatter when other people, besides the one to be flattered, are by; in that case you offend the rest, and you make even your intended dupe ashamed to be pleased.

"In general, weak minds think only of others, and yet seem only occupied with themselves; *you,* on the contrary, must appear wholly engrossed with those about you, and yet never have a single idea which does not terminate in yourself: a fool, my dear Henry, flatters himself— a wise man flatters the fool.

"God bless you, my dear child, take care of your health—don't forget Coulon; and believe me your most affectionate mother,

"F.P."

By the time I had read this letter and dressed myself for the evening, Vincent's carriage was at the *porte cocher.** I hate the affectation of keeping people waiting, and went down so quickly, that I met his facetious lordship upon the stairs. "Devilish windy," said I, as we were getting into the carriage.

"Yes," said Vincent; "but the moral Horace reminds us of our remedies as well as our misfortune—

"'Jam *galeam* Pallas, et ægida,
Currusque—parat'—[2]

viz: 'Providence that prepares the *gale,* gives us also a great coat and a carriage.'"

We were not long driving to the *Palais Royal.* Véry's was crowded to excess—"A very low set!" said Lord Vincent, (who, being half a liberal, is of course a thorough aristrocrat) looking round at the various English who occupied the apartment.

---

2. "Already Pallas readies her helmet, her aegis, her car" (Horace *Carmen* 1.15.11–12).

There was, indeed, a motley congregation; country esquires; extracts from the Universities; half-pay officers; city clerks in frogged coats and mustachios; two or three of a better looking description, but in reality half swindlers half gentlemen. All, in short, fit specimens of that wandering tribe, which spread over the continent the renown and the ridicule of good old England. I know not why it is that we should look and act so very disgracefully abroad; but I never meet in any spot out of this happy island, a single Englishman, without instinctively blushing for my native country.*

"Garçon, garçon," cried a stout gentleman, who made one of three at the table next to us. *"Donnez-nous une sole frite pour un, et des pommes de terre pour trois!"*

"Humph!" said Lord Vincent; "fine ideas of English taste these *garçons* must entertain; men who prefer fried soles and potatoes to the various delicacies they can command here, might, by the same perversion of taste, prefer Bloomfield's poems[3] to Byron's. Delicate taste depends solely upon the physical construction; and a man who has it not in cookery, must want it in literature. *Fried sole and potatoes!!* If I had written a volume, whose merit was in elegance, I would not show it to such a man!—but he might be an admirable critic upon 'Cobbett's Register,' or 'Every Man his own Brewer.' "

"Excessively true," said I; "what shall we order?"

"D'abord des huîtres d' Ostende," said Vincent; "as to the rest," taking hold of the carte, *"deliberare utilia mora utilissima est."*[4]

We were soon engaged in all the pleasures and pains of dinner.

"Petimus," said Lord Vincent, helping himself to some poulet à *l'Austerlitz, "petimus bene vivere, quod petis, hic est."*

We were not, however, assured of that fact at the termination of dinner. If half the dishes were well conceived and better executed, the other half were proportionately bad. Véry is, indeed, no longer the prince of Restaurateurs. The low English who have flocked there, have entirely ruined the place. What waiter—what cook *can* possibly respect men who take no soup, and begin with a *rôti;* who know neither what is good nor what is bad; who eat *rognons* at dinner

---

3. Robert Bloomfield (1766–1823): English poet most famous for "The Farmer's Boy: A Rural Poem" (1800). 'Cobbett's Register,' below, is the *Weekly Register,* founded in 1802 by William Cobbett (1763–1835), a radical freelance journalist best remembered for his *Rural Rides* (1830).

4. "To deliberate on things useful is the most useful delay" (Publius Syrus *Sententiae* 148). The Latin sentence spoken by Lord Vincent, below, means: "We seek to live well—what you seek is here" (Horace *Epistles* 1.11.29). [Both translations are Bulwer's; 1840 ed.]

instead of at breakfast, and fall into raptures over *sauce Robert* and *pieds de cochon;* who cannot tell, at the first taste, whether the beaune is *première qualité,* or the *fricassée* made of a yesterday's chicken; who suffer in the stomach after *champignon,* and die with indigestion of a *truffle?* O! English people, English people! why can you not stay and perish of apoplexy and Yorkshire pudding, at home?

By the time we had drank our coffee it was considerably past nine o'clock, and Vincent had business at the ambassador's before ten; we therefore parted for the night.

"What do you think of Véry's?" said I, as we were at the door.

"Why," replied Vincent, "when I recal the astonishing heat of the place, which has almost sent me to sleep; the exceeding number of times in which that *bécasse* had been re-roasted, and the extortionate length of our bills, I say of Véry's, what Hamlet said of the world, *'Weary, stale, and unprofitable!'* "[5]

CHAPTER XIII

I would fight with proad swords, and sink point on the first plood drawn like a gentleman's.

The Chronicles of the Canongate[1]

I STROLLED IDLY ALONG THE PALAIS ROYAL (WHICH English people, in some silly proverb, call the *capital* of Paris, whereas no French man of any rank, nor French woman of any respectability, are ever seen in its promenades) till, being somewhat curious to enter some of the smaller *cafés,* I went into one of the meanest of them; took up a *Journal des Spectacles,*[2] and called for some lemonade. At the next table to me sat two or three Frenchmen, evidently of inferior rank, and talking very loudly over *L'Angleterre et les Anglois.** Their attention was soon fixed upon me.

---

5. *Hamlet,* I, 2, 133.

1. Walter Scott, *Chronicles of the Canongate,* "The Two Drovers," chapter 2.

2. *Journal des Spectacles*: a journal published to describe and illustrate the shows put on in the theaters at Versailles and Fontainbleau.

Have you ever observed that if people are disposed to think ill of you, nothing so soon determines them to do so as any act of yours, which, however innocent and inoffensive, differs from their ordinary habits and customs? No sooner had my lemonade made its appearance, than I perceived an increased sensation among my neighbours of the next table. In the first place, lemonade is not much drank, as you may suppose, among the French in winter; and, in the second, my beverage had an appearance of ostentation, from being one of the dearest articles I could have called for. Unhappily, I dropped my newspaper—it fell under the Frenchmen's table; instead of calling the *garçon,* I was foolish enough to stoop for it myself. It was exactly under the feet of one of the Frenchmen; I asked him, with the greatest civility, to move: he made no reply. I could not, for the life of me, refrain from giving him a slight, very slight push; the next moment he moved in good earnest; the whole party sprung up as he set the example. The offended leg gave three terrific stamps upon the ground, and I was immediately assailed by a whole volley of unintelligible abuse. At that time I was very little accustomed to French vehemence, and perfectly unable to reply to the vituperations I received.

Instead of answering them, I therefore deliberated what was best to be done. If, thought I, I walk away, they will think me a coward, and insult me in the streets; if I challenge them, I shall have to fight with men probably no better than shopkeepers; if I strike this most noisy amongst them, he *may* be silenced, or he *may* demand satisfaction: if the former, well and good; if the latter, why I shall have a better excuse for fighting him than I should have now.

My resolution was therefore taken. I was never more free from passion in my life, and it was, therefore, with the utmost calmness and composure that, in the midst of my antagonist's harangue, I raised my hand and—quietly knocked him down.

He rose in a moment. *"Sortons,"* said he, in a low tone, "a Frenchman never forgives a blow!"

At that moment, an Englishman, who had been sitting unnoticed in an obscure corner of the *café,* came up and took me aside.

"Sir," said he, "don't think of fighting the man; he is a tradesman in the *Rue St. Honoré.* I myself have seen him behind the counter; remember that *'a ram may kill a butcher.'"* [3]

3. Popular English proverb, first collected in Ray's *Collection of English Proverbs* (1670). As the reader will discover, Thornton constantly invokes proverbial wisdom.

"Sir," I replied, "I thank you a thousand times for your information. Fight, however, I must, and I'll give you, like the Irishman, my reasons afterwards: perhaps you will be my second."

"With pleasure," said the Englishman, (*a Frenchman would have said, "with pain!"*)

We left the *café* together. My countryman asked them if he should go to the gunsmith's for the pistols.

"Pistols!" said the Frenchman's second: "we will only fight with swords."

"No, no," said my new friend. '*On ne prend le lièvre au tabourin.*'[4] We are the challenged, and therefore have the choice of weapons."

Luckily I overheard this dispute, and called to my second—"Swords or pistols," said I; "it is quite the same to me. I am not bad at either, only *do* make haste."

Swords, then, were chosen and soon procured. Frenchmen never grow cool upon their quarrels: and as it was a fine, clear, starlight night, we went forthwith to the *Bois de Boulogne*. We fixed our ground in a spot tolerably retired, and, I should think, pretty often frequented for the same purpose. I was exceedingly confident, for I knew myself to have few equals in the art of fencing; and I had all the advantage of coolness, which my hero was a great deal too much in earnest to possess. We joined swords, and in a very few moments I discovered that my opponent's life was at my disposal.

"*C'est bien,*" thought I; "for once I'll behave handsomely."

The Frenchman made a desperate lunge. I struck his sword from his hand, caught it instantly, and, presenting it to him again, said,

"I think myself peculiarly fortunate that I may now apologize for the affront I have put upon you. Will you permit my sincerest apologies to suffice? A man who can so well resent an* injury, can forgive one."

Was there ever a Frenchman not taken by a fine phrase? My hero received the sword with a low bow—the tears came into his eyes.

"Sir," said he, "you have *twice* conquered."

We left the spot with the greatest amity and affection, and re-entered, with a profusion of bows, our several *fiacres*.

"Let me," I said, when I found myself alone with my second, "let me thank you most cordially for your assistance; and allow me to cultivate an acquaintance so singularly begun. I lodge at the *Hotel de ———, Rue de Rivoli;* my name is Pelham. Your's is——"

---

4. French proverb: "A hare is not taken with a drum."

"Thornton," replied my countryman. "I will lose no time in profiting by an offer of acquaintance which does me so much honour."

With these and various other fine speeches, we employed the time till I was set down at my hotel; and my companion, drawing his cloak round him, departed on foot, to fulfill (he said, with a mysterious air) a certain assignation in the *Faubourg St. Germain.*

I said to Mr. Thornton, that I would give him my reasons for fighting *after* I had fought. As I do not remember that I ever did, and as I am very unwilling that they should be lost, I am now going to bestow them on the reader. It is true that I fought a tradesman. His rank in life made such an action perfectly gratuitous on my part, and to many people perhaps perfectly unpardonable. The following was, however, my view of the question: In striking him I had placed myself on *his* level; if I did so in order to insult him, I had a right also to do it, in order to give him the only atonement in my power: had the insult come solely from him, I might then, with some justice, have intrenched myself in my superiority of rank—contempt would have been as optional as revenge: but I had left myself no alternative in being the aggressor, for if my birth was to preserve me from redressing an injury, it was also to preserve me from committing one. I confess, that the thing would have been wholly different had it been an English, instead of a French, man; and this, because of the different view of the nature and importance of the affront, which the Englishman would take. No English tradesman has an idea of *les lois d'armes*—a blow can be *returned,* or it *can be paid for.*

But in France, neither a *set-to,* nor an action for assault, would repay the generality of any class removed from the poverty of the *bas peuple,* for so great and inexcusable an affront. In all countries it is the feelings of the *generality* of people, that courtesy, which is the essence of honour, obliges one to consult. As in England I should, therefore, have paid, so in France I fought.

If it be said, that a French gentleman would not have been equally condescending to a French tradesman, I answer that the former would never have perpetrated the only insult for which the latter might think there could be only one atonement. Besides, even if this objection held good, there is a difference between the duties of a native and a stranger. In receiving the advantages of a foreign country, one ought to be doubly careful not to give offence, and it is therefore doubly incumbent upon us to redress it when given. To the feelings of the person I had offended, there was but one redress. Who can blame me if I granted it?*

CHAPTER XIV

Erat homo ingeniosus, acutus, acer, et qui plurimum et salis haberet et fellis, nec candoris minus.

PLINY[1]

I DO NOT KNOW A MORE DIFFICULT CHARACTER TO describe than Lord Vincent's. Did I imitate certain writers, who think that the whole art of portraying individual character is to seize hold of some prominent peculiarity, and to introduce this distinguishing trait, in all times and in all scenes, the difficulty would be removed. I should only have to present to the reader a man, whose conversation was nothing but alternate jest and quotation—a due union of Yorick and Partridge.[2] This would, however, be rendering great injustice to the character I wish to delineate. There were times when Vincent was earnestly engrossed in discussion in which a jest rarely escaped him, and quotation was introduced only as a serious illustration, not as a humorous peculiarity. He possessed great miscellaneous erudition, and a memory perfectly surprising for its fidelity and extent. He was a severe critic, and had a peculiar art of quoting from each author he reviewed, some part that particularly told against him. Like most men, in the theory of philosophy he was tolerably rigid; in its practice, more than tolerably loose. By his tenets you would have considered him a very Cato for stubbornness and sternness: yet was he a very child in his concession to the whim of the moment. Fond of meditation and research, he was still fonder of mirth and amusement; and while he was among the most instructive, he was also the boonest of companions. When alone with me, or with men whom he imagined like me, his pedantry (for more or less, he always *was* pedantic) took only a jocular tone; with the *savan* or the *bel esprit*, it became

---

1. "He was a clever and able man—acute, sharp—with abundance of wit and no less candor" (Pliny the Younger *Epistles* 3.21). [Bulwer's translation; 1840 ed.]

2. Yorick and Partridge: characters in *Tristram Shandy* and *Tom Jones*, respectively.

grave, searching, and sarcastic. He was rather a contradicter than a favourer of ordinary opinions: and this, perhaps, led him not unoften into paradox; yet was there much soundness, even in his most vehement notions, and the strength of mind which made him think only for himself, was visible in all the productions it created. I have hitherto only given his conversation in one of its moods; henceforth I shall be just enough occasionally to be dull, and to present it sometimes to the reader in a graver tone.

Buried deep beneath the surface of his character, was a hidden, yet a restless ambition: but this was perhaps, at present, a secret even to himself. We know not our own characters till time teaches us self-knowledge: if we are *wise,* we may thank ourselves; if we are *great,* we must thank fortune.

It was this insight into Vincent's nature which drew us closer together. I recognized in the man, who as yet was only playing a part, a resemblance to myself, while he, perhaps, saw at times that I was somewhat better than the voluptuary, and somewhat wiser than the coxcomb, which were all that at present it suited me to appear.

In person, Vincent was short, and though not ill—yet ungracefully made—but his countenance was singularly fine. His eyes were dark, bright and penetrating, and his forehead (high and thoughtful) corrected the playful smile of his mouth, which might otherwise have given to his features too great an expression of levity. He was not positively ill dressed, yet he paid no attention to any external art, except cleanliness. His usual garb was a brown coat, much too large for him, a coloured neckcloth, a spotted waistcoat, grey trowsers, and short gaiters: add to these, gloves of most unsullied doeskin, and a curiously thick cane, and the portrait is complete.

In manners, he was civil, or rude, familiar, or distant, just as the whim seized him; never was there any address less common, and less artificial. What a rare gift, by the by, is that of manners! how difficult to define—how much more difficult to impart! Better for a man to possess them, than wealth, beauty, or talent;* they will more than supply all. No attention is too minute, no labour too exaggerated, which tends to perfect them. He who enjoys their advantages in the highest degree, viz., he who can please, penetrate, persuade, as the object may require, possesses the subtlest secret of the diplomatist and the statesman, and wants nothing but opportunity* to become "*great.*"

43

CHAPTER XV

Le plaisír de la société entre les amis se cultive par une ressemblance de goût sur ce qui regarde les mœurs, et par quelque différence d'opinions sur les sciences; par là ou l'on s'affermit dans ses sentiments, ou l'on s'exerce et l'on s'instruit par la dispute.

LA BRUYÈRE[1]

THERE WAS A PARTY AT MONSIEUR DE V——E'S, TO which Vincent and myself were the only Englishmen invited: accordingly as the Hôtel de V. was in the same street as my hotel, we dined together at my rooms, and walked from thence to the minister's house.

The party was as stiff and formal as such assemblies invariably are, and we were both delighted when we espied Monsieur d'A———, a man of much conversational talent, and some celebrity as an ultra writer, forming a little group in one corner of the room.

We took advantage of our acquaintance with the urbane Frenchman to join his party; the conversation turned almost entirely on literary subjects. Allusion being made to Schlegel's History of Literature,[2] and the severity with which he speaks of Helvétius, and the philosophers of his school, we began to discuss what harm the freethinkers in philosophy had effected.

"For my part," said Vincent, "I am not able to divine why we are supposed, in works where there is much truth, and little falsehood, much good, and a little evil, to see only the evil and the falsehood, to the utter exclusion of the truth and the good. All men whose minds are sufficiently laborious or acute to love the reading of

---

1. "The pleasure of society amongst friends is cultivated by resemblance of taste as to manners, but some difference of opinion as to mental acquisitions. Thus while it is confirmed by congeniality of sentiments, it gains exercise and instruction by intellectual discussion" (Jean de La Bruyère, *Les Caracteres,* De la Société et de la conversation," 61). [Bulwer's translation; 1840 ed.] La Bruyère (1644–96) was a writer and moralist.

2. *Geschichte der alten und neuen Literatur* by Karl Wilhelm Friederich von Schlegel (1772–1829) appeared in 1815. Below, the French utilitarian philosopher Claude Adrien Helvétius (1715–71) is referred to.

44

metaphysical inquiries, will by the *same* labour and acuteness separate the chaff from the corn—the false from the true. It is the young, the light, the superficial, who are easily misled by error, and incapable of discerning its fallacy; but tell me, if it is the light, the young, the superficial, who are in the habit of reading the abstruse and subtle speculations of the philosopher. No, no! believe me that it is *the very studies Monsieur Schlegel recommends,* which do harm to morality and virtue; *it is the study of literature itself,* the play, the poem, the novel, which all minds, however frivolous, can enjoy and understand, that constitute the real foes to religion and moral improvement."

"*Ma foi,*" cried Monsieur de G., (who was a little writer, and a great reader of romances) "why, you would not deprive us of the politer literature, you would not bid us shut up our novels, and burn our theatres."

"Certainly not!" replied Vincent: "and it is in this particular that I differ from certain modern philosophers of our own country, for whom, for the most part, I entertain the highest veneration. I would not deprive life of a single grace, or a single enjoyment, but I would counteract whatever is pernicious in whatever is elegant; if among my flowers there is a snake, I would not root up my flowers, I would kill the snake. Thus, who are they that derive from fiction and literature a prejudicial effect? We have seen already—the light and superficial;—*but* who are they that derive profit from them?—they who enjoy well regulated and discerning minds. Who pleasure?—*all mankind!* Would it not therefore be better, instead of depriving some of profit, and all of pleasure, by banishing poetry and fiction from our Utopia, to correct the minds which find evil, where, if they were properly instructed, they would find good? Whether we agree with Helvétius, that all men are born with an equal capacity of improvement, or merely go the length with all other metaphysicians, that education can improve the human mind to an extent yet incalculable, it must be quite clear, that we can give sound views instead of fallacies, and make common truths as easy to discern and adopt as common errors. But if we effect this, which we all allow is so easy, with our children; if we strengthen their minds instead of weakening them, and clear their vision, rather than confuse it, from that moment, we remove the prejudicial effects of fiction, and just as we have taught them to use a knife, without cutting their fingers, we teach them to make use of fiction without perverting it to their prejudice. *What* *philosopher* was ever hurt by reading the novels of *Crébillon,*[3]* or seeing the comedies of Molière? You understand me, then, Monsieur de G., I do, it is true, think that polite literature (as it is termed), is prejudicial to the superficial, but for that reason, I would not do away with the literature, I would do away with the superficial."

"I deny," said M. D'A———, "that this is so easy a task—you cannot make all *men* wise."

"No," replied Vincent; "but you can all *children,* at least to a certain extent. Since you cannot deny the prodigious effects of education, you *must* allow that they will, at least, give common sense; for if they cannot do this, they can do nothing. Now common sense is all that is necessary to distinguish what is good and evil, whether it be in life or in books: but then your education must not be that of public teaching and private fooling; you must not counteract the effects of common sense by instilling prejudice, or encouraging weakness; your education may not be carried to the utmost goal: but as far as it does go you must see that the road is clear. Now, for instance, with regard to fiction, you must not first, as is done in all modern education, admit the disease, and then dose with warm water to expel it; you must not put fiction into your child's hands, and not give him a single principle to guide his judgment respecting it, till his mind has got wedded to the poison, and too weak, by its long use, to digest the antidote. No; first fortify his intellect by reason, and you may then please his fancy by fiction. Do not excite his imagination with love and glory, till you can instruct his judgment as to what love and glory *are.* Teach him, in short, to *reflect,* before you permit him full indulgence to *imagine.*"

Here there was a pause. Monsieur D'A——— looked very ill-pleased, and poor Monsieur de G——— thought that somehow or other his romance writing was called into question. In order to soothe them, I introduced some subject which permitted a little national flattery; the conversation then turned insensibly on the character of the French people.

"Never," said Vincent, "has there been a character more often described—never one less understood. You have been termed superficial. I think, of all people, that you least deserve the accusation. With regard to the *few,* your philosophers, your mathematicians, your men of science, are consulted by those of other nations, as some of their

---

3. Claude-Prosper Jolyot de Crébillon (1707–77): author of some scandalous novels and stories depicting the high society of the period.

profoundest authorities. With regard to the *many*, the charge is still more unfounded. Compare your mob, whether of gentlemen or plebeians, to those of Germany, Italy—even England—and I own, in spite of my national prepossessions, that the comparison is infinitely in your favour. The country gentleman, the lawyer, the *petit maître* of England, are proverbially inane and ill-informed. With you, the classes of society that answer to those respective grades, have much information in literature, and often not a little in science. In like manner, your tradesmen, your mechanics,* your servants, are, beyond all measure, of larger, better cultivated, and less prejudiced minds than those ranks in England. The fact is, that *all* with you pretend to be *savans,* and this is the chief reason why you have been censured as shallow. We see your fine gentleman, or your *petit bourgeois,* give himself the airs of a critic or a philosopher; and because he is neither a Scaliger[4] nor a Newton, we forget that he is *only* the *bourgeois* or the *petit maître,* and set down* all your philosophers and critics with the censure of superficiality, which this shallow individual of a shallow order may justly have deserved. We, the English, it is true, do not expose ourselves thus: our dandies, our tradesmen, do not vent second rate philosophy on the human mind, nor on *les beaux arts:* but why is this? Not because they are better informed than their correspondent ciphers in France, but because they are much worse; not because they can say a great deal more on the subject, but because they can say nothing at all."

"You do us more than justice," said Monsieur D'A———, "in this instance: are you disposed to do us justice also in another? It is a favourite propensity of your countrymen to accuse us of heartlessness and want of feeling. Think you that this accusation is deserved?"

"By no means," replied Vincent. "The same cause that brought on the erroneous censure we have before mentioned, appears to me also to have created this; viz. a sort of *Palais Royal* vanity, common to all your nation, which induces you to make as much display at the shop window as possible. You show great cordiality, and even enthusiasm, to strangers; you turn your back on them—you forget them. 'How heartless!' cry we. Not at all! The English show no cordiality, no enthusiasm to strangers, it is true: but they equally turn their backs on them, and equally forget them! The only respect, therefore, in which they differ from you, is the previous kindness: now if we are

---

4. Joseph Justus Scaliger (1540–1609): Italian Protestant scholar and founder of modern chronology.

47

to receive strangers, I can really see no reason why we are not to be as civil to them as possible; and so far from imputing the desire to please them to a bad heart, I think it a thousand times more amiable and benevolent than telling them, *à l'Anglaise,* by your morosity and reserve, that you do not care a pin what becomes of them. If I am only to walk a mile with a man, why should I not make that mile as pleasant to him as I can; or why, above all, if I choose to be sulky, and tell him to go and be d——d, am I to swell out my chest, colour with conscious virtue, and cry, see what a good heart I have?[5]

"Ah, Monsieur D'A———, since benevolence is inseparable from all morality, it must be clear that there is a benevolence in little things as well as in great; and that he who strives to make his fellow creatures happy, though only for an instant, is a much better man than he who is indifferent to, or, (what is worse) despises, it. Nor do I, to say truth, see that kindness to an acquaintance is at all destructive to sincerity to a friend: on the contrary, I have yet to learn, that you are (according to the customs of your country) worse friends, worse husbands, or worse fathers than we are!"

"What!" cried I, "you forget yourself, Vincent. How can the private virtues be cultivated without a coal fire? Is not domestic affection a synonymous term with *domestic hearth? and where do* you find either, except in honest old England?"

"True," replied Vincent; "and it is certainly impossible for a father and his family to be as fond of each other on a bright day in the *Tuileries,* or at *Versailles,* with music and dancing, and fresh air, as they would be in a back parlour, by a smoky hearth, occupied entirely by *le bon père, et la bonne mère;* while the poor little children sit at the other end of the table, whispering and shivering, debarred the vent of all natural spirits, for fear of making a noise; and strangely uniting the idea of the domestic hearth with that of a hobgobblin, and the association of dear papa with that of a birch rod."

We all laughed at this reply, and Monsieur D'A———, rising to depart, said, "Well, well, *milord,* your countrymen are great generalizers in philosophy; they reduce human actions to two grand touchstones. All hilarity, they consider the sign of a shallow mind; and all kindness, the token of a false heart."

---

5. Mr. Pelham, it will be remembered, has prevised the reader, that Lord Vincent was somewhat addicted to paradox. His opinions on the French are to be taken with a certain reserve. [B-L; 1835 ed.]

CHAPTER XVI

Quis sapiens bono
Confidat fragili.
SENECA[1]
Grammatici certant et adhuc sub judice lis est.
HOR.

WHEN I FIRST WENT TO PARIS, I TOOK A FRENCH master, to perfect me in the Parisian pronunciation. This "Haberdasher of Pronouns" was a person of the name of Margot.[2] He was a tall, solemn man, with a face of the most imperturbable gravity. He would have been inestimable as an undertaker. His hair was of a pale yellow; you would have thought it had caught a bilious complaint from his complexion; the latter was, indeed, of so sombre a saffron, that it looked as if ten livers had been forced into a jaundice, in order to supply its colour. His forehead was high, bald, and very narrow. His cheekbones were extremely prominent, and his cheeks so thin, that they seemed happier than Pyramus and Thisbe, and kissed each other inside without any separation or division. His face was as sharp and almost as long as an inverted pyramid, and was garnished on either side by a miserable half starved whisker, which seemed scarcely able to maintain itself, amid the general symptoms of atrophy and decay. This charming countenance was supported by a figure so long, so straight, so shadowy, that you might have taken it for *the monument in a consumption*.

But the chief characteristic of the man was the utter and wonderful gravity I have before spoken of. You could no more have coaxed a smile out of his countenance, than you could out of the poker, and yet Monsieur Margot was by no means a melancholy man. He

---

1. "What wise man puts his trust in a good but fragile thing" (Seneca *Phaedra* 773–74). The second Latin epigraph may be translated: "Grammarians dispute and the matter is still left under the consideration of the judge" (Horace *Ars Poetica* 78). [Bulwer's translation; 1840 ed.]

2. David Margot: author of a widely used elementary French grammar.

49

loved his joke, and his wine, and his dinner, just as much as if he had been of a fatter frame; and it was a fine specimen of the practical antithesis, to hear a good story, or a jovial expression, leap friskily out of that long, curved mouth; it was at once a paradox and a bathos—it was the mouse coming out of its hole in Ely Cathedral.

I said that this gravity was M. Margot's most especial characteristic. I forgot:—he had two others equally remarkable; the one was an ardent admiration for the chivalrous, the other an ardent admiration for himself. Both of these are traits common enough in a Frenchman, but in Mons. Margot their excess rendered them *uncommon*. He was a most ultra specimen of *le chevalier amoureux*—a mixture of Don Quixote and the Duc de Lauzun.[3] Whenever he spoke of the present tense, even *en professeur,* he always gave a sigh to the preterite, and an anecdote of Bayard; whenever he conjugated a verb, he paused to tell me that the favourite one of his female pupils was *je t'aime.*

In short, he had tales of his own good fortune, and of other people's brave exploits, which, without much exaggeration, were almost as long, and had perhaps as little substance, as himself; but the former was his favourite topic: to hear him, one would have imagined that his face, in borrowing the sharpness of the needle, had borrowed also its attraction;—and then the prettiness of Mons. Margot's modesty!

"It is very extraordinary," said he, "very extraordinary, for I have no time to give myself up to those affairs; it is not, Monsieur, as if I had your leisure to employ all the little preliminary arts of creating *la belle passion. Non, Monsieur,* I go to church, to the play, to the Tuileries, for a brief relaxation—and—*me voilà partout accablé* with my good fortune. I am not handsome, Monsieur, at least, not *very;* it is true, that I have expression, a certain *air noble,* (my first cousin, Monsieur, is the Chevalier *de Margot)* and above all, *de l'âme** in my physiognomy; the women love soul, Monsieur—something intellectual and spiritual always attracts them; yet my success certainly is singular."

"*Bah! Monsieur,*" replied I: "with dignity, expression, and soul! how could the heart of any French woman resist you? No, you do yourself injustice. It was said of Caesar, that he was great without an effort; much more, then, may Monsieur Margot be happy without an exertion."

---

3. Armand Louis de Gontaut, duc de Lauzun (1747–93): notorious rake and adherent of the Orléans party. Below, Pierre Terrail, chevalier de Bayard (1475–1524): French national hero called "the knight without fear or reproach."

"Ah, Monsieur!" rejoined the Frenchman, still looking

> "As weak, as earnest, and as gravely out
> As sober Lanesbro' dancing with the gout."[4]

"ah, Monsieur, there is a depth and truth in your remarks, worthy of Montaigne. As it is impossible to account for the caprices of women, so it is impossible for ourselves to analyze the merit they discover in us; but, Monsieur, hear me—at the house where I lodge, there is an English lady *en pension. Eh bien, Monsieur,* you guess the rest: she has taken a caprice for me, and this very night she will admit me to her apartment. She is very handsome.—*Ah qu'elle est belle, une jolie petite bouche, une denture éblouissante, un nez tout à fait grec,* in fine, quite a *bouton de rose.*"[5]

I expressed my envy at Monsieur Margot's good fortune, and when he had sufficiently dilated upon it, he withdrew. Shortly afterwards Vincent entered—"I have a dinner invitation for both of us to-day," said he; "you will come?"

"Most certainly," replied I; "but who is the person we are to honour?"

"A Madame Laurent," replied Vincent; "one of those ladies only found at Paris, who live upon anything rather than their income. She keeps a tolerable table, haunted with Poles, Russians, Austrians, and idle Frenchmen, *peregrinae gentis amaenum hospitium.*[6] As yet, she has not the happiness to be acquainted with any Englishmen, (though she boards one of our countrywomen) and (as she is desirous of making her fortune as soon as possible) she is very anxious of having that honour. She has heard vast reports of our wealth and wisdom, and flatters herself that we are so many ambulatory Indies: in good truth, a Frenchwoman thinks she is never in want of a fortune as long as there is a rich fool in the world.

> " 'Stultitiam patiuntur, opes,'[7]

is her hope; and

> " 'Ut tu *fortunam,* sic nos te, Celse, feremus,

is her motto."

---

4. Alexander Pope, *Moral Essays,* 1, 230–31.

5. "Ah, sir, how beautiful she is, a pretty little mouth, dazzling teeth, a perfectly Greek nose . . . rose bud."

6. Unidentified: "a comfortable place for the traveler to stay."

7. The Latin tags in this paragraph are, respectively: "Wealth allows of folly" (Horace *Epistles* 1.18.29) and "As you bear your fortune, Celsus, so we shall bear with you" (Horace *Epistles* 1.8.17).

"Madame Laurent!" repeated I, "why, surely that is the name of Mons. Margot's landlady."

"I hope not," cried Vincent, "for the sake of our dinner; he reflects no credit on her good cheer—

"'Who eats fat dinners, should himself be fat.'"[8]

"At all events," said I, "we can try the good lady for once. I am very anxious to see a countrywoman of ours, probably the very one you speak of, whom Mons. Margot eulogizes in glowing colours, and who has, moreover, taken a violent fancy for my solemn preceptor. What think you of that, Vincent?"

"Nothing extraordinary," replied Vincent; "the lady only exclaims with the moralist—

"'Love, virtue, valour, yea, all human charms,
Are shrunk and centred *in that heap of bones.*
Oh! there are wondrous beauties in the *grave!*'"[9]

I made some punning rejoinder, and we sallied out to earn an appetite in the Tuileries for Madame Laurent's dinner.

At the hour of half-past five we repaired to our engagement. Madame Laurent received us with the most evident satisfaction, and introduced us forthwith to our countrywoman. She was a pretty, fair, shrewd looking person, with an eye and lip which, unless it greatly belied her, showed her much more inclined, as an *amante*,* to be merry and wise, than honest and true.

Presently Monsieur Margot made his appearance. Though very much surprised at seeing me, he did not appear the least jealous of my attentions to his *inamorata*. Indeed, the good gentleman was far too much pleased with himself to be susceptible of the suspicions common to less fortunate lovers. At dinner I sat next to the pretty Englishwoman, whose name was Green.

"Monsieur Margot," said I, "has often spoken to me of you before I had the happiness of being personally convinced how true and un-exaggerated were his sentiments."

"Oh!" cried Mrs. Green, with an arch laugh, "you are acquainted with Monsieur Margot, then?"

"I have that honour," said I. "I receive from him every morning lessons both in love and languages. He is a perfect master of both."

Mrs. Green burst out into one of those peals so peculiarly British.*

---

8. Parody of a remark made by Dr. Johnson and recorded in Boswell: "Who drives fat oxen should himself be fat." Johnson's remark was itself a parody of a line in a tragedy he had just seen.

9. Unidentified.

"*Ah, le pauvre Professeur!*" cried she. "He is *too* absurd!"

"He tells me," said I, gravely, "that he is quite *accablé* with his *bonnes fortunes*—possibly he flatters himself that even you are not perfectly inaccessible to his addresses."

"Tell me, Mr. Pelham," said the fair Mrs. Green, "can you pass by this street about half past twelve to-night?"

"I will make a point of doing so," replied I, not a little surprised by the remark.

"Do," said she, "and now let us talk of old England."

When we went away I told Vincent of my appointment.

"What!" said he, "eclipse Monsieur Margot! Impossible!"

You are right," replied I, "nor is it my hope; there is some trick afloat of which we may as well be spectators."

"*De tout mon coeur!*"* answered Vincent; "let us go till then to the Duchesse de G———." I assented, and we drove to the *Rue de* ———. The Duchesse de G——— was a fine relict of the *ancien régime*—tall and stately, with her own grey hair *crêpé,* and surmounted by a high cap of the most dazzling *blonde.* She had been one of the earliest emigrants, and had stayed for many months with my mother, whom she professed to rank amongst her dearest friends. The duchesse possessed to perfection that singular *mélange* of ostentation and ignorance which was so peculiar to the ante-revolutionists. She would talk of the last tragedy with the emphatic tone of a connoisseur, in the same breath that she would ask, with Marie Antoinette, why the poor people were so clamorous for *bread* when they might buy such nice cakes for two-pence a-piece? "To give you an idea of the Irish," said she one day to an inquisitive marquess, "know that they *prefer* potatoes to mutton!"

Her *soirées* were among the most agreeable at Paris—she united all the rank and talent to be found in the ultra party, for she professed to be quite a female Maecenas;[10] and whether it was a mathematician or a romance-writer, a naturalist or a poet, she held open house for all, and conversed with each with equal fluency and self-satisfaction.

A new play had just been acted, and the conversation, after a few preliminary *hoverings,* settled upon it.

"You see," said the duchesse, "that *we* have actors, *you* authors; of what avail is it that you boast of a Shakspeare, since your *Liseton,* great as he is, cannot be compared with our Talma?"[11]

---

10. Maecenas: Roman patron of letters, first century B.C.

11. John Liston (1776–1846): English actor; François-Joseph Talma (1763–1826), French tragedian.

"And yet," said I, preserving my gravity with a pertinacity, which nearly made Vincent and the rest of our compatriots assembled lose theirs, "Madame must allow, that there is a striking resemblance in their persons, and the sublimity of their acting?"

"*Pour ça, j'en conviens,*" replied this '*critique de l'Ecole des Femmes.*' "*Mais cependant Liseton n'a pas la Nature! l'âme! la grandeur de Talma!*"[12]

"And will you then allow us *no* actors of merit?" asked Vincent.

"*Mais oui!—dans le genre comique, par exemple, votre buffo Kean met dix fois plus d'esprit et de drolerie dans ses rôles que La Porte.*"[13]

"The impartial and profound judgment of Madame admits of no further discussion on this point," said I. "What does she think of the present state of our dramatic *literature?*"

"Why," replied Madame, "you have many great poets, but when they write for the stage they lose themselves entirely; your Valter Scote's play of Robe Roi is very inferior to his novel of the same name."[14]

"It is a great pity," said I, "that Byron did not turn his Childe Harold into a tragedy—it has so much *energy—action—variety!*"

"Very true," said Madame, with a sigh; "but the tragedy is, after all, only suited to our nation—we alone carry it to perfection."

"Yet," said I, "*Goldoni*[15] wrote a *few* fine *tragedies.*"

"Eh bien!" said Madame, "one rose does not constitute a garden!"

And satisfied with this remark, *la femme savante* turned to a celebrated traveller to discuss with him the chance of discovering the North Pole.

There were one or two clever Englishmen present; Vincent and I joined them.

"Have you met the Persian prince yet?" said Sir George Lynton to me; "he is a man of much talent, and great desire of knowledge. He intends to publish his observations on Paris, and I suppose we

---

12. "I grant that, but, nonetheless, Liston has not the nature, the soul, the grandeur of Talma." [Bulwer's translation; 1840 ed.]

13. "Yes, in comedy, for instance, your Kean has ten times more vivacity and drollery than Laporte." [Bulwer's translation; 1840 ed.] Edmund Kean (1787–1833): English actor; Jacques-François Rozières Laporte (b. 1776): actor and harlequinist.

14. Walter Scott never adapted *Rob Roy* for the stage, though two hack writers did. Isaac Pocock wrote a three-act comedy (published 1818) and George Soane a three-act melodrama (published 1829).

15. Carlo Goldoni (1707–93): Italian dramatist famed for his comedies.

shall have an admirable supplement to Montesquieu's *Lettres Persannes!*"[16]

"I wish we had," said Vincent: "there are few better satires on a civilized country than the observations of visitors less polished; while on the contrary the civilized traveller, in describing the manners of the American barbarian, instead of conveying ridicule upon the visited, points the sarcasm on the visitor; and Tacitus could not have thought of a finer or nobler satire on the Roman luxuries than that insinuated by his treatise on the German simplicity."

"What," said Monsieur D'E—— (an intelligent *ci-devant émigré*), "what political writer is *generally* esteemed as your best?"

"It is difficult to say," replied Vincent, "since with so many parties we have many idols; but I think I might venture to name Bolingbroke[17] as among the most popular. Perhaps, indeed, it would be difficult to select a name more frequently quoted and discussed than his; and yet his political works are the least valuable part of his remains; and though* they contain many lofty sentiments, and many beautiful yet scattered truths, they were* written when legislation, most debated, was least understood, and ought to be admired rather as excellent for the day than estimable in themselves. The life of Bolingbroke would convey a juster moral than all his writings: and the author who gives us a full and impartial memoir of that extraordinary man, will have afforded both to the philosophical and political literature of England one of its greatest desideratums."

"It seems to me," said Monsieur D'E——, "that your national literature is peculiarly deficient in biography—am I right in my opinion?"

"Indubitably!" said Vincent; "we have not a single work that can be considered a model in biography, (excepting, perhaps, Middleton's Life of Cicero).[18] This brings on a remark I have often made in distinguishing your philosophy from ours. It seems to me that you who excel so admirably in biography, memoirs, comedy, satirical observation on peculiar classes, and pointed aphorisms, are fonder of considering man in his relation to society and the active commerce of the world, than in the more abstracted and metaphysical operations of the mind. *Our* writers, on the contrary, love to indulge rather in

16. Charles de Secondat, baron de Montesquieu (1689–1755): political philosopher whose satire upon European society, *Lettres Persanes,* was published in 1721.

17. Henry St. John Bolingbroke (1678–1751): The English statesman and writer was as famous for the dissipation and extravagance of his life as for his political philosophy.

18. Conyers Middleton, *The History of the Life of Marcus Tullius Cicero* (1741).

abstruse speculations on their species—to regard man in an abstract and isolated point of view, and to see him *think* alone in his chamber, while you prefer beholding him *act* with the multitude in the world."

"It must be allowed," said Monsieur D'E——t, "that if this be true, our philosophy is the most useful, though yours may be the most profound."

Vincent did not reply.

"Yet," said Sir George Lynton, "there will be a disadvantage attending your writings of this description, which, by diminishing their general *applicability*, diminish their general *utility*. Works which treat upon man in his relation to society, can only be strictly applicable so long as that relation to society treated upon continues. For instance, the play which satirizes a particular class, however deep its reflections and accurate its knowledge upon the subject satirized, must necessarily be obsolete when the class itself has become so. The political pamphlet, admirable for one state, may be absurd in another; the novel which exactly delineates the present age may seem strange and unfamiliar to the next; and thus works which treat of men relatively, and not man *in se,* must often confine their popularity to the age and even the country in which they were written. While on the other hand, the work which treats of man himself, which seizes, discovers, analyzes the human mind, as it is, whether in the ancient or the modern, the savage or the European, must evidently be applicable, and consequently useful, to all times and all nations. He who discovers the circulation of the blood, or the origin of ideas, must be a philosopher to every people who have veins or ideas; but he who even most successfully delineates the manners of one country, or the actions of one individual, is only the philosopher of a single country, or a single age. If, Monsieur D'E——t, you will condescend to consider this, you will see perhaps that the philosophy which treats of man in his relations is *not* so useful, because neither so permanent nor so invariable, as that which treats of man in himself."[19]

---

19. Yet Hume holds the contrary opinion to this, and considers a good comedy more durable than a system of philosophy. Hume is right, if by a system of philosophy is understood—a pile of guesses, false but plausible, set up by one age to be destroyed by the next. Ingenuity cannot rescue error from oblivion; but the moment Wisdom has discovered Truth, she has obtained immortality. [B-L] But is Hume right when he says that there may come a time when Addison will be read with delight, but Locke be utterly forgotten? For my part, if the two were to be matched for posterity, I think the odds would be in favor of Locke. I very much doubt whether five hundred years hence, Addison will be read at all, and I am quite sure that, a thousand years hence, Locke will not be forgotten. [B-L; added in 1835 ed.]

I was now somewhat weary of this conversation, and though it was not yet twelve, I seized upon my appointment as an excuse to depart—accordingly I rose for that purpose. "I suppose," said I to Vincent, "that you will not leave your discussion."

"Pardon me," said he, "amusement is quite as profitable to a man of sense as metaphysics. *Allons.*"

CHAPTER XVII

I was in this terrible situation when the basket stopt.
Oriental Tales—History of the Basket[1]

WE TOOK OUR WAY TO THE STREET IN WHICH MADAME Laurent resided. Meanwhile suffer me to *get rid of myself,* and to introduce you, dear Reader, to my friend, Monsieur Margot, the whole of whose adventures were subsequently detailed to me by the garrulous Mrs. Green.

At the hour appointed he knocked at the door of my fair countrywoman, and was carefully admitted. He was attired in a dressing-gown of sea-green silk, in which his long, lean, hungry body, looked more like a river* pike than any thing human.

"Madame," said he, with a solemn air, "I return you my best thanks for the honour you have done me—behold me at your feet!" and so saying the lean lover gravely knelt down on one knee.

"Rise, Sir," said Mrs. Green, "I confess that you have won my heart; but that is not all—you have yet to show that you are worthy of the opinion I have formed of you. It is not, Monsieur Margot, your person that has won me—no! it is your chivalrous and noble sentiments—prove that these are genuine, and you may command all from my admiration."

"In what manner shall I prove it, Madame," said Monsieur Margot, rising, and gracefully drawing his sea-green gown more closely round him.

---

1. Anne Claude Philippe de Tubières, comte de Caylus (1682–1765), published his *Contes orientaux* in 1743. It was translated into English as *Oriental Tales* (1745).

"By your courage, your devotion, and your gallantry! I ask but one proof—you can give it me on the spot. You remember, Monsieur, that in the days of romance, a lady threw her glove upon the stage on which a lion was exhibited, and told her lover to pick it up. Monsieur Margot, the trial to which I shall put you is less severe. Look, (and Mrs. Green threw open the window)—look, I throw my glove out into the street—descend for it."

"Your commands are my law," said the romantic Margot. "I will go forthwith," and so saying, he went to the door.

"Hold, Sir!" said the lady, "it is not by that simple manner that you are to descend—you must go the same way as my glove, *out of the window.*"

"Out of the window, Madame!" said Monsieur Margot, with astonished solemnity; "that is impossible, because this apartment is three stories high, and consequently I shall be dashed to pieces."

"By no means," answered the dame; "in that corner of the room there is a basket, to which (already foreseeing your determination) I have affixed a rope; by that basket you shall descend. See, Monsieur, what expedients a provident love can suggest."

"H—e—m!" said, very slowly, Monsieur Margot, by no means liking the airy voyage imposed upon him; "but the rope may break, or your hand may suffer it to slip."

"Feel the rope," cried the lady, "to satisfy you as to your first doubt; and, as to the second, can you—*can* you imagine that my affections would not make me twice as careful of your person as of my own. Fie! ungrateful Monsieur Margot! fie!"

The melancholy chevalier cast a rueful look at the basket. "Madame," said he, "I own that I am very averse to the plan you propose: suffer me to go down stairs in the ordinary way; your glove can be as easily picked up whether your adorer goes out of the door or the window. It is only, Madame, when ordinary means fail that we should have recourse to the extraordinary."

"Begone, Sir!" exclaimed Mrs. Green; "begone! I now perceive that your chivalry was only a pretence. Fool that I was to love you as I have done—fool that I was to imagine a hero where I now find a ———"

"Pause, Madame, I will obey you—my heart is firm—see that the *rope* is ———"

"Gallant Monsieur Margot!" cried the lady: and going to her dressing-room, she called her woman to her assistance. The rope was of the most unquestionable thickness, the basket of the most capacious dimensions. The former was fastened to a strong hook—and the latter lowered.

"I go, Madame," said Monsieur Margot, feeling the rope; "but it really is a most dangerous exploit."

"Go, Monsieur! and the God of* St. Louis befriend you!"

"Stop!" said Monsieur Margot, "let me fetch my coat: the night is cold, and my dressing-gown thin."

"Nay, nay, my Chevalier," returned the dame, "I love you in that gown: it gives you an air of grace and dignity, quite enchanting."

"It will give me my death of cold, Madame!" said Monsieur Margot, earnestly.

"Bah!" said the Englishwoman: "what knight ever feared cold? Besides, you mistake; the night is warm, and you look so handsome in your gown."

"Do I!" said the vain Monsieur Margot, with an iron expression of satisfaction; "if that is the case, I will mind it less; but may I return by the door?"

"Yes," replied the lady; "you see that I do not require too much from your devotion—enter."

"Behold me!" said the French master, inserting his body into the basket, which immediately began to descend.

The hour and the police of course made the street empty; the lady's handkerchief waved in token of encouragement and triumph. When the basket was within five yards of the ground, Mrs. Green cried to her lover, who had hitherto been elevating his serious countenance towards her, in sober, yet gallant sadness—

"Look, look, Monsieur—straight before you."

The lover turned round, as rapidly as his habits would allow him, and at that instant the window was shut, the light extinguished, and the basket arrested. There stood Monsieur Margot, upright in the basket, and there stopped the basket, motionless in the air.

What were the exact reflections of Monsieur Margot, in that position, I cannot pretend to determine, because he never favoured me with them; but about an hour afterwards, Vincent and I (who had been delayed on the road), strolling up the street, according to our appointment, perceived, by the dim lamps, some opaque body leaning against the wall of Madame Laurent's house, at about the distance of fifteen feet from the ground.

We hastened our steps towards it; a measured and serious voice, which I well knew, accosted us—

"For God's sake, gentlemen, procure me assistance; I am the

victim of a perfidious woman, and expect every moment to be precipitated to the earth."

"Good Heavens!" said I, "surely it is Monsieur Margot, whom I hear. What are you doing there?"

"Shivering with cold," answered Monsieur Margot, in a tone tremulously slow.

"But what are you *in?* for I can see nothing but a dark substance."

"I am in a basket," replied Monsieur Margot, "and I should be very much obliged to you to let me out of it."

"Well—indeed," said Vincent, (for *I* was too much engaged in laughing to give a ready reply,) "your *Château-Margot* has but a cool cellar.[2] But there are some things in the world easier said than done. How are we to remove you to a more desirable place?"

"Ah," returned Monsieur Margot, "*how* indeed! There is to be sure a ladder in the porter's lodge long enough to deliver me; but then, think of the gibes and jeers of the porter—it will get wind—I shall be ridiculed, gentlemen—I shall be ridiculed—and what is worse, I shall lose my pupils."

"My good friend," said I, "you had better lose your pupils than your life; and the day-light will soon come, and then, instead of being ridiculed by the porter, you will be ridiculed by the whole street!"

Monsieur Margot groaned. "Go then, my friend," said he, "procure the ladder! Oh, those she devils!—what *could* make me such a fool!"

While Monsieur Margot was venting his spleen in a scarcely articulate mutter, we repaired to the lodge, knocked up the porter, communicated the *accident,* and procured the ladder. However, an observant eye had been kept upon our proceedings, and the window above was re-opened, though so silently that I only perceived the action. The porter, a jolly, bluff, hearty-looking fellow, stood grinning below with a lantern, while we set the ladder (which only just reached the basket) against the wall.

The chevalier looked wistfully forth, and then, by the light of the lantern, we had a fair view of his ridiculous figure—his teeth chattered woefully, and the united cold without and anxiety within, threw a double sadness and solemnity upon his withered countenance; the night was very windy, and every instant a rapid current seized the unhappy sea-green vesture, whirled it in the air, and threw it, as if

---

2. The punster strikes again, this time recalling the wine *Château Margaux.*

in scorn, over the very face of the miserable* professor. The constant recurrence of this sportive irreverence of the gales—the high sides of the basket, and the trembling agitation of the inmate, never too agile, rendered it a work of some time for Monsieur Margot to transfer himself from the basket to the ladder; at length, he had fairly got out one thin, shivering leg.

"Thank God!"* said the pious professor—when at that instant the thanksgiving was checked, and, to Monsieur Margot's inexpressible astonishment and dismay, the basket rose five feet from the ladder, leaving its tenant with one leg dangling out, like a flag from a balloon.

The ascent was too rapid to allow Monsieur Margot even time for an exclamation, and it was not till he had had sufficient leisure in his present elevation to perceive all its consequences, that he found words to say, with the most earnest tone of thoughtful lamentation, "One could not have foreseen this!—it is really extremely distressing— would to God that I could get my leg in, or my body out!"

While we were yet too convulsed with laughter to make any comment upon the unlooked-for ascent of the luminous Monsieur Margot, the basket descended with such force as to dash the lantern out of the hand of the porter, and to bring the professor so precipitiously to the ground, that all the bones in his skin rattled audibly!

"My God!"* said he, "I am done for!—be witness how inhumanly I have been murdered."

We pulled him out of the basket, and carried him between us into the porter's lodge; but the woes of Monsieur Margot were not yet at their termination. The room was crowded. There was Madame Laurent,—there was the German count, whom the professor was teaching French;—there was the French viscount, whom he was teaching German;—there was all his fellow-lodgers—the ladies whom he had boasted of—the men he had boasted to—Don Juan, in the infernal regions, could not have met with a more unwelcome set of old acquaintance than Monsieur Margot had the happiness of opening his bewildered eyes upon in the porter's lodge.

"What!" cried they all, "Monsieur Margot, is that you who have been frightening us so? We thought the house was attacked; the Russian general is at this very moment loading his pistols; lucky for you that you did not *choose* to stay longer in that situation. Pray, Monsieur, what could induce you to exhibit yourself so, in your dressing-gown too, and the night so cold? Ar'n't you ashamed of yourself?"

61

All this, and infinitely more, was levelled against the miserable professor, who stood shivering with cold and fright; and turning his eyes first upon one, and then on another, as the exclamations circulated round the room,

"I do assure you," at length he began.

"No, no," cried one, "it is of no use explaining now!"

"Mais, Messieurs," querulously recommenced the unhappy Margot.

"Hold your tongue," exclaimed Madame Laurent, "you have been disgracing my house."

"Mais, Madame, écoutez-moi—"

"No, no," cried one, "it is of no use explaining now!"

"Mais, Monsieur Le Comte—"

"Fie, fie!" cried the Frenchman.

"Mais, Monsieur Le Vicomte—"

At this every mouth was opened, and the patience of Monsieur Margot being by this time exhausted, he flew into a violent rage; his tormentors pretended an equal indignation, and at length he fought his way out of the room, as fast as his shattered bones would allow him, followed by the whole body, screaming, and shouting, and scolding, and laughing after him.

The next morning passed without my usual lesson from Monsieur Margot; that was natural enough: but when the next day, and the next, rolled on, and brought neither Monsieur Margot nor his excuse, I began to be uneasy for the poor man. Accordingly I sent to Madame Laurent's to inquire after him: judge of my surprise at hearing that he had, early the day after his adventure, left his lodgings with his small possession of books and clothes, leaving only a note to Madame Laurent, enclosing the amount of his debt to her, and that none had since seen or heard of him.

From that day to this I have never once beheld him. The poor professor lost even the little money due to him for lessons—so true is it, that in a man of Monsieur Margot's temper, even interest is a subordinate passion to vanity.

CHAPTER XVIII

It is good to be merry and wise,
  It's good to be honest and true;
It is good to be off with the old love
  Before you be on with the new.

Song[1]

ONE MORNING, WHEN I WAS RIDING TO THE *Bois de Boulogne* (the celebrated place of assignation), in order to meet Madame d'Anville, I saw a lady on horseback, in the most imminent danger of being thrown. Her horse had taken fright at an English tandem, *or its driver*, and was plunging violently; the lady was evidently much frightened, and lost her presence of mind more and more every moment. A man who was with her, and who could scarcely manage his own horse, appeared to be exceedingly desirous, but perfectly unable, to assist her; and a great number of people were looking on, doing nothing, and saying "Good God,* how dangerous!"

I have always had a great horror of being a hero in scenes, and a still greater antipathy to *"females in distress."* However, so great is the effect of sympathy upon the most hardened of us, that I stopped for a few moments, first to look on, and secondly to assist. Just when a moment's delay might have been dangerous, I threw myself off my horse, seized hers with one hand, by the rein which she no longer had the strength to hold, and assisted her with the other to dismount. When all the peril was over, Monsieur, her companion, managed also to find his legs; and I did not, I confess, wonder at his previous delay, when I discovered that the lady in danger had been his wife. *He* gave me a profusion of thanks, and *she* made them more than complimentary by the glance which accompanied them. Their carriage was in attendance at a short distance behind. The husband went for it—I remained with the lady.

---

1. The epigraph is from an old song, the author unknown.

"Mr. Pelham," she said, "I have heard much of you from my friend Madame D'Anville, and have long been anxious for your acquaintance. I did not think I should commence it with so great an obligation."

Flattered by being already known by name, and a subject of previous interest, you may be sure that I tried every method to improve the opportunity I had gained; and when I handed my new acquaintance into her carriage, my pressure of her hand was somewhat more than slightly returned.

"Shall you be at the English ambassador's to-night?" said the lady, as they were about to shut the door of the carriage.

"Certainly, if *you* are to be there," was my answer.

"We shall meet then," said Madame, and her look *said more*.

I rode into the *Bois;* and giving my horse to my servant, as I came near *Passy,* where I was to meet Madame D'Anville, I proceeded thither on foot. I was just in sight of the spot, and indeed of my *inamorata,* when two men passed, talking very earnestly; they did not remark me, but what individual could ever escape *my* notice? The one was Thornton; the other—who could he be? Where had I seen that pale, but more than beautiful* countenance before? I looked again. I was satisfied that I was mistaken in my first thought; the hair was of a completely different colour. "No, no," said I, "it is not he: yet how like."

I was *distrait* and absent during the whole time I was with Madame D'Anville. The face of Thornton's companion haunted me like a dream; and, to say the truth, there were also moments when the recollection of my new engagement for the evening made me tired with that which I was enjoying the troublesome honour of keeping.

Madame D'Anville was not slow in perceiving the coldness of my behaviour. Though a Frenchwoman, she was rather grieved than resentful.

"You are growing tired of me, my friend," she said: "and when I consider your youth and temptations, I cannot be surprised at it—yet, I own, that this thought gives me much greater pain than I could have supposed."

"Bah! *ma belle amie,*" cried I, "you deceive yourself—I adore you—I shall always adore you; *but it's getting very late.*"

Madame D'Anville sighed, and we parted. "She is not half so pretty or agreeable as she was," thought I, as I mounted my horse, and remembered my appointment at the ambassador's.

I took unusual pains with my appearance that evening, and drove to the ambassador's hotel in the Rue Faubourg St. Honoré, full half an hour earlier than I had ever done before. I had been some time in the rooms without discovering my heroine of the morning. The Duchess of H———n passed by.

"What a wonderfully beautiful woman," said Mr. Howard de Howard (the spectral secretary of the embassy)* to Mr. Aberton.

"Ay," answered Aberton, "but to my taste, the Duchesse de Perpignan is quite equal to her—do you know *her?*"

"No—yes!" said Mr. Howard de Howard; "that is, not exactly—not well;" an Englishman never owns that he does not know a duchess.

"Hem!" said Mr. Aberton, thrusting his large hand through his lank light hair. "Hem—could one do anything, do you think, in that quarter?"

"I should think *one* might, with a tolerable person!" answered the spectral secretary,* looking down at a pair of most shadowy supporters.

"Pray," said Aberton, "what do you think of Miss ———? they say she is an heiress."

"Think of her!" said the secretary, who was as poor as he was thin, "why, I *have* thought of her!"

"They say, that fool Pelham makes up to her." (Little did Mr. Aberton imagine, when he made this remark, that I was close behind him.)

"I should not imagine that was true," said the secretary; "he is so occupied with Madame D'Anville."

"Pooh!" said Aberton, dictatorially, *"she* never had any thing to say to him."

"Why are you so sure?" said Mr. Howard de Howard.

"Why? because he never showed any notes from her, or ever even said he had a *liaison* with her himself!"*

"Ah! that is quite enough!" said the secretary.* "But, is not that the Duchesse de Perpignan?"

Mr. Aberton turned, and so did I—our eyes met—his fell—well they might, after his courteous epithet to my name; however, I had far too good an opinion of myself to care one straw about his; besides, at that moment, I was wholly lost in my surprise and pleasure, in finding that this Duchesse de Perpignan was no other than my acquaintance of the morning. She caught my gaze and smiled as she bowed. "Now," thought I, as I approached her, "let us see if we cannot eclipse Mr. Aberton."

All love-making is just the same, and therefore, I shall spare the reader my conversation that evening. When he recollects that it was Henry Pelham who was the gallant, I am persuaded that he will be pretty certain as to the success.

CHAPTER XIX

Alea sequa vorax species certissima furti
Non contenta bonis, animum quoque perfida mergit!—
Furca, furax—infamis, iners, furiosa, ruina.

PETR. DIAL[1]

I DINED THE NEXT DAY AT THE Frères Provençaux; an excellent restaurateur's, by-the-by, where one gets irreproachable *gibier,* and meets no English.[2] After dinner, I strolled into the various gambling houses, with which the Palais Royal abounds.

In one of these, the crowd and heat were so great, that I should immediately have retired if I had not been struck with the extreme and intense expression of interest in the countenance of one of the spectators at the *rouge et noir* table. He was a man about forty years of age; his complexion was dark and sallow; the features prominent, and what are generally called handsome; but there was a certain sinister expression in his eyes and mouth, which rendered the effect of his physiognomy rather disagreeable than prepossessing. At a small distance from him, and playing, with an air which, in its carelessness and *nonchalance,* formed a remarkable contrast to the painful anxiety of the man I have just described, sate Mr. Thornton.

At first sight, these two appeared to be the only Englishmen present besides myself; I was more struck by seeing the former in that scene, than I was at meeting Thornton there; for there was something

---

1. "Gaming, that direst felon of the breast,/ Steals more than fortune from its wretched thrall,/ Spreads o'er the soul the inert devouring pest,/ And gnaws, and rots, and taints, and ruins all" (unidentified). [Bulwer's paraphrase; 1840 ed.]

2. Mr. Pelham could not say as much for the *Frères Provençaux* at present.* [B-L; 1835 ed.] The *Trois Frères Provençaux* was a restaurant in the Palais Royal very popular with French officers.

66

*distingué** in the mien of the stranger, which suited far worse with the appearance of the place, than the *bourgeois** air and dress of my *ci-devant* second.

"What! another Englishman?" thought I, as I turned round and perceived a thick, rough great coat, which could possibly belong to no continental shoulders. The wearer was standing directly opposite the seat of the swarthy stranger; his hat was slouched over his face; I moved in order to get a clearer view of his countenance. It was the same person I had seen with Thornton that morning. Never to this moment have I forgotten the stern and ferocious expression with which he was gazing upon the keen and agitated features of the gambler opposite. In the eye and lip there was neither pleasure, hatred, nor scorn, in their simple and unalloyed elements; but each seemed blent and mingled into one deadly concentration of evil passions.

This man neither played, nor spoke, nor moved. He appeared utterly insensible of every feeling in common with those around. There he stood, wrapt in his own dark and inscrutable thoughts, never, for one instant, taking his looks from the varying countenance which did not observe their gaze, nor altering the withering character of their almost demoniacal expression. I could not tear myself from the spot. I felt chained by some mysterious and undefinable interest; my attention was first diverted into a new channel, by a loud exclamation from the dark visaged gambler at the table; it was the first he had uttered, notwithstanding his anxiety; and, from the deep, thrilling tone in which it was expressed, it conveyed a keen sympathy with the overcharged feelings which it burst from.

With a trembling hand, he took from an old purse the few Napoleons that were still left there. He set them all at one hazard, on the *rouge*. He hung over the table with a dropping lip; his hands were tightly clasped in each other; his nerves seemed strained into the last agony of excitation. I ventured to raise my eyes upon the gaze, which I *felt* must still be upon the gambler—there it was fixed, and stern as before; but it now conveyed a deeper expression of joy than of the other passions which were there met.* Yet a joy so malignant and fiendish, that no look of mere anger or hatred could have so chilled my heart. I dropped my eyes. I redoubled my attention to the cards—the last two were to be turned up. A moment more!—the fortune was to the *noir*. The stranger had lost! He did not utter a single word. He looked with a vacant eye on the long mace, with which the marker had swept away his last hopes, with his last coin, and then, rising, left the room, and disappeared.

67

The other Englishman was not long in following him. He uttered a short, low, laugh, unobserved, perhaps, by any one but myself; and, pushing through the atmosphere of *sacrés* and *mille tonnerres*, which filled that pandaemonium, strode quickly to the door. I felt as if a load had been taken from my bosom, when he was gone.

CHAPTER XX

Reddere personæ scit convenientia cuique.

Hor. Ars Poet[1]

I WAS LOITERING OVER MY BREAKFAST THE NEXT morning, and thinking of the last night's scene, when Lord Vincent was announced.

"How fares the gallant Pelham?" said he, as he entered the room.

"Why, to say the truth," I replied, "I am rather under the influence of blue devils this morning, and your visit is like a sun-beam in November."

"A bright thought," said Vincent, "and I shall make you a very pretty little poet soon; publish you in a neat octavo, and dedicate you to Lady D——e. Pray, by-the-by, have you ever read her plays? You know they were only privately printed?"

"No," said I, (for in good truth, had his lordship interrogated me touching any other literary production, I should have esteemed it a part of my present character to return the same answer.)

"No!" repeated Vincent; "permit me to tell you, that you must never seem ignorant of any work *not* published. To be *recherché,** one must always know what other people don't—and then one has full liberty to sneer at the value of what other people *do* know. Renounce the threshold of knowledge. *There* every new proselyte can meet you. Boast of your acquaintance with the sanctum, and not one in ten thousand can dispute it with you. Have you read Monsieur de C———'s pamphlet?"

"Really," said I, "I have been so busy."

---

1. "To give each character his fitting part" (Horace *Ars poetica* 316).

"*Ah, mon ami!*" cried Vincent, "the greatest sign of an idle man is to complain of being busy. But you have had a loss: the pamphlet is good. C———, by the way, has an extraordinary, though not an expanded mind; it is like a citizen's garden near London: a pretty parterre here, and a Chinese pagoda there; an oak tree in one corner, and a mushroom bed in the other.* You may traverse the whole in a stride; it is the four quarters of the globe in a mole-hill. Yet every thing is good in its kind; and is neither without elegance nor design in its arrangement."

"What do you think," said I, "of the Baron de ———, the minister of ———?"

"Of him!" replied Vincent—

> " 'His soul
> Still sits at squat, and peeps not from its hole.'[2]

It is dark and bewildered—full of dim visions of the ancient *régime;*— it is a bat hovering about the chambers of an old ruin.* Poor, *antique* little soul! but I will say nothing more about it—

> 'For who would be satirical
> Upon a thing so very small'[3]

as the soul of the Baron de ———?"

Finding Lord Vincent so disposed to the biting mood, I immediately directed his *rabies* towards Mr. Aberton, for whom I had a most inexpressible contempt.*

"Aberton," said Vincent, in answer to my question,* if he knew that *aimable attaché*—"Yes! a sort of man who, speaking of the English embassy, says *we*—who sticks his *best* cards on his chimney-piece, and writes himself *billets-doux* from duchesses. A duodecimo of 'precious conceits,' bound in calf-skin—I know the man well; does he not dress decently, Pelham?"

"His clothes *are* well made," said I; "but no man *can* dress well with those hands and feet!"*

"Ah!" said Vincent, "I should think he went to the best tailor, and said, 'give me a collar like Lord So and So's,'; one who would not dare to have a new waistcoat till it had been authoritatively patronized, and who took his fashions, like his follies, from the best proficients. Such fellows are always too ashamed of themselves not to

---

2. Alexander Pope, *Moral Essays* 1, 55–56.

3. The lines are from "A Description of Dr. Delaney's Villa," lines 3–4, a poem often attributed to Swift but probably not his.

69

be proud of their clothes—like the Chinese mariners, they burn incense *before the needle!*"

"And Mr. Howard de Howard," said I, laughing, "what do you think of him?"

"What! the thin secretary?"* cried Vincent. "He is the mathematical definition of a straight line—*length without breadth.* His inseparable friend, Mr. Aberton, was running up the Rue St. Honoré yesterday in order to catch him."

"*Running!*" cried I, "just like common people—when were you or I ever seen *running?*"

"True," continued Vincent; "but* when I saw him chasing that meagre apparition, I said to Bennington, 'I have found out the real Peter Schlemil!'[4] 'Who?' (asked his grave lordship, with serious *naïveté*) 'Mr. Aberton,' said I; 'don't you see him *running after his shadow?*' But the pride of the lean thing is so amusing! He is fifteenth cousin to the duke, and so his favourite exordium is, 'Whenever I succeed to the titles of my ancestors.' It was but the other day, that he heard two or three silly young men discussing church and state, and they began by talking irreligion—(Mr. Howard de Howard is too unsubstantial not to be spiritually inclined)—however he only fidgeted in his chair. They then proceeded to be exceedingly disloyal. Mr. Howard de Howard fidgeted again;—they then passed to vituperations on the aristocracy—this the attenuated pomposity *(magni nominis umbra)*[5] could brook no longer. He rose up, cast a severe look on the abashed youths, and thus addressed them—'Gentlemen, I have sate by in silence, and heard my King derided, and my God blasphemed; but now in attacking the aristocracy, I can no longer refrain from noticing so obviously intentional an insult. *You have become personal.*' But did you know, Pelham, that he is going to be married?"

"No," said I. "I can't say that I thought such an event likely. Who is the intended?"

"A Miss ———, a girl with some fortune. '*I* can bring *her* none,' said he to the father, 'but I can make her Mrs. Howard de Howard.' "

"Alas, poor girl!" said I, "I fear that her happiness will hang *upon a slender thread.* But suppose we change the conversation: first, because the *subject* is so meagre, that we might easily *wear it out,* and secondly, because such jests may come home. I am not very corpulent myself."

---

4. Peter Schlemil: the legendary "man who sold his shadow," in Adelbert von Chamisso's "Peter Schlemihls wundersame Geschichte" (1814).

5. "Ghost of a great name" (Lucan *Bellum civile* 1.135).

"Bah!" said Vincent, "but at least you have bones and muscles. If you were to pound the poor secretary in a mortar, you might take him all up in a pinch of snuff."*

"Pray, Vincent," said I, after a short pause, "did you ever meet with a Mr. Thornton, at Paris?"

"Thornton, Thornton," said Vincent, musingly; "what, Tom Thornton?"

"I should think, very likely," I replied; "just the sort of man who would be Tom Thornton—has a broad face, with a colour, and wears a spotted neckcloth; Tom—what could his name be but Tom?"

"Is he about five-and-thirty?" asked Vincent, "rather short, and with reddish coloured hair and whiskers?"

"Precisely," said I; "are not all Toms alike?"

"Ah," said Vincent, "I know him well: he is a clever, shrewd fellow, but a most unmitigated rascal. He is the son of a steward in Lancashire, and received an attorney's education; but being a humorous, noisy fellow, he became a great favourite with his father's employer, who was a sort of Maecenas to cudgel players, boxers, and horse jockies. At his house, Thornton met many persons of rank, but of a taste similar to their host's: and they, mistaking his vulgar coarseness for honesty, and his quaint proverbs for wit, admitted him into their society. It was with one of them that I have seen him. I believe of late, that his character has been of a very indifferent odour: and whatever has brought him among the English at Paris—those white-washed abominations—those 'innocent blacknesses,'[6] as Charles Lamb calls chimney sweepers, it does not argue well for his professional occupations. I should think, however, that he manages to *live* here; for wherever there are English fools, there are fine pickings for an English rogue."

"Ay," said I, "but are there enough fools here, to feed the rogues?"

"Yes, because rogues are like spiders, and eat each other, when there is nothing else to catch; and Tom Thornton is safe, as long as the ordinary law of nature lasts, that the greater knave preys on the lesser, for there cannot possibly be a greater knave than he is. If you have made his acquaintance, my dear Pelham, I advise you most soberly to look to yourself, for if he doth not steal, beg, or borrow of you, Mr. Howard de Howard will grow fat, and even Mr. Aberton cease to be a fool. And now, most noble Pelham, farewell. *Il est plus aisé d'être sage pour les autres que de l'être pour soi-même.*"[7]

---

6. "The Praise of Chimney Sweepers," *Essays of Elia.*

7. "It is more easy to be wise for others than for oneself" (La Rochefoucauld, maxim no. 132). [Bulwer's translation; 1840 ed.]   71

CHAPTER XXI

This is a notable couple—and have met
But for some secret knavery.
The Tanner of Tyburn[1]

I HAD NOW BEEN SEVERAL WEEKS IN PARIS, AND I WAS not altogether disatisfied with the manner in which they had been spent. I had enjoyed myself to the utmost, while I had, as much as possible, combined profit with pleasure; viz. if I went to the Opera in the evening, I learned to dance in the morning; if I drove to a *soirée* at the Duchesse de Perpignan's, it was not till I had fenced an hour at the *Salon des Assauts d'Armes;* and if I made love to the duchess herself it was sure to be in a position I had been a whole week in acquiring from my master of the graces;* in short, I took the greatest pains to complete my education. I wish all young men who frequented the Continent for that purpose, could say the same.

One day (about a week after the conversation with Vincent, recorded in my last chapter) I was walking slowly along one of the paths in the *Jardin des Plantes,* meditating upon the various excellencies of the *Rocher de Cancale*[2] and the Duchesse de Perpignan, when I perceived a tall man, with a thick, rough coat, of a dark colour (which I recognized long before I did the face of the wearer) emerging from an intersecting path. He stopped for a few moments, and looked round as if expecting some one. Presently a woman, apparently about thirty, and meanly dressed, appeared in an opposite direction. She approached him; they exchanged a few words, and then, the woman taking his arm, they struck into another path, and were soon out of sight. I suppose that the reader has already discovered that this man was Thornton's companion in the Bois de Boulogne, and the hero of the Salon de Jeu,* in the Palais Royal.

---

1. Unidentified.

2. Rocher de Cancale: a restaurant kept by Borel, formerly one of Napoleon's cooks.

I could not have supposed that so noble a countenance, even in its frowns, could ever have wasted its smiles upon a mistress of that low station to which the woman who had met him evidently belonged. However, we all have our little foibles, as the Frenchman said, when he boiled his grandmother's head in a pipkin.

I myself was, at that time, the sort of person that is always taken by a pretty face, however coarse may be the garments which set it off; and although I cannot say that I ever stooped so far as to become amorous of a chambermaid, yet I could be tolerably lenient to any man under thirty who did. As a proof of this gentleness of disposition, ten minutes after I had witnessed so unsuitable a *rencontre,* I found myself following a pretty little *bourgeoise** into a small sort of *cabaret,* which was, at the time I speak of (and most probably still is), in the midst of the gardens. I sat down, and called for my favourite drink of lemonade; the little *grisette,* who was with an old woman, possibly her mother, and *un beau gros garçon,* probably her lover, sat opposite, and began, with all the ineffable coquetries of her country, to divide her attention between the said *garçon* and myself. Poor fellow, he seemed to be very little pleased by the significant glances exchanged over his right shoulder, and, at last, under pretence of screening her from the draught of the open window, placed himself exactly between us. This, however ingenious, did not at all answer his expectations; for he had not sufficiently taken into consideration, that *I* also was endowed with the power of locomotion; accordingly I shifted my chair about three feet, and entirely defeated the countermarch of the enemy.

But this flirtation did not last long; the youth and the old woman appeared very much of the same opinion as to its impropriety; and accordingly, like experienced generals, resolved to conquer by a retreat; they drank up their orgeat—paid for it—placed the wavering regiment in the middle, and left me master of* the field. I was not, however, of a disposition to break my heart at such an occurrence, and I remained by the window, drinking my lemonade, and muttering to myself, "After all, women are a great bore."

On the outside of the *cabaret,* and just under my window, was a bench, which for a certain number of *sous,* one might appropriate to the entire and unparticipated use of one's self and party. An old woman (so at least I suppose by her voice, for I did not give myself the trouble of looking, though, indeed as to that matter, it might have been the shrill treble of Mr. Howard de Howard) had been hitherto engrossing this settlement with some gallant or other. In Paris, no women are too old to get an *amant,* either by love or money. In a moment of tenderness, this couple paired off, and were immediately succeeded by another. The first tones of the man's voice, low as they were, made me start from my seat. I cast one quick glance before I resumed it. The new pair were the Englishman I had before noted in the garden, and the female companion who had joined him.

"Two hundred pounds, you say?" muttered the man; "we must have it all."

"But," said the woman, in the same whispered voice, "he says, that he will never touch another card."

The man laughed. "Fool," said he, "the passions are not so easily quelled—how many days is it since he had this remittance from England?"

"About three," replied the woman.

"And it is absolutely the very last remnant of his property?"

"The last."

"I am then to understand, that when this is spent there is nothing between him and beggary?"

"Nothing," said the woman, with a half sigh.

The man laughed again, and then rejoined in an altered tone, "Then, then will this parching thirst be quenched at last. I tell you, woman, that it is many months since I have known a day—night—hour, in which my life has been as the life of other men. My whole soul has been melted down into one burning, burning thought. Feel this hand—ay, you may well start—but what is the fever of the frame to that within?"

Here the voice sunk so low as to be inaudible. The woman seemed as if endeavouring to sooth him; at length she said—

"But poor Tyrrell—you will not, surely, suffer him to die of actual starvation?"

The man paused for a few moments, and then replied—

"Night and day, I pray to God, upon my bended knees, only one unvarying, unceasing prayer, and that is—*‘When the last agonies shall be upon that man—when, sick with weariness, pain, disease, hunger, he lies down to die—when the death-gurgle is in the throat, and the eye swims beneath the last dull film—when remembrance peoples the chamber with Hell, and his cowardice would falter forth its dastard recantation to Heaven—*then—may I be there!’ "

There was a long pause, only broken by the woman's sobs, which she appeared endeavouring to stifle. At last the man rose, and in a tone so soft that it seemed literally like music, addressed her in the

74

most endearing terms. She soon yielded to their persuasion, and replied to them with interest.

"Spite of the stings of my remorse," she said, "as long as I lose not you, I will lose life, honour, hope, even soul itself!"

They both quitted the spot as she said this.

O, that woman's love! how strong is it in its weakness! how beautiful in its guilt!*

CHAPTER XXII

At length the treacherous snare was laid,
Poor pug was caught—to town convey'd;
There sold. How envied was his doom,
Made captive in a lady's room!

GAY'S FABLES[1]

I WAS SITTING ALONE A MORNING OR TWO AFTER THIS adventure, when Bedos entering, announced *une dame*. This *dame* was a fine tall thing, dressed out like a print in the *Magasin des Modes*.[2] She sate herself down, threw up her veil, and, after a momentary pause, asked me if I liked my apartment?

"Very much," said I, somewhat surprised at the nature of the interrogatory.

"Perhaps you would wish it altered in some way?" rejoined the lady.

"*Non—mille remercimens!*" said I—"you are very good to be so interested in my accommodation."

"Those curtains might be better arranged—that sofa replaced with a more elegant one," continued my new superintendant.

"Really," said I, "I am too, too much flattered. Perhaps you would like to have my rooms altogether; if so, make at least no scruple of saying it."

---

1. John Gay, *Fables,* first series, 14, 8–10.

2. *Magasin des Modes*: an illustrated magazine begun in Paris in 1786 and continued later as *Journal de la Mode et du Goût.*

"Oh, no," replied the lady, "I have no objection to your staying here."

"You are too kind," said I, with a low bow.

There was a pause of some moments—I took advantage of it.

"I think, Madame, I have the honour of speaking to—to——"

"The mistress of the hotel," said the lady, quietly. "I merely called to ask you how you did, and hope you were well accommodated."

"Rather late, considering I have been six weeks in the house," thought I, revolving in my mind various reports I had heard of my present visitor's disposition to gallantry. However, seeing it was all over with me, I resigned myself, with the patience of a martyr, to the fate that I foresaw. I rose, approached her chair, took her hand (very hard and thin it was too), and thanked her with a most affectionate squeeze.

"I have seen much English!" said the lady, for the first time speaking in our language.

"Ah!" said I, giving another squeeze.

"You are handsome *garçon*," renewed the lady.

"I am so," I replied.

At that moment Bedos entered, and whispered that Madame D'Anville was in the anti-room.

"Good heavens!" said I, knowing her jealousy of disposition, "what is to be done? Oblige me, Madame," seizing the unfortunate mistress of the hotel, and opening the door to the back entrance—"There," said I, "you can easily escape. *Bon jour.*"

Hardly had I closed the door, and put the key in my pocket, before Madame D'Anville entered.

"Do you generally order your servants to keep me* waiting in your anti-room?" said she, haughtily.

"Not generally," I replied, endeavouring to make my peace; but all my complaisance was in vain—she was jealous of my intimacy with the Duchesse de Perpignan, and glad of any excuse to vent her pique. I am just the sort of man to bear, but never to forgive a woman's ill temper, viz.–it makes no impression on me at the time, but leaves a sore recollection of something disagreeable, which I internally resolve never again to experience. Madame D'Anville* was going to the Luxembourg; and my only chance of soothing her anger was to accompany her.

Down stairs, therefore, we went, and drove to the Luxembourg; I gave Bedos, before my departure, various little commissions, and told him he need not be at home till the evening. Long before the

76

expiration of an hour, Madame D'Anville's ill humour had given me an excuse for affecting it myself. Tired to death of her, and panting for release, I took a high tone—complained of her ill temper, and her want of love—spoke rapidly—waited for no reply, and leaving her at the Luxembourg, proceeded forthwith to Galignani's,[3] like a man just delivered from a strait waistcoat.

Leave me now, for a few minutes, in the reading-room at Galignani's, and return to the mistress of the hotel, whom I had so unceremoniously thrust out of my salon. The passage into which she had been put communicated by one door with my rooms, and by another with the staircase. Now, it had so happened, that Bedos was in the habit of locking the latter door, and keeping the key; the other egress, it will be remembered, I myself had secured; so that the unfortunate mistress of the hotel was no sooner turned into this passage than she found herself in a sort of dungeon, ten feet by five, and surrounded, like Eve in Paradise, by a whole creation—not of birds, beasts, and fishes, but of brooms, brushes, unclean linen, and a wood-basket. What she was to do in this dilemma was utterly inconceivable; scream, indeed, she might, but then the shame and ridicule of being discovered in so equivocal a situation, were somewhat more than our discreet landlady could endure. Besides, such an *exposé* might be attended with a loss the good woman valued more than reputation, viz. lodgers; for the possessors of the two best floors were both Englishwomen of a certain rank; and my landlady had heard such accounts of our national virtue, that she feared an instantaneous imigration of such inveterate prudes, if her screams and situation reached their ears.

Quietly then, and soberly, did the good lady sit, eyeing the brooms and brushes as they grew darker and darker with the approach of the evening, and consoling herself with the certainty that her release must eventually take place.

Meanwhile, to return to myself—from which dear little person, I very seldom, even in imagination, digress—* I found Lord Vincent at Galignani's, carefully looking over "Choice Extracts from the best English Authors."

"Ah, my good fellow!" said he, "I am delighted to see you; I made such a capital quotation just now: the young Benningtons were drowning a poor devil of a puppy; the youngest (to whom the mother belonged) looked on with a grave earnest face, till the last kick was over, and then burst into tears. 'Why do you cry so?' said I. 'Because

3. Galignani's was a Parisian publishing house that specialized in English reprints. It began issuing the widely read *Galignani's Messenger* in 1814.

it was so cruel in us to drown the poor puppy!' replied the juvenile Philocunos.[4] 'Pooh,' said I, "Quid juvat errores *mersâ jam puppe fateri.*' " Was it not good?—you remember it in Claudian, eh, Pelham? Think of its being thrown away on those Latinless young lubbers! Have you seen anything of Mr. Thornton lately?"

"No," said I, "I've not, but I am determined to have that pleasure soon."

"You will do as you please," said Vincent, "but you will be like the child playing with edged tools."

"I am not a child," said I, "so the simile is not good. He must be the devil himself, or a Scotchman at least, to take *me* in."

Vincent shook his head. "Come and dine with me at the Rocher," said he; "we are a party of six—choice spirits all."

"*Volontiers;* but we can stroll in the Tuileries first, if you have no other engagement?"

"None," said Vincent, putting his arm in mine.

As we passed up the Rue de la Paix, we met Sir Henry Millington, mounted on a bay horse, as stiff as himself, and cantering down the street as if he and his steed had been cut out of pasteboard together.

"I wish," said Vincent, (to borrow Luttrel's quotation), "that that master of arts would 'cleanse his bosom of that perilous stuff.'[5] I should like to know in what recess of that immense mass now cantering round the corner is the real body of Sir Henry Millington. I could fancy the poor snug little thing shrinking within, like a guilty conscience. Ah well says Juvenal,

> " 'Mors sola fatetur
> *Quantula* sint hominum corpuscula.' "

"He has a superb head, though," I replied. I like to allow that other people are handsome now and then—it looks generous."

"Yes," said Vincent, "for a barber's block: but here comes Mrs. C———me, and her beautiful daughter—*those* are people you ought to know, if you wish to see human nature a little relieved from the frivolities which make it in society so like a man milliner. Mrs. C——— has considerable genius, combined with great common sense."

---

4. Philocunos: Bulwer's unique form of the Greek *philokuon or* "lover of dogs." The Latin quotation following may be translated: "What's the pleasure in confessing one's errors when your boat has sunk?" (Claudian *In Eutropium* 2.7). Vincent puns on "puppe" (boat/puppy).

5. Henry Luttrell (1765–1851), "Advice to Julia." The Latin quotation at the end of the paragraph may be translated: "Death alone reveals how insignificant are the puny bodies of men" (Juvenal *Satires* 10.172).

"A rare union," said I.

"By no means," replied Vincent. "It is a cant antithesis in opinion to oppose them to one another; but, so far as mere theoretical common sense is concerned, I would much sooner apply to a great poet or a great orator for advice on matter of business, than any dull plodder who has passed his whole life in a counting-house. Common sense is only a modification of talent—genius is an exaltation of it: the difference is, therefore, in the degree, not nature. But to return to Mrs. C———; she writes beautiful poetry—almost impromptu; draws excellent caricatures; possesses a laugh for whatever is ridiculous, but never loses a smile for whatever is good. Placed in very peculiar situations, she has passed through each with a grace and credit which make her best eulogium. If she possesses one quality higher than intellect, it is her kindness of heart: no wonder, indeed, that she is so really clever—those trees which are the soundest at the core produce the finest fruits, and the most beautiful blossoms."

"Lord Vincent grows poetical," thought I—"how very different he really is to that which he affects to be in the world: but so it is with every one—we are all like the ancient actors: let our faces be ever so beautiful, we must still wear a mask."*

After an hour's walk, Vincent suddenly recollected that he had a commission of a very important nature in the Rue J. J. Rousseau. This was—to *buy a monkey.* "It is for Wormwood," said he, "who has written me a long letter, describing its qualities and qualifications. I suppose he wants it for some practical joke—some embodied bitterness—God* forbid I should thwart him in so charitable a design!"

"Amen," said I; and we proceeded together to the monkey-fancier. After much deliberation we at last decided upon the most hideous animal I ever beheld—it was of a—no, I will not attempt to describe it—it would be quite impossible! Vincent was so delighted with our choice that he insisted upon carrying it away immediately.

"Is it quite quiet?" I asked.

"*Comme un oiseau,*" said the man.

We called a *fiacre*—paid for monsieur Jocko, and drove to Vincent's apartments; there we found, however, that his valet had gone out and taken the key.

"Hang it," said Vincent, "it does not signify! We'll carry *le petit monsieur* with us to the Rocher."

Accordingly we all *three* once more entered the *fiacre,* and drove to the celebrated restaurateur's of the Rue Mont Orgueil. O, blissful recollections of that dinner! how at this moment you crowd upon my delighted remembrance! Lonely and sorrowful as I now sit, digesting with many a throe the iron thews of a British beef-steak—*more anglico*—immeasurably tough—I see the grateful apparitions of *Escallopes de Saumon* and *Laitances de Carps* rise in a gentle vapour before my eyes! breathing a sweet and pleasant odour, and contrasting the dream-like delicacies of their hue and aspect, with the dire and dure realities which now weigh so heavily on the region below my heart! And thou, most beautiful of all—thou evening star of *entremets*—thou that delightest in truffles, and gloriest in a dark cloud of sauces—exquisite *foie-gras!*[6]—Have I forgotten thee? Do I not, on the contrary, see thee—smell thee—taste thee—and almost die with rapture of thy possession? What, though the goose, of which thou art a part, has, indeed, been roasted alive by a slow fire, in order to increase thy divine proportions—yet has not our *Almanach*—the *Almanach des Gourmands*—truly declared that the goose rejoiced amid all her tortures—because of the glory that awaited her? Did she not, in prophetic vision, behold her enlarged and ennobled *foie* dilate into *pâtés* and steam into *sautés*—the companion of truffles—the glory of dishes—the delight—the treasure—the transport of gourmands! O, exalted among birds—apotheosised goose, did not thy heart exult even when thy liver parched and swelled within thee, from that most agonizing death; and didst thou not, like the Indian at the stake, triumph in the very torments which alone could render thee illustrious?

After dinner we grew exceedingly merry. Vincent punned and quoted; we laughed and applauded; and our Burgundy went round with an alacrity, to which every new joke gave an additional impetus. Monsieur Jocko was by no means the dullest in the party; he cracked his nuts with as much grace as we did our jests, and grinned and chatted as facetiously as the best of us. After coffee we were all so pleased with one another, that we resolved not to separate, and accordingly we adjourned to my rooms, Jocko and all, to find new revelries and grow brilliant over Curaçoa punch.

We entered my salon with a roar, and set Bedos to work at the punch forthwith. Bedos, that Ganymede of a valet, had himself but just arrived, and was unlocking the door as we entered. We soon blew up a glorious fire, and our spirits brightened in proportion.

---

6. Since *foie-gras* is made from artifically enlarged goose liver, the following comic rhapsody achieves a very real, if somewhat ghoulish, wit. The *Almanach des Gourmands,* mentioned below, was published in Paris between 1803 and 1812.

Monsieur Jocko sate on Vincent's knee—*Ne* monstrum,[7] as he classically termed it. One of our compotatores was playing with it. Jocko grew suddenly in earnest—a grin—a scratch and a bite, were the work of a moment.

"*Ne quid nimis*—now," said Vincent, gravely, instead of endeavouring to soothe the afflicted party, who grew into a towering passion. Nothing but Jocko's absolute disgrace could indeed have saved his life from the vengeance of the sufferer.

"Where shall we banish him?" said Vincent.

"Oh," I replied, "put him out in that back passage;" the outer door is shut; he'll be quite safe; and to the passage he was therefore immediately consigned.

It was in this place, the reader will remember, that the hapless Dame du Château was at that very instant in "durance vile."[8] Bedos, who took the condemned monkey, opened the door, thrust Jocko in, and closed it again. Meanwhile we resumed our merriment.

"*Nunc est bibendum*,"[9] said Vincent, as Bedos placed the punch on the table. "Give as a toast, Dartmore."

Lord Dartmore was a young man, with tremendous spirits, which made up for wit. He was just about to reply, when a loud shriek was heard from Jocko's place of banishment: a sort of scramble ensued, and the next moment the door was thrown violently open, and in rushed the terrified landlady, screaming like a sea-gull, and bearing Jocko aloft upon her shoulders, from which "bad eminence"[10] he was grinning and chattering with the fury of fifty devils. She ran twice round the room, and then sunk on the floor in hysterics. We lost no time in hastening to her assistance; but the warlike Jocko, still sitting upon her, refused to permit one of us to approach. There he sat, turning from side to side, showing his sharp, white teeth, and uttering from time to time the most menacing and diabolical sounds.

"What the deuce shall we do?" cried Dartmore.

"*Do?*" said Vincent, who was convulsed with laughter, and yet endeavouring to speak gravely; "why, watch like L. Opimius, '*ne quid respublica detrimenti caperet.*'"[11]

---

7. Another Vincentian pun apparently meaning, alternatively, "a monstrous knee" or "a real monster." In the next paragraph Lord Vincent again puns on the proverbial Latin tag meaning "nothing to excess."

8. In common use, the phrase dates back at least to 1513.

9. "Now we must drink" (Horace *Carmen* 1.37.1).

10. *Paradise Lost*, 2, line 6.

11. "Lest the republic come to harm . . . ": a formula used to declare a state of martial law. It was invoked in the second century B.C. by Consul Lucius Opimius against the elder Graccus, who led an uprising for land reform.

"By Jove, Pelham, he will scratch out the lady's *beaux yeux*," cried the good-natured Dartmore, endeavouring to seize the monkey by the tail, for which he very narrowly escaped with an unmutilated visage. But the man who had before suffered by Jocko's ferocity, and whose breast was still swelling with revenge, was glad of so favourable an opportunity and excuse for wreaking it. He seized the poker, made three strides to Jocko, who set up an ineffable cry of defiance, and with a single blow split the skull of the unhappy monkey in twain. It fell with one convulsion on the ground, and gave up the ghost.

We then raised the unfortunate landlady, placed her on the sofa, and Dartmore administered a plentiful potation of the Curaçoa punch. By slow degrees she revived, gave three most doleful suspirations, and then, starting up, gazed wildly around her. Half of us were still laughing—my unfortunate self among the number; this the enraged landlady no sooner perceived than she imagined herself the victim of some preconcerted villainy. Her lips trembled with passion—she uttered the most dreadful imprecations; and had I not retired into a corner, and armed myself with the dead body of Jocko, which I wielded with exceeding valour, she might, with the simple weapons with which nature had provided her hands, have for ever demolished the loves and graces that abide in the face of Henry Pelham.

When at last she saw that nothing hostile was at present to be effected, she drew herself up, and giving Bedos a tremendous box on the ear, as he stood grinning beside her, marched out of the room.

We then again rallied around the table, more than ever disposed to be brilliant, and kept up till daybreak a continued fire of jests upon the heroine of the passage. *"Cum quâ* (as Vincent observed) *clauditur adversis innoxia simia fatis!"*[12]

---

12. "He is shut up with a harmless ape by the hostile fates" (Juvenal *Satires* 13.155–6).

CHAPTER XXIII

"Show me not thy painted beauties,
These impostures I defy!"
GEORGE WITHERS[1]

"The cave of Falri smelt not more delicately—on every side appeared the marks of drunkenness and gluttony. At the upper end of the cave the sorcerer lay exended," &c.
Mirglip the Persian, in the Tales of the Genii

I WOKE THE NEXT MORNING WITH AN ACHING HEAD and feverish frame. Ah, those midnight carousals, how glorious they would be if there was *no* next morning! I took my *sauterne* and soda-water in my dressing-room; and, as indisposition always makes me meditative, I thought over all I had done since my arrival at Paris. I had become *(that,* God knows, I soon manage to do) rather a talked of and noted character. It is true that I was every where abused—one found fault with my neckcloth—another with my mind—the lank Mr. Aberton declared that I put my hair in papers, and the stuffed Sir Henry Millington said I was a thread-paper myself. One blamed my riding—a second my dancing—a third wondered how any woman *could* like me, and a fourth said that no woman *ever* could.

On one point, however, all—friends and foes— were alike agreed; viz. that I was a consummate puppy, and excessively well satisfied with myself. *A la vérité,** they were not much mistaken there. Why is it, by the by, that to be pleased with one's-self is the surest way of offending everybody else? If any one, male or female, an evident admirer of his or her own perfections, enter a room, how perturbed, restless, and unhappy every individual of the offender's sex instantly becomes: for them not only enjoyment but tranquillity is over, and if they could annihilate the unconscious victim of their spleen, I

---

1. From a sonnet, "Hence, away, thou siren leave me," lines 11–12, by George Withers. The second epigraph is from *Tales of the Genii* (1765), translated from the Persian by Sir Charles Morell.

fully believe no Christian toleration would come in the way of that last extreme of animosity. For a coxcomb there is no mercy—for a coquet no pardon. They are, as it were, the dissenters of society—no crime is too bad to be imputed to them; they do not believe the religion of others—they set up a deity of their own vanity—all the orthodox vanities of others are offended. Then comes the bigotry—the stake—the *auto-da-fé* of scandal. What, alas! is so implacable as the rage of vanity? What so restless as its persecution? Take from a man his fortune, his house, his reputation, but flatter his vanity in each, and he will forgive you. Heap upon him benefits, fill him with blessings: but irritate his self-love, and you have made the very best man an *ingrat*.* He will sting you if he can: you cannot blame him; you yourself have instilled the venom. This is one reason why you must not always* reckon upon gratitude in conferring an obligation. It is a very high mind to which gratitude is not a painful sensation. If you wish to please, you will find it wiser to receive—solicit even—favours, than accord them; for the vanity of the *obliger* is always flattered—that of the *obligee* rarely.

Well, this is an unforseen digression: let me return! I had mixed, of late, very little with the English. My mother's introductions had procured me the *entrée* of the best French houses; and to them, therefore, my evenings were usually devoted. Alas! that was a happy time, when my carriage used to await me at the door of the Rocher de Cancale, and then whirl me to a succession of visits, varying in their degree and nature as the whim prompted: now to the brilliant *soirées* of Madame De ———, or to the *appartemens au troisième* of some less celebrated daughter of dissipation and *écarté;* now to the literary conversaziones of the Duchesse de D———s, or the Vicomte d'A———,[2] and then to the feverish excitement of the gambling house. Passing from each with the appetite for amusement kept alive by variety; finding in none a disappointment, and in every one a welcome*; full of the health which supports, and the youth which colours all excess or excitation, I drained, with an unsparing lip, whatever that enchanting metropolis could afford.

I have hitherto said but little of the Duchesse de Perpignan; I think it necessary now to give some account of that personage. Ever

2. Bulwer's son identified these characters as "the Duchess Descazes [*sic*] and the Vicompte d'Arlincourt" (*Life . . . and Literary Remains*, II, p. 21). The duchess was the wife of Elie, duc Decazes (1780–1860), the French ambassador in London in 1820–22 and intimate friend of Louis XVIII; Charles Victor Prevôt, vicomte d'Arlincourt (1789–1856) was a fashionable French poet and novelist.

since the evening I had met her at the ambassador's, I had paid her the most unceasing attentions. I soon discovered that she had a curious sort of *liaison* with one of the *attachés*—a short, ill-made gentleman, with high shoulders, and a pale face, who wore a blue coat and buff waistcoat, wrote bad verses, and thought himself handsome. All Paris said she was excessively enamoured of this youth. As for me, I had not known her four days before I discovered that she could not be excessively enamoured of any thing but an oyster *pâté* and Lord Byron's Corsair. Her mind was the most marvellous *mélange* of sentiment and its opposite. In her amours she was Lucretia[3] herself; in her epicurism, Apicius would have yielded to her. She was pleased with sighs, but she adored suppers. She would leave every thing for her lover, except her dinner. The *attaché* soon quarrelled with her, and I was installed into the platonic honours of his office.

At first, I own that I was flattered by her choice, and though she was terribly *exigeante** of my *petits soins,* I managed to keep up her affection, and, what is still more wonderful, my own, for the better part of a month. What then cooled me was the following occurrence:

I was in her boudoir one evening, when her *femme de chambre* came to tell us that the duc was in the passage. Notwithstanding the innocence of our attachment, the duchesse was in a violent fright; a small door was at the left of the ottoman, on which we were sitting. "Oh, no, no, not there," cried the lady; but I, who saw no other refuge, entered it forthwith, and before she could ferret me out, the duc was in the room.

In the meanwhile, I amused myself by examining the wonders of the new world into which I had so abruptly immerged: on a small table before me, was deposited a remarkably constructed night-cap; I examined it as a curiosity: on each side was placed *une petite cotelette de veau cru,* sewed on with green-coloured silk (I remember even the smallest minutiae), a beautiful golden wig (the duchesse never like me to play with her hair) was on a block close by, and on another table was a set of teeth, *d'une blancheur éblouissante.* In this manufactory of a beauty I remained for a quarter of an hour; at the end of that time, the abigail (the duchesse had the grace to disappear) released me, and I flew down stairs* like a spirit from purgatory.

From that moment the duchesse honoured me with her most

---

3. Lucretia Borgia, daughter of Pope Alexander VI and duchess of Ferrara (1480–1519). In the same sentence, Apicius: first century A.D. Roman epicure who was said to have committed suicide rather than economize.

deadly abhorrence. Equally silly and wicked, her schemes of revenge were as ludicrous in their execution as remorseless in their design: at one time I narrowly escaped poison in a cup of coffee—at another, she endeavoured to stab me to the heart with a paper cutter.

Notwithstanding my preservation from these attacks, this new Messalina[4]* had resolved on my destruction, and another means of attempting it still remained, which the reader will yet have the pleasure of learning.

Mr. Thornton had called upon me twice, and twice I had returned the visit, but neither of us had been at home to benefit by these reciprocities of *politesse.** His acquaintance with my mysterious hero of the gambling house and the *Jardin des Plantes,* and the keen interest I took, in spite of myself, in that unaccountable person, whom I was persuaded I had seen before in some very different scene, and under very different circumstances, made me desirous to increase a *connoissance,** which, from Vincent's detail, I should otherwise have been anxious to avoid. I therefore resolved to make another attempt to find him at home; and my headache being somewhat better, I took my way to his apartments in the Faubourg St. Germain.

I love that *quartier*—if ever I went* to Paris again I should reside there. It is quite a different world from the streets usually known to, and tenanted by the English—*there,* indeed, you are among the French, the fossilized remains of the old *régime*—the very houses have an air of desolate, yet venerable grandeur—you never pass by the white and modern mansion of a *nouveau riche;* all, even to the ruggedness of the *pavé,* breathes a haughty disdain of innovation— you cross one of the numerous bridges, and you enter into another time—you are inhaling the atmosphere of a past century; no flaunting *boutique,* French in its trumpery, English in its prices, stares you in the face; no stiff coats and unnatural gaits are seen *anglicising* up the melancholy streets. Vast hotels, with their gloomy frontals, and magnificent contempt of comfort; shops, such as shops might have been in the aristocratic days of Louis Quatorze, ere British vulgarities* made them insolent and dear; public edifices, still redolent of the superb charities of *le grand monarque*—carriages, with their huge bodies and ample decorations; horses, with their Norman dimensions and undocked honours; men, on whose more high, though not less courteous demeanour, the revolution seems to have wrought no demo-

---

4. Messalina: notoriously corrupt first century A.D. Roman empress, wife of Claudius Caesar.

cratic plebeianism—all strike on the mind with a vague and nameless impression of antiquity; a something solemn even in gaiety, and faded in pomp, appears to linger over all you behold; there are the Great French people unadulterated by change, unsullied with the commerce of the vagrant and various tribes that throng their mighty mart of enjoyments.

The strangers who fill the *quartiers* on this side the Seine pass not there; between them and *the* Faubourg there is a gulf; the very skies seem different—your own feelings, thoughts—nature itself—alter, when you have passed that Styx which divides the wanderers from the habitants; your spirits are not so much damped, as tinged, refined, ennobled by a certain inexpressible awe—you are girt with the stateliness of Eld, and you tread the gloomy streets with the dignity of a man, who is recalling the splendours of an ancient court where he once did homage.[5]

I arrived at Thornton's chambers in the Rue St. Dominique. *"Monsieur, est-il chez lui?"* said I to the ancient porteress, who was reading one of Crébillon's novels.

"Oui, Monsieur, au quatrième," was the answer. I turned to the dark and unclean staircase, and, after incredible exertion and fatigue, arrived, at last, at the elevated abode of Mr. Thornton.

"Entrez," cried a voice, in answer to my rap. I obeyed the signal, and found myself in a room of tolerable dimensions and multiplied utilities. A decayed silk curtain of a dingy blue, drawn across a recess, separated the *chambre à coucher* from the *salon*. It was at present only half drawn, and did not, therefore, conceal the mysteries of the den within; the bed was still unmade, and apparently of no very inviting cleanliness; a red handkerchief, that served as a nightcap, hung pendant from the foot of the bed; at a little distance from it, more towards the pillow, were a shawl, a parasol, and an old slipper. On a table, which stood between the two dull, filmy windows, were placed a cracked bowl, still reeking with the lees of gin-punch, two bottles half full, a mouldy cheese, and a salad dish; on the ground beneath it lay two huge books, and a woman's bonnet.

Thornton himself sat by a small consumptive fire, in an easy-chair; another table, still spread with the appliances of breakfast, viz. a coffee-pot, a milk-jug, two cups, a broken loaf, and an empty dish, mingled with a pack of cards, *one* dice, and an open book *de mauvais goût*, stood immediately before him.

---

5. It was in 1827 that this was written;* the glory (by this time) has probably left *the* Faubourg. [B-L; 1835 ed.]

Everything around bore some testimony of the spirit of low debauchery; and the man himself, with his flushed and sensual countenance, his unwashed hands, and the slovenly rakishness of his whole appearance, made no unfitting representation of the *Genius Loci.*

All that I have described, together with a flitting shadow of feminine appearance, escaping through another door, my quick eye discovered in the same instant that I made my salutation.

Thornton rose, with an air half careless and half abashed, and expressed, in more appropriate terms than his appearance warranted, his pleasurable surprise at seeing me at last. There was, however, a singularity in his conversation, which gave it an air both of shrewdness and vulgarity. This was, as may before have been noted, a profuse intermixture of proverbs, some stale, some new, some sensible enough, and all savouring of a vocabulary carefully eschewed by every man of ordinary refinement in conversation.

"I have but a small tenement," said he, smiling; "but, thank Heaven, at Paris a man is not made by his lodgings. Small house, small care. Few *garçons* have indeed a more sumptuous apartment than myself."

"True," said I; "and if I may judge by the bottles on the opposite table, and the bonnet beneath it, you find that no abode is too humble or too exalted for the solace of the senses."

" 'Fore Gad, you are in the right, Mr. Pelham," replied Thornton, with a loud, coarse, chuckling laugh, which, more than a year's conversation could have done, let me into the secrets of his character. "I care not a rush for the decorations of the table, so that the cheer be good; nor for the gew-gaws of the head-dress, as long as the face is pretty—'the taste of the kitchen is better than the smell.' Do you go much to Madame B———'s in the Rue Gretry—eh, Mr. Pelham?—ah, I'll be bound you do."

"No," said I, with a loud laugh, but internal shiver; "but you know where to find *le bon vin et jolies filles.* As for me, I am still a stranger at Paris, and amuse myself but very indifferently."

Thornton's face brightened. "I tell you what my good fell——I beg pardon—I mean Mr. Pelham—I can shew you the best sport in the world, if you can only spare me a little of your time—this very evening, perhaps?"

"I fear," said I, "I am engaged all the present week; but I long for nothing more than to cultivate an acquaintance, seemingly *so exactly to my own taste.*"

Thornton's grey eyes twinkled. "Will you breakfast with me on Sunday?*" said he.

"I shall be *too* happy," I replied.

There was now a short pause. I took advantage of it. "I think," said I, "I have seen you once or twice with a tall, handsome man, in a loose great coat of very singular colour. Pray, if not impertinent, who is he? I am sure I have seen him before in England."

I looked full upon Thornton as I said this; he changed colour, and answered my gaze with a quick glance from his small, glittering eye, before he replied. "I scarcely know who you mean, my acquaintance is so large and miscellaneous at Paris. It might have been Johnson, or Smith, or Howard, or any body, in short."

"It is a man nearly six feet high," said I, "thin, and remarkably well made, of a pale complexion, light eyes, and very black hair, mustachios and whiskers. I saw him with you once in the Bois de Boulogne, and once in a hell[6] in the Palais Royal. Surely, *now* you will recollect who he is?"

Thornton was evidently disconcerted. "Oh!" said he, after a short pause, and another of his peculiarly quick, sly glances—"Oh, *that* man; I have known him a very short time. What *is* his name? let *me* see!" and Mr. Thornton affected to look down in a complete reverie of dim remembrances.

I saw, however, that, from time to time, his eye glanced up to me, with a restless, inquisitive expression, and as instantly retired.

"Ah," said I, carelessly, "I think I know who he is!"

"Who!" cried Thornton, eagerly, and utterly off his guard.

"And yet," I pursued, without noticing the interruption, "it scarcely can be—the colour of the hair is so very different."

Thornton again appeared to relapse into his recollections.

"War—Warbur—ah, I have it now!" cried he, "Warburton—that's it—that's the name—is it the one you supposed, Mr. Pelham?"

"No," said I, apparently perfectly satisfied. "I was quite mistaken. Good morning, I did not think it was so late. On Sunday,* then, Mr. Thornton—*au plaisir!*"

"A d——d* cunning dog!" said I to myself, as I left the apartments. "However, *on peut-être trop fin.*[7] I shall have him yet."

The surest way to make a dupe is to let your victim suppose that you are his.

---

6. A hell: slang for a gambling house.

7. "One can be *too* careful."

CHAPTER XXIV

Voilà de l'érudition.

Les Femmes Savantes[1]

I FOUND, ON MY RETURN, COVERED WITH BLOOD, AND foaming with passion, my inestimable valet—Bedos!

"What's the matter?" said I.

"Matter!" repeated Bedos, in a tone almost inarticulate with rage; and then, rejoicing at the opportunity of unbosoming his wrath, he poured a vast volley of *ivrognes* and *carognes*, against our Dame du Château, of monkey reminiscence. With great difficulty, I gathered, at last, from his vituperations, that the enraged landlady, determined to wreak her vengeance on some one, had sent for him into her *appartement*, accosted him with a smile, bade him sit down, regaled him with cold *vol-au-vent*, and a glass of Curaçoa, and, while he was felicitating himself on his good fortune, slipped out of the room: presently, three tall fellows entered with sticks.

"We'll teach you," said the biggest of them—"we'll teach you to lock up ladies, for the indulgence of your vulgar amusement;" and, without one other word, they fell upon Bedos, with incredible zeal and vigour. The valiant valet defended himself, tooth and nail, for some time, for which he only got the more soundly belaboured. In the meanwhile the landlady entered, and, with the same gentle smile as before, begged him to make no ceremony, to proceed with his present amusement, and when he was tired with the exercise, hoped he would refresh himself with another glass of Curaçoa.

"It was this," said Bedos, with a whimper, "which hurt me the most, to think she should serve me so cruelly, after I had eaten so plentifully of the *vol-au-vent;* envy and injustice I can bear, but treachery stabs me to the heart."

---

1. "There's erudition for you" (Molière, *Les Femmes savantes*, III, 2). [Bulwer's translation; 1840 ed.]

When these threshers of men were tired, the lady satisfied, and Bedos half dead, they suffered the unhappy valet to withdraw; the mistress of the hotel giving him a note, which she desired, with great civility, that he would transmit to me on my return. This, I found, inclosed my bill, and informed me that my month being out on the morrow, she was unwilling to continue me any longer,* and begged I would, therefore, have the *bonté* to choose another apartment.

"Carry my luggage forthwith," said I, "to the Hôtel de Mirabeau;" and that very evening I changed by abode.

I am happy in the opportunity this incident affords me of especially recommending the Hôtel de Mirabeau, Rue de la Paix, to any of my countrymen who are really gentlemen, and will not disgrace my recommendation. It is certainly the best caravansera in the English *quartier.**

I was engaged that day to a literary dinner at the Marquis D'Al——; and as I knew I should meet Vincent, I felt some pleasure in repairing to my entertainer's hotel. They were just going to dinner as I entered. A good many English were of the party. The good natured (in all senses of the word) Lady ———, who always affected to pet me, cried aloud, "Pelham, *mon joli petit mignon*, I have not seen you for an age—do give me your arm."

Madame D'Anville was just before me, and, as I looked at her, I saw that her eyes were full of tears; my heart smote me for my late inattention, and going up to her, I only nodded to Lady ———, and said, in reply to her invitation, "*Non, perfide*, it is *my* turn to be cruel *now*. Remember your flirtation with Mr. Howard de Howard."

"Pooh!" said Lady ———, taking Lord Vincent's arm, "your jealousy does indeed rest upon '*a trifle light as air.*' "[2]

"Do you forgive me?" whispered I to Madame D'Anville, as I handed her to the *salle à manger*.

"'Does not love forgive every thing?" was her answer.

"At least," thought I, "it never talks in those pretty phrases."

The conversation soon turned upon books. As for me, I never at that time took a share in those discussions; indeed, I have long laid it down as a rule, that a man never gains by talking to more than one person at a time. If you don't shine, you are a fool—if you do, you are a bore. You must become either ridiculous or unpopular—either hurt your own self-love by stupidity, or that of others by wit. I therefore sat in silence, looking exceedingly edified, and now and

---

2. *Othello*, III, 3, 322.

then muttering "good!" "true!" Thank heaven, however, the suspension of one faculty only increases the vivacity of the others; my eyes and ears always watch like sentinels over the repose of my lips. Careless and indifferent as I seem to all things, nothing ever escapes me: the minutest *erreur* in a dish or a domestic, the most trifling peculiarity in a criticism or a coat, my glance detects in an instant, and transmits for ever to my recollection.*

"You have seen Jouy's 'Hermite de la Chaussée D'Antin?' "[3] said our host to Lord Vincent.

"I have, and think meanly of it. There is a perpetual aim at something pointed, which as perpetually merges into something dull. He is like a bad swimmer, strikes out with great force, makes a confounded splash, and never gets a yard the further for it. It is a great effort *not to sink*. Indeed, Monsieur D'A———, your literature is at a very reduced ebb; bombastic in the drama—shallow in philosophy—mawkish in poetry, your writers of the present day seem to think, with Boileau—

> " 'Souvent de tous nos maux la raison est le pire.' "[4]

"Surely," cried Madame D'Anville, "you will allow De la Martine's poetry[5] to be beautiful?"

"I allow it," said he, "to be among the best you have; and I know very few lines in your language equal to the two first stanzas in his 'Meditation on Napoleon,' or to those exquisite verses called *'Le Lac;'* but *you* will allow also that he wants originality and nerve. His thoughts are pathetic, but not deep; he whines, but sheds no tears. He has, in his imitation of Lord Byron, reversed the great miracle: instead of turning water into wine, he has turned wine into water. Besides, he is so unpardonably obscure. He thinks, with Bacchus —(you remember, D'A———, the line in Euripides, which I will *not* quote), that 'there is something august in the shades;'[6] but he has applied this thought wrongly—in his obscurity there is nothing sublime—it is the back ground of a Dutch picture. It is only a red herring, or an old hat, which he has invested with such pomposity of shadow and darkness."

---

3. Victor Joseph Etienne de Jouy (1764–1846). *L'Ermite* (1812–14), in five volumes, is a series of satirical sketches of Parisian life.

4. "Reason is often the worst of all our ills" (Boileau, *Satires*, 4, 114).

5. Alphonse de Lamartine (1790–1869): historian, statesman, and celebrated Romantic poet.

6. *The Bacchae*, line 486.

92

"'But his verses are *so* smooth," said Lady ———.
"Ah!" answered Vincent.

> " 'Quand la rime enfin se trouve au bout des vers,
> Qu'importe que le reste y soit mis des travers.' "[7]

"*Hélas!*" said the Viscount D'A———t, an author of no small celebrity himself; "I agree with you—we shall never again see a Voltaire or a Rousseau."

"There is but little justice in those complaints, often as they are made," replied Vincent. "You may not, it is true, see a Voltaire or a Rousseau, but you will see their equals. Genius can never be exhausted by one individual. In our country, the poets after Chaucer in the fifteenth century complained of the decay of their art—they did not anticipate Shakespeare. In Hayley's time,[8] who ever dreamt of the ascension of Byron? Yet Shakspeare and Byron came like the bridegroom 'in the dead of night;'[9] and you have the same probability of producing—not, indeed, another Rousseau, but a writer to do equal honour to your literature."

"I think," said Lady ———, "that Rousseau's 'Julie' is over-rated. I had heard so much of 'La Nouvelle Héloïse' when I was a girl, and been so often told that it was destruction to read it, that I bought the book the very day after I was married. I own to you that I could not get through it."

"I am not surprised at it," answered Vincent; "but Rousseau is not the less a genius for all that; there is no story* to bear out the style, and he himself is right when he says *ce livre convient à très peu de lecteurs.*[10]* One letter would delight every one—four volumes of them are a surfeit—it is the *toujours perdrix.* But the chief beauty of that wonderful conception of an empassioned and meditative mind is to be found in the inimitable manner in which the thoughts are embodied, and in the tenderness, the truth, the profundity of the thoughts themselves: when Lord Edouard says, '*c'est le chemin des*

---

7. "No matter what the stuff, if good the rhime—/ The rubble stands cemented with the lime" (Boileau, *Satires*, 2, 83–84). [Bulwer's paraphrase; 1840 ed.]

8. William Hayley (1745–1820), minor poet now remembered as the (somewhat troublesome) friend of William Blake.

9. An allusion to the parable of the wise and foolish virgins: Matthew, chapter 25.

10. "This book will suit very few readers" (Rousseau, Preface, *Julie, ou, La Nouvelle Héloïse*).

passions qui m'a conduit à la philosophie,'[11] he inculcates, in one simple phrase, a profound and unanswerable truth. It is in these remarks that nature is chiefly found in the writings of Rousseau: too much engrossed in himself to be deeply skilled in the characters of others, that very *self-study* had yet given him a knowledge of the more hidden recesses of the heart. He could perceive at once the motive and the cause of actions, but he wanted the patience to trace the elaborate and winding progress of their effects. He saw the passions in their home, but he could not follow them abroad. He knew *mankind* in the general, but not *men* in the detail. Thus, when he makes an aphorism or reflection, it comes home at once to you as true; but when he would *analyze* that reflection, when he argues, reasons, and attempts to prove, you reject him as unnatural, or you refute him as false. It is then that he partakes of that *manie commune* which he imputes to other philosophers, *'de nier ce qui est, et d' expliquer cc qui n'est pas.'* "

There was a short pause. "I think," said Madame D'Anville, "that it is in those *pensées** which you admire so much in Rousseau, that our authors in general excel."

"You are right," said Vincent, "and for this reason—with you *les gens de lettres* are always *les gens du monde.** Hence their quick perceptions are devoted to men* as well as to books. Thy make observations acutely, and embody them with grace; but it is worth remarking, that the same cause which produced the aphorism, frequently prevents its being profound. These literary *gens du monde* have the tact to observe, but not the patience, perhaps not the time, to investigate. They make the maxim, but they never explain to you the train of reasoning which led to it. Hence they are more brilliant than true. An English writer would not dare to make a maxim, involving, perhaps, in two lines, one of the most important of moral truths, without bringing pages to support his dictum. A French essayist leaves it wholly to itself. He tells you neither how he came by his reasons, nor their conclusion, *'le plus fou souvent est le plus satisfait.'*[12] Consequently, if less tedious than the English, your reasoners are more dangerous, and ought rather to be considered as models of terseness

---

11. "It is the path of the passions which has conducted me to philosophy." The French at the end of the paragraph means: "To deny that which is and to explain that which is not." [Bulwer's translation; 1840 ed.]

12. "The most foolish is often the most satisfied." The French quotation at the end of the paragraph means: "My sweetest longing is to lose hope" (Corneille, *Le Cid,* I, 2).

than of reflection. A man might learn to *think* sooner from your writers, but he will learn to *think justly* sooner from ours. Many observations of La Bruyère and Rochefoucault—the latter especially—have obtained credit for truth solely from their point. They possess exactly the same merit as the very sensible—permit me to add—very *French* line in Corneille:—

> " 'Ma plus douce espérance est de perdre l'espoir.' "

The Marquis took advantage of the silence which followed Vincent's criticism to rise from table. We all (except Vincent, who took leave) adjourned to the salon. *"Qui est cet homme là?"* said one, *"comme il est épris de lui-même."*[13] "How silly he is," cried another—"how *ugly*," said a third. What a taste in literature—such a talker—such shallowness, and such assurance—not worth the answering—could not slip in a word—disagreeable, revolting, awkward, slovenly, were the most complimentary opinions bestowed upon the unfortunate Vincent. The women called him *un horreur,* and the men *un bête.** The old railed at his *mauvais goût,* and the young at his *mauvais coeur,* for the former always attribute whatever does not correspond with their sentiments, to a perversion of taste, and the latter whatever does not come up to their enthusiasm, to a depravity of heart.

As for me, I went home, enriched with two new observations; first, that one may not speak of any thing relative to a foreign country, as one would if one was a native. National censures become particular affronts.

Secondly, that those who know mankind in theory, seldom know it in practice; the very wisdom that conceives a rule, is accompanied with the abstraction, or the vanity, which destroys it. I mean that the philosopher of the cabinet is often too diffident to put into action his observations, or too eager for display to conceal their design. Lord Vincent values himself upon his *science du monde.* He has read much upon men, he has reflected more; he lays down aphorisms to govern or to please them. He goes into society; he is cheated by the one half, and the other half he offends. The sage in the cabinet is but a fool in the salon; and the most consummate men of the world are those who have considered the least on it.

---

13. "Who is that man? How taken he is with himself."

CHAPTER XXV

Falstaff.—What money is in my purse?
Page.—Seven groats and two-pence.
　　　　　　　2nd Part of Henry IV[1]
　　　　En iterum Crispinus.

THE NEXT DAY A NOTE WAS BROUGHT ME, WHICH HAD been sent to my former lodgings in the Hôtel de Paris: it was from Thornton.

"My dear Sir," (it began)

"I am very sorry that particular business will prevent me the pleasure of seeing you at my rooms on Sunday.* I hope to be more fortunate some other day. I should like much to introduce you, the first opportunity, to my friends in the *Rue Grétry*, for I like obliging my countrymen. I am sure, if you were to go there, you would cut and come again—one shoulder of mutton drives down another.

"I beg you to accept my repeated excuses, and remain,

　　　　　　　"Dear Sir,

　　　　　　　　"Your very obedient servant,

　　　　　　　　　"Thomas Thornton.

"Rue St. Dominique,

Friday Morning."

This letter produced in me many and manifold cogitations. What could possibly have induced Mr. Tom Thornton, rogue as he was, to postpone thus of his own accord, the plucking of a pidgeon, which he had such good reason to believe he had entrapped? There was evidently no longer the same avidity to cultivate my acquaintance as before; in putting off our appointment with so little ceremony, he did not even fix a day for another. What had altered his original

---

1. *II Henry IV*, I, 2, 262–63. The Latin epigraph may be translated: "Look, Crispinus again!" (Juvenal *Satires* 4.1).

designs towards me? for if Vincent's account was true, it was natural to suppose that he wished to profit by any acquaintance he might form with me, and therefore such an acquaintance his own interests would induce him to continue and confirm.

Either, then, he no longer had the same necessity for a dupe, or he no longer imagined I should become one. Yet neither of these suppositions was probable. It was not likely that he should grow suddenly honest, or suddenly rich: nor had I, on the other hand, given him any reason to suppose I was a jot more wary than any other individual he might have imposed upon. On the contrary, I had appeared to seek his acquaintance with an eagerness which said but little for my knowledge of the world. The more I reflected, the more I should have been puzzled, had I not connected his present back-wardness with his acquaintance with the stranger, whom he termed Warburton. It is true, that I had no reason to suppose so: it was a conjecture wholly unsupported, and, indeed, against my better sense: yet, from some unanalysed associations, I could not divest myself of the supposition.

"I will soon see," thought I; and wrapping myself in my cloak, for the day was bitterly cold, I bent my way to Thornton's lodgings. I could not explain to myself the deep interest I took in whatever was connected with (the so-called) Warburton, or whatever promised to discover more clearly any particulars respecting him. His behaviour in the gambling house; his conversation with the woman in the *Jardin des Plantes;* and the singular circumstance, that a man of so very aristocratic an appearance, should be connected with Thornton, and only seen in such low scenes, and with such low society, would not have been sufficient so strongly to occupy my mind, had it not been for certain dim recollections, and undefinable associations, that his ap-pearance when present, and my thoughts of him when absent, per-petually recalled.

As, engrossed with meditations of this nature, I was passing over the *Pont-Neuf,* I perceived the man* Warburton had so earnestly watched in the gambling house, and whom I* identified with the "Tyrrell," who had formed the subject of conversation in the *Jardin des Plantes,* pass slowly before me. There was an appearance of great exhaustion in his swarthy and strongly marked countenance. He walked carelessly on, neither looking to the right nor the left, with that air of thought and abstraction which I have remarked as* common to all men in the habit of indulging any engrossing and exciting passion.

We were just on the other side of the *Seine,* when I perceived the woman of the *Jardin des Plantes* approach. Tyrrell (for that, I afterwards discovered, was really his name) started as she came near, and asked her, in a tone of some asperity, where she had been? As I was but a few paces behind, I had a clear, full view of the woman's countenance. She was about twenty-eight or thirty years of age. Her features were decidedly handsome, though somewhat too sharp and aquiline for my individual taste.* Her eyes were light and rather sunken; and her complexion bespoke somewhat of the paleness and languor of ill-health. On the whole, the expression of her face, though decided, was not unpleasing, and when she returned Tyrrell's rather rude salutation, it was with a smile, which made her, for the moment, absolutely beautiful.

"Where have I been to?" she said, in answer to his interrogatory. "Why, I went to look at the New Church, which they told me was so *superbe."*

"Methinks," replied the man, "that ours are not precisely the circumstances in which such spectacles are amusing."

"Nay, Tyrrell," said the woman, as taking his arm they walked on together a few paces before me, "nay, we are quite rich now to what we have been; and, if you *do* play again, our two hundred pounds may swell into a fortune. Your losses have brought you skill, and you may now turn them into actual advantages."

Tyrrell did not reply exactly to these remarks, but appeared as if debating with himself. "Two hundred pounds—twenty already gone!—in a few months all will have melted away. What is it then now but a respite from starvation?—but with luck it may become a competence."

"And why not have luck? many a fortune has been made with a worse beginning," said the woman.

"True, Margaret," pursued the gambler, "and even without luck, our fate can only commence a month or two sooner—better a short doom than a lingering torture."

"What think you of trying some new game where you have more experience, or where the chances are greater than in that of *rouge et noir?*" asked the woman. "Could you not make something out of that tall, handsome man, who Thornton says is so rich?"

"Ah, if one could!" sighed Tyrrell, wistfully. "Thornton tells me, that he has won thousands from him, and that they are mere drops in his income. Thornton is a good, easy, careless fellow, and might

98

let me into a share of the booty: but then, in what games can I engage him?"

Here I passed this well-suited pair, and lost the remainder of their conversation. "Well," thought I, "if this precious personage does starve at last, he will most richly deserve it, partly for his designs on the stranger, principally for his opinion of Thornton. If he was a knave only, one might pity him; but a knave and fool both, are a combination of evil, for which there is no intermediate purgatory of opinion—nothing short of utter damnation."

I soon arrived at Mr. Thornton's abode. The same old woman, poring over the same novel of Crébillon, made me the same reply as before; and accordingly again I ascended the obscure and rugged stairs, which seemed to indicate, that the road to vice is not so easy as one generally supposes. I knocked at the door, and receiving no answering acknowledgment, opened it at once. The first thing I saw was the dark, rough coat of Warburton—that person's back was turned to me, and he was talking with some energy to Thornton (who lounged idly in his chair, with one ungartered leg thrown over the elbow).

"Ah, Mr. Pelham," exclaimed the latter, starting from his *not* very graceful position, "it gives me great pleasure to see you—Mr. Warburton, Mr. Pelham—Mr. Pelham, Mr. Warburton."

My new-made and mysterious acquaintance drew himself up to his full height, and bowed very slightly to my own acknowledgment of the introduction. A low person would have thought him rude. I only supposed him ignorant of the world. No real gentleman is uncivil. He turned round after this stiff condescension, *de sa part,** and sunk down on the sofa, with his back towards me.

"I was mistaken," thought I, "when I believed him to be above such associates as Thornton—they are well matched."

"My dear Sir," said Thornton, "I am very sorry I could not see you to breakfast—a particular engagement prevented me—*verbum sap.* Mr. Pelham, you take me, I suppose—black eyes, white skin, and such an ancle*;" and the fellow rubbed his great hands and chuckled.

"Well," said I, "I cannot blame you, whatever may be my loss— a dark eye and a straight ancle* are powerful excuses. What says Mr. Warburton to them?" and I turned to the object of my interrogatory.

"Really," he answered drily,* and without moving from his uncourteous position, "Mr. Thornton only can judge of the niceties of his peculiar tastes, or the justice of his general excuses."

Mr. Warburton said this in a sarcastic, bitter tone. Thornton bit his lip, more, I should think, at the manner than the words, and his small grey eyes sparkled with a malignant and stern expression, which suited the character of his face far better than the careless levity and *enjouement** which his glances usually denoted.

"They are no such great friends after all," thought I; and now let me change my attack. "Pray," I asked, "among all your numerous acquaintances at Paris, did you ever meet with a Mr. Tyrrell?"

Warburton started from his chair, and as instantly re-seated himself. Thornton eyed me with one of those peculiar looks which so strongly reminded me of a dog, in deliberation whether to bite or run away.

"I do know a Mr. Tyrrell!" he said, after a short pause.

"What sort of a person is he?" I asked with an indifferent air— "a great gamester, is he not?"

"He does slap it down on the colours now and then," replied Thornton. "I hope you don't know him, Mr. Pelham!"

"Why?" said I, evading the question. "His character is not affected by a propensity so common, unless, indeed, you suppose him to be more a gambler than a gamester, viz. more acute than unlucky."

"God* forbid that I should say any such thing," replied Thornton; "you won't catch an old lawyer in such imprudence."

"The greater the truth the greater the libel," said Warburton, with a sneer.

"No!" resumed Thornton, "I know nothing against Mr. Tyrrell— nothing! He *may be* a very good man, and I believe he is; but as a friend, Mr. Pelham, (and Mr. Thornton grew quite affectionate), I advise you to have as little as possible to do *with that sort of people*."

"Truly," said I, "you have now excited my curiosity. Nothing, you know, is half so inviting as mystery."

Thornton looked as if he had expected a very different reply; and Warburton said, in an abrupt tone—

"Whoever enters an unknown road in a fog may easily lose himself."

"True," said I; "but that very chance is more agreeable than a road where one knows every tree! Danger and novelty are more to my taste than safety and sameness. Besides, as I never* gamble myself, I can lose nothing* by an acquaintance with those who do."

Another pause ensued—and, finding I had got all from Mr. Thornton and his uncourteous guest that I was likely to do, I took my hat and my departure.

"I do not know," thought I, "whether I have profited much by this visit. Let me consider. In the first place, I have not ascertained why I was put off by Mr. Thornton—for as to his excuse, it could only have availed one day, and had he been anxious for my acquaintance, he would have named another. I have, however, discovered, first, that he does not wish me to form any connection with Tyrrell; secondly, from Warburton's sarcasm, and his glance of reply, that there is but little friendship between those two, whatever be the *intimacy;* and, thirdly, that Warburton, from his *dorsal* positions, so studiously preserved, either wished to be uncivil or unnoticed." The latter, after all, was the most probable;* and, upon the whole, I felt more than ever convinced that he was the person I suspected him to be.

CHAPTER XXVI

Tell how the fates my giddy course did guide,
The inconstant turns of every changing hour.
        Pierce Gaveston, by M. DRAYTON[1]
Je me retire donc.—Adieu, Paris, adieu!
                BOILEAU

WHEN I RETURNED HOME, I FOUND ON MY TABLE THE following letter from my mother:

"MY DEAR HENRY,

"I am rejoiced to hear you are so well entertained at Paris—that you have been so often to the D———s and C———s; that Coulon says you are his best pupil—that your favourite horse is so much admired—and that you have only exceeded your allowance by a £1,000; with some difficulty I have persuaded your uncle to transmit you an order for £1,500, which will, I trust, make up all your deficiencies.

"You must not, my dear child, be so extravagant for the future, and for a very good reason, viz. I do not see how you can. Your uncle,

---

1. Michael Drayton, *The Legend of Pierce Gaveston,* lines 19–20. The French epigraph may be translated: "Then I am leaving. Adieu, Paris, adieu" (Boileau, *Satires,* 1, 164).

I fear, will not again be so generous, and your father cannot assist you. You will therefore see more clearly than ever the necessity of marrying an heiress; there are only two in England (the daughters of gentlemen) worthy of you—the most deserving of these has £10,000 a year, the other has £150,000.* The former is old, ugly, and very ill tempered; the latter tolerably pretty, and agreeable, and just of age; but you will perceive the impropriety of even thinking of her till we have tried the other. I am going to ask both to my Sunday *soirées,* where I never admit any single men, so that *there,* at least, you will have no rivals.

"And now, my dear son, before I enter into a subject of great importance to you, I wish to recall to your mind that pleasure is never an end, but a means—viz. that in your horses and amusements at Paris—your visits and your *liaisons*—you have always, I trust, remembered that these were only so far desirable as the methods of shining in society. I have now a new scene on which you are to enter, with very different objects in view, and where any pleasures you may find have nothing the least in common with those you at present enjoy.

"I know that this preface will not frighten you as it might many silly young men. Your education has been too carefully attended to, for you to imagine that any step can be rough or unpleasant which raises you in the world.

"To come at once to the point. One of the seats in your uncle's borough of Buyemall is every day expected to be vacated; the present member, Mr. Toolington, cannot possibly live a week, and your uncle is very desirous that you should fill the vacancy which Mr. Toolington's death will create. Though I called it Lord Glenmorris's borough, yet it is not entirely at his disposal, which I think very strange, since my father, who was not half so rich as your uncle, could send two members to Parliament without the least trouble in the world—but I don't understand these matters. Possibly your uncle (poor man) does not manage them well. However, he says no time is to be lost. You are to return immediately to England, and come down to his house in ———shire. It is supposed you will have some contest, but be certain eventually to come in.

"You will also, in this visit to Lord Glenmorris, have an excellent opportunity of securing his affection; you know it is some time since he saw you, and the greater part of his property is unentailed. If you come into the House you must devote yourself wholly to it, and I have no fear of your succeeding; for I remember, when you were

102

quite a child, how well you spoke, 'My name is Norval,'[2] and 'Romans, countrymen, and lovers,' &c. I heard Mr. Canning speak the other day, and I think his voice is quite like yours; in short, I make no doubt of seeing you in the ministry in a very few years.

"You see, my dear son, that it is absolutely necessary you should set out immediately. You will call on Lady ———, and you will endeavour to make firm friends of the most desirable among your present acquaintance; so that you may be on the same footing you are now, should you return to Paris. This a little civility will easily do: nobody (as I before observed), except in England, ever loses by politeness; by the by, that last word is one you must never use, it is too *Gloucester-place like*.[3]

"You will also be careful, in returning to England, to make very little use of French phrases; no vulgarity is more unpleasing. I could not help being exceedingly amused by a book written the other day, which professes to give an accurate description of good society. Not knowing what to make us say in English, the author has made us talk nothing but French. I have often wondered what common people think of us, since in their novels they always affect to portray us so different from themselves. I am very much afraid we are in all things exactly like them, except in being more simple and unaffected. The higher the rank, indeed, the less pretence, because there is less to pretend *to*. This is the chief reason why our manners are better than low persons: ours are more natural, because they imitate no one else; theirs are affected, because they think to imitate ours; and whatever is evidently borrowed becomes vulgar. Original affectation is sometimes good *ton*—imitated affectation, always bad.

"Well, my dear Henry, I must now conclude this letter, already too long to be interesting. I hope to see you about ten days after you receive this; and if you could bring me a Cachemire shawl, it would give me great pleasure to see your taste in its choice. God bless you, my dear son.

"Your very affectionate
"FRANCES PELHAM."

---

2. John Home (1722–1808), *Douglas*, II, 1. The second dramatic speech referred to is from *Julius Caesar*, III, 1. Below, George Canning (1770–1827): Tory statesman.

3. Many aspirants to a place in the fashionable world bought houses in Gloucester Place, a street just off (in both a geographical and social sense) the highly fashionable Portman Square.

"P.S. I hope you go to church sometimes: I am sorry to see the young men of the present day so irreligious. Perhaps you could get my old friend, Madame De ———, to choose the Cachemire—take care of your health."

This letter, which I read carefully twice over, threw me into a most serious meditation. My first feeling was regret at leaving Paris; my second, was a certain exultation at the new prospects so unexpectedly opened to me. The great aim of a philosopher is, to reconcile every disadvantage by some counterbalance of good—where he cannot create this, he should imagine it. I began, therefore, to consider less what I should lose than what I should gain, by quitting Paris. In the first place, I was tolerably tired of its amusements: no business is half so fatiguing as pleasure. I longed for a change: behold, a change was at hand! Then, to say truth, I was heartily glad of a pretence of escaping from a numerous cohort of *folles amours,* with Madame D'Anville at the head; and the very circumstance which men who play the German flute and fall in love, would have considered the most vexatious, I regarded as the most consolatory.

There was yet another reason which reconciled me more than any other to my departure. I had, in my residence at Paris, among half wits and whole *roués,* contracted a certain—not exactly *grossièreté*—but want of refinement—a certain coarseness of expression and idea which, though slight, and easily thrown off, took in some degree from my approach to that character which I wished to become. I know nothing which would so polish the manners as continental intercourse, were it not for the English *débauchés* with which that intercourse connects one. English profligacy is always coarse, and in profligacy nothing is more contagious than its tone. One never keeps a restraint on the manner when one unbridles the passions, and one takes from the associates with whom the latter are indulged, the air and the method of the indulgence.

I was, the reader well knows, too solicitous for improvement, not to be anxious to escape from such chances of deterioration, and I therefore consoled myself with considerable facility for the pleasures and the associates I was about to forego.* My mind being thus relieved from all regret at my departure, I now suffered it to look forward to the advantages of my return to England. My love of excitement and variety made an election, in which I was to have both the importance of the contest and the certainty of the success, a very agreeable object of anticipation.

I was also by this time wearied with my attendance upon women, and eager to exchange it for the ordinary objects of ambition to men; and my vanity whispered that my success in the one was no unfavourable omen of my prosperity in the other. On my return to England, with a new scene and a new motive for conduct, I resolved that I would commence a different character to that I had hitherto assumed. How far I kept this resolution the various events hereafter to be shown, will testify. For myself, I felt that I was now about to enter a more crowded scene upon a more elevated ascent; and my previous experience of human nature was sufficient to convince me that my safety required a more continual circumspection, and my success a more dignified bearing.

CHAPTER XXVII

Je noterai cela, Madame, dans mon livre.
MOLIÈRE[1]

I AM NOT ONE OF THOSE PERSONS WHO ARE MANY days in deciding what may be effected in one. "On the third day from this," said I to Bedos, "at half past nine in the morning, I shall leave Paris for England."

"Oh, my poor wife!" said the valet, "she will break her heart if I leave her."

"Then stay," said I. Bedos shrugged his shoulders.

"I prefer being with Monsieur to all things."

"What, even to your wife?" The courteous rascal placed his hand to his heart and bowed. "You shall not suffer by your fidelity—you shall take your wife with you."

The conjugal valet's countenance fell. "No," he said, "no; he could not take advantage of Monsieur's generosity."

"I insist upon it—not another word."

"I beg a thousand pardons of Monsieur; but—but my wife is very ill, and unable to travel."

1. "Madame, I will note that in my book" (Molière, *Les Femmes savantes*, IV, 5).

"Then, in that case, so excellent a husband cannot think of leaving a sick and destitute wife."

"Poverty has no law; if I consulted my heart and stayed, I should starve, *et il faut vivre.*"

"*Je n'en vois pas la nécessité,*" replied I, as I got into my carriage. That repartee, by the way, I cannot claim as my own; it is the very unanswerable answer of a judge to an expostulating thief.

I made the round of reciprocal regrets, according to the orthodox formula. The Duchesse de Perpignan was the last—(Madame D'Anville I reserved for another day)—that virtuous and wise personage was in the *boudoir* of reception. I glanced at the fatal door as I entered. I have a great aversion, after any thing has once happened and fairly subsided, to make any allusion to its former existence. I never, therefore, talked to the Duchesse about our ancient *égaremens.* I spoke, this morning, of the marriage of one person, the death of another, and lastly, the departure of my individual self.

"When do you go?" she said, eagerly.

"In two days: my departure will be softened, if I can execute any commissions in England for Madame."

"None," said she; and then in a low tone (that none of the idlers, who were always found at her morning *levées,* should hear), she added, "you will receive a note from me this evening."

I bowed, changed the conversation, and withdrew. I dined in my own rooms, and spent the evening in looking over the various *billets-doux,* received during my *séjour* at Paris.

"Where shall I put all these locks of hair?" asked Bedos, opening a drawer full.

"Into my scrap-book."

"And all these letters?"

"Into the fire."

I was just getting into bed when the Duchesse de Perpignan's note arrived—it was as follows:—

"MY DEAR FRIEND,

"For that word, so doubtful in our language, I may at least call you in *your own.* I am unwilling that you should leave this country with those sentiments you now entertain of me, unaltered, yet I cannot imagine any form of words of sufficient magic to change them. Oh! if you knew how much I am to be pitied; if you could look for one moment into this lonely and blighted heart; if you could trace, step by step, the progress I have made in folly and sin, you would

106

see how much of what you now condemn and despise, I have owed to circumstances, rather than to the vice of my disposition. I was born to beauty, educated a beauty, owed fame, rank, power to beauty; and it is to the advantages I have derived from person that I owe the ruin of my mind. You have seen how much I now derive from art. I loathe myself as I write that sentence; but no matter: from that moment you loathed me too. You did not take into consideration, that I had been living on excitement all my youth, and that in my maturer years I could not relinquish it. I had reigned by my attractions, and I thought every art preferable to resigning my empire: but in feeding my vanity, I had not been able to stifle the dictates of my heart. Love is so natural to a woman, that she is scarcely a woman who resists it: but in me it has been a sentiment, not a passion.

"Sentiment, then, and vanity, have been my seducers. I said, that I owed my errors to circumstances, not to nature. You will say, that in confessing love and vanity to be my seducers, I contradict this assertion—you are mistaken. I mean, that though vanity and sentiment were in me, yet the scenes in which I have been placed, and the events which I have witnessed, gave to those latent currents of action a wrong and a dangerous direction. I was formed *to love;* for one whom I did love I could have made every sacrifice. I married a man I hated, and I only learnt the depths of my heart when it was too late.

"Enough of this; you will leave this country; we shall never meet again—never! You may return to Paris, but I shall then be no more; *n'importe*—I shall be unchanged to the last. *Je mourrai en reine.*

"As a latest pledge of what I have felt for you, I send you the enclosed chain and ring; as a latest favour, I request you to wear them for six months, and, above all, for two hours in the Tuileries tomorrow. You will laugh at this request: it seems idle and romantic—perhaps it is so. Love has many exaggerations in sentiment, which reason would despise. What wonder, then, that mine, above that of all others, should conceive them? You will not, I know, deny this request. Farewell!—in *this* world we shall never meet again, and I believe not in the existence of another.* Farewell!

                                                        "E. P."

"A most sensible effusion," said I to myself, when I had read this billet; "and yet, after all, it shows more feeling and more character than I could have supposed she possessed." I took up the chain: it was of Maltese workmanship; not very handsome, nor, indeed, in any way remarkable, except for a plain hair ring which was attached to it, and which I found myself unable to take off, without breaking. "It is a very singular request," thought I, "but then it comes from a very singular person; and as it rather partakes of adventure and intrigue, I shall at all events appear in the Tuileries, tomorrow, *chained* and *ringed.*"

CHAPTER XXVIII

Thy incivility shall not make me fail to do what becomes me; and since thou hast more valour than courtesy, I for thee will hazard that life which thou wouldst take from me.
—*Cassandra, "elegantly done into English by* Sir Charles Cotterell.*"*[1]

About the usual hour for the promenade in the Tuileries, I conveyed myself thither. I set the chain and ring in full display, rendered still more conspicuous by the dark coloured dress which I always wore. I had not been in the gardens ten minutes, before I perceived a young Frenchman, scarcely twenty years of age, look with a very peculiar air at my new decorations. He passed and repassed me, much oftener than the alternations of the walk warranted; and at last, taking off his hat, said in a low tone, that he wished much for the honour of exchanging a few words with me in private. I saw, at the first glance, that he was a gentleman, and accordingly withdrew with him among the trees, in the more retired part of the garden.

"Permit me," said he, "to inquire how that ring and chain came into your possession?"

"Monsieur," I replied, "you will understand me, when I say, that the honour of another person is implicated in my concealment of that secret."

"Sir," said the Frenchman, colouring violently, "I have seen them before—in a word, they belong to me!"

I smiled—my young hero fired at this. *"Oui, Monsieur,"* said he, speaking very loud, and very quick, "they belong to *me,* and I insist

1. Cotterell's translation of "The Famous Romance of Cassandra" by G. de Costes, seigneur de la Calprenède, appeared in 1661.

upon your immediately restoring them, or vindicating your claim to them by arms."

"You leave me but one answer, Monsieur," said I; "I will find a friend to wait upon you immediately. Allow me to inquire your address?" The Frenchman, who was greatly agitated, produced a card. We bowed and separated.

I was glancing over the address I held in my hand, which was— C. D'Azimart,* Rue de Bourbon, Numéro——, when my ears were saluted with—

> " 'Now do you know me?—thou shouldst be Alonzo.' "[2]

I did not require the faculty of sight to recognize Lord Vincent. "My dear fellow," said I, "I am rejoiced to see you!" and thereupon I poured into his ear the particulars of my morning adventure. Lord Vincent listened to me with much apparent interest, and spoke very unaffectedly of his readiness to serve me, and his regret at the occasion.

"Pooh!" said I, "a duel in France, is not like one in England; the former is a matter of course; a trifle of common occurrence; one makes an engagement to fight, in the same breath as an engagement to dine; but the latter is a thing of state and solemnity—long faces— early rising—and willmaking. But *do* get this business over as soon as you can, that we may dine at the Rocher afterwards."

"Well, my dear Pelham," said Vincent, "I cannot refuse you my services; and as I suppose Monsieur D'Azimart* will choose swords, I venture to augur every thing from your skill in that species of weapon. It is the first time I have ever interfered in affairs of this nature, but I hope to get well through the present.

> " 'Nobilis ornatur lauro collega *secundo*,'[3]

as Juvenal says: *au revoir*," and away went Lord Vincent, half forgetting all his late anxiety for my life, in his paternal pleasure for the delivery of his quotation.

Vincent is the only punster I ever knew with a good heart. No action to that race in general is so serious an occupation as the play upon words; and the remorseless habit of murdering a phrase, renders them perfectly obdurate to the simple death of a friend. I walked through every variety the straight paths of the Tuileries could afford,

---

2. Unidentified.

3. "His highborn colleague is decorated with the second bay" (Juvenal *Satires* 8.253).

and was beginning to get exceedingly tired, when Lord Vincent returned. He looked very grave, and I saw at once that he was come to particularize the circumstances of the last extreme. *"The Bois de Boulogne—pistols—in one hour,"* were the three leading features of his detail.

"Pistols!" said I; "well, be it so. I would rather have had swords, for the young man's sake as much as my own: but 13 paces and a steady aim will settle the business as soon. We will try a bottle of the chambertin to-day, Vincent." The punster smiled faintly, and for once in his life made no reply. We walked gravely and soberly to my lodgings for the pistols, and then proceeded to the engagement as silently as Christians* should do.

The Frenchman and his second were on the ground first. I saw that the former was pale and agitated, not, I think, from fear, but passion. When we took our ground, Vincent came to me, and said, in a low tone, "For God's* sake, suffer me to accommodate this, if possible?"

"It is not in *our* power," said I, receiving the pistol. I looked steadily at D'Azimart,* and took my aim. His pistol, owing, I suppose, to the trembling of his hand, went off a moment sooner than he had anticipated—the ball grazed my hat. My aim was more successful—I struck him in the shoulder—the exact place I had intended. He staggered a few paces, but did not fall.

We hastened towards him—his cheek assumed a still more livid hue as I approached; he muttered some half-formed curses between his teeth, and turned from me to his second.

"You will inquire whether Monsieur D'Azimart* is satisfied," said I to Vincent, and retired to a short distance.

"His second," said Vincent, (after a brief conference with that person,) "replies to my question, that Monsieur D'Azimart's* wound has left him, for the present, no alternative." Upon this answer I took Vincent's arm, and we returned forthwith to my carriage.

"I congratulate you most sincerely on the event of this duel," said Vincent. "Monsieur de M——— (D'Azimart's* second) informed me, when I waited on him, that your antagonist was one of the most celebrated pistol shots in Paris, and that a lady with whom he had been long in love, made the death of the chain-bearer the price of her favours. Devilish lucky for you, my good fellow, that his hand trembled so; but I did not know *you* were so good a shot."

"Why," I answered, "I am *not* what is vulgarly termed 'a crack shot'—I cannot split a bullet on a penknife; but I am sure of a target somewhat smaller than a man: and my hand is as certain in the field as it is in the practice-yard."

"*Le sentiment de nos forces les augmente*,"[4] replied Vincent. "Shall I tell the coachman to drive to the Rocher?"

CHAPTER XXIX

Here's a kind host, that makes the invitation,
To your own cost, to his *fort bon collation.*
                              WYCHERLY's *Gent. Dancing Master*[1]
Vous pouvez bien juger que je n'aurai pas grande peine à me con-
soler d'une chose dont je me suis déjà consolé tant de fois.
                              Lettres de BOILEAU

As I WAS WALKING HOME WITH VINCENT FROM THE Rue Mont Orgueil, I saw, on entering the Rue St. Honoré, two figures before us; the tall and noble stature of the one I could not for a moment mistake. They stopped at the door of an hotel, which opened in that noiseless manner so peculiar to the *Conciergerie* of France. I was at the *porte** the moment they disappeared, but not before I had caught a glance of the dark locks and pale countenance of Warburton—my eye fell upon the number of the hotel.

"Surely," said I, "I have been in that house before."

"Likely enough," growled Vincent, who was gloriously drunk. "It is a house of two-fold utility—you may play with cards, or coquet with women, *selon votre goût.*"*

At these words I remembered the hotel and its inmates immediately. It belonged to an old nobleman, who, though on the brink of the grave, was still grasping at the good things on the margin. He lived with a pretty and clever woman, who bore the name and

---

4. "The conviction of our forces augments them" (Vanvenargues, *Réflexions et maximes*, no. 75). [Bulwer's translation; 1840 ed.]

1. William Wycherly, *The Gentleman Dancing-Master*, I, 2. The French epigraph may be translated: "You can well understand that I will not have great difficulty consoling myself for something over which I have already consoled myself so often."

honours of his wife. They kept up two *salons,* one *pour le petit souper,* and the other *pour le petit jeu.* You saw much *écarté* and more love-making, and lost your heart and your money with equal facility. In a word, the marquis and his *jolie petite femme* were a wise and prosperous couple, who made the best of their lives, and lived decently and honourably upon other people.

"*Allons,* Pelham," cried Vincent, as I was still standing at the door in deliberation; "how much longer will you keep me to congeal in this 'eager and nipping air'[2]—'Quamdiu nostram patientiam abutêre Catilina!' "

"Let us enter," said I. "I have the run of the house, and we may find———"

" 'Some young vices—some fair iniquities,' " interrupted Vincent, with a hiccup—

> " 'Leade on, good fellowe,' quoth Robin Hood,
> Lead on, I do bid thee.' "[3]

And, with these words, the door opened in obedience to my rap, and we mounted to the marquis's tenement *au première.*

The room was pretty full—the *soi-disante* marquise was flitting from table to table—betting at each, and coquetting with all; and the marquis himself, with a moist eye and a shaking hand, was affecting the Don Juan with the various Elviras and Annas with which his *salon* was crowded. Vincent was trying to follow me through the crowd, but his confused vision and unsteady footing led him from one entanglement to another, till he was quite unable to proceed. A tall, corpulent Frenchman, six foot by five, was leaning, *(a great and weighty objection),* just before him, utterly occupied in the vicissitudes of an *écarté* table, and unconscious of Vincent's repeated efforts, first on one side, and then on the other, to pass him.

At last, the perplexed wit, getting more irascible as he grew more bewildered, suddenly seized the vast incumbrance by the arm, and said to him, in a sharp, querulous tone, "Pray, Monsieur, why are you like the lote tree in Mahomet's Seventh Heaven?"

"*Sir!*" cried the astonished Frenchman.

"Because," (continued Vincent, answering his own enigma)—"because, *beyond you there is no passing!*"

---

2. *Hamlet,* I, 4, 2. The following Latin phrase is from Cicero, badly misquoted from the first Catalinian oration, lines 1–2: "How long will you abuse our patience, Cataline?"

3. From the anonymous ballad "Robin Hood and Guy of Gisborne," lines 117–18.

The Frenchman (one of that race who always forgive any thing for a *bon-mot*) smiled, bowed, and drew himself aside. Vincent steered by, and, joining me, hiccuped out, "In rebus adversis opponite pectora fortia."[4]*

Meanwhile I had looked round the room for the objects of my pursuit: to my great surprise I could not perceive them; they may be in the other room, thought I, and to the other room I went; the supper was laid out, and an old *bonne* was quietly helping herself to some sweetmeat. All *other* human beings (if, indeed, an old woman can be called a human being) were, however, invisible, and I remained perfectly bewildered as to the nonappearance of Warburton and his companion. I entered the *Salle à Jouer** once more—I looked round in every corner—I examined every face—but in vain; and with a feeling of disappointment very disproportioned to my loss, I took Vincent's arm, and we withdrew.

The next morning I spent with Madame D'Anville. A Frenchwoman easily consoles herself for the loss of a lover—she converts him into a friend, and thinks herself (nor is she much deceived) benefited by the exchange. We talked of our grief in maxims, and bade each other adieu in antitheses. Ah! it is a pleasant thing to drink with Alcidonis (in Marmontel's Tale)[5] of the rose-coloured phial—to sport with the fancy, not to brood over the passion, of youth. There is a time when the heart, from very tenderness, runs over, and (so much do our virtues as well as vices flow from our passions) there is, perhaps, rather hope than anxiety for the future in that excess. Then, if Pleasure errs, it errs through heedlessness, not design; and Love, wandering over flowers, "proffers honey, but bears *not* a sting."[6] Ah! happy time! in the lines of one who can so well translate feeling into words—

"Fate has not darkened thee—Hope has not made
The blossoms expand it but opens to fade;
Nothing is known of those wearing fears
Which will shadow the light of *our* after years."
The Improvisatrice[7]

---

4. "And confront adversities with brave hearts" (Horace *Satires* 2.2.136). Again Bulwer badly misquotes.

5. Bulwer seems to have in mind Alcimédon in Marmontel's moral fable *Palémon*.

6. Pelham reverses a proverbial sentiment.

7. *The Improvisatrice* (1824), a romantic poem by Letitia Elizabeth Landon (1802–38). The quotation at the end of the paragraph is from *Much Ado about Nothing*, III, 3, 49.

113

Pardon this digression—not much, it must be confessed, in my ordinary strain—but let me, dear reader, very seriously advise thee not to judge of me yet. When thou hast got to the end of my book, if thou dost condemn it or its hero—why "I will let thee alone (as honest Dogberry advises) till thou art sober; and, if thou make me not, then, the better answer, thou art not the man I took thee for."

CHAPTER XXX

It must be confessed, that flattery comes mighty easily to one's mouth in the presence of royalty.

Letters of STEPHEN MONTAGUE[1]

'Tis he.—How come he thence—what doth he here?

LARA

I HAD RECEIVED FOR THAT EVENING (MY LAST AT PARIS) an invitation from the Duchesse de B———. I knew that the party was to be small, and that very few besides the royal family would compose it.[2] I had owed the honour of this invitation to my intimacy with the ———s, the great friends of the duchesse, and I promised myself some pleasure in the engagement.

There were but eight or nine persons present when I entered the royal chamber. The most *distingué** of these I recognized immediately as the ———.* He came forward with much grace as I approached, and expressed his pleasure at seeing me.

"You were presented, I think, about a month ago," added the ———, with a smile of singular fascination; "I remember it well."

I bowed low to this compliment.

"Do you propose staying long at Paris?" continued the ———.

"I protracted," I replied, "my departure solely for the honour this evening affords me. In so doing, please your ———,* I have followed the wise maxim of keeping the greatest pleasure to the last."

1. Stephen Montague: unidentified. The second epigraph is from Byron's *Lara,* 1, 426.
2. The family of Louis XVIII, the restored king of France (1814–24). Below, Pelham talks briefly with the king's brother, the comte d'Artois, who succeeded to the throne as Charles X in 1824.

114

The royal chevalier bowed to my answer with a smile still sweeter than before, and began a conversation with me which lasted for several minutes. I was much struck with the ———'s air and bearing. They possess great dignity, without any affectation of its assumption. He speaks peculiarly good English, and the compliment of addressing me in that language was therefore as judicious as delicate. His observations owed little to his rank; they would have struck you as appropriate, and the air which accompanied them pleased you as graceful, even in a simple individual. Judge, then, if they charmed me in the ———. The upper part of his countenance is prominent and handsome, and his eyes have much softness of expression. His figure is slight and particularly well knit; perhaps he is altogether more adapted to strike in private than* public effect. Upon the whole, he is one of those very few persons of great rank* whom you would have had pride in knowing as an equal, and have pleasure in acknowledging as a superior.[3]

As the ——— paused, and turned with great courtesy to the Duc de ———, I bowed my way to the Duchesse de B———. That personage, whose liveliness and piquancy of manner always make one wish for one's own sake that her rank was less exalted, was speaking with great volubility to a tall, stupid looking man, one of the ministers, and smiled most graciously upon me as I drew near. She spoke to me of our national amusements. "You are not," said she, "so fond of dancing as we are."

"We have not the same exalted example to be at once our motive and our model," said I, in allusion to the duchesse's well known attachment to that accomplishment. The Duchesse D'A——— came up as I said this, and the conversation flowed on evenly enough till the ———'s whist party was formed. His partner was Madame de la R———, the heroine of La Vendée.[4] She was a tall and very stout woman, singularly lively and entertaining, and appeared to possess both the moral and the physical energy to accomplish feats still more noble than those she performed.

---

3. The sketch of these unfortunate members of an exiled and illustrious family may not be the less interesting from the reverses which, since the first publication of this work, placed the Orleans family on the Bourbon throne. As for the erring Charles X, he was neither a great monarch nor a wise man, but he was, in air, grace, and manner, the most thorough-bred gentleman I ever met. H.P.* [B-L; 1835 ed.]

4. La Vendée: the peasant counterrevolutionary insurrection in Vendée in 1793. The heroine was the marquise de la Rochejacquelin.

115

I soon saw that it would not do for me to stay very long. I had already made a favourable impression, and, in such cases, it is my constant rule immediately to retire. Stay, if it be whole hours, until you *have* pleased, but leave the moment *after* your success. A great genius should not linger too long either in the *salon* or the world. He must quit each with *éclat*. In obedience to this rule, I no sooner found that my court had been effectually made than I rose to withdraw.

"You will return soon to Paris," said the Duchesse de B———.

"I cannot resist it," I replied. "*Mon corps reviendra pour chercher mon coeur.*"[5]

"We shall not forget you," said the duchesse.

"Your Highness has *now* given me my only inducement *not* to return," I answered, as I bowed out of the room.

It was much too early to go home; at that time I was too young and restless to sleep till long after midnight; and while I was deliberating in what manner to pass the hours, I suddenly recollected the hotel in the Rue St. Honoré, to which Vincent and I had paid so unceremonious a visit the night before. Impressed with the hope that I might be more successful in meeting Warburton than I had then been, I ordered the coachman to drive to the abode of the old Marquis ———.

The *salon* was as crowded as usual. I lost a few Napoleons at *écarté* in order to pay my *entrée,* and then commenced a desultory flirtation with one of the fair decoys. In this occupation my eye and my mind frequently wandered. I could not divest myself of the hope of once more seeing Warburton before my departure from Paris, and every reflection which confirmed my suspicions of his identity redoubled my interest in his connection with Tyrrell and the vulgar *débauché* of the Rue St. Dominique. I was making some languid reply to my Cynthia of the minute, when my ear was suddenly greeted by an English voice. I looked round, and saw Thornton in close conversation with a man whose back was turned to me, but whom I rightly conjectured to be Tyrrell.

"Oh! he'll be here soon," said the former, "and we'll *bleed him* regularly to-night. It is very singular that you who play so much better should not have *floored* him yesterday evening."

Tyrrell replied in a tone so low as to be inaudible, and a minute afterwards the door opened, and Warburton entered. He came up

---

5. "My body will return to find my heart."

instantly to Thornton and his companion; and after a few words of ordinary salutation, Warburton said, in one of those modulated tones so peculiar to himself, "I am sure, Tyrrell, that you must be eager for your revenge. To lose to such a mere Tyro as myself, is quite enough to double the pain of defeat, and the desire of retaliation."

I did not hear Tyrrell's reply, but the trio presently moved towards a door, which till then I had not noticed, and which was probably the entrance to our hostess's *boudoir*. The *soi-distant* marquise opened it herself, for which kind office Thornton gave her a leer and a wink, characteristic of his claims to gallantry. When the door was again closed upon them, I went up to the marquise, and after a few compliments, asked whether the room Messieurs les Anglois* had entered, was equally open to all guests?

"Why," said she, with a slight hesitation, "those gentlemen play for higher stakes than we usually do here, and one of them is apt to get irritated by the advice and expostulations of the lookers on; and so after they had played a short time in the *salon* last night, Monsieur Thornton, a very old friend of mine," (here the lady looked down) "asked me permission to occupy the inner room; and as I knew him so well, I could have no scruple in obliging him."

"Then, I suppose," said I, "that, as a stranger, I have not permission to intrude upon them?"

"Shall I inquire?" answered the marquise.

"No!" said I, "it is not worth while;" and accordingly I re-seated myself, and appeared once more occupied in saying *des belles choses* to my kind-hearted neighbour. I could not, however, with all my dissimulation, sustain a conversation from which my present feelings were so estranged, for more than a few minutes; and I was never more glad than when my companion, displeased with my inattention, rose, and left me to my own reflections.

What could Warburton (if he were the person I suspected) gain by the disguise he had assumed? He was too rich to profit by any sums he could win from Tyrrell, and too much removed from Thornton's station in life, to derive any pleasure or benefit from his acquaintance with that person. His dark threats of vengeance in the *Jardin des Plantes,* and his reference to the two hundred pounds Tyrrell possessed, gave me, indeed, some clue as to his real object; but then— why this disguise? Had he known Tyrrell before, in his proper semblance, and had anything passed between them, which rendered this concealment now expedient?—this, indeed, seemed probable enough;

117

but, was Thornton entrusted with the secret?—and, if revenge was the object, was that low man a partaker in its execution?—or was he not, more probably, playing the traitor to both? As for Tyrrell himself, his own designs upon Warburton were sufficient to prevent pity for any fall into the pit he had dug* for others.

Meanwhile, time passed on, the hour grew late, and the greater part of the guests were gone; still I could not tear myself away; I looked, from time to time at the door, with an indescribable feeling of anxiety. I longed, yet dreaded, for it to open; I felt as if my own fate were in some degree implicated in what was then agitating within, and I could not resolve to depart, until I had formed some conclusions on the result.

At length the door opened; Tyrrell came forth—his countenance was perfectly hueless, his cheek was sunk and hollow, the excitement of two hours had been sufficient to render it so. I observed that his teeth were set, and his hand clenched, as they are when we idly seek, by the strained and extreme tension of the nerves, to sustain the fever and the agony of the mind. Warburton and Thornton followed him; the latter with his usual air of reckless indifference—his quick rolling eye glanced from the marquis to myself, and though his colour changed slightly, his nod of recognition was made with its wonted impudence and ease; but Warburton passed on, like Tyrrell, without noticing or heeding any thing around. He fixed his large bright eye upon the figure which preceded him, without once altering its direction, and the extreme beauty of his features, which, not all the dishevelled length of his hair and whiskers could disguise, was lighted up with a joyous but savage expression, which made me turn away, almost with a sensation of fear.

Just as Tyrrell was leaving the room, Warburton put his hand upon his shoulder—"Stay," said he, "I am going your way, and will accompany you." He turned round to Thornton (who was already talking with the marquis) as he said this, and waved his hand, as if to prevent his following; the next moment, Tyrrell and himself had left the room.

I could not now remain longer. I felt a feverish restlessness, which impelled me onwards. I quitted the *salon,* and was on the *escalier** before the gamesters had descended. Warburton was, indeed, but a few steps before me; the stairs were but very dimly lighted by one expiring lamp; he did not turn round to see me, and was probably too much engrossed to hear me.

"You may yet have a favourable reverse," said he to Tyrrell.

"Impossible!" replied the latter, in a tone of such deep anguish,

118

that it thrilled me to the very heart. "I am an utter beggar—I have nothing in the world—I have no expectation but to starve!"

While he was saying this, I perceived by the faint and uncertain light, that Warburton's hand was raised to his own countenance.

"Have you *no* hope—no spot wherein to look for comfort—is beggary your absolute and only possible resource from famine?" he replied, in a low and suppressed tone.

At that moment we were just descending into the court-yard. Warburton was but one step behind Tyrrell: the latter made no answer; but as he passed from the dark staircase into the clear moonlight of the court, I caught a glimpse of the big tears which rolled heavily and silently down his cheeks. Warburton laid his hand upon him.

"Turn," he cried, suddenly, "your cup is not yet full—look upon me—and *remember!*"

I pressed forward—the light shone full upon the countenance of the speaker—the dark hair was gone—my suspicions were true—I discovered at one glance the bright locks and lofty brow of Reginald Glanville. Slowly Tyrrell gazed, as if he were endeavouring to repel some terrible remembrance, which gathered, with every instant, more fearfully upon him; until, as the stern countenance of Glanville grew darker and darker in its mingled scorn and defiance, he uttered one low cry, and sank senseless upon the earth.

CHAPTER XXXI

Well, he is gone, and with him go these thoughts.
SHAKSPEARE[1]

What ho! for England!
IBID

I HAVE ALWAYS HAD AN INSUPERABLE HORROR OF BEING placed in what the vulgar call a *predicament*. In a predicament I was most certainly placed at the present moment. A man at my feet

---

1. *King John,* III, 3, 6. The second epigraph has not been identified.

in a fit—the cause of it having very wisely disappeared, devolving upon me the charge of watching, recovering, and conducting home the afflicted person— made a concatenation of disagreeable circumstances, as much unsuited to the temper of Henry Pelham, as his evil fortune could possibly have contrived.

After a short pause of deliberation, I knocked up the porter, procured some cold water, and bathed Tyrrell's temples for several moments before he recovered. He opened his eyes slowly, and looked carefully around with a fearful and suspicious glance: "Gone—gone —(he muttered)—ay—what did he here at such a moment?—vengeance —for what?—*I* could not tell—it would have killed her—let him thank his own folly. I do not fear; I defy his malice." And with these words, Tyrrell sprung to his feet.

"Can I assist you to your home?" said I; "you are still unwell— pray suffer me to have that pleasure."

I spoke with some degree of warmth and sincerity; the unfortunate man stared wildly at me for a moment, before he replied. "Who," said he, at last, "who speaks to *me*—the lost—the guilty—the ruined, in the accents of interest and kindness?"

I placed his arm in mine, and drew him out of the yard into the open street. He looked at me with an eager and wistful survey, and then, by degrees, appearing to recover his full consciousness of the present, and recollection of the past, he pressed my hand warmly, and after a short silence, during which we moved on slowly towards the Tuileries, he said—"Pardon me, Sir, if I have not sufficiently thanked you for your kindness and attention. I am now quite restored; the close room in which I have been sitting for so many hours, and the feverish excitement of play, acting upon a frame very debilitated by ill health, occasioned my momentary indisposition. I am now, I repeat, quite recovered, and will no longer trespass upon your good nature."

"Really," said I, "you had better not discard my services yet. Do suffer me to accompany you home?"

"Home!" muttered Tyrrell, with a deep sigh; "no—no!" and then, as if recollecting himself, he said, "I thank you, Sir, but—but—"

I saw his embarrassment, and interrupted him. "Well, if I cannot assist you any further, I will take your dismissal. I trust we shall meet again under auspices better calculated for improving acquaintance."

Tyrrell bowed, once more pressed my hand, and we parted. I hurried on up the long street towards my hotel.

When I had got several paces beyond Tyrrell, I turned back to

120

look at him. He was standing in the same place in which I had left him. I saw by the moonlight that his face and hands were raised towards Heaven. It was but for a moment: his attitude changed while I was yet looking, and he slowly and calmly continued his way in the same direction as myself. When I reached my chambers, I hastened immediately to bed, but not to sleep: the extraordinary scene I had witnessed; the dark and ferocious expression of Glanville's countenance, so strongly impressed with every withering and deadly passion; the fearful and unaccountable remembrance that had seemed to gather over the livid and varying face of the gamester; the mystery of Glanville's disguise; the intensity of a revenge so terribly expressed, together with the restless and burning anxiety I felt—not from idle curiosity, but, from my early and intimate friendship for Glanville, to fathom its cause—all crowded upon my mind with a feverish confusion, that effectually banished repose.

It was with that singular sensation of pleasure which none but those who have passed frequent nights in restless and painful agitation, can recognize, that I saw the bright sun penetrate through my shutters, and heard Bedos move across my room.

"What hour will Monsieur have the post horses?" said that praiseworthy valet.

"At eleven," answered I, springing out of bed with joy at the change of scene which the very mention of my journey brought before my mind.

I was a luxurious personage in those days. I had had a bath made from my own design; across it were constructed two small frames—one for the journal of the day, another to hold my breakfast apparatus; in this manner I was accustomed to lie for about an hour, engaging the triple happiness of reading, feeding, and bathing. Owing to some unaccountable delay, Galignani's Messenger did not arrive at the ususal hour, on the morning of my departure; to finish breakfast, or bathing, without Galignani's Messenger, was perfectly impossible, so I remained, till I was half boiled, in a state of the most indolent imbecility.

At last it came: the first paragraph that struck my eyes was the following:*—"It is rumoured among the circles of the Faubourg, that a duel was fought on ———, between a young Englishman and Monsieur D———; the cause of it is said to be the pretensions of both to the beautiful Duchesse de P———, who, if report be true, cares for neither of the gallants, but lavishes her favours upon a certain *attaché* to the English embassy."

121

"Such," thought I, "are the materials for all human histories. Every one who reads, will eagerly swallow this account as true: if an author were writing the memoirs of the court, he would compile his facts and scandal from this very collection of records; and yet, though so near the truth, how totally false it is! Thank Heaven, however, that, at least, I am not suspected of the degradation of the duchesse's love:—to fight for her may make me seem a fool—to be loved by her would constitute me a villain."

The next passage in that collection of scandal which struck me was—"We understand that E.W. Howard de Howard, Esq., Secretary, &c., is shortly to lead to the hymeneal altar the daughter of Timothy Tomkins, Esq., late Consul of ———." I quite started out of my bath with delight. I scarcely suffered myself to be dried and perfumed, before I sat down to write the following congratulatory epistle to the thin man:—

"MY DEAR MR. HOWARD DE HOWARD,

"Permit me, before I leave Paris, to compliment you upon that happiness which I have just learnt is in store for you. Marriage to a man like you, who has survived the vanities of the world—who has attained that prudent age when the passions are calmed into reason, and the purer refinements of friendship succeed to the turbulent delirium of the senses—marriage, my dear Mr. Howard, to a man like you, must, indeed, be a most delicious Utopia. After all the mortifications you may meet elsewhere, whether from malicious females, or a misjudging world, what happiness to turn to one being to whom your praise is an honour, and your indignation of consequence!

"But if marriage itself be so desirable, what words shall I use sufficiently expressive of my congratulation at the particular match you have chosen, so suitable in birth and station? I can fancy you, my dear Sir, in your dignified retirement, expatiating to your admiring bride upon all the honours of your illustrious line, and receiving from her, in return, a full detail of all the civic glories that have ever graced the lineage of the Tomkins's. As the young lady is, I suppose, an heiress, I conclude you will take her name, instead of changing it. Mr. Howard de Howard de Tomkins, will sound peculiarly majestic; and when you come to the titles and possessions of your ancestors, I am persuaded that you will continue to consider your alliance with the honest citizens of London among your proudest distinctions.

"Should you have any commands in England, a letter directed to

122

me in Grosvenor-square will be sure to find me; and you may rely upon my immediately spreading among our mutual acquaintance in London, the happy measure you are about to adopt, and my opinions on its propriety.

"Adieu, my dear Sir.

"With the greatest respect and truth,

"Yours, &c.

"H. PELHAM."

"There," said I, as I sealed my letter, "I have discharged some part of that debt I owe to Mr. Howard de Howard, for an enmity towards me, which he has never affected to conceal. He prides himself on his youth—my allusions to his age will delight him! On the importance of his good or evil opinion—I have flattered him to a wonder! Of a surety, Henry Pelham, I could not have supposed you were such an adept in the art of panegyric."*

"The horses, Sir!" said Bedos; and "the bill, Sir?" said the *garçon*. Alas! that *those* and *that* should be so* coupled together; that we can never take our departure without such awful witnesses of our sojourn. Well—to be brief—the bill for once *was* discharged—the horses snorted —the carriage door was opened—I entered—Bedos mounted behind— crack went the whips—off went the steeds, and so terminated my adventures at dear Paris.

CHAPTER XXXII

O, cousin, you know him—the fine gentleman they talk of so much in town.

WYCHERLY'S *Dancing Master*[1]

BY THE BRIGHT DAYS OF MY YOUTH, THERE IS SOME-thing truly delightful in the quick motion of four* post-horses. In France, where one's steeds are none of the swiftest, the pleasures of travelling are not quite so great as in England; still, however, to a man who is tired of one scene—panting for another—in love with excitement, and not yet wearied of its pursuit—the turnpike road is more grateful than the easiest chair ever invented, and the little

1. Wycherly, *The Gentleman Dancing-Master,* I, 1.

prison we entitle a carriage, more cheerful than the state-rooms of Devonshire House.²

We reached Calais in safety, and in good time, the next day.

"Will Monsieur dine in his rooms, or at the *table d'hôte?*"

"In his rooms, of course," said Bedos, indignantly deciding the question. A French valet's dignity is always involved in his master's.

"You are too good, Bedos," said I, "I shall dine at the *table d'hôte* —who have you there in general?"

"Really," said the *garçon*, "we have such a swift succession of guests, that we seldom see the same faces two days running. We have as many changes as an English administration."

"You are facetious," said I.

"No," returned the *garçon*, who was a philosopher as well as a wit; "no, my digestive organs are very weak, and *par conséquence,* I am naturally melancholy—*Ah, ma foi très triste!*" and with these words the sentimental plate-changer placed his hand— I can scarcely say, whether on his heart, or his stomach, and sighed bitterly!

"How long," said I, "does it want to dinner?" My question restored the *garçon* to himself.

"Two hours, Monsieur, two hours," and twirling his *serviette* with an air of exceeding importance, off went my melancholy acquaintance to compliment new customers, and complain of his digestion.

After I had arranged myself and my whiskers—two very distinct affairs*—yawned three times, and drank two bottles of soda water, I strolled into the town. As I was sauntering along leisurely enough, I heard my name pronounced behind me. I turned, and saw Sir Willoughby Townshend, an old baronet of an antediluvian age—a fossil witness of the wonders of England, before the deluge of French manners swept away ancient customs, and created, out of the wrecks of what had been, a new order of things, and a new race of mankind.

"Ah! my dear Mr. Pelham, how are you? and the worthy Lady Frances, your mother, and your excellent father, all well?—I'm delighted to hear it. Russelton,"³ continued Sir Willoughby, turning

2. Devonshire House, home of the dukes of Devonshire, was probably the most fashionable house in London in the early nineteenth century. All the wits, Whigs, and *beaux esprits* of the Regency frequented the coteries and parties there. The Prince Regent was in habitual attendance. William, the sixth duke, presided at these famous entertainments.

3. Russelton: a portrait of Beau Brummell in exile at Calais after fleeing England, his debts, and the Prince Regent in 1816. Scattered throughout the Russelton episode are references to events in Brummell's life and echoes of his famous witticisms. See William Jesse's *Life of George Brummell* (London, 1884). Below, Richard Brinsley Sheridan (1751–1816): English dramatist and dandy.

to a middle-aged man, whose arm he held, "you remember Pelham—true Whig—great friend of Sheridan's?—let me introduce his son to you. Mr. Russelton, Mr. Pelham; Mr. Pelham, Mr. Russelton."

At the name of the person thus introduced to me, a thousand recollections crowded upon my mind; the contemporary and rival of Napoleon—the autocrat of the great world of fashion and cravats—the mighty genius before whom aristocracy had been humbled and *ton* abashed—at whose nod the haughtiest *noblesse* of Europe had quailed—who had introduced, by a single example, starch into neck-cloths, and had fed the pampered appetite of his boot-tops on champagne—whose coat and whose friend were cut with an equal grace—and whose name was connected with every triumph that the world's great virtue of audacity could achieve—the illustrious, the immortal Russelton, stood before me. I recognised in him a congenial, though a superior spirit, and I bowed with a profundity of veneration, with which no other human being has ever inspired me.

Mr. Russelton seemed pleased with my evident respect, and returned my salutation with a mock dignity which enchanted me. He offered me his disengaged arm; I took it with transport, and we all three proceeded up the street.

"So," said Sir Willoughby—"so, Russelton, you like your quarters here; plenty of sport among the English, I should think: you have not forgot the art of quizzing; eh, old fellow?"

"Even if I had," said Mr. Russelton, speaking very slowly, "the sight of Sir Willoughby Townshend would be quite sufficient to refresh my memory. Yes," continued the venerable wreck, after a short pause,—"yes, I like my residence pretty well; I enjoy a calm conscience, and a clean shirt: what more can man desire? I have made acquaintance with a tame parrot, and I have taught it to say, whenever an English fool with a stiff neck and a loose swagger passes him—'True Briton—true Briton.' I take care of my health, and reflect upon old age. I have read Gil Blas, and the Whole Duty of Man;[4] and, in short, what with instructing my parrot, and improving myself, I think I pass my time as creditably and decorously as the Bishop of Winchester, or my Lord of A—v—ly himself. So you have just come from Paris, I presume, Mr. Pelham?"

"I left it yesterday!"

---

4. *Gil Blas:* a picaresque novel by Le Sage, published between 1715 and 1735; *The Whole Duty of Man* (1658): a moral treatise commonly ascribed to Richard Allestree (1619–81). Below, Lord Alvanly: a notorious Regency dandy.

"Full of those horrid English, I suppose; thrusting their broad hats and narrow minds into every shop in the *Palais Royal*—winking their dull eyes at the damsels of the counter, and manufacturing their notions of French into a higgle for *sous*. Oh! the monsters!—they bring on a bilious attack whenever I think of them: the other day one of them accosted me, and talked me into a nervous fever about patriotism and roast pigs: luckily I was near my own house, and reached it before the thing became fatal; but only think, had I wandered too far, when he met me! at my time of life, the shock would have been too great; I should certainly have perished in a fit. I hope, at least, they would have put the cause of my death in my epitaph—'Died, of an Englishman, John Russelton, Esq., aged,' &c. Pah! You are not engaged, Mr. Pelham; dine with me to-day; Willoughby and his umbrella are coming."

"*Volontiers*," said I, "though I was going to make observations on men and manners at the *table d'hôte* of my hotel."

"I am most truly grieved," replied Mr. Russelton, "at depriving you of so much amusement. With me you will only find some tolerable Lafitte, and an anomalous dish my *cuisinière* calls a mutton chop. It will be curious to see what variation in the monotony of mutton she will adopt to-day. The first time I ordered "a chop," I thought I had amply explained every necessary particular; a certain portion of flesh, and a gridiron: at seven o'clock, up came a *côtelette panée, faute de mieux*. I swallowed the composition, drowned as it was, in a most pernicious sauce. I had one hour's sleep, and the nightmare, in consequence. The next day, I imagined no mistake *could* be made: sauce was strictly prohibited; all extra ingredients laid under a most special veto, and a natural gravy gently recommended: the cover was removed, and lo! a breast of mutton, all bone and gristle, like the dying gladiator![5] This time my heart was too full for wrath; I sat down and wept! To-day will be the third time I shall make the experiment, if French cooks will consent to let one starve upon nature. For my part, I have no stomach left now for art: I wore out my digestion in youth, swallowing Jack St. Leger's suppers,[6] and Sheridan's promises to pay. Pray, Mr. Pelham, did you try Staub[7] when you were at Paris?"

---

5. The Dying Gladiator: the statue in Rome's Capitoline Museum celebrated by Byron in *Childe Harold's Pilgrimage*, 4, stanzas 140–41.

6. Probably a reference to the Irish officer and dandy Colonel William St. Leger (1759–1818).

7. Staub and, in the following paragraph, Stultz were famous tailors.

"Yes; and thought him one degree better than Stultz, whom, indeed, I have long condemned, as fit only for minors at Oxford, and majors in the infantry."

"True," said Russelton, with a very faint smile at a pun, somewhat in his own way, and levelled at a tradesman, of whom he was, perhaps, a little jealous—"True; Stultz aims at making *gentlemen,* not *coats;* there is a degree of aristocratic pretension in his stitches, which is vulgar to an appalling degree. You can tell a Stultz coat any where, which is quite enough to damn it: the moment a man's known by an invariable cut, and that not original, it ought to be all over with him. Give me the man who makes the tailor, not the tailor who makes the man."

"Right, by G—!"* cried Sir Willoughby, who was as badly dressed as one of Sir E———'s dinners. "Right; just my opinion. I have always told my Schneiders to make my clothes neither in the fashion nor out of it; to copy no other man's coat, and to cut their cloth according to my natural body, not according to an isosceles triangle. Look at this coat, for instance," and Sir Willoughby Townshend made a dead halt, that we might admire his garment the more accurately.

"Coat!" said Russelton, with an appearance of the most *naïve* surprise, and taking hold of the collar, suspiciously, by the finger and thumb; "coat, Sir Willoughby! do you call *this thing a coat?*"

CHAPTER XXXIII

J'ai toujours cru que le bon n'étoit que le *beau* mis en action.

ROUSSEAU[1]

SHORTLY AFTER RUSSELTON'S ANSWER TO SIR WILLOUGH-by's eulogistic observations on his own attire, I left those two worthies till I was to join them at dinner; it wanted three hours yet to that time, and I repaired to my quarters to bathe and write letters. I scribbled one to Madame D'Anville, full of antitheses and

---

1. "I have always believed that the good was only beauty turned active." Source unidentified.

maxims, sure to charm her; another to my mother, to prepare her for my arrival; and a third to Lord Vincent, giving him certain commissions at Paris, which I had forgotten personally to execute.

My pen is not that of a ready writer; and what with yawning, stretching, admiring my rings,* and putting pen to paper, in the intervals of these more natural occupations,* it was time to bathe and dress before my letters were completed. I set off to Russelton's abode in high spirits, and fully resolved to make the most of a character so original.

It was a very small room in which I found him; he was stretched in an easy chair before the fireplace, gazing complacently at his feet, and apparently occupied in any thing but listening to Sir Willoughby Townshend, who was talking with great vehemence about politics and the corn laws.[2] Notwithstanding the heat of the weather, there was a small fire on the hearth, which, aided by the earnestness of his efforts to convince his host, put poor Sir Willoughby into a most intense perspiration. Russelton, however, seemed enviably cool, and hung over the burning wood like a cucumber on a hotbed. Sir Willoughby came to a full stop by the window, and (gasping for breath) attempted to throw it open.

"What are you doing? for Heaven's sake, what are you doing?" cried Russelton, starting up; "do you mean to kill me?"

"Kill you!" said Sir Willoughby, quite aghast.

"Yes; kill me! is it not quite cold enough already in this d——d seafaring place, without making my only retreat, humble as it is, a theatre for thorough draughts? Have I not had the rheumatism in my left shoulder, and the ague in my little finger, these last six months? and must you now terminate my miserable existence at one blow, by opening that abominable lattice? Do you think, because your great frame, fresh from the Yorkshire wolds, and compacted of such materials, that one would think, in eating your beeves, you had digested their hides into skin—do you think, because your limbs might be cut up into planks for a seventy-eight, and warranted water-proof without pitch, because of the density of their pores—do you think, because you are as impervious as an araphorostic shoe, that I, John Russelton, am equally impenetrable, and that you are to let easterly winds play about my room like children, begetting rheums and asthmas and all manner of catarrhs? I do beg, Sir Willoughby Town-

---

2. The Corn Law was passed in 1815 to protect British grain from foreign imports. It worked great hardships on the poor.

shend, that you will suffer me to die a more natural and civilized death;" and so saying, Russelton sank down into his chair, apparently in the last state of exhaustion.

Sir Willoughby, who remembered the humorist in all his departed glory, and still venerated him as a temple where the deity yet breathed, though the altar was overthrown, made to this extraordinary remonstrance no other reply than a long *whiff,* and a "Well, Russelton, dash my wig (a favourite oath of Sir W.'s)* but you're a queer fellow."

Russelton now turned to me, and invited me, with a tone of the most lady-like languor, to sit down near the fire. As I am naturally of a chilly disposition, and fond, too, of beating people in their own line, I drew a chair close to the hearth, declared the weather was very cold, and rung the bell for some more wood. Russelton stared for a moment, and then, with a politeness he had not deigned to exert before, approached his chair to mine, and began a conversation, which, in spite of his bad witticisms, and peculiarity of manner, I found singularly entertaining.

Dinner was announced, and we adjourned to another room—poor Sir Willoughby, with his waistcoat unbuttoned, and breathing like a pug in phthisis—groaned bitterly, when he discovered that this apartment was smaller and hotter than the one before. Russelton immediately helped him to some scalding soup—and said, as he told the the servant to hand Sir Willoughby the cayenne—"you will find this, my dear Townshend, a very sensible *potage* for this severe season."

Dinner went off tamely enough, with the exception of "our stout* friend's" agony, which Russelton enjoyed most luxuriously. The threatened mutton-chops did not make their appearance, and the dinner, though rather too small, was excellently cooked, and better arranged. With the dessert, the poor baronet rose, and pleading sudden indisposition, tottered out of the door.

When he was gone, Russelton threw himself back in his chair, and laughed for several minutes with a low chuckling sound, till the tears ran down his cheek. "A nice heart you must have!" thought I—(my conclusions of character are always drawn from small propensities).*

After a few jests at Sir Willoughby, our conversation turned upon other individuals. I soon saw that Russelton was a soured and disappointed man; his remarks on people were all sarcasms—his mind was overflowed with a suffusion of illnature—he bit as well as growled. No man of the world ever, I am convinced, becomes a real philosopher in retirement. People who have been employed for years upon trifles have not the greatness of mind, which could alone make them in-different to what they have coveted all their lives, as most enviable and important.

"Have you read ———'s memoirs?" said Mr. Russelton. "No! Well, I imagined every one had at least dipped into them. I have often had serious thoughts of dignifying my own retirement, by the literary em-ployment of detailing my adventures in the world. I think I could throw a new light upon things and persons, which my contemporaries will shrink back like owls at perceiving."

"Your life," said I, "must indeed furnish matter of equal instruc-tion and amusement."

"Ay," answered Russelton; "amusement to the fools, but instruc-tion to the knaves. I am, indeed, a lamentable example of the fall of ambition. I brought starch into all the neckcloths in England, and I end by tying my own at a three-inch looking-glass at Calais. You are a young man, Mr. Pelham, about to commence life, probably with the same views as (though greater advantages than) myself; perhaps in indulging my egotism, I shall not weary without recompensing you.

"I came into the world with an inordinate love of glory, and a great admiration of the original; these propensities might have made me a Shakspeare—they did more, they made me a Russelton! When I was six years old, I cut my jacket into a coat, and turned my aunt's best petticoat into a waistcoat. I disdained at eight the language of the vulgar, and when my father asked me to fetch his slippers, I replied, that my soul swelled beyond the limits of a lackey's. At nine, I was self-inoculated with propriety of ideas. I rejected malt with the air of His Majesty, and formed a violent affection for maraschino; though starving at school, I never took twice of pudding, and paid sixpence a week out of my shilling to have my shoes blacked. As I grew up, my notions expanded. I gave myself, without restraint, to the ambition that burnt within me—I cut my old friends, who were rather envious than emulous of my genius, and I employed three tradesmen to make my gloves—one for the hand, a second for the fingers, and a *third for the thumb!* These two qualities made me courted and admired by a new race—for the great secrets of being courted are, to shun others, and seem delighted with yourself. The latter is obvious enough; who the deuce *should* be pleased with you, if you yourself are not?*

"Before I left college I fell in love. Other fellows, at my age, in such a predicament, would have whined—shaved only twice a week, and written verses. I did none of the three—the last indeed I tried, but, to my infinite surprise, I found my genius was not universal. I began with

> " 'Sweet nymph, for whom I wake my muse.'

"For this, after considerable hammering, I could only think of the rhyme 'shoes'—so I began again,—

> " 'Thy praise demands much softer lutes.'

And the fellow of this verse terminated like myself in 'boots.'—Other efforts were equally successful—'bloom' suggested to my imagination no rhyme but 'perfume;'—'despair' only reminded me of my 'hair,'— and 'hope' was met at the end of the second verse, by the inharmonious antithesis of 'soap.' Finding, therefore, that my *forte* was not in the Pierian line, I redoubled my attention to my dress; I *coated,* and *cravated,* and *essenced,* and *oiled,** with all the attention the very inspiration of my rhymes seemed to advise;—in short, I thought the best pledge I could give my Dulcinea of my passion for her person, would be to show her what affectionate veneration I could pay to my own.

"My mistress could not withhold from me her admiration, but she denied me her love. She confessed Mr. Russelton was the best dressed man at the University, and had the whitest hands; and two days after this avowal, she ran away with a great rosy-cheeked extract from Leicestershire.

"I did not blame her: I pitied her too much—but I made a vow never to be in love again. In spite of all advantages I kept my oath, and avenged myself on the species for the insult of the individual.

"Before I commenced a part which was to continue through life, I considered deeply on the humours of the spectators. I saw that the character of the English* was servile to rank, and yielding to pretension—they admire you for your acquaintance, and cringe to you for your conceit. The first thing, therefore, was to know great people— the second to controul them. I dressed well, and had good horses— that was sufficient to make me sought by the young of my own sex. I talked scandal, and was never abashed—that was more than enough to make me *recherché** among the matrons of the other. It is single men, and married women, to whom are given the St. Peter's keys of Society. I was soon admitted into its heaven—I was more—I was one of its saints. I became imitated as well as initiated. I was the rage— the lion. Why?—was I better—was I richer—was I handsomer—was I cleverer, than my kind? No, no;—(and here Russelton ground his teeth with a strong and wrathful expression of scorn);—and had I been all—had I been a very concentration and monopoly of all human perfections, they would not have valued me at half the price they *did* set on me. It was—I will tell you the simple secret, Mr. Pelham—it was because *I trampled on them,* that, like crushed herbs, they sent up a grateful incense in return.

"Oh! it was balm to my bitter and loathing temper, to see those who would have spurned *me* from them, if they dared, writhe beneath my lash, as I withheld or inflicted it at will. I was the magician who held the great spirits that longed to tear me to pieces, by one simple spell which a superior hardihood had won me—and, by Heaven, I did not spare to exert it.

"Well, well, this is but an idle recollection now; all human power, says the proverb of every language, is but of short duration. Alexander did not conquer kingdoms for ever; and Russelton's good fortune deserted him at last. Napoleon died in exile, and so shall I; but we have both had our day, and mine was the brightest of the two, for it had no change till the evening. I am more happy than people would think for—*Je ne suis pas souvent où mon corps est*[3]—I live in a world of recollections, I trample again upon coronets and ermine, the glories of the small great! I give once more laws which no libertine is so hardy not to feel exalted in adopting; I hold my court, and issue my fiats; I am like the madman, and out of the very straws of my cell, I make my subjects and my realm; and when I wake from these bright visions, and see myself an old, deserted man, forgotten, and decaying inch by inch in a foreign village, I can at least summon sufficient of my ancient regality of spirit not to sink beneath the reverse. If I am inclined to be melancholy, why, I extinguish my fire, and imagine I have demolished a duchess. I steal up to my solitary chamber, to renew again, in my sleep, the phantoms of my youth; to carouse with princes; to legislate for nobles; and to wake in the morning (here Russelton's countenance and manner suddenly changed to an affectation of methodistical gravity), and thank Heaven that I have still a coat to my stomach, as well as to my back, and that I am safely delivered of such villainous company; 'to forswear sack and live cleanly,' during the rest of my sublunary existence."

After this long detail of Mr. Russelton's, the conversation was but dull and broken. I could not avoid indulging a reverie upon

***

3. "I am not often where my body is." The quotation at the end of the paragraph is from *I Henry IV,* V, 4, 168–69.

what I had heard, and my host was evidently still revolving the recollections his narration had conjured up; we sat opposite each other for several minutes as abstracted and distracted as if we had been a couple two months married; till at last I rose, and tendered my adieus. Russelton received them with his usual coldness, but more than his usual civility, for he followed me to the door.

Just as they were about to shut it, he called me back. "Mr. Pelham," said he, "Mr. Pelham, when you come back this way, do look in upon me, and—and as you will be going a good deal into society, *just find out what people say of my manner of life!*"[4]

CHAPTER XXXIV

An old worshipful gentleman, that had a great estate,
And kept a brave old house at a hospitable rate.

Old Song

I THINK I MAY, WITHOUT MUCH LOSS TO THE READER, pass in silence over my voyage, the next day, to Dover. (Horrible reminiscence!) I may also spare him an exact detail of all the inns and impositions between that sea-port and London; nor will it be absolutely necessary to the plot of this history, to linger over every milestone between the metropolis and Glenmorris Castle, where my uncle and my mother were impatiently awaiting the arrival of the candidate to be.

It was a fine bright evening when my carriage entered the park. I had not seen the place for years; and I felt my heart swell with something like family pride, as I gazed on the magnificent extent of hill and plain that opened upon me, as I passed the ancient and ivy-covered lodge. Large groups of trees, scattered on either side,

---

4. It will be perceived by those readers who are kind or patient enough to reach the conclusion of this work, that Russelton is specified as one of my few dramatis personae of which only the *first* outline is taken from real life: all the rest—all, indeed, which forms and marks the character thus briefly delineated, is drawn solely from imagination. [B-L]

seemed, in their own antiquity, the witness of that of the family which had given them existence. The sun set on the waters which lay gathered in a lake at the foot of the hill, breaking the waves into unnumbered sapphires, and tinging the dark firs that overspread the margin, with a rich and golden light, that put me excessively in mind of the Duke of ———'s livery.

When I descended at the gate, the servants, who stood arranged in an order so long that it almost startled me, received me with a visible gladness and animation, which shewed me, at one glance, the old fashioned tastes of their master. Who, in these days, ever inspires his servants with a single sentiment of regard or interest for himself or his whole race? That tribe one never, indeed, considers as possessing a life separate from their services to us: beyond that purpose of existence, we know not even if they exist. As Providence made the stars for the benefit of earth, so it made servants for the use of gentlemen; and, as neither stars nor servants appear except when we want them, so I suppose they are in a sort of suspense from *being*, except at those important and happy moments.

To return—for if I have any fault, it is too great a love for abstruse speculation and reflection—I was formally ushered through a great hall, hung round with huge antlers and rusty armour, through a lesser one, supported by large stone columns, and without any other adornment than the arms of the family; then through an anti-room, covered with tapestry, representing the gallantries of King Solomon to the Queen of Sheba; and lastly, into the apartment honoured by the august presence of Lord Glenmorris. That personage was dividing the sofa with three spaniels and a setter; he rose hastily when I was announced, and then checking the first impulse which hurried him, perhaps, into an unseemingly warmth of salutation, held out his hand with a pompous* air of kindly protection, and while he pressed mine, surveyed me from head to foot to see how far my appearance justified his condescension.

Having, at last, satisfied himself, he proceeded to inquire after the state of my appetite. He smiled benignantly when I confessed that I was excessively well prepared to testify its capacities (the first idea of all kind-hearted, old-fashioned people, is to stuff you), and, silently motioning to the grey-headed servant who stood in attendance, till, receiving the expected sign, he withdrew, Lord Glenmorris informed me that dinner was over for every one but myself, that for me it would be prepared in an instant, that Mr. Toolington had expired four days since, that my mother was, at that moment, canvassing for

134

me, and that my own electioneering qualities were to open their exhibition with the following day.

After this communication there was a short pause. "What a beautiful place this is!" said I, with great enthusiasm. Lord Glenmorris was pleased with the compliment, simple as it was.

"Yes," said he, "it is, and I have made it still more so than you have yet been able to perceive."

"You have been planting, probably, on the other side of the park?"

"No;" said my uncle, smiling; "Nature had done everything for this spot when I came to it, but one, and the addition of that one ornament is the only real triumph which art ever can achieve."

"What is it?" asked I; "oh, I know—water."

"You are mistaken," answered Lord Glenmorris; "it is the ornament of—*happy faces.*"

I looked up to my uncle's countenance in sudden surprise. I cannot explain how I was struck with the expression which it wore; so calmly bright and open!—it was as if the very daylight had settled there.

"You don't understand this at present, Henry," said he, after a moment's silence; "but you will find it, of all rules for the improvement of property, the easiest to learn. Enough of this now. Were you not *au désespoir** at leaving Paris?"

"I should have been, some months ago; but when I received my mother's summons, I found the temptations of the continent very light in comparison with those held out to me here."

"What, have you already arrived at that great epoch, when vanity casts off its *first* skin, and ambition succeeds to pleasure? Why—but thank Heaven that you have lost my moral—your dinner is announced."

Most devoutly *did* I thank Heaven, and most earnestly did I betake myself to do honour to my uncle's hospitality.

I had just finished my repast, when my mother entered. She was, as you might well expect from her maternal affection, quite overpowered with joy, *first,* at finding my hair grown so much darker, and, *secondly,* at my looking so well. We spent the whole evening in discussing the great business for which I had been summoned. Lord Glenmorris promised me money, and my mother advice; and I, in my turn, enchanted them, by promising to make the best use of both.

135

CHAPTER XXXV

Cor. Your good voice, Sir—what say you?
2nd Cit. You shall have it, worthy Sir.
                                    Coriolanus[1]

THE BOROUGH OF BUYEMALL HAD LONG BEEN IN undisputed possession of the lords of Glenmorris, till a rich banker, of the name of Lufton, had bought a large estate in the immediate neighbourhood of Glenmorris Castle. This event, which was the precursor of a mighty revolution in the borough of Buyemall, took place in the first year of my uncle's accession to his property. A few months afterwards, a vacancy in the borough occurring, my uncle procured the nomination of one of his own political party. To the great astonishment of Lord Glenmorris, and the great gratification of the burghers of Buyemall, Mr. Lufton offered himself in opposition to the Glenmorris candidate. In this age of enlightenment, innovation has no respect for the most sacred institutions of antiquity. The burghers, for the only time since their creation as a body, were cast first into doubt, and secondly into rebellion. The Lufton faction, *horresco referens,*[2] were triumphant, and the rival candidate was returned. From that hour the Borough of Buyemall was open to all the world.

My uncle, who was a good easy man, and had some strange notions of free representation, and liberty of election, professed to care very little for this event. He contented himself henceforward, with exerting his interest for one of the members, and left the other seat entirely at the disposal of the line of Lufton, which, from the time of the first competition, continued peaceably to monopolize it.

During the last two years, my uncle's candidate, the late Mr. Toolington, had been gradually dying of a dropsy, and the Luftons had been so *particularly* attentive to the honest burghers, that it was shrewdly suspected a bold push was to be made for the other seat.

---

1. *Coriolanus,* II, 3, 84–85.
2. "I tremble at the recollection" (Virgil *Aeneid* 2.204).

During the last month, these doubts were changed into certainty. Mr. Augustus Leopold Lufton, eldest son to Benjamin Lufton, Esq., had publicly declared his intention of starting at the decease of Mr. Toolington; against this personage, behold myself armed and arrayed.

Such is, in brief, the history of the borough, up to the time in which I was to take a prominent share in its interests and events.

On the second day after my arrival at the castle, the following advertisement appeared at Buyemall:—

"*To the Independent Electors of the Bourough of Buyemall.*

"Gentlemen,

"In presenting myself to your notice, I advance a claim not altogether new and unfounded. My family have for centuries been residing amongst you, and exercising that interest which reciprocal confidence, and good offices may fairly create. Should it be my good fortune to be chosen your representative, you may rely upon my utmost endeavours to deserve that honour. One word upon the principles I espouse: they are those which have found their advocates among the wisest and the best; they are those which, hostile alike to the encroachments of the crown, and the licentiousness of the people, would support the real interest of both. Upon these grounds, gentlemen, I have the honour to solicit your votes; and it is with the sincerest respect for your ancient and honourable body, that I subscribe myself your very obedient servant,

"Henry Pelham."

Glenmorris Castle," &c. &c.

Such was the first public signification of my intentions; it was drawn up by Mr. Sharpon, our lawyer, and considered by our friends as a masterpiece: for, as my mother sagely observed, it did not commit me in a single instance—espoused no principle, and yet professed what all parties would allow was the best.

At the first house where I called, the proprietor was a clergyman of good family, who had married a lady from Baker-street: of course the Reverend Combermere St. Quintin and his wife valued themselves upon being "*genteel.*" I arrived at an unlucky moment; on entering the hall, a dirty footboy was carrying a yellow-ware dish of potatoes into the back room. Another Ganymede (a sort of footboy major), who opened the door, and who was still *settling himself into his coat,* which he had slipped on at my tintinnabulary summons, ushered me

137

with a mouth full of bread and cheese into this said back room. I gave up every thing as lost, when I entered, and saw the lady helping her youngest child to some ineffable trash, which I have since heard is called "blackberry pudding." Another of the tribe was bawling out, with a loud hungry tone—"A tatoe, pa!" The father himself was carving for the little group, with a napkin stuffed into the top button-hole of his waistcoat, and the mother, with a long bib, plentifully bespattered with congealing gravy, and the nectarean liquor of the "blackberry pudding," was sitting, with a sort of presiding compla-cency, on a high stool, like Jupiter* on Olympus, enjoying rather than stilling the confused hubbub of the little domestic deities, who eat, clattered, spattered, and squabbled around her.

Amidst all this din and confusion, the candidate for the borough of Buyemall was ushered into the household privacy of the *genteel* Mr. and Mrs. St. Quintin. Up started the lady at the sound of my name. The Reverend Combermere St. Quintin seemed frozen into stone. The plate between the youngest child and the blackberry-pudding, stood as still as the sun in Ajalon.[3] The morsel between the mouth of the elder boy and his fork had a respite from mastication. The Seven Sleepers[4] could not have been spell-bound more suddenly and completely.

"Ah!" cried I, advancing eagerly, with an air of serious and yet abrupt gladness; "how deuced* lucky that I should find you all at luncheon. I was up and had finished breakfast so early this morning, that I am half famished. Only think how fortunate, Hardy (turning round to one of the members of my committee, who accompanied me); I was just saying what would I not give to find Mr. St. Quintin at luncheon. Will you allow me, Madam, to make one of your party?"

Mrs. St. Quintin coloured, and faultered, and muttered out some-thing which I was fully resolved *not* to hear. I took a chair, looked round the table, not *too* attentively, and said—"Cold veal; ah! ah! nothing I like so much. May I trouble you, Mr. St. Quintin?—Hollo, my little man, let's see if you can't give me a potatoe. There's a brave fellow. How old are you, my young hero?—to look at your mother, I should say two; to look at *you*, six."

"He is four next May," said his mother, colouring, and this time *not* painfully.

---

3. Joshua 10:12 and II Chronicles 11:10.

4. Versions of the legend of the Seven Sleepers appear in the Koran, Voragine's *Golden Legends*, Gregory of Tour's *De Gloria Martyrorum*, and the comte de Caylus's *Oriental Tales.*

"Indeed!" said I, surveying him earnestly; and then, in a graver tone, I turned to the Reverend Combermere with—"I think you have a branch of your family still settled in France. I met Monsieur St. Quintin, the Duc de Poictiers, abroad."

"Yes," said Mr. Combermere, "yes, the name is still in Normandy, but I was not aware of the title."

"No!" said I, with surprise; "and yet (with another look at the boy), it is astonishing how long family likenesses last. I was a great favourite with all the Duc's children. Do you know, I must trouble you for some more veal, it is so very good, and I am so very hungry."

"How long have you been abroad?" said Mrs. St. Quintin, who had slipped off her bib, and smoothed her ringlets; for which purposes I had been most adroitly looking in an opposite direction the last three minutes.

"About seven or eight months. The fact is, that the continent only does for us English people to see—not to inhabit; and yet, there are some advantages there, Mr. St. Quintin!—Among others, that of the due respect ancient birth is held in. Here, you know, 'money makes the man,' as the vulgar proverb has it."

"Yes," said Mr. St. Quintin, with a sigh, "it is really dreadful to see those upstarts rising around us, and throwing every thing that is respectable and ancient into the back ground. Dangerous times these, Mr. Pelham—dangerous times; nothing but innovation upon the most sacred institutions. I am sure, Mr. Pelham, that your principles must be decidedly against these new-fashioned doctrines, which lead to nothing but anarchy and confusion—absolutely nothing."

"I'm delighted to find you so much of my opinion!" said I. "I cannot endure any thing *that leads to anarchy and confusion.*"

Here Mr. Combermere glanced at his wife—who rose, called to the children, and, accompanied by them, gracefully withdrew.

"Now then," said Mr. Combermere, drawing his chair nearer to me,—"now, Mr. Pelham, we can discuss these matters. Women are no politicians,"—and at this sage aphorism, the Rev. Combermere laughed a low solemn laugh, which could have come from no other lips. After I had joined in this grave merriment for a second or two —I hemmed thrice, and with a countenance suited to the subject and the hosts, plunged at once *in medias res.*

"Mr. St. Quintin," said I, "you are already aware, I think, of my intention of offering myself as a candidate for the borough of Buye-mall. I could not think of such a measure, without calling upon you, the very first person, to solicit the honour of your vote." Mr. Combermere looked pleased, and prepared to reply. "You are the very first person I called upon," repeated I.

Mr. Combermere smiled. "Well, Mr. Pelham," said he, "our families have long been on the most intimate footing."

"Ever since," cried I, "ever since Henry the Seventh's time have the houses of St. Quintin and Glenmorris been allied. Your ancestors, you know, were settled in the county before ours, and my mother assures me that she has read in some old book or another, a long account of your forefathers' kind reception of mine at the castle of St. Quintin. I *do* trust, Sir, that we have done nothing to forfeit a support so long afforded us."

Mr. St. Quintin bowed in speechless gratification; at length he found voice. "But your principles, Mr. Pelham?"

"Quite your's, my dear Sir: *quite against anarchy and confusion.*"

"But the Catholic question, Mr. Pelham?"

"Oh! the Catholic question," repeated I, "is a question of great importance; it won't be carried—no, Mr. St. Quintin, no, it won't be carried; how *did* you think, my dear Sir, that I could, in so great a question, act against my conscience?"[5]

I said this with warmth, and Mr. St. Quintin was either too convinced or too timid to pursue so dangerous a topic any further. I blessed my stars when he paused, and not giving him time to think of another piece of debateable ground, continued, "Yes, Mr. St. Quintin, I called upon you the very first person. Your rank in the county, your ancient birth, to be sure, demanded it; but *I* only considered the long, long time the St. Quintins and Pelhams had been connected."

"Well," said the Rev. Combermere, "well, Mr. Pelham, you shall have my support; and I wish, from my very heart, all success to a young gentleman of such excellent principles."

---

5. The Catholic question involved the liberal movement to repeal the Test Act, which prevented dissenting Protestants and Catholics from holding state or municipal offices. Much to nearly everyone's surprise, and often horror, Catholic emancipation was achieved in 1829 despite the unwillingness of Wellington and his Tory cabinet.

CHAPTER XXXVI

More voices!

*   *   *   *   *

Sic. How now, my masters, have you chosen him?
Cit. He has our voices, Sir!

Coriolanus[1]

FROM MR. COMBERMERE ST. QUINTIN'S, WE WENT TO A bluff, hearty, radical wine-merchant, whom I had very little probability of gaining; but my success with the clerical Armado[2] had inspirited me, and I did not suffer myself to fear, though I could scarcely persuade myself to hope. How exceedingly impossible it is, in governing men, to lay down positive rules, even where we know the temper of the individual to be gained. "You must be very stiff and formal with the St. Quintins," said my mother. She was right in the general admonition, and had I found them all seated in the best drawing-room, Mrs. St. Quintin in her best attire, and the children on their best behaviour, I should have been as stately as Don Quixote in a brocade dressing-gown, but finding them in such dishabille, I could not affect too great a plainness and almost coarseness of bearing, as if I had never been accustomed to anything more refined than I found there; nor might I, by any appearance of pride in myself, put them in mind of the wound *their* own pride had received. The difficulty was to blend with this familiarity a certain respect, just the same as a French ambassador might have testified towards the august person of George the Third, had he found his Majesty at dinner at one o'clock, over mutton and turnips.

In overcoming this difficulty, I congratulated myself with as much zeal and fervour as if I had performed the most important victory; for, whether it be innocent or sanguinary, in war or at an election,

---

1. *Coriolanus*, II, 3, 132, 163–64.
2. Armado: the fantastical Spaniard in *Love's Labour's Lost.*

141

there is no triumph so gratifying to the viciousness of human nature, as the conquest of our fellow beings.

But I must return to my wine-merchant, Mr. Briggs. His house was at the entrance of the town of Buyemall; it stood inclosed in a small garden, flaming with crocuses and sunflowers, and exhibiting an arbour to the right, where, in the summer evenings, the respectable owner might be seen, with his waistcoat unbuttoned, in order to give that just and rational liberty to the subordinate parts of the human commonwealth which the increase of their consequence after the hour of dinner, naturally demands. Nor, in those moments of dignified ease, was the worthy burgher without the divine inspirations of complacent contemplation which the weed of Virginia bestoweth. There, as he smoked and puffed, and looked out upon the bright crocuses, and meditated over the dim recollections of the hesternal journal, did Mr. Briggs revolve in his mind the vast importance of the borough of Buyemall to the British empire, and the vast importance of John Briggs to the borough of Buyemall.

When I knocked at the door a prettyish maid-servant opened it, with a smile, and a glance which the vender of wine might probably have taught her himself after too large potations of his own spirituous manufactories. I was ushered into a small parlour—where sat, sipping brandy and water, a short, stout, *monosyllabic* sort of figure, corresponding in outward shape *to the name of Briggs*—even unto a very nicety.

"Mr. Pelham," said this gentleman, who was dressed in a brown coat, white waistcoat, buff-coloured inexpressibles,[3] with long strings, and gaiters of the same hue and substance as the breeches—"Mr. Pelham, pray be seated—excuse my rising. I'm like the bishop in the story, Mr. Pelham, too old to rise;" and Mr. Briggs grunted out a short, quick, querulous, "he—he—he," to which, of course, I replied to the best of my cachinnatory powers.

No sooner, however, did I begin to laugh, than Mr. Briggs stopped short—eyed me with a sharp, suspicious glance—shook his head, and pushed back his chair at least four feet from the spot it had hitherto occupied. Ominous signs, thought I—I must sound this gentleman a little further, before I venture to treat him as the rest of his species.

"You have a nice situation here, Mr. Briggs," said I.

"Ay, Mr. Pelham, and a nice vote too, which is somewhat more to your purpose, I believe."

---

3. Inexpressibles: trousers.

142

'Oh!' thought I, 'I see through you now, Mr. Briggs!'—you must not be too civil to one who suspects you are going to be civil, in order to take him in.*

"Why," said I, "Mr. Briggs, to be frank with you, I do call upon you for the purpose of requesting your vote; give it me, or not, just as you please. You may be sure I shall not make use of the vulgar electioneering arts to coax gentlemen out of their votes. I ask you for yours as one freeman solicits another: if you think my opponent a fitter person to represent your borough, give your support to him in God's* name; if not, and you place confidence in me, I will, at least, endeavour not to betray it."

"Well done, Mr. Pelham," exclaimed Mr. Briggs: "I love candour —you speak just after my own heart; but you must be aware that one does not like to be bamboozled out of one's right of election, by a smooth-tongued fellow, who sends one to the devil the moment the election is over—or still worse, to be frightened out of it by some stiff-necked proud coxcomb, with his pedigree in his hand, and his acres in his face, thinking he does you a marvellous honour to ask you at all. Sad times these for this free country, Mr. Pelham, when a parcel of conceited paupers, like Parson Quinny (as I call that reverend fool, Mr. Combermere St. Quintin), imagine they have a right to dictate to warm, honest men, who can buy their whole family out and out. I tell you what, Mr. Pelham, we shall never do anything for this country till we get rid of those landed aristocrats, with their ancestry and humbug. I hope you're of my mind, Mr. Pelham."

"Why," answered I, "there is certainly nothing so respectable in Great Britain as our commercial interest. A man who makes himself is worth a thousand men made by their forefathers."

"Very true, Mr. Pelham," said the wine-merchant, advancing his chair to me, and then laying a short, *thickset* finger upon my arm— he looked up in my face with an investigating air, and said:—"Parliamentary Reform—what do you say to that? you're not an advocate for ancient abuses, and modern corruption, I hope, Mr. Pelham?"[4]

"By no means," cried I, with an honest air of indignation—"I have a conscience, Mr. Briggs, I have a conscience as a public man, no less than as a private one!"

"Admirable!" cried my host.

---

4. Mr. Briggs refers to the liberal pressure to institute widespread reform in the nature of the electoral process. The first Parliamentary Reform Bill was passed in 1832.

"No," I continued, glowing as I proceeded, "no, Mr. Briggs; I disdain to talk too much about my principles before they are tried; the proper time to proclaim them is when they have effected some good by being put into action. I won't supplicate your vote, Mr. Briggs, as my opponent may do; there must be a mutual confidence between my supporters and myself. When I appear before you a second time, you will have a right to see how far I have wronged that trust reposed in me as your representative. Mr. Briggs, I dare say it may seem rude and impolitic to address you in this manner; but I am a plain, blunt man, and I disdain the vulgar arts of electioneering, Mr. Briggs."

"Give us your fist, old boy," cried the wine merchant, in a transport; "give us your fist; I promise you my support, and I am delighted to vote for *a young gentleman of such excellent principles.*"

So much, dear reader, for Mr. Briggs, who became from that interview my staunchest supporter. I will not linger longer upon this part of my career; the above conversations may serve as a sufficient sample of my electioneering qualifications: and so I shall merely add, that after the due quantum of dining, drinking, spouting, lying, equivocating, bribing, rioting, head-breaking, promise-breaking, and —thank the god Mercury, who presides over elections—*chairing* of successful candidateship, I found myself fairly chosen member for the borough of Buyemall.[5]

---

5. It is fortunate that Mr. Pelham's election was not for a rotten borough; so that the satire of this chapter is not yet obsolete nor unsalutary. Parliamentary Reform has not terminated the tricks of canvassing—and Mr. Pelham's descriptions are as applicable now as when first written. All personal canvassing is but for the convenience of cunning—the opportunity for manner to disguise principle. Public meetings, in which expositions of opinion must be clear, and will be cross examined, are the only legitimate mode of canvass. The English begin to discover this truth; may these scenes serve to quicken their apprehension. [B-L; 1835 ed.] Boroughs which continued to enjoy parliamentary representation despite the fact that population centers had shifted to other, poorly represented areas (like the industrial midlands) were called "Rotten." The reform bill of 1832 abolished these boroughs and attempted to equalize population and parliamentary representation.

CHAPTER XXXVII

Political education is like the keystone to the arch—the strength
of the whole depends upon it.

Encycl. Britt. Sup. Art. Education[1]

I WAS SITTING IN THE LIBRARY OF GLENMORRIS CASTLE,
about a week after all the bustle of contest and the *éclat* of victory
had begun to subside, and quietly *dallying* with the dry toast, which
constituted then, and does to this day, my ordinary breakfast, when
I was accosted by the following speech from my uncle.

"Henry, your success has opened to you a new career: I trust
you intend to pursue it?"

"Certainly," was my answer.

"But you know, my dear Henry, that though you have great
talents, which, I confess, I was surprised in the course of the election
to discover, yet they want that careful cultivation, which, in order
to shine in the House of Commons, they must receive. *Entre nous*,
Henry; a little reading would do you no harm."

"Very well," said I, "suppose I begin with Walter Scott's novels;
I am told they are extremely entertaining."

"True," answered my uncle, "but they don't contain the most
accurate notions of history, or the soundest principles of political
philosophy in the world. What did you think of doing to-day, Henry?"

"*Nothing!*" said I very innocently.

"I should conceive that to be an usual answer of yours, Henry,
to any similar question."

"I think it is," replied I, with great *naïveté*.

"Well, then, let us have the breakfast things taken away, and do
something this morning."

"Willingly," said I, ringing the bell.

The table was cleared, and my uncle began his examination. Little,
poor man, had he thought, from my usual bearing and the character
of my education, that in general literature there were few subjects
on which I was not to the full as well read as himself. I enjoyed his

---

1. James Mill (1773–1836), in the *Encyclopaedia Britannica Supplement* (1824),
s.v. "Education."

surprise, when little by little he began to discover the extent of my information, but I was mortified to find it was *only* surprise, *not* delight.

"You have," said he, "a considerable store of learning; far more than I could possibly have imagined you possessed; but it is *knowledge, not learning,* in which I wish you to be skilled. I would rather, in order to gift you with the former, that you were more destitute of the latter. The object of education, is to instil *principles* which are hereafter to guide and instruct us; *facts* are only desirable, so far as they illustrate those principles; principles ought therefore to precede facts! What then can we think of a system which reverses this evident order, overloads the memory with facts, and those of the most doubtful description, while it leaves us entirely in the dark with regard to the principles which could alone render this heterogeneous mass of any advantage or avail? Learning without knowledge, is but a bundle of prejudices; a lumber of inert matter set before the threshold of the understanding to the exclusion of common sense. Pause for a moment, and recal those of your contemporaries, who are generally considered well-informed; tell me if their information has made them a whit the *wiser;* if not, it is only sanctified ignorance. Tell me if names with them are not a sanction for opinion; quotations, the representatives of axioms? All they have learned only serves as an excuse for all they are ignorant of. In one month, I will engage that you shall have a juster and deeper insight into wisdom, than they have been all their lives acquiring; the great error of education is to fill the mind *first* with antiquated authors, and then to try the principles of the present day by the authorities and maxims of the past. We will pursue for our plan, the exact reverse of the ordinary method. We will learn the doctrines of the day, as the first and most necessary step, and we will then glance over those which have passed away, as researches rather curious than useful.

"You see this very small pamphlet; it is a paper by Mr. Mill, upon Government.[2] We will know this thoroughly, and when we have done so, we may rest assured that we have a far more accurate information upon the head and front of all political knowledge, than two-thirds of the young men whose cultivation of mind you have usually heard panegyrized."

So saying, my uncle opened the pamphlet. He pointed out to me its close and mathematical reasoning, in which no flaw could be

2. Mill wrote his celebrated essay on government for the *Encyclopaedia Britannica Supplement* of 1825.

detected, nor deduction controverted: and he filled up, as we proceeded, from the science of his own clear and enlarged mind, the various parts which the political logician had left for reflection to complete. My uncle had this great virtue of an *expositor,* that he never *over-explained;* he never made a parade of his lecture, nor confused what was simple by unnecessary comment.

When we broke off our first day's employment, I was quite astonished at the new light which had gleamed upon me. I felt like Sinbad, the sailor, when, in wandering through the cavern in which he had been buried alive, he caught the first glimpse of the bright day. Naturally eager in every thing I undertook, fond of application, and addicted to reflect over the various bearings of any object that once engrossed my attention, I made great advances in my new pursuit. After my uncle had brought me to be thoroughly conversant with certain and definite principles, we proceeded to illustrate them from fact. For instance, when we had finished the "Essay upon Government," we examined into the several constitutions of England, British America, and France; the three countries which pretend the most to excellence in their government: and we were enabled to perceive and judge the defects and merits of each, because we had, *previous* to our examination, established certain rules, by which they were to be investigated and tried. Here my sceptical indifference to facts was my chief reason for readily admitting knowledge. I had no prejudices to contend with; no obscure notions gleaned from the past; no popular maxims cherished as truths. Every thing was placed before me as before a wholly impartial inquirer—freed from all the decorations and delusions of sects and parties, every argument was stated with logical precision—every opinion referred to a logical test. Hence, in a very short time, I owned the justice of my uncle's assurance, as to the comparative concentration of knowledge. We went over the whole of Mill's admirable articles in the Encyclopaedia, over the more popular works of Bentham, and thence we plunged into the recesses of political economy. I know not why this study has been termed uninteresting. No sooner had I entered upon its consideration, than I could scarcely tear myself from it. Never from that moment to this have I ceased to pay it the most constant attention, not so much as a study as an amusement; but a that time my uncle's object was not to make me a profound political economist. "I wish," said he, "merely to give you an acquaintance with the principles of the science; not that you may be entitled to boast of knowledge, but that you may be enabled to avoid ignorance; not

147

that you may discover truth, but that you may detect error. Of all sciences, political economy is contained in the fewest books, and yet is the most difficult to master; because all its higher branches require earnestness of reflection, proportioned to the scantiness of reading. Mrs. Marsett's elementary work,[3]* together with some conversational enlargement on the several topics she* treats of, will be enough for our present purpose. I wish, *then,* to show you, how inseparably allied is the great science of public policy with that of private morality. And this, Henry, is the grandest object of all. Now to our *present* study."

Well, gentle Reader, (I love, by the by, as you already perceive, that old-fashioned courtesy of addressing you)—well, to finish this part of my life which, as it treats rather of my attempts at reformation than my success in error, must begin to weary you exceedingly, I acquired, more from my uncle's conversation than the books we read, a sufficient acquaintance with the elements of knowledge, to satisfy myself, and to please my instructor. And I must say, in justification of my studies and my tutor, that I derived one benefit from them which has continued with me to this hour—viz. I obtained a clear knowledge of moral principle. Before that time, the little ability I possessed only led me into acts, which, I fear, most benevolent Reader, thou hast already sufficiently condemned: my good feelings—for I was not naturally bad—never availed me the least when present temptation came into my way. I had no guide but passion; no rule but the impulse of the moment. What else could have been the result of my education? If I was immoral, it was because I was never taught morality. Nothing, perhaps, is less innate than virtue. I own that the lessons of my uncle did not work miracles—that, living in the world, I have not separated myself from its errors and its follies: the vortex was too strong—the atmosphere too contagious; but I have at least avoided the crimes into which my temper would most likely have driven me. I ceased to look upon the world as a game one was to play fairly, if possible—but where a little cheating was readily allowed; I no longer divorced the interests of other men from my own: if I endeavoured to blind them, it was neither by unlawful means, nor for a purely selfish end:—if—but come, Henry Pelham, thou hast praised thyself enough for the present; and, after all, thy future adventures will best tell if thou art really amended.

---

3. Mrs. Marsett is an invention of Bulwer's. He substituted Ricardo in the 1835 edition and included thereafter a reference to the celebrated political economist David Ricardo (1772–1823).

VOLUME TWO

CHAPTER I

Mihi jam non regia Roma
Sed vacuum Tiber placet.
HORAT[1]

"MY DEAR CHILD," SAID MY MOTHER TO ME, AFFEC-
tionately, "you must be very much bored here, *pour dire vrai,** I am
so myself. Your uncle is a very good man, but he does not make his
house pleasant; and I have, lately, been very much afraid that he
should convert you into a mere bookworm; after all, my dear Henry,
you are quite clever enough to trust to your own ability. Your great
geniuses never read."

"True, my dear mother," said I, with a most unequivocal yawn,
and depositing on the table Mr. Bentham upon Popular Fallacies;[2]
"true, and I am quite of your opinion. Did you see in the Post of
this morning, how full Cheltenham was?"

"Yes, Henry; and now you mention it, I don't think you could
do better than to go there for a month or two. As for me, I must
return to your father, whom I left at Lord H———'s, a place, *entre
nous,* very little more amusing than this—but then one does get one's
écarté table, and that dear Lady Roseville, your old acquaintance, is
staying there.

"Well," said I, musingly, "suppose we take our departure the
beginning of next week?—our way will be the same as far as London,
and the plea of attending you will be a good excuse to my uncle, for
proceeding no farther in these confounded books."

"*C'est une affaire finie,*" replied my mother, "and I will speak to
your uncle myself."

Accordingly the necessary disclosure of our intentions was made.
Lord Glenmorris received it with proper indifference, so far as my

---

1. "My pleasure today is not queenly Rome but the quiet Tiber" (Horace
Epistles 1.7.44–45).
2. Bentham's *Book of Fallacies* appeared in 1824.

151

mother was concerned; but expressed much pain at *my* leaving him so soon. However, when he found I was so much gratified as honoured by his wishes for my longer *séjour,* he gave up the point with a delicacy that enchanted me.

The morning of our departure arrived. Carriage at the door—bandboxes in the passage—breakfast on the table—myself in my great coat—my uncle in his great chair. "My dear boy," said he, " I trust we shall meet again soon: you have abilities that may make you capable of effecting much good to your fellow-creatures; but you are fond of the world, and, though not averse to application, devoted to pleasure, and likely to pervert the gifts you possess. At all events, you have now learned, both as a public character and a private individual, the difference between good and evil. Make but this distinction, that, whereas, in political science, though the rules you have learned be fixed and unerring, yet the application of them must vary with time and circumstance. We must bend, temporize, and frequently withdraw, doctrines, which, invariable in their truth, the prejudices of the time will not invariably allow, and even relinquish a faint hope of obtaining a great good, for the certainty of obtaining a lesser; yet in the science of private morals, which relate for the main part to ourselves individually, we have no right to deviate one single iota from the rule of our conduct. Neither time nor circumstance must cause us to modify or to change. Integrity knows no variation; honesty no shadow of turning. We must pursue the same course—stern and uncompromising—in the full persuasion that the path of right is like the bridge from earth to heaven, in the Mahometan creed—if we swerve but a single hair's breadth, we are irrevocably lost."

At this moment my mother joined us, with a "Well, my dear Henry, every thing is ready—we have no time to lose."

My uncle rose, pressed my hand, and left in it a pocket-book, which I afterwards discovered to be most satisfactorily furnished. We took an edifying and affectionate farewell of each other, passed through the two rows of servants, drawn up in martial array, along the great hall, entered the carriage, and *went off* with the rapidity of a novel upon "fashionable life."

CHAPTER II

Dic—si grave non est
Quæ prima iratum ventrem placaverit esca.
HORAT[1]

I DID NOT REMAIN ABOVE A DAY OR TWO IN TOWN. I had never seen much of the humours of a watering-place, and my love of observing character made me exceedingly impatient for that pleasure. Accordingly, the first bright morning I set off for Cheltenham. I was greatly struck with the entrance to that town: it is to these watering-places that a foreigner should be taken, in order to give him an adequate idea of the magnificent opulence, and universal luxury, of England. Our country has, in every province, what France only has in Paris—a capital, consecrated to gaiety, idleness, and enjoyment. London is both too busy in one class of society, and too pompous in another, to please a foreigner, who has not excellent recommendations to private circles. But at Brighton, Cheltenham, Hastings, Bath, he may, as at Paris, find all the gaieties of society without knowing a single individual.

My carriage stopped at the ——— Hotel. A corpulent and stately waiter, with gold buckles to a pair of very tight pantaloons, showed me up stairs. I found myself in a tolerable room facing the street, and garnished with two pictures of rocks and rivers, with a comely flight of crows, hovering in the horizon of both, as natural as possible, only they were a little larger than the trees. Over the chimney-piece, where I had fondly hoped to find a looking-glass, was a grave print of General Washington, with one hand stuck out like the spout of a tea-pot. Between the two windows—(unfavourable position!) was an oblong mirror, to which I immediately hastened, and had the pleasure of seeing my complexion catch the colour of the curtains that overhung the glass on each side, and exhibit the pleasing *rurality* of a pale green.

---

1. "Tell me, if you don't mind, what was the first dish that pleased a growling appetite" (Horace *Satires* 2.8.4–5).

153

I shrunk back aghast, turned, and beheld the waiter. Had I seen myself in a glass delicately shaded by rose-hued curtains, I should gently and smilingly have said, "Have the goodness to bring me the bill of fare." As it was, I growled out, "Bring me the bill, and be d——d to you."*

The stiff waiter bowed solemnly, and withdrew slowly. I looked round the room once more, and discovered the additional adornments of a tea-urn, and a book. "Thank Heaven," thought I, as I took up the latter, "it can't be one of Jeremy Bentham's." No! it was the Cheltenham Guide. I turned to the head of amusements—"Dress ball at the rooms every———" some day or other—which of the seven I utterly forget; but it was the same as that which witnessed my first arrival in the small drawing-room of the ——— Hotel.

"Thank Heaven!" said I to myself, as Bedos entered with my things, and was ordered immediately to have all in preparation for "the dress-ball at the rooms," at the hour of half-past ten. The waiter entered with the bill. "Soups, chops, cutlets, steaks, roast joints, &c. &c. —*lion, birds.*"

"Get some soup," said I, "a slice or two of lion, and half a dozen birds."

"Sir," said the solemn waiter, "you can't have less than a whole lion, and we have only two birds in the house."

"Pray," asked I, "are you in the habit of supplying your larder from Exeter 'Change, or do you breed lions here like poultry?"

"Sir," answered the grim waiter, never relaxing into a smile, "we have lions brought us from the country every day."

"What do you pay for them?" said I.

"About three and sixpence a piece, Sir."

"Humph!—market in Africa overstocked," thought I.

"Pray, how do you dress an animal of that description?"

"Roast and stuff him, Sir, and serve him up with currant jelly."

"What! like a hare?"

"It *is* a hare, Sir."

"What!"

"Yes, Sir, it is a hare!²—but we call it a lion, because of the Game Laws."

'Bright discovery,' thought I; 'they have a new language in Cheltenham: nothing's like travelling to enlarge the mind.' "And the

2. I have since learned, that this custom of calling a *hare* a *lion* is not peculiar to Cheltenham. At that time I was utterly unacquainted with the regulations of the London coffee-houses. [B-L]

154

birds," said I, aloud, "are neither humming birds, nor ostriches, I suppose?"

"No, Sir; they are partridges."

"Well, then, give me some soup; a *côtelette de mouton*,* and a 'bird,' as you term it, and be quick about it."

"It shall be done with dispatch," answered the pompous attendant, and withdrew.

Is there, in the whole course of this pleasant and varying life, which young gentlemen and ladies write verses to prove same and sorrowful,—is there, in the whole course of it, one half-hour really and genuinely disagreeable?—if so, it is the half-hour before dinner at a strange inn. Nevertheless, by the help of philosophy and the window, I managed to endure it with great patience: and though I was famishing with hunger, I pretended the indifference of a sage, even when the dinner was at length announced. I coquetted a whole minute with my napkin, before I attempted the soup, and I helped myself to the potatory food with a slow dignity that must have perfectly won the heart of the solemn waiter. The soup was a little better than hot water, and the sharp sauced *côtelette*,* than leather and vinegar; howbeit, I attacked them with the vigour of an Irishman, and washed them down with a bottle of the worst liquor ever dignified with the *venerabile nomen* of claret. The bird was tough enough to have passed for an ostrich in miniature; and I felt its ghost hopping about the stomachic sepulchre to which I consigned it the whole of that evening and a great portion of the next day, when a glass of curaçoa laid it at rest.

After this splendid repast, I flung myself back on my chair with the complacency of a man who has dined well, and dozed away the time till the hour of dressing.

"Now," thought I, as I placed myself before my glass, "shall I gently please, or sublimely astonish the 'fashionables' of Cheltenham? Ah, bah! the latter school is vulgar, Byron spoilt it. Don't put out that chain, Bedos—I wear—the black coat, waistcoat, and trowsers. Brush my hair as much *out* of curl as you can, and give an air of graceful negligence to my *tout ensemble*."

"*Oui, Monsieur, je comprends*," answered Bedos.

I was soon dressed, for it is the *design*, not the *execution*, of all great undertakings which requires deliberation and delay. *Action* cannot be too prompt. A chair was called, and Henry Pelham was conveyed to the rooms.

155

CHAPTER III

Now see, prepared to lead the sprightly dance,
The lovely nymphs, and well dressed youths advance;
The spacious room receives its jovial guest,
And the floor shakes with pleasing weight oppressed.
Art of Dancing[1]

Page. His name, my lord, is Tyrrell.
Richard III

UPON ENTERING, I SAW SEVERAL HEADS RISING AND
sinking, to the tune of "Cherry ripe." A whole row of stiff necks, in
cravats of the most unexceptionable length and breadth, were just
before me. A tall thin young man, with dark wiry hair brushed on
one side, was drawing on a pair of white Woodstock gloves, and
affecting to look round the room with the supreme indifference
of *bon ton.*

"Ah, Ritson," said another young Cheltenhamian to him of the
Woodstock gauntlets, "haven't you been dancing yet?"

"No, Smith, 'pon honour!" answered Mr. Ritson; "it is so over-
poweringly hot; no fashionable man dances now;—*it isn't the thing.*"

"Why," replied Mr. Smith, who was a good-natured looking
person, with a blue coat and brass buttons, a gold pin in his neckcloth, and knee-breeches, "Why, they dance at Almack's,[2] don't they?"

"No, 'pon honour," murmured Mr. Ritson, "no, they just walk
a quadrille or *spin a waltz,* as my friend, Lord Bobadob calls it,
nothing more—no, hang dancing, 'tis *so* vulgar."

A stout, red-faced man, about thirty, with wet auburn hair, a
marvellously fine waistcoat, and a badly-washed frill, now joined
Messrs. Ritson and Smith.

---

1. Soame Jenyns, *The Art of Dancing*, canto 2, lines 1–4. The second epigraph
is from *Richard III*, IV, 2, 40.

2. Almack's: the Regency's most exclusive club.

156

"Ah, Sir Ralph," cried Smith, "how d'ye do? been hunting all day, I suppose?"

"Yes, old cock," replied Sir Ralph; "been after the brush till I am quite done up; such a glorious run. By G—, you should have seen my grey mare, Smith. By G—, she's a glorious fencer."

"You don't hunt, do you, Ritson?" interrogated Mr. Smith.

"Yes, I do," replied Mr. Ritson, affectedly playing with his Wood-stock glove; "yes, but I only hunt in Leicestershire with my friend, Lord Bobadob; 'tis not the thing to hunt any where else, 'tis *so* vulgar."

Sir Ralph stared at the speaker with mute contempt: while Mr. Smith, like the ass between the hay, stood balancing betwixt the opposing merits of the baronet and the beau. Meanwhile, a smiling, nodding, affected female thing, in ringlets and flowers, flirted up to the trio.

"Now, reelly, Mr. Smith, you should deence; a feeshonable young man, like you—I don't know what the young leedies will say to you." And the fair seducer laughed bewitchingly.

"You are very good, Mrs. Dollimore," replied Mr. Smith, with a blush and a low bow; "but Mr. Ritson tells me it is not *the thing* to dance."

"Oh," cried Mrs. Dollimore, "but then he's seech a naughty, conceited creature—don't follow his example, Meester Smith," and again the good lady laughed immoderately.

"Nay, Mrs. Dollimore," said Mr. Ritson, passing his hand through his abominable hair, "you are too severe; but tell me, Mrs. Dollimore, is the Countess St. A——— coming here?"

"Now, reelly, Mr. Ritson, *you* who are the pink of feeshon, ought to know better than I can; but I hear so."

"Do you know the countess?" said Mr. Smith, in respectful surprise, to Ritson.

"Oh, very well," replied the Coryphaeus[3] of Cheltenham, swinging his Woodstock glove to and fro; "I have often *danced* with her at Almack's."

"Is she a good deencer?" asked Mrs. Dollimore.

"Oh, capital," responded Mr. Ritson; *"she's such a nice genteel little figure."*

Sir Ralph, apparently tired of this "feeshonable" conversation, swaggered away.

"Pray," said Mrs. Dollimore, "who is that geentleman?"

---

3. Coryphaeus: A leader, from the Greek meaning "chorus leader."

"Sir Ralph Rumford," replied Smith, eagerly, "a particular friend of mine at Cambridge."

"I wonder if he's going to make a long steey?" said Mrs. Dollimore.

"Yes, I believe so," replied Mr. Smith, "if we make it agreeable to him."

"You must poositively introduce him to me," said Mrs. Dollimore.

"I will, with great pleasure," said the good-natured Mr. Smith.

"Is Sir Ralph *a man of fashion?*" inquired Mr. Ritson.

"He's a baronet!" emphatically pronounced Mr. Smith.

"Ah!" replied Ritson, "but he may be a man of rank, without being a man of fashion."

"True," lisped Mrs. Dollimore.

"I don't know," replied Smith, with an air of puzzled wonderment, "but he has £7,000 a-year."

"Has he, indeed?" cried Mrs. Dollimore, surprised into her natural tone of voice; and, at that moment, a young lady, ringletted and flowered like herself, joined her, and accosted her by the endearing appellation of "Mamma."

"Have you been dancing, my love?" inquired Mrs. Dollimore.

"Yes, ma; with Captain Johnson."

"Oh," said the mother, with a toss of her head; and, giving her daughter a significant push, she walked away with her to another end of the room, to talk about Sir Ralph Rumford, and his seven thousand pounds a-year.

"Well!" thought I, "odd people these; let us enter a little farther into this savage country." In accordance with this reflection, I proceeded towards the middle of the room.

"Who's that?" said Mr. Smith, in a loud whisper, as I passed him.

"'Pon honour," answered Ritson, "I don't know! but he's a deuced neat looking fellow, *quite genteel.*"

"Thank you, Mr. Ritson," said my vanity, "you are not so offensive after all."

I paused to look at the dancers; a middle-aged, respectable looking gentleman was beside me. Common people, after they have passed forty, grow social. My neighbour hemmed twice, and made preparations for speaking. "I may as well encourage him," was my reflection; accordingly I turned round, with a most good-natured expression of countenance.

"A fine room this, Sir," said the man immediately.

"Very," said I, with a smile, "and extremely well filled."

"Ah, Sir," answered my neighbour, "Cheltenham is not as it used

158

to be some fifteen years ago. I have seen as many as one thousand two hundred and fifty persons within these walls;" (certain people are always so d——d particularizing), "ay, Sir," pursued my *laudator temporis acti*, "and half the peerage here into the bargain."

"Indeed!" quoth I, with an air of surprise suited to the information I received, "but the society is very good still, is it not?"

"Oh, very *genteel*," replied the man; "but not so *dashing* as it used to be." (Oh! those two horrid words! low enough to suit even the author of "———.")

"Pray," asked I, glancing at Messrs. Ritson and Smith, "do you know who those gentlemen are?"

"Extremely well!" replied my neighbour: "the tall young man is Mr. Ritson; his mother has a house in Baker-street, and gives quite *elegant* parties. He's a most *genteel* young man; but such an insufferable coxcomb."

"And the other?" said I.

"Oh! he's a Mr. Smith; his father was an eminent merchant,* and is lately dead, leaving each of his sons thirty thousand pounds; the young Smith is *a knowing hand,* and wants to spend his money with spirit. He has a great passion for '*high life,*' and *therefore* attaches himself much to Mr. Ritson, who is *quite that way inclined.*"

"He could not have selected a better model," said I.

"True," rejoined my Cheltenham Asmodeus,[4] with *naïve* simplicity; "but I hope he won't adopt his *conceit* as well as his *elegance.*"

"I shall die," said I to myself, "if I talk with this fellow any longer," and I was just going to glide away, when a tall, stately dowager, with two lean, scraggy daughters, entered the room; I could not resist pausing to inquire who they were.

My friend looked at me with a very altered and disrespectful air at this interrogation. "*Who?*" said he, "why, the Countess of Babbleton, and her two daughters, the Honourable Lady Jane Babel, and the Honourable Lady Mary Babel. They are the great people of Cheltenham," pursued he, "and it's *a fine thing* to get into their set."

Meanwhile Lady Babbleton and her two daughters swept up the room, bowing and nodding to the riven ranks on each side, who made their salutations with the most profound respect. My experienced eye detected in a moment that Lady Babbleton, in spite of her title and her stateliness, was exceedingly the reverse of good *ton,* and the daughters (who did not resemble the scrag of mutton, *but its ghost*),

---

4. Asmodeus: the demon of vanity and dress.

159

had an appearance of sour affability, which was as different from the manners of proper society, as it possibly could be.

I wondered greatly who and what they were. In the eyes of the Cheltenhamians, they were *the* countess and her daughters; and any further explanation would have been deemed quite superfluous; further explanation I was, however, determined to procure, and was walking across the room in profound meditation as to the method in which the discovery should be made, when I was startled by the voice of Sir Lionel Garrett: I turned round, and to my inexpressible joy, beheld that worthy baronet.

"God bless me, Pelham," said he, "how delighted I am to see you. Lady Harriett, here's your old favourite, Mr. Pelham."

Lady Harriett was all smiles and pleasure. "Give me your arm," said she; "I must go and speak to Lady Babbleton—odious woman!"

"Do, my dear Lady Harriett," said I, "explain to me *what* Lady Babbleton was?"

"Why—she was a milliner, and took in the late Lord, who was an idiot.—*Voilà tout!*"

"Perfectly satisfactory," replied I.

"Or, short and sweet, as Lady Babbleton would say," replied Lady Harriett, laughing.

"In antithesis to her daughters, who are long and sour."

"Oh, you satirist!" said the affected Lady Harriett (who was only three removes better than the Cheltenham countess); "but tell me how long have you been at Cheltenham?"

"About four hours and a half!"

"Then you don't know any of the lions here?"

"None."*

"Well, let me dispatch Lady Babbleton, and I'll then devote myself to being your nomenclator."

We walked up to Lady Babbleton, who had already disposed of her daughters, and was sitting in solitary dignity at the end of the room.

"My dear Lady Babbleton," cried Lady Harriett, taking both the hands of the dowager—"I am so glad to see you, and how well you are looking; and your charming daughters, how are they?—sweet girls! —and how long have you been here?"

"We have only just come," replied the *ci-devant* milliner, half rising and rustling her plumes in stately agitation, like a nervous parrot; "we must conform to modern *ours*, Lady *Arriett*, though for my part, I like the old-fashioned plan of dining early, and finishing

160

one's gaieties before midnight; but I set the fashion of good *ours* as well as I can. I think it's a duty *we* owe to society, Lady Arriett, to encourage morality by our own example. What else do we have rank for?" And, so saying, the counter countess drew herself up with a most edifying air of moral dignity.

Lady Harriett looked at me, and perceiving that my eye said "go on," as plain as eye could possibly speak, she continued—"Which of the wells do you attend, Lady Babbleton?"

"All," replied the patronizing dowager. "I like to encourage the poor people here; I've no notion of being proud because one has a title, Lady *Arriett*."

"No," rejoined the worthy helpmate of Sir Lionel Garrett; "every body talks of your condescension, Lady Babbleton; but are you not afraid of letting yourself down by going every where?"

"Oh," answered *the countess*, "I admit very few into my set, *at home*, but I *go out promiscuously;*" and then, looking at me, she said, in a whisper, to Lady Harriett, "Who is that nice young gentleman?"

"Mr. Pelham," replied Lady Harriett; and, turning to me, formally introduced us to each other.

"Are you any relation (asked the dowager) to Lady Frances Pelham?"

"Only her son," said I.

"Dear me," replied Lady Babbleton, "how odd; what a nice *elegant* woman she is! She does not go much out, does she? I don't often meet her!"

"I should not think it likely that your ladyship did meet her much. She does not visit *promiscuously*."

"Every rank has its duty," said Lady Harriett, gravely; "your mother, Mr. Pelham, may confine her circle as much as she pleases; but the high rank of Lady Babbleton requires greater condescension; just as the Dukes of Sussex and Gloucester go to many places where you and I would not."

"Very true!" said the innocent dowager; "and that's a very sensible remark! Were you at Bath last winter, Mr. Pelham?" continued *the countess*, whose thoughts wandered from subject to subject in the most *rudderless* manner.

"No, Lady Babbleton, I was unfortunately at a less distinguished place."

"What was that?"

"Paris!"

"Oh, indeed! I've never been abroad; I don't think persons of a certain rank should leave England; they should stay at home and encourage their own manufactories."

"Ah!" cried I, taking hold of Lady Babbleton's shawl, "what a pretty Manchester pattern this is."

"Manchester pattern!" exclaimed the petrified peeress; "why it is real cachemere: you don't think I wear any thing English, Mr. Pelham?"

"I beg your ladyship ten thousand pardons. I am no judge of dress; but to return—I am quite of your opinion, *that we ought to encourage our own manufactories,* and not go abroad: but one cannot stay long on the Continent, even if one is decoyed there. One soon longs for home again."

"Very sensibly remarked," rejoined Lady Babbleton: "that's what I call true patriotism and morality. I wish all the young men of the present day were like you. Oh, dear!—here's a great favourite of mine coming this way—Mr. Ritson!—do you know him; shall I introduce you?"

"God* forbid!" exclaimed I—frightened out of my wits, and my manners. "Come, Lady Harriett, let us rejoin Sir Lionel;" and, "swift at the word," Lady Harriett retook my arm, nodded her adieu to Lady Babbleton, and withdrew with me to an obscurer part of the room.

Here we gave way to our laughter for some time, till, at last, getting weary of the Cheltenham Cleopatra, I reminded Lady Harriett of her promise to name to me the various personages of the assemblage.

"Eh bien," began Lady Harriett; *"d' abord,* you observe that very short person, somewhat more than inclined to *embonpoint?"*

"What, that thing like a Chinese tumbler—that peg of old clothes—that one foot square of mortality, with an aquatic-volucrine face, like a spoonbill?"

"The very same," said Lady Harriett, laughing; "she is a Lady Gander. She professes to be a patroness of literature, and holds weekly *soirées* in London, for all the newspaper poets. She also falls in love every year, and then she employs her minstrels to write sonnets: her son has a most filial tenderness for a jointure of £10,000 a-year, which she casts away on these feasts and follies; and, in order to obtain it, declares the good lady to be insane. Half of her friends he has bribed, or persuaded, to be of his opinion; the other half stoutly maintain her rationality; and, in fact, she herself is divided in her own opinion as to the case; for she is in the habit of drinking to a most

162

unsentimental excess, and when the fit of intoxication is upon her, she confesses to the charge brought against her—supplicates for mercy and brandy, and totters to bed with the air of a Magdalene; but when she recovers the next morning, the whole scene is changed; she is an injured woman, a persecuted saint, a female Sophocles—declared to be mad only because she is a miracle. Poor Harry Darlington called upon her in town, the other day; he found her sitting in a large chair, and surrounded by a whole host of hangers-on, who were disputing by no means *sotto voce,* whether Lady Gander was mad or not? Henry was immediately appealed to:—"Now, is not this a proof of insanity?" said one.—"Is not this a mark of *compos mentis?*" cried another. "I appeal to you, Mr. Darlington," exclaimed all. Meanwhile the object of the conversation sate in a state of maudlin insensibility, turning her head, first on one side, and then on the other; and nodding to all the disputants, as if agreeing with each. But enough of her. Do you observe that lady in ——."*

"Good heavens!" exclaimed I, starting up, "is that—can that be Tyrrell?"

"What's the matter with the man?" cried Lady Harriett.

I quickly recovered my presence of mind, and reseated myself: "Pray forgive me, Lady Harriett," said I; "but I think, nay, I am sure, I see a person I once met under very particular circumstances. Do you observe that dark man in deep mourning, who has just entered the room, and is now speaking to Sir Ralph Rumford?"

"I do, it is Sir John Tyrrell!" replied Lady Harriett: "he only came to Cheltenham yesterday. His is a very singular history."

"What is it?" said I, eagerly.

"Why! he was the only son of a younger branch of the Tyrrells; a very old family, as the name denotes. He was a great deal in a certain *roué* set, for some years, and was celebrated for his *affaires de coeur.** His fortune was, however, perfectly unable to satisfy his expenses; he took to gambling, and lost the remains of his property. He went abroad, and used to be seen at the low gaming houses at Paris, earning a very degraded and precarious subsistence; till, about three months ago, two persons, who stood between him and the title and estates of the family, died, and most unexpectedly he succeeded to both. They say that he was found in the most utter penury and distress, in a small cellar at Paris; however that may be, he is now Sir John Tyrrell, with a very large income, and in spite of a certain coarseness of manner, probably acquired by the low company he

163

latterly kept, he is very much liked, and even admired by the few good people in the society of Cheltenham."

At this instant* Tyrrell passed us; he caught my eye, stopped short, and coloured violently. I bowed; he seemed undecided for a moment as to the course he should adopt; it was *but* for a moment. He returned my salutation with great appearance of cordiality; shook me warmly by the hand; expressed himself delighted to meet me; inquired where I was staying, and said he should certainly call upon me. With this promise he glided on, and was soon lost among the crowd.

"Where did you meet him?" said Lady Harriett.

"At Paris."

"What! was he in decent society there?"

"I don't know," said I. "Good night, Lady Harriett;" and, with an air of extreme lassitude, I took my hat, and vanished from that motley mixture of the *fashionably* low and the vulgarly *genteel!*

CHAPTER IV

Full many a lady
I have eyed with best regard, and many a time
The harmony of their tongues hath unto bondage
Drawn my too diligent eyes.
But you, oh! you,
So perfect and so peerless, are created
Of every creature's best.

SHAKSPEARE[1]

THOU WILT EASILY CONCEIVE, MY DEAR READER, WHO hast been in my confidence throughout the whole of this history, and whom, though as yet thou hast cause to esteem me but lightly, I already love as my familiar and my friend—thou wilt easily conceive my surprise at meeting so unexpectedly with my old hero of the gambling house. I felt indeed perfectly stunned at the shock of so singular a change in his circumstances since I had last met him. My thoughts reverted immediately to that scene, and to the mysterious

---

1. *The Tempest*, III, 1, 39–41, 46–48. Misquoted.

connection between Tyrrell and Glanville. How would the latter receive the intelligence of his enemy's good fortune? was his vengeance yet satisfied, or through what means could it now find vent?

A thousand thoughts similar to these occupied and distracted my attention till morning, when I summoned Bedos into the room to read me to sleep. He opened a play of Monsieur Delavigne's,[2] and at the beginning of the second scene I was in the land of dreams.

I woke about two o'clock; dressed, sipped my chocolate, and was on the point of arranging my hat to the best advantage, when I received the following note:

"My dear Pelham,

"*Me tibi commendo.* I heard this morning, at your hotel, that you were here; my heart was a house of joy at the intelligence. I called upon you two hours ago; but, like Antony, 'you revel long o' nights.' Ah, that I could add with Shakspeare, that you were 'notwithstanding up.'[3] I have just come from Paris, that *umbilicus terrae,* and my adventures since I saw you, for your private satisfaction, 'because I love you, I will let you know;' but you must satisfy me with a meeting. Till you do, 'the mighty gods defend you!'

"Vincent."

The hotel from which Vincent dated this epistle, was in the same street as my own caravansera, and to this hotel I immediately set off. I found my friend sitting before a huge folio, which he in vain endeavoured to persuade me that he seriously intended to read. We greeted each other with the greatest cordiality.

"But how," said Vincent, after the first warmth of welcome had subsided, "how shall I congratulate you upon your new honours? I was not prepared to find you grown from a *roué* into a senator.

" 'In gathering votes you were not slack,
Now stand as tightly by your tack,
Ne'er show your lug an' fidge your back,
    An' hum an' haw,
But raise your arm, an' tell your crack
    Before them a'.'[4]

---

2. Jean François Casimir Delavigne (1793–1843): French poet and dramatist. His comedy *Ecole des vieillards* (1823) gained his election to the French Academy in 1825.

3. *Julius Caesar,* II, 2, 6–7. The quotation in the next sentence is from Ibid., line 74, and that in the concluding sentence was a traditional leavetaking in ancient Rome.

4. Robert Burns, "The Author's Earnest Cry and Prayer," stanza 6.

165

So saith Burns; advice which, being interpreted, meaneth, that you must astonish the rats of St. Stephen's."[5]

"Alas!" said I, "all one's clap-traps in that house must be baited."

"Nay, but a rat bites at any cheese, from Gloucester to Parmasan, and you can easily scrape up a bit of some sort. Talking of the House, do you see, by the paper, that the civic senator, Alderman W——, is at Cheltenham?"

"I was not aware of it. I suppose he's cramming speeches and turtle for the next season."

"How wonderfully," said Vincent, "your city dignities unloose the tongue: directly a man has been a mayor, he thinks himself qualified for a Tully at least. Faith, Venables* asked me one day, what was the Latin for spouting? and I told him, *'hippomanes,* or a raging humour in *mayors.'* "

After I had paid, through the medium of my risible muscles, due homage to this witticism of Vincent's, he shut up his folio, called for his hat, and we sauntered down into the street. As we passed by one of the libraries, a whole mob of the dandies of the last night were lounging about the benches placed before the shop windows.

"Pray, Vincent," said I, "remark those worthies, and especially that tall meagre youth in the blue frock-coat, and the buff waistcoat; he is Mr. Ritson, the *De Rous* (viz. the finished gentleman) of the place."

"I see him," answered Vincent: "he seems a most happy mixture of native coarseness and artificial decoration. He puts me in mind of the picture of the great ox, set in a gilt frame."

"Or a made dish in Bloomsbury-square, garnished with cut carrots, by way of adornment," said I.

"Or a flannel petticoat, with a fine crape over it," added Vincent. "Well, well, these imitators are, after all, not worse than the originals.* When do you go up to town?"

"Not till my senatorial duties require me."

"Do you stay here till then?"

"As it pleases the gods. But, good Heavens, Vincent, what a beautiful girl!"

Vincent turned. *"O Dea certè,"* murmured he, and stopped.

The object of our exclamations was standing by a corner shop, apparently waiting for some one within. Her face, at the moment I first saw her, was turned full towards me. Never had I seen any

---

5. St. Stephen's Chapel, given to the Commons in 1547 by Edward VI, was destroyed by fire in 1834. St. Stephen's Hall was built on its site.

countenance half so lovely. She was apparently about twenty, her hair was of the richest chesnut, and a golden light played through its darkness, as if a sunbeam had been caught in those luxuriant tresses, and was striving in vain to escape. Her eyes were of a light hazel, large, deep, and *shaded into softness* (to use a modern expression) by long and very dark lashes. Her complexion alone would have rendered her beautiful, it was so clear—so pure; the blood blushed beneath it, like roses under a clear stream; if, in order to justify my simile, roses would have the complacency to grow in such a situation. Her nose was of that fine and accurate mould that one so seldom sees, except in the Grecian statues, which unites the clearest and most decided outline with the most feminine delicacy and softness, and the short curved arch which descended from thence to her mouth, was so fine—so *airily* and exquisitely formed, that it seemed as if Love himself had modelled the bridge which led to his most beautiful and fragrant island. On the right side of the mouth was one dimple, that corresponded so exactly with every smile and movement of those rosy lips, that you might have sworn the shadow of each passed there; it was like the rapid changes of an April heaven reflected upon a valley. She was somewhat, but not much taller, than the ordinary height; and her figure, which united all the first freshness and youth of the girl, with the more luxuriant graces of the woman, was rounded and finished so justly—so *minutely**—that the eye could glance over the whole, without discovering the least harshness, or unevenness, or atom, to be added or subtracted. But over all these was a light, a glow, a pervading spirit, of which it is impossible to convey the faintest idea. You should have seen her by the side of a shaded fountain on a summer's day. You should have watched her amidst music and flowers—and she might have seemed to you like the fairy that presided over both. So much for poetical description.*

"What think you of her, Vincent?" said I.

"I say with Theocritus, in his epithalamium of Helen———"

"Say no such thing," said I: "I will not have her presence profaned by any helps from your memory."

At that moment the girl turned round abruptly, and re-entered the shop,* at the door of which she had been standing. It was a small perfumer's shop. "Thank Heaven," said I, "that she *does* use perfumes. What scents can she now be hesitating between?—the gentle *bouquet du roi,* the cooling *esprit de Portugal,* the mingled treasures *des millefleurs,* the less distinct but agreeably adulterated *miel,* the sweet May-recalling *esprit des violets,* or the ———"

"Omnis copia narium,"[6] said Vincent; "let us enter: I want some *eau de Cologne."**

I desired no second invitation; we marched into the shop; my Armida[7] was leaning on the arm of an old lady. She blushed deeply when she saw us enter, and, as ill luck would have it, the old lady concluded her purchases the moment after, and they withdrew.

> "'Who had thought this clime had held
> A deity so unparallel'd!'"[8]

justly observed my companion.

I made no reply. All the remainder of that day I was absent and reserved; and Vincent, perceiving that I no longer laughed at his jokes, nor smiled at his quotations, told me I was sadly changed for the worse, and pretended an engagement, to rid himself of an auditor so obtuse.

CHAPTER V

Tout notre mal vient de ne pouvior être seuls; de là le jeu, le luxe, la dissipation, le vin, les femmes, l'ignorance, la médisance, l'envie, l'oubli de soi-même et de Dieu.

LA BRUYÈRE.[1]

THE NEXT DAY I RESOLVED TO CALL UPON TYRRELL, seeing that he had not yet kept his promise of anticipating me, and being very desirous not to lose any opportunity of improving my acquaintance with him; accordingly, I sent my valet to make inquiries as to his abode. I found that he lodged in the same hotel as myself;

---

6. *Omnis* etc: "An entire abundance of scents."

7. Armida: the sorceress in Tasso's *Gerusalemme Liberata*.

8. Unidentified.

1. "Every evil that befalls us comes from not being able to be alone; from this comes gaming, luxury, dissipation, wine, women, ignorance, slander, envy, forgetfulness of self and of God" (Jean de La Bruyère, *Les Caractères*, "De l'homme," 99).

and having previously ascertained that he was at home, I made up my features into their most winning expression, and was ushered by the head waiter into the gamester's apartment.

He was sitting by the fire in a listless, yet thoughtful attitude. His muscular and rather handsome person was indued in a dressing-gown of rich brocade, thrown on with a slovenly *nonchalance*. His stockings were about his heels, his hair was dishevelled, and the light streaming through the half-drawn window-curtains, rested upon the grey flakes with which its darker luxuriance was interspersed, and the cross light in which he had the imprudence or misfortune to sit (odious cross light, which even *I* already begin carefully to avoid),* fully developed the deep wrinkles which years and dissipation had planted round his eyes and mouth. I was quite startled at the *oldness* and haggardness of his appearance.

He rose gracefully enough when I was announced; and no sooner had the waiter retired, than he came up to me, shook me warmly by the hand, and said, "Let me thank you *now* for the attention you formerly shewed me, when I was less able to express my acknowledgments. I shall be proud to cultivate your intimacy."

I answered him in the same strain, and in the course of conversation, made myself so entertaining, that he agreed to spend the remainder of the day with me. We ordered our horses at three, and our dinner at seven, and I left him till the former were ready, in order to allow him time for his toilet.

During our ride we talked principally on general subjects, on the various differences of France and England, on horses, on wines, on women, on politics, on all things, except that which had created our acquaintance. His remarks were those of a strong, ill regulated mind, which had made experience supply the place of the reasoning faculties; there was a looseness in his sentiments, and a licentiousness in his opinions, which startled even me (used as I had been to rakes of all schools); his philosophy was of that species which thinks that the best maxim of wisdom is—to despise. Of men he spoke with the bitterness of hatred; of women, with the levity of contempt. France had taught him its debaucheries, but not the elegance which refines them: if his sentiments were low, the language in which they were clothed was meaner still: and that which makes the morality of the upper classes, and which no criminal is supposed to be hardy enough to reject; that religion which has no scoffers, that code which has no impugners, *that honour* among gentlemen, which constitutes the moving principle of the society in which they live, he seemed to imagine, even in its most fundamental laws, was an authority to which nothing but the inexperience of the young, and the credulity of the romantic, could accede.

Upon the whole, he seemed to me a "bold, bad man,"[2] with just enough of intellect to teach him to be a villain, without that higher degree which shews him that it is the worst course for his interest; and just enough of daring to make him indifferent to the dangers of guilt, though it was not sufficient to make him conquer and control them. For the rest, he loved trotting better than cantering—piqued himself upon being manly—wore doe-skin gloves—drank port wine, *par préférence,* and considered beef-steaks and oysters as the most delicate dish in the whole *carte.** I think, now, reader, you have a tolerably good view of his character.

After dinner, when we were discussing the second bottle, I thought it would not be a bad opportunity to question him upon his acquaintance with Glanville. His countenance fell directly I mentioned that name. However, he rallied himself. "Oh," said he, "you mean the *soi-disant* Warburton. I knew him some years back—he was a poor silly youth, half mad, I believe, and particularly hostile to me, owing to some foolish disagreement when he was quite a boy."

"What was the cause?" said I.

"Nothing—nothing of any consequence," answered Tyrrell; and then added, with an air of coxcombry, "I believe I was more fortunate than he, in an *affaire de coeur.** Poor Glanville is a little romantic you know. But enough of this now: shall we go to the rooms?"

"With pleasure," said I; and to the rooms we went.

---

2. Spenser, *The Fairie Queene,* 1, 1, stanza 37.

170

CHAPTER VI

Veteres revocavit artes.

HORACE[1]

Since I came hither I have heard strange news.

King Lear

TWO DAYS AFTER MY LONG CONVERSATION WITH
Tyrrell, I called again upon that worthy. To my great surprise he had
left Cheltenham. I then strolled to Vincent: I found him lolling on
his sofa, surrounded, as usual, with books and papers.

"Come in, Pelham," said he, as I hesitated at the threshold—
"come in. I have been delighting myself with Plato all the morning;
I scarcely know what it is that enchants us so much with the ancients.
I rather believe, with Schlegel, that it is that air of perfect repose—
the stillness of a deep soul, which rests over their writings. Whatever
would appear common-place amongst us, has with them I know not
what of sublimity and pathos. Triteness seems the profundity of truth
—wildness the daring of a luxuriant imagination. The fact is, that
in spite of every fault, you see through all the traces of original
thought; there is a contemplative grandeur in their sentiments, which
seems to have nothing borrowed in its meaning or its dress. Take, for
instance, this fragment of Mimnermus,[2] on the shortness of life,—
what subject can seem more tame?—what less striking than the feelings
he expresses?—and yet, throughout every line, there is a melancholy
depth and tenderness, which it is impossible to define. Of all English
writers who partake the most of this spirit of conveying interest and
strength to sentiments, subjects, and language,* neither novel in
themselves, nor adorned in their arrangement, I know none that equal
Byron; it is indeed the chief beauty of that extraordinary poet. Examine Childe Harold accurately, and you will be surprised to discover

---

1. "He called to mind the ancient graces" (Horace *Carmen* 4.15.12). The second
epigraph is from *King Lear,* II, 1, 88–89).

2. Mimnermus: seventh century B.C. Greek elegiac poet.

171

how very little of real depth or novelty there often is in the reflections which seem most deep and new. You are enchained by the vague but powerful beauty of the style; the strong impress of originality which breathes throughout. Like the oracle of Dodona,[3] he makes the forest his tablets, and writes his inspirations upon the leaves of the trees: but the source of that inspiration you cannot tell; it is neither the truth nor the beauty of his sayings which you admire, though you fancy that it is: it is the mystery which accompanies them."

"Pray," said I, stretching myself listlessly on the opposite sofa to Vincent,* "do you not imagine that one great cause of this spirit of which you speak, and which seems to *be nothing more than a thoughtful method of expressing all things, even to trifles,* was the great loneliness to which the ancient poets and philosophers were attached? I think (though I have not your talent for quoting) that Cicero calls the *consideratio naturae,* the *pabulum animi;*[4]* and the mind which, in solitude, is confined necessarily to a few objects, meditates more closely upon those it embraces: the habit of this meditation enters and pervades the system, and whatever afterwards emanates from it is tinctured with the thoughtful and contemplative colours it has received."

"*Heus Domine!*"* cried Vincent: "how long have you learnt to read Cicero, and talk about the mind?"

"Ah," said I, "I am perhaps less ignorant than I affect to be: it is *now* my object to be a dandy; hereafter I may aspire to be an orator— a wit, a scholar, or a Vincent. You will see then that there have been many odd quarters of an hour in my life less unprofitably wasted than you imagine."

Vincent rose in a sort of nervous excitement, and then reseating himself, fixed his dark bright eyes steadfastly upon me for some moments; his countenance all the while assuming a higher and graver expression than I had ever before seen it wear.

"Pelham," said he, at last, "it is for the sake of moments like these, when your better nature flashes out, that I have sought your society and your friendship. *I,* too, am not wholly what I appear: the world may yet see that Halifax[5] was not the only statesman whom the pursuits of literature had only formed the better for the labours of

---

3. Dodona: the most ancient oracle of Greece, located by some in Thessaly, by others in Epirus.

4. Cicero *Academica* 2.41.127.

5. George Savile, first marquess of Halifax (1633–95): English pamphleteer and statesman.

172

business. Meanwhile, let me pass for the pedant, and the bookworm: like a sturdier adventurer than myself, 'I bide my time.'[6]—Pelham—this will be a busy session! shall you prepare for it?"

"Nay," answered I, relapsing into my usual tone of languid affectation; "I shall have too much to do in attending to Stultz, and Nugee, and Tattersall and Baxter,[7] and a hundred other occupiers of spare time. Remember, this is my first season in London since my majority."

Vincent took up the newspaper with evident chagrin; however, he was too theoretically the man of the world, long to shew his displeasure. "Parr[8]—Parr—again," said he; "how they stuff the journals with that name. God* knows, I venerate learning as much as any man; but I respect it for its uses, and not for itself. However, I will not quarrel with his reputation—it is but for a day. Literary men, who leave nothing but their name to posterity, have but a short twilight of posthumous renown. *Apropos,* do you know my pun upon Parr and the Major!"

"Not I," said I, "*Majora* canamus!"[9]

"Why, Parr and I, and two or three more were dining once at poor T. M———'s, the author of 'The Indian Antiquities.'[10] Major ———, a great traveller, entered into a dispute with Parr about Babylon; the Doctor got into a violent passion, and poured out such a heap of quotations on his unfortunate antagonist, that the latter, stunned by the clamour, and terrified by the Greek, was obliged to succumb. Parr turned triumphantly to me: 'What is your opinion, my lord,' said he; 'who is in the right?'

" '*Adversis* MAJOR—PAR *secundis,*'[11] answered I."

"Vincent," I said, after I had expressed sufficient admiration at his pun—"Vincent, I begin to be weary* of this life; I shall accordingly pack up my books and myself, and go to Malvern Wells, to live quietly till I think it time for London. After to-day, you will, therefore, see me no more."

---

6. The legend on the Ravenswood family crest in Scott's *Bride of Lammermoor.*

7. Nugee: a famous Regency tailor at St. James's Street; Tattersall's: the popular gathering place for sportsmen of all sorts; Baxter: a London hatter popular with *ton.*

8. Samuel Parr (1747–1825): celebrated author, cleric, and educator, a zealous Whig.

9. "Let us sing a nobler theme" (Virgil *Eclogues* 4.1). The pun is, of course, on *majora.*

10. T. Maurice, *The Indian Antiquities* (1806).

11. Another Vincentian pun, this time upon a Latin motto meaning: "Greater than his enemies, equal to his followers."

"I cannot," answered Vincent, "contravene so laudable a purpose, however I may be the loser." And after a short and desultory conversation, I left him once more to the tranquil enjoyment of his Plato. That evening I went to Malvern, and there I remained in a monotonous state of existence, dividing my time equally between my mind and my body, and forming myself into that state of contemplative reflection, which was the object of Vincent's admiration in the writings of the ancients.

Just when I was on the point of leaving my retreat, I received an intelligence which most materially affected my future prospects. My uncle, who had arrived to the sober age of fifty, without any apparent designs of matrimony, fell suddenly in love with a lady in his immediate neighbourhood, and married her, after a courtship of three weeks.

"I should not," said my poor mother, very generously, in a subsequent letter, "so much have minded his marriage, if the lady had not thought proper to become in the family way; a thing which I do and always shall consider a most unwarrantable encroachment on your rights."

I will confess that, on first hearing this news, I experienced a bitter pang; but I reasoned it away. I was already under great obligations to my uncle, and I felt it a very unjust and ungracious assumption on my part, to affect anger at conduct I had no right to question, or mortification at the loss of pretensions I had so equivocal a privilege to form. A man of fifty has, *perhaps,* a right to consult his own happiness, almost as much as a man of thirty; and if he attracts by his choice the ridicule of those whom he has never obliged, it is at least from those persons he *has* obliged, that he is to look for countenance and defence.

Fraught with these ideas, I wrote to my uncle a sincere and warm letter of congratulation. His answer was, like himself, kind, affectionate, and generous: it informed me that he had already made over to me the annual sum of one thousand pounds; and that in case of his having a lineal heir, he had, moreover, settled upon me, after his death, two thousand a-year. He ended by assuring me, that his only regret at marrying a lady who, in *all* respects, was above *all* women, calculated to make him happy, was his unfeigned reluctance to deprive me of a station, which (he was pleased to say), I not only deserved, but should adorn.

Upon receiving this letter, I was sensibly affected with my uncle's kindness; and so far from repining at his choice, I most heartily

174

wished him every blessing it could afford him, even though an heir to the titles of Glenmorris were one of them.

I protracted my stay at Malvern some weeks longer than I had intended; the circumstance which had wrought so great a change in my fortune, wrought no less powerfully on my character. I became more thoughtfully and solidly ambitious. Instead of wasting my time in idle regrets at the station I had lost, I rather resolved to carve out for myself one still loftier and more universally acknowledged. I determined to exercise, to their utmost, the little ability and knowledge I possessed; and while the increase of income, derived from my uncle's generosity, furnished me with what was necessary for my luxury, I was resolved that it should not encourage me in the indulgence of my indolence.

In this mood and with these intentions, I repaired to the metropolis.

CHAPTER VII

Cum pulchris tunicis sumet nova consilia et spes.
HOR[1]

And look always that they be shape,
What garment that thou shalt make
Of him that can best do
With all that pertaineth thereto.
Rom. of the Rose

HOW WELL I CAN REMEMBER THE FEELINGS WITH which I entered London, and took possession of the apartments prepared for me at Mivart's.[2] A year had made a vast alteration in my mind; I had ceased to regard pleasure for its own sake, I rather coveted its enjoyments, as the great sources of worldly distinction. I was not the less a coxcomb than heretofore, nor the less a voluptuary,* nor

---

1. "Along with fine tunics he will put on new plans and hopes" (Horace *Epistles* 1.18.23). The second epigraph is from the translation of the *Romaunt of the Rose* customarily ascribed to Chaucer, lines 2259–62.

2. Mivart's: a fashionable London hotel.

the less choice in my perfumes,* nor the less fastidious in my horses and my dress; but I viewed these matters in a light wholly different from that in which I had hitherto regarded them. Beneath all the carelessness of my exterior, my mind was close, keen, and inquiring; and under the affectations of foppery, and the levity of a manner almost *unique,* for the effeminacy of its tone,* I veiled an ambition the most extensive in its object, and a resolution the most daring in the accomplishment of its means.

I was still lounging over my breakfast, on the second morning of my arrival, when Mr. N———, the tailor, was announced.

"Good morning, Mr. Pelham; happy to see you returned. Do I disturb you too early? shall I wait on you again?"

"No, Mr. N———, I am ready to receive you; you may renew my measure."

"We are a very good figure, Mr. Pelham; very good figure," replied the Schneider, surveying me from head to foot, while he was preparing his measure; "we want a little assistance though; we must be padded well here; we must have our chest thrown out, and have an additional inch across the shoulders; we must live for effect in this world, Mr. Pelham; a *leetle* tighter round the waist, eh?"

"Mr. N———," said I, "you will take, first, my exact measure, and, secondly, my exact instructions. Have you done the first?"

"We are done now, Mr. Pelham," replied my *man-maker,* in a slow, solemn tone.

"You will have the goodness then to put no stuffing of any description in my coat; you will *not* pinch me an iota tighter across the waist than is natural to that part of my body, and you will please, in your infinite mercy, to leave me as much after the fashion in which God made me, as you possibly can."

"But, Sir, we *must* be padded; we are much too thin; all the gentlemen in the Life Guards are padded, Sir."

"Mr. N———," answered I, "you will please to speak of *us,* with a separate, and not a collective pronoun; and you will let me for once have my clothes such as a gentleman, who, I beg of you to understand, is not a Life Guardsman, can wear without being mistaken for a Guy Fawkes on a fifth of November."

Mr. N——— looked very discomfited: "We shall not be liked, Sir, when we are made—we sha'n't, I assure you. I will call on Saturday at 11 o'clock. Good morning, Mr. Pelham; we shall never be done justice to, if we do not live for effect; good morning, Mr. Pelham."

Scarcely had Mr. N——— retired, before Mr.———, his rival, appeared. The silence and austerity of this importation from Austria, were very refreshing after the orations of Mr. N———.

"Two frock-coats, Mr. ———," said I, "one of them brown, velvet collar same colour; the other, dark grey, no stuffing, and finished by Wednesday. Good morning, Mr. ———."

"*Monsieur B———, un autre tailleur,*" said Bedos, opening the door after Mr. S.'s departure.

"Admit him," said I. "Now for the most difficult article of dress—the waistcoat."*

And here, as I am weary of tailors, let me reflect a little upon that divine art of which they are the professors. Alas, for the instability of all human sciences! A few short months ago, in the first edition of this memorable Work, I laid down rules for costume, the value of which, Fashion begins already to destroy. The thoughts which I shall now embody, shall be out of the reach of that great innovator, and applicable not to one age, but to all. To the sagacious reader, who has already discovered what portions of this work are writ in irony—what in earnest—I fearlessly commit these maxims; beseeching him to believe, with Sterne, that "every thing is big with jest, and has wit in it, and instruction too, if we can but find it out!"[3]

MAXIMS

1.

Do not require your dress so much to fit, as to adorn you. Nature is not to be copied, but to be exalted by art. Apelles blamed Protogenes[4] for being *too* natural.

2.

Never in your dress altogether desert that taste which is general. The world considers eccentricity in great things, genius; in small things, folly.

3.

Always remember that you dress to fascinate others, not yourself.

4.

Keep your mind free from all violent affections at the hour of the toilet. A philosophical serenity is perfectly necessary to success. Helvétius says justly, that our errors arise from our passions.

---

3. Laurence Sterne, *Tristram Shandy,* Book 5, chapter 32.

4. Apelles and Protogenes: two celebrated painters of Greek antiquity.

5.

Remember that none but those whose courage is unquestionable, can venture to be effeminate. It was only in the field that the Lacedemonians* were accustomed to use perfumes and curl their hair.

6.

Never let the finery of chains and rings seem *your own* choice; that which naturally belongs to women should appear only worn for their sake. We dignify foppery, when we invest it with a sentiment.

7.

To *win* the affection of your mistress, appear negligent in your costume—to *preserve* it, assiduous: the first is a sign of the *passion* of love; the second, of its *respect*.

8.

A man must be a profound calculator to be a consummate dresser. One must not dress the same, whether one goes to a minister or a mistress; an avaricious uncle, or an ostentatious cousin: there is no diplomacy more subtle than that of dress.

9.

Is the great man whom you would conciliate a coxcomb?—go to him in a waistcoat like his own. "Imitation," says the author of Lacon,⁵ "is the sincerest flattery."

10.

The handsome may be shewy in dress, the plain should study to be unexceptionable; just as in great men we look for something to admire—in ordinary men we ask for nothing to forgive.

11.

There is a study of dress for the aged, as well as for the young. Inattention is no less indecorous in one than in the other; we may distinguish the taste appropriate to each, by the reflection that youth is made to be loved—age, to be respected.

---

5. Rev. Caleb C. Colton, an eccentric clergyman, was the author of *Lacon: or Many things in Few Words; Addressed to Those Who Think* (1820–22), a collection of rather good apothogems.

12.

A fool may dress gaudily, but a fool cannot dress well—for to dress well requires judgment; and Rochefoucault says with truth, "*On est quelquefois un sot avec de l'esprit, mais on ne l'est jamais avec du jugement.*"[6]

13.

There may be more pathos in the fall of a collar, or the curl of a lock, than the shallow think for. Should we be so apt as we are now to compassionate the misfortunes, and to forgive the insincerity of Charles I., if his pictures had portrayed him in a bob wig and a pigtail? Vandyke was a greater sophist than Hume.

14.

The most graceful principle of dress is neatness—the most vulgar is preciseness.

15.

Dress contains the two codes of morality—private and public. Attention is the duty we owe to others—cleanliness that which we owe to ourselves.

16.

Dress so that it may never be said of you "What a well dressed man!"—but, "What a gentlemanlike man!"

17.

Avoid many colours; and seek, by some one prevalent and quiet tint, to sober down the others. Apelles used only four colours, and always subdued those which were more florid, by a darkening varnish.

18.

Nothing is superficial to a deep observer! It is in trifles that the mind betrays itself. "In what part of that letter," said a king to the wisest of living diplomatists, "did you discover irresolution?"—"In its *ns* and *gs!*" was the answer.

19.

A very benevolent man will never shock the feelings of others, by an excess either of inattention or display; you may doubt, there- fore, the philanthropy both of a sloven and a fop.

---

6. "We sometimes see a fool possessed of talent, but never of judgment" (La Rochefoucauld, maxim no. 456).

20.

There is an indifference to please in a stocking down at heel—but there may be a malevolence in a diamond ring.

21.

Inventions in dressing should resemble Addison's definition of fine writing, and consist of "refinements which are natural, without being obvious."[7]

22.

He who esteems trifles for themselves, is a trifler—he who esteems them for the conclusions to be drawn from them, or the advantage to which they can be put, is a philosopher.*

CHAPTER VIII

Tantôt, Monseigneur le Marquis à cheval—
Tantôt, Monsieur du Mazin de bout!
L'Art de se Promener à Cheval[1]

MY CABRIOLET WAS AT THE DOOR, AND I WAS PREPARING to enter, when I saw a groom managing, with difficulty, a remarkably fine and spirited horse. As, at that time, I was chiefly occupied with the desire of making as perfect an equine collection* as my fortune would allow, I sent my cab boy (*vulgo* Tiger) to inquire of the groom, whether the horse was to be sold, and to whom it belonged.

"It was not to be disposed of," was the answer, "and it belonged to Sir Reginald Glanville."

The name thrilled through me: I drove after the groom, and inquired Sir Reginald Glanville's address. His house, the groom (whose dark coloured livery was the very perfection of a right judgment)* informed me, was at No. —— Pall Mall. I resolved to call that morning, but first I drove* to Lady Roseville's to talk about Almack's and the *beau monde,* and be initiated into the newest scandal and satire of the day.

---

7. *Spectator,* no. 253 (December 20, 1711).

1. "Now my Lord the Marquis on a horse,/ Now M. du Mazin on foot" (*The Art of Riding Horseback*). Author unidentified.

Lady Roseville was at home; I found the room half full of women: the beautiful countess was one of the few persons extant who admit people of a morning. She received me with marked kindness. Seeing that ———, who was esteemed, among his friends, the handsomest man of the day, had risen from his seat, next to Lady Roseville, in order to make room for me, I negligently and quietly dropped into it, and answered his grave and angry stare at my presumption, with my very sweetest and most condescending smile. Heaven be praised, the handsomest man of the day is never the chief object in the room, when Henry Pelham and his guardian angel, termed by his enemies, his *self-esteem,* once enter it.

"Charming collection you have here, dear Lady Roseville," said I, looking round the room; "quite a museum! But who is that very polite, gentlemanlike young man, who has so kindly relinquished his seat to me,—though it quite grieves me to take it from him?" added I: at the same time leaning back, with a comfortable projection of the feet, and establishing myself more securely in my usurped chair. *"Pour l'amour de Dieu,* tell me the *on dits* of the day. Good Heavens! what an unbecoming glass that is! placed just opposite to *me,* too! Could it not be removed while I stay here? Oh! by the by, Lady Roseville, do you patronize the Bohemian glasses? For my part, I have one which I only look at when I am out of humour; it throws such a lovely flush upon the complexion, that it revives my spirits for the rest of the day. Alas! Lady Roseville, I am looking much paler than when I saw you at Garrett Park; but *you—you* are like one of those beautiful flowers, which bloom the brightest in the winter."

"Thank Heaven, Mr. Pelham," said Lady Roseville, laughing, "that you allow me at last to say one word. You have learned,* at least, the art of making the *frais* of the conversation since your visit to Paris."

"I understand you," answered I; "you mean that I talk too much; it is true—I own the offence—nothing is so unpopular! Even I, the civilest, best natured, most unaffected person in all Europe, am almost disliked, positively disliked, for that sole and simple crime. Ah! the most beloved man in society is that deaf and dumb person, *comment s'appelle-t-il?"*

"Yes," said Lady Roseville, "Popularity is a goddess best worshipped by negatives; and the fewer claims one has to be admired, the more pretensions one has to be beloved."

"Perfectly true, in general," said I—"for instance, I make the rule, and you the exception. I, a perfect paragon, am hated, because

I am one. You, a perfect paragon, are idolized in spite of it. But tell me what literary news is there. I am tired of the trouble of idleness, and in order to enjoy a little dignified leisure, intend to set up as a *savant*."

"Oh, Lady C——— B——— is going to write a Commentary on Ude; and Madame de Genlis a Proof of the Apocrypha.[2] The Duke of N———e is publishing a Treatise on 'Toleration;' and Lord L———y an Essay on 'Self-knowledge.' As for news more remote, I hear that the Dey of Algiers is finishing an 'Ode to Liberty,' and the College of Caffraria preparing a volume of voyages to the North Pole!"

"Now," said I, "if I retail this information with a serious air, I will lay a wager that I find plenty of believers—for falsehood,* uttered solemnly, is much more like probability than truth uttered doubtingly —else how do the priests of Brama and Mahomet live?"

"Ah! now you grow too profound, Mr. Pelham!"

"*C'est vrai*—but—"

"Tell me," interrupted Lady Roseville, "how it happens that you, who talk eruditely enough upon matters of erudition, should talk so lightly upon matters of levity?"

"Why," said I, rising to depart, "very great minds are apt to think that all which they set *any* value upon, is of equal importance. Thus Hesiod, who, you know, was a capital poet, though rather an imitator of Shenstone, tells us that God bestowed valour on some men, and on others a genius for dancing. It was reserved for me, Lady Roseville, to unite the two perfections. Adieu!"

"Thus," said I, when I was once more alone—"thus do we 'play the fools with the time,'[3] until Fate brings that which is better than folly; and, standing idly upon the sea-shore, till we can catch the favouring wind which is to waft the vessel of our destiny to enterprise and fortune, amuse ourselves with the weeds and the pebbles which are within our reach!"*

---

2. Louis Eustache Ude: the most famous chef of the day in England, author of *The French Cook* (1813), which went through twelve editions in twenty years; Madame de Genlis (1746–1830): author of numerous sentimental romances. Caffraria, in the last sentence of this paragraph, refers to a small eastern district of England's Cape Colony in Africa.

3. *II Henry IV*, II, 2, 153–4.

CHAPTER IX

There was a youth who, as with toil and travel,
Had grown quite weak and grey before his time;
Nor any could the restless grief unravel,
Which burned within him, withering up his prime,
And goading him, like fiends, from land to land.

P. B. Shelley[1]

From lady roseville's i went to glanville's house. He was at home. I was ushered into a beautiful apartment, hung with rich damask, and interspersed with a profusion of mirrors, which enchanted me to the heart:* beyond, to the right of this room, was a small *boudoir,** fitted up with books, and having, instead of carpets, soft cushions of dark green velvet, so as to supersede the necessity of chairs.* This room, evidently a favourite retreat, was adorned at close intervals with girandoles of silver and mother of pearl; and the interstices of the book-cases were filled with mirrors, set in silver:* the handles of the doors were of the same metal.*

Beyond this library (if such it might be called), and only divided from it by half-drawn curtains of the same colour and material as the cushion, was a bath room. The decorations of this room were of a delicate rose colour; the bath, which was of the most elaborate workmanship, represented, in the whitest marble, a shell, supported by two Tritons. There was, as Glanville afterwards explained to me, a machine in this room, which kept up a faint but perpetual breeze, and the light curtains, waving to and fro,. scattered about perfumes of the most exquisite odour.*

Through this luxurious chamber* I was led, by the obsequious and bowing valet, into a fourth room, in which, opposite to a toilet of massive gold, and* negligently robed in his dressing-gown, sate Reginald Glanville:—"Good Heavens," thought I, as I approached him, "can this be the man who made his residence *par choix,** in a

---

1. *Prince Athanase,* lines 1–5.

miserable hovel, exposed to all the damps, winds, and vapours, that the prolific generosity of an English Heaven ever begot?"

Our meeting was cordial in the extreme. Glanville, though still pale and thin, appeared in much better health than I had yet seen him since our boyhood. He was, or affected to be, in the most joyous spirits; and when his dark blue eye lighted up, in answer to the merriment of his lips, and his noble and glorious cast of countenance shone out, as if it had never been clouded by grief or passion, I thought, as I looked at him, that I had never seen so perfect a specimen of masculine beauty, at once physical and intellectual.

"My dear Pelham," said Glanville, "let us see a great deal of each other: I live very much alone: I have an excellent cook, sent me over from France, by the celebrated gourmand Maréchal de ———. I dine every day exactly at eight, and never accept an invitation to dine elsewhere. My table is always laid for three, and you will, therefore, be sure of finding a dinner here every day you have no better engagement. What think you of my taste in furnishing?"*

"I have only to say," answered I, "that since I am so often to dine with you, I hope your taste in wines will be one half as good."

"We are all," said Glanville, with a faint smile, "we are all, in the words of the true old proverb, 'children of a larger growth.' Our first toy is love—our second, display, according as our ambition prompts us to exert it. Some place it in horses—some in honours, some in feasts, and some—*voici un exemple*—in furniture.* So true it is, Pelham, that our earliest longings are the purest: in love, we covet goods for the sake of the one beloved; in display, for our own: thus, our first stratum of mind produces fruit for others; our second becomes niggardly, and bears only sufficient for ourselves. But enough of my morals—will you drive me out, if I dress quicker than you ever saw man dress before?"

"No," said I; "for I make it a rule never to drive out a badly dressed friend; take time, and I will let you accompany me."

"So be it then.* Do you ever read? If so, my books are made to be opened, and you may toss them over while I am at my toilet."

"You are very good," said I, "but I never do read."*

"Look—here," said Glanville,* "are two works, one of poetry—one on the Catholic Question—both dedicated to me. Seymour—my waistcoat. See what it is to furnish a house differently from other people; one becomes a *bel esprit*, and a Maecaenas, immediately. Believe me, if you are rich enough to afford it, that there is no passport to fame like eccentricity. Seymour—my coat. I am at your service,

184

Pelham. Believe hereafter* that one may dress well in a short time?"

"*One* may do it, but not *two—allons!*"*

I observed that Glanville was dressed in the deepest mourning, and imagined, from that circumstance, and his accession to the title I heard applied to him for the first time, that his father was only just dead. In this opinion I was soon undeceived. He had been dead for some years. Glanville spoke to me of his family;—"To my mother," said he, "I am particularly anxious to introduce you—of my sister, I say nothing; I expect you to be surprised with her. I love her more than any thing on earth *now*," and as Glanville said this, a paler shade passed over his face.

We were in the Park—Lady Roseville passed us—we both bowed to her; as she returned our greeting, I was struck with the deep and sudden blush which overspread her countenance. "Can that* be for *me?*" thought I. I looked towards Glanville: his countenance had recovered its serenity, and was settled into its usual proud, but not displeasing, calmness of expression.

"Do you know Lady Roseville well?" said I.

"Very," answered Glanville, laconically, and changed the conversation. As we were leaving the Park, through Cumberland Gate, we were stopped by a blockade of carriages; a voice, loud, harsh, and vulgarly *accented,* called out to Glanville by his name. I turned, and saw Thornton.

"For God's* sake, Pelham, drive on," cried Glanville; "let me, for once, escape that atrocious plebeian."

Thornton was crossing the road towards us; I waved my hand to him civilly enough (for I never cut any body), and drove rapidly through the other gate, without appearing to notice his design of speaking to us.

"Thank Heaven!" said Glanville, and sunk back in a reverie, from which I could not awaken him, till he was set down at his own door.

When I returned to Mivart's, I found a card from Lord Dawton, and a letter from my mother.

"MY DEAR HENRY, (began the letter),

"Lord Dawton having kindly promised to call upon you, personally, with this note, I cannot resist the opportunity that promise affords me, of saying how desirous I am that you should cultivate his acquaintance. He is, you know, among the most prominent leaders of the Opposition; and should the Whigs, by any possible chance, ever come into power, he would have a great chance of becoming prime minister. I trust, however, that you will not adopt that side of the question. The Whigs are a horrid set of people (*politically* speaking), vote for the Roman Catholics, and never get into place; they give very good dinners, however, and till you have decided upon your politics, you may as well make the most of them. I hope, by the by, that you see a great deal of Lord Vincent: every one speaks highly of his talents; and only two weeks ago, he said, publicly, that he thought you the most promising young man, and the most naturally clever person, he had ever met. I hope that you will be attentive to your parliamentary duties; and, oh, Henry, be sure that you see Cartwright, the dentist, as soon as possible.

"I intend hastening to London three weeks earlier than I had intended, in order to be useful to you. I have written already to dear Lady Roseville, begging her to *introduce* you at Lady C.'s, and Lady ———'s; the only places worth going to at present. They tell me there is a horrid, vulgar, ignorant book come out, about ———. As you ought to be well versed in modern literature, I hope you will read it, and give me your opinion. Adieu, my dear Henry, ever your affectionate mother,

"Frances Pelham."

I was still at my solitary dinner, when the following note was brought me from Lady Roseville:—

"Dear Mr. Pelham,

"Lady Frances wishes Lady C——— to be made acquainted with you; this is her night, and I therefore enclose you a card. As I dine at ——— House, I shall have an opportunity of making your *éloge* before your arrival. Your's sincerely,

"C. Roseville."

I wonder, thought I, as I made my toilet, whether or not Lady Roseville is enamoured with her new correspondent? I went very early, and before I retired, my vanity was undeceived. Lady Roseville was playing at *écarté*, when I entered. She beckoned to me to approach. I did. Her antagonist was Mr. Bedford, a natural son of the Duke of Shrewsbury, and one of the best natured and best looking dandies about town: there was, of course, a great crowd round the table. Lady Roseville played incomparably; bets were high in her favour. Suddenly her countenance changed—her hand trembled—her presence of mind forsook her. She lost the game. I looked up and saw just opposite to her, but apparently quite careless and unmoved, Reginald Glanville.

186

We had only time to exchange nods, for Lady Roseville* rose from the table, took my arm, and walked to the other end of the room, in order to introduce me to my hostess.

I spoke to her a few words, but she was absent and inattentive; my penetration required no farther proof to convince me that she was not wholly insensible to the attentions* of Glanville. Lady —— was as civil and silly as the generality of Lady Blanks are: and feeling very much bored, I soon retired to an obscurer corner of the room. Here Glanville joined me.

"It is but seldom," said he, "that I come to these places; to-night my sister persuaded me to venture forth."

"Is she here?" said I.

"She is," answered he; "she has just gone into the refreshment room with my mother, and when she returns, I will introduce you."

While Glanville was yet speaking, three middle-aged ladies, who had been talking together with great vehemence for the last ten minutes, approached us.

"Which is he?—which is he?" said two of them, in no inaudible accents.

"This," replied the third; and coming up to Glanville, she addressed him, to my great astonishment, in terms of the most hyperbolical panegyric.

"Your work is wonderful! wonderful!" said she.

"Oh! quite—quite!" echoed the other two.

"I can't say," recommenced the *Coryphoea,* "that I like the moral —at least not quite; no, not quite."

"Not quite," repeated her coadjutrices.

Glanville drew himself up with his most stately air, and after three profound bows, accompanied by a smile of the most unequivocal contempt, he turned on his heel, and sauntered away.

"Did your grace *ever* see such a bear?" said one of the echoes.

"Never," said the duchess, with a mortified air; "but I will have him yet. How handsome he is for an author!"

I was descending the stairs in the last state of *ennui,* when Glanville laid his hand on my shoulder.

"Shall I take you home?" said he: "my carriage has just drawn up."

I was too glad to answer in the affirmative.

"How long have you been an author?" said I, when we were seated in Glanville's carriage.

"Not many days," he replied. "I have tried one resource after

187

another—all—all in vain. Oh, God! that for me there *could* exist such a blessing as *fiction!* Must I be ever the martyr of one burning, lasting, indelible *truth!"*

Glanville uttered these words with a peculiar wildness and energy of tone: he then paused abruptly for a minute, and continued, with an altered voice—

"Never, my dear Pelham, be tempted by any inducement into the pleasing errors of print; from that moment you are public property; and the last monster at Exeter 'Change has more liberty than you; but here we are at Mivart's. *Addio**—I will call on you to-morrow, if my wretched state of health will allow me."

And with these words we parted.

CHAPTER X

Ambition is a lottery, where, however uneven the chances, there are *some* prizes; but in dissipation, *every* one draws a blank.

Letters of Stephen Montague[1]

THE SEASON WAS NOT FAR ADVANCED BEFORE I GREW heartily tired of what are *nicknamed* its gaieties; I shrunk, by rapid degrees, into a very small orbit, from which I rarely moved. I had already established a certain reputation for eccentricity, coxcombry,* and, to my great astonishment, also for talent; and my pride was satisfied with finding myself universally *recherché,** whilst I indulged my inclinations by rendering myself universally scarce. I saw much of Vincent, whose varied acquirements and great talents became more and more perceptible, both as my own acquaintance with him increased, and as the political events with which that year was pregnant, called forth their exertion and display. I went occasionally to Lady Roseville's, and was always treated rather as a long-known friend, than an ordinary acquaintance; nor did I undervalue this distinction, for it was part of her pride to render her house not only as splendid, but as agreeable, as her command over society enabled her to effect.

---

1. Unidentified.

188

At the House of Commons my visits would have been duly paid, but for one trifling occurrence, upon which, as it is a very sore subject, I shall dwell as briefly as possible. I had scarcely taken my seat, before I was forced to relinquish it. My unsuccessful opponent, Mr. Lufton, preferred a petition against me, for what he called undue means. God* knows what he meant;[2] I am sure the House did not, for they turned me out, and declared Mr. Lufton duly elected.

Never was there such a commotion in the Glenmorris family before. My uncle was seized with the gout in his stomach, and my mother shut herself up with Tremaine,[3] and one China monster, for a whole week. As for me, though I writhed at heart, I bore the calamity philosophically enough in external appearance, nor did I the less busy myself in political matters: with what address and success, good or bad, I endeavoured to supply the loss of my parliamentary influence, the reader will see, when it suits the plot of this history to touch upon such topics.

Glanville I saw continually. When in tolerable spirits, he was an entertaining, though never a frank nor a communicative companion. His conversation then was lively, yet without wit, and sarcastic, though without bitterness. It abounded also in philosophical reflections and terse maxims, which always brought improvement, or, at the worst, allowed discussion. He was a man of even vast powers—of deep thought —of luxuriant, though dark imagination, and of great miscellaneous, though, perhaps, ill arranged erudition. He was fond of paradoxes in reasoning, and supported them with a subtlety and strength of mind, which Vincent, who admired him greatly, told me he had never seen surpassed. He was subject, at times, to a gloom and despondency, which seemed almost like aberration of intellect. At those hours he would remain perfectly silent, and apparently forgetful of my presence, and of every object around him.

It was only then, when the play of his countenance was vanished, and his features were still and set, that you saw in their full extent, the dark and deep traces of premature decay. His cheek was hollow and hueless; his eye dim, and of that visionary and glassy aspect, which is never seen but in great mental or bodily disease, and which, according to the superstitions of some nations, implies a mysterious and unearthly communion of the soul with the beings of another world. From

---

2. He meant that Pelham was guilty of obtaining votes improperly, e.g., by fraud, bribery, misrepresentation, etc.

3. *Tremaine, or, The Man of Refinement* (1825), a popular fashionable novel by Robert Plumer Ward.

these trances he would sometimes start abruptly, and renew any conversation broken off before, as if wholly unconscious of the length of his reverie. At others, he would rise slowly from his seat, and retire into his own apartment, from which he never emerged during the rest of the day.

But the reader must bear in mind that there was nothing artificial or affected in his musings, of whatever complexion they might be. Nothing like the dramatic brown studies, and quick starts, which young gentlemen, in love with Lara and Lord Byron, are apt to practise. There never, indeed, was a character that possessed less cant of any description. His work, which was a singular, wild tale—of mingled passion and reflection—was, perhaps, of too original, certainly of too abstract a nature, to suit the ordinary novel readers of the day. It did not acquire popularity for itself, but it gained great reputation for the author. It also inspired every one who read it, with a vague and indescribable interest to see and know the person who had composed so singular a work.

This interest he was the first to laugh at, and to disappoint. He shrunk from all admiration, and from all sympathy. At the moment when a crowd assembled round him, and every ear was bent to catch the words, which came alike from so beautiful a lip, and so strange and imaginative a mind, it was his pleasure to utter some sentiment totally different from his written opinion, and utterly destructive of the sensation he had excited. But it was very rarely that he exposed himself to these "trials of an author." He went out little to any other house but Lady Roseville's, and it was seldom more than once a week that he was seen even there. Lonely, and singular in mind and habits, he lived in the world like a person occupied by a separate object, and possessed of a separate existence, from that of his fellow-beings. He was luxurious and splendid, beyond all men, in his habits, rather than his tastes. His table groaned beneath a weight of gold,* too costly for the daily service even of a prince; but he had no pleasure in surveying it. His wines and viands were of the most exquisite description; but he scarcely tasted them. Yet, what may seem inconsistent, he was averse to all ostentation and show in the eyes of others. He admitted very few into his society—no one so intimately as myself. I never once saw more than three persons at his table. He seemed, in his taste for furniture,* in his love of literature, and his pursuit after fame, to be, as he himself said, eternally endeavouring to forget, and eternally brought back to remembrance.

"I pity that man even more than I admire him," said Vincent

to me, one night when we were walking home from Glanville's house. "His is, indeed, the disease *nullâ medicabilis herbâ*.[4] Whether it is the past or the present that afflicts him—whether it is the memory of past evil, or the satiety of present good, he has taken to his heart the bitterest philosophy of life. He does not reject its blessings—he gathers them around him, but as a stone gathers moss—cold, hard, unsoftened by the freshness and the greenness which surround it. As a circle can only touch a circle in one place, every thing that life presents to him, wherever it comes from—to whatever portion of his soul it is applied—can find but one point of contact; and that is the soreness of affliction: whether it is the *oblivio* or the *otium* that he requires, he finds equally that he is for ever in want of one treasure:—'*neque gemmis neque purpurâ venale nec auro.*'"[5]

CHAPTER XI

Mons. Jourdain. Etes-vous fou de l'aller quereller' lui qui entend la tierce et la quarte, et qui sait tuer un homme par raison démonstrative?

Le Maître à Danser. Je me moque de sa raison démonstrative, et de sa tierce et de sa quarte.

MOLIÈRE[1]

"HOLLO, MY GOOD FRIEND; HOW ARE YOU?—D——D glad to see you in England," vociferated a loud, clear, good-humoured voice, one cold morning, as I was shivering down Brook-street, into Bond-street. I turned, and beheld Lord Dartmore, of Rocher de Cancale memory. I returned his greeting with the same cordiality with which it was given; and I was forthwith saddled with Dartmore's arm,

---

4. That is, love, the disease for which there is no cure. Bulwer conflates two passages from Ovid, *Epistulae* 5.149 and *Epistulae ex ponto* 1.3.25.

5. "Neither gems nor rich purple robes nor gold" (Horace *Carmen* 2.16.7).

1. "*M. Jourdain:* Are you mad to go and quarrel with a man who understands tierce and quart, and knows how to kill another by demonstrative reason? *Dancing Master:* I don't care a straw for his demonstrative reason, and his tierce and quart" (Molière, *Le Bourgeois Gentilhomme*, II, 3).

and dragged up Bond Street, into that borough of all noisy, riotous, unrefined, good fellows—yclept ———'s Hotel.[2]

Here we were soon plunged into a small, low apartment, which Dartmore informed me was his room. It was* crowded with a score of masculine looking youths, at whose very appearance my gentler frame shuddered from head to foot. However, I put as good a face on the matter as I possibly could, and affected a freedom and frankness of manner, correspondent with the unsophisticated tempers with which I was so unexpectedly brought into contact.*

Dartmore was still gloriously redolent of Oxford: his companions were all extracts from Christchurch; and his favourite occupations were boxing and hunting—scenes at the Fives' Court—nights in the Cider Cellar—and mornings at Bow-street.[3] Figure to yourself a fitter companion for the hero and writer of these adventures! The table was covered with boxing gloves, single sticks, two ponderous pair of dumb bells, a large pewter pot of porter, and four foils; one snapped in the middle.

"Well," cried Dartmore, to two strapping youths, with their coats off, "which was the conqueror?"

"Oh, it is not yet decided," was the answer; and forthwith the bigger one hit the lesser a blow, with his boxing glove, heavy enough to have felled Ulysses,[4] who, if I recollect aright, was rather 'a game blood' in such encounters.

This slight salute was forthwith the prelude to an encounter, which the whole train crowded round to witness. I, among the rest, pretending an equal ardour, and an equal interest, and hiding, like many persons in a similar predicament, a most trembling spirit beneath a most valorous exterior.

When the match (which terminated in favour of the lesser champion) was over, "Come, Pelham," said Dartmore, "let me take up the gloves with you?"

"You are too good!" said I, for the first time using my drawing-room drawl. A wink and a grin went round the room.

"Well, then, will you fence with Staunton, or play at single sticks with me?" said the short, thick, bullying, impudent, vulgar Earl of Calton.

---

2. Long's Hotel, the celebrated caravanserai.

3. The Fives' Court: a London prize-fighting center in St. Martin's Street; the Cider Cellar: a famous night house in Maiden Lane next to the stage door of the Adelphi Theatre.

4. See the *Odyssey,* Book 18.

"Why," answered I, "I am a poor hand at the foils, and a still worse at the sticks; but I have no objection to exchange a cut or two at the latter with Lord Calton."

"No, no!" said the good-natured Dartmore;— "no, Calton is the best stick-player I ever knew;" and then, whispering me, he added, "and the hardest hitter—and he never spares, either."

"Really," said I aloud, in my most affected tone, "it is a great pity, for I am excessively delicate; but as I said I would engage him, I don't like to retract. Pray let me look at the hilt: I hope the basket is strong: I would not have my knuckles rapped for the world—now for it. I'm in a deuced fright, Dartmore;" and so saying, and inwardly chuckling at the universal pleasure depicted in the countenances of Calton and the by-standers, who were all rejoiced at the idea of the "dandy being drubbed," I took the stick, and pretended great awkwardness, and lack of grace in the position I chose.

Calton placed himself in the most scientific attitude, assuming at the same time an air of *hauteur* and *nonchalance,* which seemed to call for the admiration it met.

"Do we make* hard hitting?" said I.

"Oh! by all means," answered Calton, eagerly.

"Well," said I, settling on* my own *chapeau,* "had not you better put on your hat?"

"Oh, no," answered Calton, imperiously; "I can take pretty good care of my head;" and with these words we commenced.

I remained at first nearly upright, not availing myself in the least of my superiority in height, and only acting on the defensive. Calton played well enough for a gentleman; but he was no match for one who had, at the age of thirteen, beat the Life Guardsmen at Angelo's.[5] Suddenly, when I had excited a general laugh at the clumsy success with which I warded off a most rapid attack of Calton's, I changed my position, and keeping Calton at arm's length till I had driven him towards a corner, I took advantage of a haughty imprudence on his part, and by a common enough move in the game, drew back from a stroke aimed at my limbs, and suffered the whole weight of my weapon to fall so heavily upon his head, that I felled him to the ground in an instant.

I was sorry for the severity of the stroke, the moment after it was inflicted; but never was punishment more deserved. We picked up the discomfited hero, and placed him on a chair to recover his senses;

---

5. Angelo's Fencing Rooms in St. James's Street.

meanwhile I received the congratulations of the conclave with a frank alteration of manner which delighted them: and I found it impossible to get away, till I had promised to dine with Dartmore, and spend the rest of the evening in the society of his friends.

CHAPTER XII

Heroes mischievously gay,
Lords of the street and terrors of the way,
Flush'd as they are with folly, youth, and wine.
JOHNSON's London[1]

Hol. Novi hominem tanquam te—his humour is lofty, his discourse peremptory, his tongue filed, his eye ambitious, his gait majestical, and his general behaviour vain, ridiculous, and thrasonical.
SHAKSPEARE

I WENT A LITTLE AFTER SEVEN O'CLOCK TO KEEP MY dinner engagement at ———'s; for very young men are seldom unpunctual at dinner. We sat down, six in number, to a repast at once incredibly bad, and ridiculously extravagant; turtle without fat—venison without flavour—champagne with the taste of a gooseberry, and hock with the properties of a pomegranate.[2] Such is the constant habit of young men: they think anything expensive is necessarily good, and they purchase poison at a dearer rate than the most medicine-loving hypochondriac in England.

Of course, all the knot declared the dinner was superb; called in the master to eulogize him in person, and made him, to his infinite dismay, swallow a bumper of his own hock. Poor man, they mistook his reluctance for his diffidence, and forced him to wash it away in another potation. With many a wry face of grateful humility, he left the room, and we then proceeded to pass the bottle with the *suicidal* determination of defeated Romans. You may imagine that we were not

---

1. Samuel Johnson, "London," lines 31–33. The second epigraph is from *Love's Labour's Lost,* V, 10–14.

2. [Pomum valde purgatorium. (B-L)]:* "A really hellish fruit."

long in arriving at the devoutly wished for consummation of comfortable inebriety; and with our eyes reeling, our cheeks burning, and our brave spirits full ripe for a quarrel, we sallied out at eleven o'clock, vowing death, dread, and destruction to all the sober portion of his majesty's subjects.

We came to a dead halt in Arlington-street, which, as it was the quietest spot in the neighbourhood, we deemed a fitting place for the arrangement of our forces. Dartmore, Staunton, (a tall, thin, well formed, silly youth), and myself, marched first, and the remaining three followed. We gave each other the most judicious admonitions as to propriety of conduct, and then, with a shout that alarmed the whole street, we renewed our way. We passed on safely enough till we got to Charing-Cross, having only been thrice upbraided by the watchmen, and once threatened by two carmen of prodigious size, to whose wives or sweethearts we had, to our infinite peril, made some gentle overtures. When, however, we had just passed the Opera Colonnade, we were accosted by a bevy of buxom Cyprians,[3] as merry and as drunk as ourselves. We halted for a few minutes in the midst of the kennel, to confabulate with our new friends, and a very amicable and intellectual conversation ensued. Dartmore was an adept in the art of slang, and he found himself fairly matched, by more than one of the fair and gentle creatures by whom we were surrounded. Just, however, as we were all in high glee, Staunton made a trifling discovery, which turned the merriment of the whole scene into strife, war, and confusion. A bouncing lass, whose hands were as ready as her charms, had quietly helped herself to a watch which Staunton wore, *à la mode,* in his waistcoat pocket. Drunken as the youth was at that time, and dull as he was at all others, he was not without the instinctive penetration with which all human bipeds watch over their individual goods and chattels. He sprung aside from the endearments of the syren, grasped her arm, and in a voice of querulous indignation, accused her of the theft.

> "Then rose the cry of women—shrill
> As shriek of gosshawk on the hill."[4]

Never were my ears so stunned. The angry authors in the adventures of Gil Blas,[5] were nothing to the disputants in the kennel at

---

3. Cyprians: loose women of the streets.

4. Unidentified.

5. See *Gil Blas,* book XI, chapter 119, the picaresque novel by Alan René Lesage (1668–1747).

Charing Cross; we rowed, swore, slanged with a Christian meekness and forbearance, which would have rejoiced Mr. Wilberforce[6] to the heart, and we were already preparing ourselves for a more striking engagement, when we were most unwelcomely interrupted by the presence of three watchmen.

"Take away this—this— d——d woman," hiccuped out Staunton, "She has sto—len—(hiccup)—my watch"—(hiccup).

"No such thing, watchman," halooed out the accused, "the b—— counter-skipper never *had* any watch! he only filched a twopenny-half-penny gilt chain out of his master, Levi, the pawnbroker's window, and stuck it in his *eel-skin* to make a show:[7] ye did, ye pitiful, lanky-chopped son of a dog-fish, ye did."

"Come, come," said the watchman, "move on, move on."

"You be d——d, for a Charley!"[8] said one of our gang.

"Ho! ho! master jackanapes, I shall give you a cooling in the watch-house, if you tips us any of your jaw. I dare say the young *oman* here, is quite right about ye, and ye never had any watch at all, at all."

"You are a d——d* liar," cried Staunton; "and you are all in with each other, like a pack of rogues as you are."

"I'll tell ye what, young gemman," said another watchman, who was a more potent, grave, and reverend senior than his comrades, "if you do not move on instantly, and let those decent young *omen* alone, I'll take you all up before Sir Richard.

"Charley, my boy," said Dartmore, "did you ever get thrashed for impertinence?"

The last mentioned watchman took upon himself to reply to this interrogatory by a very summary proceeding: he collared Dartmore; and his companions did the same kind office to us. This action was not committed with impunity: in an instant two of the moon's minions, staffs, lanterns, and all, were measuring their length at the foot of their namesake of royal memory; the remaining Dogberry was, however, a tougher assailant; he held Staunton so firmly in his gripe, that the poor youth could scarcely breathe out a faint and feeble d—— ye of defiance, and with his disengaged hand he made such an admirable use of his rattle, that we were surrounded in a trice.

---

6. William Wilberforce (1759–1833), philanthropist, statesman, vigorous opponent of slavery. A profound believer in human depravity, he wrote a book exposing the corruptions of the Christian churches.

7. Counter-skipper: a draper's assistant; eel-skin: very tight trousers.

8. Charley: a watchman.

As when an ant-hill is invaded, from every quarter and crevice of the mound arise and pour out an angry host, of whose previous existence the unwary assailant had not dreamt; so from every lane, and alley, and street, and crossing, came fast and far the champions of the night.

"Gentlemen," said Dartmore, "we must fly—*sauve qui peut.*" We wanted no stronger admonition, and, accordingly, all of us who were able, set off with the utmost velocity with which God had gifted us. I have some faint recollection that I myself headed the flight. I remember well that I dashed *up* the Strand, and dashed *down* a singular little shed, from which emanated the steam of tea, and a sharp, querulous scream of "All hot—all hot! a penny a pint." I see, now, by the dim light of retrospection, a vision of an old woman in the kennel, and a pewter pot of mysterious ingredients precipitated into a greengrocer's shop, *"te virides inter lauros,"* [9] as Vincent would have said. On we went, faster and faster, as the rattle rung in our ears, and the tramp of the enemy echoed after us in hot pursuit.

"The *devil* take the hindmost," said Dartmore, breathlessly (as he kept up with me).

"The watchman has saved his majesty the trouble," answered I, looking back and seeing one of our friends in the clutch of the pursuers.

"On, on!" was Dartmore's only reply.

At last, after innumerable perils, and various immersements into back passages, and courts, and alleys, which, like the chicaneries of law, preserved and befriended us, in spite of all the efforts of justice, we fairly found ourselves in safety in the midst of a great square.

Here we paused, and after ascertaining our individual safeties, we looked round to ascertain the sum total of the general loss. Alas! we were wofully shorn of our beams—we were reduced one-half: only three out of the six survived the conflict and the flight.

"Half," (said the companion of Dartmore and myself, whose name was Tringle, and who was a dabbler in science, of which he was not a little vain) "half is less worthy than the whole; but the half is more worthy than nonentity."

"An axiom," said I, "not to be disputed; but now that we are safe, and have time to think about it, are you not slightly of opinion that we behaved somewhat scurvily to our better half, in leaving it so quietly in the hands of the Philistines?"

9. "You among the green laurels" (an adaptation of passages in Virgil and Apuleius).

"By no means," answered Dartmore. "In a party, whose members make no pretensions to sobriety, it would be too hard to expect that persons who are scarcely capable of taking care of themselves, should take care of other people. No; we have, in all these exploits, only the one maxim of self-preservation."

"Allow me," said Tringle, seizing me by the coat, "to explain it to you on scientific principles. You will find, in hydrostatics, that the attraction of cohesion is far less powerful in fluids than in solids; viz. that persons who have been converting their 'solid flesh'[10] into wine skins, cannot stick so close to one another as when they are sober."

"Bravo, Tringle!" cried Dartmore; "and now, Pelham, I hope your delicate scruples are, after so luminous an *éclaircissement*, set at rest forever."

"You have convinced me," said I; "let us leave the unfortunates to their fate, and Sir Richard. What is now to be done?"

"Why, in the first place," answered Dartmore, "let us reconnoitre. Does any one know this spot?"

"Not I," said both of us. We inquired of an old fellow, who was tottering home under the same Bacchanalian auspices as ourselves, and found we were in Lincoln's Inn Fields.

"Which shall we do?" asked I, "stroll home; or parade the streets, visit the Cider-Cellar, and the Finish,[11] and kiss the first lass we meet in the morning bringing her charms and carrots to Covent Garden Market?"

"The latter," cried Dartmore and Tringle, "without doubt."

"Come, then," said I, "let us investigate Holborn, and dip into St. Giles's, and then find our way into some more known corner of the globe."

"Amen!" said Dartmore, and accordingly we renewed our march. We wound along a narrow lane, tolerably well known, I imagine, to the gentlemen of the quill, and entered Holborn. There was a beautiful moon above us, which cast its light over a drowsy stand of hackney coaches, and shed a 'silver sadness' over the thin visages and sombre vestments of two guardians of the night, who regarded us, we thought, with a very ominous aspect of suspicion.

We strolled along, leisurely enough, till we were interrupted by a miserable-looking crowd, assembled round a dull, dingy, melancholy shop, from which gleamed a solitary candle, whose long, spinster-like

---

10. *Hamlet*, I, 2, 129.

11. The Finish, like the Cider Cellar, was a notorious night house, located in St. James's Street, Covent Garden, and kept by one Jack Rowbottom.

wick was flirting away with an east wind, at a most unconscionable rate. Upon the haggard and worn countenances of the by-standers, was depicted one general and sympathizing expression of eager, envious, wistful anxiety, which predominated so far over the various characters of each, as to communicate something of a likeness to all. It was an impress of such a seal as you might imagine, not the archfiend, but one of his subordinate shepherds,* would have set upon each of his flock.

Amid this crowd, I recognized more than one face which I had often seen in my equestrian lounges through town, peering from the shoulders of some intrusive, ragmuffin, wagesless lackey, and squealing out of its wretched, unpampered mouth, the everlasting query of "*Want your oss held, Sir?*" The rest were made up of unfortunate women of the vilest and most ragged description, aged itinerants, with features seared with famine, bleared eyes, dropping jaws, shivering limbs and all the mortal signs of hopeless and aidless, and, worst of all, breadless infirmity. Here and there an Irish accent broke out in the oaths of national impatience, and was answered by the shrill, broken voice of some decrepit but indefatigable votaress of pleasure— (*Pleasure!* good God!)* but the chief character of the meeting was *silence;*—silence, eager, heavy, engrossing; and, above them all, shone out the quiet moon, so calm, so holy, so breathing of still happiness and unpolluted glory, as if it never looked upon the traces of human passion, and misery, and sin. We stood for some moments contemplating the group before us, and then, following the steps of an old, withered crone, who, with a cracked cup in her hand, was pushing her way through the throng, we found ourselves in that dreary pandaemonium, at once the origin and the refuge of humble vices— *a Gin-shop*.

"Poor devils," said Dartmore, to two or three of the nearest and eagerest among the crowd, "come in, and I will treat you."

The invitation was received with a promptness which must have been the most gratifying compliment to the inviter; and thus Want, which is the mother of Invention, does not object, now and then, to a bantling by Politeness.

We stood by the counter while our *protégés* were served, in silent observation. In low vice, to me, there is always something too gloomy, almost too *fearful* for light mirth; the contortions of the madman are stranger than those of the fool, but one does not laugh at them; the sympathy is for the cause—not the effect.*

Leaning against the counter at one corner, and fixing his eyes de-

199

liberately and unmovingly upon us, was a man about the age of fifty, dressed in a costume of singular fashion, apparently pretending to an antiquity of taste, correspondent with that of the material. This person wore a large cocked-hat, set rather jauntily on one side,—a black coat, which seemed an *omnium gatherum* of all abominations that had come in its way for the last ten years, and which appeared to advance equal claims (from the manner it was made and worn), to the several dignities of the art military and civil, the *arma* and the *toga:*—from the neck of the wearer hung a blue ribbon of amazing breadth, and of a very surprising assumption of newness and splendour, by no means in harmony with the other parts of the *tout ensemble;* this was the guardian of an eye-glass of block tin, and of dimensions correspondent with the size of the ribbon. Stuck under the right arm, and shaped fearfully like a sword, peeped out the hilt of a very large and sturdy looking stick, "in war a weapon, in peace a support."[12]

The features of the man were in keeping with his garb; they betokened an equal mixture of the traces of poverty, and the assumption of the dignities reminiscent of a better day. Two small, light-blue eyes were shaded by bushy, and rather imperious brows, which lowered from under the hat, like Cerberus out of his den. These, at present, wore the dull, fixed stare of habitual intoxication, though we were not long in discovering that they had not yet forgotten to sparkle with all the quickness, and more than the roguery of youth. His nose was large, prominent, and aristocratic; nor would it have been ill formed, had not some unknown cause pushed it a little nearer towards the left ear, than would have been thought, by an equitable judge of beauty, fair to the pretensions of the right. The lines in the countenance were marked as if in iron, and had the face been perfectly composed, must have given to it a remarkably stern and sinister appearance; but at that moment, there was an arch leer about the mouth, which softened, or at least altered, the expression the features habitually wore.

"Sir," said he, (after a few minutes of silence), "Sir," said he, approaching me, "will you do me the honour to take a pinch of snuff?" and so saying, he tapped a curious copper box, with a picture of his late majesty upon it.

"With great pleasure," answered I, bowing low, "since the act is a prelude to the pleasure of your acquaintance."

---

12. Unidentified.

My gentleman of the gin-shop opened his box with an air, as he replied—"It is but seldom that I meet, in places of this description, gentlemen of the exterior of yourself and your friends. I am not a person very easily deceived by the outward man. Horace, Sir, could not have included *me*, when he said, *specie decipimur*.[13] I perceive that you are surprised at hearing me quote Latin. Alas! Sir, in my wandering and various manner of life, I may say, with Cicero and Pliny, that the study of letters has proved my greatest consolation. '*Gaudium mihi,*' says the latter author, '*et solatium in literis: nihil tam laete quod his non laetius, nihil tam triste quod non per has sit minus triste.*' God d——n ye, you scoundrel, give me my gin! ar'nt you ashamed of keeping a gentlemen of my fashion so long waiting?" This was said to the sleepy dispenser of the spirituous potations, who looked up for a moment with a dull stare, and then replied, "Your money first, Mr. Gordon—you owe us seven-pence halfpenny already."

"Blood and confusion! speakest thou to me of halfpence! Know that thou art a mercenary varlet; yes, knave, mark that, a mercenary varlet." The sleepy Ganymede replied not, and the wrath of Mr. Gordon subsided into a low, interrupted, internal muttering of strange oaths, which rolled and grumbled, and rattled in his throat, like distant thunder.

At length he cheered up a little—"Sir," said he, addressing Dartmore, "it is a sad thing to be dependant on these low persons; the wise among the ancients were never so wrong as when they panegyrized poverty: it is the wicked man's tempter, the good man's perdition, the proud man's curse, the melancholy man's *halter*."

"You are a strange old cock," said the unsophisticated Dartmore, eyeing him from head to foot; "there's half a sovereign for you."

The blunt blue eyes of Mr. Gordon sharpened up in an instant; he seized the treasure with an avidity, of which the minute after, he seemed somewhat ashamed; for he said, playing with the coin, in an idle, indifferent manner—"Sir, you show a consideration, and, let me add, Sir, a delicacy of feeling, unusual at your years. Sir, I shall repay you at my earliest leisure, and in the meanwhile allow me to say, that I shall be proud of the honour of your acquaintance."

"Thank-ye, old boy," said Dartmore, putting on his glove before he accepted the offered hand of his new friend, which, though it was

---

13. "We are deceived by the appearance" (Horace *Ars Poetica* 25). The quotation below from Pliny the Younger, Epistles 8.19.1, may be translated: "Literature affords me both happiness and solace; nothing is so joyful that is not made more joyful by it, nothing so sad that it does not lessen my grief."

tendered with great grace and dignity, was of a marvellously dingy and soapless aspect.

"Harkye! you d——d son of a gun!" cried Mr. Gordon, abruptly turning from Dartmore, after a hearty shake of the hand, to the man at the counter—"Harkye! give me change for this half sovereign, and be d——d to you—and then tip us a double gill of your best;[14] you whey-faced, liver-drenched, pence-griping, belly-griping, pauper-cheating, sleepy-souled Arismanes of bad spirits. Come, gentlemen, if you have nothing better to do, I'll take you to my club; we are a rare knot of us, there—all choice spirits; some of them are a little uncouth, it is true, but we are not all born Chesterfields. Sir, allow me to ask the favour of your name?"

"Dartmore."

"Mr. Dartmore, you are a gentleman. Hollo! you *Liquorpond-street of a scoundrel*—having nothing of liquor but the name, you narrow, nasty, pitiful alley of a fellow, with a kennel for a body, and a sink for a soul; give me my change and my gin, you scoundrel! Humph, is that all right, you Procrustes of the counter, chopping our lawful appetites down to your rascally standard of seven-pence half-penny? Why don't you take a motto, you Paynim dog? Here's one for you— 'Measure for measure, and the devil to pay!' Humph, you pitiful toadstool of a trader, you have no more spirit than an empty water-bottle; and when you go to h—ll, they'll use you to cool the bellows. I say, you rascal, why are you worse off than the devil in a hip bath of brimstone?—because, you knave, the devil then would only be half d——d, and you are d——d all over! Come, gentlemen, I am at your service."

---

14. Flash (thieves') language meaning: "Give me a double gill-ale."

CHAPTER XIII

The history of a philosophical vagabond, pursuing novelty, and losing content.

Vicar of Wakefield[1]

WE FOLLOWED OUR STRANGE FRIEND THROUGH THE crowd at the door, which he elbowed on either side with a most aristocratic disdain, perfectly regardless of their jokes at his dress and manner; he no sooner got through the throng, than he stopped short (though in the midst of the kennel) and offered us his arm. This was an honour, of which we were by no means desirous; for, to say nothing of the shabbiness of Mr. Gordon's exterior, there was a certain odour in his garments which was possibly less displeasing to the wearer than to his acquaintance. Accordingly, we pretended not to notice this invitation, and merely said, we would follow his guidance.

He turned up a narrow street, and after passing some of the most ill-favoured alleys I ever had the happiness of beholding, he stopped at a low door; here he knocked twice, and was at last admitted by a slip-shod, yawning wench, with red arms, and a profusion of sandy hair. This Hebe, Mr. Gordon greeted with a loving kiss, which the kissee resented in a very unequivocal strain of disgustful reproach.

"Hush! my Queen of Clubs; my Sultana Sootina!" said Mr. Gordon; "hush! or these gentlemen will think you in earnest. I have brought three new customers to the club."

This speech somewhat softened the incensed Houri of Mr. Gordon's Paradise, and she very civilly asked us to enter.

"Stop!" said Mr. Gordon, with an air of importance, "I must just step in and ask the gentlemen to admit you;—merely a form—for a word from me will be quite sufficient." And so saying, he vanished for about five minutes.

On his return, he said, with a cheerful countenance, that we were free of the house, but that we must pay a shilling each as the customary

---

1. Oliver Goldsmith, *The Vicar of Wakefield,* headnote to chapter 20.

fee. This sum was soon collected, and quietly inserted in the waistcoat pocket of our chaperon, who then conducted us up the passage into a small back room, where were sitting about seven or eight men, enveloped in smoke, and moistening the fever of the Virginian plant with various preparations of malt. On entering, I observed Mr. Gordon deposit, at a sort of bar, the sum of three-pence, by which I shrewdly surmised he had gained the sum of two and nine-pence by our admission. With a very arrogant air, he proceeded to the head of the table, sat himself down with a swagger, and called out, like a lusty royster of the true kidney, for a pint of purl[2] and a pipe. Not to be out of fashion, we ordered the same articles of luxury.

After we had all commenced a couple of puffs at our pipes, I looked round at our fellow guests; they seemed in a very poor state of body, as might naturally be supposed; and, in order to ascertain how far the condition of the mind was suited to that of the frame, I turned round to Mr. Gordon, and asked him in a whisper to give us a few hints as to the genus and characteristics of the individual components of his club. Mr. Gordon declared himself delighted with the proposal, and we all adjourned to a separate table at the corner of the room, where Mr. Gordon, after a deep draught at the purl, thus began:—

"You observe yon thin, meagre, cadaverous animal, with rather an intelligent and melancholy expression of countenance—his name is Chitterling Crabtree: his father was an eminent coal-merchant, and left him £10,000. Crabtree turned politician. When fate wishes to ruin a man of moderate abilities and moderate fortune, she makes him an orator. Mr. Chitterling Crabtree attended all the meetings at the Crown and Anchor[3]—subscribed to the aid of the suffering friends of freedom—harangued, argued, sweated, wrote—was fined and imprisoned—regained his liberty, and married—his wife loved a community of goods no less than her spouse, and ran *off* with one citizen, while he was running *on* to the others. Chitterling dried his tears; and contented himself with the reflection, that, in 'a proper state of things,' such an event could not have occurred.

"Mr. Crabtree's money and life were now half gone. One does not subscribe to the friends of freedom and spout at their dinners for nothing. But the worst drop was yet in the cup. An undertaking, of the most spirited and promising nature, was conceived by the chief of the friends, and the dearest familiar of Mr. Chitterling Crabtree.

2. Purl: a mixture of hot gin and beer.
3. A tavern in the Strand which housed a number of clubs.

Our worthy embarked his fortune in a speculation so certain of success;—crash went the speculation, and off went the friend—Mr. Crabtree was ruined. He was not, however, a man to despair at trifles. What were bread, meat, and beer, to the champion of equality! He went to the meeting that very night: he said he gloried in his losses—they were for the cause: the whole conclave rang with shouts of applause, and Mr. Chitterling Crabtree went to bed happier than ever. I need not pursue history farther; *you see him here*—verbum sap. He spouts at the 'Ciceronian,' for half a crown a night, and to this day subscribes sixpence a week to the cause of 'liberty and enlightenment all over the world.' "

"By Heaven!" cried Dartmore, "he is a fine fellow, and my father shall do something for him."

Gordon pricked up his ears, and continued,—"Now, for the second person, gentlemen, whom I am about to describe to you. You see that middle-sized, stout man, with a slight squint, and a restless, lowering, cunning expression?"

"What! him in the kerseymere breeches and green jacket?" said I.

"The same," answered Gordon. "His real name, when he does not travel with an alias, is Job Jonson. He is one of the most remarkable rogues in Christendom: he is so noted a cheat, that there is not a pickpocket in England who would keep company with him if he had anything to lose. He was the favourite of his father, who intended to leave him all his fortune, which was tolerably large. He robbed him one day on the high road; his father discovered it, and disinherited him. He was placed at a merchant's office, and rose, step by step, to be head clerk, and intended son-in-law. Three nights before his marriage, he broke open the till, and was turned out of doors the next morning. If you were going to do him the greatest favour in the world, he could not keep his hands out of your pocket till you had done it. In short, he has rogued himself out of a dozen fortunes, and a hundred friends, and managed, with incredible dexterity and success, to cheat himself into beggary and a pot of beer."

"I beg your pardon," said I, "but I think a sketch of your own life must be more amusing than that of any one else: am I impertinent in asking for it?"

"Not at all," replied Mr. Gordon; "you shall have it in as few words as possible."

"I was born a gentleman, and educated with some pains; they told me I was a genius, and it was not very hard to persuade me of the truth of the assertion. I wrote verses to a wonder—robbed orchards

205

according to military tactics—never played at marbles, without explaining to my competitors the theory of attraction—and was the best informed, mischievous, little rascal in the whole school. My family were in great doubt what to do with so prodigious a wonder; one said the law, another the church, a third talked of diplomacy, and a fourth assured my mother, that if I could but be introduced at court, I should be lord chamberlain in a twelvemonth. While my friends were deliberating, I took the liberty of deciding; I enlisted, in a fit of loyal valour, in a marching regiment; my friends made the best of a bad job, and bought me an ensigncy.

"I recollect I read Plato the night before I went to battle; the next morning they told me I ran away. I am sure it was a malicious invention, for if I had, I should have recollected it; whereas I was in such a confusion that I cannot remember a single thing that happened in the whole course of that day. About six months afterwards, I found myself out of the army, and in gaol; and no sooner had my relations released me from the latter predicament, than I set off on my travels. At Dublin, I lost my heart to a rich widow (as I thought) ; I married her, and found her as poor as myself. God* knows what would have become of me, if I had not taken to drinking; my wife scorned to be outdone by me in any thing; she followed my example, and at the end of a year I followed her to the grave. Since then I have taken warning, and been scrupulously sober.—Betty, my love, another pint of purl.

"I was now once more a freeman in the prime of my life; handsome, as you see, gentlemen, and with the strength and spirit of a young Hercules. Accordingly I dried my tears, turned marker by night, at a gambling house, and buck by day, in Bond-street (for I had returned to London). I remember well one morning, that his present Majesty was pleased, *en passant,* to admire my buckskins—— *tempora mutantur.*[4] Well, gentlemen, one night at a brawl in our *salon,* my nose met with a rude hint to move to the right. I went, in a great panic to the surgeon, who mended the matter, by moving it to the left. There, thank God! it has rested in quiet ever since. It is needless to tell you the nature of the quarrel in which this accident occurred; however, my friends thought it necessary to remove me from the situation I then held. I went once more to Ireland, and was introduced to 'a friend of freedom.' I was poor: that circumstance is

---

4. "Times change." This proverbial wisdom was first found in the *Gesta Romanorum* (c.1300).

206

quite enough to make a patriot. They sent me to Paris on a secret mission, and when I returned, my friends were in prison. Being always of a free disposition, I did not envy them their situation: accordingly I returned to England. Halting at Liverpool, with a most debilitated purse, I went into a silversmith's shop to brace it, and about six months afterwards, I found myself on a marine excursion to Botany Bay. On my return from that country, I resolved to turn my literary talents to account. I went to Cambridge, wrote declamations, and translated Virgil at so much a sheet. My relations (thanks to my letters, neither few nor far between) soon found me out; they allowed me (they do so still) half a guinea a week; and upon this and my declamations, I manage to exist. Ever since, my chief residence has been at Cambridge. I am an universal favourite with both graduates and under-graduates. I have reformed my life and my manners, and have become the quiet, orderly person you behold me. Age tames the fiercest of us—

"'Non sum qualis eram.'[5]

"Betsy, bring me my purl, and be d——d to you.

"It is now vacation time, and I have come to town with the idea of holding lectures on the state of education. Mr. Dartmore, your health. Gentlemen, yours. My story is done, and I hope you will pay for the purl."[6]

---

5. "I am not what I was" (Horace *Carmen* 4.1.3).

6. "Poor Jemmy Gordon—thou art no more!—Death hath removed thee;—may it not be to that bourne where alone thy oaths can be outdone! He was indeed a singular character, that Jemmy Gordon, as many a generation of Cantabs can attest! His long stick and his cocked hat—and his tattered Lucretius, and his mighty eye-glass, how familiarly do they intermingle with our recollections of Trinity and Trumpington Street. If I have rightly heard, his death was the consequence of a fractured limb. Laid by the leg in a lofty attic, his spirit was not tamed; the noises he made were astounding to the last.—The grim foe carried him off in a whirlwind of slang! I do not say, 'Peace to his manes', for quiet would be the worst hell that could await him;—and heaven itself would be torture to Jemmy Gordon, if he were not allowed to swear in it!—Noisiest of reprobates, fare thee well!—H. P." [B-L; 1840 ed.] "Jemmy Gordon was the real name of an eccentric character at Cambridge notorious for his scraps of learning, his inebriety, and his coarseness" (*Life . . . and Literary Remains*, II, 193).

CHAPTER XIV

I hate a drunken rogue.
Twelfth Night[1]

WE TOOK AN AFFECTIONATE LEAVE OF MR. GORDON, and found ourselves once more in the open air; the smoke and the purl had contributed greatly to the continuance of our inebriety, and we were as much averse to bed as ever. We conveyed ourselves, laughing and rioting all the way, to a stand of hackney-coaches. We entered the head of the flock, and drove to Piccadilly. It set us down at the corner of the Haymarket.

"Past two!" cried the watchman, as we sauntered by him.

"You lie, you rascal," said I, "you have passed *three* now."

We were all merry enough to laugh at this sally; and seeing a light gleam from the entrance of the Royal Saloon,[2] we knocked at the door, and it was opened unto us. We sat down at the only spare table in the place, and looked round at the smug and *varment* citizens with whom the room was filled.

"Hollo, waiter!" cried Tringle, "some red wine negus—I know not why it is, but the devil himself could never cure me of thirst. Wine and I have a most chemical attraction for each other. You know that we always estimate the force of attraction between bodies by the force required to separate them!"

While we were all three as noisy and nonsensical as our best friends could have wished us, a new stranger entered, approached, looked round the room for a seat, and seeing none, walked leisurely up to our table, and accosted me with a—"Ha! Mr. Pelham, how d'ye do? Well met; by your leave I will sip my grog at your table. No offence, I hope—more the merrier, eh?—Waiter, a glass of hot brandy and water—not too weak. D'ye hear?"

Need I say that this pithy and pretty address proceeded from the mouth of Mr. Tom Thornton. He was somewhat more than half

1. *Twelfth Night*, V, 1, 207.

2. The Royal Saloon, or Astley's Amphitheatre, in Piccadilly, which offered variety shows and quasi-theatrical performances of all sorts.

drunk, and his light, prying eyes twinkled dizzily in his head. Dartmore, who was, and is, the best natured fellow alive, hailed the signs of his intoxication as a sort of freemasonry, and made way for him beside himself. I could not help remarking, that Thornton seemed singularly less sleek than heretofore; his coat was out at the elbows, his linen was torn and soiled; there was not a vestige of the vulgar spruceness about him which was formerly one of his most prominent characteristics. He had also lost a great deal of the florid health formerly visible in his face; his cheeks seemed sunk and haggard, his eyes hollow, and his complexion sallow and squalid, in spite of the flush which intemperance spread over it at the moment. However, he was in high spirits, and soon made himself so entertaining that Dartmore and Tringle grew charmed with him.

As for me, the antipathy I had to the man sobered and silenced me for the rest of the night; and finding that Dartmore and his friend were eager for an introduction to some female friends of Thornton's, whom he mentioned in terms of high praise, I tore myself from them, and made the best of my way home.

CHAPTER XV*

Illi mors gravis incubat
Qui notus nimis omnibus
Ignotus moritur sibi.
        SENECA[1]

Nous serons par nos lois les juges des ouvrages.
        Les Femmes Savantes

VINCENT CALLED ON ME THE NEXT DAY. "I HAVE NEWS for you," said he, "though somewhat of a lugubrious nature. *Lugete Veneres Cupidinesque.*[2] You remember the Duchesse de Perpignan?"
"I should think so," was my answer.

---

1. "Death weighs heavily on him who, known all too well to others, dies unknown to himself" (Seneca *Thyestes* 401–3, slightly misquoted). The second epigraph, from Molière, *Les Femmes savantes*, III, 2, may be translated: "We will judge the results by our laws."
2. "Mourne, O you Graces and Loves" (Catullus *Carmen* 3.1).

"Well then," pursued Vincent, "she is no more. Her death was worthy of her life. She was to give a brilliant entertainment to all the foreigners at Paris; the day before it took place a dreadful eruption broke over* her complexion. She sent for the doctors in despair. 'Cure me against to-morrow,' she said, 'and name your own reward.' 'Madame, it is impossible to do so with safety to your health.' '*Au diable!* with your health,' said the duchesse, 'what is health to an eruption?' The doctors took the hint; an external application was used—the duchesse woke in the morning as beautiful as ever—the entertainment took place—she was the Armida of the scene. Supper was announced. She took the arm of the ——— ambassador, and moved through the crowd amidst the audible admiration of all. She stopped for a moment at the door; all eyes were upon her. A fearful and ghastly convulsion passed over her countenance, her lips trembled, she fell on the ground with the most terrible contortions of face and frame. They carried her to bed. She remained for some days insensible; when she recovered, she asked for a looking-glass. Her whole face was drawn on one side, not a wreck of beauty was left;—that night she poisoned herself!"

I cannot express how shocked I was at this information. Much as I had cause to be disgusted with the conduct of that unhappy woman, I could find in my mind no feeling but commiseration and horror at her death; and it was with great difficulty that Vincent persuaded me to accept an invitation to Lady Roseville's for the evening, to meet Glanville and himself.

However, I cheered up as the night came on; and though my mind was still haunted with the tale of the morning, it was neither in a musing nor a melancholy mood that I entered the drawing-room at Lady Roseville's—"So runs the world away."

Glanville was there in his "customary mourning,"[3] and looking remarkably handsome.*

"Pelham," he said, when he joined me, "do you remember at Lady ———'s one night, I said I would introduce you to my sister? I had no opportunity then, for we left the house before she returned from the refreshment room. May I do so now?"

I need not say what was my answer. I followed Glanville into the next room; and to my inexpressible astonishment and delight, discovered in his sister the beautiful, the never-forgotten stranger I had seen at Cheltenham.

---

3. *Hamlet,* III, 2, 285.

210

For once in my life I was embarrassed—my bow would have shamed a major in the line, and my stuttered and irrelevant address, an alderman in the presence of His Majesty. However, a few moments sufficed to recover me, and I strained every nerve to be as agreeable and *séduisant** as possible.

After I had conversed with Miss Glanville for some time, Lady Roseville joined us. Stately and Juno-like as was that charming personage in general, she relaxed into a softness of manner to Miss Glanville, that quite won my heart. She drew her to a part of the room, where a very animated and chiefly literary conversation was going on—and I, resolving to make the best of my time, followed them, and once more found myself seated beside Miss Glanville. Lady Roseville was on the other side of my beautiful companion; and I observed that, whenever she took her eyes from Miss Glanville, they always rested upon her brother, who, in the midst of the disputation and the disputants, sat silent, gloomy, and absorbed.

The conversation turned upon Scott's novels; thence on novels in general; and finally on the particular one of Anastasius.

"It is a thousand pities," said Vincent, "that the scene of that novel is so far removed from us. Could the humour, the persons, the knowledge of character, and of the world, come home to us, in a national, not an exotic garb, it would be a more popular, as it is certainly a more gifted work, than even the exquisite novel of Gil Blas.* But it is a great misfortune for Hope that—

> " 'To *learning* he narrowed his mind,
> And gave up to the *East* what was meant for mankind.'[4]

One often loses, in admiration at the knowledge of peculiar costume, the deference one would have paid to the masterly grasp of universal character."

"It must require," said Lady Roseville, "an extraordinary combination of mental powers to produce a perfect novel."

"One so extraordinary," answered Vincent, "that, though we have one perfect epic poem, and several which pretend to perfection, we have not one perfect novel in the world.[5] Gil Blas approaches more to perfection than any other (owing to the defect I have just mentioned in Anastasius);* but it must be confessed that there is a

---

4. Thomas Hope (1770–1831): author of *Anastasius, or, Memoirs of a Modern Greek* (1819), a popular picaresque novel.

5. For Don Quixote is not what Lord Vincent terms a *novel*, viz., the actual representation of real life. [B-L; 1835 ed.]

want of dignity, of moral rectitude, and of what I may term moral beauty, throughout the whole book. If an author could combine the various excellencies of Scott and Le Sage, with a greater and more metaphysical knowledge of morals then either, we might expect from him the perfection we have not yet discovered since the days of Apuleius."

"Speaking of morals," said Lady Roseville, "do you not think every novel should have its distinct *but,** and inculcate, throughout, some one peculiar moral, such as many of Marmontel's and Miss Edgeworth's?"[6]

"No!" answered Vincent, "every good novel has one great end— the same in all—*viz.* the increasing our knowledge of the heart. It is thus that a novel writer must be a philosopher. Whoever succeeds in shewing us more accurately the nature of ourselves and species, has done science, and, consequently, virtue, the most important benefit; *for every truth is a moral. This* great and universal end, I am led to imagine, is rather crippled than extended by the rigorous attention to the *one* isolated moral you mention.

"Thus Dryden, in his Essay on the Progress of Satire, very rightly prefers Horace to Juvenal, so far as *instruction* is concerned; because the miscellaneous satires of the former are directed against every vice— the more confined ones of the latter (for the most part) only against *one*. All mankind is the field the novelist should cultivate—all truth, the moral he should strive to bring home. It is in occasional dialogue, in desultory maxims, in deductions from events, in analysis of character, that he should benefit and instruct. It is not enough—and I wish a certain novelist who has lately arisen would remember this—it is not enough for a writer to have a good heart, amiable sympathies, and what are termed high feelings, in order to shape out a moral, either true in itself, or beneficial in its inculcation. Before he touches his tale, he should be thoroughly acquainted with the intricate science of morals, and the metaphysical, as well as the more open, operations of the mind. If his knowledge is not deep and clear, his love of the good may only lead him into error; and he may pass off the prejudices of a susceptible heart for the precepts of virtue. Would to God* that people would think it necessary to be instructed before they attempt to instruct. *Dire simplement que la vertu est vertu parce qu'elle est bonne en son fonds, et le vice tout au contraire, ce n'est pas les faire*

---

6. Maria Edgeworth (1767–1849): English novelist.

connoître.[7] For me, if I was to write a novel, I would first make myself an acute, active, and vigilant observer of men and manners. Secondly, I would, after having thus noted effects by action in the world, trace the causes by books, and meditation in my closet. It is then, and not till then, that I would study the lighter graces of style and decoration; nor would I give the rein to invention, till I was convinced that it would create neither monsters of men nor falsities of truth. For my vehicles of instruction or amusement, I would have people as they are—neither worse nor better—and the moral they should convey, should be rather through jest or irony, than gravity and seriousness. There never was an imperfection corrected by portraying perfection;* and if levity or ridicule be said so easily to allure to sin, I do not see why they should not be used in defence of virtue. Of this we may be sure, that as laughter is a distinct indication of the human race, so there never was a brute mind or a savage heart that loved to indulge in it."[8]

Vincent ceased.

"Thank you, my lord," said Lady Roseville, as she took Miss Glanville's arm and moved from the table. "For once you have condescended to give us your own sense, and not other people's; you have scarce made a single quotation."

"Accept," answered Vincent, rising—

"'Accept a miracle instead of wit.'"[9]

---

7. "Say merely that virtue is virtue because it is good in its fundamentals, and that vice, on the contrary, does not manifest such fundamental principles." Unidentified.

8. The Philosopher* of Malmesbury expresses a very different opinion of the origin of laughter, and, for my part, I think his doctrine, in great measure, though not altogether—true.—See *Hobbes on Human Nature,* and the answer to him in *Campbell's Rhetoric.* [B-L] Bulwer's note refers to the Scotch divine George Campbell (1719–96), who published his *Philosophy of Rhetoric* in 1776.

9. From the couplet traditionally ascribed to Pope and said to have been written to Lord Chesterfield; however, it has never been included in Pope's authoritative corpus.

213

CHAPTER XVI

Oh! I love!—Methinks
This word of love is fit for all the world,
And that for gentle hearts, another name
Should speak of gentler thoughts than the world owns.

P. B. SHELLEY[1]

For me, I ask no more than honour gives,
To think me yours, and rank me with your friends.

SHAKSPEARE

CALLOUS AND WORLDLY AS I MAY SEEM, FROM THE TONE of these memoirs, I can say, safely, that one of the most delicious evenings I ever spent, was the first of my introduction to Miss Glanville. I went home intoxicated with a subtle spirit of enjoyment that gave a new zest and freshness to life. Two little hours seemed to have changed the whole course of my thoughts and feelings.

There was nothing about Miss Glanville like a heroine—I hate your heroines. She had none of that "modest ease," and "quiet dignity," and "English grace" (Lord help us!)* of which certain writers speak with such applause. Thank Heaven, *she was alive.* She had great sense, but the playfulness of a child; extreme rectitude of mind, but with the tenderness of a gazelle: if she laughed, all her countenance, lips, eyes, forehead, cheeks laughed too: "Paradise seemed opened in her face:"[2] if she looked grave, it was such a lofty and *upward,* yet sweet and gentle gravity, that you might (had you been gifted with the least imagination), have supposed, from the model of her countenance, a new order of angels, between the cherubim and the seraphim, the angels of Love and Wisdom. She was not, perhaps, quite so silent in society as my individual taste would desire; but when she spoke, it was with a propriety of thought and diction

---

1. Shelley, *Fragments of an Unfinished Drama,* lines 41–44. The second epigraph, attributed to Shakespeare, is unidentified.

2. Dryden, *Absalom and Achitophel,* 1, 30.

which made me lament when her voice had ceased. It was as if something beautiful in creation had stopped suddenly.

Enough of this now. I was lazily turning (the morning after Lady Roseville's) over some old books, when Vincent entered. I observed that his face was flushed, and his eyes sparkled with more than their usual brilliancy. He looked carefully round the room, and then approaching his chair towards mine, said, in a low tone—

"Pelham, I have something of importance on my mind which I wish to discuss with you; but let me entreat you to lay aside your ususal levity, and pardon me if I say affectation; meet me with the candour and plainness which are the real distinctions of your character."

"My Lord Vincent," I replied, "there is, in your words, a depth and solemnity which pierce me, through one of N——'s best stuffed coats, even to the very heart. Let me ring for my poodle and some *eau de Cologne,* and* I will hear you as you desire, from the alpha to the omega of your discourse."

Vincent bit his lip, but I rung, had my orders executed, and then settling myself and my poodle on the sofa, I declared my readiness to attend to him.*

"My dear friend," said he, "I have often seen that, in spite of all your love of pleasure, you have your mind continually turned towards higher and graver objects; and I have thought the better of your talents, and of your future success, for the little parade you make of the one, and the little care you appear to pay to the other: for

> "'tis a common proof,
> That lowliness is young Ambition's ladder.'[3]

I have also observed that you have, of late, been much to Lord Dawton's; I have even heard that you have been twice closeted with him. It is well known that that person entertains hopes of leading the Opposition to the *grata arva* of the Treasury benches; and notwithstanding the years in which the Whigs have been out of office, there are some persons who pretend to foresee the chance of a coalition between them and Mr. Gaskell, to whose principles it is also added that they have been gradually assimilating."[4]

---

3. *Julius Caesar,* II, 1, 21–22.

4. Bulwer seems to have in mind the actual coalition that was formed between the Whigs and Canning's liberal Tories. The coalition put Canning in office and split the Tory party badly.

Here Vincent paused a moment, and looked full at me. I met his eye with a glance as searching as his own. His look changed, and he continued.

"Now listen to me, Pelham: such a coalition never can take place. You smile; I repeat it. It is my object to form a third party; perhaps while the two great sects 'anticipate the cabinet designs of fate,' there may suddenly come by a third, 'to whom the whole shall be referred.'[5] Say that you think it not impossible that you may join us, and I will tell you more."

I paused for three minutes before I answered Vincent. I then said—"I thank you very sincerely for your proposal: tell me the names of two of your designed party, and I will answer you.

"Lord Lincoln and Lord Lesborough."

"What!" said I—"the Whig, who says in the Upper House, that whatever may be the distresses of the people, they shall not be gratified at the cost of one of the despotic privileges of the aristocracy. Go to!—I will have none of him. As to Lesborough, he is a fool and a boaster—who is always puffing his own vanity with the windiest pair of oratorical bellows that ever were made by air and brass, for the purpose of sound and smoke, 'signifying nothing.'[6] Go to!—I will have none of him either."

"You are right in your judgment of my *confrères*," answered Vincent; "but we must make use of bad tools for good purposes."

"No—no!" said I; "the commonest carpenter will tell you the reverse."

Vincent eyed me suspiciously. "Look you!" said he: "I know well that no man loves better than you place, power, and reputation. Do you grant this?"

"I do!" was my reply.

"Join with us; I will place you in the House of Commons immediately: if we succeed, you shall have the first and the best post I can give you. Now—'under which king, Bezonian, speak or die!'"[7]

"I answer you in the words of the same worthy you quote," said I—"A foutra for thine office.'—Do you know, Vincent, that I have, strange as it may seem to you, such a thing as a conscience? It is true I forget it now and then; but in a public capacity, the recollections of others would put me very soon in mind of it. I know your party

---

5. Unidentified.

6. *Macbeth,* V, 5, 28.

7. *As You Like It,* II, 7, 156.

well. I cannot imagine—forgive me—one more injurious to the country, nor one more revolting to myself; and I do positively affirm, that I would sooner feed my poodle on paunch and liver, instead of cream and fricassee, than be an instrument in the hands of men like Lincoln and Lesborough; who talk much, who perform nothing—who join ignorance of every principle of legislation to indifference for every benefit to the people:—who are full of 'wise saws,' but empty of 'modern instances'[8]—who level upwards, and trample downwards—and would only value the ability you are pleased to impute to me, in the exact proportion that a sportsman values the ferret, that burrows for his pleasure, and destroys for his interest. Your *party* sha'n't* stand!"

Vincent turned pale—"And how long," said he, "have you learnt 'the principles of legislation,' and this mighty affection for the 'benefit of the people?' "

"Ever since," said I, coldly, "I learnt *any* thing! The first piece of *real* knowledge I ever gained was, that my interest was incorporated with that of the beings with whom I had the chance of being cast: if I injure them, I injure myself: if I can do them any good, I receive the benefit in common with the rest. Now, as I have a great love for that personage who has now the honour of addressing you, I resolved to be honest for his sake. So much for my affection for the benefit of the people. As to the little knowledge of the principles of legislation, on which you are kind enough to compliment me, look over the books on this table, or the writings in this desk, and know, that ever since I had the misfortune of parting from you at Cheltenham, there has not been a day in which I have spent less than six hours reading and writing on that sole subject. But enough of this—will you ride to-day?"

Vincent rose slowly—

> "'Gli arditi (said he) tuoi voti
> Già noti mi sono;
> Ma invano a quel trono,
> Tu aspiri con me
> Trema per te!' "[9]

---

8. *II Henry IV,* V, 3, 119. The quotation in the next sentence is from Ibid., line 121.

9. Bulwer may not be quoting correctly. The passage seems to mean: "I have known your passionate desires; but in vain do you aspire with me toward that throne. I must fear for you." The rejoinder immediately following may be translated: "I must be afraid—of you." The opera is unidentified.

" '*Io trema*' (I replied out of the same opera)—'*Io trema—di te!*' "

"Well," answered Vincent, and his fine high nature overcame his momentary resentment and chagrin at my reception of his offer— "Well, I honour you for your sentiments, though they are opposed to my own. I may depend on your secrecy?"

"You may," said I.

"I forgive you, Pelham," rejoined Vincent: "we part friends."

"Wait one moment," said I, "and pardon me, if I venture to speak in the language of caution to one in every way so superior to myself. No one, (I say this with a safe conscience, for I never flattered my friend in my life, though I have often adulated my enemy) —no one has a greater admiration for your talents than myself; I desire eagerly to see you in the station most fit for their display; pause one moment before you link yourself, not only to a party, but to principles that cannot stand. You have only to exert yourself, and you may either lead the opposition, or be among the foremost in the administration. Take something certain, rather than what is doubtful; or at least stand alone:—such is my belief in your powers, if fairly tried, that if you were not united to those men, I would promise you faithfully to stand or fall by you alone, even if we had not through all England another soldier to our standard; but———"

"I thank you, Pelham," said Vincent, interrupting me; "till we meet in public as enemies, we are friends in private—I desire no more. —Farewell."

CHAPTER XVII

Il vaut mieux employer notre esprit à supporter les infortunes qui nous arrivent, qu'à prévoir celle qui nous peuvent arriver.

ROCHEFOUCAULT[1]

NO SOONER HAD VINCENT DEPARTED, THAN I BUTTONED my coat, and sallied out through a cold easterly wind to Lord Dawton's. It was truly said by the political quoter, that I had been often to

---

1. "It is better to use our strength to support those misfortunes which befall us than to anticipate those which might" (La Rochefoucauld, maxim no. 174).

that nobleman's, although I have not thought it advisable to speak of my political adventures hitherto. I have before said that I was ambitious; and the sagacious have probably already discovered, that I was somewhat less ignorant than it was my usual pride and pleasure to appear. Heaven knows why! but* I had established among my uncle's friends, a reputation for talent, which I by no means deserved;* and no sooner had I been personally introduced to Lord Dawton, than I found myself courted by that personage in a manner equally gratifying and uncommon. When I lost my seat in Parliament, Dawton assured me that before the session was over, I should be returned for one of his boroughs; and though my mind revolted at the idea of *becoming dependant* on any party, I made little scruple of promising *conditionally* to *ally* myself to his. So far had affairs gone, when I was honoured with Vincent's proposal. I found Lord Dawton in his library, with the Marquess of Clandonald, (Lord Dartmore's father, and, from his rank and property, classed among the highest, as, from his vanity and restlessness, he was among the most active members of the Opposition.) Clandonald left the room when I entered. Few men in office are wise enough to trust the young; as if the greater zeal and sincerity of youth did not more than compensate for its appetite for the gay, or its thoughtlessness of the serious.

When we were alone, Dawton said to me, "We are in great despair at the motion upon the ———, to be made in the Lower House. We have not a single person whom we can depend upon for the sweeping and convincing answer we ought to make; and though we should at least muster our full force in voting, our whipper-in, poor ———, is so ill, that I fear we shall make but a very pitiful figure."

"Give me," said I, "full permission to go forth into the high-ways and by-ways, and I will engage to bring a whole legion of dandies to the House door. I can go no farther; your other agents must do the rest."

"Thank you, my dear young friend," said Lord Dawton, eagerly; "thank you a thousand times: we must really get you in the House as soon as possible; you will serve us more than I can express."

I bowed, with a sneer I could not repress. Dawton pretended not to observe it. "Come," said I, "my lord, we have no time to lose. I shall meet you, perhaps, at Brookes's, to morrow evening, and report to you respecting my success."

Lord Dawton pressed my hand warmly, and followed me to the door.

"He is the best premier we could have," thought I; "but he de-

219

ceives himself, if he thinks Henry Pelham will play the jackall to his lion. He will soon see that I shall keep for myself what he thinks I hunt for him." I passed through Pall Mall, and thought of Glanville. I knocked at his door: he was at home. I found him leaning his cheek upon his hand, in a thoughtful position; an open letter was before him.

"Read that," he said, pointing to it.

I did so. It was from the agent to the Duke of ——, and contained his appointment to an opposition borough.

"A new toy, Pelham," said he, faintly smiling; "but a little longer, and they will all be broken—the *rattle* will be the last."

"My dear, dear Glanville," said I, much affected, "do not talk thus; you have every thing before you."

"Yes," interrupted Glanville, "you are right, for every thing left for me is in the grave. Do you imagine that I can taste one of the possessions which fortune has heaped upon me, that I have one healthful faculty, one sense of enjoyment, among the hundred which other men are 'heirs to?'[2] When did you ever see me for a moment happy? I live, as it were, on a rock, barren, and herbless, and sapless, and cut off from all human fellowship and intercourse. I had only a single object left to live for, when you saw me at Paris; I have gratified that, and the end and purpose of my existence is fulfilled. Heaven is merciful; but a little while, and this feverish and unquiet spirit shall be at rest."

I took his hand and pressed it.

"Feel," said he, "this dry, burning skin; count my pulse through the variations of a single minute, and you will cease either to pity me, or to speak to me of life. For months I have had, night and day, a wasting—wasting fever, of brain, and heart, and frame; the fire works well, and the fuel is nearly consumed."

He paused, and we were both silent. In fact, I was shocked at the fever of his pulse, no less than affected at the despondency of his words. At last I spoke to him of medical advice.

"'Canst thou,'" he said, with a deep solemnity of voice and manner, "'administer to a mind diseased—pluck from the memory'[3]— Ah! away with the quotation and the reflection." And he sprung from the sofa, and going to the window, opened it, and leaned out for a few moments in silence. When he turned again towards me, his manner had regained its usual quiet. He spoke about the important

---

2. *Hamlet*, III, i, 63.

3. *Macbeth*, V, 3, 40–41.

motion approaching on the ———, and promised to attend; and then, by degrees, I led him to talk of his sister.

He mentioned her with enthusiasm. "Beautiful as Ellen is," he said, "her face is the very faintest reflection of her mind. Her habits of thought are so pure, that every impulse is a virtue. Never was there a person to whom goodness was so easy. Vice seems something so opposite to her nature, that I cannot imagine it possible for her to sin."

"Will you not call with me at your mother's?" said I. "I am going there to-day."

Glanville replied in the affirmative, and we went at once to Lady Glanville's, in Berkeley-square. We were admitted into his mother's *boudoir*. She was alone with Miss Glanville. Our conversation soon turned from common-place topics to those of a graver nature; the deep melancholy of Glanville's mind imbued all his thoughts when he once suffered himself to express them.

"Why," said Lady Glanville, who seemed *painfully* fond of her son, "why do you not go more into the world? You suffer your mind to prey upon itself, till it destroys you. My dear, dear son, how very ill you seem."

Ellen, whose eyes swam in tears, as they gazed upon her brother, laid her beautiful hand upon his, and said, "For *my mother's* sake, Reginald, do take more care of yourself: you want air, and exercise, and amusement."

"No," answered Glanville, "I want nothing but occupation, and thanks to the Duke of ———, I have now got it. I am chosen member for ———."

"I am *too* happy," said the proud mother; "you will now be all I have ever predicted for you;" and, in her joy at the moment, she forgot the hectic of his cheek, and the hollowness of his eye.

"Do you remember," said Reginald, turning to his sister, "those beautiful lines in my favourite Ford—

<blockquote>
" 'Glories
Of human greatness are but pleasing dreams,
And shadows soon decaying. On the stage
Of my mortality, my youth has acted
Some scenes of vanity, drawn out at length
By varied pleasures—sweetened in the mixture,
But tragical in issue. Beauty, pomp,
With every sensuality our giddiness
Doth frame an idol—are inconstant friends
</blockquote>

221

When any troubled passion makes us halt
On the unguarded castle of the mind.' "[4]

"Your verses," said I, "are beautiful, even to me, who have no
soul for poetry, and never wrote a line in my life. But I love not
their philosophy. In all sentiments that are impregnated with melancholy, and instil sadness as a moral, I question the wisdom, and
dispute the truth. There is no situation in life which we cannot
sweeten, or embitter, at will. If the past is gloomy, I do not see the
necessity of dwelling upon it. If the mind can make one vigorous exertion, it can another: the same energy you put forth in acquiring
knowledge, would also enable you to baffle misfortune. Determine
not to think upon what is painful; resolutely turn away from every
thing that recals it; bend all your attention to some new and engrossing object; do this, and you defeat the past. You smile, as if this were
impossible; yet it is not an iota more so, than to tear one's self from a
favourite pursuit, and addict one's self to an object unwelcome to
one at first. This the mind does continually through life: so can it
also do the other, if you will but make an equal exertion. Nor does it
seem to me natural to the human heart to look *much* to the past; all
its plans, its projects, its aspirations, are for the future; it is *for* the
future, and *in* the future, that we live. Our very passions, when most
agitated, are most anticipative. Revenge, avarice, ambition, love, the
desire of good and evil, are all fixed and pointed to some distant goal:
to look backwards, is like walking backwards—against our proper
formation; the mind does not readily adopt the habit, and when once
adopted, it will readily return to its natural bias. Oblivion is, therefore,
an easier* obtained boon than we imagine. Forgetfulness of the past
is purchased by increasing our anxiety for the future."

I paused for a moment, but Glanville did not answer me; and,
encouraged by a look from Ellen, I continued—"you remember that,
according to an old creed, if we were given memory as a curse, we
were also given hope as a blessing. Counteract the one by the other.
In my own life, I have committed many weak, many* wicked actions;
I have chased away their remembrance, though I have transplanted
their warning to the future. As the body involuntarily avoids what is
hurtful to it, without tracing the association to its first experience,
so the mind insensibly shuns what has formerly afflicted it, even without palpably recalling the remembrance of the affliction. The Roman
philosopher placed the secret of human happiness in the one maxim—

---

4. John Ford, *The Broken Heart*, III, 5, 13–23.

222

'not to admire.'[5] I never could exactly comprehend the sense of the moral: my maxim for the same object, would be—'never to regret.' "

"Alas! my dear friend," said Glanville—"we are great philosophers to each other, but not to ourselves; the moment we begin to *feel* sorrow, we cease to reflect on its wisdom. Time is the only comforter; your maxims are very true, but they confirm me in my opinion— that it is in vain for us to lay down fixed precepts for the regulation of the mind, so long as it is dependent upon the body. Happiness and its reverse are constitutional in many persons, and it is then only that they are independent of circumstances. Make the health, the frames of all men alike—make their nerves of the same susceptibility— their memories of the same bluntness, or acuteness—and I will then allow, that you can give rules adapted to all men; till then, your maxim, 'never to regret,' is as idle as Horace's 'never to admire.' It may be wise to you—it is impossible to me!"

With these last words, Glanville's voice faltered, and I felt averse to push the argument further. Ellen's eye caught mine, and gave me a look so kind, and almost grateful, that I forgot every thing else in the world. A few moments afterwards a friend of Lady Glanville's was announced, and I left the room.

CHAPTER XVIII

Intus et in jecore ægro,
Nascuntur domini.
PERSIUS[1]

THE NEXT TWO OR THREE DAYS I SPENT IN VISITING ALL my male friends in the Lower House, and engaging them to dine with me, preparatory to the great act of voting on ——'s motion. I led them myself to the House of Commons, and not feeling sufficiently interested in the debate to remain, as a stranger, where I ought, in my

5. Proverbial maxim found e.g. in Horace *Epistles* 1.6.1.

1. "Masters spring up in our own breast and from a morbid liver" (Persius *Satires* 5.129–30).

own opinion, to have acted as a performer, I went to Brookes's to wait the result. Lord Gravelton, a stout, bluff, six-foot nobleman, with a voice like a Stentor, was "blowing up" the waiters in the coffee-room. Mr. ———, the author of T———, was conning the Courier in a corner; and Lord Armadilleros, the haughtiest and most honourable peer in the calendar, was monopolizing the drawing-room, with his right foot on one hob and his left on the other. I sat myself down in silence, and looked over the "crack article" in the Edinburgh. By and by, the room got fuller; every one spoke of the motion before the House, and anticipated the merits of the speeches, and the numbers of the voters.

At last a principal member entered—a crowd gathered round him. "I have heard," he said, "the most extraordinary speech, for the combination of knowledge and imagination, that I ever recollect to have listened to."

"From Gaskell, I suppose?" was the universal cry.

"No," said Mr. ———, "Gaskell has not yet spoken. It was from a young man who has only just taken his seat. It was received with the most unanimous cheers, and was, indeed, a remarkable display."

"What is his name?" I asked, already half foreboding the answer.

"I only just learnt it as I left the House," replied Mr. ———: "the speaker was Sir Reginald Glanville."

Then every one whom I had often before heard censure Glanville for his rudeness, or laugh at him for his eccentricity, opened their mouths in congratulations to their own wisdom, for having long admired his talents and predicted his success.

I left the *"turba Remi sequens fortunam;"*[2] I felt agitated and feverish; those who have unexpectedly heard of the success of a man for whom great affection is blended with greater interest, can understand the restlessness of mind with which I wandered into the streets. The air was cold and nipping. I was buttoning my coat round my chest, when I heard a voice say, "You have dropped your glove, Mr. Pelham."

The speaker was Thornton. I thanked him coldly for his civility, and was going on, when he said, "If your way is up Pall Mall, I have no objection to join you for a few minutes."

I bowed with some *hauteur;* and as I seldom refuse any opportunity of knowing more perfectly individual character, I said I should be happy of his company so long as our way lay together.

---

2. "The mob of Remus following fortune" (Juvenal *Satires* 10.73).

"It is a cold night, Mr. Pelham," said Thornton, after a pause. "I have been dining at Hatchett's, with an old Paris acquaintance: I am sorry we did not meet more often in France, but I was so taken up with my friend Mr. Warburton."

As Thornton uttered that name, he looked hard at me, and then added, "By the by, I saw you with Sir Reginald Glanville the other day; you know him well, I presume?"

"Tolerably well," said I, with indifference.

"What a strange character he is," rejoined Thornton; "*I* also have known him for some years," and again Thornton looked pryingly into my countenance. Poor fool, it was not for a penetration like his to read the *cor inscrutabile* of a man born and bred like me, in the consummate dissimulation of *bon ton*.

"He is very rich, is he not?" said Thornton, after a brief silence.

"I believe so," said I.

"Humph!" answered Thornton. "Things have grown better with him, in proportion as they grew worse with me, who have had 'as good luck as the cow that stuck herself with her own horn.' I suppose he is not too anxious to recollect me—'poverty parts fellowship.' Well, hang pride, say I; give me an honest heart all the year round, in summer or winter, drought or plenty. Would to God,* some kind friend would lend me twenty pounds."

To this wish I made no reply. Thornton sighed.

"Mr. Pelham," renewed he, "it is true I have known you but a short time—excuse the liberty I take—but if you *could* lend me a trifle, it would really assist me very much."

"Mr. Thornton," said I, "if I knew you better, and could serve you more, you might apply to me for a more real assistance than any *bagatelle* I could afford you would be. If twenty pounds would really be of service to you, I will lend it to you, upon this condition, that you never ask me for another farthing."

Thornton's face brightened. "A thousand, thousand—" he began.

"No," interrupted I, "no thanks, only your promise."

"Upon my honour," said Thornton, "I will never ask you for another farthing."

"There *is* honour among thieves," thought I, and so I took out the sum mentioned, and gave it to him. In good earnest, though I disliked the man, his threadbare garments and altered appearance moved me to compassion. While he was pocketing the money, which he did with the most unequivocal delight, a tall figure passed us rapidly. We both turned at the same instant, and recognized Glanville. He had not gone seven yards beyond us, before we observed his steps, which were very irregular, pause suddenly; a moment afterwards he fell against the iron rails of an area; we hastened towards him, he was apparently fainting. His countenance was perfectly livid, and marked with the traces of extreme exhaustion. I sent Thornton to the nearest public-house for some water; before he returned, Glanville had recovered.

"All—all—in vain," he said, slowly and unconsciously, "death is the only Lethe."

He started when he saw me. I made him lean on my arm, and we walked on slowly.

"I have already heard of your speech," said I. Glanville smiled with the usual faint and sicklied expression, which made his smile painful even in its exceeding sweetness.

"You have also already seen its effects; the excitement was too much for me."

"It must have been a proud moment when you sat down," said I.

"It was one of the bitterest I ever felt—it was fraught with the memory of the dead. What are all honours to me now?—O God! O God! have mercy upon me!"

And Glanville stopped suddenly, and put his hand to his temples.

By this time Thornton had joined us. When Glanville's eyes rested upon him, a deep hectic rose slowly and gradually over his cheeks. Thornton's lip curled with a malicious expression. Glanville marked it, and his brow grew on the moment as black as night.

"Begone!" he said, in a loud voice, and with a flashing eye, "begone instantly; I loathe the very sight of so base a thing."

Thornton's quick, restless eye, grew like a living coal, and he bit his lip so violently that the blood gushed out. He made, however, no other answer than—

"You seem agitated to-night, Sir Reginald; I wish your speedy restoration to better health. Mr. Pelham, your servant."

Glanville walked on in silence till we came to his door: we parted there; and for want of any thing better to do, I sauntered towards the M——— Hell. There were only about ten or twelve persons in the rooms, and all were gathered round the hazard table— I looked on silently, seeing the knaves devour the fools, and younger brothers make up in wit for the deficiencies of fortune.

The Honourable Mr. Blagrave came up to me; "Do you never play?" said he.

"Sometimes," was my brief reply.

226

"Lend me a hundred pounds!" rejoined my kind acquaintance.

"I was just going to make you the same request," said I.

Blagrave laughed heartily. "Well," said he, "be my security to a Jew, and I'll be yours. My fellow lends me money at only forty per cent. My governor is a d——d stingy old fellow, for I am the most moderate son in the universe. I neither hunt, nor race, nor have I any one favourite expense, except gambling, and he won't satisfy me in that—now I call such conduct shameful!"

"Unheard-of barbarity," said I; "and you do well to ruin your property by Jews, before you have it; you could not avenge yourself better on 'the governor.'"

"No, d—— me,"* said Blagrave, "leave me alone for that! Well, I have got five pounds left, I shall go and slap it down."

No sooner had he left me than I was accosted by Mr. Goren,* a handsome little adventurer, who lived the devil knew how, for the devil seemed to take excellent care of him.

"Poor Blagrave!" said he, eyeing the countenance of that ingenious youth. "He is a strange fellow—he asked me the other day, if I ever read the History of England, and told me there was a great deal in it about his ancestor, a Roman General, in the time of William the Conqueror, called Caractacus.[3] He told me at the last Newmarket, that he had made up a capital book, and it turned out that he had hedged with such dexterity, that he *must* lose one thousand pounds, and he *might* lose two. Well, well," continued Goren, with a sanctified expression; "I would sooner see those real fools here, than the confounded scoundrels, who pillage one under a false appearance. Never, Mr. Pelham, trust to a man at a gaming-house; the honestest look hides the worst sharper! Shall you try your luck to-night?"

"No," said I, "I shall only look on."

Goren sauntered to the table, and sat down next to a rich young man, of the best temper and the worst luck in the world. After a few throws, Goren said to him, "Lord ———, do put your money aside—you have so much on the table, that it interferes with mine—and that is really *so* unpleasant. Suppose you put some of it in your pocket."

Lord ——— took a handful of notes, and stuffed them carelessly in his coat pocket. Five minutes afterwards I saw Goren insert his hand, *empty*, in his neighbour's pocket, and bring it out *full*—and half an hour afterwards he handed over a fifty pound note to the marker,

---

3. Caractacus: first century A.D. British king who resisted Roman occupation.

saying, "There, Sir, is my debt to you. God bless me, Lord ———, how you *have* won; I wish you would not leave all your money about—do put it in your pocket with the rest."

Lord ——— (who had perceived the trick, though he was too indolent to resent it), laughed. "No, no, Goren," said he, "you must let me keep *some!*"

Goren coloured, and soon after rose. "D——n my luck!" said he, as he passed me. "I wonder I continue to play—but there are such sharpers in the room. Avoid a gaming house, Mr. Pelham, if you wish to live."

"And *let* live," thought I.

I was just going away, when I heard a loud laugh on the stairs, and immediately afterwards Thornton entered, joking with one of the markers. He did not see me; but approaching the table, drew out the identical twenty pound note I had given him, and asked for change with the air of a *millionnaire*. I did not wait to witness his fortune, good or ill; I cared too little about it. I descended the stairs, and the servant, on opening the door for me, admitted Sir John Tyrrell. "What," I thought, "is the habit *still* so strong?" We stopped each other, and after a few words of greeting, I went, once more, up stairs with him.

Thornton was playing eagerly with his small quota as Lord C——— was with his ten thousands. He nodded with an affected air of familiarity to Tyrrell, who returned his salutation with the most supercilious hauteur; and very soon afterwards the baronet was utterly engrossed by the chances of the game. I had, however, satisfied my curiosity, in ascertaining that there was no longer any intimacy between him and Thornton, and accordingly once more I took my departure.

CHAPTER XIX

The times have been
That when the brains were out, the man would die,
And there an end—but now they rise again.

Macbeth[1]

IT WAS A STRANGE THING TO SEE A MAN LIKE GLANVILLE, with costly tastes, luxurious habits, great talents, peculiarly calculated for display, courted by the highest members of the state, admired for his beauty and genius by half the women in London, yet living in the most ascetic seclusion from his kind, and indulging in the darkest and most morbid despondency. No female was ever seen to win even his momentary glance of admiration. All the senses seemed to have lost, for his palate, their customary allurements. He lived among his books, and seemed to make his favourite companions amidst the past. At nearly all hours of the night he was awake and occupied, and at day-break his horse was always brought to his door. He rode alone for several hours, and then, on his return, he was employed, till the hour he went to the House, in the affairs and politics of the day. Ever since his *début,* he had entered with much constancy into the more leading debates, and his speeches were invariably of the same commanding order which had characterised his first.

It was singular that, in his parliamentary display, as in his ordinary conversation, there were none of the wild and speculative opinions, or the burning enthusiasm of romance, in which the natural inclination of his mind seemed so essentially to delight. His arguments were always remarkable for the soundness of the principles on which they were based, and the logical clearness with which they were expressed. The feverish fervour of his temperament was, it is true, occasionally shown in a remarkable energy of delivery, or a sudden and unexpected burst of the more impetuous powers of oratory; but

---

1. *Macbeth,* III, 4, 78–80.

these were so evidently natural and spontaneous, and so happily adapted to be impressive of the subject, rather than irrelevant from its bearings, that they never displeased even the oldest and coldest cynics and calculators of the House.

It is no uncommon contradiction in human nature (and in Glanville it seemed peculiarly prominent) to find men of imagination and genius gifted with the strongest common sense, for the admonition or benefit of *others,* even while constantly neglecting to exert it for themselves. He was soon marked out as the most promising and important of all the junior members of the House; and the coldness with which he kept aloof from social intercourse with the party he adopted, only served to increase their respect, though it prevented their affection.

Lady Roseville's attachment to him was scarcely a secret; the celebrity of her name in the world of *ton* made her least look or action the constant subject of present remark and after conversation; and there were too many moments, even in the watchful publicity of society, when that charming but imprudent person forgot every thing but the romance of her attachment. Glanville seemed not only perfectly untouched by it, but even wholly unconcious of its existence, and preserved invariably, whenever he was forced into the crowd, the same stern, cold, unsympathizing reserve, which made him, at once, an object of universal conversation and dislike.

Three weeks after Glanville's first speech in the House, I called upon him, with a proposal from Lord Dawton. After we had discussed it, we spoke on more familiar topics, and, at last, he mentioned Thornton. It will be observed that we had never conversed respecting that person; nor had Glanville once alluded to our former meetings, or to his disguised appearance and false appellation at Paris. Whatever might be the mystery, it was evidently of a painful nature, and it was not, therefore, for me to allude to it. This day he spoke of Thornton with a tone of indifference.

"The man," he said, "I have known for some time; he was useful to me abroad, and, notwithstanding his character, I rewarded him well for his services. He has since applied to me several times for money, which is spent at the gambling-house as soon as it is obtained. I believe him to be leagued with a gang of sharpers of the lowest description; and I am really unwilling any farther to supply the vicious necessities of himself and his comrades. He is a mean, mercenary rascal, who would scruple at no enormity, provided he was paid for it!"

230

Glanville paused for a few moments, and then added, while his cheek blushed, and his voice seemed somewhat hesitating and embarrassed—

"You remember Mr. Tyrrell, at Paris?"

"Yes," said I—"he is, at present, in London, and—" Glanville started as if he had been shot.

"No no," he exclaimed, wildly—"he died at Paris, from want—from starvation."

"You are mistaken," said I; "he is now Sir John Tyrrell, and possessed of considerable property. I saw him myself, three weeks ago."

Glanville, laying his hand upon my arm, looked in my face with a long, stern, prying gaze, and his cheek grew more ghastly and livid with every moment. At last he turned, and muttered something between his teeth; and at that moment the door opened, and Thornton was announced. Glanville sprung towards him and seized him by the throat!

"Dog!" he cried, "you have deceived me—Tyrrell lives!"

"Hands off!" cried the gamester, with a savage grin of defiance—"hands off! or, by the Lord that made me, you shall have gripe for gripe!"

"Ho, wretch!" said Glanville, shaking him violently, while his worn and slender, yet still powerful frame, trembled with the excess of his passion; "dost thou dare to threaten me!" and with these words he flung Thornton against the opposite wall with such force, that the blood gushed out of his mouth and nostrils. The gambler rose slowly, and wiping the blood from his face, fixed his malignant and fiery eye upon his aggressor, with an expression of collected hate and vengeance, that made my very blood creep.

"It is not my day *now*," he said, with a calm, quiet, cold voice, and then, suddenly changing his manner, he approached me with a sort of bow, and made some remark on the weather.

Meanwhile, Glanville had sunk on the sofa, exhausted, less by his late effort than the convulsive passion which had produced it. He rose in a few moments, and said to Thornton, "Pardon my violence; let this pay your bruises;" and he placed a long and apparently well filled purse in Thornton's hand. That *veritable philosophe* took it with the same air as a dog receives the first caress from the hand which has just chastised him; and feeling the purse between his short, hard fingers, as if to ascertain the soundness of its condition, quietly slid it into his breeches pocket, which he then buttoned with care, and pulling his waistcoat down, as if for further protection to the deposit, he turned towards Glanville, and said, in his usual quaint style of vulgarity—

"Least said, Sir Reginald, the soonest mended. Gold is a good plaister for bad bruises. Now, then, your will;—ask and I will answer, unless you think Mr. Pelham *un* de trop.*"

I was already at the door, with the intention of leaving the room, when Glanville cried, "Stay, Pelham, I have but one question to ask Mr. Thornton. Is John Tyrrell still living?"

"He is!" answered Thornton, with a sardonic smile.

"And beyond all want?" resumed Glanville.

"He is!" was the tautological reply.

"Mr. Thornton," said Glanville, with a calm voice, "I have now done with you—you may leave the room!"

Thornton bowed with an air of ironical respect, and obeyed the command.

I turned to look at Glanville. His countenance, always better adapted to a stern, than a soft expression, was perfectly fearful; every line in it seemed dug into a furrow; the brows were bent over his large and flashing eyes with a painful intensity of anger and resolve; his teeth were clenched firmly as if by a vice, and the thin upper lip, which was drawn from them with a bitter curl of scorn, was as white as death. His right hand had closed upon the back of the massy* chair, over which his tall nervous frame leant, and was grasping it with an iron force, which it could not support: it snapped beneath his hand like a hazel stick. This accident, slight as it was, recalled him to himself. He apologized with apparent self-possession for his disorder; and, after a few words of fervent and affectionate farewell on my part, I left him to the solitude which I knew he desired.

232

CHAPTER XX

While I seemed only intent upon pleasure, I locked in my heart
the consciousness and vanity of power; in the levity of the lip, I disguised the knowledge and the workings of the brain; and I looked,
as with a gifted eye, upon the mysteries of the hidden depths, while I
seemed to float an idler with the herd only upon the surface of the
stream.

FALKLAND[1]

As I WALKED HOME, REVOLVING THE SCENE I HAD
witnessed, the words of Tyrrell came into my recollection—*viz.* that
the cause of Glanville's dislike to him had arisen in Tyrrell's greater
success in some youthful *liaison*. In this account I could not see much
probability. In the first place, the cause was not sufficient to produce
such an effect; and, in the second, there was little likelihood that
the young and rich Glanville, possessed of the most various accomplishments, and the most remarkable personal beauty, should be
supplanted by a needy spendthrift (as Tyrrell at that time was), of
coarse manners, and unpolished mind; with a person not, indeed,
unprepossessing, but somewhat touched by time, and never more
comparable to Glanville's than that of the Satyr to Hyperion.

While I was meditating over a mystery which excited my curiosity
more powerfully than anything, not relating to himself, ought ever
to occupy the attention of a wise man, I was accosted by Vincent:
the difference in our politics had of late much dissevered us, and
when he took my arm, and drew me up Bond-street, I was somewhat
surprised at his condescension.

"Listen to me, Pelham," he said; "once more I offer you a settlement in our colony. There will be great changes soon: trust me, so
radical a party as that you have adopted can never come in: ours, on
the contrary, is no less moderate than liberal. This is the last time of
asking; for I know you will soon have exposed your opinions in public

---

1. From Bulwer's earlier novel *Falkland* (1827), book 1, letter 6.

233

more openly than you have yet done, and then it will be too late. At present I hold, with Hudibras, and the ancients, that it is—

"'More honourable far, *servare*
Civem than slay an adversary.' "[2]

"Alas, Vincent," said I, "I am marked out for slaughter, for you cannot convince me by words, and so, I suppose, you must conquer me by blows. Adieu, this is my way to Lord Dawton's: where are you going?"

"To mount my horse, and join the *parca* juventus,"[3] said Vincent, with a laugh at his own witticism, as we shook hands, and parted.

I grieve much, my beloved reader, that I cannot unfold to thee all the particulars of my political intrigue. I am, by the very share which fell to my lot, bound over to the strictest secrecy, as to its nature, and the characters of the chief agents in its execution. Suffice it to say, that the greater part of my time was, though furtively, employed in a sort of home diplomacy, gratifying alike to the activity of my tastes, and the vanity of my mind; and there were moments when I ventured to grasp in my imagination the highest honours of the state, and the most lucrative offices of power.* I had filled Dawton, and his coadjutors, with an exaggerated opinion of my abilities; but I knew well how to sustain it. I rose by candle-light, and consumed, in the intensest application, the hours which every other individual of our party wasted in enervating slumbers, from the hesternal dissipation or debauch. Was there a question in political economy debated, mine was the readiest and the clearest reply. Did a period in our constitution become investigated, it was I to whom the duty of expositor was referred. From Madame D'Anville, with whom (though lost as a lover) I constantly corresponded as a friend, I obtained the earliest and most accurate detail of the prospects and manoeuvres of the court in which her life was spent, and in whose more secret offices her husband was employed. I spared no means of extending my knowledge of every the minutest point which could add to the reputation I enjoyed. I made myself acquainted with the individual interests and exact circumstances of all whom it was our object to intimidate or to gain. It was I who brought to the House the younger and idler members, whom no more nominally powerful agent could allure from the ball-room or the gaming-house.

In short, while, by the dignity of my birth, and the independent

---

2. Samuel Butler, *Hudibras*, 1, 3, 759–60.

3. "Stingy youth" (Horace *Satires* 2.5.79). Another Vincentian pun.

hauteur of my bearing, I preserved the rank of an equal amongst the highest of the set, I did not scruple to take upon myself the labour and activity of the most subordinate. Dawton declared me his right hand; and, though I knew myself rather his head than his hand, I pretended to feel proud of the appellation. In truth, I only waited for my *entrée* into the House, to fix my eye and grasp upon the very situation that nobleman coveted for himself.*

Meanwhile, it was my pleasure to wear in society the coxcombical and* eccentric costume of character I had first adopted, and to cultivate the arts which won from women the smile which cheered and encouraged me in my graver contest with men. It was only to Ellen Glanville, that I laid aside an affection, which I knew was little likely to attract a taste so refined and unadulterated as hers. I discovered in her a mind which, while it charmed me by its tenderness and freshness, elevated me by its loftiness of thought. She was, at heart, perhaps, as ambitious as myself; but while my aspirations were concealed by affectation, her's were softened by her timidity, and purified by her religion. There were moments when I opened myself to her, and caught a new spirit from her look of sympathy and enthusiasm.

"Yes," thought I, "I do long for honours, but it is that I may ask her to share and ennoble them." In fine, I loved as other men loved—and I fancied a perfection in her, and vowed an emulation in myself, which it was reserved for Time to ratify or deride.

Where did I leave myself? as the Irishman said—on my road to Lord Dawton's. I was lucky enough to find that personage at home; he was writing at a table covered with pamphlets and books of reference.

"Hush! Pelham," said his lordship, who is a quiet, grave, meditative little man, always ruminating on a very small cud—"hush! or *do* oblige me by looking over this history, to find out the date of the Council of Pisa."[4]

"That will do, my young friend," said his lordship, after I had furnished him with the information he required—"I wish to Heaven, I could finish this pamphlet by to-morrow: it is intended as an answer to ———. But I am so perplexed with business, that—"

"Perhaps," said I, "if you will pardon my interrupting you, I can throw your observations together—make your Sibylline leaves into a book. Your lordship will find the matter, and I will not spare the trouble."

---

4. The Council of Pisa was held between 1409 and 1414.

Lord Dawton was profuse in his thanks; he explained the subject, and left the arrangement wholly to me. He could not presume to dictate. I promised him, if he lent me the necessary books, to finish the pamphlet against the following evening.

"And now," said Lord Dawton—"that we have settled this affair—what news from France?"—

*　　*　　*　　*　　*　　*　　*

"I wish," sighed Lord Dawton, as we were calculating our forces, "that we could gain over Lord Guloseton."

"What, the facetious epicure?" said I.

"The same," answered Dawton: "we want him as a dinner-giver; and, besides, he has four votes in the Lower House."

"Well," said I, "he is indolent and independent—it is not impossible."

"Do you know him?" answered Dawton.

"No," said I.

Dawton sighed.—"And young A———?" said the statesman, after a pause.

"Has an expensive mistress, and races. Your lordship might be sure of him, were you in power, and sure not to have him while you are out of it."

"And B.?" rejoined Dawton.

*　　*　　*　　*　　*　　*　　*

CHAPTER XXI

Mangez-vous bien, Monsieur?
Oui, et bois encore mieux.
    Mons. de Porceaugnac[1]

MY PAMPHLET TOOK PRODIGIOUSLY. THE AUTHORSHIP was attributed to the most talented member of the Opposition; and though there were many errors in style, and (I *now* think)* many

---

1. "Are you enjoying your food, Sir?"—"Yes, and the drink even more" (Molière, *Monsieur de Porceaugnac*, I, 11).

sophisms in the reasoning, yet it carried the end proposed by all ambition of whatever species—and imposed upon the taste of the public.

Sometime afterwards, I was going down the stairs at Almack's, when I heard an altercation, high and grave, at the door of reception. To my surprise, I found Lord Guloseton and a very young man in great wrath; the latter had never been to Almack's before, and had forgotten his ticket. Guloseton, who belonged to a very different set to that of the Almackians, insisted that his word was enough to bear his juvenile companion through. The ticket inspector was irate and obdurate, and having seldom or ever* seen Lord Guloseton himself, paid very little respect to his authority.

As I was wrapping myself in my cloak, Guloseton turned to me, for passion makes men open their hearts: too eager for an opportunity of acquiring the epicure's acquaintance, I offered to get his friend admittance in an instant; the offer was delightedly accepted, and I soon procured a small piece of pencilled paper from Lady ———, which effectually silenced the Charon, and opened the Stygian via to the Elysium beyond.

Guloseton overwhelmed me with his thanks. I remounted the stairs with him—took every opportunity of ingratiating myself— received an invitation to dinner on the following day, and left Willis's transported at the goodness of my fortune.

At the hour of eight on the ensuing evening, I had just made my entrance into Lord Guloseton's drawing-room. It was a small apartment furnished with great luxury and some taste. A Venus of Titian's was placed over the chimney-piece, in all the gorgeous voluptuousness of her unveiled beauty—the pouting lip, not *silent* though *shut*— the eloquent lid drooping over the eye, whose *réveille** you could so easily imagine—the arms—the limbs—the attitude, so composed, yet so redolent of life—all seemed to indicate that sleep was not forgetfulness, and that the dreams of the goddess were not wholly inharmonious with the waking realities in which it was her gentle prerogative to indulge. On either side, was a picture of the delicate and golden hues of Claude; these were the only landscapes in the room; the remaining pictures were more suitable to the Venus of the luxurious Italian. Here was one of the beauties of Sir Peter Lely;[2] there was an admirable copy of the Hero and Leander. On the table

---

2. Sir Peter Lely (1617–80): English painter. In the next sentence, Johannes Secundus (1511–36): Dutch poet, whose *Basia* was published in 1539.

lay the Basia of Johannes Secundus, and a few French works on Gastronomy.

As for the *genius loci*—you must imagine a middle-sized, middle-aged man, with an air rather of delicate than florid health. But little of the effects of his good cheer were apparent in the external man. His cheeks were neither swollen nor inflated—his person, though not thin, was of no unwieldy obesity—the tip of his nasal organ was, it is true, of a more ruby tinge than the rest, and one carbuncle, of tender age and gentle dyes, diffused its mellow and moonlight influence over the physiognomical scenery—his forehead was high and bald, and the few locks which still rose above it, were carefully and gracefully curled *à l' antique*. Beneath a pair of grey shaggy brows, which their noble owner had a strange habit of raising and depressing, according to the nature of his remarks), rolled two very small, piercing, arch, restless orbs, of a tender green; and the mouth, which was wide and thick-lipped, was expressive of great sensuality, and curved upwards in a perpetual smile.

Such was Lord Guloseton. To my surprise no other guest but myself appeared.

"A new friend," said he, as we descended into the dining-room, "is like a new dish—one must have him all to oneself, thoroughly to enjoy and rightly to understand him."

"A noble precept," said I, with enthusiasm. "Of all vices, indiscriminate hospitality is the most pernicious. It allows us neither conversation nor dinner, and realizing the mythological fable of Tantalus, gives us starvation in the midst of plenty."

"You are right," said Guloseton, solemnly; "I never ask above six persons to dinner, and I never dine out; for a bad dinner, Mr. Pelham, a bad dinner is a most serious—I may add, *the* most serious calamity."

"Yes," I replied, "for it carries with it no consolation: a buried friend may be replaced—a lost mistress renewed—a slandered character be recovered—even a broken constitution restored; but a dinner, once lost, is irremediable; that day is for ever departed; an appetite once thrown away can never, till the cruel prolixity of the gastric agents is over, be regained. *'Il y a tant de maitresses,* (says the admirable Corneille), *'il n'y a qu'un diner.'* "[3]

"You speak like an oracle—*like the Cook's Oracle,* Mr. Pelham:

---

3. Bulwer has parodied a line from Corneille's *Le Cid,* III, 6: "There are so many mistresses, but there is only one dinner."

may I send you some soup, it is *à la Carmelite?* But what are you about to do with that case?"

"It contains" (said I) "my spoon, my knife, and my fork. Nature afflicted me with a propensity, which through these machines I have endeavoured to remedy by art. I eat with *too great a rapidity*. It is a most unhappy failing, for one often hurries over in *one* minute, what ought to have afforded the fullest delight for the period of *five*. It is, indeed, a vice which deadens enjoyment, as well as abbreviates it; it is a shameful waste of the gifts, and a melancholy perversion of the bounty, of Providence: my conscience tormented me; but the habit, fatally indulged in early childhood, was not easy to overcome. At last I resolved to construct a spoon of peculiarly shallow dimensions, a fork so small, that it could only raise a certain portion to my mouth, and a knife rendered blunt and jagged, so that it required a proper and just time to carve the goods 'the gods provide me.' My lord, 'the lovely Thais[4] sits beside me' in the form of a bottle of Madeira. Suffer me to take wine with you?"

"With pleasure, my good friend; let us drink to the memory of the Carmelites, to whom we are indebted for this inimitable soup."

"Yes!" I cried. "Let *us* for once shake off the prejudices of sectarian faith, and do justice to one order of those incomparable men, who, retiring from the cares of an idle and sinful world, gave themselves with undivided zeal and attention to the theory and practice of the profound science of gastronomy. It is reserved for us, my lord, to pay a grateful tribute of memory to those exalted recluses, who, through a long period of barbarism and darkness, preserved, in the solitude of their cloisters, whatever of Roman luxury and classic dainties have come down to this later age. We will drink to the Carmelites as a sect, but we will drink also to the monks as a body. Had we lived in those days, we had been monks ourselves."

"It is singular," answered Lord Guloseton— "(by the by, what think you of this turbot?)—to trace the history of the kitchen; it affords the greatest scope to the philosopher and the moralist. The ancients seemed to have been more mental, more imaginative, than we are in their dishes; they fed their bodies as well as their minds upon delusion: for instance, they esteemed beyond all price the tongues of nightingales, because they tasted the very music of the

---

4. Thais: notorious Athenian courtesan of the late fourth century B.C. This quotation and that in the previous sentence is from Dryden's "Alexander's Feast," lines 95–6.

birds in the organs of their utterance. That is what I call the poetry of gastronomy!"

"Yes," said I, with a sigh, "they certainly had, in some respects, the advantage over us. Who can pore over the suppers of Apicius without the fondest regret? The venerable Ude[5] implies, that the study has not progressed. 'Cookery (he says, in the first part of his work) posesses but few innovators.' "

"It is with the greatest diffidence," said Guloseton, (his mouth full of truth and turbot), "that we may dare to differ from so great an authority. Indeed, so high is my veneration for that wise man, that if all the evidence of my sense and reason were on one side, and the dictum of the great Ude upon the other, I should be inclined—I think, I *should be determined*—to relinquish the former, and adopt the latter."[6]

"Bravo, my lord," cried I, warmly. " '*Qu'un Cuisinier est un mortel divin!*'[7] Why should we not be proud of our knowledge in cookery? It is the soul of festivity at all times, and to all ages. How many marriages have been the consequence of meeting at dinner? How much good fortune has been the result of a good supper? At what moment of our existence are we happier than at table? There hatred and animosity are lulled to sleep, and pleasure alone reigns. Here the cook, by his skill and attention, anticipates our wishes in the happiest selection of the best dishes and decorations. Here our wants are satisfied, our minds and bodies invigorated, and ourselves qualified for the high delights of love, music, poetry, dancing, and other pleasures; and is he, whose talents have produced these happy effects, to rank no higher in the scale of man than a common servant?[8]

" 'Yes,' cries the venerable professor himself, in a virtuous and prophetic paroxysm of indignant merit—'yes, my disciples, if you adopt, and attend to the rules I have laid down, the self-love of mankind will consent at last, that cookery shall rank in the class of the sciences, and its professors deserve the name of artists!' "[9]

---

5. Q.—The venerable Bede.—*Printer's Devil.* [B-L] The Printer's Devil is Bulwer's little joke, for Ude is the person referred to; Bulwer has a fine point of wit here, however, for he wants to carry forward the running analogy between the religious temperament and the gourmand's taste. The Venerable Bede was a seventh century A.D. English theologian and historian.

6. See the speech of Mr. Brougham in honour of Mr. Fox. [B-L] Henry Brougham (1778–1868) and Charles James Fox (1749–1806) were both famous Whig statesmen.

7. "What a human divinity a chef is!"

8. Ude, verbatim. [B-L]

9. Ibid. [B-L]

"My dear, dear Sir," exclaimed Guloseton, with a kindred glow, "I discover in you a spirit similar to my own. Let us drink long life to the venerable Ude!"

"I pledge you, with all my soul," said I, filling my glass to the brim.

"What a pity," rejoined Guloseton, "that Ude, whose *practical* science was so perfect, should ever have written, or suffered others to write, the work published under his name; true it is that the opening part which you have so feelingly recited, is composed with a grace, a charm beyond the reach of art; but the instructions are vapid, and frequently so erroneous, as to make me* suspect their authenticity; but, after all, cooking is not capable of becoming a written science— it is the philosophy of practice!"

"Ah! by Lucullus,"[10] exclaimed I, interrupting my host, "what a visionary *béchamelle!* Oh, the inimitable sauce; these chickens are indeed worthy of the honour of being dressed. Never, my lord, as long as you live, eat a chicken in the country; excuse a pun, you will have *foul* fare."

> " 'J'ai toujours redouté la volaille perfide,
> Qui brave les efforts d'une dent intrépide;
> Souvent par un ami, dans ses champs entrainé,
> J'ai reconnu le soir le coq infortuné
> Qui m'avait le matin à l'aurore naissante
> Réveillé brusquement de sa voix glapissante;
> Je l'avais admiré dans le sein de la cour,
> Avec des yeux jaloux, j'avais vu son amour.
> Hélas! la malheureux, abjurant sa tendresse,
> Exerçait à souper sa fureur vengeresse.' "[11]

Pardon the prolixity of my quotation for the sake of its value."

---

10. Lucullus: first century B.C. Roman general famous for the splendid table he set.

11.
> "Ever I dread (when dup'd a day to spend
> At his snug villa, by some fatal friend)
> Grim chanticleer, whose breast, devoid of ruth,
> Braves the stout effort of the desperate tooth
> Oft have I recognized at eve, the bird,
> Whose morning notes my ear prophetic heard,
> Whose tender courtship won my pain'd regard,
> Amids't the plum'd seraglio of the yard.
> Tender no more—behold him in your plate—
> And now, while eating, you revenge his fate."

Quotation unidentified. [Bulwer's paraphrase; 1840 ed.]

"I do, I do," answered Guloseton, laughing at the humour of the lines; till, suddenly checking himself, he said, "we must be grave, Mr. Pelham, it will never do to laugh. What would become of our digestions?"

"True," said I, relapsing into seriousness; "and if you will allow me one more quotation, you will see what my author adds with regard to any abrupt interruption.

> " 'Défendez que personne au milieu d'un banquet,
> Ne vous vienne donner un avis indiscret,
> Ecartez ce fâcheux qui vers vous s'achemine,
> Rien ne doit déranger l'honnête homme qui dine."[12]

"Admirable advice," said Guloseton, toying with a *filet mignon de poulet*. "Do you remember an example in the Bailly of Suffren,[13] who, being in India, was waited upon by a deputation of natives while he was at dinner. 'Tell them,' said he, 'that the Christian religion peremptorily forbids every Christian, while at table, to occupy himself with any earthly subject, except the function of eating.' The deputation retired in the profoundest respect at the exceeding devotion of the French general."

"Well," said I, after we had chuckled gravely and quietly, with the care of our digestion before us, for a few minutes—"well, however good the invention was, the idea is not entirely new, for the Greeks esteemed eating and drinking plentifully, a sort of offering to the gods; and Aristotle explains the very word, *Thoinai*, or feasts, by an etymological exposition, *'that it was thought a duty to the gods to be drunk;'* no bad idea of our classical patterns of antiquity. Polypheme, too, in the Cyclops of Euripides, no doubt a very sound theologian, says, his stomach is his only deity; and Xenophon tells us, that as the Athenians exceeded all other people in the number of their gods, so they exceeded them also in the number of their feasts.[14] May I send your lordship an ortolan?"*

"Pelham, my boy," said Guloseton, whose eyes began to roll and

---

12. "At meals no access to the indiscreet;
    All are intruders on the wise who eat.
    In that blest hour your bore's the veriest sinner!
    Nought must disturb a man of worth—at dinner."
  Quotation unidentified. [Bulwer's paraphrase; 1840 ed.]

13. Pierre André de Suffren de Saint-Tropez (1726–88): famous French naval officer.

14. Aristotle *Problemata* 530; Euripides *Cyclops* 335; Xenophon "On the Athenian Republic."

twinkle with a brilliancy suited to the various liquids which ministered to their rejoicing orbs; "I love you for your classics. Polypheme was a wise fellow, a very wise fellow, and it was a terrible shame in Ulysses to put out his eye.[15] No wonder that the ingenious savage made a deity of his stomach; to what known and visible source, on this earth, was he indebted for a keener enjoyment—a more rapturous and a more constant delight? No wonder he honoured it with his gratitude, and supplied it with his peace-offerings;—let us imitate so great an example;—let us make our digestive receptacles a temple, to which we will consecrate the choicest goods we possess;—let us conceive no pecuniary sacrifice too great, which procures for our altar an acceptable gift;—let us deem it an impiety to hesitate, if a sauce seems extravagant, or an ortolan too dear; and let our last act in this sublunary existence, be a solemn festival in honour of our unceasing benefactor."

"Amen to your creed," said I: "edibilatory Epicurism holds the key to all morality: for do we not see now how sinful it is to yield to an obscene and exaggerated intemperance?—would it not be to the last degree ungrateful to the great source of our enjoyment, to overload it with a weight which would oppress it with languor, or harass it with pain; and finally to drench away the effects of our impiety with some nauseous potation which revolts it, tortures it, convulses, irritates, enfeebles it, through every particle of its system? How wrong in us to give way to anger, jealousy, revenge, or any evil passion; for does not all that affects the mind operate also upon the stomach; and how can we be so vicious, so obdurate, as to forget, for a momentary indulgence, our debt to what you have so justly designated our perpetual benefactor?"

"Right," said Lord Guloseton, " a bumper to the morality of the stomach."

The dessert was now on the table. "I have dined well," said Guloseton, stretching his legs with an air of supreme satisfaction; "but—" and here my philosopher sighed deeply—"we cannot *dine again till to-morrow!* Happy, happy, happy common people, who can eat supper! Would to Heaven, that I might have one boon—perpetual appetite—a digestive Houri, which renewed its virginity every time it was touched. Alas! for the instability of human enjoyment. But now that we have no immediate hope to anticipate, let us cultivate the pleasures of memory. What thought you of the *veau à la Dauphine?*"

---

15. *Odyssey,* book 9.

"Pardon me if I hesitate at giving my opinion, till I have corrected my judgment by yours."

"Why, then, I own I was somewhat displeased—disappointed as it were—with that dish; the fact is, veal ought to be killed in its very first infancy; they suffer it to grow to too great an age. It becomes a sort of *hobbydehoy,* and possesses nothing of veal but its insipidity, or of beef, but its toughness."

"Yes," said I, "it is only in their veal, that the French surpass us; their other meats want the ruby juices and elastic freshness of ours. Monsieur L——— allowed this truth, with a candour worthy of his vast mind. *Mon Dieu!* what claret!—what a body! and, let me add, what a *soul,* beneath it! Who would *drink* wine like this? it is only made to *taste.* It is like first love—too pure for the eagerness of enjoyment; the rapture it inspires is in a touch, a kiss. It is a pity, my lord, that we do not serve perfumes at dessert: it is their appropriate place. In confectionary (delicate invention of the Sylphs) we imitate the forms of the rose and the jessamine; why not their odours too? What is nature without its scents?—and as long as they are absent from our desserts, it is in vain that the Bard exclaims, that—

> ——"'L'observateur de la belle Nature,
> S'extasie en voyant des fleurs en confiture.' "[16]

"It is an exquisite idea of yours," said Guloseton—"and the next time you dine here, we will have perfumes. Dinner ought to be a reunion of all the senses—

> "'Gladness to the ear, nerve, heart, and sense.' "

There was a momentary pause. "My lord," said I, "what a lusty lusciousness in this pear! it is like the style of the old English poets. What think you of the seeming good understanding between Mr. Gaskell and the Whigs?"

"I trouble myself little about it," replied Guloseton, helping himself to some preserves—"politics disturb the digestion."

"Well," thought I, "I must ascertain some point in this man's character easier to handle than his epicurism: all men are vain: let us find out the peculiar vanity of mine host."

"The Tories,"* said I, "seem to think themselves exceedingly secure; they attach no importance to the neutral members: it was

---

16. "The observer of nature's beauty delights to see preserved flowers." This quotation and the English quotation just below have not been identified.

but the other day, Lord ——— told me that he did not care a straw for Mr. ———, notwithstanding he possessed *four* votes. Heard you ever such arrogance?"

"No, indeed," said Guloseton, with a lazy air of indifference—"are you a favourer of the olive?"

"No," said I, "I love it not; it hath an under taste of sourness, and an upper of oil, which do not make harmony to my palate. But, as I was saying, the Whigs, on the contrary, pay the utmost deference to their partizans; and a man of fortune, rank, and parliamentary influence, might have all the power without the trouble of a leader."

"Very likely," said Guloseton, drowsily.

"I must change my battery," thought I; but while I was meditating a new attack, the following note was brought me:—

"For God's sake, Pelham, come out to me: I am waiting in the street to see you; come directly, or it will be too late to render me the service I would ask of you.

"R. GLANVILLE."

I rose instantly. "You must excuse me, Lord Guloseton, I am called suddenly away."

"Ha! ha!" laughed the gourmand; "some tempting viand—*post prandia Callirhoe.*"[17]

"My good lord," said I, not heeding his insinuation—"I leave you with the greatest regret."

"And I part from you with the same; it is a real pleasure to see such a person at dinner."

"Adieu! my host—*'Je vais vivre et manger en sage.' "*[18]

---

17. "Calliroe after dinner" (Persius *Satires* 1.134).
18. "I go to live and eat wisely." Unidentified.

CHAPTER XXII

I do defy him, and I spit at him,
Call him a slanderous coward and a villain—
Which to maintain I will allow him odds.

SHAKSPEARE[1]

I FOUND GLANVILLE WALKING BEFORE THE DOOR WITH a rapid and uneven step.

"Thank Heaven!" he said, when he saw me—"I have been twice to Mivart's to find you. The second time, I saw your servant, who told me where you were gone. I knew you well enough to be sure of your kindness."

Glanville broke off abruptly: and after a short pause, said, with a quick, low, hurried tone—"The office I wish you to take upon yourself is this:—go immediately to Sir John Tyrrell, with a challenge from me. Ever since I last saw you, I have been hunting out that man, and in vain. He had then left town. He returned this evening, and quits it to-morrow: you have no time to lose."

"My dear Glanville," said I, "I have no wish to learn any secret you would conceal from me; but forgive me if I ask for some further instructions than those you have afforded me. Upon what plea am I to call out Sir John Tyrrell? and what answer am I to give to any excuses he may create?"

"I have anticipated your reply," said Glanville, with ill-subdued impatience; "you have only to give this paper: it will prevent all discussion. Read it if you will;* I have left it unsealed for that purpose."

I cast my eyes over the lines Glanville thrust into my hand; they ran thus:—

"The time has at length come for me to demand the atonement so long delayed. The bearer of this, who is, probably, known to you, will

---

1. *Richard II*, 1, 160–62.

arrange with any person you may appoint, the hour and place of our meeting. He is unacquainted with the grounds of my complaint against you, but he is satisfied of my honour: your second will, I presume, be the same with respect to *yours*. It is for me only to question the latter, and to declare you solemnly to be void alike of principle and courage, a villain, and a poltroon.

"Reginald Granville."

"You are my earliest friend," said I, when I had read this soothing epistle; "and I will not flinch from the place you assign me; but I tell you fairly and frankly, that I would sooner cut off my right hand than suffer it to give this note to Sir John Tyrrell."

Glanville made no answer; we walked on till he stopped suddenly, and said, "My carriage is at the corner of the street; you must go instantly; Tyrrell lodges at the Clarendon; you will find me at home on your return."

I pressed his hand, and hurried on my mission. It was, I own, one peculiarly unwelcome and displeasing. In the first place, I did not love to be made a party in a business of the nature of which I was so profoundly ignorant.* Besides, Glanville was more dear to me than any one, judging only of my external character, would suppose; and constitutionally indifferent as I am to danger for myself, I trembled like a woman at the peril I was instrumental in bringing upon him. But what weighed upon me far more than either of these reflections, was the recollection of Ellen. Should her brother fall in an engagement in which I was his supposed adviser, with what success could I hope for those feelings from her, which, at present, constituted the tenderest and the brightest of my hopes? In the midst of these disagreeable ideas the carriage stopped at the door of Tyrrell's Hotel.

The waiter said Sir John was in the coffee-room; thither I immediately marched. Seated in the box nearest the fire sat Tyrrell, and two men, of that old-fashioned *roué* set, whose members indulged in debauchery, as if it were an attribute of manliness, and esteemed it, as long as it were hearty and English, rather a virtue to boast of, than a vice to disown. Tyrrell nodded to me familiarly as I approached him; and I saw, by the half-emptied bottles before him, and the flush of his sallow countenance, that he had not been sparing of his libations. I whispered that I wished to speak to him on a subject of great importance; he rose with much reluctance, and, after swallowing a large tumbler-full of port wine to fortify him for the task, he led the way to a small room, where he seated himself, and asked me, with

247

his usual mixture of bluntness and good-breeding, the nature of my business. I made him no reply: I contented myself with placing Glanville's *billet doux* in his hand. The room was dimly lighted with a single candle, and the small and capricious fire, near which the gambler was seated, threw its *upward* light, by starts and intervals, over the strong features and deep lines of his countenance. It would have been a study worthy of Rembrandt.

I drew my chair near him, and half shading my eyes with my hand, sat down in silence to mark the effect the letter would produce. Tyrrell (I imagine) was a man originally of hardy nerves, and had been thrown much in the various situations of life where the disguise of all outward emotion is easily and insensibly taught; but whether his frame had been shattered by his excesses, or that the insulting language of the note touched him to the quick, he seemed perfectly unable to govern his feelings; the lines were written hastily, and the light, as I said before, was faint and imperfect, and he was forced to pause over each word as he proceeded, so that "the iron had full time to enter into his soul."[2]

Passion, however, developed itself differently in him than in Glanville: in the latter, it was a rapid transition of powerful feelings, one angry wave dashing over another; it was the passion of a strong and keenly susceptible mind, to which every sting was a dagger, and which used the force of a giant to dash away the insect which attacked it. In Tyrrell, it was passion acting on a callous mind but a broken frame—his hand trembled violently—his voice faltered—he could scarcely command the muscles which enabled him to speak; but there was no fiery start—no indignant burst—no flashing forth of the soul; in him, it was the body overcoming and paralyzing the mind. In Glanville it was the mind governing and convulsing the body.

"Mr. Pelham," he said at last, after a few preliminary efforts to clear his voice, "this note requires some consideration. I know not at present whom to appoint as my second—will you call upon me early to-morrow?"

"I am sorry," said I, "that my sole instructions were to get an immediate answer from you. Surely either of the gentlemen I saw with you would officiate as your second?"

Tyrrell made no reply for some moments. He was endeavouring to compose himself, and in some measure he succeeded. He raised his

---

2. Psalms 105:18.

248

head with a haughty air of defiance, and tearing the paper deliberately, though still with uncertain and trembling fingers, he stamped his foot upon the atoms.

"Tell your principal," said he, "that I retort upon him the foul and false words he has uttered against me; that I trample upon his assertions with the same scorn I feel towards himself; and that before this hour to-morrow, I will confront him *to* death as through life. For the rest, Mr. Pelham, I cannot name my second till the morning; leave me your address, and you shall hear from me before you are stirring. Have you any thing farther with me?"

"Nothing," said I, laying my card on the table, "I have fulfilled the most ungrateful charge ever entrusted to me. I wish you good night."

I re-entered the carriage, and drove to Glanville's. I broke into the room rather abruptly; Glanville was leaning on the table, and gazing intently on a small miniature. A pistol-case lay beside him: one of the pistols in order for use, and the other still unarranged; the room was, as usual, covered with books and papers, and on the costly cushions of the ottoman, lay the large, black dog, which I remembered well as his companion of yore, and which he kept with him constantly, as the only thing in the world whose society he could at all times bear: the animal lay curled up, with its quick, black eye fixed watchfully upon its master, and directly I entered, it uttered, though without moving, a low, warning growl.

Glanville looked up, and in some confusion thrust the picture into a drawer of the table, and asked me my news. I told him word for word what had passed. Glanville set his teeth, and clenched his hand firmly; and then, as if his anger was at once appeased, he suddenly changed the subject and tone of our conversation. He spoke with great cheerfulness and humour, on the various topics of the day; touched upon politics; laughed at Lord Guloseton, and seemed as indifferent and unconscious of the event of the morrow as my peculiar constitution would have rendered myself.

When I rose to depart, for I had too great an interest in *him* to feel much for the subjects he conversed on, he said, "I shall write one line to my mother, and another to my poor sister; you will deliver them if I fall, for I have sworn that one of us shall not quit the ground alive. I shall be all impatience to know the hour you will arrange with Tyrrell's second. God bless you, and farewell for the present."

CHAPTER XXIII

Charge, Chester, charge!
MARMION[1]

Though this was one of the first *mercantile* transactions of my life, I had no doubt about acquitting myself with reputation.

Vicar of Wakefield

THE NEXT MORNING I WAS AT BREAKFAST, WHEN A packet was brought me from Tyrrell; it contained a sealed letter to Glanville, and a brief note to myself. The latter I transcribe:—

"MY DEAR SIR,

"The enclosed letter to Sir Reginald Glanville will explain my reasons for not keeping my pledge: suffice it to state to you, that they are such as wholly to exonerate me, and fairly to satisfy Sir Reginald. It will be useless to call upon me; I leave town before you will receive this. Respect for myself obliges me to add that, although there are circumstances to forbid my meeting Sir Reginald Glanville, there are none to prevent my demanding satisfaction of any one, *whoever he may be,* who shall deem himself authorized to call my motives into question.

"I have the honour, &c.

"JOHN TYRRELL."

It was not till I had thrice read this letter that I could credit its contents. From all I had seen of Tyrrell's character, I had no reason to suspect him to be less courageous than the generality of worldly men; and the conclusion* of his letter, evidently pointed at myself, should I venture to impugn his conduct, seemed by no means favourable to any suspicion of his cowardice. And yet, when I considered the violent language of Glanville's letter, and Tyrrell's apparent resolution the night before, I scarcely knew to what more honourable

---

1. Walter Scott, *Marmion*, 6, 991. The second epigraph is from Oliver Goldsmith, *The Vicar of Wakefield*, chapter 14.

motive to attribute his conduct. However, I lost no time in despatching the whole packet to Glanville, with a few lines from myself, saying I should call in an hour.

When I fulfilled this promise, Glanville's servant told me his master had gone out immediately on reading the letters I had sent, and had merely left word that he should not return home the whole day. That night he was to have brought an important motion before the House. A message from him, pleading sudden and alarming illness, devolved this duty upon another member of our party. Lord Dawton was in despair: the motion was lost by a great majority; the papers, the whole of that week, were filled with the most triumphant abuse and ridicule of the Whigs. Never was that unhappy and persecuted party reduced to so low an ebb: never did there seem a fainter probability of their coming into power. They appeared almost annihilated— a mere *nominis umbra.*

On the eighth day from Glanville's disappearance, a sudden event in the cabinet threw the whole country into confusion; the Tories trembled to the very soles of their easy slippers of sinecure and office; the eyes of the public were turned to the Whigs; and chance seemed to effect in an instant that change in their favour, which all their toil, trouble, eloquence, and art, had been unable for so many years to render even a remote probability.

But there was a strong though secret party in the state, which reminded me of the independents in the reign of Charles the First, that, concealed under a general name, worked only for a private end, and made a progress in number and respectability, not the less sure for being but little suspected.[2] Foremost among the leaders of this party was Lord Vincent. Dawton, who knew of their existence, and regarded them with fear and jealousy, considered the struggle rather between them and himself, than any longer between himself and the Tories; and strove, while it was yet time, to reinforce himself by a body of allies, which, should the contest really take place, might be certain of giving him the superiority. The Marquis of Chester was among the most powerful of the neutral noblemen: it was of the greatest importance to gain him to the cause. He was a sturdy, sporting, independent man, who lived chiefly in the country, and

---

2. The Roundheads were originally part of the Parliamentary party, but as Charles I grew more resistant to the rights of Parliament a group of Puritan reformers formed a coalition to oppose the king more vigorously then the less radical Parliamentarians were doing. The two groups eventually became the Roundheads and the Constitutional Royalists.

turned his ambition rather towards promoting the excellence of quadrupeds, than the bad passions of men. To this personage Lord Dawton implored me to be the bearer of a letter, and to aid, with all the dexterity in my power, the purpose it was intended to effect. It was the most consequential mission yet entrusted to me, and I felt eager to turn my diplomatic energies to so good an account. Accordingly, one bright morning I wrapt myself carefully in my cloak, placed my invaluable person safely in my carriage, and set off to Chester Park, in the county of Suffolk.

CHAPTER XXIV

Hinc Canibus blandis rabies venit—
VIRGIL. *Georg.*[1]

I SHOULD HAVE MENTIONED, THAT THE DAY AFTER I sent Glanville Tyrrell's communication, I received a short and hurried note from the former, saying, that he had left London in pursuit of Tyrrell, and that he would not rest till he had brought him to account. In the hurry of the public events in which I had been of late so actively engaged, my mind had not had leisure to dwell much upon Glanville; but when I was alone in my carriage, that singular being, and the mystery which attended him, forced themselves upon my reflection, in spite of all the importance of my mission.

I was leaning back in the carriage, at (I think) Ware, while they were changing horses, when a voice, strongly associated with my meditations, struck upon my ear. I looked out, and saw Thornton standing in the yard, attired with all his original smartness of boot and breeches: he was employed in smoking a cigar, sipping brandy and water, and exercising his conversational talents in a mixture of slang and jockeyism, addressed to two or three men of his own rank of life, and seemingly his companions. His brisk eye soon discovered me, and he swaggered to the carriage door with that ineffable assurance of manner which was so peculiarly his own.

---

1. "Then madness strikes the fawning dogs" (Virgil *Georgics* 3.496).

"Ah, ah, Mr. Pelham," said he, "going to Newmarket, I suppose? bound there myself—like to be found among my *betters*. Ha, ha—excuse a pun: what odds on the favourite? What! you won't bet, Mr. Pelham? close and sly at present; well, *the silent sow sups all the broth*—eh!—"

"I'm not going to Newmarket," I replied: "I never attend races."

"Indeed!" answered Thornton. "Well, if I was as rich as you, I would soon make or spend a fortune on the course. Seen Sir John Tyrrell? No! He is to be there. Nothing can cure him of gambling—what's bred in the bone, &c. Good day, Mr. Pelham—won't keep you any longer—sharp shower coming on. 'The devil will soon be basting his wife with a leg of mutton,' as the proverb says—*au plaisir,** Mr. Pelham.''

And at these words my post-boy started, and released me from my *bête noire*. I spare my reader an account of my miscellaneous reflections on Thornton, Dawton, Vincent, politics, Glanville, and *Ellen*, and will land him, without further delay, at Chester Park.

I was ushered through a large oak hall of the reign of James the First, into a room strongly resembling the principal apartment of a club; two or three round tables were covered with newspapers, journals, racing calendars, &c. An enormous fire-place was crowded with men of all ages, I had almost said, of all ranks; but, however various they might appear in their mien and attire, they were wholly of the patrician order. One thing, however, in this room, belied its similitude* to the apartment of a club, viz., a number of dogs, that lay in scattered groups upon the floor. Before the windows were several horses, in body-cloths, led or, rode to exercise upon a plain in the park, levelled as smooth as a bowling-green at Putney; and stationed at an oriel window, in earnest attention to the scene without, were two men; the tallest of these was Lord Chester. There was a stiffness and inelegance in his address which prepossessed me strongly against him. *"Les manières que l'on néglige comme de petites choses, sont souvent ce qui fait que les hommes décident de vous en bien ou en mal."*[2]

I had long since, when I was at the University, been introduced to Lord Chester; but I had quite forgotten his person, and he the very circumstance. I said, in a low tone, that I was the bearer of a letter of some importance from our mutual friend, Lord Dawton,

2. "The manners which one neglects are often precisely those on which men decide on you favorably or the reverse" (La Bruyère, *Les Caractères*, "De la Société," no. 31). [Bulwer's translation; 1840 ed.]

and that I should request the honour of a private interview at Lord Chester's first convenience.

His lordship bowed, with an odd mixture of the civility of a jockey and the hauteur of a head groom of the stud, and led the way to a small apartment, which I afterwards discovered he called his own. (I never could make out, by the way, why, in England, the very worst room in the house is always appropriated to the master of it, and dignified by the appellation of "the gentleman's own.") I gave the Newmarket grandee the letter intended for him, and quietly seating myself, awaited the result.

He read it through slowly and silently, and then taking out a huge pocket-book, full of racing bets, horses' ages, jockey opinions, and such like memoranda, he placed it with much solemnity among this dignified company, and then said, with a cold, but would-be courteous air, "My friend, Lord Dawton, says you are entirely in his confidence, Mr. Pelham. I hope you will honour me with your company at Chester Park for two or three days, during which time I shall have leisure to reply to Lord Dawton's letter. Will you take some refreshment?"

I answered the first sentence in the affirmative, and the latter in the negative; and Lord Chester thinking it perfectly unnecessary to trouble himself with any further questions or remarks, which the whole jockey club might not hear, took me back into the room we had quitted, and left me to find, or make whatever acquaintance I could. Pampered and spoiled as I was in the most difficult circles of London, I was beyond measure indignant at the cavalier demeanour of this rustic Thane, whom I considered a being as immeasurably beneath me in every thing else, as he really was in antiquity of birth, and, I venture to hope, in cultivation of intellect.* I looked round the room, and did not recognize a being of my acquaintance: I seemed literally thrown into a new world: the very language in which the conversation was held, sounded strange to my ear. I had always transgressed my general rule of knowing all men in all grades, in the single respect of *sporting characters:* they were a species of bipeds, that I would never recognize as belonging to the human race. Alas! I now found the bitter effects of not following my usual maxims. It is a dangerous thing to encourage too great a disdain of one's inferiors: pride must have a fall.

After I had been a whole quarter of an hour in this strange place, my better genius came to my aid. Since I found no society among the two-legged brutes, I turned to the quadrupeds. At one corner of the

254

room lay a black terrier of the true English breed; at another was a short, sturdy, wirey one, of the Scotch. I soon formed a friendship with each of these *canine Pelei*, (little bodies with great souls), and then by degrees alluring them from their retreat to the centre of the room, I fairly endeavoured to set them by the ears. Thanks to the national antipathy, I succeeded to my heart's content. The contest soon aroused the other individuals of the genus—up they started from their repose, like Roderic Dhu's[3] merry men, and incontinently flocked to the scene of battle.

"To it," said I; and I took one by the leg and another by the throat, and dashing them against each other, turned all their peevish irascibility at the affront into mutual aggression.* In a very few moments, the whole room was a scene of uproarious confusion; the beasts yelled, and bit, and struggled, with the most delectable ferocity. To add to the effect, the various owners of the dogs crowded round—some to stimulate, others to appease the fury of the combatants. As for me, I flung myself into an arm chair, and gave way to an excess of merriment, which only enraged the spectators more: many were the glances of anger, many the murmurs of reproach directed against me. Lord Chester himself eyed me with an air of astonished indignation, that redoubled my hilarity:* at length, the conflict was assuaged—by dint of blows, and kicks, and remonstrances from their dignified proprietors, the dogs slowly withdrew, one with the loss of half an ear, another with a shoulder put out,* a third with a mouth increased by one-half of its natural dimensions.

In short, every one engaged in the conflict bore some token of its severity.* I did not wait for the thunder-storm I foresaw:* I rose with a *nonchalant* yawn of *ennui*—marched out of the apartment, called a servant—demanded my own room—repaired to it, and immersed the internal faculties of my head in Mignet's History of the Revolution,[4] while Bedos busied himself in its outward embellishment.

---

3. Roderick Dhu: a highland chieftain and one of the principal characters in Scott's *Lady of the Lake*.

4. Auguste Mignet (1796–1884), *Histoire de la Révolution française* (1824).

CHAPTER XXV

Noster ludos, spectaverat unà,
Luserat in campo, Fortunæ filius omnes.

HOR[1]

I DID NOT LEAVE MY ROOM TILL THE FIRST DINNER-BELL
had ceased a sufficient time to allow me the pleasing hope that I should
have but a few moments to wait in the drawing-room, previous* to
the grand epoch and ceremony of an European day. The manner most
natural to me, is one rather open and easy; but I pique myself peculiarly upon a certain (though occasional) air, which keeps impertinence aloof; in fine, I am by no means a person with whom others
would lightly take a liberty, or to whom they would readily offer or
resent an affront.* This day I assumed a double quantum of dignity,
in entering a room which I well knew must be filled with my enemies:*
there were a few women round Lady Chester, and, as I always feel
reassured by a sight of the dear sex, I walked towards them.

Judge of my delight, when I discovered amongst the group, Lady
Harriett Garrett. It is true that I had no particular predilection for
that lady, but the sight of a negress I had seen before, I should have
hailed with rapture in so desolate and inhospitable a place. If my
pleasure at seeing Lady Harriett was great, hers seemed equally so
at receiving my salutation. She asked me if I knew Lady Chester—
and on my negative reply, immediately introduced me to that personage. I now found myself quite at home; my spirits rose, and I exerted
every nerve to be as charming as possible. In youth, to endeavour is to
succeed.

I gave a most animated account of the canine battle, interspersed
with various sarcasms on the owners of the combatants, which were
by no means ill-received either by the marchioness or her companions;
and, in fact, when the dinner was announced, they all rose in a mirth,

---

1. "He has watched the games, played on the fields. Everyone calls him fortune's
darling" (Horace *Satires* 6.48–49).

256

sufficiently unrestrained to be any thing but patrician: for my part, I offered my arm to Lady Harriett, and paid her as many compliments on crossing the suite that led to the dining-room, as would have turned a much wiser head than her ladyship's.

The dinner went off agreeably enough, as long as the women stayed, but the moment they quitted the room, I experienced exactly the same feeling known unto a mother's darling, left for the first time at that strange, cold, comfortless place—ycleped a school.

I was not, however, in a mood to suffer my flowers of oratory to blush unseen. Besides, it was absolutely necessary that I should make a better impression upon my host. I leant, therefore, across the table, and listened eagerly to the various conversations afloat: at last I perceived, on the opposite side, Sir Lionel Garrett, a personage whom I had not before even inquired after, or thought of. He was busily and noisily employed in discussing the game-laws. Thank Heaven, thought I, I shall be on firm ground there. The general interest of the subject, and the loudness with which it was debated, soon drew all the scattered conversation into one focus.

"What!" said Sir Lionel, in a high voice, to a modest, shrinking youth, probably from Cambridge, who had supported the liberal side of the question—"what! are our interests to be *never* consulted? Are we to have our only amusement taken away from us? What do you imagine brings country gentlemen to their seats? Do you not know, Sir, the vast importance our residence at our country houses is to the nation? Destroy the game laws, and you destroy our very existence as a people."[2]

'Now,' thought I, 'it is my time.' "Sir Lionel," said I, speaking almost from one end of the table to the other, "I perfectly agree with your sentiments; I am entirely of opinion, first, that it is absolutely necessary for the safety of the nation that game should be preserved; secondly, that if you take away game you take away country gentlemen: no two propositions can be clearer than these; but I do differ from you with respect to the intended alterations. Let us put wholly out of the question, the interests of the poor people, or of society at large: those are minor matters, not worthy of a moment's consideration; let us only see how far *our* interests as sportsmen will be affected. I think by a very few words I can clearly prove to you, that the proposed alterations will make us much better off than we are at present."

---

2. The Game Laws protected the hunting rights of the aristocracy and imposed severe penalties for poaching. Peasants and farmers had no redress if their crops were damaged by the hunters.

I then entered shortly, yet fully enough, into the nature of the laws as they now stood, and as they were intended to be changed. I first spoke of the two great disadvantages of the present system to country gentlemen; viz. in the number of poachers, and the expense of preserving. Observing that I was generally and attentively listened to, I dwelt upon these two points with much pathetic energy; and having paused till I had got Sir Lionel and one or two of his supporters to confess that it would be highly desirable that these defects should, *if possible,* be remedied, I proceeded to show how, and in what manner it *was* possible. I argued, that to effect this possibility, was the exact object of the alterations suggested; I anticipated the objections; I answered them in the form of propositions, as clearly and concisely stated as possible; and as I spoke with great civility and conciliation, and put aside every appearance of care for any human being in the world who was not possessed of a qualification, I perceived at the conclusion of my harangue, that I had made a very favourable impression. That evening completed my triumph: for Lady Chester and Lady Harriett made so good a story of my adventure with the dogs, that the matter passed off as a famous joke, and I was soon considered by the whole knot as a devilish amusing, good-natured, sensible fellow. So true is it that there is no situation which a little tact cannot turn to our own account: manage *yourself* well, and you may manage all the world.

As for Lord Chester, I soon won his heart by a few feats of horsemanship, and a few extempore inventions respecting the sagacity of dogs. Three days after my arrival we became inseparable; and I made such good use of my time, that in two more, he spoke to me of his friendship for Dawton, and his wish for a dukedom. These motives it was easy enough to unite, and at last he promised me that his answer to my principal should be as acquiescent as I could desire; the morning after this promise commenced *the great day* at Newmarket.

Our whole party were of course bound to the race-ground, and with great reluctance I was pressed into the service. We were not many miles distant from the course, and Lord Chester mounted me on one of his horses. Our shortest way lay through rather an intricate series of cross roads: and as I was very little interested in the conversation of my companions, I paid more attention to the scenery we passed, than is my customary wont: for I study nature rather in men than fields, and find no landscape afford such variety to the eye, and such subject to the contemplation, as the inequalities of the human heart.

258

But there were to be fearful circumstances hereafter to stamp forcibly upon my remembrance some traces of the scenery which now courted and arrested my view. The chief characteristics of the country were broad, dreary plains, diversified at times by dark plantations of fir and larch; the road was rough and stony, and here and there a melancholy rivulet, swelled by the first rains of spring, crossed our path, and lost itself in the rank weeds of some inhospitable marsh.

About six miles from Chester Park, to the left of the road, stood an old house with a new face; the brown, time-honoured bricks which composed the fabric, were strongly contrasted by large Venetian windows newly inserted in frames of the most ostentatious white. A smart, green veranda, scarcely finished, ran along the low portico, and formed the termination to two thin rows of meagre and dwarfish sycamores, which did duty for an avenue, and were bounded, on the roadside, by a spruce white gate, and a sprucer lodge, so moderate in its dimensions, that it would scarcely have boiled a turnip: if a rat had got into it, he might have run away with it. The ground was dug in various places, as if for the purpose of further *improvements,* and here and there a sickly little tree was carefully hurdled round, and seemed pining its puny heart out at the confinement.

In spite of all these well-judged and well-thriving graces of art, there was such a comfortless and desolate appearance about the place, that it quite froze one to look at it; to be sure, a damp marsh on one side, and the skeleton rafters and beams of an old stable on the other, backed by a few dull and sulky-looking fir trees, might, in some measure, create, or at least considerably add to, the indescribable cheerlessness of the *tout ensemble.* While I was curiously surveying the various parts of this northern *"Délices,"*[3] and marvelling at the choice of two crows who were slowly walking over the unwholesome ground, instead of making all possible use of the black wings with which Providence had gifted them, I perceived two men on horseback wind round from the back part of the building, and proceed in a brisk trot down the avenue. We had not advanced many paces before they overtook us; the foremost of them turned round as he passed me, and pulling up his horse abruptly, discovered to my dismayed view, the features of Mr. Thornton. Nothing abashed by the slightness of my bow, or the grave stares of my lordly companions, who never forgot the dignity of their birth, in spite of the vulgarity of their tastes, Thornton instantly and familiarly accosted me.

---

3. *Délices:* the name of Voltaire's house in Ferney, on the Swiss border.

"Told you so, Mr. Pelham—*silent sow, &c.*—Sure I should have the pleasure of seeing you, though you kept it so snug. Well, will you bet *now?* No!—Ah, you're a sly one. Staying here at that *nice-looking* house—belongs to Dawson, an old friend of mine—shall *be happy to introduce you!*"

"Sir," said I, abruptly, "you are too good. Permit me to request that you will rejoin your friend Mr. Dawson."

"Oh," said the imperturbable Thornton, "it does not signify; he won't be affronted at my lagging a little. However," (and here he caught my eye, which was assuming a sternness that perhaps little pleased him), "however, as it gets late, and my mare is none of the best, I'll wish you good morning." With these words Thornton put spurs to his horse and trotted off.

"Who the devil have you got there, Pelham?" said Lord Chester.

"A person," said I, "who picked me up at Paris, and insists on the right of treasure trove to claim me in England. But will you let me ask, in my turn, whom that cheerful mansion we have just left, belongs to?"

"To a Mr. Dawson, whose father was a gentleman farmer who bred horses, a very respectable person, *for* I made one or two excellent bargains with him. The son was always on the turf, and contracted the worst of its habits. He bears but a very indifferent character, and will probably become a complete blackleg. He married, a short time since, a woman of some fortune, and I suppose it is her taste which has so altered and modernized his house. Come, gentlemen, we are on even ground, shall we trot?"

We proceeded but a few yards before we were again stopped by a precipitous ascent, and as Lord Chester was then earnestly engaged in praising his horse, to one of the cavalcade, I had time to remark the spot. At the foot of the hill we were about slowly to ascend, was a broad, uninclosed patch of waste land; a heron, flapping its enormous wings as it rose, directed my attention to a pool overgrown with rushes, and half-sheltered on one side by a decayed tree, which, if one might judge from the breadth and hollowness of its trunk, had been a refuge to the wild bird, and a shelter to the wild cattle, at a time when such were the only intruders upon its hospitality; and when the country, for miles and leagues round, was honoured by as little of man's care and cultivation as was at present the rank waste which still nourished its gnarled and venerable roots. There was something remarkably singular and grotesque in the shape and sinuosity of its naked and spectral branches: two of exceeding length

260

stretched themselves forth, in the very semblance of arms held out in the attitude of supplication; and the bend of the trunk over the desolate pond, the form of the hoary and blasted summit, and the hollow trunk, half riven asunder in the shape of limbs, seemed to favour the gigantic deception. You might have imagined it an antediluvian transformation, or a daughter of the Titan race, preserving in her metamorphosis her attitude of entreaty to the merciless Olympian.

This was the only tree visible; for a turn of the road and the unevenness of the ground, completely veiled the house we had passed, and the few low firs and sycamores which made its only plantations. The sullen pool—its ghost-like guardian—the dreary heath around, the rude features of the country beyond, and the apparent absence of all human habitation, conspired to make a scene of the most dispiriting and striking desolation. I know not how to account for it, but as I gazed around in silence, the whole place appeared to grow over my mind, as one which I had seen, though dimly and drearily, before; and a nameless and unaccountable presentiment of fear and evil sunk like ice into my heart. We ascended the hill, and the rest of the road being of a kind better adapted to expedition, we mended our pace and soon arrived at the goal of our journey.

The race-ground had its customary compliment of knaves and fools—the dupers and the duped. Poor Lady Chester, who had proceeded to the ground by the high road (for the way we had chosen was inaccessible to those who ride in chariots, and whose charioteers are set up in high places), was driving to and fro, the very picture of cold and discomfort; and the few solitary carriages which honoured the course, looked as miserable as if they were witnessing the funeral of their owner's persons, rather than the peril of their characters and purses.

As we rode along to the betting-post, Sir John Tyrrell passed us: Lord Chester accosted him familiarly, and the baronet joined us. He had been an old votary of the turf in his younger days, and he still preserved all his ancient predilection in its favour.

It seemed that Chester had not met him for many years, and after a short and characteristic conversation of "God bless me, how long since I saw you!—d——d good horse you're on—you look thin—admirable condition—what have you been doing?—grand action—a'n't we behind hand?—famous fore-hand—recollect old Queensberry?—hot in the mouth—gone to the devil—what are the odds?" Lord

Chester asked Tyrrell to go home with us. The invitation was readily accepted.

> "With impotence of will
> We wheel, tho' ghastly shadows interpose
> Round us, and round each other."[4]

Now, then, arose the noise, the clatter, the swearing, the lying, the perjury, the cheating, the crowd, the bustle, the hurry, the rush, the heat, the ardour, the impatience, the hope, the terror, the rapture, the agony of the race. Directly* the first heat was over, one asked me one thing, one bellowed another; I fled to Lord Chester, he did not heed me. I took refuge with the marchioness; she was as sullen as an east wind could make her. Lady Harriett would talk of nothing but the horses: Sir Lionel would not talk at all. I was in the lowest pit of despondency, and the devils that kept me there were as blue as Lady Chester's nose. Silent, sad, sorrowful, and sulky, I rode away from the crowd, and moralized on its vicious propensities. One grows marvellously honest when the species of cheating before us is not suited to one's self. Fortunately, my better angel reminded me, that about the distance of three miles from the course lived an old college friend, blessed, since we had met, with a parsonage and a wife. I knew his tastes too well to imagine that any allurement of an equestrian nature could have seduced him from the ease of his library and the dignity of his books; and hoping, therefore, that I should find him at home, I turned my horse's head in an opposite direction, and rejoiced at the idea of my escape, bade adieu to the course.

As I cantered across the far end of the heath, my horse started from an object upon the ground; it was a man wrapped from head to foot in a long horseman's cloak, and so well guarded as to the face, from the raw inclemency of the day, that I could not catch even a glimpse of the features, through the hat and neck-shawl which concealed them. The head was turned, with apparent anxiety, towards the distant throng; and imagining the man belonging to the lower orders, with whom I am always familiar, I addressed to him, *en passant,* some trifling remark on the event of the race. He made no answer. There was something about him which induced me to look back several moments after I had left him behind. He had not moved an atom. There is such a certain uncomfortableness always occasioned to the mind, by stillness and mystery united, that even the disguising

---

4. Percy Bysshe Shelley. [B-L] From *The Triumph of Life,* lines 170–72.

garb, and motionless silence of the man, innocent as I thought they must have been, impressed themselves disagreeably on my meditations as I rode briskly on.

It is my maxim never to be unpleasantly employed, even in thought, if I can help it; accordingly, I changed the course of my reflection, and amused myself with wondering how matrimony and clerical dignity sat on the indolent shoulders of my old acquaintance.

CHAPTER XXVI

And as for me, tho' that I can but lite
On bookes for to read I me delight,
And to hem give I faith and full credènce;
And in mine heart have hem in reverence,
So heartily that there is game none,
That fro' my bookès maketh me to gone.

CHAUCER[1]

CHRISTOPHER CLUTTERBUCK WAS A COMMON INDIVIDUAL of a common order, but little known in this busy and toiling world.[2] I cannot flatter myself that I am about to present to your notice that *rara avis,* a new character—yet there is something interesting, and even unhacknied, in the retired and simple class to which he belongs: and before I proceed to a darker periòd in my memoirs, I feel a calm and tranquillizing pleasure in the rest which a brief and imperfect delineation of my college companion, affords me. My friend came up to the University with the learning one about to quit the world might, with credit, have boasted of possessing, and the simplicity one about to enter it would have been ashamed to confess. Quiet and shy in his habits and his manners, he was never seen out of the precincts of his apartment, except in obedience to the stated calls of dinner, lectures, and chapel. Then his small and stooping form might be

---

1. *The Legend of Good Women,* lines 29–34.

2. "This strongly drawn portrait of the clerical scholar . . . was undoubtedly suggested by the wasted life of Richard Warburton Lytton [Bulwer's grandfather]" (*Life . . . and Literary Remains,* II, 192–3).

marked, crossing the quadrangle with a hurried step, and cautiously avoiding the smallest blade of the barren grass-plots, which are forbidden ground to the feet of all the lower orders of the collegiate oligarchy. Many were the smiles and the jeers, from the worse natured and better appointed students, who loitered idly along the court, at the rude garb and saturnine appearance of the humble under-graduate; and the calm countenance of the grave. but amiable man, who then bore the honour and *onus* of mathematical lecturer at our college, would soften into a glance of mingled approbation and pity, as_he noted the eagerness which spoke from the wan cheek and emaciated frame of the ablest of his pupils, hurrying—after each legitimate interruption—to the enjoyment of the crabbed characters and worm-worn volumes, which contained for him all the seductions of pleasure, and all the temptations of youth.

It is a melancholy thing, which none but those educated at a college can understand, to see the debilitated frames of the aspirants for academical honours; to mark the prime—the verdure—the glory—the life—of life wasted irrevocably away in a *labor ineptiarum,* which brings no harvest either to others or themselves. For the poet, the philosopher, the man of science, we can appreciate the recompence if we commiserate the sacrifice; from the darkness of their retreat there goes a light—from the silence of their studies there issues a voice, to illumine or convince. We can imagine them looking from their privations to the far visions of the future, and hugging to their hearts, in the strength of no unnatural vanity, the reward which their labours are certain hereafter to obtain. To those who can anticipate the vast dominions of immortality among men, what boots the sterility of the cabined and petty *present?* But the mere man of languages and learning—the machine of a memory heavily but unprofitably employed —the Columbus wasting at the galley oar the energies which should have discovered a world—for him there is no day-dream of the future, no grasp at the immortality of fame. Beyond the walls of his narrow room he knows no object; beyond the elucidation of a dead tongue he indulges no ambition; his life is one long school-day of lexicons and grammars—a fabric of ice, cautiously excluded from a single sun-beam—elaborately useless, ingeniously unprofitable; and leaving at the moment it melts away, not a single trace of the space it occupied, or the labour it cost.

At the time I went to the University, my poor collegian had attained all the honours his employment could ever procure him.

He *had been* a Pitt scholar; *he was* a senior wrangler,[3] and a Fellow of his college. It often happened that I found myself next to him at dinner, and I was struck by his abstinence, and pleased with his modesty, despite of the *gaucherie* of his manner, and the fashion of his garb. By degrees I insinuated myself into his acquaintance; and, as I had still some love of scholastic lore, I took frequent opportunities of conversing with him upon Horace, and consulting him upon Lucian.

Many a dim twilight have we sat together, reviving each other's recollection, and occasionally relaxing into the grave amusement of *capping verses*. Then, if by any chance my ingenuity or memory enabled me to puzzle my companion, his good temper would lose itself in a quaint pettishness, or he would cite* against me some line of Aristophanes, and ask me, with a raised voice, and arched brow, to give him a fitting answer to *that*. But if, as was much more frequently the case, he fairly run me down into a pause and confession of inability, he would rub his hands with a strange chuckle, and offer me, in the bounteousness of his heart, to read aloud a Greek Ode of his own, while he treated me "to a dish of tea." There was much in the good man's innocence, and guilelessness of soul, which made me love him, and I did not rest till I had procured him, before I left the University, the living which he now held. Since then, he had married the daughter of a neighbouring clergyman, an event of which he had duly informed me; but, though this great step in the life of "a reading man," had not taken place many months since, I had completely, after a hearty wish for his domestic happiness, consigned it to a dormant place in my recollection.

The house which I now began to approach was small, but comfortable; perhaps there was something *triste** in the old-fashioned hedges, cut and trimmed with mathematical precision, which surrounded the glebe, as well as in the heavy architecture and dingy bricks of the reverend recluse's habitation. To make amends for this, there was also something peculiarly still and placid about the appearance of the house, which must have suited well the tastes and habits of the owner. A small, formal lawn was adorned with a square fishpond, bricked round, and covered with the green weepings of four willows, which drooped over it, from their station, at each corner. At the opposite side of this Pierian reservoir, was a hermitage, or arbour of laurels, shaped in the stiff rusticity of the Dutch school,

3. Senior wrangler: one who places in the first class of the Mathematical tripos at Cambridge.

in the prevalence of which it was probably planted; behind this arbour, the ground, after a slight railing, terminated in an orchard.

The sound I elicited from the gate bell seemed to ring through that retired place with singular shrillness; and I observed at the opposite window, all that bustle of drawing curtains, peeping faces, and hasty retreats, which denote female anxiety and perplexity, at the unexpected approach of a stranger.

After some time the parson's single servant, a middle-aged, slovenly man, in a loose frock, and buff kerseyemere nondescripts, opened the gate, and informed me that his master *was* at home. With a few earnest admonitions to my admittor—who was, like the domestics of many richer men, both groom and valet—respecting the safety of my borrowed horse, I entered the house: the servant did not think it necessary to inquire my name, but threw open the door of the study, with the brief introduction of—"a gentleman, Sir."

Clutterbuck was standing, with his back towards me, upon a pair of library steps, turning over some dusky volumes; and below stood a pale, cadaverous youth, with a set and serious countenance, that bore no small likeness to Clutterbuck himself.

"*Mon Dieu,*" thought I, "he cannot have made such good use of his matrimonial state as to have raised this lanky impression of himself in the space of seven months?" The good man turned round, and almost fell off the steps with the nervous shock of beholding me so near him: he descended with precipitation, and shook me so warmly and tightly by the hand, that he brought tears into my eyes, as well as his own.

"Gently, my good friend," said I—"*parce precor,*[4] or you will force me to say, '*ibimus una ambo, flentes valido connexi foedere.*'"

Clutterbuck's eyes watered still more, when he heard the grateful sounds of what to him was the mother tongue. He surveyed me from head to foot with an air of benign and fatherly complacency, and dragging forth from its sullen rest a large arm chair, on whose cushions of rusty horse-hair sat an eternal cloud of classic dust, too sacred to be disturbed, he *plumped* me down upon it, before I was aware of the cruel hospitality.

"Oh! my nether garments," thought I. "*Quantus sudor inerit Bedoso,*[5] to restore you to your pristine purity."

---

4. "Have mercy, please!" (Horace *Carmen* 4.1.2). The quotation immediately following may be translated: "We will go together, weeping and bound to each other by a strong compact." Unidentified.

5. "How much sweat is in Bedosus." Unidentified.

"But, whence come you?" said my host, who cherished rather a formal and antiquated method of speech.

"From the Pythian games," said I. "The campus hight Newmarket. Do I see right, or is not yon *insignis juvenis* marvellously like you? Of a surety he rivals the Titans, if he is only a seven months' child!"

"Now, truly, my worthy friend," answered Clutterbuck, "you indulge in jesting! The boy is my nephew, a goodly child, and a painstaking. I hope he will thrive at our gentle mother. He goes to Trinity next October. Benjamin Jeremiah, my lad, this is my worthy friend and benefactor, of whom I have often spoken; go, and order him of our best—he will partake of our repast!"

"No, really," I began; but Clutterbuck gently placed the hand, whose strength of affection I had already so forcibly experienced, upon my mouth. "Pardon me, my friend," said he. "No *stranger* should depart till he had broken bread with us, how much more then a friend! Go, Benjamin Jeremiah, and tell your aunt that Mr. Pelham will dine with us; and order, furthermore, that the barrel of oysters sent unto us as a present, by my worthy friend Dr. Swallow'em, be dressed in the fashion that seemeth best; they are a classic dainty, and we shall think of our great masters the ancients whilst we devour them. And—stop, Benjamin Jeremiah, see that we have the wine with the black seal; and—now—go, Benjamin Jeremiah!"

"Well, my old friend," said I, when the door closed upon the sallow and smileless nephew, "how do you love the *connubiale jugum?** Do you give the same advice as Socrates? I hope, at least, it is not from the same experience."[6]

"Hem!" answered the grave Christopher, in a tone that struck me as somewhat nervous and uneasy, "you are become quite a humourist since we parted. I suppose you have been warming your wit by the lambent fires of Horace and Aristophanes!"

"No," said I, "the living allow those whose toilsome lot it is to mix constantly with them, but little time to study the monuments of the dead. But, in sober earnest, are you as happy as I wish you?"

Clutterbuck looked down for a moment, and then, turning towards the table, laid one hand upon a MS., and pointed with the other to his books. "With this society," said he, "how can I be otherwise?"

I gave him no reply, but put my hand upon his MS. He made a modest and coy effort to detain it, but I knew that writers were like

---

6. Socrates' own wife was apparently something of a shrew, and the philosopher advised others to marry a difficult woman in order to ensure for themselves a sort of constant moral self-discipline. See Xenophon's "Banquet of Xenophon."

women, and making use of no displeasing force, I possessed myself of the paper.

It was a treatise on the Greek participle. My heart sickened within me; but, as I caught the eager glance of the poor author, I brightened up my countenance into an expression of pleasure, and appeared to read and comment upon the *difficiles nugae* with an interest commensurate to his own. Meanwhile the youth returned. He had much of that delicacy of sentiment which always accompanies mental cultivation, of whatever sort it may be. He went, with a scarlet blush over his thin face, to his uncle, and whispered something in his ear, which, from the angry embarrassment it appeared to occasion, I was at no loss to divine.

"Come," said I, "we are too long acquainted for ceremony. Your *placens uxor,* like all ladies in the same predicament, thinks your invitation a little unadvised; and, in real earnest, I have so long a ride to perform, that I would rather eat your oysters another day!"

"No, no," said Clutterbuck, with greater eagerness than his even temperament was often hurried into betraying—"no, I will go and reason with her myself. 'Wives, obey your husbands,'[7] saith the preacher!" And the quondam senior wrangler almost upset his chair in the perturbation with which he arose from it.

I laid my hand upon him. "Let me go myself," said I, "since you *will* have me dine with you. 'The sex is ever to a stranger kind,'[8] and I shall probably be more persuasive than you, in despite of your legitimate authority."

So saying, I left the room, with a curiosity more painful than pleasing, to see the collegian's wife. I arrested the man servant, and ordered him to usher and announce me.

I was led instanter into the apartment where I had discovered all the signs of female inquisitiveness, which I have before detailed. There I discovered a small woman, in a robe equally slatternly and fine, with a sharp pointed nose, small, cold, grey eyes, and a complexion high towards the cheek bones, but waxing of a light green before it reached the wide and querulous mouth, which, well I ween, seldom opened to smile upon the unfortunate possessor of her charms. She, like the Rev. Christopher, was not without her companions; a tall meagre woman, of advanced age, and a girl, some years younger than herself, were introduced to me as her mother and sister.

---

7. Epistle to the Ephesians 5:22.
8. Adapted from Pope's translation of the *Odyssey,* book 14.

My *entrée* occasioned no little confusion, but I knew well how to remedy that. I held out my hand so cordially to the wife, that I enticed, though with evident reluctance, two bony fingers into my own, which I did not dismiss without a most mollifying and affectionate squeeze; and drawing my chair close towards her, began conversing as familiarly as if I had known the whole triad for years. I declared my joy at seeing my old friend so happily settled—commented on the improvement of his looks—ventured a sly joke at the good effects of matrimony—praised a cat couchant, worked in worsted by the venerable hand of the eldest matron—offered to procure her a *real* cat of the true Persian breed, black ears four inches long, with a tail like a squirrel's; and then slid, all at once, into the unauthorized invitation of the good man of the house.

"Clutterbuck," said I, "has asked me very warmly to stay dinner; but, before I accepted his offer, I insisted upon coming to see how far it was confirmed by you. Gentlemen, you are aware, my dear Madam, know nothing of these matters, and I never accept a married man's invitation till it has the sanction of his lady: I have an example of that at home. My mother (Lady Frances) is the best-tempered woman in the world: but my father could no more take the liberty (for I may truly call it such) to ask even his oldest friend to dinner, without consulting the mistress of the house, than he could think of flying. No one (says my mother, and she says what is very true), can tell about the household affairs, but those who have the management of them; and in pursuance of this aphorism, I dare not accept any invitation in this house, except from its mistress."

"Really," said Mrs. Clutterbuck, colouring, with mingled embarrassment and gratification, "you are very considerate and polite, Mr. Pelham: I only wish Mr. Clutterbuck had half your attention to these things; nobody can tell the trouble and inconvenience he puts me to. If I *had* known, a little time before, that you were coming—but now I fear we have nothing in the house; but if you can partake of our fare, such as it is, Mr. Pelham—"

"Your kindness enchants me," I exclaimed, "and I no longer scruple to confess the pleasure I have in accepting my old friend's offer."

This affair being settled, I continued to converse for some minutes with as much vivacity as I could summon to my aid, and when I went once more to the library, it was with the comfortable impression of having left those as friends, whom I had visited as foes.

The dinner hour was four, and till it came, Clutterbuck and I

269

amused ourselves "in commune wise and sage." There was something high in the sentiments and generous in the feelings of this man, which made me the more regret the bias of mind which rendered them so unavailing. At college he had never *(illis dissimilis in nostro tempore natis)*[9] cringed to the possessors of clerical power. In the duties of his station, as dean of the college, he was equally strict to the black cap and the lordly hat. Nay, when one of his private pupils, whose father was possessed of more church preferment than any nobleman in the peerage, disobeyed his repeated summons, and constantly neglected to attend his instructions, he sent for him, resigned his tuition, and refused any longer to accept a salary which the negligence of his pupil would not allow him to requite. In his clerical tenets he was high: in his judgment of others he was mild. His knowledge of the liberty of Greece was not drawn from the ignorant historian of her republics;[10] nor did he find in the contemplative mildness and gentle philosophy of the ancients, nothing but a sanction for modern bigotry and existing abuses.

It was a remarkable trait in his conversation, that though he indulged in many references to the old authors, and allusions to classic customs, he never deviated into the innumerable quotations with which his memory was stored. No words, in spite of all the quaintness and antiquity of his dialect, purely Latin or Greek, ever escaped his lips, except in our engagements at capping verses, or when he was allured into accepting a challenge of learning from some of its pretenders; then, indeed, he could pour forth such a torrent of authorities as effectually silenced his opponent; but these contests were rarely entered into, and these triumphs moderately indulged. Yet he loved the use of quotations in others, and I knew the greatest pleasure I could give him was in the frequent use of them. Perhaps he thought it would seem like an empty parade of learning in one who so confessedly possessed it, to deal in the strange words of another tongue, and consequently rejected them, while, with an innocent inconsistency, characteristic of the man, it never occurred to him that there was any thing, either in the quaintness of his dialect or the occupations of his leisure, which might subject him to the same imputation of pedantry.

---

9. "How unlike them are the men born in our degenerate days (Juvenal *Satires* 15.68). Bulwer's quotation is badly corrupt.

10. It is really a disgrace to the University, that any of its colleges should accept as a reference, or even tolerate as an author, the presumptuous bigot who has bequeathed to us, in his History of Greece, the masterpiece of a declaimer without energy, and of a pedant without learning. [B-L] William Mitford (1744–1827) published his five-volume *History of Greece* between 1784 and 1810.

And yet, at times, when he warmed in his subject, there was a tone in his language as well as sentiment, which might not be improperly termed eloquent; and the real modesty and quiet enthusiasm of his nature, took away from the impression he made, the feeling of pomposity and affectation with which otherwise he might have inspired you.

"You have a calm and quiet habitation here," said I; "the very rooks seem to have something lulling in that venerable caw which it always does me such good to hear."

"Yes," answered Clutterbuck, "I own that there is much that is grateful to the temper of my mind in this retired spot. I fancy that I can the better give myself up to the contemplation which makes, as it were, my intellectual element and food. And yet I dare say that in this (as in all other things) I do strongly err; for I remember that during my only sojourn in London, I was wont to feel the sound of wheels and of the throng of steps shake the windows of my lodging in the Strand, as if it were but a warning to recal my mind more closely to its studies—of a verity that noisy evidence of man's labour reminded me how little the great interests of this rolling world were to me, and the feeling of solitude amongst the crowds without, made me cling more fondly to the company I found within. For it seems that the mind is ever addicted to contraries, and that when it be transplanted into a soil where all its neighbours do produce a certain fruit, it doth, from a strange perversity, bring forth one of a different sort. You would little believe, my honoured friend, that in this lonely seclusion, I cannot at all times prohibit my thoughts from wandering to that gay world of London, which, during my tarry therein, occupied them in so partial a degree. You smile, my friend, nevertheless it is true; and when you reflect that I dwelt in the western department of the metropolis, near unto the noble mansion of Somerset House,[11] and consequently in the very centre of what the idle call Fashion, you will not be so surprised at the occasional migration of my thoughts."

Here the worthy Clutterbuck paused and sighed slightly. "Do you farm or cultivate your garden," said I; "they are no ignoble nor unclassical employments?"

"Unhappily," answered Clutterbuck, "I am inclined to neither; my chest pains me with a sharp and piercing pang when I attempt to stoop, and my respiration is short and asthmatic; and, in truth, I seldom love to stir from my books and papers. I go with Pliny to his

---

11. The Royal Academy was at Somerset House from 1780 to 1838.

garden, and with Virgil to his farm; those mental excursions are the sole ones I indulge in; and when I think of my appetite for application, and my love of idleness, I am tempted to wax proud of the propensities which reverse the censure of Tacitus on our German ancestors, and incline so fondly to quiet, while they turn so restlessly from sloth."

Here the speaker was interrupted by a long, low, dry cough, which penetrated me to the heart. 'Alas!' thought I, as I heard it, and looked upon my poor friend's hectic and hollow cheek, 'it is not only his mind that will be the victim to the fatality of his studies.'

It was some moments before I renewed the conversation, and I had scarcely done so before I was interrupted by the entrance of Benjamin Jeremiah, with a message from his aunt that dinner would be ready in a few minutes. Another long whisper to Christopher succeeded. The *ci-devant* fellow of Trinity looked down at his garments with a perplexed air. I saw at once that he had received a hint on the propriety of a change of raiment. To give him due leisure for this, I asked the youth to shew me a room in which I might perform the usual ablutions previous to dinner, and followed him upstairs to a comfortless sort of dressing-room, without a fire-place, where I found a yellow ware jug and basin, and a towel, of so coarse a huckaback, that I did not dare adventure its rough texture next my complexion— my skin is not made for such rude fellowship. While I was tenderly and daintily anointing my hands with some hard water, of no Blandusian spring, and that vile composition entitled Windsor soap, I heard the difficult breathing of poor Clutterbuck on the stairs, and soon after he entered the adjacent room. Two minutes more, and his servant joined him, for I heard the rough voice of the domestic say, "There is no more of the wine with the black seal left, Sir!"

"No more, good Dixon; you mistake grievously. I had two dozen not a week since."

"Don't know, I'm sure, Sir!" answered Dixon, with a careless and half impertinent accent; "but there are great things, *like alligators,* in the cellar, which break all the bottles!"

"Alligators in my cellar!" said the astonished Clutterbuck.

"Yes, Sir—at least a venomous sort of reptile like them, which the people about here call *efts!*"

"What!" said Clutterbuck, innocently, and evidently not seeing the irony of his own question; "What! have the efts broken two dozen bottles in a week? Of an exceeding surety, it is strange that a little creature of the lizard species should be so destructive—perchance they

272

have an antipathy to the vinous smell; I will confer with my learned friend, Dr. Dissectall, touching their strength and habits. Bring up some of the port, then, good Dixon."

"Yes, Sir. All the corn is out; I had none for the gentleman's horse."

"Why, Dixon, my memory fails me strangely, or I paid you the sum of four pounds odd shillings for corn on Friday last."

"Yes, Sir: but your cow and the chickens eat so much, and then blind Dobbin has four feeds a day, and Farmer Johnson always puts his horse in our stable, and Mrs. Clutterbuck and the ladies fed the jackass the other day in the hired donkey chaise; besides, the rats and mice are always at it."

"It is a marvel unto me," answered Clutterbuck, "how detrimental the vermin race are; they seem to have noted my poor possessions as their especial prey; remind me that I write to Dr. Dissectall to-morrow, good Dixon."

"Yes, Sir, and now I think of it——" but here Mr. Dixon was cut short in his items, by the entrance of a third person, who proved to be Mrs. Clutterbuck.

"What, not dressed yet, Mr. Clutterbuck; what a dawdler you are! —and do look—was ever woman so used? you have wiped your razor upon my nightcap—you dirty, slovenly ———"

"I crave you many pardons; I own my error!" said Clutterbuck, in a nervous tone of interruption.

"Error, indeed!" cried Mrs. Clutterbuck, in a sharp, overstretched, querulous falsetto, suited to the occasion: "but this is always the case— I am sure, my poor temper is tried to the utmost—and Lord help thee, idiot! you have thrust those spindle legs of yours into your coat-sleeves instead of your breeches!"

"Of a truth, good wife, your eyes are more discerning than mine; and my legs, which are, as you say, somewhat thin, have indued themselves in what appertaineth not unto them; but for all that, Dorothea, I am not deserving of the epithet of idiot, with which you have been pleased to favour me; although my humble faculties are indeed of no eminent or surpassing order———"

"Pooh! pooh! Mr. Clutterbuck, I am sure, I don't know what else you are, muddling your head all day with those good-for-nothing books. And now do tell me, how you could think of asking Mr. Pelham to dinner, when you knew we had nothing in the world but hashed mutton and an apple pudding? Is that the way, Sir, you disgrace your wife, after her condescension in marrying you?"

"Really," answered the patient Clutterbuck, "I was forgetful of

273

those matters; but my friend cares as little as myself, about the grosser tastes of the table; and the feast of intellectual converse is all that he desires in his brief sojourn beneath our roof."

"Feast of fiddlesticks, Mr. Clutterbuck! did ever man talk such nonsense?"

"Besides," rejoined the *master* of the house, unheeding this interruption, "we have a luxury even of the palate, than which there are none more delicate, and unto which he, as well as myself, is, I know, somewhat unphilosophically given; I speak of the oysters, sent here by our good friend, Dr. Swallow'em."

"What do you mean, Mr. Clutterbuck? My poor mother and I had those oysters last night for our supper. I am sure she as well as my sister are almost starved; but you are always wanting to be pampered up above us all."

"Nay, nay," answered Clutterbuck, "you know you accuse me wrongfully, Dorothea; but now I think of it, would it not be better to modulate the tone of our conversation, seeing that our guest, (a circumstance which until now quite escaped my recollection), was shown into the next room, for the purpose of washing his hands, the which, from their notable cleanliness, seemed to me wholly unnecessary. I would not have him overhear you, Dorothea, lest his kind heart should imagine me less happy than—than it wishes me."

"Good God, Mr. Clutterbuck!" were the only words I heard farther: and with tears in my eyes, and a suffocating feeling in my throat, for the matrimonial situation of my unfortunate friend, I descended into the drawing-room. The only one yet there, was the pale nephew; he was bending painfully over a book; I took it from him, it was "Bentley upon Phalaris."[12] I could scarcely refrain from throwing it into the fire—another victim, thought I—oh, the curse of an English education! By and by, down came the mother and the sister, then Clutterbuck, and lastly, bedizened out with gewgaws and trumpery—the wife. Born and nurtured as I was in the art of the *volto sciolto pensieri stretti*,[13] I had seldom found a more arduous task of dissimulation than that which I experienced now. However, the hope to benefit my friend's situation assisted me; the best way, I thought, of obtaining him more respect from his wife, would be by showing her the respect he meets with from others: accordingly, I sat down by her,

---

12. *Dissertation on the Epistles of Phalaris* (1697) by Richard Bentley (1662–1742), English scholar and critic.

13. "An open face and closed thoughts" (proverbial expression).

and having first conciliated her attention by some of that coin, termed compliments, in which there is no counterfeit that does not have the universal effect of real, I spoke with the most profound veneration of the talents and learning of Clutterbuck—I dilated upon the high reputation he enjoyed—upon the general esteem in which he was held —upon the kindness of his heart—the sincerity of his modesty—the integrity of his honour—in short, whatever I thought likely to affect her; most of all, I insisted upon the high panegyrics bestowed upon him, by Lord this, and the Earl that, and wound up, with adding that I was certain he would die a bishop. My eloquence had its effect; all dinner time, Mrs. Clutterbuck treated her husband with even striking consideration: my words seemed to have gifted her with a new light, and to have wrought a thorough transformation in her view of her lord and master's character. Who knows not the truth, that we have dim and short-sighted eyes to estimate the nature of our own kin, and that we borrow the spectacles which alone enable us to discern their merits or their failings from the opinion of strangers! It may be readily supposed that the dinner did not pass without its share of the ludicrous—that the waiter and the dishes, the family and the host, would have afforded ample materials, no less for the student of nature in Hogarth, than of caricature in Bunbury;[14] but I was too seriously occupied in pursuing my object, and marking its success, to have time even for a smile. Ah! if ever you would allure your son to diplomacy, show him how subservient he may make it to benevolence.

When the women had retired, we drew our chairs near to each other, and laying down my watch on the table, as I looked out upon the declining day, I said, "Let us make the best of our time, I can only linger here one half hour longer."

"And how, my friend," said Clutterbuck, "shall we learn the method of making the best use of time? *there*, whether it be in the larger segments, or the petty subdivisions of our life, rests the great enigma of our being. Who is there that has ever exclaimed—(pardon my pedantry, I am for once *driven* into Greek)—Eureka! to this most difficult of the sciences?"

"Come," said I, "it is not for you, the favoured scholar—the honoured academician—whose hours are never idly employed, to ask this question!"

"Your friendship makes too flattering the acumen of your judg-

---

14. Henry William Bunbury (1750–1811): English caricaturist.

ment," answered the modest Clutterbuck. "It has indeed been my lot to cultivate the fields of truth, as transmitted unto our hands by the wise men of old; and I have much to be thankful for, that I have, in the employ, been neither curtailed in my leisure, nor abased in my independence—the two great goods of a calm and meditative mind; yet are there moments in which I am led to doubt of the wisdom of my pursuits: and when, with a feverish and shaking hand, I put aside the books which have detained me from my rest till the morning hour, and repair unto a couch often baffled of slumber by the pains and discomforts of this worn and feeble frame, I almost wish I could purchase the rude health of the peasant by the exchange of an idle and imperfect learning for the ignorance, content with the narrow world it possesses, because unconscious of the limitless creation beyond. Yet, my dear and esteemed friend, there is a dignified and tranquillizing philosophy in the writings of the ancients which ought to teach me a better condition of mind; and when I have risen from the lofty, albeit, somewhat melancholy strain, which swells through the essays of the graceful and tender Cicero, I have indeed felt a momentary satisfaction at my studies, and an elation even at the petty success with which I have cherished them. But these are brief and fleeting moments, and deserve chastisement for their pride. There is one thing, my Pelham, which has grieved me bitterly of late, and that is, that in the earnest attention which it is the—perhaps fastidious—custom of our University, to pay to the minutiae of classic lore, I do now oftentimes lose the spirit and beauty of the general bearing; nay, I derive a far greater pleasure from the ingenious amendment of a perverted text, than from all the turn and thought of the sense itself: while I am straightening a crooked nail in the wine-cask, I suffer the wine to evaporate; but to this I am somewhat reconciled, when I reflect that it was also the misfortune of the great Porson,[15] and the elaborate Parr, men with whom I blush to find myself included in the same sentence."

"My friend," said I, "I wish neither to wound your modesty, nor to impugn your pursuits; but think you not that it would be better, both for men and for yourself, that, while you are yet in the vigour of your age and reason, you occupy your ingenuity and application in some more useful and lofty work, than that which you suffered me to glance at in your library; and moreover, as the great object of him who would perfect his mind, is first to strengthen the faculties of

---

15. Richard Porson (1759–1808): English classical scholar.

his body, would it not be prudent in you to lessen for a time your devotion to books; to exercise yourself in the fresh air—to relax the bow, by loosing the string; to mix more with the living, and impart to men in conversation, as well as in writing, whatever the incessant labour of many years may have hoarded? Come, if not to town, at least to its vicinity; the profits of your living, if even tolerably managed, will enable you to do so without inconvenience. Leave your books to their shelves, and your flock to their curate, and—you shake your head—do I displease you?"

"No, no, my kind and generous adviser—but as the twig was set, the tree must grow. I have not been without that ambition which, however vain and sinful, is the first passion to enter the wayward and tossing vessel of our soul, and the last to leave its stranded and shattered wreck; but mine found and attained its object at an age, when in others it is, as yet, a vague and unsettled feeling; and it feeds now rather upon the recollections of what has been, than ventures forward on a sea of untried and strange expectation. As for my studies! how can you, who have, and in no moderate draught, drank of the old stream of Castaly, how can *you* ask me *now* to change them? Are not the ancients my food, my aliment, my solace in sorrow—my sympathizers, my very benefactors, in joy? Take them away from me, and you take away the very winds which purify and give motion to the obscure and silent current of my life. Besides, my Pelham, it cannot have escaped your observation, that there is little in my present state which promises a long increase of days: the few that remain to me must glide away like their predecessors; and whatever be the infirmities of my body, and the little harassments which, I am led to suspect, do occasionally molest the most fortunate, who link themselves unto the unstable and fluctuating part of creation, which we term women, more especially in an hymeneal capacity—whatever these may be, I have my refuge and my comforter in the golden-souled and dreaming Plato, and the sententious wisdom of the less imaginative Seneca. Nor, when I am reminded of my approaching dissolution by the symptoms which do mostly at the midnight hour press them selves upon me, is there a small and inglorious pleasure in the hope that I may meet hereafter, in those islands of the blest which they dimly dreamt of, but which are opened unto *my* vision, without a cloud, or mist, or shadow of uncertainty and doubt, with those bright spirits which we do now converse with so imperfectly; that I may catch from the very lips of Homer the unclouded gorgeousness of fiction, and from the accents of Archimedes, the unadulterated calculations of truth."

277

Clutterbuck ceased, and the glow of his enthusiasm diffused itself over his sunken eye and consumptive cheek. The boy, who had sat apart, and silent, during our discourse, laid his head upon the table, and sobbed audibly; and I rose, deeply affected, to offer to one for whom they were, indeed, unavailing, the wishes and blessing of an eager, but not hardened disciple of the world. We parted: on this earth we can never meet again. The light has wasted itself away beneath the bushel. It will be six weeks to-morrow since the meek and noble-minded academician breathed his last.*

CHAPTER XXVII

'Tis but a single murder.
LILLO's *Fatal Curiosity*[1]

IT WAS IN A MELANCHOLY AND THOUGHTFUL MOOD that I rode away from the parsonage. Numerous and hearty were the maledictions I bestowed upon a system of education which, while it was so ineffective with the many, was so pernicious to the few. Miserable delusion (thought I), that encourages the ruin of health and the perversion of intellect by studies that are as unprofitable to the world as they are destructive to the possessor—that incapacitate him for public, and unfit him for private life—and that, while they expose him to the ridicule of strangers, render him the victim of his wife, and the prey of his domestic.

Busied in such reflections, I rode quickly on till I found myself once more on the heath. I looked anxiously round for the conspicuous equipage of Lady Chester, but in vain—the ground was thin—nearly all the higher orders had retired—the common people, grouped together, and clamouring noisily, were withdrawing: and the shrill voices of the itinerant hawkers of cards and bills had at length subsided into silence. I rode over the ground, in the hope of finding some solitary straggler of our party. Alas! there was not one; and, with much reluctance at, and distaste to, my lonely retreat, I turned in a homeward direction from the course.

---

1. George Lillo, *The Fatal Curiosity*, III, 1, 169–70.

The evening had already set in, but there was a moon in the cold grey sky, that I could almost have thanked in a sonnet for a light which I felt was never more welcomely dispensed, when I thought of the cross roads and the dreary country I had to pass before I reached the longed-for haven of Chester Park. After I had left the direct road, the wind, which had before been piercingly keen, fell, and I perceived a dark cloud behind, which began slowly to overtake my steps. I care little, in general, for the discomfort of a shower; yet, as when we are in one misfortune we always exaggerate the consequence of a new one, I looked upon my dark pursuer with a very impatient and petulant frown, and set my horse on a trot, much more suitable to my inclination than his own. Indeed, he seemed fully alive to the cornless state of the parson's stable, and evinced his sense of the circumstance by a very languid mode of progression, and a constant attempt, whenever his pace abated, and I suffered the rein to slumber upon his neck, to crop the rank grass that sprung up on either side of our road. I had proceeded about three miles on my way, when I heard the clatter of hoofs behind me. My even pace soon suffered me to be overtaken, and, as the stranger checked his horse when he was nearly by my side, I turned towards him, and beheld Sir John Tyrrell.

"Well," said he, "this is really fortunate—for I began to fear I should have my ride, this cold evening, entirely to myself."

"I imagined that you had long reached Chester Park by this time," said I. "Did not you leave the course with our party?"

"No," answered Tyrrell, "I had business, at Newmarket, with a rascally fellow of the name of Dawson. He lost to me rather a considerable wager, and asked me to come to the town with him after the race, in order to pay me. As he said he lived on the direct road to Chester Park, and would direct, and even accompany me, through all the difficult part of the ride, I the less regretted not joining Chester and his party; and you know, Pelham, that when pleasure pulls one way, and money another, it is all over with the first. Well—to return to my rascal—would you believe, that when we got to Newmarket, he left me at the inn, in order, he said, to fetch the money; and after having kept me in a cold room, with a smoky chimney, for more than an hour, without making his appearance, I sallied out into the town, and found Mr. Dawson quietly seated in a hell with that scoundrel Thornton, whom I did not conceive, till then, he was acquainted with. It seems that he was to win, at hazard, sufficient to pay his wager. You may fancy my anger, and the consequent increase to it, when he rose

279

from the table, approached me, expressed his sorrow, d——d his ill luck, and informed me that he could not pay me for three months. You know that I could not ride home with such a fellow—he might have robbed me by the way—so I returned to my inn—dined—ordered my horse, set off—*en cavalier seul**—inquired my way of every passenger I passed, and after innumerable misdirections—here I am."

"I cannot sympathise with you," said I, "since I am benefited by your misfortunes. But do you think it very necessary to trot so fast? I fear my horse can scarcely keep up with yours."

Tyrrell cast an impatient glance at my panting steed. "It is cursed unlucky you should be so badly mounted, and we shall have a pelting shower presently."

In complaisance to Tyrrell, I endeavoured to accelerate my steed. The roads were rough and stony, and I had scarcely got the tired animal into a sharper trot, before—whether or no by some wrench among the deep ruts and flinty causeway—he fell suddenly lame. The impetuosity of Tyrrell broke out in oaths, and we both dismounted to examine the cause of my horse's hurt, in the hope that it might only be the intrusion of some pebble between the shoe and the hoof. While we were yet investigating the cause of our misfortune, two men on horseback overtook us. Tyrrell looked up. "By Heaven," said he, in a low tone, "it's that dog Dawson, and his worthy coadjutor, Tom Thornton."

"What's the matter, gentlemen?" cried the bluff voice of the latter. "Can I be of any assistance?" and without waiting our reply, he dismounted, and came up to us. He had no sooner felt the horse's leg, than he assured us it was a most severe strain, and that the utmost I could effect would be to walk the brute gently home.

As Tyrrell broke out into impatient violence at this speech, the sharper looked up at him with an expression of countenance I by no means liked; but in a very civil, and even respectful tone, said, "If you want, Sir John, to reach Chester Park sooner than Mr. Pelham can possibly do, suppose you ride on with us, I will put you in the direct road before I quit you." (Good breeding, thought I, to propose leaving me to find my own way through this labyrinth of ruts and stones!) However, Tyrrell, who was in a vile humour, in no very courteous manner, refused the offer, and added that he should continue with me as long as he could, and did not doubt that when he left me he should be able to find his own way. Thornton pressed the invitation still closer, and even offered, *sotto voce,* to send Dawson on before, should the baronet object to his company.

280

"Pray, Sir," said Tyrrell, "leave me alone, and busy yourself about your own affairs." After so tart a reply, Thornton thought it useless to say more; he remounted, and with a silent and swaggering nod of familiarity, soon rode away with his companion.

"I am sorry," said I, as we were slowly proceeding, "that you rejected Thornton's offer."

"Why, to say truth," answered Tyrrell, "I have so very bad an opinion of him, that I was almost afraid to trust myself in his company on so dreary a road. I have nearly (and he knows it), to the amount of two thousand pounds about me; for I was very fortunate in my betting-book to-day."

"I know nothing about racing regulations," said I; "but I thought one never paid sums of that amount upon the ground?"

"Ah!" answered Tyrrell, "but I won this sum, which is £1,800, of a country squire from Norfolk, who said he did not know when he should see me again, and insisted on paying me on the spot: 'faith I was not nice in the matter. Thornton was standing by at the time, and I did not half like the turn of his eye when he saw me put it up. Do you know, too," continued Tyrrell, after a pause, "that I have had a d——d fellow dodging me all day, and yesterday too; wherever I go, I am sure to see him. He seems constantly, though distantly, to follow me; and what is worse, he wraps himself up so well, and keeps at so cautious a distance, that I can never catch a glimpse of his face."

I know not why, but at that moment the recollection of the muffled figure I had seen upon the course, flashed upon me.

"Does he wear a long horseman's cloak?" said I.

"He does," answered Tyrrell, in surprise: "have you observed him?"

"I saw such a person on the race ground," replied I; "but only for an instant!"

Farther conversation was suspended by a few heavy drops which fell upon us; the cloud had passed over the moon, and was hastening rapidly and loweringly over our heads. Tyrrell was neither of an age, a frame, nor a temper, to be so indifferent to a hearty wetting as myself.

"God!"* he cried, "you *must* put on that beast of your's—I can't get wet, for all the horses in the world."

I was not much pleased with the dictatorial tone of this remark. "It is impossible," said I, "especially as the horse is not my own, and seems considerably lamer than at first; but let me not detain you."

"Well!" cried Tyrrell, in a raised and angry voice, which pleased

281

me still less than his former remark; "but how am I to find my way, if I leave you?"

"Keep straight on," said I, "for a mile farther, then a sign-post will direct you to the left; after a short time, you will have a steep hill to descend, at the bottom of which is a large pool, and a singularly shaped tree; then keep straight on, till you pass a house belonging to Mr. Dawson ———"

"Come, come, Pelham, make haste!" exclaimed Tyrrell, impatiently, as the rain began now to descend fast and heavy.

"When you have passed that house," I resumed coolly, rather enjoying his petulance, "you must bear to the right for six miles, and you will be at Chester Park in less than an hour.

Tyrrell made no reply, but put spurs to his horse. The pattering rain and the angry heavens soon drowned the last echoes of the receding hoof-clang.

For myself, I looked in vain for a tree; not even a shrub was to be found; the fields lay bare on either side, with no other partition but a dead hedge, and a deep dyke. *"Patientia fit melius,"*[2] &c. thought I, as Horace said, and Vincent *would* say; and in order to divert my thoughts from my situation, I turned them towards my diplomatic success with Lord Chester. Presently, for I think scarcely five minutes had elapsed since Tyrrell's departure, a horseman passed me at a sharp pace; the moon was hid by the dense cloud, and the night, though not wholly dark, was dim and obscured, so that I could only catch the outline of the flitting figure. A thrill of fear crept over me, when I saw that it was enveloped in a horseman's cloak. I soon rallied —"There are more cloaks in the world than one," said I to myself: "besides, even if it be Tyrrell's dodger, as he calls him, the baronet is better mounted than any highwayman since the days of Du Val;[3] and is, moreover, strong enough and cunning enough to take admirable care of himself." With this reflection I dismissed the occurrence from my thoughts, and once more returned to self-congratulations upon my own incomparable genius. "I shall now," I thought, " have well earned my seat in parliament; Dawton will indisputably be, if not the prime, the principal minister in rank and influence. He cannot fail to promote me for his own sake, as well as mine; and when I have once fairly got my legs in St. Stephen's, I shall soon have my hands in office: 'power,' says some one, 'is a snake that when it once finds a

2. "Patience makes it easier" (Horace *Carmen* 1.24.19). Misquoted.

3. Claude Duval (1643–70): notorious highwayman whose adventures formed the subject of numerous stories and poems.

hole into which it can introduce its head, soon manages to wriggle in the rest of its body.' "[4] With such meditations I endeavoured to beguile the time and cheat myself into forgetfulness of the lameness of my horse, and the dripping wetness of his rider. At last the storm began sullenly to subside: one impetuous torrent, ten-fold more violent than those that had preceded it, was followed by a momentary stillness, which was again broken by a short relapse of a less formidable severity, and the moment it ceased, the beautiful moon broke out, the cloud rolled heavily away, and the sky shone forth, as fair and smiling as Lady ———at a ball, after she has been beating her husband at home.

But at that instant, or perhaps a second before the storm ceased, I thought I heard the sound of a human cry. I paused, and my heart stood still—I could have heard a gnat hum: the sound was not repeated; my ear caught nothing but the plashing of the rain drops from the dead hedges, and the murmur of the swollen dykes, as the waters pent within them rolled hurriedly on. By and by, an owl came suddenly from behind me, and screamed as it flapped across my path; that, too, went rapidly away: and with a smile, at what I deemed my own fancy, I renewed my journey. I soon came to the precipitous descent I have before mentioned; I dismounted, for safety, from my drooping and jaded horse, and led him down the hill. At a distance beyond I saw something dark moving on the grass which bordered the road; as I advanced, it started forth from the shadow, and fled rapidly before me, in the moonshine—it was a riderless horse. A chilling foreboding seized me: I looked round for some weapon, such as the hedge might afford; and finding a strong stick of tolerable weight and thickness, I proceeded more cautiously, but more fearlessly than before. As I wound down the hill, the moonlight fell full upon the remarkable and lonely tree I had observed in the morning. Bare, wan, and giant-like, as it rose amidst the surrounding waste, it borrowed even a more startling and ghostly appearance from the cold and lifeless moonbeams which fell around and upon it like a shroud. The retreating animal* I had driven before me, paused by this tree. I hastened my steps, as if by an involuntary impulse, as well as the enfeebled animal I was leading would allow me, and discovered a horseman galloping across the waste at full speed. The ground over which he passed was steeped in the moonshine, and I saw the long and disguising cloak, in which he

---

4. Unidentified.

was enveloped, as clearly as by the light of day. I paused; and as I was following him with my looks, my eye fell upon some obscure object by the left side of the pool. I threw my horse's rein over the hedge, and firmly grasping my stick, hastened to the spot. As I approached the object, I perceived that it was a human figure; it was lying still and motionless; the limbs were half immersed in the water—the face was turned upwards—the side and throat were wet with a deep red stain—it was of blood; the thin, dark hairs of the head, were clotted together over a frightful and disfiguring contusion. I bent over the face in a shuddering and freezing silence. It was the countenance of Sir John Tyrrell!

VOLUME THREE

CHAPTER I

Marry, he was dead—
And the right valiant Banquot walked too late,
Whom, you may say, if it please you, Fleance killed,
For Fleance fled!

Macbeth[1]

IT IS A FEARFUL THING, EVEN TO THE HARDIEST NERVES, to find ourselves suddenly alone with the dead. How much more so, if we have, but a breathing interval before, moved and conversed with the warm and living likeness of the motionless clay before us!

And this was the man from whom I had parted in coldness— almost in anger—at a word—a breath! I took up the heavy hand—it fell from my grasp, and as it did so, I thought a change passed over the livid countenance. I was deceived; it was but a light cloud flitting over the moon;—it rolled away, and the placid and guiltless light shone over that scene of dread and blood, making more wild and chilling the eternal contrast of earth and heaven—man and his Maker— passion and immutability—dust and immortality.*

But that was not a moment for reflection—a thousand thoughts hurried upon me, and departed as swift and confusedly as they came. My mind seemed a jarring and benighted chaos of the faculties which were its elements; and I had stood several minutes over the corpse before, by a vigorous effort, I shook off the stupor that possessed me, and began to think of the course that it now behoved me to pursue.

The house I had noted in the morning was, I knew, within a few minutes' walk of the spot; but it belonged to Dawson, upon whom the first weight of my suspicions rested. I called to mind the disreputable character of that man, and the still more daring and hardened one of his companion Thornton. I remembered the reluctance of the deceased to accompany them, and the well-grounded reason he

---

1. *Macbeth*, III, 6, 4–7.

assigned; and my suspicions amounting to certainty, I resolved rather to proceed to Chester Park, and there give the alarm, than to run the unnecessary risk of interrupting the murderers in the very lair of their retreat. And yet, thought I, as I turned slowly away, how, if *they* were the villains, is the appearance and flight of the disguised horseman to be accounted for.

Then flashed upon my recollection all that Tyrrell had said of the dogged pursuit of that mysterious person, and the circumstance of his having passed me upon the road so immediately after Tyrrell had quitted me. These reflections (associated with a name that* I did not dare breathe even to myself, although I could not suppress a suspicion which accounted at once for the pursuit, and even for the deed), made me waver in, and almost renounce my former condemnation of Thornton and his friend: and by the time I reached the white gate and dwarfish avenue which led to Dawson's house, I resolved, at all events, to halt at the solitary mansion, and mark the effect my information would cause.

A momentary fear for my own safety came across me, but was as instantly dismissed;—for even supposing the friends were guilty, still it would be no object to them to extend their remorseless villany to me; and I knew that I could sufficiently command my own thoughts to prevent any suspicion I might form, from mounting to my countenance, or discovering itself in my manner.

There was a light in the upper story; it burned still and motionless. How holy seemed the tranquillity of life, to the forced and fearful silence of the death scene I had just witnessed! I rung twice at the door—no one came to answer my summons, but the light in the upper window moved hurriedly to and fro.

"They are coming," said I to myself. No such thing—the casement above was opened—I looked up, and discovered, to my infinite comfort and delight, a blunderbuss protruded eight inches out of the window in a direct line with my head; I receded close to the wall with no common precipitation.

"Get away, you rascal," said a gruff, but trembling voice, "or I'll blow your brains out."

"My good Sir," I replied, still keeping my situation, "I come on urgent business, either to Mr. Thornton or Mr. Dawson; and you had better, therefore, if the delay is not very inconvenient, defer the honour you offer me, till I have delivered my message."

"Master and 'Squire Thornton are not returned from Newmarket, and we cannot let any one in till they come home," replied the voice, in a tone somewhat mollified by my rational remonstrance; and while I was deliberating what rejoinder to make, a rough, red head, like Liston's, in a farce, poked itself cautiously out under cover of the blunderbuss, and seemed to reconnoitre my horse and myself. Presently another head, but attired in the more civilized gear of a cap and flowers, peeped over the first person's left shoulder; the view appeared to reassure them both.

"Sir," said the female, "my husband and Mr. Thornton are not returned; and we have been so much alarmed of late, by an attack on the house, that I cannot admit any one till their return."

"Madam," I replied, reverently doffing my hat, "I do not like to alarm you by mentioning the information I should have given to Mr. Dawson; only oblige me by telling them, on their return, to look beside the pool on the common; they will then do as best pleases them."

Upon this speech, which certainly was of no agreeable tendency, the blunderbuss palpitated so violently, that I thought it highly imprudent to tarry any longer in so perilous a vicinity; accordingly, I made the best of my way out of the avenue, and once more resumed my road to Chester Park.

I arrived there at length; the gentlemen were still in the dining-room. I sent out for Lord Chester, and communicated the scene I had witnessed, and the cause of my delay.

"What, Brown Bob lamed?" said he, "and Tyrrell—poor—poor fellow, how shocking! We must send instantly. Here, John! Tom! Wilson!" and his lordship shouted and rung the bell in an indescribable agitation.

The under butler appeared, and Lord Chester began—"My head groom—Sir John Tyrrell is murdered—violent sprain in off leg—send lights with Mr. Pelham—poor gentleman—and express instantly to Dr. Physicon—Mr. Pelham will tell you all—Brown Bob—his throat cut from ear to ear—what shall be done?" and with this coherent and explanatory harangue, the marquis sunk down in his chair in a sort of hysteric.

The under butler looked at him in suspicious bewilderment. "Come," said I, "I will explain what his lordship means:" and, taking the man out of the room, I gave him, in brief, the necessary particulars. I ordered a fresh horse for myself, and four horsemen to accompany me. While these were preparing, the news was rapidly spreading, and I was soon surrounded by the whole house. Many of the men wished to accompany me; and Lord Chester, who had at last recovered from his stupor, insisted upon heading the search. We set off,

289

to the number of fourteen, and soon arrived at Dawson's house: the light in the upper room was still burning. We rang, and after a brief pause, Thornton himself opened the door to us. He looked pale and agitated.

"How shocking!" he said directly—"we are only just returned from the spot."

"Accompany us, Mr. Thornton," said I, sternly, and fixing my eye upon him.

"Certainly," was his immediate answer, without testifying any confusion—"I will fetch my hat." He went into the house for a moment.

"Do you suspect these people?" whispered Lord Chester.

"Not suspect," said I, "but *doubt*."

We proceeded down the avenue: "Where is Mr. Dawson?" said I to Thornton.

"Oh, within!" answered Thornton. "Shall I fetch him?"

"Do," was my brief reply.

Thornton was absent some minutes; when he re-appeared, Dawson was following him. "Poor fellow," said he to me in a low tone—"he was so shocked by the sight, that he is still all in a panic; besides, as you will see, he is half drunk still."

I made no answer, but looked narrowly at Dawson; he was evidently, as Thornton said, greatly intoxicated: his eyes swam, and his feet staggered as he approached us; yet, through all the natural effects of drunkenness, he seemed nervous and frightened. This, however, might be the natural, and consequently innocent effect, of the mere sight of an object so full of horror; and, accordingly, I laid little stress upon it.

We reached the fatal spot: the body seemed perfectly unmoved. "Why," said I, apart to Thornton, while all the rest were crowding fearfully round the corpse—"why did you not take the body within?"

"I was going to return here with our servant for that purpose," answered the gambler; "for poor Dawson was both too drunk and too nervous to give me any assistance."

"And how came it," I rejoined, eyeing him searchingly, "that you and your friend had not returned home when I called there, although you had both long since passed me on the road, and I had never overtaken you?"

Thornton, without any hesitation, replied—"Because, during the violence of the shower, we cut across the fields to an old shed, which we recollected, and we remained there till the rain had ceased."

"They are probably innocent," thought I—and I turned to look once more at the body which our companions had now raised. There was upon the head a strong contusion, as if inflicted by some blunt and heavy instrument. The fingers of the right hand were deeply gashed, and one of them almost dissevered: the unfortunate man had, in all probability, grasped the sharp weapon from which his other wounds proceeded; these were one wide cut along the throat, and another in the side; either of them would have occasioned his death.

In loosening the clothes, another wound was discovered, but apparently of a less fatal nature; and in lifting the body, the broken blade of a long sharp instrument, like a case-knife, was discovered. It was the opinion of the surgeon, who afterwards examined the body, that the blade had been broken by coming in contact with one of the rib bones; and it was by this that he accounted for the slightness of the last mentioned wound. I looked carefully among the fern and long grass, to see if I could discover any other token of the murderer: Thornton assisted me. At the distance of some feet from the body, I thought I perceived something glitter. I hastened to the place, and picked up a miniature. I was just going to cry out, when Thornton whispered—"Hush! I know the picture; it is as I suspected."

An icy thrill ran through my very heart. With a desperate but trembling hand, I cleansed from the picture the blood, in which, notwithstanding its distance from the corpse, the greater part of it was bathed. I looked upon the features; they were those of a young and singularly beautiful female. I recognized them not: I turned to the other side of the miniature; upon it were braided two locks of hair—one was the long, dark ringlet of a woman, the other was of a light auburn. Beneath were four letters. I looked eagerly at them. "My eyes are dim," said I, in a low tone to Thornton, "I cannot trace the initials."

"But *I* can," replied he, in the same whispered key, but with a savage exultation, which made my heart stand still—"they are G. D., R. G.; they are the initials of Gertrude Douglas and *Reginald Glanville.*"

I looked up at the speaker—our eyes met—I grasped his hand vehemently. He understood me. "Put it up," said he; "we will keep the secret." All this, so long in the recital, passed in the rapidity of a moment.

"Have you found any thing there, Pelham?" shouted one of our companions.

291

"No!" cried I, thrusting the miniature in my bosom, and turning unconcernedly away.

We carried the corpse to Dawson's house. The poor wife was in fits. We heard her scream as we laid the body upon a table in the parlour.

"What more can be done?" said Lord Chester.

"Nothing," was the general answer. No excitation makes the English people* insensible to the chance of catching cold!

"Let us go home, then, and send to the nearest magistrate," exclaimed our host: and this proposal required no repetition.

On our way, Chester said to me, "That fellow Dawson looked devilish uneasy—don't you still suspect him and his friend?"

"*I do not!*" answered I, emphatically.

CHAPTER II

And now I'm in the world alone,

*   *   *   *   *

But why for others should I groan,
When none will sigh for me?

BYRON[1]

THE WHOLE COUNTRY WAS IN CONFUSION AT THE NEWS of the murder. All the myrmidons of justice were employed in the most active research for the murderers. Some few persons were taken up on suspicion, but were as instantly discharged. Thornton and Dawson underwent a long and rigorous examination; but no single tittle of evidence against them appeared: they were consequently dismissed. The only suspicious circumstance against them, was their delay on the road; but the cause given, the same as Thornton had at first assigned to me, was probable and natural. The shed was indicated, and, as if to confirm Thornton's account, a glove belonging to that person was found there. To crown all, my own evidence, in which I was constrained to mention the circumstance of the muffled horse-

---

1. Byron, *Childe Harold's Pilgrimage,* canto 1, lines 182, 184–85.

man having passed me on the road, and being found by me on the spot itself, threw the whole weight of suspicion upon that man, whoever he might be.

All attempts, however, to discover him were in vain. It was ascertained that a man, muffled in a cloak, was *seen* at Newmarket, but not remarkably observed; it was also discovered, that a person so habited had put up a grey horse to bait in one of the inns at Newmarket; but in the throng of strangers, neither the horse nor its owner had drawn down any particular remark.

On further inquiry, testimony differed; *four* or *five* men, in cloaks, had left their horses at the stables; one ostler changed the colour of the steed to brown, a second to black, a third deposed that the gentleman was remarkably tall, and the waiter swore solemnly he had given a glass of brandy and water to an *unked*[2] looking gentleman, in a cloak, who was remarkably short. In fine, no material point could be proved, and though the officers were still employed in active search, they could trace nothing that promised a speedy discovery.

As for myself, as soon as I decently could, I left Chester Park, with a most satisfactory despatch in my pocket, from its possessor to Lord Dawton, and found myself once more on the road to London.

Alas! how different were my thoughts, how changed the temper of my mind, since I had last travelled that road! Then I was full of hope, energy, ambition—of interest for Reginald Glanville—of adoration for his sister; and *now*, I leaned back listless and dispirited, without a single feeling to gladden the restless and feverish despair which, ever since *that* night, had possessed me. What was ambition henceforth to me? The most selfish amongst us must have some human being *to* whom to refer—*with* whom to connect—to associate—to treasure the triumphs and gratifications of self. Where now for my heart was such a being? My earliest friend, for whom my esteem was the greater for his sorrows, my interest the keener for his mystery, Reginald Glanville, was a murderer! a dastardly, a barbarous felon, whom the chance of an instant might convict!—and she—she, the only woman in the world I had ever really loved—who had ever pierced the thousand folds of my ambitious and scheming heart—*she* was the sister of the assassin!

Then came over my mind the savage and exulting eye of Thornton, when it read the damning record of Glanville's guilt; and in spite of my horror at the crime of my former friend, I trembled for his safety:

---

2. Unked: unfamiliar, strange.

293

nor was I satisfied with myself at my prevarication as a witness. It is true that I had told the truth, but I had concealed *all* the truth; my heart swelled proudly and bitterly against the miniature which I still concealed in my bosom.

Light as I may seem to the reader, bent upon the pleasures and the honours of the great world, as I really was, there had never, since I had recognized and formed a decided code of principles, been a single moment in which I had transgressed it: and perhaps I was sterner and more inflexible in the tenets of my morality, such as they were, than even the most zealous worshipper of the letter, as well as the spirit of the law and the prophets, would require. Certainly there were many pangs within me, when I reflected, that* to save a criminal, in whose safety I was selfishly concerned, I had tampered with my honour, paltered with the truth, and broken what I felt to be a peremptory and inviolable duty. Let it be for ever remembered, that once acknowledge and ascertain that a principle is publicly good, and no possible private motive should ever induce you to depart from it.*

It was with a heightened pulse, and a burning cheek, that I entered London: before midnight I was in a high fever; they sent for the vultures of physic—I was bled copiously—I was kept quiet in bed for six days; at the end of that time, my constitution and youth restored me. I took up one of the newspapers listlessly; Glanville's name struck me; I read the paragraph which contained it—it was a high-flown and fustian panegyric on his genius and promise. I turned to another column, it contained a long speech he had the night before made in the House of Commons.

"Can such things be?" thought I; yea, and thereby hangs a secret and an anomaly in the human heart. A man may commit the greatest of crimes, and (if no other succeed to it) it changes not the current of his being; to all the world—to all intents—for all objects he may be the same. He may equally serve his country—equally benefit his friends—be generous—brave—benevolent, all that he was before. *One* crime, however heinous, makes no revolution in the system—it is only the *perpetual* course of sins, vices, follies, however insignificant they may seem, which alters the nature and hardens the heart.

My mother was out of town when I returned there. They had written to her during my illness, and while I was yet musing over the day's journal, a letter from her was put into my hand. I transcribe it.

294

"My dearest Henry,

"How dreadfully uneasy I am about you: write to me directly. I would come to town myself, but am staying with dear Lady Dawton, who will not hear of my going; and I cannot offend her for *your* sake. By the by, why have you not called upon Lord Dawton? but, I forgot, you have been ill. My dear, dear child, I am wretched about you, and how pale your illness will make you look! just too, as the best part of the season is coming on. How unlucky! Pray, don't wear a black cravat when you next call on Lady Roseville; but choose a very fine *baptiste* one—it will make you look rather delicate than ill. What physician do you have? I hope, in God, that it is Sir Henry Halford.[3] I shall be too miserable if it is not. I am sure no one can conceive the anguish I suffer. Your father, too, poor man, has been laid up with the gout for the last three days. Keep up your spirits, my dearest child, and get some light books to entertain you: but, pray, as soon as you *are* well, do go to Lord Dawton's—he is dying to see you; but be sure not to catch cold. How did you like Lady Chester? Pray take the greatest care of yourself, and write soon to

"Your wretched, and most
"Affectionate Mother,
"F. P.

"P.S. How dreadfully shocking about that poor Sir John Tyrrell!"

I tossed the letter from me. Heaven pardon me if the misanthropy of my mood made me less grateful for the maternal solicitude than I should otherwise have been.

I took up one of the numerous books with which my table was covered; it was a worldly work of one of the French reasoners; it gave a new turn to my thoughts—my mind reverted to its former projects of ambition. Who does not know what active citizens private misfortune makes us? The public is like the pools of Bethesda[4]—we all hasten there, to plunge in and rid ourselves of our afflictions.

I drew my *portefeuille** to me, and wrote to Lord Dawton. Three hours after I had sent the note, he called upon me. I gave him Lord Chester's letter, but he had already received from that nobleman a notification of my success. He was profuse in his compliments and thanks.

"And, do you know," added the statesman, "that you have quite

---

3. Sir Henry Halford (1766–1844) was one of George III's consulting physicians.
4. John 5:2–4.

made a conquest of Lord Guloseton? He speaks of you publicly in the highest terms: I wish we could get him and his votes. We *must* be strengthened, my dear Pelham; every thing depends on the crisis."

"Are you certain of the cabinet?" I asked.

"Yes; it is not yet publicly announced, but it is fully known amongst us, who comes in, and who stays out. I am to have the place of ———."

"I congratulate your lordship from my heart. What post do you design for me?"

Lord Dawton changed countenance. "Why—really—Pelham, we have not yet filled up the lesser appointments, but you shall be well remembered—*well,* my dear Pelham—be sure of it."

I looked at the noble speaker with a glance which, I flatter myself, is peculiar to me. If, thought I, the embryo minister is playing upon me as upon one of his dependant characters; if he dares forget what he owes to my birth and zeal, I will grind myself to powder but I will shake him out of his seat.* The anger of the moment passed away.

"Lord Dawton," said I, "one word, and I have done discussing my claims for the present. Do you mean to place me in Parliament as soon as you are in the cabinet? What else you intend for me, I question not."

"Yes, assuredly, Pelham. How can you doubt it?"

"Enough!—and now read this letter from France."

*   *   *   *   *   *   *

Two days after my interview with Lord Dawton, as I was riding leisurely through the Green Park, in no very bright and social mood, one of the favoured carriages, whose owners are permitted to say, *"Hic iter est nobis,"*[5] overtook me. A sweet voice ordered the coachman to stop, and then addressed itself to me.

"What, the hero of Chester Park returned, without having once narrated his adventures to me?"

"Beautiful Lady Roseville," said I, "I plead guilty of negligence—not treason. I forgot, it is true, to appear before you, but I forget not the devotion of my duty now that I behold you. Command, and I obey."

"See, Ellen," said Lady Roseville, turning to a bending and blushing countenance beside her, which I then first perceived—"see what it is to be a knight-errant; even his language is worthy of Amadis of

---

5. "This road is ours." Apparently adapted from Horace *Satires* 1.9.16. See also *Aeneid* 9.321.

Gaul[6]—but—(again addressing me) your adventures are really too shocking a subject to treat lightly. We lay our serious orders on you to come to our castle this night: we shall be alone."

"Willingly shall I repair to your bower, fayre ladie; but tell me, I beseech you, how many persons are signified in the word 'alone?' "

"Why," answered Lady Roseville, "I fear we *may* have two or three people with us; but I think, Ellen, we may promise our chevalier that the number shall not exceed twelve."

I bowed and rode on. What worlds would I not have given to have touched the hand of the countess's companion, though only for an instant. But—and that fearful *but,* chilled me, like an ice-bolt. I put spurs to my horse, and dashed fiercely onwards. There was rather a high wind stirring, and I bent my face from it, so as scarcely to see the course of my spirited and impatient horse.

"What ho, Sir!—what ho!" cried a shrill voice—"for God's sake, don't ride over me *before* dinner, whatever you do after it!"

I pulled up. "Ah, Lord Guloseton! how happy I am to see you; pray forgive my blindness, and my horse's stupidity."

" 'Tis an ill wind," answered the noble gourmand, "which blows nobody good. An excellent proverb, the veracity of which is daily attested; for, however unpleasant a keen wind may be, there is no doubt of its being a marvellous whetter of that greatest of Heaven's blessings—*an appetite.* Little, however, did I expect, that besides blowing me a relish for my *sauté de foie gras,* it would also blow me one who might, probably, be a partaker of my enjoyment. Honour me with your company at dinner to-day."

"What saloon will you dine in, my Lord Lucullus?" said I, in allusion to the custom of the epicure, by whose name I addressed him.

"The saloon of Diana," replied Guloseton—"for she must certainly have shot the fine buck of which Lord H. sent me the haunch that we shall have to-day. It is the true old Meynell breed. I ask you not to meet Mr. So-and-so, and Lord What-d'ye-call-him: I ask you to meet a *sauté de foie gras,* and a haunch of venison."

"I will most certainly pay them my respects. Never did I know before how far *things* were better company than *persons.* Your lordship has taught me that great truth."

"God bless me!" cried Guloseton, with an air of vexation, "here comes the Duke of Stilton, a horrid person, who told me the other

<hr>

6. The hero of the chivalric romance *Amadis of Gaul* (thirteenth or fourteenth century, Spanish or Portuguese).

day, at my *petit diner,* when I apologized to him for some strange error of my *artiste's,* by which common vinegar had been substituted for Chili—who told me—what think you he told me? You cannot guess, he told me, forsooth, that he did not care what he eat; and, for his part, he could make a very good dinner off a beef-steak! Why the deuce, then, did he come and dine with *me?* Could he have said any thing more cutting? Imagine my indignation, when I looked round my table and saw so many good things thrown away upon such an idiot."

Scarcely was the last word out of the gourmand's mouth before the noble personage so designated, joined us. It amused me to see Guloseton's contempt (which he scarcely took the pains to suppress) of a person whom all Europe honoured, and his evident weariness of a companion, whose society every one else would have coveted as the *summum bonum* of wordly distinction. As for me, feeling any thing but social, I soon left the ill-matched pair, and rode into the other park.

Just as I entered it, I perceived, on a dull, yet cross-looking pony, Mr. Wormwood, of bitter memory. Although we had not met since our mutual sojourn at Sir Lionel Garrett's, and were then upon very cool terms of acquaintance, he seemed resolved to recognize and claim me.

"My dear Sir," said he, with a ghastly smile, "I am rejoiced once more to see you; bless me, how pale you look. I heard you had been very ill. Pray, have you been yet to that man who professes to cure consumption in the worst stages?"

"Yes," said I, "he read me two or three letters of reference from the patients he had cured. His last, he said, was a gentleman very far gone—a Mr. Wormwood."

"Oh, you are pleased to be facetious," said the cynic, coldly—"but pray do tell me about that horrid affair at Chester Park. How disagreeable it must have been to you to be taken up *on suspicion of the murder.*"

"Sir," said I, haughtily, "what do you mean?"

"Oh, you were not—wer'n't you? Well, I always thought it unlikely; but every one says so———"

"My dear Sir," I rejoined, "how long is it since you have minded what every body says? If I were so foolish, I should not be riding with you now; but *I* have always said, *in contradiction to every body,* and even in spite of being universally laughed at for my singular opinion, that you, my dear Mr. Wormwood, were by no means silly, nor ignorant, nor insolent, nor intrusive; that you were, on the contrary, a very decent author, and a very good sort of man; and that you were so benevolent, that you daily granted to some one or other, the greatest happiness in your power: it is a happiness I am now about to enjoy, and it consists in wishing you *'good by!'*" And without waiting for Mr. Wormwood's answer, I gave the rein to my horse, and was soon lost among the crowd, which had now begun to assemble.

Hyde Park is a stupid place. The English* make business an enjoyment, and enjoyment a business: they are born without a smile; they rove about public places like so many easterly winds—cold, sharp, and cutting; or like a group of fogs on a frosty day, sent out of his hall by Boreas for the express purpose of *looking black at one another.* When they ask you, "how do you do," you would think they were measuring the length of your coffin. They are ever, it is true, *labouring* to be agreeable; but they are like Sisyphus, the stone they roll up the hill with so much toil, runs down again, and hits you a thump on the legs. They are sometimes *polite,* but invariably *uncivil;* their warmth is always artificial—their cold never; they are stiff without dignity, and cringing without manners. They offer you an affront, and call it "plain truth," they wound your feelings, and tell you it is manly "to speak their minds;" at the same time, while they have neglected all the graces and charities of artifice, they have adopted all its falsehood and deceit. While they profess to abhor servility, they adulate the peerage—while they tell you they care not a rush for the minister, they move heaven and earth for an invitation from the minister's wife. There is not another court in Europe where such systematized meanness is carried on,—where they will even believe you, when you assert that it exists. Abroad, you can smile at the vanity of one class, and the flattery of another: the first is too well bred to affront, the latter too graceful to disgust; but *here,* the pride of a *noblesse,* (by the way, the most mushroom in Europe), knocks you down in a hail-storm, and the fawning of the *bourgeois* makes you sick with hot water.* Then their amusements—the heat—the dust— the sameness—the slowness of that odious park in the morning; and the same exquisite scene repeated in the evening, on the condensed stage of a rout-room, where one has more heat, with less air, and a narrower dungeon, with diminished possibility of escape!—we wander about like the damned in the story of Vathek, and we pass our lives, like the royal philosopher of Prussia,[7] in conjugating the verb, *Je m'ennuis.*

7. William Beckford published his gothic tale *Vathek* in 1786; the "royal philosopher" is Frederick II (the Great) of Prussia.

CHAPTER III

In solo vivendi causa palato est.

JUVENAL[1]

They would talk of nothing but high life, and high-lived company; with other fashionable topics, such as pictures, taste, Shakspeare, and the musical glasses.

Vicar of Wakefield

THE REFLECTIONS WHICH CLOSED THE LAST CHAPTER, will serve to show that I was in no very amiable or convivial temper, when I drove to Lord Guloseton's dinner. However, in the world, it matters little what may be our real mood, the mask hides the bent brow and the writhing lip.

Guloseton was stretched on his sofa, gazing with upward eye at the beautiful Venus which hung above his hearth. "You are welcome, Pelham; I am worshipping my household divinity!"

I prostrated myself on the opposite sofa, and made some answer to the classical epicure, which made us both laugh heartily. We then talked of pictures, painters, poets, the ancients, and Dr. Henderson on Wines;[2] we gave ourselves up, without restraint, to the enchanting fascination of the last-named subject, and our mutual enthusiasm confirming our cordiality, we went down stairs to our dinner, as charmed with each other as boon companions always should be.

"This is *comme il faut*,"* said I, looking round at the well filled table, and the sparkling spirits immersed in the ice-pails, "a genuine *friendly* dinner. It is very rarely that I dare entrust myself to such extempore hospitality—*miserum est alienâ vivere quadrâ*[3]—a friendly dinner, a family meal, are things from which I fly with undisguised

---

1. "The pleasures of the palate are their only reasons for living" (Juvenal *Satires* 11.11). The second epigraph is from Goldsmith, *The Vicar of Wakefield*, chapter 9.

2. Dr. Alexander Henderson, *The History of Ancient and Modern Wines* (1824).

3. "It is miserable to live at another's expense" (Juvenal *Satires* 5.2).

aversion. It is very hard, that in England, one cannot have a friend on pain of being shot or poisoned; if you refuse his familiar invitations, he thinks you mean to affront him, and says something rude, for which you are forced to challenge him; if you accept them, you perish beneath the weight of boiled mutton and turnips, or——"

"My dear friend," interrupted Guloseton, with his mouth full, "it is very true; but this is no time for talking, *let us eat.*"

I acknowledged the justice of the rebuke, and we did not interchange another word beyond the exclamations of surprise, pleasure, admiration, or dissatisfaction, called up by the objects which engrossed our attention, till we found ourselves alone with our dessert.

When I thought my host had imbibed a sufficient quantity of wine, I once more renewed my attack. I had tried him before upon that point of vanity which is centred in power, and political consideration, but in vain; I now bethought me of another.

"How few persons there are," said I, "capable of giving even a tolerable dinner—how many capable of admiring one worthy of estimation! I could imagine no greater triumph for the ambitious epicure, than to see at his board the first and most honoured persons of the state, all lost in wonder at the depth, the variety, the purity, the munificence of his taste; all forgetting, in the extorted respect which a gratified palate never fails to produce, the more visionary schemes and projects which usually occupy their thoughts;—to find those whom all England are soliciting for posts and power, become, in their turn, eager and craving aspirants for places at his table;—to know that all the grand movements of the ministerial body are planned and agitated over the inspirations of his viands and the excitement of his wine. From a haunch of venison, like the one of which we have partaken to-day, what noble and substantial measures might arise! From a *sauté de foie,* what delicate subtleties of finesse might have their origin! From a ragout *à la financière,* what godlike improvements in taxation! Oh, could such a lot be mine, I would envy neither Napoleon for the goodness of his fortune, nor S—— for the grandeur of his genius."

Guloseton laughed. "The ardour of your enthusiasm blinds your philosophy, my dear Pelham; like Montesquieu, the liveliness of your fancy often makes you advance paradoxes which the consideration of your judgment would afterwards condemn. For instance, you must allow, that if one had all those fine persons at one's table, one would be forced to talk more, and consequently to eat less; moreover, you would either be excited by your triumph, or you would not, that is

301

indisputable; if you are not excited, you have the bore for nothing; if you are excited, you spoil your digestion: nothing is so detrimental to the stomach as the feverish inquietude of the passions. All philosophies recommend calm as to the *to kalon*[4] of their code; and you must perceive, that if, in the course you advise, one has occasional opportunities of pride, one also has those of mortification. Mortification! terrible word; how many apoplexies have arisen from its source! No, Pelham, away with ambition; fill your glass, and learn, at last, the secret of real philosophy."

"Confound the man!" was my *mental* anathema.—"Long life to the Solomon of *sautés,*" was my *audible* exclamation.

"There is something," resumed Guloseton, "in your countenance and manner, at once so frank, lively, and ingenuous, that one is not only prepossessed in your favour, but desirous of your friendship. I tell you, therefore, in confidence, that nothing more amuses me than to see the courtship I receive from each party. I laugh at all the unwise and passionate contests in which others are engaged, and I would as soon think of entering into the chivalry of Don Quixote, or attacking the visionary enemies of the Bedlamite, as of taking part in the fury of politicians. At present, looking afar off at their delirium, I can ridicule it; were I to engage in it, I should be hurt by it. I have no wish to become the weeping, instead of the laughing, philosopher. I sleep well now—I have no desire to sleep ill. I eat well—Why should I lose my appetite? I am undisturbed and unattacked in the enjoyments best suited to my taste—for what purpose should I be hurried into the abuse of the journalists and the witticisms of pamphleteers? I can ask those whom I like to my house—why should I be forced into asking those whom I do not like? In fine, my good Pelham, why should I sour my temper and shorten my life, put my green old age into flannel and physic, and become, from the happiest of sages, the most miserable of fools? Ambition reminds me of what Bacon says of anger—'It is like rain, it breaks itself upon that which it falls on.'[5] Pelham, my boy, taste the *Château Margôt.*"

However hurt my vanity might be in having so ill succeeded in my object, I could not help smiling with satisfaction at my entertainer's principles of wisdom. My diplomatic honour, however, was concerned, and I resolved yet to gain him. If, hereafter, I succeeded, it was by a very different method than I had yet taken; meanwhile,

---

4. Literally, "the Beautiful." A common Greek expression for the highest ideal.
5. Francis Bacon, *Essays,* "Of Anger," 57.

I departed from the house of this modern Apicius with a new insight into the great book of mankind, and a new conclusion from its pages; viz. that no virtue can make so perfect a philosopher as the senses. There is no content like that of the epicure—no active code of morals so difficult to conquer as the inertness of his indolence; he is the only being in the world for whom the present has a supremer gratification than the future.

My cabriolet soon whirled me to Lady Roseville's door; the first person I saw in the drawing-room, was Ellen. She lifted up her eyes with that familiar sweetness with which they had long since begun to welcome me. "Her brother may perish on the gibbet!"* was the thought that curdled my blood, and I bowed distantly and passed on.

I met Vincent. He seemed dispirited and dejected. He already saw how ill his party had succeeded; above all, he was enraged at the idea of the person assigned by rumour to fill the place he had intended for himself. This person was a sort of rival to his lordship, a man of quaintness and quotation, with as much learning as Vincent, equal wit, and—but that personage is still in office, and I will say no more, lest he should think I flatter.

To our subject. It has probably been observed that Lord Vincent had indulged less of late in that peculiar strain of learned humour formerly his wont. The fact is, that he had been playing another part; he wished to remove from his character that appearance of literary coxcombry with which he was accused. He knew well how necessary, in the game of politics, it is to appear no less a man of the world than of books; and though he was not averse to display his clerkship and scholastic information, yet he endeavoured to make them seem rather valuable for their weight, than curious for their fashion. How few there are in the world who retain, after a certain age, the character originally natural to them! We all get, as it were, a second skin; the little foibles, propensities, eccentricities, we first indulged through affectation, conglomerate and encrust till the artificiality grows into nature.

"Pelham," said Vincent, with a cold smile, "the day will be yours; the battle is not to the strong—the Whigs will triumph. *'Fugere Pudor, verumque, fidesque; in quorum subiere locum fraudesque dolique insidioeque et vis et amor sceleratus habendi.'* "6

---

6. "Shame, Truth, and Faith have flown; in their stead creep in frauds, craft, snares, force, and the rascally love of gain" (Ovid *Metamorphoses* 1.129–31). [Bulwer's translation; 1840 ed.]

"A pretty modest quotation," said I. "You must allow, at least, that the *amor sceleratus habendi* was also, in some moderate degree, shared by the *Pudor* and *Fides* which characterize your party; otherwise, I am at a loss how to account for the tough struggle against us we have lately had the honour of resisting."

"Never mind," replied Vincent, "I will not refute you,

"'La richesse permet une juste fierté,
Mais il faut être souple avec la pauvreté.'[7]*

It is not for us, the defeated, to argue with you, the victors. But pray, (continued Vincent, with a sneer which pleased me not), pray, among this windfall of the Hesperian fruit, what nice little apple will fall to your share?"

"My good Vincent, don't let us anticipate; if any such apple should come into my lap, let it not be that of discord between us."

"Who talks of discord?" asked Lady Roseville, joining us.

"Lord Vincent," said I, "fancies himself the celebrated fruit, on which was written, *datur pulchriori*, to be given to the fairest.[8] Suffer me, therefore, to make him a present to your ladyship."

Vincent muttered something which, as I really liked and esteemed him, I was resolved not to hear; accordingly I turned to another part of the room: there I found Lady Dawton—she was a tall, handsome woman, as proud as a liberal's wife ought to be. She received me with unusual graciousness, and I sat myself beside her. Three dowagers, and an old beau of the old school, were already sharing the conversation with the haughty countess. I found that the topic was society.

"No," said the old beau, who was entitled Mr. Clarendon, "society is very different from what it was in my younger days. You remember, Lady Paulet, those delightful parties at D ——— House? Where shall we ever find any thing like them? Such ease, such company—even the mixture was so piquant, if one chanced to sit next a *bourgeois,* he was sure to be distinguished for his wit or talent. People were not tolerated, as now, merely for their riches."

"True," cried Lady Dawton, "it is the introduction of low persons, without any single pretension, which spoils the society of the present day!" And the three dowagers sighed amen, to this remark.

---

7. "Riches permit a just pride, but you must be pliable if you are poor" (Boileau, *Satires,* 1, 59–60).

8. "Let it be given to the most beautiful." Pelham refers, of course, to Paris and the apple of discord.

"And yet," said I, "since I may safely say so *here* without being suspected of a personality in the shape of a compliment, don't you think, that without any such mixture, we should be very indifferent company? Do we not find those dinners and *soirées* the pleasantest where we see a minister next to a punster, a poet to a prince, and a coxcomb like me next to a beauty like Lady Dawton? The more variety there is in the conversation, the more agreeable it becomes."

"Very just," answered Mr. Clarendon; "but it is precisely because I wish for that variety that I dislike a miscellaneous society. If one does not know the person beside whom one has the happiness of sitting, what possible subject can one broach with any prudence. I put politics aside, because, thanks to party spirit, we rarely meet those we are strongly opposed to; but if we sneer at the methodists, our neighbour may be a saint—if we abuse a new book, he may have written it—if we observe that the tone of the piano-forte is bad, his father may have made it—if we complain of the uncertainty of the banking* interest, his uncle may have been gazetted last week. I name no exaggerated instances; on the contrary, I refer these general remarks to particular individuals, whom all of us have probably met. Thus, you see, that a variety of topics is prescribed in a mixed company, because some one or other of them will be certain to offend."

Perceiving that we listened to him with attention, Mr. Clarendon continued—"Nor is this more than a minor objection to the great mixture prevalent amongst us: a more important one may be found in the universal imitation it produces. The influx of common persons being once permitted, certain sets recede, as it were, from the con-tamination, and contract into very diminished coteries. *Living familiarly solely* amongst themselves, however they may be forced into *visiting promiscuously*, they imbibe certain manners, certain peculiarities in mode and words—even in an accent or a pronunciation, which are confined to themselves: and whatever differs from these little eccentricities, they are apt to condemn as vulgar and suburban. Now, the fastidiousness of these sets making them difficult of intimate access, even to many of their superiors in actual rank, those very superiors, by a natural feeling in human nature, of prizing what is rare, even if it is worthless, are the first to solicit their acquaintance; and, as a sign that they enjoy it, to *imitate* those peculiarities which are the especial hieroglyphics of this sacred few. The lower grades catch the contagion, and *imitate* those they imagine most likely to know the *propriétés** of the mode; and thus manners, unnatural to all, are transmitted second-hand, third-hand, fourth-hand, till they are

305

ultimately filtered into something worse than no manners at all. Hence, you perceive all people timid, stiff, unnatural, and ill at ease; they are dressed up in a garb which does not fit them, to which they have never been accustomed, and are as little at home as the wild Indian in the boots and garments of the more civilized European."

"And hence," said I, "springs that universal vulgarity of idea, as well as manner, which pervades all society—for nothing is so plebian as imitation."

"A very evident truism!" said Clarendon. "What I lament most, is the injudicious method certain persons took to change this order of things, and diminish the *désagrémens* of the mixture we speak of. I remember well, when Almack's was first set up, the intention was to keep away the rich *roturiers* from a place, the tone of which was also intended to be contrary to their own. For this purpose the patronesses were instituted,[9] the price of admission made extremely low, and all ostentatious refreshments discarded: it was an admirable institution for the interests of the little oligarchy who ruled it—but it has only increased the general imitation and vulgarity. Perhaps the records of that institution contain things more disgraceful to the aristocracy of England, than the whole history of Europe can furnish. And how could the Monsieur and Madame Jourdains help following the servile and debasing example of *Monseigneur le Duc et Pair?*"[10]

"How strange it is," said one of the dowagers, "that of all the novels on society with which we are annually inundated, there is scarcely one which gives even a tolerable description of it!"

"*Not* strange," said Clarendon, with a formal smile, "if your ladyship will condescend to reflect. Most of the writers upon our little, great world, have seen nothing of it: at most, they have been occasionally admitted into the routs of the B.'s and C.'s of the second, or rather the third set. A very few are, it is true, gentlemen; but gentlemen, who are not writers, are as bad as writers who are not gentlemen. In one work, which, since it is popular, I will not name,[11] there is a stiffness and stiltedness in the dialogue and descriptions, perfectly ridiculous. The author makes his countesses always talking of their family, and his earls always quoting the peerage. There is as much fuss about state, and dignity, and pride, as if the greatest amongst

---

9. The six despotic patronesses of Almack's were Lady Castlereagh, Princess Esterhazy, Lady Cowper, Lady Jersey, Mrs. Drummond Burrell (later Lady Sefton), and the Princess Lieven.

10. See Molière's *Le Bourgeois Gentilhomme*.

11. Pelham is referring to Disraeli's *Vivian Grey* (1826).

us were not far too busy with the petty affairs of the world to have time for such lofty vanities. There is only one rule necessary for a clever writer who wishes to delineate the *beau monde*. It is this: let him consider that 'dukes, and lords, and noble princes,'[12] eat, drink, talk, move, exactly the same as any other class of civilized people—nay, the very subjects in conversation are, for the most part, the same in all sets—only, perhaps, they are somewhat more familiarly and easily treated than among the lower orders, who fancy rank is distinguished by pomposity, and that state affairs are discussed with the solemnity of a tragedy—that we are always my lording and my ladying each other—that we ridicule commoners, and curl our hair with Debrett's Peerage."

We all laughed at this speech, the truth of which we readily acknowledged.

"Nothing," said Lady Dawton, "amuses me more than to see the great distinction which novel writers make between the titled and the untitled; they seem to be perfectly unaware, that a commoner, of ancient family and large fortune, is very often of far more real rank and estimation, and even *weight,* in what they are pleased to term *fashion,* than many of the members of the Upper House. And what amuses me as much, is the *no* distinction they make between all people who have titles—Lord A——, the little baron, is exactly the same as Lord Z——, the great marquess, equally haughty and equally important."

"*Mais, mon Dieu,*" said a little French count, who had just joined us; "how is it that you can expect to find a description of society entertaining, when the society itself is so dull?—the closer the copy, the more tiresome it must be. Your manner, *pour vous amuser,* consists in standing on a crowded staircase, and complaining that you are terribly bored. *L'on s'accoutume difficilement à une vie qui se passe sur l'escalier.*"[13]

"It is very true," said Clarendon, "we cannot defend ourselves. We are a very sensible, thinking, brave, sagacious, generous, industrious, noble-minded people; but it must be confessed, that we are terrible bores to ourselves and all the rest of the world. Lady Paulet, if you *are* going so soon, honour me by accepting my arm."

"You should say your *hand,*" said the Frenchman.

---

12. See *Richard III,* II, 1, 68 and *Henry V,* III, 5, 46.

13. "It is difficult to accustom oneself to a life that passes on the staircase" (unidentified).

"Pardon me," answered the gallant old beau; "I say, with your brave countryman when he lost his legs in battle, and was asked by a lady, like the one who now leans on me, whether he would not sooner have lost his arms? 'No, Madam,' said he, (and this, Monsieur le Comte, is the answer I give to your rebuke), 'I want my hands to guard my heart.' "

Finding our little knot was now broken up, I went into another part of the room, and joined Vincent, Lady Roseville, Ellen, and one or two other persons who were assembled round a table covered with books and prints. Ellen was sitting on one side of Lady Roseville; there was a vacant chair next her, but I avoided it, and seated myself on the other side of Lady Roseville.

"Pray, Miss Glanville," said Lord Vincent, taking up a thin volume, "do you greatly admire the poems of this lady?"

"What, Mrs. Hemans?"[14] answered Ellen. "I am more enchanted with her poetry than I can express: if that is 'The Forest Sanctuary' which you have taken up, I am sure you will bear me out in my admiration."

Vincent turned over the leaves with the quiet cynicism of manner habitual to him; but his countenance grew animated after he had read two pages. "This is, indeed, beautiful," said he, "really and genuinely beautiful. How singular that such a work should not be more known! I never met with it before. But whose pencil-marks are these?"

"Mine, I believe," said Ellen, modestly.

And Lady Roseville turned the conversation upon Lord Byron.*

"I must confess, for my part," said Lord Edward Neville (an author of some celebrity and more merit), "that I was exceedingly weary of those doleful ditties with which we were favoured for so many years. No sooner had Lord Byron declared himself unhappy, than every young gentleman with a pale face and dark hair, used to think himself justified in frowning in the glass and writing Odes to Despair. All persons who could scribble two lines were sure to make them into rhymes of 'blight' and 'night.' Never was there so grand a *penchant* for the *triste*."

"It would be interesting enough," observed Vincent, "to trace the origin of this melancholy mania. People are wrong to attribute it to poor Lord Byron—it certainly came from Germany; perhaps Werter was the first hero of that school."

---

14. Mrs. Felicia Hemans (1794–1835). *The Forest Sanctuary*, referred to in the next sentence, appeared in 1826.

308

"There seems," said I, "an unaccountable prepossession among all persons, to imagine that whatever seems gloomy must be profound, and whatever is cheerful must be shallow. They have put poor Philosophy into deep mourning, and given her a coffin for a writing-desk, and a skull for an inkstand."

"Oh," cried Vincent, "I remember some lines so applicable to your remark, that I must forthwith interrupt you, in order to introduce them. Madame de Staël said, in one of her works, that melancholy was a source of perfection.[15] Listen now to my author—

> " 'Une femme nous dit, et nous prouve en effet,
> Qu'avant quelques mille ans l'homme sera parfait,
> Qu'il devra cet état à la *mélancolie.*
> On *sait que la tristesse annonce le génie;*
> Nous avons déjà fait des progrès étonnans,
> Que de tristes écrits—que de tristes romans!
> Des plus noires horreurs nous sommes idolâtres,
> Et la mélancolie a gagné nos théâtres.' "[16]

"What!" cried I, "are you so well acquainted with my favourite book?"

"Yours!" exclaimed Vincent. "Gods, what a sympathy; it has long been my most familiar acquaintance; but—

> " 'Tell us what hath chanced to-day,
> That Cæsar looks so sad?' "[17]

My eye followed Vincent's to ascertain the meaning of this question, and rested upon Glanville, who had that moment entered the room. I might have known that he was expected, by Lady Roseville's abstraction, the restlessness with which she started at times from her seat, and as instantly resumed it; and the fond expecting looks

---

15. See, e.g., *De la littérature,* 1, 11.

16. La Gastronomie, Poëme, par J. Berchoux. [B-L] The complete title of Berchoux's charming book, published in 1801, is *Gastronomie ou l'homme des champs à table.* The lines, in Bulwer's paraphrase (1840 ed.), are:
> A woman tells us, and in fact she proves
> That man, though slowly, to perfection moves;
> But to be perfect, first we must be sad;
> Genius, we know, is melancholy and mad.
> Already time our startling progress hails;
> What cheerless essays! What disastrous tales!
> Horror has grown the amusement of the age,
> And mirth despairing yawns and flies the stage.

17. *Julius Caesar,* I, 2, 16–17.

towards the door, every time it shut or opened, which denote so strongly the absent and dreaming heart of the woman who loves.

Glanville seemed paler than usual, and perhaps even sadder; but he was less *distrait* and abstracted: no sooner did he see, than he approached me, and extended his hand with great cordiality. *His* hand, thought I, and I could not bring myself to accept it; I merely addressed him in the common-place salutation. He looked hard and inquisitively at me, and then turned abruptly away. Lady Roseville had risen from her chair—her eyes followed him. He had thrown himself on a settee near the window. She went up to him, and sate herself by his side. I turned—my face burnt—my heart beat—I was now next to Ellen Glanville; she was looking down, apparently employed with some engravings, but I thought her hand (that small, delicate, *Titania* hand),* trembled.

There was a pause. Vincent was talking with the other occupiers of the table; a woman, at such times, is always the first to speak. "We have not seen you, Mr. Pelham," said Ellen, "since your return to town."

"I have been very ill," I answered, and I felt my voice falter. Ellen looked up anxiously at my face; I could not brook those large, deep, tender eyes, and it now became my turn to occupy myself with the prints.

"You *do* look pale," she said, in a low voice. I did not trust myself with a further remark—dissimulator as I was to others, I was like a guilty child before the woman I loved. There was another pause—at last Ellen said, "How do you think my brother looks?"

I started; yes, he *was* her brother, and I was once more myself at that thought. I answered so coldly and almost haughtily, that Ellen coloured, and said with some dignity, that she should join Lady Roseville. I bowed slightly, and she withdrew to the countess. I seized my hat and departed—but not utterly alone—I had managed to secrete the book which Ellen's hand had marked; through many a bitter day and sleepless night, that book has been my only companion; I have it before me now, and it is open at a page which is yet blistered with the traces of former tears.

310

CHAPTER IV

Our mistress is a little given to philosophy: what disputations shall we have here by and by?

GIL BLAS[1]

IT WAS NOW BUT SELDOM THAT I MET ELLEN, FOR I went little into general society, and grew every day more engrossed in political affairs. Sometimes, however, when, wearied of myself, and my graver occupations, I yielded to my mother's solicitations, and went to one of the nightly haunts of the goddess *we* term *Pleasure,* and the Greeks *Moria,* the game of dissipation (to use a Spanish proverb) shuffled us together. It was then that I had the most difficult task of my life to learn and to perform; to check the lip—the eye—the soul—to heap curb on curb, upon the gushings of the heart, which daily and hourly yearned to overflow; and to feel, that while the mighty and restless tides of passion were thus fettered and restrained, all within was a parched and arid wilderness, that wasted itself, for want of very moisture, away. Yet there was something grateful in the sadness with which I watched her form in the dance, or listened to her voice in the song; and I felt soothed, and even happy, when my fancy flattered itself, that her step never now seemed so light, as it was wont to be when in harmony with mine, nor the songs that pleased her most, so gay as those that were formerly her choice.

Distant and unobserved, I loved to feed my eyes upon her pale and downcast cheek; to note the abstraction that came over her at moments, even when her glance seemed brightest, and her lip most fluent; and to know, that while a fearful mystery might for ever forbid the union of our hands, there was an invisible, but electric chain, which connected the sympathies of our hearts.

Ah! why is it, that the noblest of our passions should be also the most selfish?—that while we would make all earthly sacrifice for the one we love, we are perpetually demanding a sacrifice in return;

---

1. *Gil Blas,* book IV, chapter 8.

that if we cannot have the rapture of blessing, we find a consolation in the power to afflict; and that we acknowledge, while we reprobate, the maxim of the sage: *"L'on veut faire tout le bonheur, ou, si cela ne se peut ainsi, tout le malheur de ce qu'on aime."*[2]

The beauty of Ellen was not of that nature which rests solely upon the freshness of youth, nor even the magic of expression; it was as faultless as it was dazzling; no one could deny its excess or its perfection; her praises came constantly to my ear into whatever society I went. Say what we will of the power of love, it borrows greatly from opinion; pride, above all things, sanctions and strengthens affection. When all voices were united to panegyrize her beauty—when I knew, that the powers of her wit—the charms of her conversation—the accurate judgment, united to the sparkling imagination, were even more remarkable characteristics of her *mind,* than loveliness of her *person,* I could not but feel my ambition, as well as my tenderness, excited: I dwelt with a double intensity on my choice, and with a tenfold bitterness on the obstacle* which forbade me to indulge it.

Yet there was one circumstance, to which, in spite of all the evidence against Reginald, my mind still fondly and eagerly clung. In searching the pockets of the unfortunate Tyrrell, the money he had mentioned to me as being in his possession, could not be discovered. Had Glanville been the murderer, at all events he could not have been the robber. It was true that in the death scuffle, which in all probability took place, the money might have fallen from the person of the deceased, either among the long grass which grew rankly and luxuriantly around, or in the sullen and slimy pool, close to which the murder was perpetrated; it was also possible, that Thornton, knowing the deceased had so large a sum about him, and not being aware that the circumstance had been communicated to me or any one else, might not have been able (when he and Dawson first went to the spot), to resist so great a temptation. However, there was a slight crevice in this fact, for a sunbeam of hope to enter, and I was too sanguine, by habitual temperament and present passion, not to turn towards it from the general darkness of my thoughts.

With Glanville I was often brought into immediate contact. Both united in the same party, and engaged in concerting the same measures, we frequently met in public, and sometimes even alone. However, I was invariably cold and distant, and Glanville confirmed rather than

---

2. "One wishes to make all the happiness, or, if that is forbidden, all the unhappiness of the being we love!" (La Bruyère, *Les Caractères,* "Du coeur," no. 39).

diminished my suspicions, by making no commentary on my behaviour, and imitating it in the indifference of his own. Yet, it was with a painful and aching heart, that I marked, in his emaciated form and sunken cheek, the gradual, but certain progress of disease and death; and while all England rung with the renown of the young, but almost unrivalled orator, and both parties united in anticipating the certainty and brilliancy of his success, I felt how improbable it was, that, even if his crime escaped the unceasing vigilance of justice, this living world would long possess any traces of his genius but the remembrance of his name. There was something in his love of letters, his habits of luxury and expense, the energy of his mind—the solitude, the darkness, the hauteur, the reserve of his manners and life, which reminded me of the German Wallenstein;[3] nor was he altogether without the superstition of that evil, but extraordinary man. It is true, that he was not addicted to the romantic fables of astrology, but he was an earnest, though secret, advocate of the world of spirits. He did not utterly disbelieve the various stories of their return to earth and their visits to the living; and it would have been astonishing to me, had I been a less diligent observer of human inconsistencies, to mark a mind otherwise so reasoning and strong, in this respect so credulous and weak; and to witness its reception of a belief, not only so adverse to ordinary reflection, but so absolutely contradictory to the philosophy it passionately cultivated, and the principles it obstinately espoused.

One evening, I, Vincent, and Clarendon, were alone at Lady Roseville's, when Reginald and his sister entered. I rose to depart; *la belle Comtesse** would not suffer it; and when I looked at Ellen, and saw her blush at my glance, the weakness of my heart conquered, and I remained.

Our conversation turned partly upon books, and principally on the science *du coeur et du monde,* for Lady Roseville was *un peu philosophe,* as well as more than *un peu littéraire;* and her house, like those of the Du Deffands and D'Epinays[4] of the old French régime, was one where serious subjects were cultivated, as well as the lighter ones; where it was the mode to treat no less upon *things* than to scandalize *persons;* and where maxims on men and reflections on manners,

---

3. Albrecht von Wallenstein (1583–1634): Austrian general, the melancholy hero of Schiller's dramatic trilogy *Wallenstein* (1798–99).

4. Marquise du Deffand (1697–1780): prominent member of French literary and philosophical circles; Louise d'Epinay (1726–83): French author, intimate friend of Rousseau.

were as much in their places, as strictures on the Opera and invitations to balls.

All who were now assembled were more or less suited to one another; all were people of the world, and yet occasional students of the closet; but all had a different method of expressing their learning or their observations. Clarendon was dry, formal, shrewd, and possessed of the suspicious philosophy common to men hacknied in the world. Vincent relieved his learning by the quotation, or metaphor, or originality of some sort with which it was expressed. Lady Roseville seldom spoke much, but when she did, it was rather with grace than solidity. She was naturally melancholy and pensive, and her observations partook of the colourings of her mind; but she was also a *dame de la cour,* accustomed to conceal, and her language was gay and trifling, while the sentiments it clothed were pensive and sad.

Ellen Glanville was an attentive listener, but a diffident speaker. Though her knowledge was even masculine for its variety and extent, she was averse to displaying it; the childish, the lively, the tender, were the outward traits of her character—the flowers were above, but the mine was beneath; one noted the beauty of the former—one seldom dreamt of the value of the latter.

Glanville's favourite method of expressing himself was terse and sententious. He did not love the labour of detail: he conveyed the knowledge of years in a problem. Sometimes he was fanciful, sometimes false; but, generally, dark, melancholy, and bitter.

As for me, I entered more into conversation at Lady Roseville's than I usually do elsewhere; being, according to my favourite philosophy, gay on the serious, and serious on the gay; and, perhaps, this is a juster method of treating the two than would be readily imagined: for things which are usually treated with importance, are, for the most part, deserving of ridicule; and those which we receive as trifles, swell themselves into a consequence we little dreamt of, before they depart.

Vincent took up a volume: it was Shelley's Posthumous Poems.[5] "How fine," said he, "some of these are; but they are fine fragments of an architecture in bad taste: they are imperfect in themselves, and faulty in the school they belonged to; yet, such as they are, the master-hand is evident upon them. They are like the pictures of Paul Veronese—often offending the eye, often irritating the judgment, but breathing of something vast and lofty—their very faults are majestic—

5. *Posthumous Poems* was published in 1824.

314

this age, perhaps no other will ever do them justice—but the disciples of future schools will make glorious pillage of their remains. The writings of Shelley would furnish matter for a hundred volumes: they are an admirable museum of ill-arranged curiosities—they are diamonds, awkwardly set; but one of them, in the hands of a skilful jeweller, would be inestimable: and the poet of the future, will serve him as Mercury did the tortoise in his own translation from Homer—make him 'sing sweetly when he's dead!'[6] Their lyres will be made out of his *shell.*"

"If I judge rightly," said Clarendon, "his literary faults were these: he was too learned in his poetry, and to poetical in his learning. Learning is the bane of a poet. Imagine how beautiful Petrarch would be without his platonic conceits: fancy the luxuriant imagination of Cowley, left to run wild among the lofty objects of nature, not the minute peculiarities of art. Even Milton, who made a more graceful and gorgeous use of learning than, perhaps, any other poet, would have been far more popular if he had been more familiar. Poetry is for the multitude—erudition for the few. In proportion as you mix them, erudition will gain in readers, and poetry lose."

"True," said Glanville; "and thus the poetical, among philosophers, are the most popular of their time; and the philosophical among poets, the least popular of theirs."

"Take care," said Vincent, smiling, "that we are not misled by the *point* of your deduction; the remark is true, but with a certain reservation, viz. that the philosophy which renders a poet less popular, must be the philosophy of *learning,* not of *wisdom.* Wherever it consists in the knowledge of the *plainer* springs of the heart, and not in *abstruse* inquiry into its metaphysical and hidden subtleties, it necessarily increases the popularity of the poem; because, instead of being limited to the few, it comes home to every one. Thus it is the philosophy of Shakspeare, which puts him into every one's hands and hearts —while that of Lucretius, wonderful poet as he is, makes us often throw down the book, because it fatigues us with the scholar. Philosophy, therefore, only sins in poetry, when, in the severe garb of learning, it becomes 'harsh and crabbed,' and *not* 'musical, as is Apollo's lute.' "[7]

"Alas!" said I, "how much more difficult than of yore education is become: formerly, it had only one object—to acquire learning; and

6. Shelley's translation of "Hymn to Mercury," line 44.
7. Milton, *Comus,* lines 477–78.

315

now, we have not only to acquire it, but to know what to do with it when we have—nay, there are not a few cases where the very perfection of learning will be to *appear* ignorant."

"Perhaps," said Glanville, "the very perfection of *wisdom* may consist in *retaining* actual ignorance. Where was there ever the individual who, after consuming years, life, health, in the pursuit of science, rested satisfied with its success, or rewarded by its triumph? Common sense tells us that the best method of employing life is to *enjoy* it. Common sense tells us, also, the ordinary means of this enjoyment; health, competence, and the indulgence, but the *moderate* indulgence, of our passions. What have these to do with science?"

"I might tell you," replied Vincent, "that I myself have been no idle nor inactive seeker after the hidden treasures of mind; and that, from my own experience, I could speak of pleasure, pride, complacency, in the pursuit, that were no inconsiderable augmenters of my stock of enjoyment: but I have the candour to confess, also, that I have known disappointment, mortification, despondency of mind, and infirmity of body, that did more than balance the account. The fact is, in my opinion, that the individual is a sufferer for his toils, but then the mass is benefited by his success. It is we who reap, in idle gratification, what the husbandman has sown in the bitterness of labour. Genius did not save Milton from poverty and blindness—nor Tasso from the madhouse—nor Galileo from the inquisition; *they* were the sufferers, but posterity the gainers. The literary empire reverses the political; it is not the many made for one—it is the one made for many. Wisdom and Genius must have their martyrs as well as Religion, and with the same results, viz. *semen ecclesiæ est sanguis martyrorum.*[8] And this reflection must console us for their misfortunes, for, perhaps, it was sufficient to console *them*. In the midst of the most affecting passage in the most wonderful work, perhaps, ever produced, for the mixture of universal thought with individual interest—I mean the two last cantos of Childe Harold—the poet warms from himself at his hopes of being remembered

" 'In his line
" 'With his land's language.'[9]

And who can read the noble and heart-speaking apology of Algernon

---

8. "The blood of martyrs is the seed of the church" (Tertullian *Apologeticus.* 48). Misquoted.

9. Byron, *Childe Harold's Pilgrimage,* canto 4, lines 77–78.

Sidney,[10] without entering into his consolation no less than his misfortunes? Speaking of the law being turned into a snare instead of a protection, and instancing its uncertainty and danger in the times of Richard the Second, he says, 'God only knows what will be the issue of the like practices in these our days; perhaps he will in his mercy speedily visit his afflicted people; *I die in the faith that he will do it, though I know not the time or ways.*' "

"I love," said Clarendon, "the enthusiasm which places comfort in so noble a source; but, is vanity, think you, a less powerful agent than philanthropy? Is it not the desire of shining before men that prompts us to whatever may effect it? and if it can *create*, can it not also *support?* I mean, that if you allow that to shine, to dazzle, to enjoy praise, is no ordinary incentive to the commencement of great works, the conviction of future success for this desire becomes no inconsiderable reward. Grant, for instance, that this desire produced the 'Paradise Lost,' and you will not deny that it might also support the poet through his misfortunes. Do you think that he thought rather of the pleasure *his* work should afford to posterity, than of the praises *posterity* should extend to his work? Had not Cicero left us such frank confessions of himself, how patriotic, how philanthropic we should have esteemed him! *Now* we know both his motive and meed was vanity, may we not extend the knowledge of human nature which we have gained in this instance by applying it to others? For my part, I should be loth to inquire how great a quantum of vanity mingled with the haughty patriotism of Sidney, or the unconquered spirit of Cato."

Glanville bowed his head in approval.

"But," observed I,* "why be so uncharitable to this poor and persecuted principle, since none of you deny the good and great actions it effects; why stigmatize vanity as a vice, when it creates, or, at least, participates in, so many virtues? I wonder the ancients did not erect the choicest of their temples to is worship. *Quant à moi,** I shall henceforth only speak of it as the *primum mobile* of whatever we venerate and admire, and shall think it the highest compliment I can pay to a man, to tell him *he is eminently vain.*"

"I incline to your opinion," cried Vincent, laughing. "The reason we dislike vanity in others, is because it is perpetually hurting our

---

10. Algernon Sidney (1623–83): English statesman celebrated as a martyr for liberty. The quotation in the next sentence is from the peroration of his *Apology in the Day of His Death,* his public declaration of his innocence of the charge of treason.

own. Of all passions (if for the moment I may call it such) it is the most indiscreet; it is for ever blabbing out its own secrets. If it would but keep its counsel, it would be as graciously received in society, as any other well-dressed and well-bred intruder of quality. Its garrulity makes it despised. But in truth it must be clear, that vanity in itself is neither a vice nor a virtue, any more than this knife, in itself, is dangerous or useful; the person who employs gives it its qualities: thus, for instance, a great mind desires to shine, *or is vain,* in great actions; a frivolous one, in frivolities; and so on through the varieties of the human intellect. But I cannot agree with Mr. Clarendon, that my admiration of Algernon Sidney (Cato I never *did* admire) would be at all lessened by the discovery, that his resistance to tyranny in a great measure originated in vanity, or that the same vanity consoled him, when he fell a victim to that resistance; for what does it prove but this, that, among the various feelings of his soul, indignation at oppression, (so common to all men)—enthusiasm for liberty, (so predominant in him)—the love of benefiting others—the noble pride of being, in death, consistent with himself; among all these feelings, among a crowd of others equally honourable and pure—there was also one, and perhaps no inconsiderable feeling of desire, that his life and death should be hereafter appreciated justly—*contemptu famae, contemni virtutes*[11]*—contempt of fame is the contempt of virtue? Never consider that vanity an offense which limits itself to wishing for the praise of good men for good actions: 'next to our own esteem,' says the best of the Roman philosophers, 'it is a virtue to desire the esteem of others.' "[12]

"By your emphasis on the word *esteem,*" said Lady Roseville, "I suppose you attach some peculiar importance to the word?"

"I do," answered Vincent. "I use it in contradistinction to *admiration.* We may covet general admiration for a *bad* action—(for many bad actions have the *clinquant,* which passes for real gold)—but one can expect general *esteem* only for a *good* one."

"From this distinction," said Ellen, modestly, "may we not draw an inference, which will greatly help us in our consideration of vanity; may we not deem that vanity, which desires only the *esteem* of others, to be invariably a virtue, and that which only longs for *admiration* to be frequently a vice?"-

"We *may* admit your inference," said Vincent; "and before I leave

---

11. "To despise fame is to despise merit" (Tacitus *Annals* 4.88).
12. Cicero *De officiis.*

this question, I cannot help remarking upon the folly of the superficial, who imagine, by studying human motives, that philosophers wish to depreciate human actions. To direct our admiration to a proper point, is surely not to destroy it; yet how angry inconsiderate enthusiasts are, when we assign real, in the place of exaggerated feelings. Thus the advocates for the doctrine of utility—the most benevolent, because the most indulgent, of all philosophies—are branded with the epithets of selfish and interested; decriers of moral excellence, and disbelievers in generous actions. Vice has no friend like the prejudices which call themselves virtue. *La prétexte ordinaire de ceux qui font le malheur des autres est qu'ils veulent leur bien.*[13]

My eyes were accidentally fixed on Glanville as Vincent ceased; he looked up, and coloured faintly as he met my look; but he did not withdraw his own—keenly and steadily we gazed upon each other, till Ellen, turning round suddenly, remarked the unwonted meaning of our looks, and placed her hand in her brother's, with a sort of fear.

It was late; he rose to withdraw, and passing me, said in a low tone, "A little while, and you shall know all." I made no answer— he left the room with Ellen.

"Lady Roseville has had but a dull evening, I fear, with our stupid saws and *ancient* instances," said Vincent. The eyes of the person he addressed were fixed upon the door; I was standing close by her, and as the words struck her ear, she turned abruptly;—a tear fell upon my hand—she perceived it, and though I *would not* look upon her *face,* I saw that her very *neck* blushed; but she, like me, if she gave way to feeling, had learnt too deep a lesson from the world, not readily to resume her self-command; she answered Vincent railingly, upon his bad compliment to us, and received our adieus with all her customary grace, and more than her customary gaiety.

---

13. "The ordinary pretext of those who make the misery of others is that they wish for their good" (Vauvenargues, *Réflexions et maximes,* no. 160).

CHAPTER V

Ah! Sir, had I but bestowed half the pains in learning a trade, that I have in learning to be a scoundrel, I might have been a rich man at this day; but, rogue as I am, still I may be your friend, and that, perhaps, when you least expect it.

Vicar of Wakefield[1]

WHAT WITH THE ANXIETY AND UNCERTAINTY OF MY political prospects, the continued dissipation* in which I lived, and, above all, the unpropitious state of my *belle passion,* my health gave way; my appetite forsook me—my sleep failed me—a wrinkle settled itself under my left eye,* and my mother declared, that I should have no chance with an heiress: all these circumstances together were not without their weight. So I set out one morning to Hampton Court, (with a volume of Bishop Berkeley, and a bottle of wrinkle water),* for the benefit of the country air.

It is by no means an unpleasant thing to turn one's back upon the great city, in the height of its festivities. Misanthropy is a charming feeling for a short time, and one inhales the country, and animadverts on the town, with the most melancholy satisfaction in the world. I sat myself down at a pretty little cottage, a mile out of the town. From the window of my drawing-room I revelled in the luxurious contemplation of three pigs, one cow, and a straw-yard; and I could get to the Thames in a walk of five minutes, by a short cut through a lime-kiln. Such pleasing opportunities of enjoying the beauties of nature, are not often to be met with: you may be sure, therefore, that I made the most of them. I rose early, walked before breakfast, *pour ma santé,*, and came back with a most satisfactory head-ache, *pour mes peines.* I read for just three hours, walked for two more, thought over Abernethy,[2] dyspepsia, and blue pills, till dinner; and absolutely forgot Lord Dawton, ambition, Guloseton, epicurism—ay, all but—of

---

1. Oliver Goldsmith, *The Vicar of Wakefield,* chapter 25.
2. John Abernethy (1763–1831): doctor and writer on medical subjects.

320

course, reader, you know whom I am about to except—the ladye of my love.

One bright, laughing day, I threw down my book an hour sooner than usual, and sallied out with a lightness of foot and exhilaration of spirit, to which I had long been a stranger. I had just sprung over a stile that led into one of those green shady lanes, which make us feel that the old poets who loved, and lived for Nature, were right in calling our island "the merry England"—when I was startled by a short, quick bark, on one side of the hedge. I turned sharply round; and, seated upon the sward, was a man, apparently of the pedlar profession; a large deal box was lying open before him; a few articles of linen, and female dress, were scattered round, and the man himself appeared earnestly occupied in examining the deeper recesses of his itinerant warehouse. A small black terrier flew towards me with no friendly growl. "Down," said I: "all strangers are not foes, though the English generally think so."

The man hastily looked up; perhaps he was struck with the quaintness of my remonstrance to his canine companion; for, touching his hat, civilly, he said—"The dog, Sir, is very quiet; he only means to give *me* the alarm by giving it to *you;* for dogs seem to have no despicable insight into human nature, and know well that the best of us may be taken by surprise."

"You are a moralist," said I, not a little astonished in my turn by such an address from such a person. "I could not have expected to stumble upon a philosopher so easily. Have you any wares in your box likely to suit me? if so, I should like to purchase of so moralizing a vendor?"

"No, Sir," said the seeming pedlar, smiling, and yet at the same time hurrying his goods into his box, and carefully turning the key— "no, Sir, I am only a bearer of other men's goods; my morals are all that I can call my own, and those I will sell you at your own price."

"You are candid, my friend," said I, "and your frankness, alone, would be inestimable in this age of deceit, and country of hypocrisy."

"Ah, Sir!" said my new acquaintance, "I see already that you are one of those persons who look to the dark side of things; for my part, I think the present age the best that ever existed, and our own country the most virtuous in Europe."

"I congratulate you, Mr. Optimist, on your opinions," quoth I; "but your observation leads me to suppose, that you are both an historian and a traveller: am I right?"

"Why," answered the box-bearer, "*I have* dabbled a little in books,

321

and wandered *not* a little among men. I am just returned from Germany, and am now going to my friends in London. I am charged with this box of goods; God send me the luck to deliver it safe."

"Amen," said I; "and with that prayer and this trifle, I wish you a good morning."

"Thank you a thousand times, Sir, for both," replied the man— "but do add to your favours by informing me of the right road to the town of * * * * "

"I am going in that direction myself: if you choose to accompany me part of the way, I can ensure your not missing the rest."

"Your honour is too good!" returned he of the box, rising, and slinging his fardel across him—"it is but seldom that a gentleman of your rank will condescend to walk three paces with *one* of mine. You smile, Sir; perhaps you think I should not class myself among gentlemen; and yet I have as good a right to the name as most of the set. I belong to no trade—I follow no calling: I rove where I list, and rest where I please: in short, I know no occupation but my indolence, and no law but my will. Now, Sir, may I not call myself a gentleman?"

"Of a surety!" quoth I. "You seem to me to hold a middle rank between a half-pay captain and the king of the gipsies."

"You have hit it, Sir," rejoined my companion, with a slight laugh. He was now by my side, and as we walked on, I had leisure more minutely to examine him. He was a middle-sized, and rather athletic man, apparently about the age of thirty-eight. He was attired in a dark blue frock coat, which was neither shabby nor new, but ill made, and much too large and long for its present possessor; beneath this was a faded velvet waistcoat, that had formerly, like the Persian ambassador's tunic, "blushed with crimson, and blazed with gold;" but which might now have been advantageously exchanged in Monmouth-street for the lawful sum of two shillings and nine-pence; under this was an inner vest of the cashmere shawl pattern, which seemed much too new for the rest of the dress. Though his shirt was of a very unwashed hue, I remarked, with some suspicion, that it was of a very respectable fineness; and a pin, which might be paste, or could be diamond, peeped below a tattered and dingy black kid stock, like a gipsy's eye beneath her hair.

His trowsers were of a light grey, and the justice of Providence, or of the tailor, avenged itself upon them, for the prodigal length bestowed upon their ill-sorted companion, the coat; for they were much too tight for the muscular limbs they concealed, and rising

322

far above the ankle, exhibited the whole of a thick Wellington boot, which was the very picture of Italy upon the map.

The face of the man was common-place and ordinary; one sees a hundred such, every day, in Fleet-street or the 'Change; the features were small, irregular, and somewhat flat: yet, when you looked twice upon the countenance, there was something marked and singular in the expression, which fully atoned for the commonness of the features. The right eye turned away from the left, in that watchful squint which seems constructed on the same considerate plan as those Irish guns, made for shooting round a corner; his eye-brows were large and shaggy, and greatly resembled bramble bushes, in which his fox-like eyes had taken refuge. Round these vulpine retreats was a labyrinthean maze of those wrinkles, vulgarly called crow's-feet; deep, intricate, and intersected, they seemed for all the world like the web of a Chancery suit. Singular enough, the rest of the countenance was perfectly smooth and unindented; even the lines from the nostril to the corners of the mouth, usually so deeply traced in men of his age, were scarcely more apparent than in a boy of eighteen.

His smile was frank—his voice clear and hearty—his address open, and much superior to his apparent rank of life, claiming somewhat of equality, yet conceding a great deal of respect; but, notwithstanding all these certainly favourable points, there was a sly and cunning expression in his perverse and vigilant eye and all the wrinkled demesnes in its vicinity, that made me mistrust even while I liked my companion; perhaps, indeed, he was too frank, too familiar, too dégagé, to be quite natural. Your honest men soon buy reserve by experience. Rogues are communicative and open, because confidence and openness cost them nothing. To finish the description of my new acquaintance, I should observe, that there was something in his countenance, which struck me as not wholly unfamiliar; it was one of those which we have not, in all human probability, seen before, and yet, which (perhaps from their very commonness) we imagine we have encountered a hundred times.

We walked on briskly, notwithstanding the warmth of the day; in fact, the air was so pure, the grass so green, the laughing noonday so full of the hum, the motion, and the life of creation, that the feeling produced was rather that of freshness and invigoration, than of languor and heat.

"We have a beautiful country, Sir," said my hero of the box. "It is like walking through a garden, after the more sterile and sullen features of the Continent. A pure mind, Sir, loves the country; for

323

my part, I am always disposed to burst out in thanksgiving to Providence when I behold its works, and, like the valleys in the psalm, I am ready to laugh and sing."[3]

"An enthusiast," said I, "as well as a philosopher!—perhaps (and I believed it likely), I have the honour of addressing a poet also."

"Why, Sir," replied the man, "I have made verses in my life; in short, there is little I have not done, for I was always a lover of variety; but, perhaps, your honour will let me return the suspicion. Are *you* not a favourite of the muse?"

"I cannot say that I am," said I. "I value myself only on my common sense—the very antipodes to genius, you know, according to the orthodox belief."

"Common sense!" repeated my companion, with a singular and meaning smile, and a twinkle with his left eye. "Common sense! Ah, that is not my *forte*, Sir. You, I dare say, are one of those gentlemen whom it is very difficult to take in, either passively or actively, by appearance, or in act? For my part, I have been a dupe all my life—a child might cheat me! I am the most unsuspicious person in the world."

"Too candid by half," thought I. "The man is certainly a rascal; but what is that to me? I shall never see him again;" and true to my love of never losing an opportunity of ascertaining individual character, I observed, that I thought such an acquaintance very valuable, especially if he were in trade; it was a pity, therefore, for my sake, that my companion had informed me that he followed no calling.

"Why, Sir," said he, "I *am* occasionally in employment; my nominal profession is that of a broker. I buy shawls and handkerchiefs of poor countesses, and retail them to rich plebeians. I fit up new married couples with linen, at a more moderate rate than the shops, and procure the bridegroom his present of jewels, at forty per cent, less than the jewellers; nay, I am as friendly to an intrigue as a marriage; and when I cannot sell my jewels, I will my good offices. A gentleman so handsome as your honour, may have an affair upon your hands: if so, you may rely upon my secrecy and zeal. In short, I am an innocent, good-natured fellow, who does harm to no one for nothing, and good to every one for something."

"I admire your code," quoth I, "and whenever I want a mediator between Venus and myself, will employ you. Have you always followed your present idle profession, or were you brought up to any other?"

---

3. Psalms 65:13

324

"I was intended for a silversmith," answered my friend; "but Providence willed it otherwise: they taught me from childhood to repeat the Lord's prayer; Heaven heard me, and delivered me from temptation—there is, indeed, something terribly seducing in the face of a silver spoon!"

"Well," said I, "you are the honestest knave I ever met, and one would trust you with one's purse for the ingenuousness with which you own you would steal it. Pray, think you it is probable that I have ever had the happiness to meet you before? I cannot help fancying so—yet as I have never been in the watch-house, or the Old Bailey, my reason tells me that I must be mistaken."

"Not at all, Sir," returned my worthy: "I remember you well, for I never saw a face like yours that I did *not* remember. I had the honour of sipping some British liquors, in the same room with yourself one evening; you were then in company with my friend Mr. Gordon."

"Ha!" said I, "I thank you for the hint. I now remember well, by the same token, that he told me you were the most ingenious gentleman in England; and that you had a happy propensity of mistaking other people's possessions for your own. I congratulate myself upon so desirable an acquaintance."[4]

My friend, who was indeed no other than Mr. Job Jonson, smiled with his usual blandness, and made me a low bow of acknowledgment before he resumed:

"No doubt, Sir, Mr. Gordon informed you right. I flatter myself few gentlemen understand better than myself, the art of *appropriation;* though I say it who should not say it, I deserve the reputation I have acquired. Sir, I have always had ill fortune to struggle against, and have always remedied it by two virtues—perseverance and ingenuity. To give you an idea of my ill fortune, know that I have been taken up twenty-three times, on suspicion; of my perseverance, know that twenty-three times I have been taken up *justly;* and of my ingenuity, know that I have been twenty-three times let off, because there was not a tittle of legal evidence against me."

"I venerate your talents, Mr. Jonson," replied I, "if by the name of Jonson, it pleaseth you to be called, although, like the heathen deities, I presume that you have many other titles, whereof some are more grateful to your ears than others."

---

4. See page 205. [B-L] "Mr. Job Jonson . . . had his prototype in a member of the swell-mob known to the author" (*Life . . . and Literary Remains,* II, 193).

"Nay," answered the man of two virtues—"I am never ashamed of my name; indeed, I have never done any thing to disgrace me. I have never indulged in low company, nor profligate debauchery: whatever I have executed by way of profession, has been done in a superior and artist-like manner; not in the rude, bungling fashion of other adventurers. Moreover, I have always had a taste for polite literature, and went once as an apprentice to a publishing bookseller, for the sole purpose of reading the new works before they came out. In fine, I have never neglected any opportunity of improving my mind; and the worst that can be said against me is, that I have remembered my catechism, and taken all possible pains 'to learn and labour truly, to get my living, and do my duty in that state of life, to which it has pleased Providence to call me.' "[5]

"I have often heard," answered I, "that there is *honour* among thieves; I am happy to learn from you, that there is also religion: your baptismal sponsors must be proud of so diligent a godson."

"They ought to be, Sir," replied Mr. Jonson, "for I gave *them* the first specimens of my address: the story is long, but if you ever give me an opportunity, I will relate it."

"Thank you," said I; "meanwhile I must wish you good morning: your road now lies to the right. I return you my best thanks for your condescension, in accompanying so undistinguished an individual as myself."

"Oh, never mention it; your honour," rejoined Mr. Jonson. "I am always too happy to walk with a gentleman of your 'common sense.' Farewell, Sir; may we meet again."

So saying, Mr. Jonson struck into his new road, and we parted.[6]

I went home, musing on my adventure, and delighted with my adventurer. When I was about three paces from the door of my home, I was accosted, in a most pitiful tone, by a poor old beggar, apparently in the last extreme of misery and disease. Notwithstanding my political economy, I was moved into alms-giving by a spectacle so wretched. I put my hand into my pocket, my purse was gone; and, on searching the other, lo— my handkerchief, my pocket-book, and a gold bracelet,* which had belonged to Madame D'Anville, had vanished too.

One does not keep company with men of two virtues, and receive compliments upon one's common sense for nothing!

---

5. *The Book of Common Prayer. The Catechism.*

6. If anyone should think this sketch from nature exaggerated, I refer him to the "Memoirs of James Hardy Vaux." [B-L] The work referred to is *Memoirs of the First Thirty-one Years of the Life of J. H. V.*, ed. B. Field (1819).

The beggar still continued to importune me.

"Give him some food and half a crown," said I, to my landlady. Two hours afterwards, she came up to me—"Oh, Sir! my silver tea-pot—*that villain, the beggar!*"

A light flashed upon me—"Ah, Mr. Job Jonson! Mr. Job Jonson!" cried I, in an indescribable rage; "out of my sight, woman! out of my sight!" I stopped short; my speech failed me. Never tell me that shame is the companion of guilt—the sinful knave is never so ashamed of himself as is the innocent fool who suffers by him.

CHAPTER VI

Then must I plunge again into the crowd,
And follow all that peace disdains to seek.
BYRON[1]

IN THE QUIET OF MY RETREAT I REMAINED FOR EIGHT days—during which time I never looked once at a newspaper—imagine how great was my philosophy! On the ninth, I began to think it high time I should hear from Dawton; and finding that I had eaten two rolls for breakfast, and that my untimely wrinkle* began to assume a more mitigated appearance, I bethought me once more of the "Beauties of Babylon."

While I was in this kindly mood towards the great city and its inhabitants, my landlady put two letters in my hand—one was from my mother, the other from Guloseton. I opened the latter first; it ran thus—

"DEAR PELHAM,

"I was very sorry to hear you had left town—and so unexpectedly too. I obtained your address at Mivart's, and hasten to avail myself of it. Pray come to town immediately. I have received some *chevreuil* as a present, and long for your opinion, it is too nice to keep: for all things nice were made but to grow bad when nicest; as Moore, I

---

1. *Childe Harold's Pilgrimage,* canto 2, lines 909–10.

believe, says of flowers, substituting sweet and fleetest, for bad and nicest;[2] so, you see, you must come without loss of time.

"But *you,* my friend—how *can* you possibly have been spending your time? I was kept awake all last night, by thinking what you *could* have for dinner. Fish is out of the question in the country; chickens die of the pip every where but in London; game is out of season; it is impossible to send to Giblett's for meat; it is equally impossible to get it any where else; and as for the only two natural productions of the country, vegetables and eggs, I need no extraordinary penetration to be certain that your cook cannot *transmute* the latter into an *omelette aux huîtres,* or the former into *légumes à la crême.*

"Thus, you see, by a series of undeniable demonstrations, you *must* absolutely be in a state of starvation. At this thought, the tears rush into my eyes: for Heaven's sake, for my sake, for your own sake, but *above all,* for the sake of the *chevreuil,* hasten to London. I figure you to myself in the last stage of atrophy—airy as a trifle, thin as the ghost of a greyhound.

"I need say no more on the subject. I may rely on your own discretion to procure me the immediate pleasure of your company. Indeed, were I to dwell longer on your melancholy situation, my feelings would overcome me—*Mais revenons à nos moutons*[3]—(a most pertinent phrase, by the by—oh! the French excel us in every thing, from the paramount science of cookery, to the little art of conversation).

"You must tell me your candid, your unbiassed, your deliberate opinion of *chevreuil.* For my part, I should not wonder at the mythology of the northern heathen nations, which places hunting among the chief enjoyments of their heaven, were *chevreuil* the object of their chace; but *nihil est omni parte beatum,*[4] it wants *fat,* my dear Pelham, it wants fat: nor do I see how to remedy this defect; for were we by art to supply the *fat,* we should deprive ourselves of the *flavour* bestowed by nature; and this, my dear Pelham, was always my great argument for liberty. Cooped, chained, and confined in cities, and slavery, all things lose the fresh and *generous tastes,* which it is the peculiar blessing of freedom and the country to afford.

"Tell me, my friend, what has been the late subject of your

2. An allusion to "All that's bright must fade," in Thomas Moore's *National Airs.*

3. Lord Guloseton is punning on *moutons* (sheep). The phrase means: "But let us return to our subject."

4. "There is no such thing as an unmixed good" (Horace *Carmen* 2.16.27). Slightly misquoted.

328

reflections? *My* thoughts have dwelt much, and seriously, on the 'terra incognita,' the undiscovered tracts in the *pays culinaire,* which the profoundest investigators have left untouched and unexplored in——veal. But more of this hereafter;—the lightness of a letter is ill suited to the depths of philosophical research.

"Lord Dawton sounded me upon my votes yesterday. 'A thousand pities too,' said he, 'that *you* never speak in the House of Lords.' —'Orator *fit,*' said I—*orators are subject to apoplexy.*[5]

"Adieu, my dear friend, for friend you are, if the philosopher was right in defining true friendship to consist in liking and disliking the same things.[6]* You hate parsnips *au naturel*—so do I; you love *pâtés du foie gras, et moi aussi—nous voilà donc les meilleurs amis du monde.*[7]

"GULOSETON."

So much for my friend, thought I—and now for my mother, opening the maternal epistle, which I herewith transcribe:

"MY DEAR HENRY,

"Lose no time in coming to town. Every day the ministers are filling up the minor places, and it requires a great stretch of recollection in a politician to remember the absent. Mr. V—— said yesterday, at a dinner party where I was present, that Lord Dawton had promised him the Borough of ——. Now you know, my dear Henry, that was the very borough he promised to you: you must see further into this. Lord Dawton is a good sort of man enough, but refused once to fight a duel; therefore, if he has disregarded his honour in one instance, he may do so in another: at all events, you have no time to lose.

"The young Duke of —— gives a ball to-morrow evening: Mrs. —— pays all the expenses, and I know for a certainty that she will marry him in a week; this as yet is a secret. There will be a great mixture, but the ball will be worth going to. I have a card for you.

"Lady Huffemall and I think that we shall not patronize the future duchess; but have not yet made up our minds. Lady Roseville, however, speaks of the intended match with great respect, and says that since we admit *convenance,* as the chief rule in matrimony, she never remembers an instance in which it has been more consulted.

---

5. "The orator is made." Part of an old proverb: "The poet is born, the orator is made." Guloseton puns again, this time on *fit* (made) in order to suggest, as he says, that "orators are subject to apoplexy."
6. See Sallust *Catalina* 20.4.
7. "And I do too—thus we are clearly the best friends in the world."

"There are to be several promotions in the peerage. Lord H———'s friends wish to give out that he will have a dukedom; *Mais j'en doute.* However, he has well deserved it; for he not only gives the best dinners in town, but the best account of them in the Morning Post, afterwards; which I think is very properly upholding the dignity of our order.

"I hope most earnestly that you do not (in your country retreat) neglect your health; nor, I may add, your mind; and that you take an opportunity every other day of practising waltzing, which you can very well do, with the help of an arm-chair. I would send you down (did I not expect you here so soon) Lord Mount E———'s Musical Reminiscences;[8] not only because it is a very entertaining book, but because I wish you to pay much greater attention to music than you seem inclined to do. * * * * * * who is never very refined in his *bons mots,* says, that Lord M. seems to have considered the world a concert, in which the best performer plays first fiddle. It is, indeed, quite delightful to see the veneration our musical friend has for the orchestra and its occupants. I wish to heaven, my dear Henry, he could instil into you a little of his ardour. I am quite mortified at times by your ignorance of tunes and operas: nothing tells better in conversation than a knowledge of music, as you will one day or other discover.

"God bless you, my dearest Henry. Fully expecting you, I have sent to engage your former rooms at Mivart's; do not let me be disappointed.

"Yours, &c.

"F. P."

I read the above letter twice over, and felt my cheek glow and my heart swell as I passed the passage relative to Lord Dawton and the borough. The new minister had certainly, for some weeks since, been playing a double part with me: it would long ago have been easy to procure me a subordinate situation—still easier to place me in parliament; yet he had contented himself with doubtful promises and idle civilities. What, however, seemed to me most unaccountable was, his motive in breaking or paltering with his engagement: he knew that I had served him and his party better than half his corps; he professed, not only to me, but to society, the highest opinion of my abilities, knowledge, and application: he saw, consequently, how serviceable I could be as a friend; and from the same qualities, joined

---

8. Lord Mount Edgecumb's *Musical Reminiscences of an Old Amateur* (1827).

to the rank of my birth and connections, and the high and resentful temper of my mind, he might readily augur that I could be equally influential as a foe.

With this reflection, I stilled the beating of my heart, and the fever of my pulse. I crushed the obnoxious letter in my hand, walked thrice up and down my room, paused at the bell—rung it violently—ordered post horses instantly, and in less than an hour was on the road to London.

How different is the human mind, according to the difference of place. In our passions, as in our creeds, we are the mere dependents of geographical situation. Nay, the trifling variation of a single mile will revolutionize the whole tides and torrents of our hearts. The man who is meek, generous, benevolent, and kind in the country, enters the scene of contest, and becomes forthwith fiery or mean, selfish or stern, just as if the virtues were only for solitude, and the vices for the city. I have ill expressed the above reflection; *n'importe*—so much the better shall I explain my feelings at the time I speak of—for I was then too eager and engrossed to attend to the niceties of words. On my arrival at Mivart's, I scarcely allowed myself time to change my dress before I set out to Lord Dawton. He shall afford me an explanation, I thought, or a recompence, *or a revenge*. I knocked at the door—the minister was out. "Give him this card," said I, to the porter, "and say I shall call to-morrow at three."

I walked to Brookes's—there I met Mr. V———. My acquaintance with him was small, but he was a man of talent, and, what was more to my purpose, of open manners. I went up to him, and we entered into conversation. "Is it true," said I, "that I am to congratulate you upon the certainty of your return for Lord Dawton's borough of ———?"

"I believe so," replied V———. "Lord Dawton engaged it to me last week, and Mr. H———, the present member, has accepted the Chiltern Hundreds. You know all our family support Lord Dawton warmly on the present crisis, and my return for this borough was materially insisted upon. Such things are, you see, Mr. Pelham, even in these virtuous days of parliamentary purity."

"True," said I, dissembling my chagrin, "yourself and Dawton have made an admirable exchange. Think you the ministry can be said to be fairly seated?"

"By no means; every thing depends upon the motion of ———, brought on next week. Dawton looks to that as to the decisive battle for this session."

Lord Gavelton now joined us, and I sauntered away with the utmost (seeming) indifference. At the top of St. James's-street, Lady Roseville's well known carriage passed me—she stopped for a moment. "We shall meet at the Duke of ———'s to-night," said she, "shall we not?"

"If *you* go—certainly," I replied.

I went home to my solitary apartment, and if I suffered somewhat of the torments of baffled hope and foiled ambition, the pang is not for the spectator. My lighter moments are for the world—my deeper for myself; and, like the Spartan boy, I would keep, even in the pangs of death, a mantle over the teeth and fangs which are fastening upon my breast.

CHAPTER VII

Nocet empta dolore voluptas.

OVID[1]

THE FIRST PERSON I SAW AT THE DUKE OF ———'S WAS Mr. Mivart—he officiated as gentleman usher: the *second* was my mother—she was, as usual, surrounded by men, "the shades of heroes that have been,"[2] remnants of a former day, when the feet of the young and fair Lady Frances were as light as her head, and she might have rivalled in the science *de la danse,* even the graceful Duchess of B———d. Over the dandies of her own time she still preserved her ancient empire; and it was amusing enough to hear the address of the *ci-devant jeunes hommes,* who continued, through habit, the compliments began thirty years since, through admiration.

My mother was, indeed, what the world calls a very charming, agreeable woman. Few person were more popular in society: her manners were perfection—her smile enchantment: she lived, moved, breathed, only for the world, and the world was not ungrateful for

1. "Pleasure bought by pain is harmful" (Horace *Epistles* 1.2.55). Incorrectly attributed to Ovid.

2. Unidentified.

the constancy of her devotion. Yet, if her letters have given my readers any idea of her character, they will perceive that the very desire of supremacy in *ton,* gave (God* forgive my filial impiety!) a sort of demi-vulgarism to her ideas; for they who live wholly for the opinion of others, always want that self-dignity which alone confers a high cast upon the sentiments; and the most really unexceptionable in mode, are frequently the least genuinely patrician in mind.

I joined the maternal party, and Lady Frances soon took an opportunity of whispering, "You are looking very well, and very handsome; I declare you are *not* unlike me, especially about the eyes. I have just heard that Miss Glanville will be a great heiress, for poor Sir Reginald cannot live much longer. She is here to-night; pray do not lose the opportunity."

My cheek burnt like fire at this speech, and my mother, quietly observing that I had a beautiful colour, and ought therefore *immediately* to find out Miss Glanville, lest it should vanish by the least delay, turned from me to speak of a public breakfast about shortly to be given. I passed into the dancing-room; there I found Vincent; he was in unusually good spirits.

"Well," said he, with a sneer, "you have not taken your seat yet. I suppose Lord Dawton's representative, whose place you are to supply, is like Theseus, *sedet eternumque* sedebit.³ A thousand pities you can't come in before next week; we shall then have fiery *motions* in the *Lower House,* as the astrologers say."

I smiled. '*Ah, mon cher!*" said I, "Sparta hath many a worthier son than me!⁴ Meanwhile, how get on the noble Lords Lesborough and Lincoln? 'sure such a pair were never seen, so justly formed to meet by nature!' "⁵

"Pooh!" said Vincent, coarsely, "they shall get *on* well enough, before you get *in.* Look to yourself, and remember that 'Caesar plays the ingrate.' "

Vincent turned away; my eyes were rivetted on the ground; the beautiful Lady ——— passed by me: "What, *you* in a reverie?" said she, laughing; "our very host will turn thoughtful next!"

"Nay," said I, "in your absence would you have me glad? However, if Moore's mythology be true—Beauty loves Folly the better for

---

3. "He sits and will continue to sit forever" (Virgil *Aeneid* 6.617).

4. The remark of the mother of Brasidas, a Lacedaemonian general, to the strangers who praised the memory of her son. See Plutarch's *Moralia* and Byron's *Childe Harold's Pilgrimage,* canto 4.

5. This quotation and the one immediately following are unidentified.

borrowing something from Reason;[6] but, come, this is a place not for the grave, but the *giddy*. Let us join the waltzers."

"I am engaged."

"I know it! do you think I would dance with any woman who was *not* engaged?—there would be no triumph to one's vanity in that case. *Allons, ma belle*, you *must* prefer me to an engagement;" and so saying, I led off my prize.

Her intended partner was Mr. V———; just as we had joined the dancers, he spied us out, and approached with his long, serious, respectful face; the music struck *up*, and the next moment poor V. was very nearly struck *down*. Fraught with the most political spite, I whirled up against him; apologized with my blandest smile, and left him wiping his mouth, and rubbing his shoulder, the most forlorn picture of Hope in adversity, that can possibly be conceived.

I soon grew wearied of my partner, and leaving her to fate, rambled into another room. There, seated alone, was Lady Roseville. I placed myself beside her; there was a sort of freemasonry between her and myself; each knew something more of the other than the world did, and read his or her heart, by other signs than words. I soon saw that she was in no mirthful mood; so much the better—she was the fitter companion for a baffled aspirant like me.

The room we were in was almost deserted, and finding ourselves uninterrupted, the stream of our conversation flowed into sentiment.

"How little," said Lady Roseville, "can the crowd know of the individuals who compose it. As the most opposite colours may be blended into one, and so lose their individual hues, and be classed under a single name, so every one here will go home, and speak of the '*gay scene*,' without thinking for a moment, how many breaking hearts may have composed it."

"I have often thought," said I, "how harsh we are in our judgments of others—how often we accuse those persons of being worldly, who merely seem so to the world; who, for instance, that saw you in your brightest moments, would ever suppose that you could make the confession you have just made?"

"I would *not* make such a confession to many beside yourself," answered Lady Roseville. "Nay, you need not thank me. I am some years older than you; I have lived longer in the world; I have seen much of its various characters; and my experience has taught me to penetrate and prize a character like yours. While you seem frivolous

---

6. A paraphrase of the last stanza of Thomas Moore's "Reason, Folly, and Beauty" in his *National Airs*.

to the superficial, I know you to have a mind not only capable of the most solid and important affairs, but habituated by reflection to consider them. You appear effeminate, I know that none are more daring—indolent, none are more actively ambitious—utterly selfish, and I know that no earthly interest could bribe you into meanness or injustice—no, nor even into a venial dereliction of principle. It is from this estimate of your character, that I am frank and open to you. Besides, I recognize something in the careful pride with which you conceal your higher and deeper feelings, resembling the strongest actuating principle in my own mind. All this interests me warmly in your fate; may it be as bright as my presentiments forebode."

I looked into the beautiful face of the speaker as she concluded; perhaps, at that solitary moment, my heart was unfaithful to Ellen; but the infidelity passed away like the breath from the mirror. Coxcomb as I was, I knew well how passionless was the interest expressed for me. Libertine* as I had been, I knew, also, how pure may be the friendship of a woman, *provided she loves another.*

I thanked Lady Roseville, warmly, for her opinion. "Perhaps," I added, "dared I solicit your advice, you would not find me wholly undeserving of your esteem."

"My advice," answered Lady Roseville, "would be, indeed, worse than useless, were it not regulated by a certain knowledge which, perhaps, you do not possess. You seem surprised. *Eh bien;* listen to me—are you not in no small degree *lié* with Lord Dawton?—do you not expect something from him worthy of your rank and merit?"

"You do, indeed, surprise me," said I. "However close my connection with Lord Dawton may be, I thought it much more secret than it appears to be. However, I own that I have *a right* to expect from Lord Dawton, not, perhaps, a recompense of service, but, at least, a fulfillment of promises. In this expectation I begin to believe I shall be deceived."

"You will!" answered Lady Roseville. "Bend your head lower—the walls have ears. You have a friend, an unwearied and earnest friend, with those now in power; directly he heard that Mr. V——— was promised the borough, which he knew had been long engaged to you, he went straight to Lord Dawton. He found him with Lord Clandonald; however, he opened the matter immediately. He spoke with great warmth of your claims—he did more—he incorporated them with his own, which are of no mean order, and asked no other recompense for himself than the fulfillment of a long made promise to you. Dawton was greatly confused, and Lord Clandonald replied,

335

for him, that certainly there was no denying your talents—that they were very great—that you had, unquestionably, been of much service to their party, and that, consequently, it must be politic to attach you to their interests; but that there was a certain *fierté*, and assumption, and he might say (mark the climax) *independence* about you, which could not but be highly displeasing in one so young; moreover, that it was impossible to trust to you—that you pledged yourself to no party—that you spoke only of conditions and terms—that you treated the proposal of placing you in Parliament rather as a matter of favour on your part, than on Lord Dawton's—and, in a word, that there was no relying upon you. Lord Dawton then took courage, and chimed in with a long panegyric on V———, and a long account of what was due to him, and to the zeal of his family: adding, that in a crisis like this, it was absolutely necessary to engage a certain rather than a doubtful and undecided support; that, for his part, if he placed you in Parliament, he thought you quite as likely to prove a foe as a friend; that, owing to the marriage of your uncle, your expectations were by no means commensurate with your presumption, and that the same talents which made your claims to favour as an ally, created also no small danger in placing you in any situation where you could become hurtful as an enemy. All this, and much more to the same purpose, was strenuously insisted upon by the worthy pair; and your friend was obliged to take his leave, perfectly convinced that, unless you assumed a more complaisant bearing, or gave a more decided pledge, to the new minister, it was hopeless for you to expect any thing from him, at least, for the present. The fact is, he stands too much in awe of you, and would rather keep you out of the House than contribute an iota towards obtaining you a seat. Upon all this, you may rely as certain."

"I thank you from my heart," said I, warmly, seizing and pressing Lady Roseville's hand. "You tell me what I have long suspected; I am now upon my guard, and they shall find that I can *offend* as well as *defend*. But it is no time for me to boast; oblige me by informing me of the name of my unknown friend; I little thought there was a being in the world who would stir three steps for Henry Pelham."

"That friend," replied Lady Roseville, with a faltering voice and a glowing cheek, "was Sir Reginald Glanville."

"What!" cried I, "repeat the name to me again, or—" I paused, and recovered myself. "Sir Reginald Glanville," I resumed, haughtily, "is too gracious to enter into my affairs. I must be strangely altered if I need the officious zeal of *any* intermeddler to redress my wrongs."

336

"Nay, Mr. Pelham," said the countess, hastily, "you do Glanville—you do yourself injustice. For him, there never passes a day in which he does not mention you with the highest encomiums and the most affectionate regard. He says, of late, that you have altered towards him, but that he is not surprised at the change—he never mentions the cause; if I am not intruding, suffer me to inquire into it; perhaps (oh! how happy it would make me) I may be able to reconcile you; if you knew—if you could but guess half of the noble and lofty character of Reginald Glanville, you would suffer no petty difference to divide you."

"It is no *petty* difference," said I, rising, "nor am I permitted to mention the cause. Meanwhile, may God bless you, dearest Lady Roseville, and preserve that kind and generous heart from *worse* pangs than those of disappointed ambition, or betrayed trust."

Lady Roseville looked down—her bosom heaved violently; she felt the meaning of my words. I left her and St. J——'s-square. I returned home to court sleep as vainly as the monarch in the tragedy, and to exclaim as idly as the peasant in the farce, "Oh! that there were no House of Commons in the world!"[7]*

CHAPTER VIII

Good Mr. Knave, give me my due,
I like a tart as well as you;
But I would starve on good roast beef,
Ere I would look so like a thief.
        The Queen of Hearts[1]

—— Nunc vino pellite curas;
Cras ingens iterabimus æquor.
                HORAT.

THE NEXT MORNING I RECEIVED A NOTE FROM Guloseton, asking me to dine with him at eight, to *meet* his *chevreuil*.

7. The tragedy is *Macbeth,* the farce is unidentified.

1. The first epigraph is from the famous nursery rhyme. The Latin epigraph may be translated: "Now drown cares in wine; tomorrow we cross the wide sea" (Horace *Carmen* 1.7.32–33).

337

I sent back an answer in the affirmative, and then gave myself wholly up to considering what was the best line of conduct to pursue with regard to Lord Dawton. "It would be pleasant enough," said Anger, "to go to him, to ask him boldly for the borough so often pledged to you, and in case of his refusal, to confront, to taunt, and to break with him." "True," replied that more homely and less stage effect arguer, which we term* Knowledge of the World; "but this would be neither useful nor dignified—common sense never quarrels with any one. Call upon Lord Dawton, if you will—ask him for his promise, with your second best smile, and receive his excuses with your very best. Then do as you please—break with him or not—you can do either with grace and quiet; never make a scene about any thing—reproach and anger always *do* make a scene." "Very true," said I, in answer to the latter suggestion—and having made up my mind, I repaired a quarter before three to Lord Dawton's House.

"Ah, Pelham," said the little minister, "delighted to see you look so much the better from the country air; you will stay in town now, I hope, till the end of the season?"

"Certainly, my lord,* or, at all events, till the prorogation of Parliament; how, indeed, could I do otherwise with your lordship's kind promise before my eyes. Mr. ———, the member for your borough of ———, has, I believe, accepted the Chiltern Hundreds? I feel truly obliged to you for so promptly fulfilling your promise to me."

"Hem! my dear Pelham, hem!" murmured Lord Dawton. I bent forward as if in the attitude of listening respect, but really the more clearly to perceive, and closely to enjoy his confusion. He looked up and caught my eye, and not being too much gratified with its involuntary expression, he grew more and more embarrassed; at last he summoned courage.

"Why, my dear Sir," he said, "I did, it is true, promise you that borough; but individual friendship must frequently be sacrificed to the public good. All our party insisted upon returning Mr. V——— in place of the late member: what could I do? I mentioned your claims; they all, to a man, enlarged upon your rival's: to be sure, he *is* an older person, and his family *is* very powerful in the Lower House; in short, you perceive, my dear Pelham—that is, you are aware—you can feel for the delicacy of my situation—one could not appear too eager for one's own friends at first, and I was *forced* to concede."

Lord Dawton was now fairly delivered of his speech; it was, therefore, only left me to congratulate him on his offspring.

"My dear lord," I began, "you could not have pleased me better:

338

Mr. V——— is a most estimable man, and I would not, for the world, have had you suspected of placing such a trifle as your own honour—that is to say—your promise to me, before the commands—that is to say, the interests—of your party; but no more of this now. Was your lordship at the Duke of ———'s last night?"

Dawton seized joyfully the opportunity of changing the conversation, and we talked and laughed on in different matters till I thought it time to withdraw; this I did with the most cordial appearance of regard and esteem; nor was it till I had fairly set my foot out of his door, that I suffered myself to indulge the "black bile," at my breast. I turned towards the Green Park, and was walking slowly along the principal mall with my hands behind me, and my eyes on the ground, when I heard my own name uttered. On looking back, I perceived Lord Vincent on horseback; he stopped, and conversed with me. In the humour I was in with Lord Dawton, I received him with greater warmth than I had done of late; and he also, being in a social mood, seemed so well satisfied with our *rencontre,* and my behaviour, that he dismounted to walk with me.

"This park is a very different scene now," said Vincent, "from what it was in the times of 'The Merry Monarch!'[2] yet it is still a spot much more to my taste, than its more gaudy and less classical brother of Hyde. There is something pleasingly melancholy, in walking over places haunted by history; for all of us live more in the past than the present."

"And how exactly alike in all ages," said I, "men have been. On the very spot we are on now, how many have been actuated by the same feelings that now actuate us—how many have made perhaps exactly the same remark just made by you. It is this universal identity, which forms our most powerful link with those that have been—there is a satisfaction in seeing how closely we resemble the Agamemnons of gone times, and we take care to lose none of it, by thinking how closely we also resemble the *sordidi** Thersites.[3]

"True," replied Vincent: "if wise and great men did but know how little difference there is between them and the foolish or the mean, they would not take such pains to be wise and great; to use the Chinese proverb, 'they sacrifice a picture to get possession of its ashes.' It is almost a pity that the desire to progress* should be so necessary to our being; ambition is often a fine, but never a felicitous

2. 'The Merry Monarch': Charles II of England.

3. Thersites: in mythology a foul-mouthed Greek who rails at Agamemnon until beaten into silence by Odysseus. See *Iliad,* book 2.

feeling. Cyprian, in a beautiful passage on envy, calls it 'the moth of the soul:' but perhaps, even that passion is less gnawing, less a *'tabes pectoris,'*[4] than ambition. You are surprised at my heat—the fact is, I am enraged at thinking how much we forfeit, when we look *up* only, and trample unconsciously, in the blindness of our aspiration, on the affections which strew our path. Now, you and I have been utterly estranged from each other of late. Why?—for any dispute—any disagreement in private—any discovery of meanness—treachery, unworthiness in the other? No! merely because I dine with Lord Lincoln, and you with Lord Dawton, *voilà tout*. Well say the Jesuits, that they who live for the public, must renounce all private ties; the very day we become citizens, we are to cease to be men. Our privacy is like *Leo Decimus;* directly it dies, all peace, comfort, joy, and sociality are to die with it; and an iron age, *'barbara vis et dira malorum omnium incommoda'*[5] to succeed."

"It is a pity that we struck into different paths," said I; "no pleasure would have been to me greater than making our political interests the same; but ———"

"Perhaps there is *no* but," interrupted Vincent; "perhaps, like the two knights in the hacknied story, we are only giving different names to the same shield, because we view it on different sides; let us also imitate them in their reconciliation, as well as their quarrel, and since we have already run our lances against each other, be convinced of our error, and make up our difference."

I was silent; indeed, I did not like to trust myself to speak. Vincent continued:

"I know," said he, "and it is in vain for you to conceal it, that you have been ill-used by Dawton. Mr. V——— is my first cousin; he came to me the day after the borough was given to him, and told me all that Clandonald and Dawton had said to him at the time. Believe me, they did not spare *you;*—the former, you have grievously offended: you know that he has quarrelled irremediably with his son Dartmore, and he insists that you are the friend and abettor of that ingenuous youth, in all his debaucheries and extravagance—*tu illum corrumpi sinis.*[6] I tell you this without hesitation, for I know you are less vain than ambitious, and I do not care about hurting you

---

4. "A wasting of the heart" (St. Cyprian *De zelotypia et livore* 7). In the same passage Cyprian calls envy the moth of the soul.

5. See Jovius. [B-L] "A barbarous, terrible, and troublesome force of every sort of evil" (Paolo Giovio, Bishop of Nocera [1483–1552]).

6. "You said that he was corrupted" (Terence *Adelphoe* 97).

in the one point, if I advance you in the other. As for me, I own to you candidly and frankly, that there are no pains I would spare to secure you to our party. Join us, and you shall, as I have often said, be on the parliamentary benches of our corps, without a moment of unnecessary delay. More I *cannot* promise you, because I cannot promise more to myself; but from that instant your fortune, if I augur aught aright from your ability, will be in your hands. You shake your head—surely you must see, that there is not a difference between two vehemently opposite parties to be reconciled—*aut numen aut Nebuchadnezar.** There is but a *verbal* disagreement between us, and we must own the wisdom of the sentence recorded in Aulus Gellius, that 'he is but a madman, who splits the weight of things upon the hair-breadths of words.'[7] You laugh at the quaintness of the quotation; quaint proverbs are often the truest."

If my reader should think lightly of me, when I own that I felt wavering and irresolute at the end of this speech, let him for a moment place himself in my situation—let him feel indignant at the treachery, the injustice, the ingratitude of one man; and, at the very height of his resentment, let him be soothed, flattered, courted, by the offered friendship and favour of another. Let him personally despise the former, and esteem the latter; and let him, above all, be *convinced* as well as *persuaded* of the truth of Vincent's remark, viz. that no sacrifice of principle, nor of measures, was required—nothing but an alliance against *men,* not measures. And who were those men? bound to me by a single tie—meriting from my gratitude a single consideration? No! the men, above all others, who had offered me the greatest affront, and deserved from me the smallest esteem.

But, however human feelings might induce me to waver, I felt that it was not by them only I was to decide. I am not a man whose vices or virtues are regulated by the impulse and passion of the moment; if I am quick to act, I am habitually slow to deliberate. I turned to Vincent, and pressed his hand: "I dare not trust myself to answer you now," said I: "give me till to-morrow; I shall then have both considered and determined."

I did not wait for his reply. I sprung from him, turned down the passage which leads to Pall Mall, and hastened home once more to commune with my own heart, and—*not* to be still.

In these confessions I have made no scruple of owning my errors and my foibles; all that could occasion mirth or benefit to the reader

---

7. Aulus Gellius *Noctes Attica* 1.15.1.

were his own. I have kept a veil over the darker and stormier emotions of my soul; all that could neither amuse nor instruct him *are mine!*

Hours passed on—it became time to dress—I rung for Bedos—dressed with my usual elaborateness of pains*—great emotions interfere little with the mechanical operations of life—and drove to Guloseton's.

He was unusually entertaining; the dinner too was unusually good; but, thinking that I was sufficiently intimate with my host not to be obliged to belie my feelings, I remained *distrait,* absent, and dull.

"What is the matter with you, my friend?" said the good-natured epicure; "you have neither applauded my jokes, nor tasted my *escallopes;* and your behaviour has trifled alike with my *chevreuil* and my feelings?" The proverb is right, in saying 'Grief is communicative.' I confess that I was eager to unbosom myself to one upon whose confidence I could depend. Guloseton heard me with great attention and interest—"Little," said he, kindly, "little as I care for these matters myself, I can feel for those who do: I wish I could serve you better than by advice. However, you cannot, I imagine, hesitate to accept Vincent's offer. What matters it whether you sit on one bench or on another, so that you do not sit in a thorough draught—or dine at Lord Lincoln's, or Lord Dawton's, so long as the cooks are equally good? As for Dawton, I always thought him a shuffling, mean fellow, who buys his wines at the second price, and sells his offices at the first. Come, my dear fellow, let us drink to his confusion."

So saying, Guloseton filled my glass to the brim. He had sympathized with me—I thought it, therefore, my duty to sympathize with him; nor did we part till the eyes of the *bon vivant* saw more things in heaven and earth, than are dreamt of in the philosophy of the sober.[8]

---

8. *Hamlet,* I, 5, 166–67.

CHAPTER IX

Si ad honestatem nati sumus ea aut sola expetenda est, aut
certe omni pondere gravior est habenda quam reliqua omnia.

TULLY[1]

Cas. Brutus, I do observe you now of late:
I have not from your eyes that gentleness,
And show of love as I was wont to have.

Julius Cæsar.

I ROSE AT MY USUAL EARLY HOUR; SLEEP HAD TENDED
to calm, and, I hope, also, to better my feelings. I had now leisure to
reflect, that I had not embraced my party from any private or interested motive; it was not, therefore, from a private or interested motive
that I was justified in deserting it. Our passions are terrible sophists!
When Vincent had told me, the day before, that it was from men,
not measures, that I was to change, and that such a change could
scarcely deserve the name, my heart adopted the assertion, and fancied
it into truth.

I now began to perceive the delusion; were government as mechanically perfect as it has never yet been (but as I trust it may yet be),
it would signify little who were the mere machines that regulated its
springs: but in a constitution like ours, the chief character of which
—pardon me, ye De Lolmites[2]—is its uncertainty; where men invariably
make the measures square to the dimensions of their own talent or
desire; and where, reversing the maxim of the tailor, the measures
so rarely make the men; it required no penetration to see how dangerous it was to entrust to the aristocratic prejudice of Lincoln, or
the vehement imbecility of Lesborough, the execution of the very same
measures which might safely be committed to the plain sense of

---

1. "If we are born for the practice of virtue, it ought either to be our only
object, or at least deemed of far more weighty importance than anything else"
(Cicero *De officiis* 3.35). The second epigraph is from *Julius Caesar,* I, 2, 31–33.

2. Students of Jean Louis Delolme (1740–1806), author of the *Constitution de
l'Angleterre* (1771).

Dawton, and, above all, to the great and various talents of his co-adjutors. But what made the vital difference between the two parties was less in the leaders than the body. In the Dawton faction, the best, the purest, the wisest of the day were enrolled; they took upon themselves the origin of all the active measures, and Lord Dawton was the mere channel through which those measures flowed; the plain, the unpretending, and somewhat feeble character of Lord Dawton's mind, readily conceded to the abler components of his party, the authority it was so desirable that they should exert. In Vincent's party, with the exception of himself, there was scarcely an individual with the honesty requisite for loving the projects they affected to propose, or the talents that were necessary for carrying them into effect, even were their wishes sincere; nor were either the haughty Lincoln, or his noisy and overbearing companion, Lesborough, at all of a temper to suffer that quiet, yet powerful interference of others, to which Dawton unhesitatingly submitted.

I was the more resolved to do all possible justice to Dawton's party, from the inclination I naturally had to lean towards the other; and in all matters, where private pique or self-interest can possibly penetrate, it has ever been the object of my *maturer* consideration to direct my particular attention to that side of the question which such undue partizans are the least likely to espouse. While I was gradually, but clearly, feeling my way to a decision, I received the following note from Guloseton:—

"I said nothing to you last night of what is now to be the subject of my letter, lest you should suppose it arose rather from the heat of an extempore conviviality, than its real source, viz. a sincere esteem for your mind, a sincere affection for your heart, and a sincere sympathy in your resentment and your interest.

"They tell me that Lord Dawton's triumph or discomfiture rests entirely upon the success of the motion upon ———, brought before the House of Commons, on the ———. I care, you know, very little, for my *own* part, which way this question is decided; do not think, therefore, that I make any sacrifice when I request you to suffer me to follow your advice in the disposal of my four votes. I imagine, of course, that you would wish them to adopt the contrary side to Lord Dawton; and upon receiving a line from you to that effect, they shall be empowered to do so.

"Pray oblige me also by taking the merit of this measure upon yourself, and saying (wherever it may be useful to you), how entirely, both the voters and their influence are at your disposal. I trust we

344

shall yet play the Bel to this Dragon,[3] and fell him from his high places.

"Pity me, my dear friend; I dine out to-day, and feel already, by an intuitive shudder, that the soup will be cold, and the sherry hot. Adieu.

"Ever yours,
"GULOSETON."

Now, then, my triumph, my vanity, and my revenge might be fully gratified. I had before me a golden opportunity of displaying my own power, and of humbling that of the minister. My heart swelled high at the thought. Let it be forgiven me, if, for a single moment, my previous calculations and morality vanished from my mind, and I saw only the offer of Vincent, and the generosity of Guloseton. But I checked the risings of my heart, and compelled my proud spirit to obedience.

I placed Guloseton's letter before me, and as I read it once more in order to reply to it, the disinterested kindness and delicacy of one, whom I had long, in the injustice of my thoughts, censured as selfish, came over me so forcibly, and contrasted so deeply with the hollowness of friends more sounding, alike in their profession and their creeds, that the tears streamed fast and gushingly from my eyes.

A thousand misfortunes are less affecting than a single kindness.

I wrote, in answer, a warm and earnest letter of thanks for an offer, the kindness of which penetrated me to the soul. I detailed, at some length, the reasons which induced me to the decision I had taken; I sketched also the nature of the very important motion about to be brought before the House, and deduced from that sketch the impossibility of conscientiously opposing Lord Dawton's party in the debate. I concluded with repeating the expressions my gratitude suggested; and after declining all interference with Lord Guloseton's votes, ventured to add, that *had* I interfered, it would have been in support of Dawton; not as a man, but a minister—not as an individual friend, but a public servant.

I had just despatched this letter when Vincent entered: I acquainted him, though in the most respectful and friendly terms, with my determination. He seemed greatly disappointed, and endeavoured to shake my resolution; finding this was in vain, he appeared at last satisfied, and even affected with my reasons. When we

---

3. Daniel, chapter 14 (western canon).

parted, it was with a promise, confirmed by both, that no public variance should ever again alter our private opinion* of each other.

When I was once more alone, and saw myself brought back to the very foot of the ladder I had so far and so fortunately climbed; when I saw that, in rejecting all the overtures of my friends, I was left utterly solitary and unaided among my foes—when I looked beyond, and saw no faint loophole of hope, no single stepping stone on which to recommence my broken but unwearied career—perhaps one pang of regret and repentance at my determination came across me: but there is something marvellously restorative in a good conscience, and one soon learns to look with hope to the future, when one can feel justified in turning with pride to the past.

My horse came to the door at my usual hour for riding: with what gladness I sprung upon his back, felt the free wind freshening over my fevered cheek, and turned my rein towards the green lanes that border the great city on its western side. I know few counsellors more exhilarating than a spirited horse. I do not wonder that the Roman emperor made a consul of his steed.[4] On horseback I always best feel my powers, and survey my resources: on horseback I always originate my subtlest schemes, and plan their ablest execution. Give me but a light rein, and a free bound, and I am Cicero—Cato—Caesar; dismount me, and I become a mere clod of the earth which you condemn me to touch; fire, energy, *ethereality* have departed; I am the soil without the sun—the cask without the wine—the garments without the man.

I returned homewards with increased spirits and collected thoughts: I urged my mind from my own situation, and suffered it to rest upon what Lady Roseville had told me of Reginald Glanville's interference in my behalf. That extraordinary man still continued powerfully to excite my interest; nor could I dwell, without some yearning of the kindlier affections, upon his unsolicited, and, but for Lady Roseville's communication, unknown exertions in my cause. Although the officers of justice were still actively employed in the pursuit of Tyrrell's murderer, and although the newspapers were still full of speculations on their indifferent success, public curiosity had begun to flag upon the inquiry. I had, once or twice, been in Glanville's company when the murder was brought upon the tapis, and narrowly examined his behaviour upon a subject which touched him so fearfully. I could not, however, note any extraordinary confusion or change in his

---

4. The emperor was Caligula, the horse Incitatus.

countenance; perhaps the pale cheek grew somewhat paler, the dreaming eye more abstracted, and the absent spirit more wandering than before; but many other causes than guilt could account for signs so doubtful and minute.

"You shall soon know all," the last words which he had addressed to me, yet rang in my ears; and most intensely did I anticipate the fulfilment of this promise. My hopes too—those flatterers, so often the pleasing antitheses of reason—whispered that this was not the pledge of a guilty man; and yet he had said to Lady Roseville, that he did not wonder at my estrangement from him: such words seemed to require a less favourable construction than those he had addressed to me; and, in making this mental remark, another, of no flattering nature to Glanville's disinterestedness, suggested itself: might not his interference for me with Lord Dawton, arise rather from policy than friendship; might it not occur to him, if, as I surmised, he was acquainted with my suspicions, and acknowledged their dreadful justice, that it would be advisable to propitiate my silence? Such were among the thousand thoughts which flashed across me, and left my speculations in debate and doubt.

Nor did my reflections pass unnoticed the nature of Lady Roseville's affection for Glanville. From the seeming coldness and austerity of Sir Reginald's temperament, it was likely that this was innocent, at least in act; and there was also something guileless in the manner in which she appeared rather to exult in, than to conceal, her attachment. True that she was bound to no ties; she had neither husband nor children, for whose sake love became a crime: free and unfettered, if she gave her heart to Glanville, it was also allowable to render the gift lawful and perpetual by the blessing of the church.

Alas! how little can woman, shut up in her narrow and limited circle of duties, know of the wandering life and various actions of her lover. Little, indeed, could Lady Roseville, when, in the heat of her enthusiasm, she spoke of the lofty and generous character of Glanville, dream of the foul and dastardly crime of which he was more than suspected; nor, while it was, perhaps, her fondest wish to ally herself to his destiny, could her wildest fancies anticipate the felon's fate, which, if death came not in an hastier and kinder shape, must sooner or later await him.

Of Thornton I had neither seen nor heard aught since my departure from Lord Chester's; that reprieve was, however, shortly to expire. I had scarcely got into Oxford-street, in my way homeward, when I perceived him crossing the street with another man. I turned round

347

to scrutinize the features of his companion, and, in spite of a great change of dress, a huge pair of false whiskers, and an artificial appearance of increased age, my habit of observing countenances enabled me to recognize, on the instant, my intellectual and virtuous friend, Mr. Job Jonson. They disappeared in a shop, nor did I think it worth while further to observe them, though I still bore a reminiscitory spite against Mr. Job Jonson, which I was fully resolved to wreak, at the first favourable opportunity.

I passed by Lady Roseville's door. Though the hour was late, and I had, therefore, but a slight chance of finding her at home, yet I thought the chance worth the trouble of inquiry. To my agreeable surprise, I was admitted: no one was in the drawing-room. The servant said, Lady Roseville was at that moment engaged, but would very shortly see me, and begged I would wait.

Agitated as I was by various reflections, I walked (in the restlessness of my mood) to and fro the spacious rooms which formed Lady Roseville's apartments of reception. At the far end was a small *boudoir,* where none but the goddess's favoured few were admitted. As I approached towards it, I heard voices, and the next moment recognised the deep tones of Glanville. I turned hastily away, lest I should overhear the discourse; but I had scarcely got three steps, when the convulsed sound of a woman's sob came upon my ear. Shortly afterwards, steps descended the stairs, and the street door opened.

The minutes rolled on, and I became impatient. The servant re-entered—Lady Roseville was so suddenly and seriously indisposed, that she was unable to see me. I left the house, and, full of bewildered conjectures, returned to my apartments.

The next day was one of the most important in my life. I was standing wistfully by my fireplace, listening, with the most mournful attention, to a broken-winded hurdy-gurdy, stationed opposite to my window, when Bedos announced Sir Reginald Glanville. It so happened, that I had that morning taken the miniature I had found in the fatal field, from the secret place in which I usually kept it, in order more closely to examine it, lest any more convincing proof of its owner, than the initials and Thornton's interpretation, might be discovered by a minuter investigation.

The picture was lying on the table when Glanville entered: my first impulse was to seize and secrete it; my second to suffer it to remain, and to watch the effect the sight of it might produce. In following the latter, I thought it, however, as well to choose my own time for discovering the miniature; and as I moved to the table, I threw my handkerchief carelessly over it. Glanville came up to me at once, and his countenance, usually close and reserved in its expression, assumed a franker and bolder aspect.

"You have lately changed towards me," he said:—"mindful of our former friendship, I have come to demand the reason."

"Can Sir Reginald Glanville's memory," answered I, "supply him with no probable cause?"

"It can," replied Glanville, "but I would not trust *only* to that. Sit down, Pelham, and listen to me. I can read your thoughts, and I might affect to despise their import—perhaps two years since I should—at present I can pity and excuse them. I have come to you now, in the love and confidence of our early days, to claim, as then, your good opinion and esteem. If you require any explanation at my hands, it shall be given. My days are approaching their end. I have made up my accounts with others—I would do so with you. I confess that I would fain leave behind me in your breast, the same affectionate remembrance I might heretofore have claimed, and which, whatever be your suspicions, I have done nothing to forfeit. I have, moreover, a dearer interest than my own to consult in this wish—you colour, Pelham—you know to whom I allude; for my sister's sake, if not for my own, you will hear me."

Glanville paused for a moment. I raised the handkerchief from the miniature—I pushed the latter towards him—"Do you remember this!" said I, in a low tone.

With a wild cry, which thrilled through my heart, Glanville sprung forward and seized it. He gazed eagerly and intensely upon it, and his cheek flushed—his eyes sparkled—his breast heaved. The next moment he fell back in his chair, in one of the half swoons, to which, upon any sudden and violent emotion, the debilitating effects of his disease subjected him.

Before I could come to his assistance he had recovered. He looked wildly and fiercely upon me. "Speak," he cried, "speak—where got you this—where?—answer, for mercy's sake!"

"Recollect yourself," said I, sternly. "I found that token of your presence upon the spot where Tyrrell was murdered."

"True, true," said Glanville, slowly, and in an absent and abstracted tone. He ceased abruptly, and covered his face with his hands; from this attitude he started with some sudden impulse.

"And tell me," he said, in a low, inward, exulting tone, "was it—was it red with the blood of the murdered man?"

"Wretch!" I exclaimed, "do you glory in your guilt?"

349

"Hold!" said Glanville, rising, with an altered and haughty air; "it is not to your accusations that I am now to listen: if you are yet desirous of weighing their justice before you decide upon them, you will have the opportunity: I shall be at home at ten this night; come to me, and *you shall know all.* At present, the sight of this picture has unnerved me. Shall I see you?"

I made no other rejoinder than the brief expression of my assent, and Glanville instantly left the room.

During the whole of that day, my mind was wrought up into a state of feverish and preternatural excitation. I could not remain in the same spot for an instant; my pulse beat with the irregularity of delirium. For the last hour I placed my watch before me, and kept my eyes constantly fixed upon it. Should any one think this exaggerated, let him remember, that* it was not *only* Glanville's confession that I was to hear; my own fate, my future connection with Ellen, rested upon the story of that night. For myself, when I called to mind Glanville's acknowledgment of the picture, and his slow and involuntary remembrance of the spot where it was found, I scarcely allowed my temper, sanguine as it was, to hope.

Some minutes before the hour of ten I repaired to Glanville's house. He was alone—the picture was before him.

I drew my chair towards him in silence, and accidentally lifting up my eyes, encountered the opposite mirror. I started at my own face; the intensity and fearfulness of my interest had rendered it even more hueless than that of my companion.

There was a pause for some moments, at the end of which Glanville thus began:—

350

CHAPTER X

I do but hide
Under these words, like embers, every spark
Of that which has consumed me. Quick and dark
The grave is yawning;—as its roof shall cover
My limbs with dust and worms, under and over,
So let oblivion hide this grief.

Julian and Maddalo[1]

With thee, the very future fled,
   I stand amid the past alone;
A tomb which still shall guard the dead,
   Tho' every earthlier trace be flown,
A tomb o'er which the weeds that love
   Decay—their wild luxuriance wreathe!
The cold and callous stone above—
   And only thou and Death beneath.

From Unpublished Poems by——

THE HISTORY OF SIR REGINALD GLANVILLE

"YOU REMEMBER MY CHARACTER AT SCHOOL—THE difficulty with which you drew me from the visionary and abstracted loneliness which, even at that time, was more consonant to my taste, than all the sports and society resorted to by other boys—and the deep, and, to you, inexplicable delight with which I returned to my reveries and solitude again. That character has continued through life the same; circumstances have strengthened, not altered it. So has it been with *you;* the temper, the habits, the tastes, so strongly contrasted with mine in boyhood, have lost nothing of that contrast. Your ardour for the various ambitions of life is still the antipodes to my indifference; your daring, restless, thoughtful resolution in the pursuit, still shames my indolence and abstraction. You are still the votary of the

---

1. Shelley, "Julian and Maddalo," lines 503–8. The second epigraph is from Bulwer's poem "To Thee," in the privately printed volume *Weeds and Wildflowers* (Paris, 1826), lines 29–36.

world, but will become its conqueror—I its fugitive—and shall die its victim.

"After we parted at school. I went for a short time to a tutor's in ——shire. Of this place I soon grew weary; and my father's death leaving me in a great measure at my own disposal,* I lost no time in leaving it. I was seized with that mania for travel common enough to all persons of my youth and disposition. My mother allowed me an almost unlimited command over the fortune hereafter* to be my own; and, yielding to my wishes, rather than her fears, she suffered me, at the age of eighteen, to set out for the Continent alone. Perhaps the quiet and reserve of my character made her think me less exposed to the dangers of youth, than if I had been of a more active and versatile temper. This is no uncommon mistake; a serious and contemplative disposition is, however, often the worst formed to acquire readily the knowledge of the world, and always the most calculated to suffer deeply from the experience.

"I took up my residence for some time at Spa. It is, you know, perhaps, a place dull enough to make gambling the only amusement; every one played—and I did not escape the contagion; nor did I wish it: for, like the minister Godolphin,[2] my habitual silence made me love gaming for its own sake, because it was a substitute for conversation. This pursuit* brought me acquainted with Mr. Tyrrell, who was then staying at Spa; he had not, at that time, quite dissipated his fortune, but was daily progressing to so desirable a consummation. A gambler's acquaintance is readily made, and easily kept, provided you gamble too.

"We became as intimate as the reserve of my habits ever suffered me to become with any one but you. He was many years older than me—had seen a great deal of the world—had mixed much in its best societies, and at that time, whatever was the *grossièreté** of his mind, had little of the coarseness of *manner* which very soon afterwards distinguished him; evil communication works rapidly in its results. Our acquaintance was, therefore, natural enough, especially when it is considered that my purse was entirely at his disposal—for borrowing is, 'twice blessed,' in him that takes and him that gives—the receiver becomes complaisant and conceding, and the lender thinks favourably of one he has obliged.

"We parted at Spa, under a mutual promise to write. I forget if this promise was kept—probably not; we were not, however, the

---

2. Sidney Godolphin (1645–1712): English statesman.

worst friends for being bad correspondents. I continued my travels for about another year; I then returned to England, the same melancholy and dreaming enthusiast as before. It is true that we are the creatures of circumstances; but circumstances are also, in a great measure, the creatures of *us*. I mean, they receive their colour from the previous bent of our own minds; what raises one would depress another, and what vitiates my neighbor might correct me. Thus the experience of the world makes some persons more worldly—others more abstracted, and the indulgence of the senses becomes a violence to one mind, and a second nature to another. As for me, I had tasted all the pleasures youth and opulence can purchase, and was more averse to them than ever. I had mixed with many varieties of men— I was still more rivetted to the *monotony* of *self*.

"I cannot hope, while I mention these peculiarities, that I am a very uncommon character: I believe the present age has produced many such. Some time hence, it will be a curious inquiry to ascertain the causes of that acute and sensitive morbidity of mind, which has been, and still is, so epidemic a disease. You know me well enough to believe, that I am not fond of the cant of assuming an artificial character, or of creating a fictitious interest; and I am far from wishing to impose upon you a malady of constitution for a dignity of mind. You must pardon my prolixity. I own that it is very painful to me to come to the main part of my confessions, and I am endeavouring to prepare myself by lingering over the prelude."

Glanville paused here for a few moments. In spite of the sententious coolness with which he pretended to speak, I saw that he was powerfully and painfully affected.

"Well," he continued, "to resume the thread of my narrative; after I had stayed some weeks with my mother and sister, I took advantage of their departure for the Continent, and resolved to make a tour through England. Rich people, and I have always been very rich, grow exceedingly tired of the embarrassment of their riches. I seized with delight at the idea of travelling without carriages and servants; I took merely a favourite horse, and the black dog, poor Terror, which you see now at my feet.

"The day I commenced this plan was to me the epoch of a new and terrible existence. However, you must pardon me if I am not here sufficiently diffuse. Suffice it, that I became acquainted with a being whom, for the first and only time in my life, I loved! This miniature attempts to express her likeness; the initials at the back, interwoven with my own, are hers."

353

"Yes," said I, incautiously, "they are the initials of Gertrude Douglas."

"What!" cried Glanville, in a loud tone, which he instantly checked, and continued in an indrawn, muttered whisper: "How long is it since I heard that name! and now—now—" he broke off abruptly, and then said, with a calmer voice, "I know not how you have learnt *her* name; perhaps you will explain?"

"From Thornton," said I.

"And has he told you more?" cried Glanville, as if gasping for breath—"the history—the dreadful——"

"Not a word," said I, hastily; "he was with me when I found the picture, and he explained the initials."

"It is well!" answered Glanville, recovering himself; "you will see presently if I have reason to love that those foul and sordid lips should profane the story I am about to relate. Gertrude was an only daughter; though of gentle blood, she was no match for me, either in rank or fortune. Did I say just now that the world had not altered me? See my folly; one year before I saw her, and I should not have thought *her*, but *myself*, honoured by a marriage;—twelve little months had sufficed to—God forgive me! I took advantage of her love—her youth—her innocence—she fled with me—*but not to the altar!*"

Again Glanville paused, and again, by a violent effort, conquered his emotion, and proceeded:

"Never let vice be done by halves—never let a man invest all his purer affections in the woman he ruins—never let him cherish the kindness, if he gratifies the selfishness, of his heart. A profligate, who really loves his victim, is one of the most wretched of beings. In spite of my successful and triumphant passion—in spite of the first intoxication of possession, and the better and deeper delight of a reciprocity of thought—feeling, sympathy, for the first time, found;—in the midst of all the luxuries my wealth could produce, and of the voluptuous and spring-like hues with which youth, health, and first love, clothe the earth which the loved one treads, and the air which she inhales: in spite of these, in spite of all, I was any thing but happy. If Gertrude's cheek seemed a shade more pale, or her eye less bright, I remembered the sacrifice she had made me, and believed that *she* felt it too. It was in vain, that, with the tender and generous devotion —never found but in woman—she assured me that my love was a recompense for all; the more touching was her tenderness, the more poignant was my remorse. I never loved but her; I have never, therefore, entered into the common-place of passion, and I cannot, even

354

to this day, look upon her sex as ours do in general. I thought, I think so still, that ingratitude to a woman is often a more odious offence—I am sure it contains a more painful penalty—than ingratitude to a man. But enough of this; if you know me, you can penetrate the nature of my feelings—if not, it is in vain to expect your sympathy.

"I never loved living long in one place. We travelled over the greater part of England and France. What must be the enchantment of love, when accompanied with innocence and joy, when, even in sin, in remorse, in grief, it brings us a rapture to which all other things are tame. Oh! those were moments steeped in the very elixir of life; overflowing with the hoarded fondness and sympathies of hearts too full for words, and yet too agitated for silence, when we journeyed alone, and at night, and as the shadows and stillness of the waning hours gathered round us, drew closer to each other, and concentrated this breathing world in the deep and embracing sentiment of our mutual love! It was then that I laid my burning temples on her bosom, and felt, while my hand clasped her's, that my visions were realized, and my wandering spirit had sunk unto its rest.

"I remember well that, one night, we were travelling through one of the most beautiful parts of England; it was in the very height and flush of summer, and the moon (what scene of love—whether in reality, or romance—has any thing of tenderness, or passion, or divinity, where her light is not!) filled the intense skies of June with her presence, and cast a sadder and paler beauty over Gertrude's cheek. She was always of a melancholy and despondent temper; perhaps, for that reason, she was more congenial to my own; and when I gazed upon her that night, I was not surprised to see her eyes filled with tears. 'You will laugh at me,' she said, as I kissed them off, and inquired into the cause; 'but I feel a presentiment that I cannot shake off; it tells me that you will travel this road again before many months are past, and that I shall not be with you, perhaps not upon the earth.' She was right in all her forebodings, but the suggestion of her death; —*that* came later.

"We took up our residence for some time at a beautiful situation, a short distance from a small watering place. Here,* to my great surprise, I met with Tyrrell. He had come there partly to see a relation from whom he had some expectations, and partly to recruit his health, which was much broken by his irregularities and excesses. I could not refuse to renew my old acquaintance with him; and, indeed, I thought him too much of a man of the world, and of society, to feel with him that particular delicacy, in regard to Gertrude, which made

355

me in general shun all intercourse with my former friends. He was in great pecuniary embarassment—much more deeply so than I then imagined; for I believed the embarrassment to be only temporary. However, my purse was then, as before, at his disposal, and he did not scruple to avail himself very largely of my offers. He came frequently to our house; and poor Gertrude, who thought I had, for her sake, made a real sacrifice in renouncing my acquaintance, endeavoured to conquer her usual diffidence, and that more painful feeling than diffidence, natural to her station, and even to affect a pleasure in the society of *my* friend, which she was very far from feeling.

"I was detained at ——— for several weeks by Gertrude's confinement. The child—happy being!—died a week after its birth. Gertrude was still in bed, and unable to leave it, when I received a letter from Ellen, to say, that my mother was then staying at Toulouse, and dangerously ill; if I wished once more to see her, Ellen besought me to lose no time in setting off for the continent. You may imagine my situation, or rather you cannot, for you cannot conceive the smallest particle of that intense love I bore to Gertrude. To you—to any other man, it might seem no extraordinary hardship to leave her even for an uncertain period—to me it was like tearing away the very life from my heart.

"I procured her a sort of half companion, and half nurse; I provided for her every thing that the most anxious and fearful love could suggest; and with a mind full of forebodings too darkly to be realized hereafter, I hastened to the nearest seaport, and set sail for France.

"When I arrived at Toulouse my mother was much better, but still in a very uncertain and dangerous state of health. I stayed with her for more than a month, during which time every post brought me a line from Gertrude, and bore back a message from 'my heart to hers' in return. This was no mean consolation, more especially when each letter spoke of increasing health and strength. At the month's end, I was preparing to return—my mother was slowly recovering, and I no longer had any fears on her account; but, there are links in our destiny fearfully interwoven with each other, and ending only in the anguish of our ultimate doom. The day before that fixed for my departure, I had been into a house where an epidemic disease raged; that night I complained of oppressive and deadly illness—before morning I was in a high fever.

"During the time I was sensible of my state, I wrote constantly to Gertrude, and carefully concealed my illness; but for several days I was delirious. When I recovered I called eagerly for my letters—*there were none—none!* I could not believe I was yet awake; but days still passed on, and not a line from England—from Gertrude. The instant I was able, I insisted upon putting horses to my carriage; I could bear no longer the torture of my suspense. By the most rapid journeys my debility would allow me to bear, I arrived in England. I travelled down to ——— by the same road that I had gone over with her! the words of her foreboding, at that time, sunk like ice into my heart, 'You will travel this road again before many months are past, and I shall not be with you: perhaps, I shall not be upon the earth.' At that thought I could have called unto the grave to open for me. Her unaccountable and lengthened silence, in spite of all the urgency and entreaties of my letters for a reply, filled me with presentiments the most fearful. Oh, God—oh, God, they were nothing to the truth!

"At last I arrived at ———; my carriage stopped at the very house—my whole frame was perfectly frozen with dread—I trembled from limb to limb—the ice of a thousand winters seemed curdling through my blood. The bell rung—once, twice—no answer. I would have leaped out of the carriage—I would have forced an entrance, but I was unable to move. A man fettered and spellbound by an incubus, is less helpless than I was. At last, an old female I had never seen before, appeared.

" ' Where is she? How!' I could utter no more—my eyes were fixed upon the inquisitive and frightened countenance opposite to my own. Those eyes, I thought, might have said all that my lips could not; I was deceived—the old woman understood me no more than I did her; another person appeared—I recognized the face—it was that of a girl, who had been one of our attendants. Will you believe, that at that sight, the sight of one I had seen before, and could associate with the remembrance of the breathing, the living, the present Gertrude, a thrill of joy flashed across me—my fears seemed to vanish—my spell to cease?

"I sprung from the carriage; I caught the girl by the robe. 'Your mistress,' said I, 'your mistress—she is well—she is alive—speak, speak?' The girl shrieked out; my eagerness, and, perhaps, my emaciated and altered appearance, terrified her; but she had the strong nerves of youth, and was soon re-assured. She requested me to step in, and she would tell me all. My wife (Gertrude always went by that name) *was* alive, and, she believed, well, but she had left that place some weeks since. Trembling, and still fearful, but, comparatively, in heaven, to my former agony, I followed the girl and the old woman into the house.

"The former got me some water. 'Now,' said I, when I had drank a long and hearty draught, 'I am ready to hear *all*—my wife has left this house, you say—for what place?' The girl hesitated and looked down; the old woman, who was somewhat deaf, and did not rightly understand my questions, or the nature of the personal interest I had in the reply, answered,—'What does the gentleman want? the poor young lady who was last here? Lord help her!'

" 'What of her?' I called out, in a new alarm. 'What of her? Where has she gone? Who took her away?'

" 'Who took her?' mumbled the old woman, fretful at my impatient tone; 'Who took her? *why, the mad doctor, to be sure!'*

"I heard no more; my frame could support no longer the agonies my mind had undergone; I fell lifeless on the ground.

"When I recovered, it was at the dead of night. I was in bed, the old woman and the girl were at my side. I rose slowly and calmly. You know, all men who have ever suffered much, know the strange anomalies of despair—the quiet of our veriest anguish. Deceived by my bearing, I learned, by degrees, from my attendants, that Gertrude had some weeks since betrayed sudden symptoms of insanity; that these, in a very few hours, arose to an alarming pitch.—From some reason the woman could not explain, she had, a short time before, discarded the companion I had left with her; she was, therefore, alone among servants. They sent for the ignorant practitioners of the place; they tried their nostrums without success; her madness increased; her attendants, with that superstitious horror of insanity, common to the lower classes, became more and more violently alarmed; the landlady insisted on her removal; and—and—I told you, Pelham—I told you— they sent her away—sent her to a madhouse! All this I listened to— all!—ay, and patiently! I noted down the address of her present abode: it was about the distance of twenty miles from ———. I ordered fresh horses and set off immediately.

"I arrived there at day-break. It was a large, old house, which, like a French hotel, seemed to have no visible door; dark and gloomy, the pile appeared worthy of the purpose to which it was devoted. It was a long time before we aroused any one to answer our call; at length, I was ushered into a small parlour—how minutely I remember every article in the room! what varieties there are in the extreme passions! sometimes the same feeling will deaden all the senses— sometimes render them a hundredfold more acute?

358

"At last, a man of a smiling and rosy aspect appeared. He pointed to a chair—rubbed his hands—and begged me to unfold my business; few words sufficed to do that. I requested to see his patient; I demanded by what authority she had been put under his care. The man's face altered. He was but little pleased with the nature of my visit. 'The lady,' he said, coolly, 'had been entrusted to his care, with an adequate remuneration, by Mr. Tyrrell; without that gentleman's permission he could not think even of suffering me to see her.' I controlled my passion; I knew something, if not of the nature of private madhouses, at least of that of mankind. I claimed his patient as my wife; I expressed myself obliged by his care, and begged his acceptance of a further remuneration, which I tendered, and which was eagerly accepted. The way was now cleared—there is no hell to which a golden branch will not win your admittance.

"The man detained me no longer; he hastened to lead the way. We passed through various long passages; sometimes the low moan of pain and weakness came upon my ear—sometimes the confused murmur of the idiot's drivelling soliloquy. From one passage, at right angles with the one through which we proceeded, came a fierce and thrilling shriek; it sunk at once into silence—*perhaps beneath the lash!*

"We were now in a different department of the building—all was silence—hushed—deep—breathless: this seemed to me more awful than the terrible sounds I had just heard. My guide went slowly on, sometimes breaking the stillness of the dim gallery by the jingle of his keys—sometimes by a muttered panegyric on himself and his humanity. I neither heeded nor answered him.

"We read in the annals of the Inquisition, of every limb, nerve, sinew of the victim, being so nicely and accurately strained to their utmost, that the frame would not bear the additional screwing of a single hair breadth. Such seemed *my* state. We came to a small door, at the right hand; it was the last but one in the passage. We paused before it. 'Stop,' said I, 'for one moment:' and I was so faint and sick at heart, that I leaned against the wall to recover myself, before I let him open the door: when he did, it was a greater relief than I can express, to see that all was utterly dark. 'Wait, Sir,' said the guide, as he entered; and a sullen noise told me that he was unbarring the heavy shutter.

"Slowly the grey cold light of the morning broke in: a dark figure was stretched upon a wretched bed, at the far end of the room. She raised herself at the sound. She turned her face towards me; I did not fall, nor faint, nor shriek; I stood motionless, as if fixed into stone; and yet it was Gertrude upon whom I gazed! Oh, Heaven! who but myself could have recognized her? Her cheek was as the cheek of the dead—the hueless skin clung to the bone—the eye was dull and glassy for one moment, the next it became terribly and preternaturally bright—but not with the ray of intellect, or consciousness, or recognition. She looked long and hard at me; a voice, hollow and broken, but which still penetrated my heart, came forth through the wan lips, that scarcely moved with the exertion. 'I am very cold,' it said—'but if I complain, you will beat me.' She fell down again upon the bed, and hid her face.

"My guide, who was leaning carelessly by the window, turned to me with a sort of smirk—'This is her way, Sir,' he said; 'her madness is of a very singular description: we have not, as yet, been able to discover how far it extends; sometimes she seems conscious of the past, sometimes utterly oblivious of every thing: for days she is perfectly silent, or, at least, says nothing more than you have just heard; but, at times, she raves so violently, that—that—*but I never use force where it can be helped.*'

"I looked at the man, but I could not answer, unless I had torn him to pieces on the spot. I turned away hastily from the room; but I did not quit the house without Gertrude—I placed her in the carriage, by my side—notwithstanding all the protestations and fears of the keeper; these were readily silenced by the sum I gave him; it was large enough to have liberated half his household. In fact, I gathered from his conversation, that Tyrrell had spoken of Gertrude as an unhappy female whom he himself had seduced, and would now be rid of. I thank you, Pelham, for that frown, but keep your indignation till a fitter season for it.

"I took *my* victim, for I then regarded her as such, to a secluded and lonely spot: I procured for her whatever advice England could afford; all was in vain. Night and day I was by her side, but she never, for a moment, seemed to recollect me: yet were there times of fierce and overpowering delirium, when my name was uttered in the transport of the most passionate enthusiasm—when my features as absent, though not present, were recalled and dwelt upon with all the minuteness of the most faithful detail; and I knelt by her in all those moments, when no other human being was near, and clasped her wan hand, and wiped the dew from her forehead, and gazed upon her convulsed and changing face, and called upon her in a voice which could once have allayed her wildest emotions; and had

360

the agony of seeing her eye dwell upon me with the most estranged indifference or the most vehement and fearful aversion. But, ever and anon, she uttered words which chilled the very marrow of my bones; words which I would not, dared not believe, had any meaning or method in their madness—but which entered into my own brain, and preyed there like the devouring of a fire. There *was* a truth in those ravings—a reason in that incoherence—and my cup was not yet full.

"At last, one physician, who appeared to me to have more knowl-edge than the rest of the mysterious workings of her dreadful disease, advised me to take her to the scenes of her first childhood: 'Those scenes,' said he, justly, 'are in all stages of life, the most fondly re-membered; and I have noted, that in many cases of insanity, places are easier recalled than persons; perhaps, if we can once awaken one link in the chain, it will communicate to the rest.'

"I took this advice, and set off to Norfolk. Her early home was not many miles distant from the churchyard where you once met me, and in that churchyard her mother was buried. *She* had died before Gertrude's flight; the father's death had followed it: perhaps my sufferings were a just retribution. The house had gone into other hands, and I had no difficulty in engaging it. Thank Heaven, I was spared the pain of seeing any of Gertrude's relations.

"It was night when we moved to the house. I had placed within the room where she used to sleep, all the furniture and books, with which it appeared, from my inquiries, to have been formerly filled. We laid her in the bed that had held that faded and altered form, in its freshest and purest years. I shrouded myself in one corner of the room, and counted the dull minutes till the daylight dawned. I pass over the detail of my recital—the experiment partially suc-ceeded—would to God that it had not! would that she had gone down to her grave with her dreadful secret unrevealed! would—but——"

Here Glanville's voice failed him, and there was a brief silence before he recommenced.

"Gertrude now had many lucid intervals; but these my presence were always sufficient to change into a delirous raving, even more incoherent than her insanity had ever yet been. She would fly from me with the most fearful cries, bury her face in her hands, and seem like one oppressed and haunted by a supernatural visitation, as long as I remained in the room; the moment I left her, she began, though slowly, to recover.

"This was to me the bitterest affliction of all—to be forbidden to nurse, to cherish, to tend her, was like taking from me my last hope!

361

But little can the thoughtless or the worldly dream of the depths of a real love; I used to wait all day by her door, and it was luxury enough to me to catch her accents, or hear her move, or sigh, or even weep; and all night, when she could not know of my presence, I used to lie down by her bedside; and when I sank into a short and convulsed sleep, I saw her once more, in my brief and fleeting dreams, in all the devoted love, and glowing beauty, which had once constituted the whole of my happiness, and *my world.*

"One day I had been called from my post by her door. They came to me hastily—she was in strong convulsions. I flew up stairs, and supported her in my arms till the fits had ceased: we then placed her in bed; she never rose from it again; but on that bed of death, the words, as well as the cause of her former insanity, were explained—the mystery was unravelled.

"It was a still and breathless night. The moon, which was at its decrease, came through the half-closed shutters, and beneath its solemn and eternal light, she yielded to my entreaties, and revealed all. The man—my friend—Tyrrell—had polluted her ear with his addresses, and when forbidden the house, had bribed the woman I had left with her, to convey his letters—she was discharged—but Tyrrell was no ordinary villain; he entered the house one evening, when no one but Gertrude was there.—Come near me, Pelham—nearer—bend down your ear—he used force, violence! That night Gertrude's senses deserted her—you know the rest.

"The moment that I gathered, from Gertrude's broken sentences, their meaning, that moment the demon entered into my soul. All human feelings seemed to fly from my heart; it shrunk into one burning, and thirsty, and fiery want—and that want was for revenge. I would have sprung from the bedside, but Gertrude's hand clung to me, and detained me; the damp, chill grasp, grew colder and colder—it ceased—the hand fell—I turned—one slight, but awful shudder, went over that face, made yet more wan by the light of the waning and ghastly moon—one convulsion shook the limbs—one murmur passed the falling and hueless lips. I cannot tell you the rest—you know—you can guess it.

"That day week we buried her in the lonely churchyard—where she had, in her lucid moments, wished to lie—by the side of her mother.

CHAPTER XI

I breathed,
But not the breath of human life;
A serpent round my heart was wreathed,
And stung my every thought to strife.
The Giaour[1]

"THANK HEAVEN, THE MOST PAINFUL PART OF MY story is at an end. You will now be able to account for our meeting in the churchyard at ———. I secured myself a lodging at a cottage not far from the spot which held Gertrude's remains. Night after night I wandered to that lonely place, and longed for a couch beside the sleeper, whom I mourned in the selfishness of my soul. I prostrated myself on the mound: I humbled myself to tears. In the overflowing anguish of my heart I forgot all that had aroused its stormier passions into life. Revenge, hatred, all vanished. I lifted up my face to the tender heavens: I called aloud to the silent and placid air; and when I turned again to that unconscious mound, I thought of nothing but the sweetness of our early love and the bitterness of her early death. It was in such moments that your footstep broke upon my grief: the instant others had seen me—other eyes penetrated the sanctity of my regret—from that instant, whatever was more soft and holy in the passions and darkness of my mind seemed to vanish away like a scroll. I again returned to the intense and withering remembrance which was henceforward to make the very key and pivot of my existence. I again recalled the last night of Gertrude's life; I again shuddered at the low, murmured sounds, whose dreadful sense broke slowly upon my soul. I again felt the cold—cold, slimy grasp of those wan and dying fingers; and I again nerved my heart to an iron strength, and vowed deep, deep-rooted, endless, implacable revenge.

"The morning after the night you saw me, I left my abode. I went to London, and attempted to methodize my plans of vengeance.

1. Byron, *The Giaour*, lines 1192–95.

The first thing to discover, was Tyrrell's present residence. By accident, I heard he was at Paris, and within two hours of receiving the intelligence, I set off for that city. On arriving there, the habits of the gambler soon discovered him to my search. I saw him one night at a hell. He was evidently in distressed circumstances, and the fortune of the table was against him. Unperceived by him, I feasted my eyes on his changing countenance, as those deadly and wearing transitions of feeling, only to be produced by the gaming-table, passed over it. While I gazed upon him, a thought of more exquisite and refined revenge, than had yet occurred to me, flashed upon my mind. Occupied with the ideas it gave rise to, I went into the adjoining room, which was quite empty. There I seated myself, and endeavoured to develop, more fully, the rude and imperfect outline of my scheme.

"The arch tempter favoured me with a trusty coadjutor in my designs. I was lost in a reverie, when I heard myself accosted by name. I looked up, and beheld a man whom I had often seen with Tyrrell, both at Spa, and ——— (the watering-place where, with Gertrude, I had met the latter).* He was a person of low birth and character; but esteemed, from his love of coarse humour, and vulgar enterprise, a man of infinite parts—a sort of Yorick—by the set most congenial to Tyrrell's tastes. By this undue reputation, and the *levelling* habit of gaming, to which he was addicted, he was raised, in certain societies, much above his proper rank: need I say that this man was Thornton. I was but slightly acquainted with him; however, he accosted me cordially, and endeavoured to draw me into conversation.

" 'Have you seen Tyrrell?' said he; 'he is at it again; what's bred in the bone, you know, &c.' I turned pale with the mention of Tyrrell's name, and replied very laconically, to what purpose, I forget.—'Ah! ah!' rejoined Thornton, eyeing me with an air of impertinent familiarity— 'I see you have not forgiven him; he played you but a shabby trick at ———; seduced your mistress, or something of that sort; he told me all about it: pray, how is the poor girl now?'

"I made no reply; I sunk down and gasped for breath. All I had suffered, seemed nothing to the indignity I then endured. *She—she—* who had *once* been my pride—my honour—life—to be thus spoken of— and——. I could not pursue the idea. I rose hastily, looked at Thornton with a glance, which might have abashed a man less shameless and callous than himself, and left the room.

"That night, as I tossed restless and feverish on my bed of thorns, I saw how useful Thornton might be to me in the prosecution of the scheme I had entered into; and the next morning I sought him out, and purchased (no very difficult matter) both his secrecy and his assistance. My plan of vengeance, to one who had seen and observed less of the varieties of human nature than you have done, might seem far-fetched and unnatural; for while the superficial are ready to allow eccentricity as natural in the coolness of ordinary life, they never suppose it can exist in the heat of the passions—as if, in such moments, any thing was ever considered absurd in the means which was favourable to the end. Were the secrets of one passionate and irregulated heart laid bare, there would be more romance in them, than in all the fables which we turn from with incredulity and disdain, as exaggerated and overdrawn.

"Among the thousand schemes for retribution which had chased each other across my mind, the death of my victim was only the ulterior object. Death, indeed—the pang of one moment—appeared to me but very feeble justice for the life of lingering and restless anguish to which his treachery had condemned *me;* but *my* penance, *my* doom, I could have forgiven: it was the fate of a more innocent and injured being which irritated the sting and fed the venom of my revenge. That revenge no ordinary punishment could appease. If fanaticism can only be satisfied by the rack and the flames, you may readily conceive a like unappeasable fury, in a hatred so deadly, so concentrated, and so just as mine—and if fanaticism persuades itself into a virtue, so also did my hatred.

"The scheme which I resolved upon was, to attach Tyrrell more and more to the gaming-table, to be present at his infatuation, to feast my eyes upon the feverish intensity of his suspence—to reduce him, step by step, to the lowest abyss of poverty—to glut my soul with the abjectness and humiliation of his penury—to strip him of all aid, consolation, sympathy, and friendship—to follow him, unseen, to his wretched and squalid home—to mark the struggles of the craving nature with the loathing pride—and, finally, to watch the frame wear, the eye sink, the lip grow livid, and all the terrible and torturing progress of gnawing want, to utter starvation. Then, in that last state, but not before, I might reveal myself—stand by the hopeless and succourless bed of death—shriek out in the dizzy ear a name, which could treble the horrors of remembrance—snatch from the struggling and agonizing conscience the last plank, the last straw, to which, in its madness, it could cling, and blacken the shadows of departing life, by opening to the shuddering sense the threshold of an impatient and yawning hell.

"Hurried away by the unhallowed fever of these projects, I thought of nothing but their accomplishment. I employed Thornton, who still maintained his intimacy with Tyrrell, to decoy him more and more to the gambling-house; and as the unequal chances of the public table were not rapid enough in their termination to consummate the ruin even of an impetuous and vehement gamester, like Tyrrell, so soon as my impatience desired, Thornton took every opportunity of engaging him in private play, and accelerating my object by the unlawful arts of which he was master. My enemy was every day approaching the farthest verge of ruin; near relations he had none, all his distant ones he had disobliged; all his friends, and even his acquaintance, he had fatigued by his importunity, or disgusted by his conduct. In the whole world there seemed not a being who would stretch forth a helping hand to save him from the total and pennyless beggary to which he was hopelessly advancing. Out of the wrecks of his former property, and the generosity of former friends, whatever he had already wrung, had been immediately staked at the gaming house, and as immediately lost.

"Perhaps this would not so soon have been the case, if Thornton had not artfully fed and sustained his expectations. He had been long employed by Tyrrell in a professional capacity, and he knew well all the gamester's domestic affairs; and when he promised, should things come to the worst, to find some expedient to restore them, Tyrrell easily adopted so flattering a belief.

"Meanwhile, I had taken the name and disguise under favour of which you met me at Paris, and Thornton had introduced me to Tyrrell as a young Englishman of great wealth, and still greater inexperience. The gambler grasped eagerly at an acquaintance, which Thornton readily persuaded him he could turn to such account; and I had thus every facility of marking, day by day, how my plot thickened, and my vengeance hastened to its triumph.

"This was not all. I said, there was not in the wide world a being who would have saved Tyrrell from the fate he deserved and was approaching. I forgot there *was* one who still clung to him with affection, and for whom he still seemed to harbour the better and purer feelings of less degraded and guilty times. This person (you will guess readily it was a woman) I made it my especial business and care to wean away from my prey; I would not suffer him a consolation he had denied to me. I used all the arts of seduction to obtain the transfer of her affections. Whatever promises and vows—whether of love or wealth—could effect, were tried; nor, at last, without success —*I* triumphed. The woman became my slave. It was she who, when-

366

ever Tyrrell faltered in his course to destruction, combated his scruples, and urged on his reluctance; it was she who informed me minutely of his pitiful finances, and assisted, to her utmost, in expediting their decay. The still more bitter treachery of deserting him in his veriest want I reserved till the fittest occasion, and contemplated with a savage delight.

"I was embarrassed in my scheme by two circumstances: first, Thornton's acquaintance with you; and, secondly, Tyrrell's receipt (some time afterwards) of a very unexpected sum of two hundred pounds, in return for renouncing all further and *possible* claim on the purchasers of his estate. To the former, so far as it might interfere with my plans, or lead to my detection, you must pardon me for having put a speedy termination; the latter threw me into great consternation—for Tyrrell's first idea was to renounce the gaming table, and endeavour to live upon the trifling pittance he had acquired, as long as the utmost economy would permit.

"This idea, Margaret, the woman I spoke of, according to my instructions, so artfully and successfully combated, that Tyrrell yielded to his natural inclination, and returned once more to the infatuation of his favourite pursuit. However, I had become restlessly impatient for the termination to this prefatory part of my revenge, and, accordingly, Thornton and myself arranged that Tyrrell should be persuaded by the former to risk all, even to his vary last farthing, in a private game with me. Tyrrell, who believed he should readily recruit himself by my unskilfulness in the game, fell easily into the snare; and on the second night of our engagement, he not only had lost the whole of his remaining pittance, but had signed bonds owning to a debt of far greater amount than he, at that time, could ever even have dreamt of possessing.

"Flushed, heated, almost maddened with my triumph, I yielded to the exultation of the moment. I did not know you were so near—I discovered myself—you remember the scene. I went joyfully home: and for the first time since Gertrude's death, I was happy; but there I imagined my vengeance only would begin; I revelled in the burning hope of marking the hunger and extremity that must ensue. The next day, when Tyrrell turned round, in his despair, for one momentary word of comfort from the lips to which he believed, in the fond credulity of his heart, falsehood and treachery never came, his last earthly friend taunted and deserted him. Mark me, Pelham, I *was by, and heard her.*

"But here my power of retribution was to close: from the thirst still unslaked and unappeased, the cup was abruptly snatched. Tyrrell disappeared—no one knew whither. I set Thornton's inquiries at work. A week afterwards he brought me word that Tyrrell had died in extreme want, and from very despair. Will you credit, that at hearing this news, my first sensations were only rage and disappointment. True, he had died, died in all the misery my heart could wish, but *I had not seen* him die; and the death-bed seemed to me robbed of its bitterest pang.

"I know not to this day, though I have often questioned him, what interest Thornton had in deceiving me by this tale; for my own part, I believe that he himself was deceived;[2] certain it is (for I inquired) that a person, very much answering to Tyrrell's description, had perished in the state Thornton mentioned, and this might, therefore, in all probability, have misled him.

"I left Paris, and returned, through Normandy, to England (where I remained some weeks); there we again met: but I think we did *not* meet till I had been persecuted by the insolence and importunity of Thornton. The tools of our passions cut both ways; like the monarch, who employed strange beasts in his army, we find our treacherous allies less destructive to others than ourselves.[3] But I was not of a temper to brook the tauntings, or the encroachment of my own creature; it had been with but an ill grace that I had endured his familiarity, when I absolutely required his services, much less could I suffer his intrusion when those services—services not of love, but hire—were no longer necessary. Thornton, like all persons of his stamp, has a low pride, which I was constantly offending. He had mixed with men, more than my equals in rank, on a familiar footing, and he could ill brook the hauteur with which my disgust at his character absolutely constrained me to treat him. It is true, that the profuseness of my liberality was such, that the mean wretch stomached affronts for which he was so largely paid; but with the cunning and malicious spite natural to him, he knew well how to repay them in kind. While he assisted, he affected to ridicule my revenge; and though he soon saw that he durst not, for his very life, breathe a syllable openly against Gertrude, or her memory, yet he contrived, by general remarks, and covert insinuations, to gall me to the very quick, and in the very tenderest point. Thus a deep and cordial antipathy to each

2. It seems (from subsequent investigation) that this was really the case. [B-L]

3. Bulwer refers to Porus (d. 321 B.C.), an Indian king who bravely but unsuccessfully resisted the advance of Alexander the Great in 327 B.C. Alexander used fire to turn the elephants in Porus's army against him.

other arose, and grew, and strengthened, till, I believe, like the fiends in hell, our mutual hatred became our common punishment.

"No sooner had I returned to England, than I found him here, awaiting my arrival. He favoured me with frequent visits and requests for money. Although not possessed of any secret really important, affecting my character, he knew well, that he was possessed of one important to my quiet; and he availed himself to the utmost of my strong and deep aversion even to the most delicate recurrence to my love to Gertrude, and its unhallowed and disastrous termination. At length, however, he wearied me. I found that he was sinking into the very dregs and refuse of society, and I could not longer brook the idea of enduring his familiarity and feeding his vices.

"I pass over any detail of my own feelings, as well as my *outward* and *worldly* history. Over my mind, a great change had passed; I was no longer torn by violent and contending passions; upon the tumultuous sea a dead and heavy torpor had fallen; the very winds, necessary for health, had ceased;*

'I slept on the abyss without a surge.'[4]

One violent and engrossing passion is among the worst of all *immoralities,* for it leaves the mind too stagnant and exhausted for those activities and energies which constitute our real duties. However, now that the tyrant feeling of my mind was removed, I endeavoured to shake off the apathy it had produced, and return to the various occupations and business of life. Whatever could divert me from my own dark memories, or give a momentary motion to the stagnation of my mind, I grasped at with the fondness and eagerness of a child. Thus you found me, surrounding myself with luxuries which palled upon my taste the instant that their novelty had passed: *now* striving for the vanity of literary frame; *now,* for the emptier baubles which riches could procure. At one time I shrouded myself in my closet, and brooded over the dogmas of the learned, and the errors of the wise; at another, I plunged into the more engrossing and active pursuits of the living crowd which rolled around me, and flattered my heart, that amidst the applause of senators, and the whirlpool of affairs, I could lull to rest the voices of the past, and the spectre of the dead.

"Whether these hopes were effectual, and the struggle not in vain, this haggard and wasting form, drooping day by day into the grave, can declare; but I said I would not dwell long upon this part of my

---

4. Byron, "Darkness," line 77.

369

history, nor is it necessary. Of one thing only, not connected with the main part of my confessions, it is right, for the sake of one tender and guiltless being, that I should speak.

"In the cold and friendless world with which I mixed, there was a heart which had years ago given itself wholly up to me. At that time I was ignorant of the gift I so little deserved, or (for it was before I knew Gertrude) I might have returned it, and been saved years of crime and anguish. Since then, the person I allude to had married, and by the death of her husband, was once more free. Intimate with my family, and more especially with my sister, she now met me constantly; her compassion for the change she perceived in me, both in mind and person, was stronger than even her reserve, and this is the only reason why I speak of an attachment which ought otherwise to be concealed: I believe that you already understand to whom I allude, and since you have discovered her weakness, it is right that you should know also of her virtue; it is right that you should learn, that it was not in her the fantasy, or passion of a moment, but a long and secreted love; that you should learn, that it was her pity and no unfeminine disregard to opinion which betrayed her into imprudence, and that she is, at this moment, innocent of every thing, but the folly of loving *me*.

"I pass on to the time, when I discovered that I had been, either intentionally or unconsciously, deceived, and that my enemy yet lived! *lived* in honour, prosperity, and the world's blessings. This information was like removing a barrier from a stream hitherto pent into quiet and restraint. All the stormy thoughts, feelings, and passions, so long at rest, rushed again into a terrible and tumultuous action. The newly formed stratum of my mind was swept away, every thing seemed a wreck, a chaos, a convulsion of jarring elements; but this is a trite and tame description of my feelings; words would be but common-place to express the revulsion which I experienced: yet, amidst all, there was one paramount and presiding thought, to which the rest were as atoms in the heap—the awakened thought of vengeance!—but how was it to be gratified?

"Placed as Tyrrell now was in the scale of society, every method of retribution but the one formerly rejected, seemed at an end. To that one, therefore, weak and merciful as it appeared to me, I resorted —you took my challenge to Tyrrell—you remember his behaviour— Conscience doth indeed make cowards of us all![5] The letter inclosed

---

5. *Hamlet,* III, 1, 83.

to me in his to you, contained only the common-place argument urged so often by those who have injured us; viz. the reluctance to attempting our life after having ruined our happiness. When I found that he had left London, my rage knew no bounds; I was absolutely frantic with indignation; the earth reeled before my eyes; I was almost suffocated by the violence—*the whirlpool*—of my emotions. I gave myself no time to think, I wrote you a hurried line to acquaint you with my resolution, and left town in pursuit of my foe.

"I found that—still addicted, though, I believe, not so madly as before, to his old amusements—he was in the neighborhood of Newmarket, awaiting the races shortly to ensue. No sooner did I find his address, than I wrote him another challenge, still more forcibly and insultingly worded than the one you took. In this I said that his refusal was of no avail; that I had sworn that my vengeance should overtake him; and that, sooner or later, in the face of heaven and despite of hell, my oath should be fulfilled. Remember those words, Pelham, I shall refer to them hereafter.

"Tyrrell's reply was short and contemptuous; he affected to treat me as a madman. Perhaps (and I confess that the incoherence of my letter authorized such suspicion) he believed I really was one. He concluded by saying, that if he received more of my letters, he should shelter himself from my aggressions by the protection of the law.

"On receiving this reply, a stern, sullen, iron spirit entered into my bosom. I betrayed no external mark of passion; I sat down in silence—I placed the letter and Gertrude's picture before me. There, still and motionless, I remained for hours. I remember well, I was awakened from my gloomy reverie by the clock, as it struck the first hour of the morning. At that lone and ominous sound, the associations of romance and dread which the fables of our childhood connect with it, rushed coldly and fearfully into my mind; the damp dews broke out upon my forehead, and the blood curdled in my limbs. In that moment I knelt down and vowed a frantic and deadly oath— the words of which* I would not dare now to repeat—that before three days expired, hell should no longer be cheated of its prey. I rose—I flung myself on my bed, *and slept.*

"The next day I left my abode. I purchased a strong and swift horse, and, disguising myself from head to foot in a long horseman's cloak, I set off alone, locking in my heart the calm and cold conviction, that my oath should be kept. I placed, concealed in my dress, two pistols; my intention was to follow Tyrrell wherever he went, till we could find ourselves alone, and without the chance of intrusion.

371

It was then my determination to *force* him into a contest, and that no trembling of the hand, no error of the swimming sight, might betray my purpose, to place foot to foot, and the mouth of each pistol almost to the very temple of each antagonist. Nor was I deterred for a moment from this resolution by the knowledge that my own death must be as certain as my victim's. On the contrary, I looked forward to dying thus, and so baffling the more lingering, but not less sure, disease, which was daily wasting me away, with the same fierce, yet not unquiet delight with which men have rushed into battle, and sought out a death less bitter to them than life.

"For two days, though I each day saw Tyrrell, fate threw into my way no opportunity of executing my design. The morning of the third came—Tyrrell was on the race ground: sure that he would remain there for some hours, I put up my wearied horse in the town, and seating myself in an obscure corner of the course, was contented with watching, as the serpent does his victim, the distant motions of my enemy. Perhaps you can recollect passing a man seated on the ground and robed in a horseman's cloak. I need not tell you that it was I whom you passed and accosted. I saw you ride by me; but the moment you were gone I forgot the occurrence. I looked upon the rolling and distant crowd, as a child views the figures of the phantasmagoria, scarcely knowing if my eyes deceived me, feeling impressed with some stupifying and ghastly sensation of dread, and cherishing the conviction that my life was not as the life of the creatures that passed before me.

"The day waned—I went back for my horse—I returned to the course, and keeping at a distance as little suspicious as possible, followed the motions of Tyrrell. He went back to the town—rested there —repaired to a gaming table—stayed in it a short time—returned to his inn, ordered his horse.

"In all these motions I followed the object of my pursuit; and my heart bounded with joy when I, at last, saw him set out alone, and in the advancing twilight. I followed him till he left the main road. Now, I thought, was my time. I redoubled my pace, and had nearly reached him, when some horsemen appearing, constrained me again to slacken my pace. Various other similar interruptions occurred to delay my plot. At length all was undisturbed. I spurred my horse, and was nearly on the heels of my enemy, when I perceived him join another man—this was *you*—I clenched my teeth, and drew my breath, as I once more retreated to a distance. In a short time two men passed me, and I found, that owing to some accident on the

372

road, they stopped to assist you. It appears by your evidence on a subsequent event, that these men were Thornton and his friend Dawson; at the time, they passed too rapidly, and I was too much occupied in my own dark thoughts, to observe them: still I kept up to you and Tyrrell, sometimes catching the outline of your figures through the moon-light, at others, (with the acute sense of anxiety), only just distinguishing the clang of your horses' hoofs on the stony ground. At last, a heavy shower came on; imagine my joy, when Tyrrell left you and rode off alone.

"I passed you, and followed my enemy as fast as my horse would permit; but it was not equal to Tyrrell's, which was almost at its full speed. However, I came, at last, to a very steep, and almost precipitous, descent. I was forced to ride slowly and cautiously; this, however, I the less regarded, from my conviction that Tyrrell must be obliged to use the same precaution. My hand was on my pistol with the grasp of premeditated revenge, when a shrill, sharp, solitary cry, broke on my ear.

"No sound followed—all was silence. I was just approaching towards the close of the descent, when a horse without its rider passed me. The shower had ceased, and the moon broken from the cloud some minutes before; by its light, I recognized the horse rode by Tyrrell; perhaps, I thought, it has thrown its master, and my victim will now be utterly in my power. I pushed hastily forward in spite of the hill, not yet wholly passed. I came to a spot of singular desolation —it was a broad patch of waste land, a pool of water was on the right, and a remarkable and withered tree hung over it. I looked round, but saw nothing of life stirring. A dark and imperfectly developed object lay by the side of the pond—I pressed forward—merciful God! my enemy had escaped my hand, and lay in the stillness of death before me!"

"What!" I exclaimed, interrupting Glanville, for I could contain myself no longer, "it was not by *you* then that Tyrrell fell?" With these words I grasped his hand; and, excited as I had been by my painful and wrought up interest in his recital, I burst into tears of gratitude and joy. Reginald Glanville was innocent—Ellen was not the sister of an assassin.

After a short pause, Glanville continued—

"I gazed upon the upward and distorted face, in a deep and sickening silence; an awe, dark and undefined, crept over my heart; I stood beneath the solemn and sacred heavens, and felt that the hand of God was upon me—that a mysterious and fearful edict had gone

373

forth—that my headlong and unholy wrath had, in the very midst of
its fury, been checked, as if but the idle anger of a child—that the
plan I had laid in the foolish wisdom of my heart, had been traced,
step by step, by an all seeing eye, and baffled in the moment of its
fancied success, by an inscrutable and awful doom. I had wished the
death of my enemy—lo! my wish was accomplished—*how*, I neither
knew nor guessed—there, a still and senseless clod of earth, without
power of offence or injury, he lay beneath my feet—it seemed as if,
in the moment of my uplifted arm, the Divine Avenger had asserted
his prerogative—as if the Angel which had smitten the Assyrian, had
again swept forth, though against a meaner victim—and while he
punished the guilt of an human criminal, had set an eternal barrier
to the vengeance of an human foe.

"I dismounted from my horse, and bent over the murdered man.
I drew from my bosom the miniature, which never forsook me, and
bathed the lifeless resemblance of Gertrude in the blood of her be-
trayer. Scarcely had I done so, before my ear caught the sound of
steps; hastily I thrust, as I thought, the miniature in my bosom, remounted, and rode hurriedly away. At that hour, and for many which
succeeded to it, I believe that all sense was suspended. I was like a
man haunted by a dream, and wandering under its influence; or as
one whom a spectre pursues, and for whose eye, the breathing and
busy world is but as a land of unreal forms and flitting shadows,
teeming with the monsters of darkness, and the terrors of the tomb.

"It was not till the next day that I missed the picture. I returned
to the spot—searched it carefully, but in vain—the miniature could not
be found; I returned to town, and shortly afterwards the newspapers
informed me of what had subsequently occurred. I saw, with dismay,
that all appearances pointed to me as the criminal, and that the
officers of justice were at that moment tracing the clue which my
cloak, and the colour of my horse, afforded them. My mysterious
pursuit of Tyrrell; the disguise I had assumed; the circumstance of
my passing you on the road, and of my flight when you approached,
all spoke volumes against me. A stronger evidence yet remained, and
it was reserved for Thornton to indicate it—at this moment my life
is in his hands. Shortly after my return to town, he forced his way
into my room, shut the door—bolted it—and the moment we were
alone, said, with a savage and fiendish grin of exultation and defiance,
—'Sir Reginald Glanville, you have many a time and oft insulted me
with your pride, and more with your gifts: now it is my time to insult

and triumph over you—know that one word of mine could sentence you to the gibbet.'

"He then minutely summed up the evidence against me, and drew from his pocket the threatening letter I had last written to Tyrrell. You remember that therein I said my vengeance was sworn against him, and that, sooner or later, it should overtake him. 'Couple,' said Thornton, coldly, as he replaced the letter in his pocket—'couple these words with the evidence already against you, and I would not buy your life at a farthing's value.'

"How Thornton came by this paper, so important to my safety, I know not: but when he read it, I was startled by the danger it brought upon me: one glance sufficed to shew me that I was utterly at the mercy of the villain who stood before me: he saw and enjoyed my struggles.

" 'Now,' said he, 'we know each other—at present I want a thousand pounds; you will not refuse it me, I am sure; when it is gone, I shall call again: till then you can do without me.' I flung him a note* for the money, and he departed.

"You may conceive the mortification I endured, in this sacrifice of pride to prudence: but those were no ordinary motives which induced me to submit to it. Fast approaching to the grave, it mattered to me but little whether a violent death should shorten a life to which a limit was already set, and which I was far from being anxious to retain: but I could not endure the thought of bringing upon my mother and my sister, the wretchedness and shame which the mere suspicion of a crime so enormous, would occasion them; and when my eye caught all the circumstances arrayed against me, my pride seemed to suffer a less mortification even in the course I adopted, than in the thought of the felon's gaol, and the criminal's trial; the hoots and execrations of the mob, and the death and ignominious remembrance of the murderer.

"Stronger than either of these motives was my shrinking and loathing aversion to whatever seemed likely to unrip the secret history of the past. I sickened at the thought of Gertrude's name and fate being bared to the vulgar eye, and exposed to the comment, the strictures, the ridicule of the gaping and curious public. It seemed to me, therefore, but a very poor exertion of philosophy to conquer my feelings of humiliation at Thornton's insolence and triumph, and to console myself with the reflection, that a few months must rid me alike of his exactions and my life.

"But, of late, Thornton's persecutions and demands, have risen to such a height, that I have been scarcely able to restrain my indignation and controul myself into compliance. The struggle is too powerful for my frame; it is rapidly bringing on the fiercest and the last contest I shall suffer, before 'the wicked shall cease from troubling, and the weary be at rest.'[6] Some days since, I came to a resolution, which I am now about to execute: it is to leave this country, and take refuge on the continent. There I shall screen myself from Thornton's pursuit, and the danger which it entails upon me; and there, unknown and undisturbed, I shall await the termination of my disease.

"But two duties remained to me to fulfill before I departed; I have now discharged them both. One was due to the warm-hearted and noble being who honoured me with her interest and affection—the other to you. I went yesterday to the former; I sketched the outline of that history which I have detailed to you. I shewed her the waste of my barren heart, and spoke to her of the disease which was wearing me away. How beautiful is the love of woman. She would have followed me over the world—received my last sigh, and seen me to the rest I shall find, at length; and this without a hope, or thought of recompense, even from the worthlessness of my love.

"But, enough!—of her my farewell has been taken. Your suspicions I have long seen and forgiven—for they were natural; it was due to me to remove them: the pressure of your hand tells me, that I have done so; but I had another reason for my confessions. I have filtered* away the romance of my heart, and I have now no indulgence for the little delicacies and petty scruples which often stand in the way of our real happiness. I have marked your former addresses to Ellen, and I confess, with great joy; for I know, amidst all your worldly ambition, and the encrusted artificiality of your exterior, how warm and generous is your real heart—how noble and intellectual is your real mind: and were my sister tenfold more perfect than I believe her, I do not desire to find on earth one more deserving of her than yourself. I have remarked your late estrangement from Ellen; and, while I *guessed,* I felt that, however painful to me, I ought to *remove* the cause: she loves you—though, perhaps, you know it not—much and truly; and since my earlier life has been passed in a selfish inactivity, I would fain let it close with the reflection of having served two beings, whom I prize so dearly, and the hope that their happiness will commence with my death.

---

6. Job 3:17.

"And now, Pelham, I have done; I am weak and exhausted, and cannot bear more—even of your society now. Think over what I have last said, and let me see you again to-morrow; on the day after, I leave England for ever."

CHAPTER XII

But wilt thou accept not
The worship the heart lifts above,
    And the Heavens reject not,
The desire of the moth for the star,
    Of the night for the morrow,
The devotion to something afar
    From the sphere of our sorrow?
                    P. B. SHELLEY[1]

IT WAS NOT WITH A LIGHT HEART—FOR I LOVED Glanville too well, not to be powerfully affected by his history and approaching fate*—but with a chastised and sober joy, that I now beheld my friend innocent of the guilt my suspicions had accused him of, and the only obstacle to my marriage with his sister removed. True it was that the sword yet hung over his head, and that while he lived, there could be no rational assurance of his safety from the disgrace and death of the felon. In the world's eye, therefore, the barrier to my union with Ellen would have been far from being wholly removed; but, at that moment, my disappointments had disgusted me with the world, and I turned with a double yearning of heart to her whose pure and holy love could be at once my recompence and retreat.

Nor was this selfish consideration my only motive in the conduct I was resolved to adopt; on the contrary, it was scarcely more prominent in my mind, than those derived from giving to a friend who was now dearer to me than ever, his only consolation on this earth, and to Ellen, the safest protection, in case of any danger to her brother. With these, it is true, were mingled feelings which, in happier

---

1. Shelley, "One word is too often profaned," lines 13–16.

circumstances might have been those of transport at a bright and successful termination to a deep and devoted love; but these I had, while Glanville's very life was so doubtful, little right to indulge, and I checked them as soon as they arose.

After a sleepless night, I repaired to Lady Glanville's house. It was long since I had been there, and the servant who admitted me, seemed somewhat surprised at the earliness of my visit. I desired to see the mother, and waited in the parlour till she came. I made but a scanty exordium to my speech. In very few words I expressed my love to Ellen, and besought her mediation in my behalf; nor did I think it would be a slight consideration in my favour, with the fond mother, to mention Glanville's concurrence with* my suit.

"Ellen is up stairs in the drawing-room," said Lady Glanville. "I will go and prepare her to receive you—if you have her consent, you have mine."

"Will you suffer me, then," said I, "to forestal you? Forgive my impatience, and let me see her before you do."

Lady Glanville was a woman of the good old school, and stood somewhat upon forms and ceremonies. I did not, therefore, await the answer, which I foresaw might not be favourable to my success, but with my customary assurance, left the room, and hastened up stairs. I entered the drawing-room, and shut the door. Ellen was at the far end; and as I entered with a light step, she did not perceive me till I was close by.

She started when she saw me; and her cheek, before very pale, deepened into crimson. "Good Heavens! is it you?" she said falteringly. "I—I thought—but—but—excuse me for an instant, I will call my mother."

"Stay for one instant, I beseech you—it is from your mother that I come—she has referred me to you." And with a trembling and hurried voice, for all my usual boldness forsook me, I poured forth, in rapid and burning words, the history of my secret and hoarded love—its doubts, fears and hopes.

Ellen sunk back on her chair, overpowered and silent by her feelings, and the vehemence of my own. I knelt, and took her hand; I covered it with my kisses—it was not withdrawn from them. I raised my eyes, and beheld in hers all that my heart had hoped, but did not dare to portray.

"You—you," said she—when at last she found words—"I imagined that you only thought of ambition and the world—I could not have dreamt of this." She ceased, blushing and embarrassed.

378

"It is true," said I, "that you had a right to think so, for, till this moment, I have never opened to you even a glimpse of my veiled heart, and its secret and wild desires; but, do you think that my love was the less a treasure, because it was hidden? or the less deep, because it was cherished at the bottom of my soul? No—no; believe me, *that* love was not to be mingled with the ordinary objects of life—it was too pure to be profaned by the levities and follies which are all of my nature that I have permitted myself to develop to the world. Do not imagine, that, because I have seemed an idler with the idle—selfish with the interested—and cold, and vain, and frivolous, with those to whom such qualities were both a passport and a virtue; do not imagine that I have concealed within me nothing more worthy of you and of myself; my very love for you shews, that I am wiser and better than I have seemed. Speak to me, Ellen—may I call you by that name—one word—one syllable! speak to me, and tell me that you have read my heart, and that you will not reject it!"

There came no answer from those dear lips; but their soft and tender smile told me that I might hope. That hour I still recal and bless! that hour was the happiest of my life.

CHAPTER XIII

A thousand crowns, or else lay down your head.
2nd Part of Henry VI[1]

FROM ELLEN, I HASTENED TO THE HOUSE OF SIR Reginald. The hall was in all the confusion of approaching departure. I sprang over the paraphernalia of books and boxes which obstructed my way, and bounded up the stairs. Glanville was, as usual, alone: his countenance was less pale than it had been lately, and when I saw it brighten as I approached, I hoped, in the new happiness of my heart, that he might baffle both his enemy and his disease.

I told him all that had just occurred between Ellen and myself. "And now," said I, as I clasped his hand, "I have a proposal to make,

---

1. *II Henry VI*, IV, 1, 16.

to which you must accede: let me accompany you abroad; I will go with you to whatever corner of the world you may select. We will plan together every possible method of concealing our retreat. Upon the past I will never speak to you. In your hours of solitude I will never disturb you by an unwelcome and ill-timed sympathy. I will tend upon you, watch over you, bear with you, with more than the love and tenderness of a brother. You shall see me only when you wish it. Your loneliness shall never be invaded. When you get better, as I presage you will, I will leave you to come back to England, and provide for the worst, by ensuring your sister a protector. I will then return to you alone, that your seclusion may not be endangered by the knowledge, even of Ellen, and you shall have me by your side tili—till—"

"The last!" interrupted Glanville. "Too—too generous Pelham, I feel—these tears (the first I have shed for a long, long time) tell you, that I feel to the heart—your friendship and disinterested attachment; but* the moment your love for Ellen has become successful, I will not tear you from its enjoyment. Believe me, all that I could derive from your society, could not afford me half the happiness I should have in knowing that you and Ellen were blest in each other. No—no, my solitude will, at that reflection, be deprived of its sting. You shall hear from me once again; my letter shall contain a request, and your executing that last favour must console and satisfy the kindness of your heart. For myself, I shall die as I have lived—*alone*. All fellow-ship with my griefs would seem to me strange and unwelcome."

I would not suffer Glanville to proceed. I interrupted him with fresh arguments and entreaties, to which he seemed at last to submit, and I was in the firm hope of having conquered his determination, when we were startled by a sudden and violent noise in the hall.

"It is Thornton," said Glanville, calmly. "I told them not to admit him, and he is forcing his way."

Scarcely had Sir Reginald said this, before Thornton burst abruptly into the room.

Although it was scarcely noon, he was more than half intoxicated, and his eyes swam in his head with a maudlin expression of triumph and insolence, as he rolled towards us.

"Oh, oh! Sir Reginald," he said, "thought of giving me the slip, eh? Your d——d servants said you were out; but I soon silenced them. 'Egad I made them *as nimble as cows in a cage*—I have not learnt the use of my fists for nothing. So, you're going abroad to-morrow; without my leave, too—pretty good joke that, indeed. Come, come,

380

my brave fellow, you need not scowl at me in that way. Why, you look *as surly as a butcher's dog with a broken head.*"

Glanville, who was livid with ill-suppressed rage, rose haughtily.

"Mr. Thornton," he said, in a calm voice, although he was trembling in his extreme passion, from head to foot, "I am not now prepared to submit to your insolence and intrusion. You will leave this room instantly. If you have any further demands upon me, I will hear them to-night, at any hour you please to appoint."

"No, no, my fine fellow," said Thornton, with a coarse chuckle; "you have as much *wit as three folks, two fools, and a madman;* but you won't *do me,* for all that. The instant my back is turned, yours will be turned too; and by the time I call again, your honour will be half way to Calais. But—bless my stars, Mr. Pelham, is that you? I really did not see you before; I suppose you are not in the secret?"

"I have *no* secrets from Mr. Pelham," said Glanville; "nor do I care if you discuss the whole of your nefarious transactions with me in his presence. Since you doubt my word, it is beneath my dignity to vindicate it, and your business can as well be despatched now, as hereafter. You have heard rightly, that I intend leaving England to-morrow: and now, Sir, what is your will?"

"By G—d, Sir Reginald Glanville!" exclaimed Thornton, who seemed stung to the quick by Glanville's contemptuous coldness, "you shall *not* leave England without my leave. Ay, you may frown, but I say you shall not; nay, you shall not budge a foot from this very room unless I cry, 'Be it so!' "

Glanville could no longer restrain himself. He would have sprung towards Thornton, but I seized and arrested him. I read, in the malignant and incensed countenance of his persecutor, all the danger to which a single imprudence would have exposed him, and I trembled for his safety.

I whispered, as I forced him again to his seat, "Leave me alone to settle with this man, and I will endeavour to free you from him." I did not tarry for his answer; but turning to Thornton, said to him coolly but civilly: "Sir Reginald Glanville has acquainted me with the nature of your very extraordinary demands upon him. Did he adopt my advice, he would immediately place the affair in the hands of his legal advisers. His ill health, however, his anxiety to leave England, and his wish to sacrifice almost every thing to quiet, induce him, rather than take this alternative, to silence your importunities, by acceding to claims, however illegal and unjust. If, therefore, you now favour Sir Reginald with your visit, for the purpose of making

381

a demand previous to his quitting England, and which consequently, will be the last to which he will concede, you will have the goodness to name the amount of your claim, and should it be reasonable, I think Sir Reginald will authorize me to say, that it shall be granted."

"Well, now!" cried Thornton, "that's what I call talking like a sensible man; and though I am not fond of speaking to a third person, when the principal is present, yet as you have always been very civil to me, I have no objection to treating with you. Please to give Sir Reginald this paper: if he will but take the trouble to sign it, he may go to the Falls of Niagara for me! I won't interrupt him—so he had better put pen to paper, and get rid of me at once, for I know I am *as welcome as snow in harvest.*"

I took the paper, which was folded up, and gave it to Glanville, who leant back on his chair, half exhausted by rage. He glanced his eye over it, and then tore it into a thousand pieces, and trampled it beneath his feet: "Go!" exclaimed he, "go, rascal, and do your worst! I will not make myself a beggar to enrich you. My whole fortune would but answer this demand."

"Do as you please, Sir Reginald," answered Thornton grinning, "do as you please. It's not a long walk from hence to Bow-street, nor a long swing from Newgate to the gallows; do as you please, Sir Reginald, do as you please!" and the villain flung himself at full length on the costly* ottoman, and eyed Glanville's countenance with an easy and malicious effrontery, which seemed to say, "I know you will struggle, but you cannot help yourself."

I took Glanville aside: "My dear friend," said I, "believe me, that I share your indignation to the utmost; but we must do any thing rather than incense this wretch: what is his demand?"

"I speak literally," replied Glanville, "when I say, that it covers nearly the whole of my fortune; for my habits of extravagance have very much curtailed my means: it is the exact sum I had set apart, for a marriage gift to my sister, in addition to her own fortune."

"Then," said I, "you shall give it him; your sister has no longer any necessity for a portion: her marriage with me prevents *that*—and with regard to yourself, your wants are not many—such as it is, you can share *my* fortune."

"No—no—no!" cried Glanville; and his generous nature lashing him into fresh rage, he broke from my grasp, and moved menacingly to Thornton. That person still lay on the ottoman, regarding as with an air half contemptuous, half exulting.

"Leave the room instantly," said Glanville, "or you will repent it!"

382

"What! another murder, Sir Reginald!" said Thornton. "No, I am not a sparrow, to have my neck wrenched by a woman's hand like yours. Give me my demand—sign the paper, and I will leave you for ever and a day."

"I will commit no such folly," answered Glanville. "If you will accept five thousand pounds, you shall have that sum; but were the rope on my neck, you should not wring from me a farthing more!"

"Five thousand!" repeated Thornton: "a mere drop—a child's toy— why, you are playing with me, Sir Reginald—nay, I am a reasonable man, and will abate a trifle or so of my just claims, but you must not take advantage of my good nature. Make me snug and easy for life— let me keep a brace of hunters—a cosey box—a bit of land to it, and a girl after my own heart, and I'll say quits with you. Now, Mr. Pelham, who is a long-headed gentleman, and does not *spit on his own blanket,* knows well enough that one can't do all this for five thousand pounds; make it a thousand a year—that is, give me a cool twenty thousand—and I won't exact another sous. Egad, this drinking makes one deuced thirsty—Mr. Pelham, just reach me that glass of water— *I hear bees in my head!*"

Seeing that I did not stir, Thornton rose, with an oath against pride; and swaggering towards the table, took up a tumbler of water, which happened accidentally to be there: close by it was the picture of the ill-fated Gertrude. The gambler, who was evidently so intoxicated as to be scarcely conscious of his motions or words, (otherwise, in all probability, he would, to borrow from himself a proverb illustrative of his profession, have played his cards better), took up the portrait.

Glanville saw the action, and was by his side in an instant. "Touch it not with your accursed hands!" he cried, in an ungovernable fury. "Leave your hold this instant, or I will dash you to pieces!"

Thornton kept a firm gripe of the picture. "Here's a to-do!" said he, tauntingly: "was there ever such work about a poor ——— (using a word too coarse for repetition) before?"

The word had scarcely passed his lips, when he was stretched full length upon the ground. Nor did Glanville stop there. With all the strength of his nervous and Herculean frame, fully requited for the debility of disease by the fury of the moment, he seized the gamester as if he had been an infant, and dragged him to the door: the next moment I heard his heavy frame rolling down the stairs with no decorous slowness of descent.

Glanville re-appeared. "Good God!"* I cried, "what have you

383

done?" But he was too lost in his still unappeased rage to heed me. He leaned, panting and breathless, against the wall, with clenched teeth, and a flashing eye, rendered more terribly bright by the feverish lustre natural to his disease.

Presently I heard Thornton re-ascend the stairs: he opened the door, and entered but one pace. Never did human face wear a more fiendish expression of malevolence and wrath. "Sir Reginald Glanville," he said, "I thank you heartily. *He must have iron nails who scratches a bear.* You have sent me a challenge, and the hangman shall bring you my answer. Good day, Sir Reginald—good day, Mr. Pelham;" and so saying, he shut the door, and rapidly descending the stairs, was out of the house in an instant.

"There is no time to be lost," said I, "order post horses to your carriage, and be gone instantly."

"You are wrong," replied Glanville, slowly recovering himself. "I must not fly; it would be worse than useless; it would seem the strongest argument against me. Remember that if Thornton has really gone to inform against me, the officers of justice would arrest me long before I reached Calais; or even if I did elude their pursuit so far, I should be as much in their power in France as in England: but to tell you the truth, I do not think Thornton *will* inform. Money, to a temper like his, is a stronger temptation than revenge; and, before he has been three minutes in the air, he will perceive the folly of losing the golden harvest he may yet make of me for the sake of a momentary passion. No—my best plan will be to wait here till to-morrow, as I originally intended. In the meanwhile he will, in all probability, pay me another visit, and I will make a compromise with his demands."

Despite of my fears, I could not but see the justice of these observations, the more especially as a still stronger argument than any urged by Glanville, forced itself on my mind; this was my internal conviction, that Thornton himself was guilty of the murder of Tyrrell, and that, therefore, he would, for his own sake, avoid the new and particularizing scrutiny into that dreadful event, which his accusation of Glanville would necessarily occasion.

Both of us were wrong. Villains have passions as well as honest men; and they will, therefore, forfeit their own interest in obedience to those passions, while the calculations of prudence invariably suppose, that that interest is their *only* rule.[2]

2. I mean "interest" in the general, not the utilitarian, signification of the word. [B-L]*

Glanville was so enfeebled by his late excitation*, that he besought me once more to leave him to himself. I did so, under a promise that he would admit me again in the evening; for notwithstanding my persuasion that Thornton would not put his threats into execution, I could not conquer a latent foreboding of dread and evil.

CHAPTER XIV

Away with him to prison—where is the provost?
Measure for Measure[1]

I RETURNED HOME, PERPLEXED BY A THOUSAND CON-tradictory thoughts upon the scene I had just witnessed; the more I reflected, the more I regretted the fatality of the circumstances that had tempted Glanville to accede to Thornton's demand. True it was, that Thornton's self-regard might be deemed a sufficient guarantee for his concealment of such extortionate transactions: moreover, it was difficult to say, when the formidable array of appearances against Glanville was considered, whether any other line of conduct than that which he had adopted, could, with safety,* have been pursued.

His feelings too, with regard to the unfortunate Gertrude, I could fully enter into, and sympathize with; but, in spite of all these considerations, it was with an inexpressible aversion that I contemplated the idea of that tacit confession of guilt, which his compliance with Thornton's exactions so unhappily implied; it was, therefore, a thought of some satisfaction, that my rash and hasty advice, of a still further concession to those extortions, had not been acceded to. My present intention was, in the event of Glanville's persevering to reject my offer of accompanying him, to remain in England, for the purpose of sifting the murder, nor did I despair of accomplishing this most desirable end, through the means of Dawson; for there was but little doubt in my own mind that Thornton and himself were the murderers, and I hoped that address or intimidation might win a confession from Dawson, although it might probably be unavailing with his hardened and crafty associate.

---

1. *Measure for Measure,* V, 1, 350.

Occupied with these thoughts, I endeavoured to while away the hours till the evening summoned me once more to the principal object of my reflections. Directly* Glanville's door was opened, I saw by one glance, that I had come too late; the whole house was in confusion; several of the servants were in the hall, conferring with each other, with that mingled mystery and agitation which always accompany the fears and conjectures of the lower classes. I took aside the valet, who had lived with Glanville for some years, and who was remarkably attached to his master, and learnt, that somewhat more than an hour before, Mr. Thornton had returned to the house accompanied by three men of very suspicious appearance. "In short, Sir," said the man, lowering his voice to a whisper, "I knew one of them by sight; he was Mr. S., the Bow-street officer; with these men, Sir Reginald left the house, merely saying, in his usual quiet manner, that he did not know when he should return."

I concealed my perturbation, and endeavoured, as far as I was able, to quiet the evident apprehensions of the servant. "At all events, Seymour," said I, "I know that I may trust you sufficiently to warn you against mentioning the circumstance any farther; above all, let me beg of you to stop the mouths of those idle loiterers in the hall—and be sure that you do not give any unnecessary alarm to Lady and Miss Glanville."

The poor man promised, with tears in his eyes, that he would obey my injunctions; and with a calm face, but a sickening heart, I turned away from the house. I knew not where to direct my wanderings; fortunately, I recollected that I should, in all probability, be among the first witnesses summoned on Glanville's examination, and that, perhaps, by the time I reached home, I might already receive an intimation to that effect; accordingly, I retraced my steps, and, on re-entering my hotel, was told by the waiter, with a mysterious air, that a gentleman was waiting to see me. Seated by the window in my room, and wiping his forehead with a red silk pocket-handkerchief, was a short, thickset man, with a fiery and rugose complexion, not altogether unlike the aspect of a mulberry; from underneath a pair of shaggy brows, peeped two singularly small eyes, which made ample amends by their fire, for their deficiency in size—they were black, brisk, and somewhat fierce in their expression; a nose, of that shape, vulgarly termed bottle, formed the "arch sublime," the bridge, the twilight as it were, between the purple sun-set of one cheek, and the glowing sun-rise of the other. His mouth was small, and drawn up at each corner, like a purse—there was something sour and crabbed about it;

386

if it *was* like a purse, it was the purse of a miser: a fair round chin had not been condemned to single blessedness—on the contrary, it was like a farmer's pillion, and carried double; on either side of a very low forehead, hedged round by closely mowed bristles, of a dingy black, was an enormous ear,* of the same intensely rubicund colour as that inflamed pendant of flesh which adorns the throat of an enraged turkey-cock; ears so large, and so red, I never beheld before—they were something preposterous.

This enchanting figure, which was attired in a sober suit of leaden black, relieved by a long gold watch-chain, and a plentiful decoration of seals, rose at my entrance with a solemn grunt, and a still more solemn bow. I shut the door carefully, and asked him his business. As I had foreseen, it was a request from the magistrate at ———, to attend a private examination on the ensuing day.

"Sad thing, Sir, sad thing," said Mr. ———, "it would be quite shocking to hang a gentleman of Sir Reginald Glanville's quality—so distinguished an orator too; sad thing, Sir,—very sad thing."

"Oh!" said I, quietly, "there is not a doubt as to Sir Reginald's innocence of the crime laid to him; and, probably, Mr. ———, I may call in your assistance to-morrow, to ascertain the real murderers—I think I am possessed of some clue."

Mr. ——— pricked up his ears—those enormous ears. "Sir," he said, "I shall be happy to accompany you—very happy; give me the clue you speak of, and I will soon find the villains. Horrid thing, Sir, murder—very horrid. It's too hard that a gentleman cannot take his ride home from a race, or a merry-making, but he must have his throat cut from ear to ear—ear to ear, Sir;" and with these words, the speaker's own auricular protuberances seemed to glow, as if in conscious horror,* with a double carnation.

"Very true, Mr. ———!" said I; "say I will certainly attend the examination—till then, good by!" At this hint, my fiery faced friend made me a low bow, and blazed out of the room, like the ghost of a kitchen fire.

Left to myself, I revolved, earnestly and anxiously, every thing that could tend to diminish the appearances against Glanville, and direct suspicion to that quarter where I was confident the guilt rested. In this endeavour I passed the time till morning, when I fell into an uneasy slumber, which lasted some hours; when I awoke, it was almost time to attend the magistrate's appointment. I dressed hastily, and soon found myself in the room of inquisition.

It is impossible to conceive a more courteous, and yet more

387

equitable man, than the magistrate whom I had the honour of attending. He spoke with great feeling on the subject for which I was summoned—owned to me, that Thornton's statement was very clear and forcible—trusted that my evidence would contradict an account which he was very loth to believe; and then proceeded to the question. I saw, with an agony which I can scarcely express, that all my answers made powerfully against the cause I endeavoured to support. I was obliged to own, that a man on horseback passed me soon after Tyrrell had quitted me; that, on coming to the spot where the deceased was found, I saw the same horseman on the very place; that I believed, nay, that I was sure (how could I evade this), that the man was Sir Reginald Glanville.

Farther evidence, Thornton had already offered to adduce. He could prove, that the said horseman had been mounted on a grey horse, sold to a person answering exactly to the description of Sir Reginald Glanville; moreover, that that horse was yet in the stables of the prisoner. He produced a letter, which, he said, he had found upon the person of the deceased, signed by Sir Reginald Glanville, and containing the most deadly threats against Sir John Tyrrell's* life; and, to crown all, he called upon me to witness, that we had both discovered upon the spot where the murder was committed, a picture belonging to the prisoner, since restored to him, and now in his possession.

The magistrate shook his head, in evident distress! "I have known Sir Reginald Glanville personally," said he: "in private as in public life, I have always thought him the most upright and honourable of men. I feel the greatest pain in saying, that it will be my duty fully to commit him for trial."

I interrupted the magistrate; I demanded that Dawson should be produced. "I have already," said he, "inquired of Thornton respecting that person, whose testimony is of evident importance; he tells me, that Dawson has left the country, and can give me no clues to his address."

"He lies!" cried I, in the abrupt anguish of my heart; "his associate *shall* be produced. Hear me: I have been, next to Thornton, the chief witness against the prisoner, and when I swear to you, that, in spite of all appearances, I most solemnly believe in his innocence, you may rely on my assurance, that there are circumstances in his favour, which have not yet been considered, but which I will pledge myself hereafter to adduce." I then related to the private ear of the magistrate, my firm conviction of the guilt of the accuser himself. I dwelt forcibly upon the circumstance of Tyrrell's having mentioned to me, that Thornton was aware of the large sum he had on his person, and of the strange disappearance of that sum, when his body was examined in the fatal field. After noting how impossible it was that Glanville could have stolen this money, I insisted strongly on the distressed circumstances—the dissolute habits, and the hardened character of Thornton—I recalled to the mind of the magistrate, the singularity of Thornton's absence from home when I called there, and the doubtful nature of his excuse: much more I said, but all equally in vain. The only point where I was successful, was in pressing for a delay, which was granted to the passionate manner in which I expressed my persuasion that I could confirm my suspicions by much stronger data before the reprieve expired.

"It is very true," said the righteous magistrate, "that there are appearances somewhat against the witness; but certainly not tantamount to any thing above a slight suspicion. If, however, you positively think you can ascertain any facts, to elucidate this mysterious crime, and point the inquiries of justice to another quarter, I will so far strain the question, as to remand the prisoner to another day—let us say the day after to-morrow. If nothing important can before then be found in his favour, he *must* be committed for trial."

CHAPTER XV

Nihil est furacius illo,

Non fuit Autolyci tam piceati manus.

MARTIAL[1]

Quo teneam vultus mutantem Protea nodo?

HORAT.

WHEN I LEFT THE MAGISTRATE, I KNEW NOT WHITHER my next step should tend. There was, however, no time to indulge the idle stupor, which Glanville's situation at first occasioned; with a

---

1. "There is nothing more grasping than he; not even the hand of Autolycus was as gluey as his" (Martial *Epigrammaton* 8.59.3–4). The second epigraph may be translated: "In what noose shall I hold this Proteus, who is always changing his appearance" (Horace *Epistles* 1.1.90).

violent effort, I shook it off, and bent all my mind to discover the best method to avail myself, to the utmost, of the short reprieve I had succeeded in obtaining; at length, one of those sudden thoughts which, from their suddenness appear more brilliant than they really are, flashed upon my mind. I remembered the accomplished character of Mr. Job Jonson, and the circumstance of my having seen him in company with Thornton. Now, although it was not very likely that Thornton should have made Mr. Jonson his confidant, in any of those affairs which it was so essentially his advantage to confine exclusively to himself; yet the acuteness and penetration visible in the character of the worthy Job, might not have lain so fallow during his companionship with Thornton, but that it might have made some discoveries which would considerably assist me in my researches; besides, as it is literally true in the systematized roguery of London, that "birds of a feather flock together," it was by no means unlikely that the honest Job might be honoured with the friendship of Mr. Dawson, as well as the company of Mr. Thornton; in which case I looked forward with greater confidence to the detection of the notable pair.

I could not, however, conceal from myself, that this was but a very unstable and ill-linked chain of reasoning, and there were moments, when the appearances against Glanville wore so close a semblance of truth, that all my friendship could scarcely drive from my mind an intrusive suspicion that he might have deceived me, and that the accusation might not be groundless.

This unwelcome idea did not, however, at all lessen the rapidity with which I hastened towards the memorable gin shop, where I had whilom met Mr. Gordon: there I hoped to find either the address of that gentleman, or of the "Club," to which he had taken me, in company with Tringle and Dartmore: either at this said club, or of that said gentleman, I thought it not unlikely that I might hear some tidings of the person of Mr. Job Jonson—if not, I was resolved to return to the office, and employ Mr. ———, my mulberry-cheeked acquaintance of the last night, in a search after the holy Job.

Fate saved me a world of trouble: as I was hastily walking onwards, I happened to turn my eyes on the opposite side of the way, and discovered a man dressed, in what the newspapers term, the very height of the fashion, viz.: in the most ostentatious attire that ever flaunted at Margate, or blazed in the *Palais Royal*. The nether garments of this *petit maître*, consisted of a pair of light blue tight pantaloons, profusely braided, and terminating in Hessian boots, adorned with brass spurs of the most burnished resplendency; a black velvet waist-coat, studded with gold stars, was *backed* by a green frock coat, covered, notwithstanding the heat of the weather, with fur, and frogged and *cordonné* with the most lordly indifference, both as to taste and expense: a small French hat, which might not have been much too large for my lord of P———, was set jauntily in the centre of a system of long black curls, which my eye, long accustomed to penetrate the arcana of habilatory art, discovered at once to be a wig. A fierce black mustachio, very much curled, wandered lovingly from the upper lip, towards the eyes, which had an unfortunate pre-possession for eccentricity in their direction. To complete the picture, we must suppose some colouring—and this consisted in a very nice and delicate touch of the *rouge* pot, which could not be called by so harsh a term as paint; say, rather that it was a *tinge*.

No sooner had I set my eyes upon this figure, than I crossed over to the side of the way which it was adorning, and followed its motions at a respectful but observant distance.

At length my *freluquet* marched into a jeweller's shop in Oxford-street; with a careless air, I affected two minutes afterwards, to saunter into the same shop; the shopman was shewing his *bijouterie* to him of the Hessians with the greatest respect; and, beguiled by the splen-dour of the wig and waistcoat, turned me over to his apprentice. Another time, I might have been indignant at perceiving that the *air noble,* on which I picqued myself far more than all other gifts of nature, personal or mental, was by no means so universally acknowl-edged as I had vainly imagined—at that moment I was too occupied to think of my insulted dignity. While I was pretending to appear wholly engrossed with some seals, I kept a vigilant eye on my superb fellow customer: at last, I saw him secrete a diamond ring, and thrust it, by a singular movement of the fore finger, up the fur cuff of his capacious sleeve; presently, some other article of minute size disap-peared in the like manner.

The *gentleman* then rose, expressed himself *very well satisfied* by the great taste of the jeweller, said he should look in again on Saturday, when he hoped the set he had ordered would be completed, and gravely took his departure amidst the prodigal bows of the shopman and his helpmates; meanwhile, I bought a seal of small value, paid for it, and followed my old acquaintance, for the reader has doubtless discovered, long before this, that *the gentleman* was no other than Mr. Job Jonson.

Slowly and struttingly did the man of two virtues perform the whole pilgrimage of Oxford-street. He stopped at Cumberland-gate, and, looking round, with an air of gentlemanlike indecision, seemed to consider whether or not he should join the loungers in the park: fortunately for that well bred set, his doubts terminated in their favour, and Mr. Job Jonson entered the park. Every one happened to be thronging to Kensington Gardens, and the man of two virtues accordingly cut across the park, as the shortest, but the least frequented way thither, in order to confer upon the seekers of pleasure the dangerous honour of his company.

Directly* I perceived that there were but few persons in the immediate locality to observe me, and that those consisted of a tall guardsman and his wife, a family of young children, with their nursery-maid, and a debilitated East India captain, walking for the sake of his liver, I overtook the incomparable Job, made him a low bow, and thus reverently accosted him—

"Mr. Jonson, I am delighted once more to meet you—suffer me to remind you of the very pleasant morning I passed with you in the neighbourhood of Hampton Court. I perceive, by your mustachios and military dress, that you have entered the army, since that day; I congratulate the British troops on such an admirable acquisition."

Mr. Jonson's assurance forsook him for a moment, but he lost no time in regaining a quality which was so natural to his character. He assumed a fierce look, and *relevant sa moustache, sourit amèrement,* like Voltaire's governor[2]—"D—mee, Sir," he cried, "do you mean to insult me? I know none of your Mr. Jonsons, and I never set my eyes upon you before."

"Lookye, my dear Mr. Job Jonson," replied I, "as I can prove not only all I say, but much more that I shall not say—such as your little mistakes just now, at the jeweller's shop in Oxford-street, &c. &c., perhaps it would be better for you not to oblige me to create a mob, and give you in charge—pardon my abruptness of speech—*to a constable!*—Surely there will be no need of such a disagreeable occurrence, when I assure you, in the first place, that I perfectly forgive you for ridding me of the unnecessary comforts of a pocket-book and handkerchief, the unphilosophical appendage of a purse, and the effeminate *gage d'amour** of a gold bracelet;* nor is this all—it is perfectly indifferent to me, whether you levy contributions on jewellers or gentlemen, and I am very far from wishing to intrude upon your harmless occupations, or to interfere with your innocent amusements. I see,

---

2. Don Fernand d'Ibarra, in the "Candide." [B-L]

Mr. Jonson, that you are beginning to understand me; let me facilitate so desirable an end by an additional information, that, since it is preceded with a promise to open my purse, may tend somewhat to open your heart; I am at this moment, in great want of your assistance —favour me with it, and I will pay you to your soul's content. Are we friends now, Mr. Job Jonson?"

My old friend burst out into a loud laugh. "Well, Sir, I must say that your frankness enchants me. I can no longer dissemble with you; indeed, I perceive, it would be useless; besides, I always adored candour—it is my favourite virtue. Tell me how I can help you, and you may command my services."

"One word," said I: "will you be open and ingenuous with me? I shall ask you certain questions, not in the least affecting your own safety, but to which, if you would serve me, you must give me (and since candour is your favorite virtue, this will be no difficult task) your most candid replies. To strengthen you in so righteous a course, know also, that the said replies will come verbatim before a court of law, and that, therefore, it will be a matter of prudence to shape them as closely to the truth as your inclinations will allow. To counterbalance this information, which, I own, is not very inviting, I repeat that the questions asked you will be wholly foreign to your own affairs, and that, should you prove of that assistance to me which I anticipate, I will so testify my gratitude as to place you beyond the necessity of pillaging rural young gentlemen and credulous shopkeepers for the future;—all your present pursuits need only be carried on for your private amusement."

"I repeat, that you may command me," returned Mr. Jonson, gracefully putting his hand to his heart.

"Pray, then," said I, "to come at once to the point, how long have you been acquainted with Mr. Thomas Thornton?"

"For some months only," returned Job, without the least embarrassment.

"And Mr. Dawson?" said I.

A slight change came over Jonson's countenance: he hesitated. "Excuse me, Sir," said he; "but I am, really, perfectly unacquainted with you, and I may be falling into some trap of the law, of which, Heaven knows, I am as ignorant as a babe unborn."

I saw the knavish justice of this remark: and in my predominating zeal to serve Glanville, I looked upon the *inconvenience* of discovering myself to a pickpocket and sharper, as a consideration not worth attending to. In order, therefore, to remove his doubts, and, at the

393

same time, to have a more secret and undisturbed place for our conference, I proposed to him to accompany me home; at first Mr. Jonson demurred, but I soon half persuaded and half intimidated him into compliance.

Not particularly liking to be publicly seen with a person of his splendid description and celebrated character, I made him walk before me to Mivart's, and I followed him closely, never turning my eye, either to the right or to the left, lest he should endeavour to escape me. There was no fear of this, for Mr. Jonson was both a bold and a crafty man, and it required, perhaps, but little of his penetration to discover that I was no officer or informer, and that my communication had been of a nature likely enough to terminate in his advantage; there was, therefore, but little need of his courage in accompanying me to my hotel.

There were a good many foreigners of rank at Mivart's, and the waiters took my companion for an ambassador at least:—he received their homage with the mingled dignity and condescension natural to so great a man.

As the day was now far advanced, I deemed it but hospitable to offer Mr. Job Jonson some edible refreshment. With the frankness on which he so justly valued himself, he accepted my proposal. I ordered some cold meat, and two bottles of wine; and, mindful of old maxims, deferred my business till his repast was over. I conversed with him merely upon ordinary topics, and, at another time, should have been much amused by the singular mixture of impudence and shrewdness which formed the stratum of his character.

At length his appetite was satisfied, and one of the bottles emptied; with the other before him, his body easily reclining on my library chair, his eyes apparently cast downwards, but ever and anon glancing up at my countenance with a searching and curious look, Mr. Job Jonson prepared himself for our conference; accordingly I began.

"You say that you *are* acquainted with Mr. Dawson; where is he at present?"

"I don't know," answered Jonson laconically.

"Come," said I, "no trifling—if you do not know, you can learn."

"Possibly I can, in the course of time," replied honest Job.

"If you cannot tell me his residence at once," said I, "our conference is at an end; that is a leading feature in my inquiries."

Jonson paused before he replied—"You have spoken to me frankly, let us do nothing by halves—tell me, at once, the nature of the service

394

I can do you, and the amount of my reward, and then you shall have my answer. With respect to Dawson, I will confess to you that I did once know him well, and that we have done many a mad prank together, which I should not like the bugaboos and bulkies[3] to know; you will, therefore, see that I am naturally reluctant to tell you any thing about him, unless your honour will inform me of the why and the wherefore."

I was somewhat startled by this speech, and by the shrewd, cunning eye which dwelt upon me, as it was uttered; but, however, I was by no means sure, that acceding to his proposal would not be my readiest and wisest way to the object I had in view. Nevertheless, there were some preliminary questions to be got over first: perhaps Dawson might be too dear a friend to the candid Job, for the latter to endanger his safety: or perhaps, (and this was more probable), Jonson might be perfectly ignorant of any thing likely to aid me: in this case my communication would be useless; accordingly I said, after a short consideration—

"Patience, my dear Mr. Jonson—patience, you shall know all in good time; meanwhile I must—even for Dawson's sake—question you blindfold. What, now, if your poor friend Dawson were in imminent danger, and you had, if it so pleased you, the power to save him, would you not do all you could?

The small, coarse features of Mr. Job grew blank with a curious sort of disappointment: "Is that all?" said he. "No! unless I were well paid for my pains in his behalf, he might go to Botany Bay, for all I care."

"What!" I cried, in a tone of reproach, "is this your friendship? I thought, just now, that you said Dawson had been an old and firm associate of yours."

"An old one, your honour; but not a firm one. A short time ago, I was in great distress, and he and Thornton had, God* knows how! about two thousand pounds between them; but I could not worm a stiver[4] out of Dawson—that gripe-all, Thornton, got it all from him."

"Two thousand pounds!" said I, in a calm voice, though my heart beat violently; "that's a great sum for a poor fellow like Dawson. How long ago is it since he had it?"

"About two or three months," answered Jonson.

"Pray, have you seen much of Dawson lately?" I asked.

---

3. Bugaboos and bulkies: slang for sheriff's officers and police constables, respectively.

4. Stiver: slang for a small amount of cash.

"I have," replied Jonson.

"Indeed!" said I. "I thought you told me, just now, that you were unacquainted with his residence?"

'So I am," replied Jonson, coldly, "it is not at his own house that I ever see him."

I was silent, for I was now rapidly and minutely weighing the benefits and disadvantages of trusting Jonson as he had desired me to do.

To reduce the question to the simplest form of logic, he had either the power of assisting my investigation, or he had not: if not, neither could he much impede it, and therefore, it mattered little whether he was in my confidence or not; if he *had* the power, the doubt was, whether it would be better for me to benefit by it openly, or by stratagem; that is—whether it were wiser to state the whole case to him, or continue to gain whatever I was able by dint of a blind examination. Now, the disadvantage of candour was, that if it were his wish to screen Dawson and his friend, he would be prepared to do so, and even to put them on their guard against my suspicions; but the indifference he had testified with regard to Dawson seemed to render this probability very small. The benefits of candour were more prominent: Job would then be fully aware that his own safety was not at stake; and should I make it more his interest to serve the innocent than the guilty, I should have the entire advantage, not only of any actual information he might possess, but of his skill and shrewdness in providing additional proof, or at least suggesting advantageous hints. Moreover, in spite of my vanity and opinion of my own penetration, I could not but confess, that it was unlikely that my cross-examination should be very successful with so old and experienced a sinner as Mr. Jonson. "Set a thief to catch a thief," is among the wisest of wise sayings, and accordingly I resolved in favour of a disclosure.

Drawing my chair close to Jonson's, fixing my eye upon his countenance, and throwing into my own the most open, yet earnest expression I could summon, I briefly proceeded to sketch Glanville's situation (only concealing his name), and Thornton's charges. I mentioned my own suspicions of the accuser, and my desire of discovering Dawson, whom Thornton appeared to me artfully to secrete. Lastly, I concluded, with a solemn promise, that if my listener could, by any zeal, exertion, knowledge, or contrivance of his own, procure the detection of the men who I was convinced were the murderers, a pension of three hundred pounds a-year should be immediately settled upon him.

396

During my communication, the patient Job sat mute and still, fixing his eyes on the ground, and only betraying, by an occasional elevation of the brows, that he took the slightest interest in the tale: when, however, I touched upon the peroration, which so tenderly concluded with the mention of three hundred pounds a-year, a visible change came over the countenance of Mr. Jonson. He rubbed his hands with an air of great content, and one sudden smile broke over his features, and almost buried his eyes amid the intricate host of wrinkles it called forth: the smile vanished as rapidly as it came, and Mr. Job turned round to me with a solemn and sedate aspect.

"Well, your honour," said he, "I'm glad you've told me all; we must see what can be done. As for Thornton, I'm afraid we shan't make much out of him, for he's an old offender, whose conscience is as hard as a brick-bat; but, of Dawson, I hope better things. However, you must let me go now, for this is a matter that requires a vast deal of private consideration. I shall call upon you to-morrow, Sir, before ten o'clock, since you say matters are so pressing; and, I trust, you will then see that you have no reason to repent of the confidence you have placed in a man of *honour*."

So saying, Mr. Job Jonson emptied the remainder of the bottle into his tumbler, held it up to the light with the *gusto* of a connoisseur, and concluded his potations with a hearty smack of the lips, followed by a long sigh.

"Ah, your honour!" said he, "good wine is a marvellous whetter of the intellect; but your true philosopher is always moderate: for my part, I never exceed my two bottles."

And with these words, this true philosopher took his departure.

No sooner was I freed from his presence, than my thoughts flew to Ellen: I had neither been able to call nor write the whole of the day; and I was painfully fearful, lest my precautions with Sir Reginald's valet had been frustrated, and the alarm of his imprisonment had reached her and Lady Glanville. Harassed by this fear, I disregarded the lateness of the hour, and immediately repaired to Berkeley-square.

Lady and Miss Glanville were alone and at dinner: the servant spoke with his usual unconcern. "They are quite well?" said I, relieved, but still anxious: and the servant replying in the affirmative, I again returned home, and wrote a long, and, I hope, consoling letter to Sir Reginald.

CHAPTER XVI

K. Henry. Lord Say, Jack Cade hath sworn to have thy head.
Say. Ay, but I hope your Highness shall have his.
2nd Part of Henry IV[1]

PUNCTUAL TO HIS APPOINTMENT, THE NEXT MORNING came Mr. Job Jonson. I had been on the rack of expectation for the last three hours previous to his arrival, and the warmth of my welcome must have removed any little diffidence with which so shamefaced a gentleman might possibly have been troubled.

At my request, he sat himself down, and seeing that my breakfast things were on the table, remarked what a famous appetite the fresh air always gave him. I took the hint, and pushed the rolls towards him. He immediately fell to work, and for the next quarter of an hour, his mouth was far too well occupied for the intrusive impertinence of words. At last the things were removed, and Mr. Jonson began.

"I have thought well over the matter, your honour, and I believe we can manage to trounce the rascals—for I agree with you, that there is not a doubt that Thornton and Dawson are the real criminals; but the affair, Sir, is one of the greatest difficulty and importance—nay, of the greatest personal danger. My life may be the forfeit of my desire to serve you—you will not, therefore, be surprised at my accepting your liberal offer of three hundred a year, should I be successful; although I do assure you, Sir, that it was my original intention to reject all recompense, for I am naturally benevolent, and love doing a good action. Indeed, Sir, if I were alone in the world, I should scorn any remuneration, for virtue is its own reward; but a real moralist, your honour, must not forget his duties on any consideration, and I have a little family to whom my loss would be an irreparable injury; this, upon my honour, is my only inducement for taking advantage of your generosity;" and as the moralist ceased, he took out of his

---

1. *II Henry IV*, IV, 4, 19.

waistcoat pocket a paper, which he handed to me with his usual bow of deference.

I glanced over it—it was a bond, apparently drawn up in all the legal formalities, pledging myself, in case Job Jonson, before the expiration of three days, gave that information which should lead to the detection and punishment of the true murderers of Sir John Tyrrell, deceased, to ensure to the said Job Jonson the yearly annuity of three hundred pounds.

"It is with much pleasure that I shall sign this paper," said I; "but allow me *(par parenthèse)* to observe, that since you only accept the annuity for the sake of benefiting your little family, in case of your death, this annuity ceasing with your life, will leave your children as pennyless as at present."

"Pardon me, your honour," rejoined Job, not a whit daunted at the truth of my remark, *"I can insure!"*

"I forgot that," said I, signing, and restoring the paper; "and now to business."

Jonson gravely and carefully looked over the interesting document I returned to him, and carefully lapping it in three envelops, inserted it in a huge red pocket-book, which he thrust into an innermost pocket in his waistcoat.

"Right, Sir," said he, slowly, "to business. Before I begin, you must, however, promise me, upon your honour as a gentleman, the strictest secrecy, as to my communications."

I readily agreed to this, so far as that secrecy did not impede my present object; and Job being content with this condition, resumed.

"You must forgive me, if, in order to arrive at the point in question, I set out from one which may seem to you a little distant."

I nodded my assent, and Job continued.

"I have known Dawson for some years; my acquaintance with him commenced at Newmarket, for I have always had a slight tendency to the turf. He was a wild, foolish fellow, easily led into any mischief, but ever the first to sneak out of it; in short, when he became one of *us,* which his extravagance soon compelled him to do, we considered him as a very serviceable tool, but one who, while he was quite wicked enough to begin a bad action, was much too weak to go through with it; accordingly he was often employed, but never trusted. By the word *us,* which I see has excited your curiosity, I merely mean a body corporate, established furtively, and restricted *solely* to exploits on the turf. I think it right to mention this,* because I have the honour to belong to many other societies to which Dawson could

399

never have been admitted. Well Sir, our club was at last broken up, and Dawson was left to shift for himself. His father was still alive, and the young hopeful having quarrelled with him, was in the greatest distress. He came to me with a pitiful story, and a more pitiful face; so I took compassion upon the poor devil, and procured him, by dint of great interest, admission into a knot of good fellows, whom I visited, by the way, last night. Here I took him under my special care; and as far as I could, with such a dull-headed dromedary, taught him some of the most elegant arts of my profession. However, the ungrateful dog soon stole back to his old courses, and robbed me of half my share of a booty to which I had helped him myself. I hate treachery and ingratitude, your honour; they are so terribly ungentlemanlike.

"I then lost sight of him, till between two and three months ago, when he returned to town, and attended our meetings with Tom Thornton, who had been chosen a member of the club some months before. Since we had met, Dawson's father had died, and I thought his flash appearance in town arose from his new inheritance. I was mistaken: old Dawson had tied up the property so tightly, that the young one could not scrape enough to pay his debts; accordingly, before he came to town he gave up his life interest in the property to his creditors. However that be, Master Dawson seemed at the top of Fortune's wheel. He kept his horses, and sported the set to champagne and venison; in short, there would have been no end to his extravagance, had not Thornton sucked him like a leech.

"It was about that time, that I asked Dawson for a trifle to keep me from jail; for I was ill in bed, and could not help myself. Will you believe, Sir, that the rascal told me to go and be d——d, and Thornton said, amen? I did not forget the ingratitude of my *protégé*, though when I recovered I appeared entirely to do so. No sooner could I walk about, than I relieved all my necessities. He is but a fool who starves, with all London before him. In proportion as my finances increased, Dawson's visibly decayed. With them, decreased also his spirits. He became pensive and downcast; never joined any of our parties, and gradually grew quite a useless member of the corporation. To add to his melancholy, he was one morning present at the execution of an unfortunate associate of ours: this made a deep impression upon him; from that moment, he became thoroughly moody and despondent. He was frequently heard talking to himself, could not endure to be left alone in the dark, and began rapidly to pine away.

"One night, when he and I were seated together, he asked me if I never repented of my sins, and then added, with a groan, that I had

400

never committed the heinous crime he had. I pressed him to confess, but he would not. However, I coupled that half avowal with his sudden riches and the mysterious circumstances of Sir John Tyrrell's death, and dark suspicions came into my mind. At that time, and indeed ever since Dawson re-appeared, we were often in the habit of discussing the notorious murder which then engrossed public attention; and as Dawson and Thornton had been witnesses on the inquest, we frequently referred to them respecting it. Dawson always turned pale, and avoided the subject; Thornton, on the contrary, brazened it out with his usual impudence. Dawson's aversion to the mention of the murder now came into my remembrance with double weight to strengthen my suspicions; and, on conversing with one or two of our comrades, I found that my doubts were more than shared, and that Dawson had frequently, when unusually oppressed with his hypochondria, hinted at his committal of some dreadful crime, and at his unceasing remorse for it.

"By degrees, Dawson grew worse and worse—his health decayed, he started at a shadow—drank deeply, and spoke, in his intoxication, words that made the hairs of our *green men*[2] stand on end.

" 'We must not suffer this,' said Thornton, whose hardy effrontery enabled him to lord it over the jolly boys, as if he were their dimber-damber:[3]* 'his ravings and humdurgeon will unman all our youngsters.'[4] And so, under this pretence, Thornton had the unhappy man conveyed away to a secret asylum, known only to the chiefs of the gang, and appropriated to the reception of persons who, from the same weakness as Dawson, were likely to endanger others, or themselves. There many a poor wretch has been secretly immured, and never suffered to revisit the light of Heaven. The moon's minions, as well as the monarch's, must have their state prisoners, and their state victims.

"Well, Sir, I shall not detain you much longer. Last night, after your obliging confidence, I repaired to the meeting; Thornton was there, and very much out of humour. When our messmates dropped off, and we were alone, at one corner of the room, I began talking to him carelessly about his accusation of your friend, who I have since learnt is Sir Reginald Glanville—an old friend of mine too; ay, you may look, Sir, but I can stake my life to having picked his pocket one night at the Opera. Thornton was greatly surprised at my early in-

2. *Green men* are inexperienced.
3. Dimber-damber: slang for thief.
4. *I Henry IV*, I, 2, 30.

telligence of a fact, hitherto kept so profound a secret: however, I explained it away by a boast of my skill in acquiring information: and he then incautiously let out, that he was exceedingly vexed with himself for the charge he had made against the prisoner, and very uneasy at the urgent inquiries set on foot for Dawson. More and more convinced of his guilt, I quitted the meeting, and went to Dawson's retreat.

"For fear of his escape, Thornton had had him closely confined to one of the most secret rooms in the house. His solitude and the darkness of the place, combined with his remorse, had worked upon a mind, never too strong, almost to insanity. He was writhing with the most acute and morbid pangs of conscience that my experience, which has been pretty ample, ever witnessed. The old hag, who is the Hecate (you see, Sir, I have had a classical education) of the place, was very loth to admit me to him, for Thornton had bullied her into a great fear of the consequences of disobeying his instructions; but she did not dare to resist my orders. Accordingly I had a long interview with the unfortunate man; he firmly believes that Thornton intends to murder him; and says, that if he could escape from his dungeon, he would surrender himself up* to the first magistrate he could find.

"I told him that an innocent man had been apprehended for the crime of which *I knew* he and Thornton were guilty; and then taking upon myself the office of a preacher, I exhorted him to atone, as far as possible, for his past crime, by a full and faithful confession, that would deliver the innocent and punish the guilty. I held out to him the hope that this confession might perhaps serve the purpose of king's evidence, and obtain him a pardon for his crime; and I promised to use my utmost zeal and diligence to promote his escape from his present den.

"He said, in answer, that he did not wish to live; that he suffered the greatest tortures of mind; and that the only comfort earth held out to him would be to ease his remorse by a full acknowledgment of his crime, and to hope for future mercy by expiating his offense on the scaffold; all this, and much more, to the same purpose, the hen-hearted fellow told me with sighs and groans. I would fain have taken his confession on the spot, and carried it away with me, but he refused to give it to me, or to any one but a parson, whose services he implored me to procure him. I told him, at first, that the thing was impossible; but, moved by his distress and remorse, I promised, at last, to bring one to-night, who should both administer spiritual

402

comfort to him and receive his deposition. My idea at the moment was to disguise *myself* in the dress of the *pater cove*,[5] and perform the double job—since then I have thought of a better scheme.

"As my character, you see, your honour, is not so highly prized by the magistrates as it ought to be, any confession made to me might not be of the same value as if it were made to any one else—to a gentleman like you, for instance; and, moreover, it will not do for me to appear in evidence against any of the fraternity; and for two reasons: first, because I have taken a solemn oath never to do so; and, secondly, because I have a very fair chance of joining Sir John Tyrrell in kingdom come if I do. My present plan, therefore, if it meets your concurrence, would be to introduce your honour as the parson, and for you to receive the confession, which, indeed, you might take down in writing. This plan, I candidly confess, is not without great diffi-culty, and some danger; for I have not only to impose you upon Dawson as a priest, but also upon Brimstone Bess as one of our jolly boys; for I need not tell you that any real parson might knock a long time at her door before it would be opened to him. You must, there-fore, be as mum as a mole, unless she *cants* to you, and your answers must then be such as I shall dictate, otherwise she may detect you, and, should any of the true men be in the house, we should both come off worse than we went in."

"My dear Mr. Job," replied I, "there appears to me to be a much easier plan than all this; and that is, simply to tell the Bow-street officers where Dawson may be found, and I think they would be able to carry him away from the arms of Mrs. Brimstone Bess without any great difficulty or danger."

Jonson smiled.

"I should not long enjoy my annuity, your honour, if I were to set the runners upon our best hive. I should be stung to death before the week was out. Even you, should you accompany me to-night, will never know where the spot is situated, nor would you discover it again if you searched all London, with the whole police at your back. Besides, Dawson is not the only person in the house for whom the law is hunting—there are a score of others whom I have no desire to give up to the gallows—hid among the odds and ends of the house, as snug as plums in a pudding. God forbid that I should betray them, *and for nothing too!* No, your honour, the only plan I can think of is the one I proposed; if you do not approve of it, and it certainly

---

5. A parson, or minister—but generally applied to a priest of the lowest order.*
[B-L]

is open to exception, I must devise some other: but that may require delay."

"No my good Job," replied I, "I am ready to attend you: but could we not manage to release Dawson, as well as take his deposition? —his personal evidence is worth all the written ones in the world."

"Very true," answered Job, "and if it be possible to give Bess the slip, we will. However, let us not lose what we may get by grasping at what we may not; let us have the confession first, and we'll try for the release afterwards. I have another reason for this, Sir, which, if you knew as much of penitent prigs as I do, you would easily understand. However, it may be explained by the old proverb, of 'the devil was sick,' &c. As long as Dawson is stowed away in a dark hole, and fancies devils in every corner, he may be very anxious to make confessions, which, in broad day-light, might not seem to him so desirable. Darkness and solitude are strange stimulants to the conscience, and we may as well not lose any advantage they give us.

"You are an admirable reasoner," cried I, "and I am impatient to accompany you—at what hour shall it be?"

"Not much before midnight," answered Jonson; "but your honour must go back to school and learn lessons before then. Suppose Bess were to address you thus: 'Well, you parish bull prigs, are you for lushing jackey, or pattering in the hum box?'[6] I'll be bound you would not know how to answer."

"I am afraid you are right, Mr. Jonson," said I, in a tone of self-humiliation.

"Never mind," replied the compassionate Job, "we are all born ignorant—knowledge is not learnt in a day. A few of the most common and necessary words in our St. Giles's Greek, I shall be able to teach you before night; and I will, beforehand, prepare the old lady for seeing a young hand in the profession. As I must disguise you before we go, and that cannot well be done here, suppose you dine with me at my lodgings."

"I shall be too happy," said I, not a little surprised at the offer.

"I am in Charlotte-street, Bloomsbury, No ———. You must ask for me by the name of Captain Douglas,"* said Job, with dignity: "and we'll dine at five, in order to have time for your preliminary initiation."

"With all my heart," said I; and Mr. Job Jonson then rose, and reminding me of my promise of secrecy, took his departure.

---

6. Well, you parson thief, are you for drinking gin, or talking in the pulpit? [B-L]

CHAPTER XVII

Pectus præceptis format amicis.
                    HORAT.[1]
Est quodam prodire tenus, si non datur ultra.
                    HORAT.[1]

WITH ALL MY LOVE OF ENTERPISE AND ADVENTURE, I cannot say that I should have particularly chosen the project before me for my evening's amusement, had I been left solely to my own will; but Glanville's situation forbade me to think of self: and so far from shrinking at the danger to which I was about to be exposed, I looked forward with the utmost impatience to the hour of rejoining Jonson.

There was yet a long time upon my hands before five o'clock; and the thought of Ellen left me no doubt how it should be passed. I went to Berkeley-square; Lady Glanville rose eagerly when I entered the drawing-room.

"Have you seen Reginald?" said she, "or do you know where he has gone to?"

I answered, carelessly, that he had left town for a few days, and, I believed, merely upon a vague excursion, for the benefit of the country air.

"You reassure us," said Lady Glanville; "we have been quite alarmed by Seymour's manner. He appeared so confused when he told us Reginald had left town, that I really thought some accident had happened to him."

I sate myself by Ellen, who appeared wholly occupied in the formation of a purse. While I was whispering into her ear words, which brought a thousand blushes to her cheek, Lady Glanville interrupted me, by an exclamation of "Have you seen the papers to-day, Mr. Pelham?" and on my reply in the negative, she pointed to an

---

1. "He influences the mind by friendly precepts" (Horace *Epistles* 2.1.128). The second epigraph, also from the *Epistles* (1.1.32), may be translated: "It is something to have gotten this far, even if we go no further."

article in the Morning Herald, which she said had occupied their conjectures all the morning—it ran thus:—

"The evening before last, a person of rank and celebrity, was privately carried before the Magistrate at ———. Since then, he has undergone an examination, the nature of which, as well as the name of the individual, is as yet kept a profound secret."

I believe that I have so firm a command over my countenance, that I should not change tint nor muscle, to hear of the greatest calamity that could happen to me. I did not therefore betray a single one of the emotions this paragraph excited within me, but appeared, on the contrary, as much at a loss as Lady Glanville, and wondered and guessed with her, till she remembered my present situation in the family, and left me alone with Ellen.

Why should the *tête-à-tête* of lovers be so uninteresting to the world—when there is scarcely a being in it who has not loved? The expressions of every other feeling come home to us all—the expressions of love weary and fatigue us. But the interview of that morning was far from resembling those delicious meetings which the history of love at the early period of its existence so often delineates.* I could not give myself up to happiness which a moment might destroy: and though I veiled my anxiety and coldness from Ellen, I felt it as a crime to indulge even in the appearance of transport, while Glanville lay alone, and in prison, with the charges* of murder yet uncontroverted, and the chances of its doom undiminished.

The clock had struck four before I left Ellen, and without returning to my hotel, I threw myself into a hackney coach, and drove to Charlotte-street. The worthy Job received me with his wonted dignity and ease; his lodgings consisted of a first floor, furnished according to all the notions of Bloomsbury elegance—viz. new, glaring Brussels carpeting; convex mirrors, with massy gilt frames, and eagles at the summit; rosewood chairs, with chintz cushions; bright grates, with a flower-pot, cut out of yellow paper, in each; in short, all that especial neatness of upholstering paraphernalia, which Vincent used, not inaptly, to designate by the title of "the tea-chest taste." Jonson seemed not a little proud of his apartments—accordingly, I complimented him upon their elegance.

"Under the rose be it spoken," said he, "the landlady, who is a widow, believes me to be an officer on half pay, and thinks I wish to marry her; poor woman, my black locks and green coat have a witchery that surprises even me: who would be a slovenly thief, when there are such advantages in being a smart one?"

406

"Right, Mr. Jonson!" said I; "but shall I own to you that I am surprised that a gentleman of your talents should stoop to the lower arts of the profession. I always imagined that pickpocketing* was a part of your business left only to the plebeian purloiner; now I know, to my cost, that you do not disdain that manual accomplishment."

"Your honour speaks like a judge," answered Job: "the fact is, that I *should* despise what you rightly designate 'the lower arts of the profession,' if I did not value myself upon giving them a charm, and investing them with a dignity, never bestowed upon them before. To give you an idea of the superior dexterity with which I manage my sleight of hand, know, that four times I have been in that shop where you saw me *borrow* the diamond ring, which you now remark upon my little finger; and four times have I brought back some token of my visitations; nay, the shopman is so far from suspecting me, that he has twice favoured me with the piteous tale of the very losses I myself brought upon him; and I make no doubt that I shall hear in a few days, the whole history of the departed diamond, now in my keeping, coupled with *your* honour's appearance and custom. Allow that it would be a pity to suffer pride to stand in the way of the talents with which Providence has blest me; to scorn the little *delicacies* of art, which I execute so well, would, in my opinion, be as absurd as for an epic poet to disdain the composition of a perfect epigram, or a consummate musician the melody of a faultless song."

"Bravo! Mr. Job," said I; "a truly great man, you see, can confer honour upon trifles." More I might have said, but was stopt short by the entrance of the landlady, who was a fine, fair, well dressed, comely woman, of about thirty-nine years and eleven months; or, to speak less precisely, *between thirty and forty*. She came to announce that dinner was served below. We descended, and found a sumptuous repast of roast beef and fish; this primary course was succeeded by that great dainty with common people—a duck and green peas.

"Upon my word, Mr. Jonson," said I, "you fare like a prince; your weekly expenditure must be pretty considerable for a single gentleman."

"I don't know," answered Jonson, with an air of lordly indifference—"I have never paid my good hostess any coin but compliments, and, in all probability, never shall."

Was there ever a better illustration of Moore's admonition—

'O ladies, beware of a gay young knight,' &c.[2]

---

2. Unidentified: not in Thomas Moore.

After dinner, we remounted to the apartments Job emphatically called *his own;* and he then proceeded to initiate me in those phrases of the noble language of "Flash," which might best serve my necessities on the approaching occasion. The slang part of my Cambridge education had made me acquainted with some little elementary knowledge, which rendered Jonson's precepts less strange and abstruse. In this lecture, "sweet and holy," the hours pased away till it became time for me to dress. Mr. Jonson then took me into the penetralia of his bed-room. I stumbled against an enormous trunk. On hearing the involuntary anathema which this accident conjured up to my lips, Jonson said—"Ah, Sir!—*do* oblige me by trying to move that box."

I did so, but could not stir it an inch.

"Your honour never saw a *jewel box* so heavy before, I think," said Jonson, with a smile.

"A jewel box!" I repeated.

"Yes," returned Jonson—"a jewel box, for it is full of *precious stones!* When I go away—not a little in my good landlady's books—I shall desire her, very importantly, to take the greatest care of '*my box.*' Egad! it would be a treasure to MacAdam:[3] he might pound its flinty contents into a street."

With these words, Mr. Jonson unlocked a wardrobe in the room, and produced a full suit of rusty black.

"There!" said he, with an air of satisfaction—"there! this will be your first step to the pulpit."

I doffed my own attire, and with "some natural sighs,"[4] at the deformity of my approaching metamorphosis, I slowly indued myself in the clerical garments: they were much too wide, and a little too short for me; but Jonson turned me round, as if I were his eldest son, breeched for the first time—and declared, with an emphatical oath, that the clothes fitted me to a hair.

My host next opened a tin dressing box, of large dimensions, from which he took sundry powders, lotions, and paints. Nothing but my extreme friendship for Glanville could ever have supported me through the operation I then underwent. My poor complexion, thought I, with tears in my eyes, it is ruined for ever! To crown all—Jonson robbed me, by four clips of his scissars, of the luxuriant locks which, from the pampered indulgence so long accorded to them, might have rebelled against the new dynasty, which Jonson now

---

3. John Loudon MacAdam (1756–1836): authority on road building.

4. In common use. See, for example, Thomas Shadwell, *Psyche,* Act III.

elected to *the crown*. This dynasty consisted of a shaggy, but admirably made wig, of a sandy colour. When I was thus completely attired from head to foot, Job displayed me to myself before a full length looking-glass.

Had I gazed at the reflection for ever, I should not have recognized either my form or visage. I thought my soul had undergone a real transmigration, and not carried to its new body a particle of the original one. What appeared the most singular was, that I did not seem even to myself at all a ridiculous or *outré* figure; so admirably had the skill of Mr. Jonson been employed. I overwhelmed him with encomiums, which he took *au pied de la lettre*. Never, indeed, was there a man so vain of being a rogue.

"But," said I, "why this disguise? Your friends will, probably, be well versed enough in the mysteries of metamorphosis, to see even through your arts; and, as they have never beheld me before, it would very little matter if I went in *propriâ personâ.*"

"True," answered Job, "but you don't reflect that without disguise you may hereafter be recognized; our friends walk in Bond-street, as well as your honour; and, in that case, you might be shot without a second, as the saying is."

"You have convinced me," said I; "and now, before we start, let me say one word further respecting our *object*. I tell you, fairly, that I think Dawson's written deposition but a secondary point; and, for this reason, should it not be supported by any *circumstantial* or *local* evidence, hereafter to be ascertained, it may be quite in-sufficient fully to acquit Glanville (in spite of all appearances), and criminate the real murderers. If, therefore, it be *possible* to carry off Dawson, *after* having secured his confession, we must. I think it right to insist more particularly on this point, as you appeared to me rather averse to it this morning."

"I say ditto to your honour," returned Job; "and you may [be] sure that I shall do all in my power to effect your object, not only from that love of virtue which is implanted in my mind, when no stronger inducement leads me astray, but from the more worldly reminiscence, that the annuity we have agreed upon is only to be given in case of *success*—not merely for *well meaning attempts*. To say that I have no objection to the release of Dawson, would be to deceive your honour; I own that I have; and the objection is, first, my fear lest he should *peach* respecting other affairs besides the mur-der of Sir John Tyrrell; and, secondly, my scruples as to *appearing* to interfere with his escape. Both of these chances expose me to great

409

danger; however, one does not get three hundred a year for washing one's hands, and I must balance the one by the other."

"You are a sensible man, Mr. Job," said I; "and I am sure you will richly earn, and long enjoy your annuity."

As I said this, the watchman beneath our window, called "past eleven;" and Jonson, starting up, hastily changed his own gay gear for a more simple dress, and throwing over all a Scotch plaid, gave me a similar one, in which I closely wrapped myself. We descended the stairs softly, and Jonson *let us out* into the street, by the "open sesame" of a key, which he retained about his person.

CHAPTER XVIII

Et *cantare* pares, et respondere parati.
VIRGIL[1]

As we walked on into Tottenham-court-road, where we expected to find a hackney-coach, my companion earnestly and strenuously impressed on my mind, the necessity of implicitly obeying any instructions or hints he might give me in the course of our adventure. "Remember," said he, forcibly, "that the least deviation from them, will not only defeat our object of removing Dawson, but even expose our lives to the most imminent peril." I faithfully promised to conform to the minutest tittle of his instructions.

We came to a stand of coaches. Jonson selected one, and gave the coachman an order; he took care it should not reach my ears. During the half hour we passed in this vehicle, Job examined and re-examined me in my "canting catechism," as he termed it. He expressed himself much pleased with the quickness of my parts, and honoured me with an assurance that in less than three months he would engage to make me as complete a ruffler as *ever nailed a swell.*

To this gratifying compliment I made the best return in my power.

---

1. "Ready both to sing and make reply" (Virgil *Eclogues* 7.5).

410

"You must not suppose," said Jonson—some minutes afterwards, "from our use of this language, that our club consists of the lower order of thieves—quite the contrary: we are a knot of gentlemen adventurers who wear the best clothes, ride the best hacks, frequent the best gaming houses, as well as the *genteelest* haunts, and sometimes keep *the first company*—in London. We are limited in number: we have nothing in common with ordinary prigs, and should my own little private amusements (as you appropriately term them) be known in the set, I should have a very fair chance of being expelled for *ungentlemanlike* practices. We rarely condescend to speak 'flash' to each other in our ordinary meetings, but we find it necessary, for many shifts to which fortune sometimes drives us. The house you are going this night to visit, is a sort of colony we have established for whatever persons amongst us are in danger of blood-money.[2] There they sometimes lie concealed for weeks together, and are at last shipped off for the continent, or enter the world under a new alias. To this refuge of the distressed we also send any of the mess, who, like Dawson, are troubled with qualms of conscience, which are likely to endanger the commonwealth; there they remain, as in a hospital, till death, or a cure; in short, we put the house, like its inmates, to any purposes likely to frustrate our enemies, and serve ourselves. Old Brimstone Bess, to whom I shall introduce you, is, as I before said, the guardian of the place; and the language that respectable lady chiefly indulges in, is the one into which you have just acquired so good an insight. Partly in compliment to her, and partly from inclination, the dialect adopted in her house is almost entirely 'flash;' and you, therefore, perceive the necessity of appearing not utterly ignorant of a tongue, which is not only the language of the country, but one with which no true boy, however high in his profession, is ever unacquainted."

By the time Jonson had finished this speech, the coach stopped— I looked eagerly out—Jonson observed the motion: "We have not got half-way yet, your honour," said he. We left the coach, which Jonson requested me to pay, and walked on.

"Tell me frankly, Sir," said Job, "do you know where you are?"

"Not in the least," replied I, looking wistfully up a long, dull, ill-lighted street.

Job rolled his sinister eye towards me with a searching look, and then turning abruptly to the right, penetrated into a sort of covered

2. Rewards for the apprehension of thieves, &c. [B-L]

lane, or court, which terminated in an alley, that brought us suddenly to a stand of three coaches; one of these Job hailed—we entered it— a secret direction was given, and we drove furiously on, faster than I should think the crazy body of hackney chariot ever drove before. I observed, that we had now entered a part of the town, which was singularly strange to me; the houses were old, and for the most part of the meanest description; we appeared to me to be threading a labyrinth of alleys; once, I imagined that I caught, through a sudden opening, a glimpse of the river, but we passed so rapidly, that my eye might have deceived me. At length we stopped: the coachman was again dismissed, and I again walked onwards, under the guidance, and almost at the mercy of my honest companion.

Jonson did not address me—he was silent and absorbed, and I had therefore full leisure to consider my present situation. Though (thanks to my physical constitution) I am as callous to fear as most men, a few chilling apprehensions certainly flitted across my mind, when I looked around at the dim and dreary sheds—houses they were not—which were on either side of our path; only, here and there, a single lamp shed a sickly light upon the dismal and intersecting lanes (though lane is too lofty a word), through which our footsteps woke a solitary sound. Sometimes this feeble light was altogether withheld, and I could scarcely catch even the outline of my companion's muscular frame. However, he strode on through the darkness, with the mechanical rapidity of one to whom every stone is familiar. I listened eagerly for the sound of the watchman's voice, in vain—that note was never heard in those desolate recesses. My ear drank in nothing but the sound of our own footsteps, or the occasional burst of obscene and unholy merriment from some half-closed hovel, where Infamy and Vice were holding revels. Now and then, a wretched thing, in the vilest extreme of want, and loathsomeness, and rags, loitered by the unfrequent lamps, and interrupted our progress with solicitations, which made my blood run cold. By degrees even these tokens of life ceased—the last lamp was entirely shut from our view—we were in utter darkness.

"We are near our journey's end now," whispered Jonson.

At these words a thousand unwelcome reflections forced themselves involuntarily on my mind: I was about to plunge into the most secret retreat of men whom long habits of villainy and desperate abandonment, had hardened into a nature which had scarcely a sympathy with my own; unarmed and defenceless, I was going to penetrate a concealment upon which their lives perhaps depended; what could

412

I anticipate from their vengeance, but the sure hand and the deadly knife, which their self-preservation would more than justify to such lawless reasoners? And who was my companion? One who literally gloried in the perfection of his nefarious practices; and who, if he had stopped short of the worst enormities, seemed neither to disown the principle upon which they were committed, nor to balance for a moment between his interest and his conscience.

Nor did he attempt to conceal from me the danger to which I was exposed; much as his daring habits of life, and the good fortune which had attended him, must have hardened his nerves, even *he* seemed fully sensible of the peril he incurred—a peril certainly considerably less than that which attended my temerity. Bitterly did I repent, as these reflections rapidly passed my mind, my negligence in not providing myself with a single weapon in case of need: the worst pang of death is the falling without a struggle.

However, it was no moment for the indulgence of fear, it was rather one of those eventful periods which so rarely occur in the monotony of common life, when our minds are sounded to their utmost depths: and energies, of which we dreamt not when at rest in their secret retreats, arise like spirits at the summons of the wizard, and bring to the invoking mind an unlooked for and preternatural aid.

There was something too in the disposition of my guide, which gave me a confidence in him, not warranted by the occupations of his life; an easy and frank boldness, an ingenuous vanity of abilities, skilfully, though dishonestly exerted, which had nothing of the meanness and mystery of an ordinary villain, and which being equally prominent with the rascality they adorned, prevented the attention from dwelling only upon the darker shades of his character. Besides, I had so closely entwined his interest with my own, that I felt there could be no possible ground either for suspecting him of any deceit towards me, or of omitting any art or exertion which could conduce to our mutual safety, or our common end.

Forcing myself to dwell solely upon the more encouraging side of the enterprise I had undertaken, I continued to move on with my worthy comrade,* silent and in darkness, for some minutes longer—Jonson then halted.

"Are you quite prepared, Sir?" said he, in a whisper: "if your heart fails, in God's name let us turn back: the least evident terror will be as much as your life is worth."

My thoughts were upon Sir Reginald and Ellen, as I replied—

413

"You have *convinced* me that I may trust in you, and I have no fears; my present object is one as strong to me as life."

"I would we had a *glim*," rejoined Job, musingly; "I should like to see your face; but will you give me your hand, Sir?"

I did, and Jonson held it in his own for more than a minute.

" 'Fore Heaven,* Sir," said he, at last, "I would you were one of us. You would live a brave man and die a game one. Your pulse is like iron; and your hand does not sway—no—not so much as to wave a dove's feather; it would be a burning shame if harm came to so stout a heart." Job moved on a few steps. "Now, Sir," he whispered, "remember your flash; do exactly as I may have occasion to tell you; and be sure to sit away from the light, should we be in company.

With these words he stopped. I perceived by the touch, for it was too dark to see, that he was leaning down,* apparently in a listening attitude; presently, he tapped five times at what I supposed was a door, though I afterwards discovered it was the shutter to a window; upon this, a faint light broke through the crevices of the boards, and a low voice uttered some sound, which my ear did not catch. Job replied in the same key, and in words which were perfectly unintelligible to me; the light disappeared; Job moved round, as if turning a corner. I heard the heavy bolts and bars of a door slowly withdraw; and in a few moments, a harsh voice said, in the thieves' dialect,

"Ruffling Job, my prince of prigs, is that you? are you come to the ken alone, or do you carry double?"

"Ah, Bess, my covess, strike me blind if my sees don't tout your bingo muns in spite of the darkmans. Egad, you carry a bene blink aloft. Come to the ken alone—no! my blowen; did not I tell you I should bring a pater cove, to chop up the whiners for Dawson?"[3]

"Stubble it, you ben, you deserve to cly the jerk for your patter; come in, and be d——d to you."

Upon this invitation, Jonson, seizing me by the arm, pushed me into the house, and followed. "Go for a glim, Bess, to light in the parish bull* with proper respect. I'll close the gig of the crib."

At this order, delivered in an authoritative tone, the old woman, mumbling "strange oaths"[4] to herself, moved away; when she was out of hearing, Job whispered,

---

3. This speech and the one that follows are couched in flash language. Bulwer's translation (1840 ed.) is: "Strike me blind if my eyes don't see your brandy face in spite of the night. . . . Come to the house alone—no! my woman; did I not tell you I should bring a parson—to say prayers for Dawson?—"Hold your tongue, fool, you deserve to be whipped for your chatter."

4. *As You Like It*, II, 7, 150.

414

"Mark, I shall leave the bolts undrawn; the door opens, with a latch, which you press *thus*—do not forget the spring; it is easy, but peculiar; should you be forced to run for it, you will also remember, above all, when you are out of the door, to turn *to the right,* and go straight forwards."

The old woman now reappeared with a light, and Jonson ceased, and moved hastily towards her: I followed. The old woman asked whether the door had been carefully closed, and Jonson, with an oath at her doubts of such a matter, answered in the affirmative.

We proceeded onwards, through a long and very narrow passage, till Bess opened a small door to the right, and introduced us into a large room, which, to my great dismay, I found already occupied by four men, who were sitting, half immersed in smoke, by an oak table, with a capacious bowl of hot liquor before them. At the back ground of this room, which resembled the kitchen of a public house, was an enormous screen, of antique fashion; a low fire burnt sullenly in the grate, and beside it was one of those high-backed chairs, seen frequently in old houses and old pictures. A clock stood in one corner, and in the opposite nook was a flight of narrow stairs, which led downwards, probably to a cellar. On a row of shelves, were various bottles of the different liquors generally in request among the "flash" gentry, together with an old-fashioned fiddle, two bridles, and some strange looking tools, probably of more use to true boys than to* honest men.

Brimstone Bess was a woman about the middle size, but with bones and sinews which would not have disgraced a prize-fighter; a cap, that *might* have been cleaner, was rather *thrown* than *put* on the back of her head, developing, to full advantage, the few scanty locks of grizzled ebon which adorned her countenance. Her eyes, large, black, and prominent, sparkled with a fire half vivacious, half vixen. The nasal feature was broad and *fungous,* and, as well as the whole of her capacious physiognomy, blushed with the deepest scarlet: it was evident to see that many a full bottle of "British compounds" had contributed to the feeding of that burning and phosphoric illumination which was, indeed, "the outward and visible sign of an inward and *spiritual grace.*"[5]

The expression of the countenance was not wholly bad. Amidst the deep traces of searing vice and unrestrained passion—amidst all that was bold, and unfeminine, and fierce, and crafty, there was a latent look of coarse good humour, a twinkle of the eye that bespoke

---

5. *Book of Common Prayer. The Catechism.*

a tendency to mirth and drollery, and an upward curve of the lip that shewed, however the human creature might be debased, it still cherished its grand characteristic—the propensity to laughter.

The garb of this dame Leonarda was by no means of that humble nature which one might have supposed. A gown of crimson silk, flounced and furbelowed to the knees, was tastefully relieved by a bright yellow shawl; and a pair of heavy pendants glittered in her ears, which were of the size proper to receive "the big words"[6] they were in the habit of hearing. Probably this finery had its origin in the policy of her guests, who had seen enough of life to know that age, which tames all other passions, never tames the passion of dress in a woman's mind.*

No sooner did the four revellers set their eyes upon me than they all rose.

"Zounds, Bess!" cried the tallest of them, "what cull's this? Is this a bowsing ken for every cove to shove his trunk in?"

"What ho, my kiddy!" cried Job, "don't be glimflashy: why you'd cry beef on a blater: the cove is a bob cull, and a pal of my own;[7] and, moreover, is as pretty a Tyburn blossom as ever was brought up to ride a horse foaled by an acorn."

Upon this commendatory introduction I was forthwith surrounded, and one of the four proposed that I should be immediately "elected."

This motion, which was probably no gratifying ceremony, Job negatived with a dictatorial air, and reminded his comrades that however they might find it convenient to lower themselves occasionally, yet that they were gentlemen sharpers, and not vulgar cracksmen and cly-fakers,[8] and that, therefore, they ought to welcome me with the good breeding appropriate to their station.

Upon this hint, which was received with mingled laughter and deference, (for Job seemed to be a man of might among these Philistines), the tallest of the set, who bore the euphonious appelation of Spider-shanks, politely asked me if I would "blow a cloud with him?" and, upon my assent, (for I thought such an occupation would be the best excuse for silence), he presented me with a pipe of tobacco, to which dame Brimstone applied a light, and I soon lent my best endeavours to darken still further the atmosphere around us.

---

6. See Boswell's *Life of Johnson*, 6 August 1763.

7. "Don't be angry! Why you'd cry beef on a calf—the man is a good fellow, and a comrade of my own." [Bulwer's translation; 1840 ed.]

8. Cracksmen and cly-fakers; housebreakers and pickpockets, respectively.

Mr. Job Jonson then began artfully to turn the conversation away from me to the elder confederates of his crew; these were all spoken under certain singular appellations which might well baffle impertinent curiosity. The name of one was "the Gimblet," another "Crack Crib," a third, the "Magician," a fourth, "Cherry-coloured Jowl." The tallest of the present company was called (as I before said) "Spider-shanks," and the shortest, "Fib Fakescrew;" Job himself was honoured by the *venerabile nomen* of "Guinea Pig." At last Job explained the cause of my appearance; *viz.* his wish to pacify Dawson's conscience by dressing up one of the pals, whom the sinner could not recognize, as an "autem bawler,"[9] and so obtaining him the benefit of the clergy without endangering the gang by his confession. This detail was received with great good humour, and Job, watching his opportunity, soon after rose, and, turning to me, said—

"Toddle, my bob cull—we must track up the dancers and tout the sinner."[10]

I wanted no other hint to leave my present situation.

"The ruffian cly thee, Guinea Pig, for stashing the lush,"[11] said Spider-shanks, helping himself out of the bowl, which was nearly empty.

"Stash the lush!" cried Mrs. Brimstone, "ay, and toddle off to Ruggins. Why, you would not be boosing till lightman's in a square crib like mine, as if you were a flash panny."

"That's bang up, mort!" cried Fib. "A square crib, indeed! ay, square as Mr. Newman's courtyard—ding-boys on three sides, and the crap on the fourth!"[12]

This characteristic witticism was received with great applause; and Jonson, taking a candlestick from the fair fingers of the exasperated Mrs. Brimstone, the hand thus conveniently released immediately transferred itself to Fib's cheeks, with so hearty a concussion that it almost brought the rash jester to the ground. Jonson and I lost not a moment in taking advantage of the confusion this gentle remonstrance appeared to occasion; but instantly left the room and closed the door.

9. "autem bawler": a parson.

10. "Move, my good fellow, we must go upstairs, and look at the sinner." [Bulwer's translation; 1840 ed.]

11. "The devil take thee, for stopping the drink." [Bulwer's translation; 1840 ed.]

12. "Stop the drink, ay, and be off to bed. You would be drinking till day—in an honest house like mine, as if you were in a disreputable place."—"That's capital. A square crib (honest house)! Ay, square as Newgate coachyard—rogues on three sides, and the gallows on the fourth." [Bulwer's translation; 1840 ed.]

CHAPTER XIX

'Tis true that we are in great danger:
The greater, therefore, should our courage be.
SHAKSPEARE[1]

WE PROCEEDED A SHORT WAY, WHEN WE WERE STOPPED by a door; this Job opened, and a narrow staircase, lighted from above by a dim lamp, was before us. We ascended, and found ourselves in a sort of gallery: here hung another lamp, beneath which Job opened a closet.

"This is the place where Bess generally leaves the keys," said he; "we shall find them here, I hope."

So saying, Master Job entered, leaving me in the passage; but soon returned with a disappointed air.

"The old harridan has left them below," said he; "I must go down for them; your honour will wait here till I return."

Suiting the action to the word, honest Job immediately descended, leaving me alone with my own reflections. Just opposite to the closet was the door of some apartment; I leant accidentally against it; it was only a-jar, and gave way; the ordinary consequence in such accidents, is a certain precipitation from the centre of gravity. I am not exempt from the general lot; and accordingly entered the room in a manner entirely contrary to that which my natural inclination would have prompted me to adopt. My ear was accosted by a faint voice, which proceeded from a bed at the opposite corner; it asked, in the thieves' dialect, and in the feeble accents of bodily weakness, who was there? I did not judge it necessary to make any reply, but was withdrawing as gently as possible, when my eye rested upon a table at the foot of the bed, upon which, among two or three miscellaneous articles, were deposited a brace of pistols, and one of those admirable swords, made according to the modern military regulation, for the united purpose of cut and thrust. The light which enabled me to

---

1. *Henry V,* IV, 1, 1–2.

418

discover the contents of the room, proceeded from a rush-light placed in the grate; this general symptom of a valetudinarian, together with some other little odd matters (combined with the weak voice of the speaker), impressed me with the idea of having intruded into the chamber of some sick member of the crew. Emboldened by this notion, and by perceiving that the curtains were drawn closely around the bed, so that the inmate could have optical discernment of nothing that occurred without, I could not resist taking two soft steps to the table, and quietly removing a weapon whose bright face seemed to invite me as a long known and long tried friend.

This was not, however done in so noiseless a manner, but what the voice again addressed me, in a somewhat louder key, by the appellation of "Brimstone Bess," asking, with sundry oaths, "What was the matter?" and requesting something to drink. I need scarcely say that, as before, I made no reply, but crept out of the room as gently as possible, blessing my good fortune for having thrown into my way a weapon with the use of which, above all others, I was best* acquainted. Scarcely had I regained the passage, before Jonson reappeared with the keys; I showed him my treasure (for indeed it was of no size to conceal).

"Are you mad, Sir?" said he, "or do you think that the best way to avoid suspicion is to walk about with a drawn sword in your hand? I would not have Bess see you for the best diamond I ever *borrowed.*" With these words Job took the sword from my reluctant hand.

"Where did you get it?" said he.

I explained in a whisper, and Job, re-opening the door I had so unceremoniously entered, laid the weapon softly *on a chair that stood within reach.* The sick man, whose senses were of course rendered doubly acute by illness, once more demanded in a fretful tone, who was there? And Job replied, in the flash language, that Bess had sent him up to look for her keys, which she imagined she had left there. The invalid rejoined, by a request to Jonson to reach him a draught, and we had to undergo a farther delay until his petition was complied with; we then proceeded up the passage, till we came to another flight of steps, which led to a door: Job opened it, and we entered a room of no common dimensions.

"This," said he, "is Bess Brimstone's sleeping apartment; whoever goes into the passage that leads not only to Dawson's room, but to the several other chambers occupied by such of the gang as require *particular care,* must pass first through this room. You see that bell by the bedside—I assure you it is no ordinary tintinnabulum; it

419

communicates with every sleeping apartment in the house, and is only rung in cases of great alarm, when every boy must look well to himself; there are two more of this description, one in the room which we have just left, another in the one occupied by Spider-shanks, who is our watch-dog, and keeps his kennel below. Those steps in the common room, which seem to lead to a cellar, conduct to his den. As we shall have to come back through this room, you see the difficulty of smuggling Dawson—and if the old dame rung the alarm, the whole hive would be out in a moment."

After this speech, Job led me from the room, by a door at the opposite end, which shewed us a passage, similar in extent and fashion to the one we had left below; at the very extremity of this was the entrance to an apartment at which Jonson stopped.

"Here," said he, taking from his pocket a small paper book and an ink-horn; "here, your honour, take these, you may want to note the heads of Dawson's confession, we are now at his door." Job then applied one of the keys of a tolerably sized bunch to the door, and the next moment we were in Dawson's apartment.

The room which, though low and narrow, was of considerable length, was in utter darkness, and the dim and flickering light Jonson held, only struggled with, rather than penetrated the thick gloom. About the centre of the room stood the bed, and sitting upright on it, with a wan and hollow countenance, bent eagerly towards us, was a meagre, attenuated figure. My recollection of Dawson, whom, it will be remembered, I had only seen once before, was extremely faint, but it had impressed me with the idea of a middle-sized and rather athletic man, with a fair and florid complexion: the creature I now saw was totally the reverse of this idea. His cheeks were yellow and drawn in: his hand, which was raised, in the act of holding aside the curtains, was like the talons of a famished vulture, so thin was it, so long, so withered in its hue and texture.

No sooner did the advancing light allow him to see us distinctly, than he half sprung from the bed, and cried, in the peculiar tone of joy which seems to throw off the breast a suffocating weight of previous terror and suspense, "Thank God, thank God! it is you at last; and you have brought the clergyman—God bless you, Jonson, you are a true friend to me."

"Cheer up, Dawson," said Job; "I have smuggled in this worthy gentleman, who, I have no doubt, will be of great comfort to you—but you must be open with him, and tell all."

"That I will—that I will," cried Dawson, with a wild and vin-

420

dictive expression of countenance—"if it be only to hang *him*. Here, Jonson, give me your hand, bring the light nearer—I say—*he*, the devil—the fiend—has been here to-day, and threatened to murder me; and I have listened, and listened, all night, and thought I heard his step along the passage, and up the stairs, and at the door; but it was nothing, Job, nothing—and you are come at last, good, kind, worthy Job. Oh! 'tis so horrible to be left in the dark, and not sleep—and in this large, large room, which looks like eternity at night—and one does fancy such sights, Job—such horrid, horrid sights. Feel my wrist-band, Jonson, and here at my back, you would think they had been pouring water over me, but it's only the cold sweat. Oh! it is a fearful thing to have a bad conscience, Job; but you won't leave me till day-light, now, that's a dear, good Job!"

"For shame, Dawson," said Jonson; "pluck up, and be a man; you are like a baby frightened by its nurse. Here's the clergyman come to heal your poor wounded conscience, will you hear him *now?*"

"Yes," said Dawson; "yes!—but go out of the room—I can't tell all if you're here; go, Job, go!—but you're not angry with me—I don't mean to offend you."

"Angry!" said Job, "Lord help the poor fellow! no, to be sure not. I'll stay outside the door till you've done with the clergyman—but make haste, for the night's almost over, and it's as much as the parson's life is worth to stay here after daybreak."

"I *will* make haste," said the guilty man, tremulously; "but, Job, where are you going—what are you doing? *leave the light!—here,* Job, by the bed-side."

Job did as he was desired, and quitted the room, leaving the door not so firmly shut but that he might hear, if the penitent spoke aloud, every particular of his confession.

I seated myself on the side of the bed, and taking the skeleton hand of the unhappy man, spoke to him in the most consolatory and comforting words I could summon to my assistance. He seemed greatly soothed by my efforts, and at last implored me to let him join me in prayer. I knelt down, and my lips readily found words for that language, which, whatever be the formula of our faith, seems, in all emotions which come home to our hearts, the most natural method of expressing them. It is *here,* by the bed of sickness, or re-morse, that the ministers of God have their real power! it is here that their office is indeed a divine and unearthly mission; and that, in breathing balm and comfort, in healing the broken heart, in raising the crushed and degraded spirit—they are the voice and oracle of

421

the FATHER, who made us in benevolence, and will judge of us in mercy! I rose, and after a short pause, Dawson, who expressed himself impatient of the comfort of confession, thus began—

"I have no time, Sir, to speak of the earlier part of my life. I passed it upon the race-course, and at the gaming-table—all that was, I know, very wrong, and wicked; but I was a wild, idle boy, and eager for any thing like enterprise or mischief. Well, Sir, it is now more than three years ago since I first met one Tom Thornton; it was at a boxing match. Tom was chosen chairman, at a sort of club of the farmers and yeomen; and being a lively, amusing fellow, and accustomed to the company of gentlemen, was a great favourite with all of us. He was very civil to me, and I was quite pleased with his notice. I did not, however, see much of him then, nor for more than two years afterwards; but some months ago we met again. I was in very poor circumstances, so was he, and this made us closer friends than we might otherwise have been. He lived a great deal at the gambling-houses, and fancied he had discovered a certain method of winning[2] at hazard. So, whenever he could not find a gentleman whom he could cheat with false dice, tricks at cards, &c., he would go into any hell to try his infallible game. I did not, however, perceive, that he made a good livelihood* by it: and though sometimes, either by that method or some other, he had large sums of money in his possession, yet they were spent as soon as acquired. The fact was, that he was not a man who could ever grow rich; he was extremely extravagant in all things—loved women and drinking, and was always striving to get into the society of people above him. In order to do this, he affected great carelessness of money; and if, at a race or a cock-fight, any real gentlemen would go home with him, he would insist upon treating them to the very best of every thing.

"Thus, Sir, he was always poor, and at his wit's end, for means to supply his extravagance. He introduced me to three or four *gentlemen,* as he called them, but whom I have since found to be markers, sharpers, and black-legs; and this set soon dissipated the little honesty my own habits of life had left me. They never spoke of things by their right names; and, therefore, those things never seemed so bad as they really were—to swindle a gentleman did not sound a crime when it was called 'macing a swell'—nor transportation a punishment, when it was termed, with a laugh, 'lagging a cove.' Thus, insensibly, my ideas of right and wrong, always obscure, became perfectly con-

---

2. A very common delusion, both among sharpers and their prey. [B-L]

fused: and the habit of treating all crimes as subjects of jest in familiar conversation, soon made me regard them as matters of very trifling importance.

"Well, Sir, at Newmarket races, this Spring meeting, Thornton and I were on *the look out.* He had come down to stay, during the races, at a house I had just inherited from my father, but which was rather an expense to me than an advantage; especially as my wife, who was an inn-keeper's daughter, was very careless and extravagant. It so happened that we were both taken in by a jockey, whom we had bribed very largely, and were losers to a very considerable amount. Among other people, I lost to a Sir John Tyrrell. I expressed my vexation to Thornton, who told me not to mind it, but to tell Sir John that I would pay him if he came to the town; and that he was quite sure we could win enough, by his certain game at hazard, to pay off my debt. He was so very urgent, that I allowed myself to be persuaded; though Thornton has since told me, that his only motive was, to prevent Sir John's going to the Marquess of Chester's (where he was invited) with my lord's party; and so to have an opportunity of accomplishing the crime he then meditated.

"Accordingly, as Thornton desired, I asked Sir John Tyrrell to come with me to Newmarket. He did so. I left him, joined Thornton, and went to the gambling-house. Here we were engaged in Thornton's sure game, when Sir John entered. I went up and apologized for not paying, and said I would pay him in three months. However, Sir John was very angry, and treated me with such rudeness, that the whole table remarked it. When he was gone, I told Thornton how hurt and indignant I was at Sir John's treatment. He incensed me still more—exaggerated Sir John's conduct—said that I had suffered the grossest insult, and, at last, put me into such a passion, that I said, that if I was a gentleman, I would fight Sir John Tyrrell across the table.

"When Thornton saw I was so moved, he took me out of the room, and carried me to an inn. Here he ordered dinner, and several bottles of wine. I never could bear much drink: he knew this, and artfully plied me with wine till I scarcely knew what I did or said. He then talked much of our destitute situation—affected to put himself out of the question—said he was a single man, and could easily make shift upon a potatoe—but that I was encumbered with a wife and child, whom I could not suffer to starve. He then said, that Sir John Tyrrell had publicly disgraced me—that I should be blown upon the course—that no gentleman would bet with me again, and

423

a great deal more of the same sort. Seeing what an effect he had produced upon me, he then told me that he had seen Sir John receive a large sum of money, which would more than pay our debts, and set us up like gentlemen; and, at last, he proposed to me to rob him. Intoxicated as I was, I was somewhat startled at this proposition. However, the slang terms in which Thornton disguised the greatness and danger of the offence, very much diminished both in my eyes—so at length I consented.

"We went to Sir John's inn, and learnt that he had just set out; accordingly, we mounted our horses, and rode after him. The night had already closed in. After we had got some distance from the main road, into a lane, which led both to my house and to Chester Park—for the former was on the direct way to my lord's—we passed a man on horseback. I only observed that he was wrapped in a cloak—but Thornton said, directly we had passed him, 'I know that man well—he has been following Tyrrell all day—and though he attempts to screen himself, I have penetrated his disguise; he is Tyrrell's mortal enemy.'

" 'Should the worst come to the worst,' added Thornton, (words which I did not at that moment understand), 'we can make *him* bear the blame.'

"When we had got some way further, we came up to Tyrrell and a gentleman, whom, to our great dismay, we found that Sir John had joined—the gentleman's horse had met with an accident, and Thornton dismounted to offer assistance. He assured the gentleman, who proved afterwards to be a Mr. Pelham, that the horse was quite lame, and that he would scarcely be able to get it home; and he then proposed to Sir John to accompany us, and said that we would put him in the right road; this offer Sir John rejected very haughtily, and we rode on.

" 'It's all up with us,' said I; 'since he has joined another person.'

" 'Not at all,' replied Thornton; 'for I managed to give the horse a sly poke with my knife; and if I know any thing of Sir John Tyrrell, he is much too impatient a spark to crawl along, a snail's pace, with any companion, especially with this heavy shower coming on.'

" 'But,' said I, for I now began to recover from my intoxication, and to be sensible of the nature of our undertaking, 'the moon is up, and unless this shower conceals it, Sir John will recognize us; so you see, even if he leaves the gentleman, it will be no use, and we had much better make haste home and go to bed.'

"Upon this, Thornton cursed me for a faint-hearted fellow, and

424

said that the cloud would effectually hide the moon—or, if not—he added—'I know how to silence a prating tongue.' At these words I was greatly alarmed, and said, that if he meditated murder as well as robbery, I would have nothing further to do with it. Thornton laughed, and told me not to be a fool. While we were thus debating, a heavy shower came on; we rode hastily to a large tree, by the side of a pond—which, though bare and withered, was the nearest shelter the country afforded, and was only a very short distance from my house. I wished to go home—but Thornton would not let me, and as I was always in the habit of yielding, I remained with him, though very reluctantly, under the tree.

"Presently, we heard the trampling of a horse.

" 'It is he—it is he,' cried Thornton with a savage tone of exultation—'and alone!—Be ready—we must make a rush—I will be the one to bid him to deliver—you hold your tongue.'

"The clouds and rain had so overcast the night, that, although it was not *perfectly* dark, it was sufficiently obscure to screen our countenances. Just as Tyrrell approached, Thornton dashed forward, and cried, in a feigned voice—'Stand, on your peril!' I followed, and we were now both by Sir John's side.

"He attempted to push by us—but Thornton seized him by the arm—there was a stout struggle, in which, as yet, I had no share;—at last, Tyrrell got loose from Thornton, and I seized him—he set spurs to his horse, which was a very spirited and strong animal—it reared upwards, and very nearly brought me and *my* horse to the ground —at that instant, Thornton struck the unfortunate man a violent blow across the head with the butt end of his heavy whip—Sir John's hat had fallen before in the struggle, and the blow was so stunning that it felled him upon the spot. Thornton dismounted, and made me do the same—'There is no time to lose,' said he; 'let us drag him from the road-side, and rifle him.' We accordingly carried him (he was still senseless) to the side of the pond before mentioned. While we were searching for the money Thornton spoke of, the storm ceased, and the moon broke out—we were detained some moments by the accident of Tyrrell's having transferred his pocket-book from the pocket Thornton had seen him put it in on the race-ground to an inner one.

"We had just discovered, and seized the pocket-book, when Sir John awoke from his swoon, and his eyes opened upon Thornton, who was still bending over him, and looking at the contents of the book to see that all was right; the moonlight left Tyrrell in no doubt

425

as to our persons; and struggling hard to get up, he cried, 'I know you! I know you! you shall hang for this.' No sooner had he uttered this imprudence, than it was all over with him. 'We will see that, Sir John,' said Thornton, setting his knee upon Tyrrell's chest, and nailing him down. While thus employed, he told me to feel in his coat-pocket for a case-knife.

" 'For God's sake,' cried Tyrrell, with a tone of agonizing terror which haunts me still, 'spare my life!'

" 'It is too late,' said Thornton, deliberately, and taking the knife from my hands, he plunged it into Sir John's side, and as the blade was too short to reach the vitals, Thornton drew it backwards and forwards to widen the wound. Tyrrell was a strong man, and still continued to struggle and call out for mercy—Thornton drew out the knife—Tyrrell seized it by the blade, and his fingers were cut through before Thornton could snatch it from his grasp; the wretched gentleman then saw all hope was over: he uttered one loud, sharp cry of despair. Thornton put one hand to his mouth, and with the other gashed his throat from ear to ear.[3]

" 'You have done for him and for us now,' said I, as Thornton slowly rose from the body. 'No,' replied he, 'look, he still moves;' and sure enough he did, but it was in the last agony. However, Thornton, to make all sure, plunged the knife again into his body: the blade came in contact with a bone, and snapped in two; so great was the violence of the blow, that, instead of remaining in the flesh, the broken piece fell upon the ground among the long fern and grass.

"While we were employed in searching for it, Thornton, whose ears were much sharper than mine, caught the sound of a horse. 'Mount! mount!' he cried, 'and let us be off!' We sprung up on our horses, and rode away as fast as we could. I wished to go home, as it was so near at hand; but Thornton insisted on making to an old shed, about a quarter of a mile across the fields: thither, therefore, we went."

"Stop," said I; "what did Thornton do with the remaining part of the case-knife? Did he throw it away, or carry it with him?"

"He took it with him," answered Dawson, "for his name was engraved on a silver plate on the handle; and he was therefore afraid of throwing it into the pond, as I advised, lest at any time it should be discovered. Close by the shed there is a plantation of young firs

---

3. "The murder of Tyrrell in the novel was founded on the murder of Weare in 1824, by Thurtell, a low gambler like Thornton" (*Life . . . and Literary Remains,* II, 193).

426

of some extent: Thornton and I entered, and he dug a hole with the broken blade of the knife, and buried it, covering up the hole again with the earth."

"Describe the place," said I. Dawson paused, and seemed to recollect. I was on the very tenterhooks of suspense, for I saw with one glance all the importance of his reply.

After some moments, he shook his head: "I *cannot* describe the place," said he, "for the wood is so thick: yet I know the exact spot so well, that, were I in any part of the plantation, I could point it out immediately."

I told him to pause again, and recollect himself; and, at all events, *to try* to indicate the place. However, his account was so confused and perplexed, that I was forced to give up the point in despair, and he continued.

"After we had done this, Thornton told me to hold the horses, and said he would go alone, to spy whether we might return: accordingly he did so, and brought back word, in about half an hour, that he had crept cautiously along till in sight of the place, and then, throwing himself down on his face by the ridge of a bank, had observed a man (who he was sure was the person with a cloak we had passed, and who, he said, was Sir Reginald Glanville) mount his horse on the very spot of the murder, and ride off, while another person (Mr. Pelham) appeared, and also discovered the fatal place.

" 'There is no doubt now,' said he, 'that we shall have the hue-and-cry upon us. However, if you are staunch and stout-hearted, no possible danger can come to us; for you may leave me alone to throw the whole guilt upon Sir Reginald Glanville.'

"We then mounted, and rode home. We stole up stairs by the back way. Thornton's linen and hands were stained with blood. The former he took off, locked up carefully, and burnt the first opportunity: the latter he washed; and, that the water might not lead to detection, *drank it*. We then appeared as if nothing had occurred, and learnt that Mr. Pelham had been to the house; but as, very fortunately, our out-buildings had been lately robbed by some idle people, my wife and servants had refused to admit him. I was thrown into great agitation, and was extremely frightened. However, as Mr. Pelham had left a message that we were to go to the pond, Thornton insisted upon our repairing there to avoid suspicion."

Dawson then proceeded to say, that, on their return, as he was still exceedingly nervous, Thornton insisted on his going to bed. When our party from Lord Chester's came to the house, Thornton went into Dawson's room, and made him swallow a large tumbler of brandy;[4] this intoxicated him so as to make him less sensible to his dangerous situation. Afterwards, when the picture was found, which circumstance Thornton communicated to him, along with that of the threatening letter sent by Glanville to the deceased, which was discovered in Tyrrell's pocket-book, Dawson recovered courage; and justice being entirely thrown on a wrong scent, he managed to pass his examination without suspicion. He then went to town with Thornton, and constantly attended "the club" to which Jonson had before introduced him; at first, among his new comrades, and while the novel flush of the money he had so fearfully acquired, lasted, he partially succeeded in stifling his remorse. But the success of the crime is too contrary to nature to continue long; his poor wife, whom, in spite of *her* extravagant, and *his* dissolute habits, he seemed really to love, fell ill, and died; on her deathbed she revealed the suspicions she had formed of his crime, and said, that those suspicions had preyed upon, and finally destroyed her health: this awoke him from the guilty torpor of his conscience. His share of the money, too, the greater part of which Thornton had bullied out of him, was gone. He fell, as Job had said, into despondency and gloom, and often spoke to Thornton so forcibly of his remorse, and so earnestly of his gnawing and restless desire to appease his mind, by surrendering himself to justice, that the fears of that villain grew, at length, so thoroughly alarmed, as to procure his removal to his present abode.

It was here that his real punishment commenced; closely confined to his apartment, at the remotest corner of the house, his solitude was never broken but by the short and hurried visits of his female gaoler, and (worse even than loneliness) the occasional invasions of Thornton. There appeared to be in that abandoned wretch what, for the honour of human nature is but rarely found, viz. a love of sin, not for its objects, but itself. With a malignity, doubly fiendish from its inutility, he forbade Dawson the only indulgence he craved—a light during the dark hours; and not only insulted him for his cowardice, but even added to his terrors, by threats of effectually silencing them.

These fears had so wildly worked upon the man's mind, that prison itself appeared to him an elysium to the hell he endured; and when his confession was ended, and* I said, "If you can be freed from this place, would you repeat before a magistrate all that you

---

4. A common practice with thieves, who fear the weak nerves of their accomplices. [B-L]

have now told me?" he started up in delight at the very thought. In truth, besides his remorse, and that inward and impelling voice which, in all the annals of murder, seems to urge the criminal onwards to the last expiation of his guilt—besides these, there mingled in his mind a sentiment of bitter, yet cowardly, vengeance, against his inhuman accomplice; and perhaps he found consolation for his own fate, in the hope of wreaking upon Thornton's head somewhat of the tortures that ruffian had inflicted upon him.

I had taken down in my book the heads of the confession, and I now hastened to Jonson, who, waiting without the door, had (as I had anticipated) heard all.

"You see," said I, "that, however satisfactory this recital has been, it contains no secondary or innate proofs to confirm it; the only evedince with which it could furnish us, would be the remnant of the broken knife, engraved with Thornton's name, but you have heard from Dawson's account, how impossible it would be in an extensive wood, for any one to discover the spot but himself. You will agree with me, therefore, that we must not leave this house without Dawson."

Job changed colour slightly.

"I see as clearly as you do," said he, "that it will be necessary for my annuity, and your friend's full acquittal, to procure Dawson's personal evidence, but it is late now; the men may be still drinking below; Bess may be still awake, and stirring; even if she sleeps, how could we pass her room without disturbing her? I own that I do not see a chance of effecting his escape to-night, without incurring the most probable peril of having our throats cut. Leave it, therefore, to me to procure his release as soon as possible—probably to-morrow, and let us now quietly retire, content with what we have yet got."

Hitherto I had implicitly obeyed Job; it was now *my* turn to command. "Look you," said I, calmly, but sternly, "I have come into this house under your guidance, solely to procure the evidence of that man; the evidence he has, as yet, given may not be worth a straw; and, since I have ventured among the knives of your associates, it shall be for some purpose. I tell you fairly that, whether you befriend or betray me, I will either leave these walls with Dawson, or remain in them a corpse."

"You are a bold blade, Sir," said Jonson, who seemed rather to respect than resent the determination of my tone, "and we will see what can be done: wait here, your honour, while I go down to see if the boys are gone to bed, and the coast is clear."

429

Job descended, and I re-entered Dawson's room. When I told him that we were resolved, if possible, to effect his escape, nothing could exceed his transport and gratitude; this was, indeed, expressed in so mean and servile a manner, mixed with so many petty threats of vengeance against Thornton, that I could scarcely conceal my disgust.

Jonson returned, and beckoned me out of the room.

"They are all in bed, Sir," said he—"Bess as well as the rest; indeed, the old girl has lushed so well at the bingo, that she sleeps as if her next morrow was the day of judgment. I have, also, seen that the street door is still unbarred, so that, upon the whole, we have, perhaps, as good a chance to-night as we may ever have again. All my fear is about that cowardly lubber. I have left both Bess's doors wide open, so we have nothing to do but creep through; as for me, I am an old file, and could steal my way through a sick man's room, like a sunbeam through a keyhole."

"Well," said I, in the same strain, "I am no elephant, and my dancing master used to tell me I might tread on a butterfly's wing without brushing off a tint: poor Coulon! he little thought of the use his lessons would be to me hereafter!—so let us be quick, Master Job."

"Stop," said Jonson; "I have yet a ceremony to perform with our caged bird. I must put a fresh gag on his mouth; for though, if he escapes, I must leave England, perhaps, for ever, for fear of the jolly boys, and, therefore, care not what he blabs about me; yet there are a few fine fellows amongst the club, whom I would not have hurt for the Indies; so I shall make Master Dawson take *our last oath*—the Devil himself would not break that, I think! Your honour will stay outside the door, for we can have no witness while it is administered.

Job then entered; I stood without;—in a few minutes I heard Dawson's voice in the accents of supplication. Soon after Job returned. "The craven dog won't take the oath," said he, "and may my right hand rot above ground before it shall turn key for him unless he does." But when Dawson saw that Job had left the room, and withdrawn the light, the conscience-stricken coward came to the door, and implored Job to return. "Will you swear then?" said Jonson; "I will, I will," was the answer.

Job then re-entered—minutes passed away—Job re-appeared, and Dawson was dressed, and clinging hold of him—"All's right!" said he to me, with a satisfied air.

The oath had been taken—what it was I know not—*but it was never broken.*[5]

Dawson and Job went first—I followed—we passed the passage, and came to the chamber of the sleeping Mrs. Brimstone. Job leant eagerly forward to listen, before we entered; he took hold of Dawson's arm, and beckoning to me to follow, stole, with a step that the blind mole would not have heard, across the room. Carefully did the practised thief veil the candle he carried, with his hand, as he now began to pass by the bed. I saw that Dawson trembled like a leaf, and the palpitation of his limbs made his step audible and heavy. Just as they had half-way passed the bed, I turned my look on Brimstone Bess, and observed, with a shuddering thrill, her eyes slowly open, and fix upon the forms of my companions. Dawson's gaze had been bent in the same direction, and when he met the full, glassy stare of the beldame's eyes, he uttered a faint scream. This completed our danger: had it not been for the exclamation, Bess might, in the uncertain vision of drowsiness, have passed over the third person, and fancied it was only myself and Jonson, in our way from Dawson's apartment; but no sooner had her ear caught the sound, than she started up, and sat erect on her bed, gazing at us in mingled wrath and astonishment.

That was a fearful moment—we stood rivetted to the spot! "Oh, my kiddies," cried Bess, at last finding speech, "you are in Queer-street, I trow! Plant your stumps, Master Guinea Pig; you are going to stall off the Daw's baby in prime twig, eh? But Bess stags you, my cove! Bess stags you."[6]

Jonson looked irresolute for one instant; but the next he had decided. "Run, run," cried he, "for your lives;" and he and Dawson (to whom, fear did indeed lend wings) were out of the room in an instant. I lost no time in following their example; but the vigilant and incensed hag was too quick for me; she pulled violently the bell, on which she had already placed her hand: the alarm rang like an echo in a cavern; below—around—far—near—from wall to wall—from chamber to chamber, the sound seemed multipled and repeated! and in the same breathing point of time, she sprang from her bed, and seized me, just as I had reached the door.

---

5. Those conversant with the annals of Newgate, well know how religiously the oaths of these fearful Freemasonries are kept. [B-L]

6. Halt, Master Guinea Pig; you are going to steal Dawson away, eh? But Bess sees you, my man, Bess sees you! [Bulwer's translation; 1840 ed.]

"On, on, on," cried Jonson's voice to Dawson, as they had already gained the passage, and left the whole room, and the staircase beyond, in utter darkness.

With a firm, muscular, nervous gripe, which almost shewed a masculine strength, the hag clung to my throat and breast; behind, among some of the numerous rooms in the passage we had left, I heard sounds, which told too plainly how rapidly the alarm had spread. A door opened—steps approached—my fate seemed fixed; but despair gave me energy: it was no time for the ceremonials due to the *beau sexe*. I dashed Bess to the ground, tore myself from her relaxing grasp, and fled down the steps with all the precipitation the darkness would allow. I gained the passage, at the far end of which hung the lamp, now weak and waning in its socket; which, it will be remembered, burnt close by the sick man's chamber that I had so unintentionally entered. A thought flashed upon my mind, and lent me new nerves and fresh speed; I flew along the passage, guided by the dying light. The staircase I had left, shook with the footsteps of my pursuers. I was at the door of the sick thief—I burst it open—seized the sword as it lay within reach on the chair, where Jonson had placed it, and feeling, at the touch of the familiar weapon, as if the might of ten men had been transferred to my single arm, I bounded down the stairs before me—passed the door at the bottom, which Dawson had fortunately left open—flung it back almost upon the face of my advancing enemies, and found myself in the long passage which led to the street-door, in safety, but in the thickest darkness. A light flashed from a door to the left; the door was that of the "Common Room" which we had first entered; it opened, and Spider-shanks, with one of his comrades, looked forth; the former holding the light. I darted by them, and, guided by their lamp, fled along the passage, and reached the door. Imagine my dismay! when, either through accident, or by the desire of my fugitive companions to impede pursuit, I found it unexpectedly closed.

The two villains had now come up to me, close at their heels were two more, probably my pursuers, from the upper apartments. Providentially the passage was (as I before said) extremely narrow, and as long as no fire-arms were used, nor a general rush resorted to, I had little doubt of being able to keep the ruffians at bay, until I had hit upon the method of springing the latch, and so winning my escape from the house.

While my left hand was employed in feeling the latch, I made such good use of my right, as to keep my antagonists at a safe distance. The one who was nearest to me, was Fib Fakescrew; he was armed with a weapon exactly similar to my own. The whole passage rung with oaths and threats. "Crash the cull—down with him—down with him, before he dubs the jigger. Tip him the degan, Fib, fake him through and through; if he pikes, we shall all be scragged."[7]

Hitherto, in the confusion, I had not been able to recall Job's instructions in opening the latch; at last I remembered, and pressed, the screw—the latch rose—I opened the door; but not wide enough to escape through the aperture. The ruffians saw my escape at hand, "Rush the b——— cove! rush him!" cried the loud voice of one behind; and at the word, Fib was thrown forwards upon the extended edge of my blade: scarcely with an effort of my own arm, the sword entered his bosom, and he fell at my feet bathed in blood; the motion which the men thought would prove my destruction, became my salvation; staggered by the fall of their companion, they gave way: I seized advantage of the momentary confusion—threw open the door, and, mindful of Job's admonition, *turned to the right,* and fled onwards, with a rapidity which baffled and mocked pursuit.

CHAPTER XX

Ille viam secat ad naves, sociosque revisit.
VIRGIL[1]

THE DAY HAD ALREADY DAWNED, BUT ALL WAS STILL and silent; my footsteps smote the solitary pavement with a strange and unanswered sound. Nevertheless, though all pursuit had long ceased, I still continued to run mechanically, till faint and breathless, I was forced into pausing.* I looked round, but could recognize nothing familiar in the narrow and filthy streets; even the names of them were to me like an unknown language. After a brief rest I

---

7. Kill the fellow, down with him before he opens the door. Stab him through and through; if he gets off, we shall all be hanged. [Bulwer's translation; 1840 ed.]

1. "He speeds along to the ships and revisits his comrades" (Virgil *Aeneid* 6.899).

renewed my wanderings, and at length came to an alley, called River Lane; the name did not deceive me, but brought me, after a short walk, to the Thames; there, to my inexpressible joy, I discovered a solitary boatman, and transported myself forthwith to the Whitehall-stairs.

Never, I ween, did gay gallant, in the decaying part of the season, arrive at those stairs for the sweet purpose of accompanying his own mistress, or another's wife, to green Richmond, or sunny Hampton, with more eager and animated delight than I felt at rejecting the arm of the rough boatman, and leaping on the well-known stones. I hastened to that stand of "jarvies" which has often been the hope and shelter of belated members of St. Stephen's, or bewetted fugitives from the Opera. I startled* a sleeping coachman, flung myself into his vehicle, and descended at Mivart's.

The drowsy porter surveyed, and told me to be gone; I had forgotten* my strange attire. "Pooh, my friend," said I, "may not Mr. Pelham go to a masquerade as well as his betters?" My voice and words undeceived my Cerberus, and I was admitted; I hastened to bed, and no sooner had I laid my head on my pillow, than I fell fast asleep. It must be confessed, that I had deserved "tired Nature's sweet restorer."[2]

I had not been above a couple of hours in the land of dreams, when I was awakened by some one grasping my arm; the events of the past night were so fresh in my memory, that I sprung up, as if the knife was at my throat—my eyes opened upon the peaceful countenance of Mr. Job Jonson.

"Thank Heaven, Sir, you are safe! I had but a very faint hope of finding you here when I came."

"Why," said I, rubbing my eyes, "it is very true that I am safe, honest Job: but, I believe, I have few thanks to give *you* for a circumstance so peculiarly agreeable to myself. It would have saved me much trouble, and your worthy friend, Mr. Fib Fakescrew, some pain, if you had left the door open instead of shutting me up with your *club,* as you are pleased to call it."

"Very true, Sir," said Job, "and I am extremely sorry at the accident; it was Dawson who shut the door, through utter unconsciousness, though I told him especially not to do it—the poor dog did not know whether he was on his head or his heels."

"You have got him safe," said I, quickly.

---

2. Edward Young, *Night Thoughts,* 1.1.

434

"Ay, trust me for that, your honour. I have locked him up at home while I came here to look for you."

"We will lose no time in transferring him to safer custody," said I, leaping out of bed; "but be off to ——— Street directly."

"Slow and sure, Sir," answered Jonson. "It is for you to do whatever you please, but my part of the business is over. I shall sleep at Dover to-night, and breakfast at Calais to-morrow. Perhaps it will not be very inconvenient to your honour to furnish me with my first quarter's annuity in advance, and to see that the rest is duly paid into Lafitte's, at Paris,[3] for the use of Captain Douglas.* Where I shall live hereafter is at present uncertain; but I dare say there will be few corners except old England and *new* England, in which I shall not make merry on your honour's bounty."

"Pooh! my good fellow," rejoined I, "never desert a country to which your talents do such credit; stay here, and reform on your annuity. If ever I can accomplish my own wishes, I will consult yours still farther; for I shall always think of your services with gratitude, though you *did* shut the door in my face."

"No, Sir," replied Job—"life is a blessing I would fain enjoy a few years longer; and, at present, my sojourn in England would put it woefully in danger of '*club law.*' Besides, I begin to think that a good character is a very agreeable thing, when not too troublesome: and, as I have none left in England, I may as well make the experiment abroad. If your honour will call at the magistrate's, and take a warrant and an officer, for the purpose of ridding me of my charge, at the very instant I see my responsibility at an end I will have the honour of bidding you adieu."

"Well, as you please," said I. "Curse your scoundrel's cosmetics! How the deuce am I ever to regain my natural complexion? Look ye, sirrah! you have painted me with a long wrinkle on the left side of my mouth, big enough to engulf all the beauty I ever had. Why, water seems to have no effect upon it!"

"To be sure not, Sir," said Job, calmly—"I should be but a poor dauber, if my paints washed off with a wet sponge."

"Grant me patience," cried I, in a real panic; "how, in the name of Heaven, *are* they to wash off? Am I, before I have reached my twenty-third year, to look like a methodist parson on the wrong side of forty, you rascal!"

"The latter question, your honour can best answer," returned Job.

---

3. Charles Lafitte, a Paris banker.

"With regard to the former, I have an unguent here, if you will suffer me to apply it, which will remove all other colours than those which nature has bestowed upon you."

With that, Job produced a small box; and, after a brief submission to his skill, I had the ineffable joy of beholding myself restored to my original state. Nevertheless, my delight was somewhat checked by the loss of my ringlets:* I thanked Heaven, however, that the damage had been sustained *after* Ellen's acceptation of my addresses. A lover confined to one, should not be too destructive, for fear of the consequences to the remainder of the female world: compassion is ever due to the fair sex.

My toilet being concluded, Jonson and I repaired to the magistrate's. He waited at the corner of the street, while I entered the house—

> "Twere vain to tell what shook the holy man,
> Who looked, not lovingly, at that divan."[4]

Having summoned to my aid the redoubted Mr. ———, of mulberry-cheeked recollection, we entered a hackney coach, and drove to Jonson's lodgings, Job mounting guard on the box.

"I think, Sir," said Mr. ———, looking up at the man of two virtues, "that I have had the pleasure of seeing that gentleman before."

"Very likely," said I; "he is a young man greatly about town."

When we had safely lodged Dawson (who seemed more collected, and even courageous, than I had expected) in the coach, Job beckoned me into a little parlour. I signed him a draught on my bankers for one hundred pounds—though at that time it was like letting the last drop from my veins—and faithfully promised, should Dawson's evidence procure the desired end, of which, indeed, there was no doubt), that the annuity should be regularly paid, as he desired. We then took an affectionate farewell of each other.

"Adieu, Sir!" said Job, "I depart into a new world—that of honest men!"

"If so," said I, "adieu indeed!—for on this earth we shall never meet again!"

We returned to ——— Street. As I was descending from the coach, a female, wrapped from head to foot in a cloak, came eagerly up to me, and seized me by the arm. "For God's sake," said she, in a low, hurried voice, "come aside, and speak to me for a single moment." Consigning Dawson to the sole charge of the officer, I did as I was

---

4. Unidentified.

436

desired. When we had gone some paces down the street, the female stopped. Though she held her veil closely drawn over her face, her voice and air were not to be mistaken: I knew her at once. "Glanville," said she, with great agitation, "Sir Reginald Glanville! tell me, is he in real danger?" She stopped short—she could say no more.

"I trust not!" said I, appearing not to recognize the speaker.

"I trust not!" she repeated; "is that all!" And then the passionate feelings of her sex overcoming every other consideration, she seized me by the hand, and said—"Oh, Mr. Pelham, for mercy's sake, tell me, is he in the power of that villain Thornton? You need disguise nothing from me; I know all the fatal history."

"Compose yourself, dear, dear Lady Roseville," said I, soothingly; "for it is in vain any longer to affect not to know you. Glanville *is* safe; I have brought with me a witness whose testimony *must* release him."

"God bless you, God bless you!" said Lady Roseville, and she burst into tears; but she dried them directly, and recovering some portion of that dignity which never long forsakes a woman of virtuous and educated mind, she resumed, proudly, yet bitterly—"It is no ordinary motive, no motive which you might reasonably impute to me, that has brought me here. Sir Reginald Glanville can never be any thing more to me than a friend—but, of all friends, the most known and valued. I learned from his servant of his disappearance; and my acquaintance with his secret history enabled me to account for it in the most fearful manner. In short, I—I—but explanations are idle now; you will never say that you have seen me here, Mr. Pelham: you will endeavour even to forget it—farewell."

Lady Roseville, then drawing her cloak closely round her, left me with a fleet and light step, and turning the corner of the street, disappeared.

I returned to my charge: I demanded an immediate interview with the magistrate. "I have come," said I, "to redeem my pledge, and procure the acquittal of the innocent." I then briefly related my adventures, only concealing (according to my promise) all description of my help-mate, Job; and prepared the worthy magistrate for the confession and testimony of Dawson. That unhappy man had just concluded his narration, when an officer entered, and whispered the magistrate that Thornton was in waiting.

"Admit him," said Mr. ———, aloud. Thornton entered with his usual easy and staggering air of effrontery: but no sooner did he set his eyes upon Dawson, than a deadly and withering change passed

437

over his countenance. Dawson could not bridle the cowardly petulance of his spite—"They know all, Thornton!" said he, with a look of triumph. The villain turned slowly from him to us, muttering something we could not hear. He saw upon my face, upon the magistrate's, that his doom was sealed: his desperation gave him presence of mind, and he made a sudden rush to the door; the officers in waiting seized him. Why should I detail the rest of the scene? He was that day fully committed for trial, and Sir Reginald Glanville honourably released, and unhesitatingly acquitted.

CHAPTER XXI

Un hymen qu'on souhaite
Entre les gens comme nous est chose bientôt faite,
Je te veux; me veux-tu de même?
                                                MOLIÈRE[1]
So may he rest, his faults lie gently on him.
                                                SHAKSPEARE

THE MAIN INTEREST OF MY ADVENTURES—IF, INDEED, I may flatter myself that they ever contained any—is now over; the mystery is explained, the innocent acquitted, and the guilty condemned. Moreover, all obstacles between the marriage of the unworthy hero, with the peerless heroine, being removed, it would be but an idle prolixity to linger over the preliminary details of an orthodox and customary courtship. Nor is it for me to dilate upon the exaggerated expressions of gratitude, in which the affectionate heart of Glanville found vent for my fortunate exertions on his behalf. He was not willing that any praise to which I might be entitled for them, should be lost. He narrated to Lady Glanville and Ellen my adventures with the comrades of the worthy Job; from the lips of the mother, and the eyes of the dear sister, came my sweetest addition to the good fortune which had made me the instrument of

---

1. "When people like us want to get married the thing is soon done. I will have you; will you have me?" (Molière, *Le Dépit amoureux*, I, 2). The second epigraph is from *Henry VIII*, IV, 2, 31.

Glanville's safety and acquittal. I was not condemned to a long protraction of that time, which, if it be justly termed the happiest of our lives, *we,* (viz. all true lovers), through that perversity common to human nature, most ardently wish to terminate.

On that day month which saw Glanville's release, my bridals were appointed. Reginald was even more eager than myself in pressing for an early day: firmly persuaded that his end was rapidly approaching, his most prevailing desire was to witness our union. This wish, and the interest he took in our happiness, gave him an energy and animation which impressed us with the deepest hopes for his ultimate recovery; and the fatal disease to which he was a prey, nursed the fondness of our hearts by the bloom of cheek, and brightness of eye, with which it veiled its desolating and gathering progress.

From the eventful day on which I had seen Lady Roseville, in ——— Street, we had not met. She had shut herself up in her splendid home, and the newspapers teemed with regret at the reported illness and certain seclusion of one, whose *fêtes* and gaieties had furnished them with their brightest pages. The only one admitted to her was Ellen. To her, she had for some time made no secret of her attachment—and of her the daily news of Sir Reginald's health was ascertained. Several times, when at a late hour I left Glanville's apartments, I passed the figure of a woman, closely muffled, and apparently watching before his windows—which, owing to the advance of summer, were never closed—to catch, perhaps, a view of his room, or a passing glimpse of his emaciated and fading figure. If that sad and lonely vigil was kept by her whom I suspected, deep, indeed, and mighty was the love, which could so humble the heart, and possess the spirit, of the haughty and high-born Countess of Roseville.

I turn to a very different personage in this *véritable histoire.* My father and mother were absent, at Lady H.'s, when my marriage was fixed; to both of them I wrote for their approbation of my choice. From Lady Frances I received the answer which I subjoin:—

"MY DEAREST SON,

"Your father desires me to add his congratulations to mine, upon the election you have made. I shall hasten to London, to be present at the ceremony. Although you must not be offended with me, if I say, that with your person, accomplishments, birth, and (above all) high *ton,* you might have chosen among the loftiest and wealthiest families in the country; yet I am by no means displeased or disappointed with your future wife. To say nothing of the antiquity of

439

her name, (the Glanvilles intermarried with the Pelhams, in the reign of Henry II) it is a great step to future distinction to marry a beauty, especially one so celebrated as Miss Glanville—perhaps it is among the surest ways to the cabinet. The forty thousand pounds which you say Miss Glanville is to receive, make, to be sure, but a slender income; though, when added to your own fortune,* that sum in ready money would have been a great addition to the Glenmorris property, if your uncle—I have no patience with him—had not married again.

"However, you will lose no time in getting into the House—at all events, the capital will ensure your return for a borough, and maintain you comfortably, till you are in the administration; when of course it matters very little what your fortune may be—tradesmen will be too happy to have your name in their books; be sure, therefore, that the money is not tied up. Miss Glanville must see that her own interest, as well as yours, is concerned in your having the unfettered disposal of a fortune, which if restricted, you would find it impossible to live upon. Pray, how is Sir Reginald Glanville? Is his cough as bad as ever? He has no entailed property, I think?*

"Will you order Stonor to have the house ready for us on Friday, when I shall return home in time for dinner? Let me again congratulate you, most sincerely, on your choice. I always thought you had more common sense, as well as genius, than any young man I ever knew: you have shown it in this important step. Domestic happiness, my dearest Henry, ought to be peculiarly sought for by every Englishman, however elevated his station; and when I reflect upon Miss Glanville's qualifications, and her celebrity as a beauty,* I have no doubt of your possessing the felicity you deserve. But be sure that the fortune is not settled away from you; poor Sir Reginald is not (I believe) at all covetous or worldly, and will not, therefore, insist upon the point.

"God bless you, and grant you every happiness.
"Ever, my dear Henry,
"Your very affectionate Mother,
"F. PELHAM."

"P.S. I think it will be better to give out that Miss Glanville has eighty thousand pounds. Be sure, therefore, that you do not contradict me."

The days, the weeks flew away. Ah, happy days! yet, I do not regret while I recal you! He that loves much, fears even in his best founded hopes. What were the anxious longings for a treasure—in my view only, not in my possession—to the deep joy of finding it for ever my own!

The day arrived—I was yet at my toilet, and Bedos, in the greatest confusion (poor fellow, he was as happy as myself), when a letter was brought me, stamped with the foreign post-mark. It was from the exemplary Job Jonson; and though I did not even open it on that day, yet it shall be more favoured by the reader—viz, if he will not pass over, without reading, the following effusion.

"Rue des Moulins, No.—, Paris.

"HONOURED SIR,

"I arrived in Paris safely, and reading in the English papers the full success of our enterprise, as well as in the Morning Post of the ——th, your approaching marriage with Miss Glanville, I cannot refrain from the liberty of congratulating you upon both, as well as of reminding you of the exact day on which the first quarter of my annuity will be paid*—it is the ——— of ———; for, I presume, your honour kindly made me a present of the draught of one hundred pounds, in order to pay my traveling expenses.

"I find that the boys are greatly incensed against me; but as Dawson was too much bound by his oath, to betray a tittle against them, I trust I shall, ultimately, pacify the club, and return to England. A true patriot, Sir, never loves to leave his native country. Even were I compelled to visit Van Diemen's Land, the ties of birth-place would be so strong as to induce me to seize the first opportunity of returning. I am not, your honour, very fond of the French—they are an idle, frivolous, penurious, *poor* nation. Only think, Sir, the other day I saw a gentleman of the most noble air secrete something at a *café,* which I could not clearly discern; as he wrapped it carefully in paper, before he placed it in his pocket. I judged that it was a silver cream ewer, at least; accordingly, I followed him out, and from pure curiosity—I do assure your honour, it was from no other motive —I transferred this purloined treasure to my own pocket. You will imagine, Sir, the interest with which I hastened to a lonely spot in the Tuileries, and carefully taking out the little packet, unfolded paper by paper, till I came—yes, Sir, till I came to—*five lumps of sugar!* Oh, the French are a mean people—a very mean people—I hope I shall soon be able to return to England. Meanwhile, I am going into Holland, to see how those rich burghers spend their time and their money. I suppose poor Dawson, as well as the rascal Thorn-

441

ton, will be hung before you receive this—they deserve it richly—it is such fellows who disgrace the profession. He is but a very poor bungler who is forced to cut throats as well as pockets. And now, your honour, wishing you all happiness with your lady,

"I beg to remain,

"Your very obedient humble Servant,

"FERDINAND DOUGLAS,* &c. &c."

Struck with the joyous countenance of my honest valet, as I took my gloves and hat from his hand, I could not help wishing to bestow upon him a blessing similar to that I was about to possess. "Bedos," said I, "Bedos, my good fellow, you left your wife to come to me; you shall not suffer by your fidelity: send for her—we will find room for her in our future establishment."

The smiling face of the Frenchman underwent a rapid change. *"Ma foi,"* said he, in his own tongue; "Monsieur is too good. An excess of happiness hardens the heart; and so, for fear of forgetting my gratitude to Providence, I will, with Monsieur's permission, suffer my adored wife to remain where she is."

After so pious a reply, I should have been worse than wicked had I pressed the matter any farther.

I found all ready at Berkeley-square. Lady Glanville is one of those good persons, who think a marriage out of church is no marriage at all; to church, therefore, we went. Although Sir Reginald was now so reduced that he could scarcely support the least fatigue, he insisted on giving Ellen away. He was that morning, and had been, for the last two or three days, considerably better, and our happiness seemed to grow less selfish in our increasing hope of his recovery.

When we returned from church, our intention was to set off immediately to ——— Hall, a seat which I had hired for our reception. On re-entering the house, Glanville called me aside—I followed his infirm and tremulous steps into a private apartment.

"Pelham," said he, "we shall never meet again! No matter—*you* are now happy, and I shall shortly be so. But there is one office I have yet to request from your friendship; when I am dead, let me be buried by *her* side, and let one tombstone cover both."

I pressed his hand, and, with tears in my eyes, made him the promise he required.

"It is enough," said he; "I have no farther business with life. God bless you, my friend—my brother; do not let a thought of me cloud your happiness."

442

He rose, and we turned to quit the room; Glanville was leaning on my arm; when we had moved a few paces towards the door, he stopped abruptly. Imagining that the pause proceeded from pain or debility, I turned my eyes upon his countenance—a fearful and convulsive change was rapidly passing over it—his eyes stared wildly upon vacancy.

"Merciful God—is it—can it be?" he said, in a low, inward tone.

Before I could speak, I felt his hand* relax its grasp upon my arm—he fell upon the floor—I raised him—a smile of ineffable serenity and peace was upon his lips; his face was as the face of an angel, but the spirit had passed away!

CHAPTER XXII

Now haveth good day, good men all,
Haveth good day, young and old;
Haveth good day, both great and small,
And graunt merci a thousand fold!
Gif ever I might full fain I wold,
Do nought that were unto your leve,
Christ keep you out of cares cold,
For now 'tis time to take my leave.

Old Song[1]

SEVERAL MONTHS HAVE NOW ELAPSED SINCE MY marriage. I am living quietly in the country, among my books, and looking forward with calmness, rather than impatience, to the time which shall again bring me before the world. Marriage with me is not that sepulchre of all human hope and energy which it often is with others. I am not more partial to my arm chair, nor more averse to shaving, than of yore. I do not bound my prospects to the dinner-hour, nor my projects to "migrations from the blue bed to the brown."[2] Matrimony found me ambitious; it has not cured me of the passion: but it has concentrated what was scattered, and determined what

1. Anonymous.
2. Goldsmith, *The Vicar of Wakefield,* chapter 1.

was vague. If I am less anxious than formerly for the reputation to be acquired in society, I am more eager for honour in the world; and instead of amusing my enemies, and the saloon, I trust yet to be useful to my friends and to mankind.

Whether this is a hope, altogether vain and idle; whether I have, in the self-conceit common to all men, (thou wilt perchance add, peculiarly prominent in myself),* overrated both the power and the integrity of my mind (for the one is bootless without the other), neither I nor the world can yet tell. "Time," says one of the fathers, "is the only touchstone which distinguishes the prophet from the boaster."³

Meanwhile, gentle reader, during the two years which I purpose devoting to solitude and study, I shall not be so occupied with my fields and folios, as to become uncourteous to thee. If ever thou hast known me in the city, I give thee a hearty invitation to come and visit me in the country. I promise thee, that my wines and viands shall not disgrace the companion of Guloseton; nor my conversation be much duller than my book. I will compliment thee on thy horses, thou shalt congratulate me upon my wife. Over old wine we will talk over new events; and if we flag at the latter, why, we will make ourselves amends with the former. In short, if thou art neither very silly nor very wise, it shall be thine own fault if we are not excellent friends.

I feel that it would be but poor courtesy in me, after having kept company with Lord Vincent, through the tedious journey of three volumes,* to dismiss him now without one word of valediction. May he, in the political course he has adopted, find all the admiration which his talents deserve; and if ever we meet as foes, let our heaviest weapon be a quotation, and our bitterest vengeance a jest.

Lord Guloseton regularly corresponds with me, and his last letter contained a promise to visit me in the course of the month, in order to recover his appetite (which has been much relaxed of late) by the country air.

My uncle wrote to me, three weeks since, announcing the death of the infant Lady Glenmorris had brought him. Sincerely do I wish that his loss may be supplied. I have already sufficient fortune for my wants, and sufficient *hope* for my desires.

Thornton died as he had lived—the reprobate and the ruffian. "Pooh," said he, in his quaint brutality, to the worthy clergyman, who

---

3. Unidentified.

attended his last moments with more zeal than success; "Pooh, what's the difference between gospel and go—spell? we agree like a bell and its clapper—you're prating while I'm *hanging*."

Dawson died in prison, penitent and in peace. Cowardice, which spoils the honest man, often ameliorates* the knave.

From Lord Dawton I have received a letter, requesting me to accept a borough (in his gift), just vacated. It is a pity that generosity—such a prodigal to those who do not want it—should often be such a niggard to those who do. I need not specify my answer. One may as well be free as dependant, when *one can afford it;* and* I hope yet to teach Lord Dawton, that to forgive the minister is not to forget the affront. Meanwhile, I am content to bury myself in my retreat with my mute teachers of logic and legislature, in order, hereafter, to justify his lordship's good opinion of my senatorial* abilities. Farewell, Brutus, we shall meet at Philippi![4]

It is some months since Lady Roseville left England; the last news we received of her, informed us, that she was living in Sienna, in utter seclusion, and very infirm health.

> "The day drags thro', though storms keep out the sun,
> And thus the heart will break, yet brokenly live on."[5]

Poor Lady Glanville! the mother of one so beautiful, so gifted, and so lost. What can I say of her which "you, and you, and you ——" all who are parents, cannot feel, a thousand times more acutely, in those recesses of the heart too deep for words or tears.[6] There are yet many hours in which I find the sister of the departed in grief that even her husband cannot console; and I —— *I* —— my friend, my brother, have I forgotten thee in death? I lay down the pen, I turn from my employment—thy dog is at my feet, and looking at me, as if conscious of my thoughts, with an eye almost as tearful as my own.

But it is not thus that I will part from my Reader; our greeting was not in sorrow, neither shall be our adieux. For thee, who hast gone with me through the motley course of my confessions, I would fain trust that I have sometimes hinted at thy instruction when only appearing to strive for thy amusement. But on this I will not dwell; for the moral *insisted upon* often loses its effect, and all that I will venture to hope is, that I have opened to thee one true, and not utterly hacknied, page in the various and mighty volume of mankind. In this

---

4. *Julius Caesar*, IV, 3.

5. *Childe Harold's Pilgrimage*, canto 3, line 289.

6. Wordsworth, "Ode: Intimations of Immortality," lines 203–4.

445

busy and restless world I have not been a vague speculator, nor an idle actor. While all around me were vigilant, I have not laid me down to sleep—even for the luxury of a poet's dream. Like the school boy, I have considered study *as* study, but action as delight.

Nevertheless, whatever I have seen, or heard, or felt, has been treasured in my memory, and brooded over by my thoughts. I now place the result before you,

"Sicut meus est mos,
Nescio quid meditans nugarum; totus in illis."[7]*

Whatever society—whether in a higher or lower grade—I have portrayed, my sketches have been taken rather as a witness than a copyist; for I have never shunned that circle, nor that individual, which presented life in a fresh view, or a man in a new relation. It is right, however, that I should add, that as I have not wished to be an individual satirist, rather than a general observer, I have occasionally, in the subordinate characters (such as Russelton and Gordon), taken only the outline from truth, and filled up the colours at my leisure and my will.[8]

With regard to myself I have been more candid. I have not only shewn—*non parcâ manu*[9]—my faults, but (grant that this is a much rarer exposure) my *foibles;* and, in my anxiety for your entertainment, I have not grudged you the pleasure of a laugh—even at my own expense. Forgive me, then, if I am not a fashionable hero—forgive me if I have not wept over a *"blighted spirit,"* nor boasted of a *"British heart;"* and allow that a man who, in these days of alternate Werters

---

7. "Meditating on some trifle or other, as is my habit, and totally absorbed in it" (Horace *Carmen* 1.9.2).

8. May the Author as well as the Hero, be permitted upon this point to solicit attention and belief. In all the lesser characters, of which the *first* idea was taken from life, especially those referred to in the text, he has, for reasons perhaps obvious enough without the tedium of recital, *purposely* introduced sufficient variation and addition to remove, in his opinion, the odium either of a copy or of a caricature. The Author thinks it the more necessary *in the present* edition to insist upon this, with all honest and sincere earnestness, because *in the first* it was too much the custom of criticism to judge of his sketches from a resemblance to some supposed originals, and not from adherence to that sole source of all legitimate imitation—Nature;—Nature as exhibited in the general mass, not in the isolated instance. It is the duty of the Novelist rather to abstract than to copy:—all humours—all individual peculiarities are his appropriate and fair materials: not so are the *humourist* and the *individual!* Observation should resemble the eastern bird, and while it nourishes itself upon the suction of a *thousand* flowers, never be seen to settle upon *one!* [B-L]

9. "With no unsparing hand" (Horace *Carmen* 3.16.44).

and Worthies, is neither the one nor the other, is, at least, a novelty in print, though, I fear, common enough in life.

And now, my kind reader, having remembered the proverb, and, in saying one word to thee, having said two for myself, I will no longer detain thee. Whatever thou mayest think of me and my thousand faults, both as an author and a man, believe me it is with a sincere and affectionate wish for the accomplishment of my parting words, that I bid thee—*farewell*.

THE END

APPENDIX A

Preface to the Edition of 1840[1]

The holiday time of life, in which this novel was written, while accounting, perhaps in a certain gayety of tone, for the popularity it has received, may perhaps also excuse, in some measure, its more evident deficiences and faults. Although I trust the time has passed when it might seem necessary to protest against those critical assumptions which so long confounded the author with the hero; although I equally trust that, even were such assumptions true, it would be scarcely necessary to dispute the justice of visiting upon later and more sobered life the supposed foibles and levities of that thoughtless age of eighteen in which this fiction was first begun,—yet, perhaps, some short sketch of the origin of a work, however idle, the success of which determined the literary career of the author, may not be considered altogether presumptuous or irrelevant.*

While, yet, then a boy in years, but with some experience of the world, which I entered prematurely, I had the good fortune to be confined to my room by a severe illness, towards the end of a London season. All my friends were out of town, and I was left to such resources as solitude can suggest to the tedium of sickness. I amused myelf by writing with incredible difficulty and labor (for till then prose was a country almost as unknown to myself as to Monsieur Jourdain) some half a dozen tales and sketches. Among them was a story called "Mortimer, or the Memoirs of a Gentleman."[2] Its commencement was almost word for word the same as that of "Pelham"; but the design was exactly opposite to that of the latter and later work. "Mortimer" was intended to show the manner in which the world deteriorates its votary, and "Pelham," on the contrary, conveys the newer, and I believe, sounder moral, of showing how a man of sense can subject the usages of the world to himself instead of being conquered by them, and gradually grow wise by the very foibles of his youth.

This tale, with the sketches written at the same period, was sent anonymously to a celebrated publisher, who considered the volume of too slight a nature for separate publication, and recommended me to select the best of the papers for a magazine. I was not at that time much inclined to a periodical

---

1. Viz., in the first collected edition of the Author's prose works. [B-L]

2. "Mortimer" was reprinted in the 1835 edition of *Pelham*.

449

mode of publishing, and thought no more of what, if *nugae*[3] to the reader, had indeed been *difficiles* to the author. Soon afterwards I went abroad. On my return I sent a collection of letters to Mr. Colburn for publication, which, for various reasons, I afterwards worked up into a fiction, and which (greatly altered from their original form) are now known to the public under the name of "Falkland."

While correcting the sheets of that tale for the press, I was made aware of many of its faults. But it was not till it had been fairly before the public that I was sensible of its greatest, namely, a sombre coloring of life; and the indulgence of a vein of sentiment which, though common enough to all very young minds in their first bitter experience of the disappointments of the world, had certainly ceased to be new in its expression, and had never been true in its philosophy.

The effect which the composition of that work produced upon my mind was exactly similar to that which (if I may reverently quote so illustrious an example) Goethe informs us the writing of "Werter" produced upon his own. I had rid my bosom of its "perilous stuff"; I had confessed my sins, and was absolved; I could return to real life and its wholesome objects. Encouraged by the reception which "Falkland" met with, flattering though not brilliant, I resolved to undertake a new and more important fiction. I had long been impressed with the truth of an observation of Madame de Staël, that a character at once gay and sentimental is always successful on the stage. I resolved to attempt a similar character for a novel, making the sentiment, however, infinitely less prominent than the gayety. My boyish attempt at the "Memoirs of a Gentleman" occurred to me, and I resolved upon this foundation to build my fiction. After a little consideration I determined, however, to enlarge and ennoble the original character: the character itself, of the clever man of the world corrupted *by* the world, was not new; it had already been represented by Mackenzie, by Moore in "Zeluco," and in some measure by the master-genius of Richardson itself, in the incomparable portraiture of Lovelace. The moral to be derived from such a creation seemed to me also equivocal and dubious. It is a moral of a gloomy and hopeless school. We live *in* the world; the great majority of us, in a state of civilization, must, more or less, *be* men *of* the world. It struck me that it would be a new, an useful, and perhaps a happy, moral, to show in what manner we might redeem and brighten the commonplaces of life; to prove (what is really the fact) that the lessons of society do not necessarily corrupt, and that we may be both men of the world, and even, to a certain degree, men of pleasure, and yet be something wiser—nobler—better. With this idea I formed in my mind the character of Pelham; revolving its qualities long and seriously before I attempted to describe them on paper. For the formation of my story I studied with no slight attention the

---

3. *Nugae,* trifles; *difficiles,* difficult. [B-L]

great works of my predecessors, and attempted to derive from that study certain rules and canons to serve me a guide; and if some of my younger contemporaries whom I could name would only condescend to take the same preliminary pains that I did, I am sure that the result would be much more brilliant. It often happens to me to be consulted by persons about to attempt fiction, and I invariably find that they imagine they have only to sit down and write. They forget that art does not come by inspiration, and that the novelist, dealing constantly with contrast and effect, must, in the widest and deepest sense of the word, study to be an *artist*. They paint pictures for Posterity without having learned to draw.

Few critics have, hitherto, sufficiently considered, and none, perhaps, have accurately defined, the peculiar characteristics of prose fiction in its distinct schools and multiform varieties: of the two principal species, the Narrative and Dramatic, I chose for "Pelham" my models in the former; and when it was objected, at the first appearance of that work, that the plot was not carried on through every incident and every scene, the critics evidently confounded the two classes of fiction I have referred to, and asked from a work in one what ought only to be the attributes of a work in the other; the dazzling celebrity of Scott, who deals almost solely with the dramatic species of fiction, made them forgetful of the examples, equally illustrious, in the narrative form of romance, to be found in Smollett, in Fielding, and Le Sage. Perhaps, indeed, there is in "Pelham" more of plot and of continued interest, and less of those incidents that do not either bring out the character of the hero, or conduce to the catastrophe, than the narrative order may be said to require, or than is warranted by the great examples I have ventured to name.

After due preparation, I commenced and finished the first volume of "Pelham." Various circumstances then suspended my labors, till several months afterwards I found myself quietly buried in the country, and with so much leisure on my hands that I was driven, almost in self-defence from *ennui,* to continue and conclude my attempt.

It may serve perhaps to stimulate the courage and sustain the hopes of others to remark that "the Reader" to whom the MS was submitted by the publisher, pronounced the most unfavorable and damning opinion upon its chances of success,—an opinion fortunately reversed by Mr. Ollier, the able and ingenious author of "Inesilla," to whom it was then referred. The book was published, and I may add, that for about two months it appeared in a fair way of perishing prematurely in its cradle. With the exception of two most flattering and generously indulgent notices in the *Literary Gazette* and the *Examiner* and a very encouraging and friendly criticism in the *Atlas,* it was received by the critics with indifference or abuse. They mistook its purport, and translated its satire literally. But about the third month it rose rapidly into the favor it has since continued to maintain. Whether it answered all the objects it attempted I cannot pretend to say; one at least

451

I imagine that it did answer: I think, above most works it contributed to put an end to the Satanic mania,—to turn the thoughts and ambition of young gentlemen without neckcloths, and young clerks who were sallow, from playing the Corsair, and boasting that they were villains. If, mistaking the irony of Pelham, they went to the extreme of emulating the foibles which that hero attributes to himself, those were foibles at least more harmless, and even more manly and noble, than the conceit of a general detestation of mankind, or the vanity of storming our pity by lamentations over imaginary sorrows, and sombre hints at the fatal burthen of inexpiable crimes.[4]

Such was the history of a publication which, if not actually my first, was the one whose fate was always intended to decide me whether to conclude or continue my attempts as an author.

I can repeat, unaffectedly, that I have indulged this egotism, not only as a gratification to that common curiosity which is felt by all relative to the early works of an author, who, whatever be his faults and demerits, has once obtained the popular ear; but also as affording, perhaps, the following lessons to younger writers of less experience, but of more genius, than myself. First, in attempting fiction, it may serve to show the use of a critical study of its rules, for to that study I owe every success in literature I have obtained; and in the mere art of composition, if I have now attained to even too rapid a facility, I must own that that facility has been purchased by a most laborious slowness in the first commencement, and a resolute refusal to write a second sentence until I had expressed my meaning in the best manner I could in the first. And, secondly, it may prove the very little value of those "cheers," of the want of which Sir Egerton Brydges[5] so feelingly complains, and which he considers so necessary towards the obtaining for an author, no matter what his talents, his proper share of popularity. I knew not a single critic, and scarcely a single author, when I began to write. I have never received to this day a single word of encouragement from any of those writers who were considered at one time the dispensers of reputation. Long after my name was not quite unknown in every other country where English literature is received, the great quarterly journals of my own disdained to recognize my existence. Let no man cry out then "for cheers," or for literary patronage, and let those aspirants, who are often now pleased to write to me lamenting their want of interest and their non-acquaintance with critics, learn from the author (insignificant though he be) who addresses them in sympathy and fellowship, that a man's labors are his best patrons; that the public is the only critic that has no interest and no motive in underrating him; that the world of an author is a mighty

---

4. Sir Reginald Glanville was drawn purposely of the would-be Byron School as a foil to Pelham. For one who would think of imitating the first, then a thousand would be unawares attracted to the last. [B-L]

5. In the melancholy and painful pages of his autobiography. [B-L]

circle, of which enmity and envy can penerate but a petty segment, and that the pride of carving with our hands our own name is worth all the "cheers" in the world. Long live Sidney's gallant and lofty motto, "Aut viam inveniam aut faciam!"[6]

---

6. I will either find a way or make it. [B-L]

APPENDIX B

Advertisement to Edition of 1849

No!—you cannot guess, my dear reader how long my pen has rested over the virgin surface of this paper, before even that "No," which now stands out so fluffly and manfully, took heart and stept forth. If, peradventure, thou shouldst, O reader, be that rarity in these days—a reader who has never been an author—thou canst form no conception of the strange aspect which the first page of a premeditated composition will often present to the curious investigator into the initials of things. There is a sad mania nowadays for collecting autographs—would that some such collector would devote his researches to the first pages of auctorial manuscripts! He would then form some idea of the felicitous significance of that idiomatic phrase, "to cudgel the brains!" Out of what grotesque zig-zags, and fantastic arabesques; out of what irrelevant, dreamy illustrations from the sister art,—houses and trees, and profile sketches of men, nightmares, and chimeras; out of what massacres of whole lines, prematurely and timidly ventured forth as forlorn hopes,— would he see the first intelligible words creep into actual life—shy streaks of light, emerging from the chaos! For that rash promise of mine that each work in this edition of works so numerous, shall have its own new and special Preface, seems to me hard, in this instance, to fulfill. Another Preface! What for? Two Prefaces to "Pelham" already exist, wherein all that I would say is said! And in going back through that long and crowded interval of twenty years since the first appearance of this work, what shadows rise to beckon me away through the glades and alleys in that dim labyrinth of the Past! Infant Hopes, scarce born ere fated, poor innocents, to die—gazing upon me with reproachful eyes, as if I myself had been their unfeeling butcher; audacious Enterprises boldly begun, to cease in abrupt whim or chilling doubt—looking now through the mists, zoophital or amphibious, like those borderers on the animal and vegetable life, which flash on us with the seeming flutter of a wing, to subside away into rooted stems and withering leaves. How can I escape the phantom throng? How return to the starting post, and recall the ardent emotions with which youth sprang forth to the goal? To write fitting Preface to this work, which if not my first, was the first which won an audience and secured a reader, I must myself become a

454

phantom, with the phantom crowd. It is the ghost of my youth that I must call up. What we are alone hath flesh and blood—what we have been, like what we shall be, is an idea; and no more! An idea how dim and impalpable! This our sense of identity, this "I" of ours, which is the single thread that continues from first to last—single thread that binds flowers changed every day, and withered every night—how thin and meagre is it of itself! How difficult to lay hold of! When we say "I remember," how vague a sentiment we utter! How different it is to say, "I *feel!*" And when in this effort of memory we travel back all the shadowland of years—when we say "I remember," what is it we retain but some poor solitary fibre in the airy mesh of that old gossamer, which floated between earth and heaven, moist with the dews and sparkling in the dawn? Some one incident, some one affection we recall, but not all the associations that surrounded it, all the companions of the brain or the heart, with which it formed one of harmonious contemporaneous ring. Scarcely even have we traced and seized one fine filament in the broken web ere it is lost again. In the inextricable confusion of old ideas, many that seem of the time we seek to grasp again, but were not so, seize and distract us. From the clear effort we sink into the vague revery; the Present hastens to recall and dash us onward, and few, leaving the actual world around them when they say "I remember," do not wake as from a dream, with a baffled sigh, and murmur "No, I forget." And therefore, if a new Preface to a work written twenty years ago, should contain some elucidation of the aims and objects with which it was composed, or convey some idea of the writer's mind at that time, my pen might well rest long over the blank page; and houses and trees, and profile sketches of men, nightmares and chimeras, and whole passages scrawled and erased, might well illustrate the barren travail of one who sits down to say "I remember!"

What changes in the outer world since this book was written. What changes of thrones and dynasties! Through what cycles of hope and fear has a generation gone! And in that inner world of Thought what old ideas have returned to claim the royalty of new ones! What new ones (new ones then) have receded out of sight, in the ebb and flow of the human mind, which, whatever the cant phrase may imply, advances in no direct steadfast progress, but gains here to lose there—a tide, not a march. So, too, in that slight surface of either world, "the manners," superficies alike of the action and the thought of an age, the ploughshares of twenty years have turned up a new soil.

The popular changes in the Constitution have brought the several classes more intimately into connection with each other; most of the old affectations of fashion and exclusiveness are out of date. We have not talked of equality, like our neighbors, the French, but, insensibly and naturally, the tone of manners has admitted much of the frankness of the principle, without the unnecessary rudeness of the pretence. I am not old enough yet to be among the indiscriminate praisers of the past, and therefore I recognize cheerfully an extraordinary improvement in the intellectual and moral features of the English world, since I first entered it as an observer. There is a far greater earnestness of purpose, a higher culture, more generous and genial views, amongst the young men of the rising generation than were common in the last. The old divisions of party politics remain; but among all divisions there is greater desire of identification with the people. Rank is more sensible of its responsibilities, Property of its duties. Amongst the clergy of all sects the improvement in zeal, in education, in active care for their flocks is strikingly noticeable; the middle class have become more instructed and refined, and yet (while fused with the highest in their intellectual tendencies, reading the same books, cultivating the same accomplishments) they have extended their sympathies more largely among the humblest. And, in our towns especially, what advances have been made amongst the operative population! I do not here refer to that branch of cultivation which comprises the questions that belong to political inquiry, but to the general growth of more refined and less polemical knowledge. Cheap books have come in vogue as a fashion during the last twenty years—books addressed, not as cheap books were once, to the passions, but to the understanding and the taste—books not written down to the supposed level of uninformed and humble readers, but such books as refine the gentleman and instruct the scholar. The arts of design have been more appreciated—the Beautiful has been admitted into the pursuits of labor as a principle—Religion has been regaining the ground it lost in the latter half of the last century. What is technically called education (education of the school and the schoolmaster), has made less progress than it might. But that inexpressible diffusion of *oral* information which is the only culture the old Athenians knew, and which, in the ready transmission of ideas, travels like light from lip to lip, has been insensibly educating the adult generation. In spite of all the dangers that menace the advance of the present century, I am convinced that classes amongst us are far more united than they were in the latter years of George the Fourth. A vast mass of discontent exists amongst the operatives, it is true, and Chartism is but one of its symptoms; yet that that discontent is more obvious than formerly is a proof that men's eyes and men's ears are more open to acknowledge its existence—to examine and listen to its causes. Thinking persons now occupy themselves with that great reality—the People; and questions concerning their social welfare, their health, their education, their interests, their rights, which philosophers alone entertained twenty years ago, are now on the lips of practical men and in the hearts of all. It is this greater earnestness, this profounder gravity of purpose and of view, which forms the most cheering characteristic of the present time; and though that time has its peculiar faults and vices, this is not the place to enlarge on them. I have done, and may yet do so, elsewhere. This work is the picture of manners in certain classes of society twenty years ago, and in that respect I believe it to be true and faithful.

Nor the less so, that under the frivolities of the hero it is easy to recognize the substance of those more serious and solid qualities which Time has educed from the generation and the class he represents. Mr. Pelham studying Mill on Government and the Political Economists, was thought by some an incongruity in character at the day in which Mr. Pelham first appeared; the truth of that conception is apparent now, at least to the observant. The fine gentlemen of that day were preparing themselves for the after things, which were already foreshadowed; and some of those, then best known in clubs and drawing-rooms, have been since foremost and boldest, nor least instructed, in the great struggles of public life.

I trust that this work may now be read without prejudice from that silly error that long sought to identify the author with the hero.

Rarely indeed, if ever, can we detect the real likeness of an author of fiction in any single one of his creations. He may live in each of them, but only for the time. He migrates into a new form with every new character he creates. He may have in himself a quality, here and there, in common with each, but others so widely opposite, as to destroy all the resemblance you fancy for a moment you have discovered. However this be, the author has the advantage over his work—that the last remains stationary, with its faults or merits, and the former has the power to improve. The one remains the index of its day, the other advances with the century. That in a book written in extreme youth there may be much that I would not write now in mature manhood, is obvious; that, in spite of its defects, the work should have retained to this day the popularity it enjoyed in the first six months of its birth, is the best apology that can be made for its defects.

LONDON, 1848.   E.B.L.

TEXTUAL NOTES

Listed here are the variant readings from the texts of the first edition of 1828 and the editions of 1835 and 1840. The first reference number, preceding the colon, gives the page number in this book; the numbers following the colon give the line or lines. The edition from which the variant is taken is shown in parentheses at the end of the entry. I have not invariably recorded the alteration in punctuation and capitalization in cases where a deletion required a change from a comma or semicolon to a period and capitalization of the first word following.

4:22	encounter FOR *rencontre* (1840)
4:23	since FOR for (1840)
4:26	confounded FOR d——d (1840)
4:30	I have . . . divorced.: DELETED (1840)
5:3	rather justly FOR justly (1835)
5:5	this FOR these (1840)
5:10	whist FOR Brookes's (1840)
5:11	conceive FOR take (1840)
5:16	Epigraph from Horace DELETED (1840)
6:17	attractive FOR *recherché* (1840)
7:9–12	while there was that in his courage and will which, despite his reserve and unpopularity, always marked him out as a leader in those enterprises wherein we test as boys the qualities which chiefly contribute to secure hereafter our position amongst men FOR and his skill . . . tempted him to dare (1840)
7:20	fifty FOR twenty (1835)
7:24	technically called a crib FOR at the bottom of the page (1840)
7:25	been only FOR only been (1835)
9:18	with FOR in (1835)
11:7	elegant FOR *distingué* (1840)
11:27	which put . . . arm-chair: DELETED (1840)
11:34	*actually came* FOR *came actually* (1835)
12:3	sought after FOR *recherché* (1840)
12:4	in England: DELETED (1840)
12:14	particular taste for the fine arts FOR great *penchant* . . . *hommes* (1840)

12:34	literary persons FOR *literati* (1840)
13:4	my lord: DELETED (1840)
13:22	You know Jekyl, of course? FOR Do you remember Jekyl? (1835)
14:8	politics FOR indecorums (1840)
14:25	blue FOR green (1835)
14:27	distinguished FOR *distingué* (1840)
15:3	most whom FOR all (1840)
15:35	and adjusted my *best curl:* DELETED (1840)
16:6	interrupted I: DELETED (1835)
19:14	with the divine sex FOR *auprès des dames* (1840)
19:36	a FOR *une* (1835)
22:22	utterly: DELETED (1840)
23:5	cabin FOR *cabaret* (1840)
24:3	He stayed nearly a month.: ADDED (1835)
24:33	made the sole inscription on the stone FOR were all . . . stone (1840)
26:11	modified FOR mollified (1835)
27:15	myself FOR me (1840)
27:19	for instance FOR *par exemple* (1840)
27:29	shaving soap FOR almond paste (1840)
28:6	despite FOR *malgré* (1840)
29:19	procure FOR produce (1835)
30:10	obnoxious to men FOR remarkable among men (1840)
30:24	Mr. Aberton FOR the *attaché* (1840)
31:1	(here I played with my best ringlet): DELETED (1835)
31:6	in exactly FOR exactly in (1840)
31:19	"What do you think . . . *screamed for assistance.":* DELETED (1835)
31:23	seemed to consider me impertinent enough to become the rage FOR looked at me . . . done before. (1835)
32:3	on the second floor FOR *au second* (1840)
32:5	on the third FOR *au troisième* (1840)
33:28	since FOR just (1835)
33:38	dilapidated: DELETED (1840)
34:10	almost Parisian FOR *presque Parisien* (1840)
35:37	neglect FOR *impolitesse* (1840)
36:2-3	no one, if he pleased, could be at once so brilliantly original, yet so completely *bon ton* FOR you had . . . *usage du monde* (1835)
36:5	much in vogue FOR *répandu* (1840)
36:23	door FOR *porte cocher* (1835)
37:9	I know not why . . . my native country.: DELETED (1835)
38:27	England and the English FOR *L'Angleterre et les Anglois* (1840)

40:29	any FOR an (1840)
41:7–41	I said to Mr. Thornton . . . if I granted it?: DELETED (1840)
43:33	even talent, if it fall short of genius FOR talent (1840)
43:38	luck and opportunity FOR opportunity (1840)
46:1	L*** FOR Crébillon (1835)
47:9	your mechanics,: DELETED (1835)
47:16	brand FOR set down (1835)
50:30	soul FOR de l'âme (1835)
52:22	as an *amante:* DELETED (1835)
52:37	laughing FOR into one of those peals so peculiarly British (1840)
53:14	with all my heart FOR *De tout mon coeur* (1840)
55:16–17	are not very valuable for political knowledge:—FOR are the least . . . and though (1835)
55:18	but they were FOR they were (1835)
57:18	starved FOR river (1835)
59:5	the God of: DELETED (1840)
61:1	unhappy FOR miserable (1828 first ed.)
61:7	Heaven FOR God (1840)
61:23	*Mon Dieu* FOR My God (1840)
63:16	*Mon Dieu* FOR Good God (1840)
64:20	and remarkable FOR but more than beautiful (1835)
65:7	legation FOR embassy (1828 first ed.)
65:7	a lean gentleman, who valued himself on his ancestors FOR (the spectral secretary of the embassy) (1840)
65:16	aristocrat FOR secretary (1840)
65:31	himself: DELETED (1835)
65:32	Mr. Howard de Howard FOR the secretary (1840)
66:31	THE NOTE ALSO INCLUDED THE FOLLOWING SENTENCE, DELETED IN 1840: Since he has been pleased to point it out to the notice of his countrymen, it has become thronged with English, and degenerated in its kitchen.
67:1	distinguished FOR *distingué* (1835)
67:2	*bourgeois:* DELETED (1840)
67:33–34	than it had hitherto assumed FOR than of the other . . . met (1835)
68:24	admired FOR *recherché* (1840)
69:6	and, above all, a Gothic ruin opposite the bay-window: ADDED (1835)
69:16	cells of an old abbey FOR chambers of an old ruin (1835)
69:23	dislike FOR contempt (1835)
69:22–23	for whom . . . contempt: DELETED (1840)
69:24	asking FOR question (1828 first ed.)
69:25	aimiable *attaché* FOR *aimable attaché* (1835); amiable young gentleman FOR aimiable *attaché* (1840)

69:30–31	candidly FOR "but no man . . . hands and feet!" (1840)
70:5	Eupatrid FOR secretary (1840)
70:9–11	"Running!" cried I . . . but: DELETED (1840)
70:27–71:3	But did you know . . . pinch of snuff.": DELETED (1840)
72:11–13	and if I made love . . . master of the graces;: DELETED (1840)
72:29	gaming-house FOR Salon de Jeu (1840)
73:12	grisette FOR bourgeoise (1840)
73:31	quitted FOR left me master of (1840)
74:29–33	suffer him to starve, to die of actual want, abandoned and alone!" "Alone! no! cried her companion fiercely. FOR suffer him to die . . . prayer, and that is (1840)
75:7	O, that woman's . . . in its guilt!: DELETED (1835)
76:28	Is it by your order that your servant keeps me FOR Do you . . . keep me (1840)
76:36	Fortunately, however, she FOR I am just . . . Madame D'Anville (1840)
77:31–32	from which . . . digress—: DELETED (1835)
78:17–79:20	As we passed up the Rue de la Paix . . . still wear a mask.": DELETED (1840)
79:26	Heaven FOR God (1840)
83:23	Perhaps FOR A la vérité, (1835)
84:12	ungrateful FOR an ingrat (1835)
84:14	rarely FOR not always (1835)
84:32	and enjoyment: ADDED (1835)
85:16	exacting FOR exigeante (1840)
85:37	the stairs FOR stairs (1840)
86:6	my fair enemy FOR this new Messalina (1840)
86:11	politeness FOR politesse (1840)
86:16	an acquaintance FOR a connoissance (1835)
86:20	go FOR went (1835)
86:33	contamination FOR vulgarities (1835)
87:40	first published FOR was written (1840)
89:2	Saturday FOR Sunday (1840)
89:33	Saturday FOR Sunday (1840)
89:35	d——d: DELETED (1840)
91:6	had promised my rooms to a particular friend FOR was unwilling . . . longer (1840)
91:14	I am happy . . . English quartier.: DELETED (1835)
92:4–7	I have two peculiarities which serve me, it may be, instead of talent; I observe, and I remember FOR the minutest erreur . . . my recollection (1835)
93:24	plot FOR story (1840)
93:26	this book will suit few readers FOR ce livre . . . de lecteurs (1840)
94:18	reflections FOR pensées (?1840)

94:21	men of letters are always men of the world FOR *les gens de lettres* are always *les gens du monde* (1840)
94:22	human beings FOR men (1840)
95:16	The women called . . . *un bête:* DELETED (1840)
96:10	Saturday FOR Sunday (1840)
97:33	the man whom FOR the man (1840)
97:34	my conjecture FOR I (1840)
97:39	which I have remarked as: DELETED (1835)
98:8	for my individual taste: DELETED (1840)
99:26	*de sa part,:* DELETED (1840)
99:33	ankle FOR ancle (1835)
99:35	ankle FOR ancle (1835)
99:38	(but in a voice that struck me as feigned and artificial): ADDED (1835)
100:4	and *enjouement:* DELETED (1840)
100:20	Heaven FOR God (1840)
100:36	rarely FOR never (1840)
100:37	little FOR nothing (1840)
101:10	probable supposition FOR most probable (1835)
102:4–5	£100,000 a year, the other has £10,000 FOR £10,000 a year, the other has £150,000 (1840)
104:35	There was yet . . . about to forego.: DELETED (1840)
107:34	and I believe not . . . of another: DELETED (1840)
109:8	*C. de Vautran* FOR *C. D'Azimart* (1840)
109:23	de Vautran FOR D'Azimart (1840)
110:12	philosophers FOR Christians (1840)
110:16	Heaven's FOR God's (1840)
110:19	de Vautran FOR D'Azimart (1840)
110:27, 30, 34	de Vautran FOR D'Azimart (1840)
111:17	door FOR *porte* (1840)
111:23	which you please FOR *selon votre goût* (1840)
113:4	Fortiaque adversis opponite pectora rebus FOR In rebus adversis . . . fortia (1835)
113:12	gaming-room FOR *Salle à Jouer* (1840)
114:20	distinguished FOR *distingué* (1840)
114:21	(the present ———): DELETED FROM 1828 FIRST ED.
114:28	Royal Highness FOR ——— (1828 first ed.)
115:13	with FOR in (1835)
115:14	of great rank: NOT IN 1828 FIRST ED.
115:38	THE NOTE CONTINUED WITH THE FOLLOWING SENTENCE, DELETED IN 1840: The old lady (a profound critic in such matters) has told me that George the Fourth—the Prince of Wales in the zenith of his popularity and personal advantages—and despite all the *prestige* in his favor, seemed positively vulgar by the side of the Count d'Artois—it was

	the difference between what was then called the "dashing blood"— and the fine gentleman.
117:13	Anglais FOR Anglois (1835)
118:5	digged FOR dug (1840)
118:35	staircase FOR *escalier* (1840)
121:36	I was turning listlessly, as I sate at breakfast over the pages of Galignani's Messenger, when the following paragraph caught my attention FOR I was a luxurious . . . was the following (1835)
122:9–123:15	The next passage . . . art of panegyric.": DELETED (1840)
123:17	so: DELETED (1835)
123:28	four, ay, or even two FOR four (1835)
124:23–24	After I had arranged my *toilette* FOR After I had arranged myself and my whiskers—two very distinct affairs (1840)
127:13	Jove FOR G—! (1840)
128:5	admiring my rings: DELETED (1840)
128:6	in the intervals of these more natural occupations: DELETED (1840)
129:8	damme FOR dash . . . Sir W.'s) (1835)
129:25	fat FOR stout (1840)
129:35	"A nice . . . propensities).: DELETED (1840)
130:38	if you are not pleased with yourself FOR if you yourself are not? (1840)
131:13	and *essenced,* and *oiled,*: DELETED (1840)
131:28	of the more fashionable of the English FOR of the English (1835)
131:34	admired FOR *recherché* (1840)
134:30	stately FOR pompous (1835)
135:22	in despair FOR *au désespoir* (1840)
138:10	Juno FOR Jupiter (1840)
138:23	deuced: DELETED (1840)
143:3	'Oh!' thought I . . . take him in.: DELETED (1840)
143:10	Heaven's FOR God's (1840)
148:5	Ricardo's work FOR Mrs. Marsett's elementary work (1835)
148:6	he FOR she (1835)
151:6	to say truth FOR *pour dire vrai* (1840)
154:5	and be d——d to you: DELETED (1840)
155:4	cutlet FOR *côtelette de mouton* (1835)
155:19	cutlet FOR *côtelette* (1835)
159:17	brewer FOR merchant (1840)
160:28	"None, except (I added to myself) the lion I had for dinner." FOR "None." (1835)
162:19	Heaven FOR God (1840)
162:24–163:16	till, at last, getting weary . . . that lady in—": DELETED (1840)
163:31	gallantries FOR *affaires de coeur* (1840)

464

164:3	moment FOR instant (1840)
166:12	the Lord Mayor FOR Venables (1840)
166:17–31	As we passed . . . the originals.: DELETED (1840)
167:23	—so *minutely*—: DELETED (1840)
167:30	It is not my *forte!* ADDED (1835)
167:36	stationer's shop FOR shop (1840)
167:36–168:1	It was a small . . . *copia narium:* DELETED (1840)
168:2	sealing wax FOR *eau de Cologne* (1840)
169:11	(odious cross light . . . to avoid): DELETED (1835)
170:12	bill of fare FOR whole *carte* (1840)
170:24	a certain intrigue FOR an *affaire de coeur* (1835)
171:26	sentiments and subjects FOR sentiments, subjects, and language (1840)
172:9–10	stretching . . . to Vincent: DELETED (1835)
172:15	the consideration of nature . . . the food of the mind FOR *consideratio naturae . . . pabulum animi* (1840)
172:21	Wonderful FOR *Heus Domine* (1840)
173:11	Heaven FOR God (1840)
173:28	aweary FOR weary (1828 first ed.)
175:28	nor the less a voluptuary,: DELETED (1840)
176:1	nor the less choice in my perfumes,: DELETED (1835)
176:6	manner FOR a manner almost . . . its tone (1835)
176:41–177:9	Scarcely had . . . the waistcoat.": DELETED (1835)
177:10–180:11	And here, as I am weary . . . is a philosopher.: THIS SECTION WAS SUBSTITUTED FOR THE FOLLOWING PASSAGE FROM THE 1828 FIRST EDITION. And here, as I am wearied of speaking of tailors, let us reflect a little upon their works. In the first place, I deem it the supreme excellence of coats, not to be *too* well made; they should have nothing of the triangle about them; at the same time, wrinkles should be carefully avoided; the coat should fit exactly, though without effort; I hold it as a decisive opinion, that this can never be the case where any padding, (beyond one thin sheet of buckram, placed smoothly under the shoulders, and sloping gradually away towards the chest), is admitted. The collar is a very important point, to which too much attention cannot be given. I think I would lay down, as a general rule, (of course dependent upon the model), that it should be rather low behind, broad, short, and slightly rolled. The tail of the coat must on no account be broad or square, unless the figure be much too thin;—no license of fashion can allow a man of delicate taste to adopt, and imitate the posterial luxuriance of a Hottentot. On the contrary, I would lean to the other extreme, and think myself safe in a swallow tail. With respect to the length allotted to the

waist, I can give no better rule than always to adopt that proportion granted us by nature. The *gigot* sleeve is an abominable fashion; anything tight across the wrist is ungraceful to the last degree; moreover such tightness does not suffer the wristband to lie smooth and unwrinkled, and has the effect of giving a large and clumsy appearance to the hand.

Speaking of the hand, I would observe, that it should never be utterly *ringless,* but whatever ornament of that description it does wear, should be distinguished by a remarkable fastidiousness of taste. I know nothing in which the good sense of a gentleman is more finely developed than in his rings; for my part, I carefully eschew all mourning rings, all hoops of *embossed* gold, all diamonds, and *very* precious stones, and all antiques, unless they are peculiarly fine. One may never be ashamed of a seal ring, nor of a very plain gold one, like that worn by married women; rings should in general be simple, but singular, and bear the semblance of a *gage d'amour.* One should never be supposed to buy a ring, unless it is a seal one.

Pardon this digression. One word now for the waistcoat; this, though apparently the least observable article in dress, is one which influences the whole appearance more than anyone not profoundly versed in the habilatory art would suppose. Besides, it is the only main portion of our attire in which we have full opportunity for the display of a graceful and well cultivated taste. Of an evening, I am by no means averse to a very rich and ornate species of vest; but the extremest caution is necessary in the selectio of the spot, the stripe, the sprig, which forms the principal decoration—nothing tawdy—nothing common must be permitted; if you wear a fine waistcoat, and see another person with one resembling it, forthwith bestow it upon your valet. A white waistcoat with a black coat and trowsers, and a small chain of dead gold, only partially seen, is never within the bann of the learned in such matters; but beware, oh, beware your linen, your neckcloth, your collar, your frill, on the day in which you are tempted to the decent perpetration of a white waistcoat! All things depend upon *their* arrangement; in a black waistcoat, the sins of a tie, or the soils of a shirtbosom, escape detection; with a white one, there is no hope. If, therefore, you are hurried in your toilette, or in a misanthropic humour at the moment of settling your cravat, let no inducement suffer you to wear a vesture which, were all else suitable, would be the most unexceptionable you could assume.

Times, by the bye, are greatly changed since Brummell interdicted white waistcoats *of a morning*. I do not know whether, during the heat of the season, you could induct yourself in a more gentle and courtly garment. The dress waistcoat should generally possess a rolling and open form, giving the fullest opening for the display of the shirt, which cannot be too curiously fine; if a frill is exquisitely washed, it is the most polished form in which your bosom appurtenances should be moulded; if not, if, indeed, your own valet, or your mistress does not superintend their lavations, I would advise a simple plait of the plainest fashion.

With regard to the trowsers, be sure that you have them exceedingly tight across the hips; if you are well made, you may then leave their further disposition to Providence, until they reach the ankle. There you must pause, and consider well whether you will have them short, so as to develope the fineness of the *bas de soie,* or whether you will continue them so as to kiss your very shoe tie; in the latter form, which is indisputably the most graceful, you must be especially careful that they flow down, as it were, in an easy and loose (but, above all, not *baggy*) fall, and that the shoestrings are arranged in the *dernier façon* of a bow and end. Of a morning, the trowsers cannot be too long or too easy, so that they avoid every *outré* and singular excess.

As to the choice of colours, in clothing, it is scarcely possible to fix any certain and definite rule. Among all persons, there should be little variety of colour, either in the morning or the evening; but fair people, with good complexions, may, if their port and bearing be genuinely aristocratic, wear light or showy colours—a taste cautiously to be shunned by the dark, the pale, the meagre, and the suburban in mien.

For the rest, I cannot sufficiently impress upon your mind the most thoughtful consideration to the minutiae of dress, such as the glove, the button, the boot, the shape of the hat, &c.; above all, the most scrupulous attention to cleanliness is an invariable sign of a polished and elegant taste, and is the life and soul of the greatest of all sciences— the science of dress.

178:3	Spartans FOR Lacedemonians (1840)
180:19	a stud FOR an equine collection (1835)
180:26–27	(whose dark coloured livery . . . right judgment): DELETED (1835)

180:28	but as the groom said he was rarely at home till late in the afternoon, I drove first FOR but first I drove (1840)
181:12–28	I rattled on through a variety of subjects till Lady Roseville at last said, laughingly, "I see, Mr. Pelham, that you have learned FOR "Charming collection . . . say one word. You have learned (1840)
181:37–182:31	"Yes," said Lady Roseville, . . . within our reach!": THIS SECTION WAS SUBSTITUTED FOR THE FOLLOWING FROM THE 1828 FIRST EDITION.

At this moment an elderly gentleman, who had been lounging on a *chaise longue* near the window, and who was the only person in the room inattentive to my display, called out,

"For God's sake come here! a poor man will certainly be thrown from his horse! Will nobody help him?"

"That will I," I cried, starting up, all the groupe [*sic*] crowding after me. One glance was sufficient to show me, that the horse was the one of Glanville's I had so lately admired, and that his rider (the groom I had spoken to) was in the most imminent danger of being dashed to pieces. He was already half off his seat, and with his head hanging down, and clinging to the mane and neck only by one hand. I sprang to the door, cleared the stairs at a bound, rushed through the hall door, and caught the enraged animal (whom no one else, of all the surrounding loiterers, dared approach), by the rein. The check, momentary as it was, gave the man, who had not lost all presence of mind, time to extricate himself from his situation, and the next instant I had sprung into the saddle. I found all my attention requisite to soothe my Bucephalus, who had recommenced kicking and plunging with redoubled vigour. There was never any situation of life in which I have lost the possession of myself. At first I was contented with bending my limbs and body, with every motion of the horse; nor was it till after several minutes of intense exercise on his part, that I used any evident authority upon my own; ten minutes were sufficed to begin and complete my triumph. I dismounted at the door with my usual air of *nonchalance,* and giving the panting, but now tractable, animal to the groom, I re-entered the hall.

The "mob of gentlemen" and gentlewomen gathered round me as I sauntered into the drawing-room. Lady Roseville gave me a smile that weighed more with me than the compliments and congratulations of all the rest.

"Believe me," said I, escaping from them all, and throwing myself on a sofa in the next room, "riding is too severe an exercise for men, it is only fit for the robuster nerves of women. Will any gentleman present lend me his essence bottle?"

182:12	fiction FOR falsehood (1835)
183:11	which enchanted me to the heart: DELETED (1835)
183:12	closet FOR boudoir (1835)
183:12–14	and having, . . . of chairs.: DELETED (1835)
183:16	and the interstices . . . set in silver: DELETED (1835)
183:17	material FOR metal (1835)
183:18–26	This closet opened upon a spacious and lofty saloon, the walls of which were covered with the masterpieces of Flemish and Italian art FOR Beyond this library . . . of the most exquisite odour (1835)
183:27	apartment FOR luxurious chamber (1835)
183:28–29	opposite to . . . gold, and: DELETED (1835)
183:31	by choice FOR *par choix* (1840)
184:17	pictures FOR furnishing (1835)
184:24	furniture or pictures FOR furniture (1835)
184:33	"Pelham, you are in a grievous error," said Glanville. "Men are like game, and are best dressed in a short time. Ask my cook if I am wrong FOR So be it then (1828 first ed.)
184:35	"You are . . . never do read.": DELETED (1840)
184:36	," said Glanville,: DELETED (1840)
185:1	Say, did I not tell you rightly FOR Believe hereafter (1828 first ed.)
185:2	"You did," said I. FOR "*One* may . . . —*allons!*" (1828 first ed.)
185:14	That can't FOR Can that . . . ? (1835)
185:24	Heaven's FOR God's (1840)
187:1	Lady R. FOR Lady Roseville (1828 first ed.)
187:6	attractions FOR attentions (1840)
188:10	Adieu FOR *Addio* (1840)
188:20	fashion FOR coxcombry (1835)
188:22	run after FOR *recherché* (1840)
189:6	Heaven FOR God (1840)
190:31	silver FOR gold (1840)
190:38	the arts FOR furniture (1835)
192:4	and which was FOR It was (1835)
192:5–9	of the most stalwart looking youths that I ever saw out of a marching regiment FOR of masculine looking youths . . . into contact (1835)
193:19	allow FOR make (1840)
193:21	on: DELETED (1840)

194:32	Which is *not* an astringent fruit FOR Pomum . . . purgatorium (1835)
196:19	d——d: DELETED (1840)
199:6–7	the arch-fiend FOR not the archfiend . . . shepherds, (1828 first ed.)
199:20	good God!: DELETED (1840)
199:40	the effect—not the cause FOR the cause—not the effect (1828 first ed.)
206:19	Heaven FOR God (1840)
209:19	THE FOLLOWING EPIGRAPH WAS ADDED IN 1840:

> Whilst we do speak, our fire
> Doth into ice expire;
> Flames turn to frost,
> And, ere we can
> Know how our crow turns swan,
> Or how a silver snow
> Springs there, where jet did grow,
> Our fading spring is in dull winter lost.
>
> *Jasper Mayne*

210:4	out on FOR over (1840)
210:31	and looking remarkably handsome: DELETED (1835)
211:5	and *séduisant:* DELETED (1840)
211:20–24	Could the humour . . . novel of Gil Blas.: DELETED (1835)
211:35–36	(owing to . . . Anastasius): DELETED (1835)
212:8	object FOR *but* (1840)
212:35	Heaven FOR God (1840)
213:12	THE FOLLOWING NOTE WAS ADDED TO THE TEXT IN 1835 BUT DROPPED IN 1840:

Loquitur Lord Vincent. For my own part, I think it often desirable to paint men better and higher than they ordinarily are. The reader will perceive that this conversation is retailed by Mr. Pelham in order quietly to hint at the canons of criticism by which he probably composed his own memoirs.

213:27	Sage FOR Philosopher (1840)
214:18	"English grace" (Lord help us!): DELETED (1840)
215:15–16	Let me ring for my poodle, and some *eau de cologne,* and: DELETED (1840)
215:18–20	Vincent bit his lip . . . attend to him.: DELETED (1840)
217:12	can't FOR sha'n't (1835)
219:5	Heaven knows why! but: DELETED (1840)
219:6	, which I by no means deserved: DELETED (1840)
222:27	a more easily FOR an easier (1835)
222:33	perhaps many FOR many (1835)
225:21	Heaven FOR God (1840)

227:12	hang it FOR d—— me (1840)
227:14	Mr. —— FOR Mr. Goren (1840). THIS CHANGE APPLIES THROUGHOUT THE CHAPTER.
232:5	*un:* DELETED (1840)
232:23	massy: DELETED (1835)
234:17–19	; and there were moments . . . of power: DELETED (1835)
235:5–7	In truth . . . for himself.: DELETED (1835)
235:8–9	coxcombical and: DELETED (1835)
236:30	—then I did not, or I should not have written them: ADDED WITHIN THE PARENTHESIS (1835)
237:11	never FOR ever (1835)
237:29	glances FOR *réveille* (1840)
241:11	us FOR me (1835)
242:31	quail FOR ortolan (1840)
244:35	ultra-Tories FOR Tories (1840)
246:25	if you will: DELETED (1835)
247:19	Secondly, if the affair terminated fatally, the world would not lightly condemn me for conveying to a gentleman of birth and fortune, a letter so insulting, and for causes of which I was so ignorant.: ADDED (1835)
250:25	worldly men. And yet FOR worldly men; and the conclusion . . . his cowardice. And yet (1835)
253:12	servant FOR *au plaisir* (1840)
253:25	likeness FOR similitude (1840)
254:27–29	who, despite his marquisate and his acres, was not less below me in the aristocracy of ancient birth, than in that of cultivated intellect FOR whom I considered . . . of intellect (1840)
255:10–12	The example became contagious FOR "To it . . . mutual aggression (1840)
255:16–21	combatants. At length FOR combatants. As for me, . . . hilarity: (1840)
255:24	another with a shoulder put out,: DELETED (1840)
255:26–27	dimensions, and, in short, every one of the combatants with some token of the severity of the conflict FOR dimensions. In short . . . severity (1840)
255:27	in the inquiry as to the origin of the war: ADDED (1840)
256:7	previously FOR previous (1835)
	aloof. This day FOR aloof; in fine, I am . . . affront. (1835)
256:14	would not be filled with my admirers FOR must be filled with my enemies (1840)
262:9	The instant FOR directly (1835)
265:13	hurl FOR cite (1835)
265:29	melancholy FOR *triste* (1840)
267:24–25	connubial yoke FOR *connubiale jugum* (1835)

"Well," said Lady Roseville, "I fear we shall never have any popular poet in our time, now that Lord Byron is dead." "So the booksellers say," replied Vincent; "but I doubt it: there will always be a certain interregnum after the death of a great poet, during which poetry will be received with distaste, and chiefly for this reason, that nearly all poetry about the same period, will be of the same school as the most popular author. Now the public soon wearies of this monotony; and no poetry, even equally beautiful with that of the most approved writer, will become popular, unless it has the charm of variety. It must not be perfect in the old school, it must be daring in a new one;—it must effect a thorough revolution in taste, and build itself a temple out of the ruins of the old worship. All this a great genius may do, if he will take the pains to alter, *radically,* the style he may have formed already. He must stoop to the apprenticeship before he *comme de faire une pendule.''*

310:14	(that small, delicate, *Titania* hand,): DELETED (1840)
312:17	obstacles FOR obstacle (1828 first ed.)
313:27	the beautiful countess FOR *la belle Comtesse* (1835)
317:28	observed I ironically FOR observed I (1835)
317:32	As for me FOR *Quant à moi* (1840)
318:21–22	justly? Contempt of fame . . . virtue. FOR justly—*contemptu* . . . virtue? (1835)
320:8	whirlpool FOR dissipation (1835)
320:11	I lost my good looks FOR a wrinkle settled under my left eye (1840)
320:14	(with a volume of Bishop Berkeley, and a bottle of wrinkle water,): DELETED (1835)
320:27	for my health FOR *pour ma santé* (1840)
320:28	for my pains FOR *pour mes peines* (1840)
326:35	locket FOR bracelet (1835)
327:18	certain untimely wrinkles FOR that my untimely wrinkle (1840)
329:11	FOOTNOTE IN THE 1828 FIRST EDITION: Seneca.
330:14	T. H—— FOR * * * * * (1828 first ed.)
333:3	Heaven FOR God (1840)
333:22	*in aeternumque* FOR *eternumque* (1840)
335:16	Rover FOR Libertine (1840)
337:18–19	and returned home. FOR and . . . in the world!'' (1835)
338:7	we might term FOR we term (1840)
338:19	Lord Dawton FOR my lord (1840)
339:32	*sordidi:* DELETED (1840)
339:37	advance FOR progress (1840)
341:8–10	that our differences are not vehement—it is a difference not of measures, but of men FOR that there is not a difference . . . *aut Nebuchadnezar* (1835)
342:4	dressed as usual FOR dressed with . . . pains (1835)
346:2	opinions FOR opinion (1828 first ed.)
350:13–14	Should any one . . . remember, that: DELETED (1835)
352:5	my own master FOR at my own disposal (1835)
352:8	eventually FOR hereafter (1840)

473

352:22	habit FOR pursuit (1828 first ed.)
352:30	vulgarity FOR *grossièreté* (1840)
355:35	At this watering place FOR Here (1835)
364:18	Tyrrell FOR the latter (1835)
369:17	THIS PASSAGE APPEARED IN AN EXPANDED FORM, AS FOLLOWS, IN THE 1828 FIRST EDITION.

and like the ocean, in the powerful sketch of 'Darkness,'
'All stood still,
And nothing stirred within their silent depths:
I slept on the abyss without a surge.'

371:33	whose words FOR the words of which (1828 first ed.)
375:17	cheque FOR note (1840)
376:24	worn FOR filtered (1840)
377:15–16	awful history FOR history and approaching fate (1835)
378:12	approbation of FOR concurrence with (1840)
380:17	but in FOR but (1835)
382:23	costly: DELETED (1835)
383:41	Heavens FOR God (1840)
384:41	DELETED: (1835)
385:1	excitement FOR excitation (1840)
385:17	with any safety FOR with safety (1828 first ed.)
386:3	The instant FOR Directly (1835)
387:5	were two enormous ears FOR was an enormous ear (1828 first ed.)
387:28–29	seemed, as in conscious horror, to glow FOR seemed . . . horror (1835)
388:20	his FOR Sir John Tyrell's (1828 first ed.)
392:10	As soon as FOR Directly (1835)
392:36	love-token FOR *gage d'amour* (1840)
392:36	locket FOR bracelet (1835)
395:31	deuce FOR God (1840)
399:40	(continued Mr. Jonson, aristocratically),: ADDED (1835)
401:22	chief FOR dimber-damber (1840)
402:20	up: DELETED (1835)
403:40	Gipsy slang: ADDED BEFORE *A parson* (1840)
404:35	De Courcy FOR Douglas (1835)
406:18–19	which the maxims of love at that early period of its existence would assert FOR which the history . . . delineates (1828 first ed.)
406:23	charge FOR charges (1835)
407:3	pocket picking FOR pickpocketing (1840)
413:35–36	we continued to move on FOR I continued . . . comrade (1828 first ed.)
414:6	Gad FOR Heaven (1840)

414:13–14	By the touch (for it was too dark to see) I felt that he was bending down FOR I perceived . . . leaning down (1835)
414:33	black 'un FOR parish bull (1835)
415:23	than FOR than to (1828 first ed.)
416:12	heart FOR mind (1840)
419:17	best: DELETED (1840)
422:21	living FOR livelihood (1835)
428:37	I said FOR and I said (1828 first ed.)
433:26	to pause FOR into pausing (1840)
434:13	started FOR startled (1840).
434:16	forgotten till then FOR forgotten (1835)
435:10	de Courcy FOR Douglas (1835)
436:7	curls FOR ringlets (1835)
440:6	your own FOR your own fortune (1828 first ed.)
440:19	By the bye, how is his property entailed? FOR He has no . . . I think? (1840)
440:27	her *renommée* as a *belle celebrée* FOR her celebrity as a beauty (1828 first ed.)
441:17	due FOR paid (1835)
442:7	De Courcy FOR Douglas (1835)
443:8	Before I could speak, I felt his hand: THESE WORDS REPLACED THE FOLLOWING PASSAGE IN THE 1828 FIRST EDITION.

At that moment, I solemnly declare, whether from my sympathy with his feelings, or from some more mysterious and indefinable cause, my whole frame shuddered from limb to limb. I saw nothing—I heard nothing; but I *felt,* as it were, within me some awful and ghostly presence, which had power to curdle my blood into ice, and cramp my sinews into impotence; it was as if some preternatural and shadowy object darkened across the mirror of my soul—as if, without the medium of my corporeal senses, a spirit spoke to, and was answered by, a spirit.

The moment was over. I felt Glanville's hand

444:6–7	peculiarly prominent in myself FOR (thou wilt perchance add, peculiarly prominent in myself) (1828 first ed.)
444:26	of two volumes FOR of three volumes (1835); of these pages FOR of two volumes (1840)
445:5	redeems FOR ameliorates (1840)
445:9–10	One may as well be . . . *can afford it;* and: DELETED (1835)
445:14	senatorial: DELETED (1835)
446:9	*Nescio quid meditans nugarum;—* but not, perhaps, *—totus in illis* FOR Nescio . . . illis (1840)

449:13   THE ORIGINAL VERSION OF THIS PREFACE, WHICH APPEARED IN THE 1835 EDITION, SHOWS A NUMBER OF MINOR VARIATIONS FROM THE VERSION REPRINTED. THE MOST SIGNIFICANT ARE THE FOLLOWING TWO PARAGRAPHS, WHICH WERE REPLACED BY THE FIRST PARAGRAPH IN THE 1840 EDITION.

When a certain wit was informed how St. Denis took a walk with his head under his arm, he wisely observed, that it was one of those cases in which the first step was half the journey. Now this observation is almost equally true with respect to the progress of a novel in the pilgrimage to Posterity. The fiction, that, in these days, amidst so great a crowd of competitors, and so general a desire for novelty, is still read and still alive at the end of six years, has a very tolerable chance of being still read and still alive at the end of sixty. It is one of those cases in which the first step is half the journey!

The favour which *Pelham* has met with and retained, may, perhaps, render a short sketch of its origin and history not without interest to the reader; and that account of his labours which would have been uncalled for, if not presumptuous, in a young author, is natural enough in one who has served an apprenticeship as long as that of the ingenious Wilhelm Meister; and who has arrived at a period of his literary life, when, in gratifying a common curiosity among readers, he may throw out some hints not without use to those of his brethren who are entering the same career.

ACKNOWLEDGMENTS

I owe a debt of thanks to a great many people for their help in preparing this edition. The book would never have appeared were it not for the learning and encouragement of Cecil Lang and Virgil Burnett. The staff of the George Arents Research Library, Syracuse University, was also a great help to me, as was the editorial staff of the University of Nebraska Press. I must also mention those people whose knowledge supplemented my ignorance in various ways: Richard Bruere, Arthur Friedman, Donald Bond, Wells Chamberlin, Nicholas Rudall, Stuart Tave, Michael Murrin, Hoover H. Jordan, and Peter White. I want to thank Jennifer Bell, for her typing and, perhaps most of all, for her patience. My wife, Anne, in her customary fashion, triumphed coolly over all of my disorder.

J. J. M.

The University of Nebraska Press wishes to thank Walter F. Wright, Marie Kotouc Roberts Professor of English, University of Nebraska, and Bernice Slote, Professor of English, University of Nebraska, for reading the introduction to this book in manuscript, and for their advice on preparing the edition. We also are indebted to Professor Slote for some detective work in regard to textual variants. We are grateful to Cecil Lang, Professor of English, University of Virginia, for proposing this project, and to Julius P. Barclay, Chief, Division of Special Collections, The Stanford University Libraries, who assisted us in procuring a microfilm and positive prints of the 1828 second edition of *Pelham*.